PENGUIN BOOKS

THE PENGUIN BOOK OF BRITISH COMIC STORIES

Patricia Craig is the co-author (with Mary Cadogan) of three critical studies, including *The Lady Investigates: Women Detectives and Spies in Fiction*, and has written a biography of Elizabeth Bowen for the Penguin Lives of Modern Women series. She is editor of *The Oxford Book of English Detective Stories* and a freelance critic and regular contributor to *The Times Literary Supplement*. She was born and grew up in Belfast, and now lives in London.

THE PENGUIN BOOK OF
BRITISH COMIC STORIES

COMPILED AND WITH AN
INTRODUCTION BY PATRICIA CRAIG

PENGUIN BOOKS

PENGUIN BOOKS

Published by the Penguin Group
Penguin Books Ltd, 27 Wrights Lane, London W8 5TZ, England
Penguin Books USA Inc., 375 Hudson Street, New York, New York 10014, USA
Penguin Books Australia Ltd, Ringwood, Victoria, Australia
Penguin Books Canada Ltd, 10 Alcorn Avenue, Toronto, Ontario, Canada M4V 3B2
Penguin Books (NZ) Ltd, 182–190 Wairau Road, Auckland 10, New Zealand

Penguin Books Ltd, Registered Offices: Harmondsworth, Middlesex, England

First published in Viking 1990
Published in Penguin Books 1991
10 9 8 7 6 5 4 3 2

Printed in England by Clays Ltd, St Ives plc

Contents

Contents

Introduction

The English comic story from the British Isles belongs to the twentieth century, but has deep roots in the past; from Chaucer on, the genre of English humour shows distinctive characteristics, such as irony and aplomb. It has thrown up some monumental oddities – for example, *Tristram Shandy*, which lets us know, among other things, what a would-be philosopher in a household of blockheads is up against: 'Cursed luck! – said he ... for a man to be master of one of the finest chains of reasoning in nature, – and have a wife at the same time with such a headpiece, that he cannot hang up a single inference within side of it, to save his soul from destruction ...' And alongside Sterne we have Thomas Love Peacock, eschewing with gusto the principle of straightforward narration and furnishing us instead with unending sportive disputation and unerring *bon mots*, with authoritative illogic playing its part.

When we come to Dickens we note a fundamental distinction between the humour of the past and that of the present; when Dickens turns to humour, it is his characters, by and large, who are cast in a comic mould, while modern authors favour the risible situation. We have only to think of the ludicrous jams into which the characters of P. G. Wodehouse (for example) are for ever precipitating themselves – 'Too late, I endeavoured to go to earth behind the chandler, only to discover that there was no chandler there' – to appreciate the role of the contretemps in contemporary hilarity.

As the short story developed strengths of its own, becoming not just an abbreviated means of recounting a full plot, but making the most of such factors as mood and angle of vision, the comic story came into its own. As we think of it, it's essentially an up-to-date form; and bearing this in mind, I have confined myself to the twentieth century in making this selection – with one exorbitant piece of tosh (from Amanda McKittrick Ros) throwing all the rest into light relief.

Some way behind the Wodehouse heroes, but conceived in a similar impulse of levity, is Richmal Crompton's William Brown,* whose exploits all lead in one way or another to an absurd predicament – 'It was, he was sure, contrary to all rules of etiquette to go out to tea accompanied by a cow.'

Writers like Wodehouse and Richmal Crompton are distinguished by a benign attitude; they locate their creations in an endlessly sunny world that is saved from cloying by the comic artificiality of its construction. There are others who go in for comic artifice (as opposed to comic realism) to a comparable degree, but opt for an altogether sharper approach: 'Saki' (H. H. Munro), for one, with his urbane ferocity and icy repartee. There is humour that reassures and humour that disturbs, and Saki's – for all its blitheness – comes into the second category.

English† humour, as embodied in the short story, comes in many varieties, from the sedate to the anarchic, but generally it depends for its effects on exactitude of style and a fair amount of insight into social mores. There are occasions, however, when both these qualities fly out of the window, with side-splitting results. I am thinking in particular of the egregious Northern Irish author Amanda McKittrick Ros, whose aberrant verbosity made her into something of a cult figure during the early part of the century. She stands, among other things, for the fullest achievement of unwitting funniness – and as one of my aims in compiling this anthology is to show the range of British comic writing, I have included an extract from her book *Helen Huddleson* (unfinished when she died in 1939, and not published for

---

* The 'William' stories, incidentally, were originally intended for an adult readership, and published in the *Happy Magazine*, before discerning children latched on to them.

† I am using this term rather loosely to denote the kinds of humour peculiar to the British Isles; there's a strong Celtic element in the anthology, with Scotland, Wales and Ireland well represented.

another thirty years). Humorists by inadvertence are humorists none the less.

Amanda Ros's innocent invective is at the opposite extreme from the needle-sharp tracts for the times – modern times, 1970s and 1980s – composed by Fay Weldon in a mood of sardonic disaffection and caustic feyness. This author uncovers and neatly serves up whole areas of contemporary awfulness – political futility, makeshift ideologies and all. She means to alert us to society's abuses by holding a few of them up to ridicule. Humour in the interests of social comment, indeed, is a major resource of present-day writing; you could claim that humour of a kind (sometimes an oblique kind) is manifested by nearly every writer of note, since an ironic detachment, at the very least, is likely to inform their observations. It's a rare blurb that fails to place humour among an author's assets. With a good deal of recent fiction, though, it's true to say that the wish to entertain is secondary to an expository drive on the part of the authors – and in selecting the stories which make up this collection, I have kept, as far as possible, to those which seem to me to show a definite comic purpose, and not just an ironic manner; though sometimes it is hard to decide exactly where one ends and the other begins. A lot of social realists, for example, are very funny indeed. Verisimilitude gains an extra dimension when it is given a comic slant; what is all-important is the narrative tone. The stories by Kingsley Amis, Beryl Bainbridge and Henry Green, for instance, exemplify the humour of incorrigibility, domestic aggravation and inconsequentiality – with the last in particular getting to grips with the queerness of everyday life. Eavesdroppers like Green and Beryl Bainbridge make an impact by imposing a comic superstructure on what they overhear. Then there are those who go in for a kind of dislocation. Samuel Beckett in 'Fingal' makes us laugh by inducing a measure of bewilderment; the enigmatic actions of his hero Belacqua aren't amenable to any cut-and-dried interpretation.

A number of funny stories are constructed along the lines of a joke, with everything tending towards an inspired punch-line. (Robert Graves's delectable 'Period Piece' is a good example of this, and Richmal Crompton's 'William and the Young Man' also reserves its most felicitous observation for the final line.) In most, however, the humour pervades the text, rather than building up to an invigorating climax. Take the Somerset Maugham story, for example, 'The Facts of Life'. This entertains by positing a desirable outcome to the breaking of some ordinary decent rules of conduct. It cocks a snook at the old moral tale, greatly to our enjoyment. And J. I. M. Stewart's marvellous 'Teddy Lester's Schooldays', in which a blameless book-collector lays himself open to a dark suspicion, plays with the humour of misunderstanding – the discrepancy between an imagined situation, and the less startling actual state of affairs.

William Trevor, in his early work at least, makes something of a feature of the frightful disclosure – the moment of truth-telling when something previously unmentionable is blurted out. The effect of this crucial indiscretion isn't always comic, but it reaches an apex of social comedy in the wonderful 'Raymond Bamber and Mrs Fitch', a story of a confrontation between a man with a nanny-complex and a drunken woman under stress. Letting the cat out of the bag: this harks back to Saki's talking cat Tobermory, in the story of that title. Tobermory, having learnt to speak, isn't bound by the conventions of polite dissembling. 'When your inclusion in this houseparty was suggested,' he informs a weekend guest, 'Sir Wilfred protested that you were the most brainless woman of his acquaintance, and that there was a wide distinction between hospitality and the care of the feeble-minded.' ('Tobermory' is not, in fact, the Saki story I've chosen for this collection; it is very well known, for a start, and on top of that I've found sufficient cats creeping in elsewhere – in the charming story by Sylvia Townsend Warner, for instance, and in P. G. Wodehouse's account of a frightful weekend.).

Some authors entertain us by providing an odd angle on things – Benedict Kiely, for example, who frequently approaches his subject matter sideways, as it were, as in 'Eton Crop', with its strange opening – 'I had an uncle once, a man of three score years and three, and when my reason's dawn began he'd take me on his knee . . .' – and subsequent ebullience.

And then we have the parodists, led by Max Beerbohm, whose *Christmas Garland* of 1912 illumines (by overdoing) the styles of several contemporary authors. His Henry James parody, 'The Mote in the Middle Distance', is a beautifully realized *jeu d'esprit*. Less admiration, and more a spirit of mockery, impelled Stella Gibbons to take on the whole genre of fearfully rural fiction, which she did to perfection in *Cold Comfort Farm*. Her story, 'Christmas at Cold Comfort Farm', isn't nearly as well known as the novel itself, but deserves the strongest applause for its enticing supplementary glimpse into the home life of the Howling Starkadders. ' "Who has the coffin-nail? Speak, you draf-saks!" . . . demanded Mrs Doom.'

Literary criticism by means of deflation is at the centre of Michael Foley's 'Dympna', in which the pretensions of an author like Villiers de Lisle-Adam are nicely highlighted. John Morrow (another Ulsterman, and a superb anecdotalist) has a lot of fun describing the untoward effects of looking distinctive in Belfast, while Gwyn Thomas ('An Ample Wish') gets to grips with a bit of innocent Welsh braggadocio. In 'The Martyr's Crown' we find Flann O'Brien once again at the business of mocking Irish nationalist pieties, with his customary cogency. And E. M. Delafield, with her 'Provincial Lady' pieces (originally issued bit by bit in the magazine *Time & Tide*), takes the shortcomings and annoyances of everyday life and turns the lot of them into a hilarious undertaking – cooks, exploding boilers, unforthcoming husband and all. She isn't alone in being endlessly sardonic about the daily round, but no one else, I think, achieved such an agreeable blend of cynicism and high spirits. The phoney war, when it came, was a gift to this author: the scene shifts to London, where a kind of crackpot urgency prevails, and ladies wearing slacks and turbans are trying to get in on the war effort and being thwarted at every turn.

Evelyn Waugh (another who presented the phoney war as a funny war) was something of a specialist in the humour of fortuitous conjunction, and this device is once again brought into play in the splendid late story, 'Basil Seal Rides Again', in which the amiable old handful proves as adept as ever at coming out on top. Who else do we find upholding and extending the English comic tradition? Muriel Spark, for one, whose ingenious and ironical 'The First Year of My Life' recalls Stevie Smith's lines: 'It was a cynical babe/Not without cause'.

Humour, to endure, seems to require above all a robust outlook combined with lightness of touch; nothing goes out of date more swiftly than the ponderous or otherwise ill-judged attempt at an amusing manner. We have only to look at certain collections of funny stuff brought out during the 1920s and 1930s to realize that genuine humour, as opposed to the ephemeral sort, has little to do with any vogue of the moment, including inappropriate behaviour in aunts or clergymen's quirks (not that these can't be funny, treated in the right way). It cuts out anything facetious or soft-centred – that way deadliness lies. Proper humour, you might say, is almost a by-product of an idiosyncratic vision on the part of the author, along with ease of manner and a strict control. It makes us see as striking or peculiar something we might otherwise have classed as mundane. What, for example, could be odder than the world of Wodehouse, with its burbling young blades and chaste infatuations? Well, perhaps Henry Green's transcription of singular, throwaway working-men's exchanges runs it close. Or Elizabeth Bowen's evocation of wartime England and a spirited cook, leaving messages in the fish-kettle: 'Mr and the 2 Misses Rangerton-Karney can boil their heads. This holds 3.' Or we might think of Frank O'Connor turning his pinched Cork childhood into a comedy of Catholicism and over-crowding. Or Graham Greene envisaging an exorbitant hazard for the visitor to Naples ...

All comic writing asserts a kind of sanity, by being bound up with watchfulness and proportion; if it is subversive in intent, it is always some enormity, such as cant or smugness, that is being undermined. The effect is always to raise the spirits, even if a slight lugubriousness or a grim jocularity comes into the picture. What else? Well, the knowing presentation of an innocent scenario is always funny, as we find in the stories by V. S. Naipaul and Dylan Thomas (not to mention Gwyn Thomas). Angus Wilson (in 'Crazy Crowd') takes a moderately unnerving social occasion and lets it run its course. George MacDonald

Fraser gets close to slapstick, but keeps his wits about him. And Julian Maclaren Ross gets at the essence of a particular period – the era of the de-mob suit – while chronicling its vagaries, both lightly and delightfully.

All kinds of humour, black, deadpan, subtle, hearty and heady, are (I hope) represented in this anthology; I am confident that every reader will light on something, in the course of the book, to bring on an outbreak of laughing. Some of the stories, it's true, may raise no more than a smile, but the smile, as a response to a comic stimulus, is not to be sneezed at. It is, of course, a personal selection, and perhaps at least one omission ought to be explained. Unlike a lot of people, I hold no affection for the R.M. stories of Somerville and Ross, which seem to me to make a wearisome business of the Irish antics they go in for; it's also against the spirit of the present to use dialect as the object, rather than the means, of ridicule, as they do. I have tried to choose stories that will indicate the variety of tones and devices available to the comic writer, as well as providing merriment, pleasure, surprise and exhilaration.

In finding the stories and assembling the collection I have had the greatest help from three individuals in particular – Jeffrey Morgan, Nigel May and Gerry Keenan; thanks are also due to many others, including John Gross, Nora T. Craig, Barbara Harris, Val Warner and Robert Johnstone, for offering some invaluable suggestions and advice. And I am greatly indebted to Hilary Rittner for lending me her copy of the *Strand* magazine with the Ordizzone watercolour which is reproduced on the cover.

Patricia Craig
London 1990

Amanda McKittrick Ros

from *Helen Huddleson*

Helen Huddleson awoke. Her power of perception seemed cleansed forever from that dull deadly dew which hitherto blinded her, as mist from a mountain top, during these hours of despair she so recently had passed through. Alert now to all that was going on around her, her planning organ did not fail her in this her hour of blatant betrayal.

While Lord Rasberry was doing 'the brigade-man' on Sir Peter Plum, Helen, with her little satchel on her arm, was hurrying down the stair of escape, along the pebbled path so recently trodden on by him who, a few moments before, had shuddered over its shifting surface.

Out into the darkness, then passing through a gate, she ran along, led by the lighted lamps stuck against huge posts whose lights glimmered darkly against a wealth of trees. Two great pillars with a large iron gate hanging on each next met her view, a bright light with a globe of dull green surrounding each top. She turned towards the gate to move up the avenue but it was locked. Inside to the right stood a neat little lodge, circular in form, whose door was ajar. She called at the top of her voice.

'Anyone there, please? Come, come, fast, fast.'

The door was soon flung open when a beardy man ran out asking:

'What's the matter, little lady? Have you lost your way?'

'Open, open, open the gate, dear good man,' Helen cried. 'O, sir, let me into your wee house. I'm a stranger here. Let me come in, sir, do, I pray you. My name is Helen Huddleson from Crow Cottage near Ballynahinch – Lord Rasberry will chase me and capture me – and – and –'

Fainting at the gate, the beardy man removed her carefully

into his little abode, otherwise an infant gate-lodge. He laid her on a soft couch in the little room beside the kitchen, slipped a spoonful of brandy between her lips which apparently seemed closed in death, then locked the door lest he whom she had mentioned and of whom she seemed in terror, might possibly find his way in.

Father Guerdo, who had come to her rescue, was a dissipated priest who once held a large stock of parishers within his tyrannical control. He was educated at a National school in the city of Dublin, receiving his final gloss at Maynooth, and like a good many more who have been registered as dispensers of divinity in disguise, was promoted to a comfortable living which he abused in many ways, drawing the censure of those in authority over him to such a degree that he was bereaved of his sinecure as one unfit to maintain the office of priesthood.

Threatening to disclose some unpleasant duties imposed on him while being initiated into the mysteries of the Roman fold, he was accordingly installed as porter at the gate-lodge attached to the Convent of St Iscariot.

Hearing footsteps approach the door, he instantly extinguished the light a small lamp cast forth, suspended by a chain from the centre of the kitchen's ceiling of polished pitch pine. By this time the sound of carriage wheels was heard, then ceased before the huge iron gate through which Helen had been so recently carried. A loud rapping was next heard at the lodge door which continued for a goodly time, then a voice rang forth.

'Porter, porter, just a moment, please. I am Lord Rasberry. Open the door, please, do.'

Father Guerdo remained obstinate and silent. After some time elapsed, retreating footsteps were heard, when the carriage wheels hurled forth bearing their load of titled trustlessness, depositing it at the Great Northern Railway station.

A sigh of relief escaped from Father Guerdo's lips as he drew over the kitchen window a jet black blind. Awaking from a state edging distraction, Helen's energies grew fortified more and more, strengthened by the thought that for a time at least she would be safe from duplicity and distrust.

To analyse her feelings at that moment she felt it would have been her wish to swim the Atlantic, nevertheless there was a strange sweetness mingled in her cell of sorrow. She was satisfied that one true clean mind twined her own, that he who probably sat waiting for her away in a foreign land was rejoicing that soon he would clasp her to his bosom. With this thought her reflective faculties appeared as if she had surmounted one great obstacle in order to cross over a dangerous chasm and still fight with deadly might for her honour.

Father Guerdo now opened the door and bending over her he had rescued from tyranny, he exclaimed 'Laus Deo', clasping his hands and turning his eyes northwards. He at once saw Helen had overcome the struggle that raged within her. Gently assisting her to a comfortable armchair deeply and softly cushioned, which he used himself in moods of deep melancholy, reflecting over a dissipated past he inwardly abhorred, to allow its pages to master him so as to tear his thoughts from this beautiful vision of loveliness so rare to be seen in the path Rome would fain make you believe you must track.

Gazing at her as she sat before before a fire of logs that flamed within a well-groomed grate, all thoughts of his past were buried beneath her glance. Priest though he was and supposed to be proof against admiration either of mistress or maid, all heresy became instantly drowned in the great tide of passion that raged within him.

Although doing penance for the past seven years by acting in the capacity of lodge porter, he still felt inclined to follow the professional routine which Roman tyranny imposes on her sons of heresy, mockery and idolatry, all of which he was sworn to support once he emitted from Maynooth, carrying them with him in his reticule of thoughts.

He had obtained a promise from the bishop to be reinitiated as parish priest as soon as a suitable vacancy conveniently occurred. He had waited seven years, still there was no appointment for him. This piqued him unpardonably and now he felt a false air blow round him and was likely to still keep blowing until his expectations became dulled, his energy impaired, his desires more limited without that distinction he had been falsely led to believe pervaded parish-priestdom.

Wavering under the spell of his misfortune and excited by the beauty of the little stranger who kept nervously wringing her hands, he asked her to give him a meagre narrative of the day's events and her reason for seeking his timely succour, which when ended he wept as never before. Her confidence in disclosing him the horror that still haunted her made him more anxious to determine her faith.

'What persuasion are you?' he asked, his voice sounding softly.

'I am a Presbyterian,' Helen Huddleson answered, 'and worship in Third Ballynahinch Presbyterian Church, once sitting under the late Reverend John Davis, a great and good man.'

Father Guerdo's face darkened some-what, his thin lips parted, exposing two rows of irregularly-set yellow-usefuls, while he drew down his brow, instantly impressing her by the fact that he felt displeased.

'In what county,' he inquired, 'did this divine try to instruct you on matters relating to your soul's welfare?'

'In County Down, sir,' replied Helen in a nervous strain.

'Say, Father, please, when addressing me,' spake he in a grim, imposing manner.

'Oh, no, no, no,' Helen answered, 'I can't call you "Father" at all, at all. I was never taught to call anybody "father", but my own dear parent, Peter Huddleson of Crow Cottage, about a mile outside Ballynahinch, near the graveyard, sir.'

' "Father", please, when addressing me,' speaking in a remonstrating tone.

'Are you a priest then?' Helen queried, her eyes glaring at his, burning with a fierce glow.

'I AM a priest,' he naively replied in a low voice.

'And what is your name, please, sir?'

'Father Guerdo,' he answered quickly.

'Then why are you living in this wee place? I thought all priests had big houses like they have in Ballynahinch.'

A sarcastic smile crept swiftly over his features.

'What a monstrous pity,' he said, 'to see a nice modest girl such as you and so beautiful, I must add, walking on the broad

road to destruction instead of on the narrow path that leadeth to life everlasting. You say you are a Presbyterian. Then you are a lost sinner. No one on earth is saved from everlasting fire, only those who belong to the one and only church and that is the Roman Catholic. All others are mere shams whose worshippers pair off in small sections here and there throughout the world, every section adopting a different name, no two of which agree in principle. But, my dear girl, they will find out on the great Day of Judgement that the Roman Catholic religion was the true and only means by which all mankind could rest forever in the angelic Mansions of Eternal Glory.

'This, I ask you, what will you think when you see your father and mother and alas yourself all branded as subjects of sin and told to move down to Hell, there to remain in everlasting punishment and torment, while the Roman Catholics will all be in heaven singing carols along with the other angels all day long (for there is no night there) and peeking upon you and your father and mother roasting, I say ROASTING, in an eternal region of flame?'

Helen's face darkened, a choking seemed to grasp her throat with a deadly grip. She closed her eyes, clasped her hands, her pale lips moving as she prayed in low, fervent tones tinged with that modest vehemence a distressed and anxious mind alone can master. Her prayer ended, she opened her eyes, fixing them steadily on the priest.

'You have been praying,' he observed, tightening his bereaved upper lip.

'Yes,' replied Helen. 'I was taught from infancy to pray when in doubt or dread.'

'Who taught you to pray, may I inquire?' asked Father Guerdo, his large dark eyes closed, his long black lashes reposing uncomfortably on his inflamed cheeks.

'The Reverend John Davis, D.D., of Third Ballynahinch Presbyterian Church,' Helen answered, 'who baptised me and my dear father and mother. He took the palm for offering up prayer.

'Let it be said here,' she continued, 'that no clergyman occupying a pulpit throughout the British Isles could toe the line

with him at offering up prayer. He had no rival during his day
for expounding holy scripture and stood as the brightest gem
in the crown of gospeldom. He was different from the majority
of holy-tooters who swim round the hives of humanity at the
present day. He never earned a shilling he didn't work for hard
and he instructed his beloved flock more for a shilling than the
clergy of to-day would for a hundred pounds.'

Father Guerdo observed a stern silence as she continued:

'It is patent to me, sir, that the present day expounders of
religion are merely a clique of unholy stockbrokers, acting as
financial props to safeguard their own comforts than as divine
messengers whose duty it is to gather the fallen of their flocks
endeavouring therefore to use every artifice within their combined power to draw them back to heavenly tutelage.'

Helen eyed him impatiently, lifting her little sailor hat and
satchel, readying herself to move on to some proper shelter for
the night.

'My dear girl,' said Father Guerdo, 'sit down. You must
remain where you are for the night at any rate. I have but one
bed, nevertheless, I'll gladly share it with you, as no harm can
befall you while you remain under the roof of a chosen disciple
of the Pope.'

'No, no, sir,' Helen said stubbornly. 'I have never been absent
from my dear home at Crow Cottage where I was born. I can
sleep tonight beneath one of those large trees bordering the
south of your window blind.'

Putting on her little sailor hat, Father Guerdo stood facing
the rustic ruby, then moved forward and locked the door of his
menial menage of misery.

Father Guerdo resorted to his powers of reasoning with Helen
Huddleson, pointing out the dangers that awaited her if she
persisted in resting for the night upon a bed of grass with her
head on a pillow of withered leaves. He stipulated strongly the
result of such an inhuman venture, proferring at the same time
to make her comfortable in his bed, but she steadfastly refused
to abide within the lodge. Being mistress of her own mind she
acted on its whisperings.

Father Guerdo smiled contemptuously as she looked at him pleadingly, tendering her best thanks for his timely succour, at the same time extending her hand, she bade him 'Good night'.

'No, no, my dear girl,' he remarked. 'I cannot possibly accede to your strange wish to glide out into the darkness, friendless and alone. There would be no valour left within me if I acted so callously towards one so beautiful, so charming, so sorrow-stricken, so betrayed. You, I repeat, must remain under my protection for this night, while I rest on this couch here. You, if I may say so, doubtless have a nightdress with you.'

Picking up her little satchel, he continued:

'To allow you to walk about or maybe sleep underneath the shelter of the trees in this avenue I guard so zealously I must actually forbid.'

'Oh, sir,' cried Helen, 'I must leave here at once and follow the dictates of a mind already clouded with horrid happenings. Please open the door. I saw you locked it. Then I shall move on and perchance secure proper shelter,' her face ashen, her beautifully-moulded lips, so natural in hue, trembling, her eyes smothered in tears that trickled down her cheeks in profusion.

Bearing up with a faculty of a strong resolution she stood on, though her tired frame shook visibly as if electrified or suddenly excited by a shock of dread that seemed to haunt her in a marked degree.

Father Guerdo, drawing his fringed lids over his two orbs fired with the inevitable, was blind to her entreaty, still ruminating over a wish – suppressed. He suddenly arose and clasped her tiny form, imprinting on both cheeks moist with nature's dew – a kiss. She tore herself from his grasp and stood facing him.

'Sir. Are you a betrayer of trust also? Priest though you were – and expect to be again – there isn't one trait of Christ in your action towards me. I sought your protection from one who practically stole me this day, thereby debarring me from entering the ring of holy matrimony with him I adore above all men – Maurice Munro. I unfolded my sorrowful tale to you concerning this day's horrible proceedings. I sought your shelter for a short time and when I now demand to be released from this, your present abode, instead of liberating me to shield myself from abject misery you not only debar me from vacating your home in order to evade capture but resort to assaulting me as you have done, which I resent.'

Glaring angrily at him she inquired in a somewhat raised tone of voice.

'Sir, are you going to open your door? I am more than ready to take my chance of shelter for the night outside these walls that seem to crush instead of protecting me, since you have so daringly manifested a desire to enrol me on your already smoked list of "passionists", not being whole or partly cognisant of my calibre. Suffice it is for me to say if you fail to liberate me I shall cry "Murder" until I obtain release.'

His countenance grew gloomy and ere he had time to reply Helen shivered somewhat and dropped into a chair. Just then the bell rang softly, when a low voice whispered through the key-hole.

'Saint Cecilia – from the convent.'

Helen felt that relief might now be at hand. Sitting spell-bound in the chair, Father Guerdo opened the door and admit-ted Saint Cecilia. Helen rushed past him and in haste knocked the nun down, leaving Father Guerdo to give her the rites usually administered in such circumstances.

The gate stood ajar while Helen passed out quickly through, heading for the city of Belfast to walk to Crow Cottage, a distance of some fourteen miles. Out into the little suburban streets, she strode exhaustively, looking behind at every lamp-post lest Father Guerdo might follow her and bring her back to his den of undignity.

Arriving at a small green oasis, she sat down on a stone wall. Her eye-lids fell down unconsciously, her head drooped dizzily. Her heart ticking tinily, her mind a maze of mystery, moulding into cinders of sorrow, her brain clouded with the fumes of frenzy. She was in this state when a man on horse-back stopped beside her. Pulling up he instantly dismounted, casting over her a flashlight, he at once knew he had triumphed on behalf of his master, Lord Rasberry, he being Sydney Sylvester, private valet to what should have been a great nobleman.

'Oh, sir,' Helen implored. 'I am feeling tired and sleepy. Can you bring me to some safe place where I can rest peacefully for this night before returning to my home at Crow Cottage near Ballynahinch?'

Knowing that his mission had been fulfilled and a reward certain from his master, this menial minion of lordly servitude, being of the Romish persuasion, could think of only one place in the vicinity where the now-captured girl-bride could be safely secreted – the convent of St Iscariot, where Father Guerdo now felt fired by the blood of defeat of Helen Huddleson's swift exit.

The veins of his face and neck expressed the anger he silently did his utmost to conceal from the alert Saint Cecilia, whose colour came and went, settling into a spot of cardinal on both her cheeks as she stood staring at the priest with a pair of deep blue eyes that strongly exhibited the jealousy of an army at losing a battle. Addressing Father Guerdo she said:

'Have a seat, please,' at the same time placing a chair beside where he stood apparently in great unrest, but he refused the proferred offer, pushing the chair from him without uttering a word.

Saint Cecilia, who seemed charged with pique, instantly arose and banging the door after her returned to the convent in a very melancholy manner.

Father Guerdo's countenance at this stage was one mass of furrowed flame. He seemed as he stood trembling in poplar-leaf fashion to impress one his reason had gone, his nerves being disobedient to nature ostensibly, while his eyes kept rolling restlessly as if he were in deep distress.

After some time, a gentle knock being heard, he approached the door and a low, soft voice whispered:

'Father Guerdo. It is Saint Maria. Be not afraid.'

Immediately the lodge door was thrown open when Saint Maria entered, Lord Rasberry following her closely and, gently closing the door, reached forth his hand and shook that of Father Guerdo warmly.

'My lord,' said the priest. 'Your loved one has gone I know not whither. I feel your reason for visiting me at this hour is your great and undying love for this beautiful and chaste creation of

Providence. Ah, my Lord, I pity you from my heart and, if I can render you any assistance, I am at your service.'

Signing dumb, Lord Rasberry waited for Father Guerdo to continue.

'Yes, my Lord, priest though I am and sworn against matrimony, as are all righteous servants of the ruling head of our church – the Pope, I must express to you my views on such a law as patronized by St Paul of apostolic fame and faith. I, my Lord, have had the pleasure to behold tonight the most perfect specimen of the work of the Creator it has ever been mine to witness. Helen Huddleson is a miraculous gem in nature's crown, born to adorn the noblest position in which the proudest in Britain would place her, born, my Lord, to display a dignity built by purity of mind, cleanliness which so few possess in this country of ours.'

Lord Rasberry seemed visibly affected by this torrent of praise, this tribute of truth trickled from the tongue of a renegade priest. A grateful smile sunning his features, Lord Rasberry spake:

'Tell me, please, where I shall find my wife? Helen, my loved one, my own. O, where?'

Saint Maria, who at this iota of time, felt deeply interested, arose and bowed lowly to Lord Rasberry.

'My Lord,' she nervously began, 'we admitted on horseback an hour ago within our holy convent, quite adjacent and within these grounds that surround us, one young yet beautiful girl, who gave the name of Helen to our Superioress, Mother Senate, who was feeling dreadfully fatigued and in a state of collapse, certainly requiring rest for the night. She has been put to bed and I firmly believe this is she whom you seek.'

'She is my wife,' cried Lord Rasberry, growing crimson. 'Please convey me to her.'

'No, no,' expostulated Saint Maria. 'She must rest. The man, Sydney Sylvester, a disciple of Rome, who brought her to us, is keeping guard outside, since nobody of masculine gender is permitted within our walls. I have spoken.'

Feeling like a second trump in opposition to this nunnish authority, Lord Rasberry replied:

'Instruct my valet, please, to bring my coach to this sacred spot. Let my rustic wife rest. Then with the assistance of this good priest, I shall come to claim her as my own.'

When Saint Maria had left them, Father Guerdo related as much as he wished to remember of the day's proceedings to Lord Rasberry who, when ended, became deluged in tears, then pulling the ancestral ring, the omen of disaster, from his finger placed it on that of Father Guerdo, wishing him to have many happy years ahead to wear such an historic gem that had graced the finger originally of a queen's consort.

Taking Father Guerdo's hand, on which this tribute shone dully, Lord Rasberry alluded to his position in life being blanked by one in power, at the same time making strict inquiries concerning the means of the priest. Straightening himself to attract attention, Father Guerdo replied with a blister of anger on his tongue.

'My noble Lord, my means hang on the lowest rung of the monetary ladder.'

'Speak on,' commanded Lord Rasberry.

'I have but a bare pittance,' said Father Guerdo. 'See this shabby garb Lazarus would have spurned and I am supposed to look decent in for the past seven years. It is as green as the fields of Ireland and as bare of colour as the top-coat of a tramp. I feel heart-sick at this degraded mode of servitude and would gladly court the whistle of change,' wiping his sallow brow on which rested some of sweat's cold crystals.

Placing his hand on Father Guerdo's shoulder, Lord Rasberry exclaimed:

'Arise and come with me.'

Father Guerdo's visage vibrated vastly at the Christlike command of the Christless lord. As soon as all his features sat once more within their varied beds, he glared with glee at Lord Rasberry, arose instantly and packed his 'alls' into a long narrow reticule, a dear old friend had presented him with when a youth, being the handiwork of his mother.

Then, settling down, he drew from a small bureau a sheet of paper which had mourned his fate since he was silenced from the fold of priestdom, wrote a page in haste to Saint Cecilia and

Saint Maria, dropping a tear of evident joy upon both nuns and, enveloping it hastily with a gummy lip, placed it upon a little walnut table, hexagonal in shape, bidding adieu forever to the coop he naturally loathed.

Taking his reticule in one hand and a blackthorn stick in the other, Lord Rasberry bade the penitent priest follow him, then dragging the door after them, creating a bang hard to twin, both left the lodge together, wending their way to the convent where rested restlessly the queen of both their hearts.

Rudyard Kipling

The Last Term

It was within a few days of the holidays, the term-end examinations, and, more important still, the issue of the College paper which Beetle edited. He had been cajoled into that office by the blandishments of Stalky and M'Turk and the extreme rigour of study law. Once installed, he discovered, as others have done before him, that his duty was to do the work while his friends criticized. Stalky christened it the *Swillingford Patriot*, in pious memory of Sponge – and M'Turk compared the output unfavourably with Ruskin and De Quincey. Only the Head took an interest in the publication, and his methods were peculiar. He gave Beetle the run of his brown-bound, tobacco-scented library; prohibiting nothing, recommending nothing. There Beetle found a fat armchair, a silver inkstand, and unlimited pens and paper. There were scores and scores of ancient dramatists; there were Hakluyt, his voyages; French translations of Muscovite authors called Pushkin and Lermontoff, little tales of a heady and bewildering nature, interspersed with unusual songs – Peacock was that writer's name; there was Borrow's *Lavengro;* an odd theme, purporting to be a translation of something called a 'Rubáiyát', which the Head said was a poem not yet come to its own; there were hundreds of volumes of verse – Crashaw; Dryden; Alexander Smith; L.E.L.; Lydia Sigourney; Fletcher and a purple island; Donne; Marlowe's *Faust*; and – this made M'Turk (to whom Beetle conveyed it) sheer drunk for three days – Ossian: *The Earthly Paradise*; *Atalanta in Calydon*; and Rossetti – to name only a few. Then the Head, drifting in under pretence of playing censor to the paper, would read here a verse and here another of these poets; opening up avenues. And, slow breathing, with half-shut eyes above his cigar, would he speak of great men living, and journals, long dead, founded in their riotous youth; of years when all the planets were little new-lit stars trying to find their places in the uncaring void, and he, the Head, knew them as young men know one another. So the regular work went to the dogs, Beetle being full of other matters and metres, hoarded in secret and only told to M'Turk of an afternoon, on the sands, walking high and disposedly round the wreck of the Armada galleon, shouting and declaiming against the long-ridged seas.

Thanks in large part to their house-master's experienced distrust, the three for three consecutive terms had been passed over for promotion to the rank of prefect – an office that went by merit, and carried with it the honour of the ground-ash, and liberty, under restrictions, to use it.

'*But*,' said Stalky, 'come to think of it, we've done more giddy jesting with the Sixth since we've been passed over than anyone else in the last seven years.'

He touched his neck proudly. It was encircled by the stiffest of stick-up collars, which custom decreed could be worn only by the Sixth. And the Sixth saw those collars and said no word. 'Pussy' Abanazar or Dick Four of a year ago would have seen them discarded in five minutes or ... But the Sixth of that term was made up mostly of young but brilliantly clever boys, pets of the house-masters, too anxious for their dignity to care to come to open odds with the resourceful three. So they crammed their caps at the extreme back of their heads, instead of a trifle over one eye as the Fifth should, and rejoiced in patent-leather boots on week-days, and marvellous made-up ties on Sundays – no man rebuking. M'Turk was going up for Cooper's Hill, and Stalky for Sandhurst, in the spring; and the Head had told them both that, unless they absolutely collapsed during the holidays, they were safe. As a trainer of colts, the Head seldom erred in an estimate of form.

He had taken Beetle aside that day and given him much good advice, not one word of which did Beetle remember when he dashed up to the study, white with excitement, and poured out the wondrous tale. It demanded a great belief.

'You begin on a hundred a year?' said M'Turk unsympathetically. 'Rot!'

'And my passage out! It's all settled. The Head says he's been breaking me in for this for ever so long, and I never knew – I never knew. One don't begin with writing straight off, y'know. Begin by filling in telegrams and cutting things out o' papers with scissors.'

'Oh. Scissors! What an ungodly mess you'll make of it,' said Stalky. 'But, anyhow, this will be your last term, too. Seven years, my dearly beloved 'earers – though not prefects.'

'Not half bad years, either,' said M'Turk. 'I shall be sorry to leave the old Coll.; shan't you?'

They looked out over the sea creaming along the Pebble Ridge in the clear winter light. 'Wonder where we shall all be this time next year?' said Stalky absently.

'This time five years,' said M'Turk.

'Oh,' said Beetle, 'my leavin's between ourselves. The Head hasn't told anyone. I know he hasn't, because Prout grunted at me today that if I were more reasonable – yah! – I might be a prefect next term. I suppose he's hard up for his prefects.'

'Let's finish up with a row with the Sixth,' suggested M'Turk.

'Dirty little schoolboys!' said Stalky, who already saw himself a Sandhurst cadet. 'What's the use?'

'Moral effect,' quoth M'Turk. 'Leave an imperishable tradition, and all the rest of it.'

'Better go into Bideford an' pay up our debts,' said Stalky. 'I've got three quid out of my father – *ad hoc*. Don't owe more than thirty bob, either. Cut along, Beetle, and ask the Head for leave. Say you want to correct the *Swillingford Patriot*.'

'Well, I do,' said Beetle. 'It'll be my last issue, and I'd like it to look decent. I'll catch him before he goes to his lunch.'

Ten minutes later they wheeled out in line, by grace released from five o'clock call-over, and all the afternoon lay before them. So also unluckily did King, who never passed without witticisms. But brigades of Kings could not have ruffled Beetle that day.

'Aha! Enjoying the study of light literature, my friends,' said

15

he, rubbing his hands. 'Common mathematics are not for such soaring minds as yours, are they?'

('One hundred a year,' thought Beetle, smiling into vacancy.)

'Our open incompetence takes refuge in the flowery paths of inaccurate fiction. But a day of reckoning approaches, Beetle mine. I myself have prepared a few trifling foolish questions in Latin prose which can hardly be evaded even by your practised arts of deception. Ye-es, Latin prose. I think, if I may say so – but we shall see when the papers are set – "Ulpian serves *your* need." "Aha! *Elucescebat*, quoth our friend." We shall see! We shall see!'

Still no sign from Beetle. He was on a steamer, his passage paid into the wide and wonderful world – a thousand leagues beyond Lundy Island.

King dropped him with a snarl.

'He doesn't know. He'll go on correctin' exercises an' jawin' an' showin' off before the little boys next term – and next.' Beetle hurried after his companions up the steep path of the furze-clad hill behind the College.

They were throwing pebbles on the top of the gasometer, and the grimy gas-man in charge bade them desist. They watched him oil a turncock sunk in the ground between two furze-bushes.

'Cokey, what's that for?' said Stalky.

'To turn the gas on to the kitchens,' said Cokey. 'If so be I didn't turn her on, yeou young gen'lemen 'ud be larnin' your book by candlelight.'

'Um!' said Stalky, and was silent for at least a minute.

'Hallo! Where are you chaps going?'

A bend of the lane brought them face to face with Tulke, senior prefect of King's house – a smallish, white-haired boy, of the type that must be promoted on account of its intellect, and ever afterwards appeals to the Head to support its authority when zeal has outrun discretion.

The three took no sort of notice. They were on lawful pass. Tulke repeated his question hotly, for he had suffered many slights from Number Five study, and fancied that he had at last caught them tripping.

'What the devil is that to you?' Stalky replied, with his sweetest smile.

'Look here, I'm not goin' – I'm not goin' to be sworn at by the Fifth!' sputtered Tulke.

'Then cut along and call a prefects' meeting,' said M'Turk, knowing Tulke's weakness.

The prefect became inarticulate with rage.

'Mustn't yell at the Fifth that way,' said Stalky. 'It's vile bad form.'

'Cough it up, ducky!' M'Turk said calmly.

'I – I want to know what you chaps are doing out of bounds?' This with an important flourish of his ground-ash.

'Ah!' said Stalky. 'Now we're gettin' at it. Why didn't you ask that before?'

'Well, I ask it now. What are you doing?'

'We're admiring you, Tulke,' said Stalky. 'We think you're no end of a fine chap, don't we?'

'We do! We do!' A dog-cart with some girls in it swept round the corner, and Stalky promptly kneeled before Tulke in the attitude of prayer; so Tulke turned a colour.

'I've reason to believe –' he began.

'Oyez! Oyez! Oyez!' shouted Beetle, after the manner of Bideford's town-crier, 'Tulke has reason to believe! Three cheers for Tulke!'

They were given. 'It's all our giddy admiration,' said Stalky. 'You know how we love you, Tulke. We love you so much we think you ought to go home and die. You're too good to live, Tulke.'

'Yes,' said M'Turk. '*Do* oblige us by dyin'. Think how lovely you'd look stuffed!'

Tulke swept up the road with an unpleasant glare in his eye.

'That means a prefects' meeting – sure pop,' said Stalky. 'Honour of the Sixth involved, and all the rest of it. Tulke'll write notes all this afternoon, and Carson will call us up after tea. They daren't overlook that.'

'Bet you a bob he follows us!' said M'Turk. 'He's King's pet, and it's scalps to both of 'em if we're caught out. We must be virtuous.'

'Then I move we go to Mother Yeo's for a last gorge. We owe her about ten bob, and Mary'll weep sore when she knows we're leaving,' said Beetle.

'She gave me an awful wipe on the head last time – Mary,' said Stalky.

'She does if you don't duck,' said M'Turk. 'But she generally kisses one back. Let's try Mother Yeo.'

They sought a little bottle-windowed half-dairy, half-restaurant, a dark-browed, two-hundred-year-old house, at the head of a narrow side street. They had patronized it from the days of their fagdom, and were very much friends at home.

'We've come to pay our debts, mother,' said Stalky, sliding his arm round the fifty-six-inch waist of the mistress of the establishment. 'To pay our debts and say goodbye – and – and we're awf'ly hungry.'

'Aie!' said Mother Yeo, 'makkin' love to me! I'm shaamed of 'ee.'

'Rackon us wouldn't du no such thing if Mary was here,' said M'Turk, lapsing into the broad North Devon that the boys used on their campaigns.

'Who'm takin' my name in vain?' The inner door opened, and Mary, fair-haired, blue-eyed, and apple-cheeked, entered with a bowl of cream in her hands. M'Turk kissed her. Beetle followed suit, with exemplary calm. Both boys were promptly cuffed.

'Niver kiss the maid when 'e can kiss the mistress,' said Stalky, shamelessly winking at Mother Yeo, as he investigated a shelf of jams.

'Glad to see one of 'ee don't want his head slapped no more?' said Mary invitingly, in that direction.

'Neu! Reckon I can get 'em give me,' said Stalky, his back turned.

'Not by me – yeou little masterpiece!'

'Niver asked 'ee. There's maids to Northam. Yiss – an' Appledore.' An unreproducible sniff, half contempt, half reminiscence, rounded the retort.

'Aie! Yeou won't niver come to no good end. Whutt be 'baout, smellin' the cream?'

' 'Tees bad,' said Stalky. 'Zmell 'un.'

Incautiously Mary did as she was bid.

'Bidevoor kiss.'

'Niver amiss,' said Stalky, taking it without injury.

'Yeou – yeou – yeou —' Mary began, bubbling with mirth.

'They'm better to Northam – more rich, laike – an' us gets them give back again,' he said, while M'Turk solemnly waltzed Mother Yeo out of breath, and Beetle told Mary the sad news, as they sat down to clotted cream, jam, and hot bread.

'Yiss. Yeou'll niver zee us no more, Mary. We'm goin' to be passons an' missioners.'

'Steady the Buffs!' said M'Turk, looking through the blind. 'Tulke has followed us. He's comin' up the street now.'

'They've niver put us out o' bounds,' said Mother Yeo. 'Bide yeou still, my little dearrs.' She rolled into the inner room to make the score.

'Mary,' said Stalky suddenly, with tragic intensity. 'Do 'ee lov' me, Mary?'

'Iss – fai! Talled 'ee zo since yeou was zo high!' the damsel replied.

'Zee 'un comin' up street, then?' Stalky pointed to the unconscious Tulke. 'He've niver been kissed by no sort or manner o' maid in hees borned laife, Mary. Oh, 'tees shaamful!'

'Whutt's to do with me? 'Twill come to 'un in the way o' nature, I rackon.' She nodded her head sagaciously. 'You niver want me to kiss un – sure-*ly?*'

'Give 'ee half-a-crown if 'ee will,' said Stalky, exhibiting the coin.

Half-a-crown was much to Mary Yeo, and a jest was more; but —

'Yeu'm afraid,' said M'Turk, at the psychological moment.

'Aie!' Beetle echoed, knowing her weak point. 'There's not a maid to Northam 'ud think twice. An' yeou such a fine maid, tu!'

M'Turk planted one foot firmly against the inner door lest Mother Yeo should return inopportunely, for Mary's face was set. It was then that Tulke found his way blocked by a tall daughter of Devon – that county of easy kisses, the pleasantest under the sun. He dodged aside politely. She reflected a moment, and laid a vast hand upon his shoulder.

'Wher be 'ee gwaine tu, my dearr?' said she.

Over the handkerchief he had crammed into his mouth Stalky could see the boy turn scarlet.

'Gie I a kiss! Don't they larn 'ee manners to College?'

Tulke gasped and wheeled. Solemnly and conscientiously Mary kissed him twice, and the luckless prefect fled.

She stepped into the shop, her eyes full of simple wonder.

'Kissed 'un?' said Stalky, handing over the money.

'Iss, fai! But, oh, my little body, *he*'m no Colleger. Zeemed tu-minded to cry, laike.'

'Well, we won't. You couldn't make us cry that way,' said M'Turk. 'Try.'

Whereupon Mary cuffed them all round.

As they went out with tingling ears, said Stalky generally, 'Don't think there'll be much of a prefects' meeting.'

'Won't there, just!' said Beetle. 'Look here. If he kissed her – which is our tack – he is a cynically immoral hog, and his conduct is blatant indecency. *Confer orationes Regis furiosissimi* when he collared me readin' "Don Juan".'

'Course he kissed her,' said M'Turk. 'In the middle of the street. With his house-cap on!'

'Time, 3.57 p.m. Make a note o' that. What d'you mean, Beetle?' said Stalky.

'Well! He's a truthful little beast. He may say he was kissed.'

'And then?'

'Why, then!' Beetle capered at the mere thought of it. 'Don't you see? The corollary to the giddy proposition is that the Sixth can't protect 'emselves from outrages an' ravishin's. Want nursemaids to look after 'em! We've only got to whisper that to the Coll. Jam for the Sixth! Jam for us! Either way it's jammy!'

'By Gum!' said Stalky. 'Our last term's endin' well. Now you cut along an' finish up your old rag, and Turkey and me will help. We'll go in the back way. No need to bother Randall.'

'Don't play the giddy garden-goat, then?' Beetle knew what help meant, though he was by no means averse to showing his importance before his allies. The little loft behind Randall's printing-office was his own territory, where he saw himself already controlling the *Times*. Here, under the guidance of the inky apprentice, he had learned to find his way more or less circuitously about the case, and considered himself an expert compositor.

The school paper in its locked formes lay on a stone-topped table, a proof by the side; but not for worlds would Beetle have corrected from the mere proof. With a mallet and a pair of tweezers, he knocked out mysterious wedges of wood that released the forme, picked a letter here and inserted a letter there, reading as he went along and stopping much to chuckle over his own contributions.

'You won't show off like that,' said M'Turk, 'when you've got to do it for your living. Upside down and backwards, isn't it? Let's see if I can read it.'

'Get out!' said Beetle. 'Go and read those formes in the rack there, if you think you know so much.'

'Formes in a rack! What's that? Don't be so beastly professional.'

M'Turk drew off with Stalky to prowl about the office. They left little unturned.

'Come here a shake, Beetle. What's this thing?' said Stalky, in a few minutes. 'Looks familiar.'

Said Beetle, after a glance: 'It's King's Latin prose exam. paper. *In – In Verrem: actio prima.* What a lark!'

'Think o' the pure-souled, high-minded boys who'd give their eyes for a squint at it!' said M'Turk.

'No, Willie dear,' said Stalky; 'that would be wrong and painful to our kind teachers. You wouldn't crib, Willie, would you?'

'Can't read the beastly stuff, anyhow,' was the reply. 'Besides, we're leavin' at the end o' the term, so it makes no difference to us.'

''Member what the Considerate Bloomer did to Spraggon's account of the Puffin'ton Hounds? We must sugar Mr King's milk for him,' said Stalky, all lighted from within by a devilish joy. 'Let's see what Beetle can do with those forceps he's so proud of.'

' 'Don't see how you can make Latin prose much more cock-eye than it is, but we'll try,' said Beetle, transposing an *aliud* and *Asiæ* from two sentences. 'Let's see! We'll put that full-stop a little further on, and begin the sentence with the next capital. Hurrah! Here's three lines that can move up all in a lump.'

'"One of those scientific rests for which this eminent hunts-man is so justly celebrated."' Stalky knew the Puffington run by heart.

'Hold on! Here's a *vol – voluntate quidnam* all by itself,' said M'Turk.

'I'll attend to her in a shake. *Quidnam* goes after *Dolabella*.'

'Good old Dolabella,' murmured Stalky. 'Don't break him. Vile prose Cicero wrote, didn't he? He ought to be grateful for —'

'Hallo!' said M'Turk, over another forme. 'What price a giddy ode? *Qui – quis* – oh, it's *Quis multa gracilis*, o' course.'

'Bring it along. We've sugared the milk here,' said Stalky, after a few minutes' zealous toil. 'Never thrash your hounds unnecessarily.'

'*Quis munditiis?* I swear that's not bad,' began Beetle, plying the tweezers. 'Don't that interrogation look pretty? *Heu quoties fidem!* That sounds as if the chap were anxious an' excited. *Cui flavam religas in rosa* – Whose flavour is relegated to a rose. *Mutatosque Deos flebit in antro*.'

'Mute gods weepin' in a cave,' suggested Stalky. ''Pon my Sam, Horace needs as much lookin' after as – Tulke.'

They edited him faithfully till it was too dark to see.

'"Aha! *Elucescebat*, quoth our friend." Ulpian serves my need, does it? If King can make anything out of *that*, I'm a blue-eyed squatteroo,' said Beetle, as they slid out of the loft window into a back alley of old acquaintance and started on a three-mile trot to the College. But the revision of the classics had detained them over long. They halted, blown and breathless, in the furze at the back of the gasometer, the College lights twinkling below, ten minutes at least late for tea and lock-up.

'It's no good,' puffed M'Turk. 'Bet a bob Foxy is waiting for defaulters under the lamp by the Fives Court. It's a nuisance, too, because the Head gave us long leave, and one doesn't like to break it.'

'"Let me now from the bonded ware'ouse of my knowledge,"' began Stalky.

'Oh, rot! Don't Jorrock. Can we make a run for it?' snapped M'Turk.

'"Bishops' boots Mr Radcliffe also condemned, an' spoke 'ighly in favour of tops cleaned with champagne an' abricot jam." Where's that thing Cokey was twiddlin' this afternoon?'

They heard him groping in the wet, and presently beheld a great miracle. The lights of the Coastguard cottages near the sea went out; the brilliantly illuminated windows of the Golf Club disappeared, and were followed by the frontages of the two hotels. Scattered villas dulled, twinkled, and vanished. Last of all, the College lights died also. They were left in the pitchy darkness of a windy winter's night.

'"Blister my kidneys. It *is* a frost. The dahlias are dead!"' said Stalky. 'Bunk!'

They squattered through the dripping gorse as the College hummed like an angry hive and the dining-rooms chorussed, 'Gas! gas! gas!' till they came to the edge of the sunk path that divided them from their study. Dropping that ha-ha like bullets, and rebounding like boys, they dashed to their study, in less than two minutes had changed into dry trousers and coat, and, ostentatiously slippered, joined the mob in the dining-hall, which resembled the storm-centre of a South American revolution.

'"Hellish dark and smells of cheese."' Stalky elbowed his way into the press, howling lustily for gas. 'Cokey must have gone for a walk. Foxy'll have to find him.'

Prout, as the nearest house-master, was trying to restore order, for rude boys were flicking butter-pats across chaos, and M'Turk had turned on the fags' tea-urn, so that many were parboiled and wept with an unfeigned dolor. The Fourth and Upper Third broke into the school song, the '*Vive la Compagnie*', to the accompaniment of drumming knife-handles; and the junior forms shrilled bat-like shrieks and raided one another's victuals. Two hundred and fifty boys in high condition, seeking for more light, are truly earnest inquirers.

When a most vile smell of gas told them that supplies had been renewed, Stalky, waistcoat unbuttoned, sat gorgedly over what might have been his fourth cup of tea. 'And that's all right,' he said. 'Hallo! 'Ere's Pomponius Ego!'

It was Carson, the head of the school, a simple, straight-minded soul, and a pillar of the First Fifteen, who crossed over from the prefects' table and in a husky, official voice invited the three to attend in his study in half an hour.

'Prefects' meetin'! Prefects' meetin'!' hissed the tables, and they imitated barbarically the actions and effects of the ground-ash.

'How are we goin' to jest with 'em?' said Stalky, turning half-face to Beetle. 'It's your play this time!'

'Look here,' was the answer, 'all I want you to do is not to laugh. I'm goin' to take charge o' young Tulke's immorality – *à la* King, and it's goin' to be serious. If you can't help laughin' don't look at me, or I'll go pop.'

'I see. All right,' said Stalky.

M'Turk's lank frame stiffened in every muscle and his eyelids dropped half over his eyes. That last was a war-signal.

The eight or nine seniors, their faces very set and sober, were ranged in chairs round Carson's severely Philistine study. Tulke was not popular among them, and a few who had had experience of Stalky & Company doubted that he might, perhaps, have made an ass of himself. But the dignity of the Sixth was to be upheld. So Carson began hurriedly:

'Look here, you chaps, I've – we've sent for you to tell you you're a good deal too cheeky to the Sixth – have been for some time – and – and we've stood about as much as we're goin' to, and it seems you've been cursin' and swearin' at Tulke on the Bideford road this afternoon, and we're goin' to show you you can't do it. That's all.'

'Well, that's awfully good of you,' said Stalky, 'but we happen to have a few rights of our own, too. You can't, just because you happen to be made prefects, haul up seniors and jaw 'em on spec, like a house-master. *We* aren't fags, Carson. This kind of thing may do for Davies tertius, but it won't do for us.'

'It's only old Prout's lunacy that we weren't prefects long ago. You know that,' said M'Turk. 'You haven't any tact.'

'Hold on,' said Beetle. 'A prefects' meetin' has to be reported to the Head. I want to know if the Head backs Tulke in this business?'

'Well – well, it isn't exactly a prefects' meeting,' said Carson. 'We only called you in to warn you.'

'But all the prefects are here,' Beetle insisted. 'Where's the difference?'

'My Gum!' said Stalky. 'Do you mean to say you've just called us in for a jaw – after comin' to us before the whole school at tea an' givin' 'em the impression it was a prefects' meeting? 'Pon my Sam, Carson, you'll get into trouble, you will.'

'Hole-an'-corner business – hole-an'-corner business,' said M'Turk, wagging his head. 'Beastly suspicious.'

The Sixth looked at each other uneasily. Tulke had called three prefects' meetings in two terms, till the Head had informed the Sixth that they were expected to maintain discipline without the recurrent menace of his authority. Now, it seemed that they had made a blunder at the outset, but any right-minded boy would have sunk the legality and been properly impressed by the Court. Beetle's protest was distinct 'cheek'.

'Well, you chaps deserve a lickin',' cried one Naughten incautiously. Then was Beetle filled with a noble inspiration.

'For interferin' with Tulke's amours, eh?' Tulke turned a rich sloe colour. 'Oh no, you don't!' Beetle went on. 'You've had your innings. We've been sent up for cursing and swearing at you, and we're going to be let off with a warning! *Are* we? Now then, you're going to catch it.'

'I – I – I —' Tulke began. 'Don't let that young devil start jawing.'

'If you've anything to say, you must say it decently,' said Carson.

'Decently? I will. Now look here. When we went into Bideford we met this ornament of the Sixth – is that decent enough? – hanging about on the road with a nasty look in his eye. We didn't know *then* why he was so anxious to stop us, *but* at five minutes to four, when we were in Yeo's shop, we saw Tulke *in* broad daylight, *with* his house-cap on, kissin' an' huggin' a woman *on* the pavement. Is that decent enough for you?'

'I didn't – I wasn't.'

'We saw you!' said Beetle. 'And now – I'll be decent, Carson – you sneak back with her kisses' (not for nothing had Beetle perused the later poets) 'hot on your lips and call prefects' meetings, which aren't prefects' meetings, to uphold the honour of the Sixth.' A new and heaven-cleft path opened before him that instant. 'And how do we know,' he shouted – 'how do we know how many of the Sixth are mixed up in this abominable affair?'

'Yes, that's what we want to know,' said M'Turk, with simple dignity.

'We meant to come to you about it quietly, Carson, but you *would* have the meeting,' said Stalky sympathetically.

The Sixth were too taken aback to reply. So, carefully modelling his rhetoric on King, Beetle followed up the attack, surpassing and surprising himself.

'It – it isn't so much the cynical immorality of the biznai, as the blatant indecency of it, that's so awful. As far as we can see, it's impossible for us to go into Bideford without runnin' up against some prefect's unwholesome amours. There's nothing to snigger over, Naughten. *I* don't pretend to know much about these things – but it seems to me a chap must be pretty far dead in sin' (that was a quotation from the school Chaplain) 'when he takes to embracing his paramours' (that was Hakluyt) 'before all the city' (a reminiscence of Milton). 'He might at least have the decency – you're authorities on decency, I believe – to wait till dark. But he didn't. You didn't! Oh, Tulke. You – you incontinent little animal!'

'Here, shut up a minute. What's all this about, Tulke?' said Carson.

'I – look here. I'm awfully sorry. I never thought Beetle would take this line.'

'Because – you've – no decency – you – thought – I hadn't,' cried Beetle all in one breath.

'Tried to cover it all up with a conspiracy, did you?' said Stalky.

'Direct insult to all three of us,' said M'Turk. 'A most filthy mind you have, Tulke.'

'I'll shove you fellows outside the door if you go on like this,' said Carson angrily.

'That proves it's a conspiracy,' said Stalky, with the air of a virgin martyr.

'I – I was goin' along the street – I swear I was,' cried Tulke, 'and – and I'm awfully sorry about it – a woman came up and kissed me. I swear I didn't kiss her.'

There was a pause, filled by Stalky's long, liquid whistle of contempt, amazement, and derision.

'On my honour,' gulped the persecuted one. 'Oh, do stop him jawing.'

'Very good,' M'Turk interjected. 'We are compelled, of course, to accept your statement.'

'Confound it!' roared Naughten. 'You aren't head-prefect here, M'Turk.'

'Oh, well,' returned the Irishman, 'you know Tulke better than we do. I am only speaking for ourselves. *We* accept Tulke's word. But all I can say is that if I'd been collared in a similarly disgustin' situation, and had offered the same explanation Tulke has, I – I wonder what you'd have said. However, it seems on Tulke's word of honour —'

'And Tulkus – beg pardon – *kiss*, of course – Tulkiss is an honourable man,' put in Stalky.

' — that the Sixth can't protect 'emselves from bein' kissed when they go for a walk!' cried Beetle, taking up the running with a rush. 'Sweet business, isn't it? Cheerful thing to tell the fags, ain't it? We aren't prefects, of course, but we aren't kissed very much. Don't think that sort of thing ever enters our heads; does it, Stalky?'

'Oh no!' said Stalky, turning aside to hide his emotions. M'Turk's face merely expressed lofty contempt and a little weariness.

'Well, you seem to know a lot about it,' interposed a prefect.

'Can't help it – when you chaps shove it under our noses.'

Beetle dropped into a drawling parody of King's most biting colloquial style – the gentle rain after the thunderstorm. 'Well, it's all very sufficiently vile and disgraceful, isn't it? I don't know who comes out of it worst: Tulke, who happens to have been caught; or the other fellows who haven't. And we' – here he wheeled fiercely on the other two – 'we've got to stand up and be jawed by them because we've disturbed their intrigues.'

'Hang it! I only wanted to give you a word of warning,' said Carson, thereby handing himself bound to the enemy.

'Warn? You?' This with the air of one who finds loathsome gifts in his locker. 'Carson, *would* you be good enough to tell us what conceivable thing there is that you are entitled to warn us about after this exposure? Warn? Oh, it's a little too much! Let's go somewhere where it's clean.'

The door banged behind their outraged innocence.

'Oh, Beetle! Beetle! Beetle! Golden Beetle!' sobbed Stalky, hurling himself on Beetle's panting bosom as soon as they reached the study. 'However did you do it?'

'Dear-r man!' said M'Turk, embracing Beetle's head with both arms, while he swayed it to and fro on the neck, in time to this ancient burden –

> *'Pretty lips – sweeter than – cherry or plum,*
> *Always look – jolly and – never look glum;*
> *Seem to say – Come away. Kissy! – come, come!*
> *Yummy-yum! Yummy-yum! Yummy-yum-yum!'*

'Look out. You'll smash my gig-lamps,' puffed Beetle, emerging. 'Wasn't it glorious? Didn't I "Eric" 'em splendidly? Did you spot my cribs from King? Oh, blow!' His countenance clouded. 'There's one adjective I didn't use – obscene. Don't know how I forgot that. It's one of King's pet ones, too.'

'Never mind. They'll be sendin' ambassadors round in half a shake to beg us not to tell the school. It's a deuced serious business for them,' said M'Turk. 'Poor Sixth – poor old Sixth!'

'Immoral young rips,' Stalky snorted. 'What an example to pure-souled boys like you and me!'

And the Sixth in Carson's study stood aghast, glowering at Tulke, who was on the edge of tears.

'Well,' said the head-prefect acidly. 'You've made a pretty average ghastly mess of it, Tulke.'

'Why – why didn't you lick that young devil Beetle before he began jawing?' Tulke wailed.

'I knew there'd be a row,' said a prefect of Prout's house. 'But you would insist on the meeting, Tulke.'

'Yes, and a fat lot of good it's done us,' said Naughten. 'They come in here and jaw our heads off when we ought to be jawin' them. Beetle talks to us as if we were a lot of blackguards and – and all that. And when they've hung us up to dry, they go out and slam the door like a house-master. All your fault, Tulke.'

'But I didn't kiss her.'

'You ass! If you'd said you *had* and stuck to it, it would have been ten times better than what you did,' Naughten retorted. 'Now they'll tell the whole school – and Beetle'll make up a lot of beastly rhymes and nick-names.'

'But, hang it, she kissed me!' Outside his work, Tulke's mind moved slowly.

'I'm not thinking of you. I'm thinking of us. I'll go up to their study and see if I can make 'em keep quiet!'

'Tulke's awf'ly cut up about this business,' Naughten began, ingratiatingly, when he found Beetle.

'Who's kissed him this time?'

'— and I've come to ask you chaps, and especially you, Beetle, not to let the thing be known all over the school. Of course, fellows as senior as you are can easily see why.'

'Um!' said Beetle, with the cold reluctance of one who faces an unpleasant public duty. 'I suppose I must go and talk to the Sixth again.'

'Not the least need, my dear chap, I assure you,' said Naughten hastily. 'I'll take any message you care to send.'

But the chance of supplying the missing adjective was too tempting. So Naughten returned to that still undissolved meeting, Beetle, white, icy, and aloof, at his heels.

'There seems,' he began, with laboriously crisp articulation, 'there seems to be a certain amount of uneasiness among you as to the steps we may think fit to take in regard to this last revelation of the – ah – obscene. If it is any consolation to you to know that we have decided – for the honour of the school, you understand – to keep our mouths shut as to these – ah – obscenities, you – ah – have it.'

He wheeled, his head among the stars, and strode statelily back to his study, where Stalky and M'Turk lay side by side upon the table wiping their tearful eyes – too weak to move.

The Latin prose paper was a success beyond their wildest dreams. Stalky and M'Turk were, of course, out of all examinations (they did extra-tuition with the Head), but Beetle attended with zeal.

'This, I presume, is a par-ergon on your part,' said King, as he dealt out the papers. 'One final exhibition ere you are translated to loftier spheres? A last attack on the classics? It seems to confound you already.'

Beetle studied the print with knit brows. 'I can't make head or tail of it,' he murmured. 'What does it mean?'

'No, no!' said King, with scholastic coquetry. 'We depend upon you to give us the meaning. This is an examination, Beetle mine, not a guessing-competition. You will find your associates have no difficulty in —'

Tulke left his place and laid the paper on the desk. King looked, read, and turned a ghastly green.

'Stalky's missing a heap,' thought Beetle. 'Wonder how King'll get out of it?'

'There seems,' King began with a gulp, 'a certain modicum of truth in our Beetle's remark. I am – er – inclined to believe that the worthy Randall must have dropped this in forme – if you know what that means. Beetle, you purport to be an editor. Perhaps you can enlighten the form as to formes.'

'What, sir? Whose form? I don't see that there's any verb in this sentence at all, an' – an' – the Ode is all different, somehow.'

'I was about to say, before you volunteered your criticism, that an accident must have befallen the paper in type, and that the printer reset it by the light of nature. No –' he held the thing at arm's length – 'our Randall is not an authority on Cicero or Horace.'

'Rather mean to shove it off on Randall,' whispered Beetle to his neighbour. 'King must ha' been as screwed as an owl when he wrote it out.'

'But we can amend the error by dictating it.'

'No, sir.' The answer came pat from a dozen throats at once. 'That cuts the time for the exam. Only two hours allowed, sir. 'Tisn't fair. It's a printed-paper exam. How're we goin' to be marked for it? It's all Randall's fault. It isn't *our* fault, anyhow. An exam.'s an exam.,' etc., etc.

Naturally Mr King considered this was an attempt to undermine his authority, and, instead of beginning dictation at once, delivered a lecture on the spirit in which examinations should be approached. As the storm subsided, Beetle fanned it afresh.

'Eh? What? What was that you were saying to MacLagan?'

'I only said I thought the papers ought to have been looked at before they were given out, sir.'

'Hear, hear!' from a back bench.

Mr King wished to know whether Beetle took it upon himself personally to conduct the traditions of the school. His zeal for knowledge ate up another fifteen minutes, during which the prefects showed unmistakable signs of boredom.

'Oh, it was a giddy time,' said Beetle, afterwards, in dismantled Number Five. 'He gibbered a bit, and I kept him on the gibber, and then he dictated about half of Dolabella & Co.'

'Good old Dolabella! Friend of mine. Yes?' said Stalky tenderly.

'Then we had to ask him how every other word was spelt, of course, and he gibbered a lot more. He cursed me and MacLagan (Mac played up like a trump) and Randall, and the "materialized ignorance of the unscholarly middle classes", "lust for mere marks", and all the rest. It was what you might call a final exhibition – a last attack – a giddy par-ergon.'

'But of course he was blind squiffy when he wrote the paper. I hope you explained *that*?' said Stalky.

'Oh yes. I told Tulke so. I said an immoral prefect an' a

drunken house-master were legitimate inferences. Tulke nearly blubbed. He's awfully shy of us since Mary's time.'

Tulke preserved that modesty till the last moment – till the journey-money had been paid, and the boys were filling the brakes that took them to the station. Then the three happily constrained him to wait awhile.

'You see, Tulke, you may be a prefect,' said Stalky, 'but I've left the Coll. Do you see, Tulke, dear?'

'Yes, I see. Don't bear malice, Stalky.'

'Stalky? Curse your impudence, you young cub,' shouted Stalky, magnificent in top-hat, stiff collar, spats, and high-waisted, snuff-coloured ulster. 'I want you to understand that *I'm* Mister Corkran, an' you're a dirty little schoolboy.'

'Besides bein' frabjously immoral,' said M'Turk. 'Wonder you aren't ashamed to foist your company on pure-minded boys like us!'

'Come on, Tulke,' cried Naughten, from the prefects' brake.

'Yes, we're comin'. Shove up and make room, you Collegers. You've all got to be back next term, with your "Yes, sir", and "Oh, sir", an' "No, sir", an' "Please, sir"; but before we say goodbye we're going to tell you a little story. Go on, Dickie' (this to the driver); 'we're quite ready. Kick that hat-box under the seat, an' don't crowd your Uncle Stalky.'

'As nice a lot of high-minded youngsters as you'd wish to see,' said M'Turk, gazing round with bland patronage. 'A trifle immoral, but then – boys will be boys. It's no good tryin' to look stuffy, Carson. Mister Corkran will now oblige with the story of Tulke an' Mary Yeo!'

Kathleen Fitzpatrick

The English Aunt

Nobody had invited the English aunt to come over to Ireland, so when a letter arrived one morning to tell them she would arrive next day everyone was surprised. The children were delighted. They had thought Aunt Mary was the only relative they possessed, but it seemed they had an English aunt as well, who was their mother's sister, and she was called Aunt Charlotte. Patsy said she would be sure to bring them presents in her trunk. But Lull went about the house preparing for her, getting her room ready, airing sheets and blankets, dusting the drawing-room, and opening the windows with a look in her eyes that would sour cream.

'Don't you want Aunt Charlotte to come?' Jane asked her.

'Want her? Why couldn't she come when she was wanted sore? What kept her in England then – and me prayin' night and day for her to come?'

Jane stopped in the middle of the drawing-room with a soup tureen full of dog daisies in her hands.

'There, I'll quit blethering,' Lull added. 'None of yous mind them days, thanks be to God; but if it had been me that had a young sister struck dumb in morshal agony, haythen Turks couldn't have kept me from her.'

Lull flounced out, and Jane was left standing in the middle of the room dumbfounded. She had never before in her life heard Lull speak like that. A young sister? – but their mother was the only sister Aunt Charlotte had got. When was their mother struck dumb in agony and Aunt Charlotte wouldn't come to her? She put the soup tureen on the middle of the table, and went out to the stable where Andy Graham was putting the horse into the car to go to meet Aunt Charlotte at the railway station. Honeybird was brushing his hat for him at the far end of the stable, but Jane did not see her.

'Andy, when was mother struck dumb in morshal agony?'

Andy dropped the end of the trace he had in his hand.

'By the holy poker, what put that into your head, Miss Jane?'

'Lull said Aunt Charlotte wouldn't come when she was wanted sore, and her young sister struck dumb in morshal agony.'

'And a fine auld clashbag Lull was to say it,' said Andy picking up the trace.

'Tell me, Andy, and I'll never name it to a soul.'

'See here, Miss Jane,' said Andy. 'It's no talk for the likes of you to be hearin'. Sure, there's niver a wan would name it if it wasn't for that auld targe of a Lull, and it be to be as far back as Noah's flood for her to forget it.'

'Go on, Andy; tell a body and I won't come over it to a living soul.'

'Sure, you know as much as I know. The mistress was terrible bad, and they telegramed for your Aunt Charlotte, but she wouldn't come.'

'Why wouldn't she?'

'God only knows. The country was disturbed. Lull was clean demented for want of her; and I'm tellin' you it got your Aunt Charlotte a bad name about the place. There's many the wan among the neighbours has it agin' her to this day.'

'Have *you*, Andy?'

'Is it me? God forgive you, I never could bear no malice. And see and forget it yourself, for she'll be the good aunt to yous all yet.'

Jane walked slowly back to the house. She would have liked to consult Mick about this news, but she had promised not to tell. The only thing to do was to wait till she could ask Aunt Charlotte herself.

Mick went to the railway station with Andy to meet Aunt Charlotte. The others waited at the gate, two on each stone lion to give a cheer when she arrived.

It was a long drive from the station, and they were stiff and cramped before the car came back, but Jane would not let them get down for fear the car would turn the corner while they were down, and Aunt Charlotte would not get a proper welcome.

At last they heard the car coming along the road. They hurrahed at the top of their voices. Then the car turned the corner. Aunt Charlotte sat on one side and Mick on the other. There was a tin trunk between them on the well of the car. As it came nearer they could see that Mick was making signs to them, shaking his head and frowning. When it turned in at the gate Aunt Charlotte looked straight in front of her and did not even glance at the welcoming party on the lions.

They got down and followed the car up the avenue. In a minute or two they were joined by Mick.

'Let's hide,' he said; 'she's an old divil.'

Silently they turned away from the house, across the lawn, and dropped over the wall into the road. They went up the road till they came to an opening in the wall on the other side where they filed through and struck out across the fields. Sheep were feeding on the spongy grass, and as they got farther away from home, rocks and boulders began to appear, and at last a long line of clear blue sea. Mick led the way till they came to a flat rock jutting out like a shelf over the sea, and here they sat down.

'What did she do?' Jane asked.

'She said I was no gentleman.'

'What for?'

Mick began his tale.

'When the train came in I went up to her and said "How are you?" Said she "Who are *you*?" Said I "I'm Michael Darragh." "Is it possible?" said she, and you should have seen the old face of her. "The car's waiting for you outside," said I. "Then tell the coachman to come in for my luggage," said she.'

'Oh, Mick!' Jane gasped, 'what did you do?'

'I didn't know what to do. I didn't like to say right out that Andy had no livery for his legs, and daren't strip off the rug. So I said "I'll get a porter to carry out your trunk." "No," said she, "I'd have to tip him – tell the coachman to come."'

'As mean as dirt,' said Patsy.

'"He can't come off the dicky," said I. "What is the matter

with him!" says she. I was afraid I'd tell a lie, so I thought a bit, and then I said, "He's disable." '

'Good for you, Micky Free!' Jane shouted.

'But it wasn't good, for when we started she began to ask him what ailed him. Andy said he was in the best of good health. "My nephew tells me you are disabled," says she. "Divil a foot, mem," says Andy. "I'm as well as you are yourself." She got as red as fire. "No gentleman tells lies, Michael," she said.' Mick's face was white with anger.

'But you told no lie, Micky dear,' said Fly.

'And you couldn't tell her Andy had no white breeches,' said Patsy.

'Dear forgive her!' said Jane bitterly; 'and we thought she was an aunt.'

They did not go home till the evening was growing dark, and then they went into the house by the back door.

Lull was sitting by the kitchen fire.

'Well!' she said, 'did you see your Aunt Charlotte? She's out looking for you.'

'She can look till she's black in the face for all we care,' said Jane.

Their mother was sitting up in bed when they went in to bid her good night. They could see she had been crying.

'You are the best children in the world,' she said, 'but your Aunt Charlotte thinks you are barbarians.'

'She's an old divil and we hate the sight of her,' said Patsy.

' 'Deed there is more than *yous* does that,' said Lull.

'Hush! Lull,' said their mother; 'after all, she is my sister.'

'Purty sister!' Lull snorted, 'comin' where she is not wanted and upsettin' everybuddy with her talk of ruination.'

'It's true, it's true,' Mrs Darragh wailed, and began to cry again.

Lull hurried the children out of the room; as they went down the passage they could hear her comforting their mother.

They went to bed with heavy hearts. Fly said her prayers three times over, and then cried herself to sleep.

Next morning Aunt Charlotte was down early. Fly and Patsy,

who had been out early to see if the gooseberries were ripe, met her in the hall as they came back.

'Good morning. I don't think I saw you yesterday,' she said. 'What are your names?'

'I'm Fly, and he's Patsy,' Fly answered.

'What?' said Aunt Charlotte.

'Fly and Patsy,' Fly repeated, and was going past when Aunt Charlotte pounced on the gooseberries Fly had in the lap of her pinafore.

'What are you going to do with these?'

'Ripen them,' said Patsy, trying to get past.

'You cannot ripen green gooseberries off the bushes,' said Aunt Charlotte.

''Deed you just can,' said Fly. 'You squeeze them till they are soft, and then you suck them till they are sweet.'

'I am sure your nurse cannot allow you to do anything so disgusting,' said Aunt Charlotte.

At this moment Lull came out of the schoolroom where she had been laying the table for breakfast.

'McLeary, surely you do not allow the children to eat such poisonous stuff as green gooseberries?'

They had never heard Lull called that name till now. Lull's eyes flashed fire for a second.

'You leave them to me,' she said, and took Fly and Patsy off to the kitchen where they squeezed and sucked the green gooseberries in peace.

At breakfast Aunt Charlotte asked questions about everything; who were their friends? where did they visit? how far away was the Protestant church?

'You see,' she said, 'I have not been here before, so you must tell me everything about your neighbourhood now.'

'Why didn't you come before?' Jane asked, 'when you were wanted sore – what kept you then?'

'Little girls cannot understand the motives of their elders,' Aunt Charlotte replied sharply. 'I was far from well, and the country was disturbed.'

'What's disturbed?' Patsy asked.

Her back stiffened.

'Your fellow countrymen were in a state of rebellion against the powers ordained by God.'

'But who wouldn't fight the police?' said Patsy. 'You should have seen the grand fight there was here on the last twelfth of July.'

'I understood that everything was quiet,' Aunt Charlotte murmured.

'Lull was praying night and day for you to come. She was clean demented for the want of you,' Jane went on, hoping Aunt Charlotte would explain. But Aunt Charlotte did nothing of the kind. She wiped her nose instead.

'We will not discuss the matter; I have told you that it was impossible for me to come.'

'I can tell you it got you an ill name about the place,' said Honeybird, looking up from her porridge. 'There is many a one has it against you to this day.'

The others looked at each other in surprise. Honeybird had a way of repeating gossip she had picked up; but only Jane knew where she could have heard this, and a kick from Jane told her to be quiet.

Aunt Charlotte's knife and fork dropped with a clatter on her plate. Her face was as white as chalk. For a minute or two no one spoke. Aunt Charlotte sipped a little coffee, and then shut her eyes. The children thought she must have forgotten to say her grace till now; they went on with their breakfast, and in a few minutes she spoke again.

'I suppose you all like toys,' she said.

The younger ones brightened up.

'You know there are beautiful toys to be had in London, and I did think of bringing over some for you; but then I thought that out here in the country, with so many trees and flowers to make you happy, it would be like bringing coals to Newcastle.'

They understood that she had brought no presents. Mick and Jane looked relieved, but Honeybird's eyes filled with tears.

'Never a wee dawl?' she asked.

'What does she mean?' said Aunt Charlotte. 'Oh, a little doll – the child speaks like a peasant.'

No one answered. Honeybird's few tears dropped into her

lap. Fly passed her a ripened green gooseberry under the table.

After breakfast Aunt Charlotte said they must show her the garden and the grounds. They had meant to go out bathing and to stay away all day, but there was no escaping from her, so they started off first to the stables to see Andy.

Aunt Charlotte shook her head over everything. 'Disgraceful neglect!' they heard her say.

'We'll soon make it grand again when our ship comes in,' said Jane.

'What a strange expression!' said Aunt Charlotte. 'And when, pray, will that be?'

'God knows, for I don't,' said Honeybird, repeating what Andy Graham always said when they asked him that question.

Aunt Charlotte looked at Honeybird, who was playing with the cat.

'Do you not know that you have taken your Maker's name in vain? Go back to the house at once, you wicked child.'

Honeybird stared, her grey eyes growing wider and wider.

'Do you hear me?' Aunt Charlotte repeated. 'Go into the house at once.'

With a gasp of bewilderment Honeybird turned back across the yard; they heard her go in at the kitchen door sobbing, 'Poor, poor wee me!'

'Now take me to the vegetable garden,' said Aunt Charlotte.

'Auld Davy will be cross if we do,' said Jane.

'I wish you would speak more distinctly,' said Aunt Charlotte, 'I cannot hear what you say.'

'I only said auld Davy would be cross.'

'Who is he, what is his name?'

'Indeed he is just the gardener, but he's a cankersome old man and he doesn't like people to come into the garden.'

'Such nonsense! Tell him to come here to speak to me at once.'

But old Davy spoke for himself.

'Be off wid you, trampin' over me beds! If I catch the hould of you I'll break your legs.' He came out from behind the bushes with a bill hook in his hand. Aunt Charlotte turned back to the house, hurrying as fast as her legs could carry her.

'She's afraid of him,' said Jane joyfully.

Patsy danced on the path.

'It would be fun to take her to see Jane Dwyer.'

They laughed at the thought of it till they had to sit down. Old Davy came down the path with a handful of ripe gooseberries for them.

'You frightened the wits out of Aunt Charlotte,' said Mick.

'What call had yous to bring the woman into the garden at this time of day, and me with my boots off havin' a bite of meat?'

'We're going to take her to see Jane Dwyer,' said Patsy.

'Yous are always at some divilment,' said old Davy as he turned away.

'I wish I could come with you,' said Jane, 'but auld Jane's friends with me now.'

'No, you'll have to stay at home; she wouldn't lift a hand to us if she saw you with us,' said Mick.

'It's all because I took those old boots,' said Jane; 'but you three can go, and mind that you run the minute she throws the first clod, for if you stand and face her she'll be as quiet as a lamb.'

A few minutes later Mick and Patsy and Fly came into the drawing-room to ask Aunt Charlotte if she would like to go for a walk. They were going down to the sea, they said.

Aunt Charlotte said she would be glad to go. She put on her hat and gloves, and they started out.

On each side of the road there was a wall of loose stones bound together by moss and brambles. In the distance at their right rose the mountains; a turn of the road about a mile from the house brought them within sight of the sea. They passed through the village – a long row of whitewashed cottages with here and there a fuchsia bush by a door, a line of bright nasturtiums under a window, or a potato patch dotted with kale by the side of a house.

Farther down the street the church stood back from the road in a graveyard full of tombstones and weeds. Aunt Charlotte said she was interested in churches, so they stopped to look at it. Coming back through the graveyard Mick showed her the tombstones of the rebels, with skull and crossbones on the top, and the grave of a great-uncle of theirs who had been hanged at the time of the rebellion.

'Serve him right, the old traitor!' said Patsy.

Aunt Charlotte was shocked.

'If he was your great-uncle, you should think of him with respect,' she said.

'And him an informer!' said Mick; ' 'deed I would have killed him myself. Andy Graham says he would have jabbed the brains out of him.'

'Lull says she would have rapped him on the head with a blackthorn stick,' said Fly; 'but whisht! – I do believe the old ruffian is lying in his grave listening to us.'

Aunt Charlotte shivered.

As they were going down the churchyard steps Patsy stopped.

'Look at those two old rats sitting on the wall like wee old men. They're just saying which of us will be brought there first.'

Aunt Charlotte gave a little scream, and hurried out on to the road.

'You children have morbid minds, you have made me quite nervous.'

About five minutes' walk from the village they came to a lane that ran down to the sea – black mud underfoot and a stone wall on either side. The lane widened into a small farmyard. There was a low, whitewashed cottage with a sodden thatched roof, a stack of peat at one side, and a few hens picking about in the mud.

'What a squalid scene!' said Aunt Charlotte; 'is it possible that any human being can live there?'

The children did not answer, for to their disappointment the door was shut.

'She's out,' said Mick.

A few yards from the cottage the land ended on the seashore. The sand was covered with brown seaweed; a cart filled with it was propped up with stones. Bits of cork and wood were strewn about in every direction; and beyond the line of dry seaweed there were big round stones covered with golden brown seaweed still wet, for the tide was only halfway out.

Aunt Charlotte did not like the seashore. She said it was so untidy; not even the beautiful green crabs that Fly caught for her under the wet seaweed pleased her, so after a few minutes they turned back. They were sure Jane Dwyer would not be back yet; but just as they were passing her cottage Aunt Charlotte gripped Mick's arm.

'Who is that?' she said sharply, 'there – coming down the lane.'

Fly smothered an hysterical giggle.

A tall figure dressed in an old green coat tied in round the waist by a dirty apron was coming towards them; white hair fell about its white face, and its big bare feet splashed in the mud. As it came nearer it muttered and scowled and shook its fist.

'Who is it, I say?' said Aunt Charlotte.

'It is Jane Dwyer.'

She came swinging along muttering and cursing to herself, stopping here and there to pick up a stone till her apron was full. Then with a sudden leap in the air she aimed. The stone hit Fly on the shin, who gave a scream of pain and was over the wall in a second. The boys followed her, while a volley of stones and curses came from the lane.

Aunt Charlotte was left behind. They heard her scrambling over the wall, the loose stones rolling off as she scrambled; and as they ran they could hear her screaming, 'My God, my God, this is terrible!'

Two fields away the boys found Fly sitting on a bank nursing her sore leg.

'Did you hear her taking her Maker's name in vain?' said Patsy. He rolled over on the grass with laughter.

'I never saw old Jane in better fettle,' said Mick.

'If we'd had any wit we would have taken her to see Sammy too!' said Fly.

'We'll do it yet,' said Patsy; and then they began to run like hares along the road where Sammy lived.

Sammy was an Innocent. He lived in a one-roomed cottage on the roadside almost entirely hidden from sight by rowan trees that grew round it. He was a dwarf about four feet high with a head too big for his body, and a thatch of coarse black hair. He spent his days looking after his sister's pig, trotting along by its side in his bare feet through the muddy lanes where the mud squelched up between his toes. There was not a more peaceable creature in the country, but on the future fate of the pig he could be roused to fury. He talked to it, sang to it and fed it out of his hand. When he walked about the fields the pig followed at his heels; when he sat on the doorstep it lay at his feet. But if one of the village children threw a stone at it, or if a neighbour threatened in joke to send for the butcher, Sammy was beside himself with rage.

Twice a week he came to Rowallan for the refuse and broken meat; and next to the pig he loved the children.

'M-m-mornin',' he stammered when they ran into the muddy lane.

They were out of breath and could hardly speak. Sammy looked frightened; it was easy to scare his few wits away.

'Oh, Sammy, she's coming after your pig,' Fly panted.

'Wh-wh-when?' Sammy shouted.

'Along the road,' said Patsy. 'She'll be here in a minute, a long string of a woman with a black dress on. She's clean mad to get at it. You'd better be out and chase her.'

'L-l-l-let me at her!' roared Sammy, picking up his bucket.

'She's come all the way from England to do it,' said Mick.

Sammy was dancing on the doorstep with the bucket in his hand.

'Hide down behind the wall till she comes,' said Patsy. 'Whisht! Sammy man, be quiet till she comes. I'll give you the word when I see her.'

In about five minutes Aunt Charlotte came in sight. They saw her through the hole in the wall walking slowly and looking back every few steps. Her hair was down, and she was trying to fasten it up. Mick nudged Fly and Patsy not to speak and gave Aunt Charlotte plenty of time to get past the cottage before he said, 'Here she comes, Sammy.'

Sammy jumped up and ran out on the road waving his bucket over his head and roaring, 'Ould butcher! English butcher! I'll – I'll – I'll bite you!'

There was a stifled scream as Aunt Charlotte turned for a second. In the next moment she was out of sight.

Sammy danced on the road and shouted after her till he was hoarse; then he came back to where the children were crouched down behind the wall.

'S-s-s-she was off like the wind before I could touch her,' he said. They shook hands with him and told him he was a brave man. Then they went down to the sea, and bathed and stayed out till bedtime. Jane and Honeybird met them at the door.

'She's away back to England,' they chanted.

The others could hardly believe their ears.

'She came back all mud and dirt,' Jane told them, 'with her hair hanging over her eyes, and said we were all heathens and savages, and she would not stay another night in this blackguardly country!'

Lull questioned them while they were having supper.

'What and ever did yous do to send your Aunt Charlotte home in that state?'

' 'Deed we just took her to see Jane Dwyer,' said Patsy.

Lull looked at him for a while.

'There's a heap of wisdom in a child,' she said at last. 'I hope and trust that will be the last we'll see of your grand relations from England.'

Saki

The Secret Sin of Septimus Brope

'Who and what is Mr Brope?' demanded the aunt of Clovis suddenly.

Mrs Riversedge, who had been snipping off the heads of defunct roses, and thinking of nothing in particular, sprang hurriedly to mental attention. She was one of those old-fashioned hostesses who consider that one ought to know something about one's guests, and that the something ought to be to their credit.

'I believe he comes from Leighton Buzzard,' she observed by way of preliminary explanation.

'In these days of rapid and convenient travel,' said Clovis, who was dispersing a colony of green-fly with visitations of cigarette smoke, 'to come from Leighton Buzzard does not necessarily denote any great strength of character. It might only mean mere restlessness. Now if he had left it under a cloud, or as a protest against the incurable and heartless frivolity of its inhabitants, that would tell us something about the man and his mission in life.'

'What does he do?' pursued Mrs Troyle magisterially.

'He edits the *Cathedral Monthly*,' said her hostess, 'and he's enormously learned about memorial brasses and transepts and the influence of Byzantine worship on modern liturgy, and all those sort of things. Perhaps he is just a little bit heavy and immersed in one range of subjects, but it takes all sorts to make a good house-party, you know. You don't find him *too* dull, do you?'

'Dullness I could overlook,' said the aunt of Clovis: 'what I cannot forgive is his making love to my maid.'

'My dear Mrs Troyle,' gasped the hostess, 'what an extra-ordinary idea! I assure you Mr Brope would not dream of doing such a thing.'

'His dreams are a matter of indifference to me; for all I care his slumbers may be one long indiscretion of unsuitable erotic advances, in which the entire servants' hall may be involved. But in his waking hours he shall not make love to my maid. It's no use arguing about it, I'm firm on the point.'

'But you must be mistaken,' persisted Mrs Riversedge; 'Mr Brope would be the last person to do such a thing.'

'He is the first person to do such a thing, as far as my information goes, and if I have any voice in the matter he certainly shall be the last. Of course, I am not referring to respectably intentioned lovers.'

'I simply cannot think that a man who writes so charmingly and informingly about transepts and Byzantine influences would behave in such an unprincipled manner,' said Mrs Riversedge; 'what evidence have you that he's doing any-thing of the sort? I don't want to doubt your word, of course, but we mustn't be too ready to condemn him unheard, must we?'

'Whether we condemn him or not, he has certainly not been unheard. He has the room next to my dressing-room, and on two occasions, when I dare say he thought I was absent, I have plainly heard him announcing through the wall, "I love you, Florrie." Those partition walls upstairs are very thin; one can almost hear a watch ticking in the next room.'

'Is your maid called Florence?'

'Her name is Florinda.'

'What an extraordinary name to give a maid!'

'I did not give it to her; she arrived in my service already christened.'

'What I mean is,' said Mrs Riversedge, 'that when I get maids with unsuitable names I call them Jane; they soon get used to it.'

'An excellent plan,' said the aunt of Clovis coldly; 'unfor-tunately I have got used to being called Jane myself. It happens to be my name.'

She cut short Mrs Riversedge's flood of apologies by abruptly remarking:

'The question is not whether I'm to call my maid Florinda, but whether Mr Brope is to be permitted to call her Florrie. I am strongly of opinion that he shall not.'

'He may have been repeating the words of some song,' said Mrs Riversedge hopefully; 'there are lots of those sorts of silly refrains with girls' names,' she continued, turning to Clovis as a possible authority on the subject. ' "You mustn't call me Mary —" '

'I shouldn't think of doing so,' Clovis assured her; 'in the first place, I've always understood that your name was Henrietta; and then I hardly know you well enough to take such a liberty.'

'I mean there's a *song* with that refrain,' hurriedly explained Mrs Riversedge, 'and there's "Rhoda, Rhoda kept a pagoda", and "Maisie is a daisy", and heaps of others. Certainly it doesn't sound like Mr Brope to be singing such songs, but I think we ought to give him the benefit of the doubt.'

'I had already done so,' said Mrs Troyle, 'until further evidence came my way.'

She shut her lips with the resolute finality of one who enjoys the blessed certainty of being implored to open them again.

'Further evidence!' exclaimed her hostess; 'do tell me!'

'As I was coming upstairs after breakfast Mr Brope was just passing my room. In the most natural way in the world a piece of paper dropped out of a packet that he held in his hand and fluttered to the ground just at my door. I was going to call out to him "You've dropped something," and then for some reason I held back and didn't show myself till he was safely in his room. You see it occurred to me that I was very seldom in my room just at that hour, and that Florinda was almost always there tidying up things about that time. So I picked up that innocent-looking piece of paper.'

Mrs Troyle paused again, with the self-applauding air of one who has detected an asp lurking in an apple-charlotte.

Mrs Riversedge snipped vigorously at the nearest rose bush, incidentally decapitating a Viscountess Folkestone that was just coming into bloom.

'What was on the paper?' she asked.

'Just the words in pencil, "I love you, Florrie," and then underneath, crossed out with a faint line, but perfectly plain to read, "Meet me in the garden by the yew."'

'There *is* a yew at the bottom of my garden,' admitted Mrs Riversedge.

'At any rate he appears to be truthful,' commented Clovis.

'To think that a scandal of this sort should be going on under my roof!' said Mrs Riversedge indignantly.

'I wonder why it is that scandal seems so much worse under a roof,' observed Clovis; 'I've always regarded it as a proof of the superior delicacy of the cat tribe that it conducts most of its scandals above the slates.'

'Now I come to think of it,' resumed Mrs Riversedge, 'there are things about Mr Brope that I've never been able to account for. His income, for instance: he only gets two hundred pounds a year as editor of the *Cathedral Monthly*, and I know that his people are quite poor, and he hasn't any private means. Yet he manages to afford a flat somewhere in Westminster, and he goes abroad to Bruges and those sorts of places every year, and always dresses well, and gives quite nice luncheon-parties in the season. You can't do all that on two hundred a year, can you?'

'Does he write for any other papers?' queried Mrs Troyle.

'No, you see he specializes so entirely on liturgy and ecclesiastical architecture that his field is rather restricted. He once tried the *Sporting and Dramatic* with an article on church edifices in famous fox-hunting centres, but it wasn't considered of sufficient general interest to be accepted. No, I don't see how he can support himself in his present style merely by what he writes.'

'Perhaps he sells spurious transepts to American enthusiasts,' suggested Clovis.

'How could you sell a transept?' said Mrs Riversedge; 'such a thing would be impossible.'

'Whatever he may do to eke out his income,' interrupted Mrs Troyle, 'he is certainly not going to fill in his leisure moments by making love to my maid.'

'Of course not,' agreed her hostess; 'that must be put a stop to at once. But I don't quite know what we ought to do.'

'You might put a barbed wire entanglement round the yew tree as a precautionary measure,' said Clovis.

'I don't think that the disagreeable situation that has arisen is improved by flippancy,' said Mrs Riversedge; 'a good maid is a treasure —'

'I am sure I don't know what I should do without Florinda,' admitted Mrs Troyle; 'she understands my hair. I've long ago given up trying to do anything with it myself. I regard one's hair as I regard husbands: as long as one is seen together in public one's private divergences don't matter. Surely that was the luncheon gong.'

Septimus Brope and Clovis had the smoking-room to themselves after lunch. The former seemed restless and preoccupied, the latter quietly observant.

'What is a lorry?' asked Septimus suddenly; 'I don't mean the thing on wheels, of course I know what that is, but isn't there a bird with a name like that, the larger form of lorikeet?'

'I fancy it's a lory, with one "r",' said Clovis lazily, 'in which case it's no good to you.'

Septimus Brope stared in some astonishment.

'How do you mean, no good to me?' he asked, with more than a trace of uneasiness in his voice.

'Won't rhyme with Florrie,' explained Clovis briefly.

Septimus sat upright in his chair, with unmistakable alarm on his face.

'How did you find out? I mean how did you know I was trying to get a rhyme to Florrie?' he asked sharply.

'I didn't know,' said Clovis, 'I only guessed. When you wanted to turn the prosaic lorry of commerce into a feathered poem flitting through the verdure of a tropical forest, I knew you must be working up a sonnet, and Florrie was the only female name that suggested itself as rhyming with lorry.'

Septimus still looked uneasy.

'I believe you know more,' he said.

Clovis laughed quietly, but said nothing.

'How much do you know?' Septimus asked desperately.

'The yew tree in the garden,' said Clovis.

'There! I felt certain I'd dropped it somewhere. But you must have guessed something before. Look here, you have surprised my secret. You won't give me away, will you? It is nothing to be ashamed of, but it wouldn't do for the editor of the *Cathedral Monthly* to go in openly for that sort of thing, would it?'

'Well, I suppose not,' admitted Clovis.

'You see,' continued Septimus, 'I get quite a decent lot of money out of it. I could never live in the style I do on what I get as editor of the *Cathedral Monthly*.'

Clovis was even more startled than Septimus had been earlier in conversation, but he was better skilled in repressing surprise.

'Do you mean to say you get money out of – Florrie?' he asked.

'Not out of Florrie, as yet,' said Septimus; 'in fact, I don't mind saying that I'm having a good deal of trouble over Florrie. But there are lots of others.'

Clovis's cigarette went out.

'This is *very* interesting,' he said slowly. And then, with Septimus Brope's next words, illumination dawned on him.

'There are heaps of others; for instance:

> ' "*Cora with the lips of coral,*
> *You and I will never quarrel.*"

That was one of my earliest successes, and it still brings me in royalties. And there is – "Esmeralda, when I first beheld her", and "Fair Teresa, how I love to please her", both of those have been fairly popular. And there is one rather dreadful one,' continued Septimus, flushing deep carmine, 'which has brought me in more more money than any of the others:

> ' "*Lively little Lucie*
> *With her naughty nez retrousse.*"

Of course, I loathe the whole lot of them; in fact, I'm rapidly becoming something of a woman-hater under their influence, but I can't afford to disregard the financial aspect of the matter. And at the same time you can understand that my position as an authority on ecclesiastical architecture and liturgical subjects would be weakened, if not altogether ruined, if it once got about that I was the author of "Cora with the lips of coral" and all the rest of them.'

Clovis had recovered sufficiently to ask in a sympathetic, if rather unsteady, voice what was the special trouble with 'Florrie'.

'I can't get her into lyric shape, try as I will,' said Septimus mournfully. 'You see, one has to work in a lot of sentimental, sugary compliment with a catchy rhyme, and a certain amount of personal biography or prophecy. They've all of them got to have a long string of past successes recorded about them, or else you've got to foretell blissful things about them and yourself in the future. For instance, there is:

> ' "*Dainty little girlie Mavis,*
> *She is such a rara avis,*
> *All the money I can save is*
> *All to be for Mavis mine.*"

It goes to a sickening namby-pamby waltz tune, and for months nothing else was sung and hummed in Blackpool and other popular centres.'

This time Clovis's self-control broke down badly.

'Please excuse me,' he gurgled, 'but I can't help it when I remember the awful solemnity of that article of yours that you so kindly read us last night, on the Coptic Church in its relation to early Christian worship.'

Septimus groaned.

'You see how it would be,' he said; 'as soon as people knew me to be the author of that miserable sentimental twaddle, all respect for the serious labours of my life would be gone. I dare say I know more about memorial brasses than any one living, in fact I hope one day to publish a monograph on the subject, but I should be pointed out everywhere as the man whose ditties were in the mouths of nigger minstrels along the entire coast-line of our Island home. Can you wonder that I positively hate Florrie all the time that I'm trying to grind out sugar-coated rhapsodies about her?'

'Why not give free play to your emotions, and be brutally

abusive? An uncomplimentary refrain would have an instant success as a novelty if you were sufficiently outspoken.'

'I've never thought of that,' said Septimus, 'and I'm afraid I couldn't break away from the habit of fulsome adulation and suddenly change my style.'

'You needn't change your style in the least,' said Clovis; 'merely reverse the sentiment and keep to the inane phraseology of the thing. If you'll do the body of the song I'll knock off the refrain, which is the thing that principally matters, I believe. I shall charge half-shares in the royalties, and throw in my silence as to your guilty secret. In the eyes of the world you shall still be the man who has devoted his life to the study of transepts and Byzantine ritual; only sometimes, in the long winter evenings, when the wind howls drearily down the chimney and the rain beats against the windows, I shall think of you as the author of "Cora with the lips of coral". Of course, if in sheer gratitude at my silence you like to take me for a much-needed holiday to the Adriatic or somewhere equally interesting, paying all expenses, I shouldn't dream of refusing.'

Later in the afternoon Clovis found his aunt and Mrs River-sedge indulging in gentle exercise in the Jacobean garden.

'I've spoken to Mr Brope about F.,' he announced.

'How splendid of you! What did he say?' came in a quick chorus from the two ladies.

'He was quite frank and straightforward with me when he saw that I knew his secret,' said Clovis, 'and it seems that his intentions were quite serious, if slightly unsuitable. I tried to show him the impracticability of the course that he was follow-ing. He said he wanted to be understood, and he seemed to think that Florinda would excel in that requirement, but I pointed out that there were probably dozens of delicately nur-tured, pure-hearted young English girls who would be capable of understanding him, while Florinda was the only person in the world who understood my aunt's hair. That rather weighed with him, for he's not really a selfish animal, if you take him in the right way, and when I appealed to the memory of his happy childish days, spent amid the daisied fields of Leighton Buzzard (I suppose daisies do grow there), he was obviously affected.

Anyhow, he gave me his word that he would put Florinda absolutely out of his mind, and he has agreed to go for a short trip abroad as the best distraction for his thoughts. I am going with him as far as Ragusa. If my aunt should wish to give me a really nice scarf-pin (to be chosen by myself), as a small recognition of the very considerable service I have done her, I shouldn't dream of refusing. I'm not one of those who think that because one is abroad one can go about dressed anyhow.'

A few weeks later in Blackpool and places where they sing, the following refrain held undisputed sway:

> '*How you bore me, Florrie,*
> *With those eyes of vacant blue;*
> *You'll be very sorry, Florrie,*
> *If I marry you.*
> *Though I'm easy-goin', Florrie,*
> *This I swear is true,*
> *I'll throw you down a quarry, Florrie.*
> *If I marry you.*'

Max Beerbohm

The Mote in the Middle Distance

By H*nry J*m*s

It was with the sense of a, for him, very memorable something
that he peered now into the immediate future, and tried, not
without compunction, to take that period up where he had,
prospectively, left it. But just where the deuce *had* he left it?
The consciousness of dubiety was, for our friend, not, this
morning, quite yet clean-cut enough to outline the figures on
what she had called his 'horizon', between which and himself
the twilight was indeed of a quality somewhat intimidating. He
had run up, in the course of time, against a good number of
'teasers'; and the function of teasing them back – of, as it were,
giving them, every now and then, 'what for' – was in him so
much a habit that he would have been at a loss had there been,
on the face of it, nothing to lose. Oh, he always had offered
rewards, of course – had ever so liberally pasted the windows
of his soul with staring appeals, minute descriptions, promises
that knew no bounds. But the actual recovery of the article –
the business of drawing and crossing the cheque, blotched
though this were with tears of joy – had blankly appeared to
him rather in the light of a sacrilege, casting, he sometimes felt,
a palpable chill on the fervour of the next quest. It was just this
fervour that was threatened as, raising himself on his elbow, he
stared at the foot of his bed. That his eyes refused to rest there
for more than the fraction of an instant, may be taken – *was*,
even then, taken by Keith Tantalus – as a hint of his recollection
that after all the phenomenon wasn't to be singular. Thus the
exact repetition, at the foot of Eva's bed, of the shape pendulous
at the foot of *his* was hardly enough to account for the fixity

with which he envisaged it, and for which he was to find, some years later, a motive in the (as it turned out) hardly generous fear that Eva had already made the great investigation 'on her own'. Her very regular breathing presently reassured him that, if she *had* peeped into 'her' stocking, she must have done so in sleep. Whether he should wake her now, or wait for their nurse to wake them both in due course, was a problem presently solved by a new development. It was plain that his sister was now watching him between her eyelashes. He had half expected that. She really was – he had often told her that she really was – magnificent; and her magnificence was never more obvious than in the pause that elapsed before she all of a sudden remarked, 'They so very indubitably *are*, you know!'

It occurred to him as befitting Eva's remoteness, which was a part of Eva's magnificence, that her voice emerged somewhat muffled by the bed-clothes. She was ever, indeed, the most telephonic of her sex. In talking to Eva you always had, as it were, your lips to the receiver. If you didn't try to meet her fine eyes, it was that you simply couldn't hope to: there were too many dark, too many buzzing and bewildering and all frankly not negotiable leagues in between. Snatches of other voices seemed often to intertrude themselves in the parley; and your loyal effort not to overhear these was complicated by your fear of missing what Eva might be twittering. 'Oh, you certainly haven't, my dear, the trick of propinquity!' was a thrust she had once parried by saying that, in that case, *he* hadn't – to which his unspoken rejoinder that she had caught her tone from the peevish young women at the Central seemed to him (if not perhaps in the last, certainly in the last but one, analysis) to lack finality. With Eva, he had found, it was always safest to 'ring off'. It was with a certain sense of his rashness in the matter, therefore, that he now, with an air of feverishly 'holding the line', said, 'Oh, as to that!'

Had *she*, he presently asked himself, 'rung off'? It was characteristic of our friend – was indeed 'him all over' – that his fear of what she was going to say was as nothing to his fear of what she might be going to leave unsaid. He had, in his converse with her, been never so conscious as now of the intervening leagues;

they had never so insistently beaten the drum of his ear; and he caught himself in the act of awfully computing, with a certain statistical passion, the distance between Rome and Boston. He has never been able to decide which of these points he was psychically the nearer to at the moment when Eva, replying, 'Well, one does, anyhow, leave a margin for the pretext, you know!' made him, for the first time in his life, wonder whether she were not more magnificent than even he had ever given her credit for being. Perhaps it was to test this theory, or perhaps merely to gain time, that he now raised himself to his knees, and, leaning with outstretched arm towards the foot of his bed, made as though to touch the stocking which Santa Claus had, overnight, left dangling there. His posture, as he stared obliquely at Eva, with a sort of beaming defiance, recalled to him something seen in an 'illustration'. This reminiscence, however – if such it was, save in the scarred, the poor dear old woebegone and so very beguilingly *not* refractive mirror of the moment – took a peculiar twist from Eva's behaviour. She had, with startling suddenness, sat bolt upright, and looked at him as if she were overhearing some tragedy at the other end of the wire, where, in the nature of things, she was unable to arrest it. The gaze she fixed on her extravagant kinsman was of a kind to make him wonder how he contrived to remain, as he beautifully did, rigid. His prop was possibly the reflection that flashed on him that, if *she* abounded in attenuations, well, hang it all, so did *he*! It was simply a difference of plane. Readjust the 'values', as painters say, and there you were! He was to feel that he was only too crudely 'there' when, leaning further forward, he laid a chubby forefinger on the stocking, causing that receptacle to rock ponderously to and fro. This effect was more expected than the tears which started to Eva's eyes and the intensity with which 'Don't you,' she exclaimed, '*see?*'

'The mote in the middle distance?' he asked. 'Did you ever, my dear, know me to see anything else? I tell you it blocks out everything. It's a cathedral, it's a herd of elephants, it's the whole habitable globe. Oh, it's, believe me, of an obsessiveness!' But his sense of the one thing it *didn't* block out from his purview enabled him to launch at Eva a speculation as to just how far Santa Claus had, for the particular occasion, gone. The gauge, for both of them, of this seasonable distance seemed almost blatantly suspended in the silhouettes of the two stockings. Over and above the basis of (presumably) sweetmeats in the toes and heels, certain extrusions stood for a very plenary fulfilment of desire. And since Eva *had* set her heart on a doll of ample proportions and practicable eyelids – *had* asked that most admirable of her sex, their mother, for it with not less directness than he himself had put into his demand for a sword and helmet – her coyness now struck Keith as lying near to, at indeed a hardly measurable distance from, the border line of his patience. If she didn't *want* the doll, why the deuce had she made such a point of getting it? He was perhaps on the verge of putting this question to her, when, waving her hand to include both stockings, she said, 'Of course, my dear, you *do* see. There they are, and you know I know you know we wouldn't, either of us, dip a finger into them.' With a vibrancy of tone that seemed to bring her voice quite close to him, 'One doesn't,' she added, 'violate the shrine – pick the pearl from the shell!'

Even had the answering question 'Doesn't one just?' which for an instant hovered on the tip of his tongue, been uttered, it could not have obscured for Keith the change which her magnificence had wrought in him. Something, perhaps, of the bigotry of the convert was already discernible in the way that, averting his eyes, he said, 'One doesn't even peer.' As to whether, in the years that have elapsed since he said this, either of our friends (now adult) has, in fact, 'peered', is a question which, whenever I call at the house, I am tempted to put to one or other of them. But any regret I may feel in my invariable failure to 'come up to the scratch' of yielding to this temptation is balanced, for me, by my impression – my sometimes all but throned and anointed certainty – that the answer, if vouchsafed, would be in the negative.

W. Somerset Maugham

The Facts of Life

It was Henry Garnet's habit on leaving the city of an afternoon to drop in at his club and play bridge before going home to dinner. He was a pleasant man to play with. He knew the game well and you could be sure that he would make the best of his cards. He was a good loser; and when he won was more inclined to ascribe his success to his luck than to his skill. He was indulgent, and if his partner made a mistake could be trusted to find an excuse for him. It was surprising then on this occasion to hear him telling his partner with unnecessary sharpness that he had never seen a hand worse played; and it was more surprising still to see him not only make a grave error himself, an error of which you would never have thought him capable, but when his partner, not unwilling to get a little of his own back, pointed it out, insist against all reason and with considerable heat that he was perfectly right. But they were all old friends, the men he was playing with, and none of them took his ill-humour very seriously. Henry Garnet was a broker, a partner in a firm of repute, and it occurred to one of them that something had gone wrong with some stock he was interested in.

'How's the market today?' he asked.

'Booming. Even the suckers are making money.'

It was evident that stocks and shares had nothing to do with Henry Garnet's vexation; but something was the matter; that was evident too. He was a hearty fellow, who enjoyed excellent health; he had plenty of money; he was fond of his wife and devoted to his children. As a rule he had high spirits, and he laughed easily at the nonsense they were apt to talk while they played; but today he sat glum and silent. His brows were crossly puckered and there was a sulky look about his mouth. Presently, to ease the tension, one of the others mentioned a subject upon which they all knew Henry Garnet was glad to speak.

'How's your boy, Henry? I see he's done pretty well in the tournament.'

Henry Garnet's frown grew darker.

'He's done no better than I expected him to.'

'When does he come back from Monte?'

'He got back last night.'

'Did he enjoy himself?'

'I suppose so; all I know is that he made a damned fool of himself.'

'Oh. How?'

'I'd rather not talk about it if you don't mind.'

The three men looked at him with curiosity. Henry Garnet scowled at the green baize.

'Sorry, old boy. Your call.'

The game proceeded in a strained silence. Garnet got his bid, and when he played his cards so badly that he went three down not a word was said. Another rubber was begun and in the second game Garnet denied a suit.

'Having none?' his partner asked him.

Garnet's irritability was such that he did not even reply, and when at the end of the hand it appeared that he had revoked, and that his revoke cost the rubber, it was not to be expected that his partner should let his carelessness go without remark.

'What the devil's the matter with you, Henry?' he said. 'You're playing like a fool.'

Garnet was disconcerted. He did not so much mind losing a big rubber himself, but he was sore that his inattention should have made his partner lose too. He pulled himself together.

'I'd better not play any more. I thought a few rubbers would calm me, but the fact is I can't give my mind to the game. To tell you the truth I'm in a hell of a temper.'

They all burst out laughing.

'You don't have to tell us that, old boy. It's obvious.'

Garnet gave them a rueful smile.

'Well, I bet you'd be in a temper if what's happened to me had happened to you. As a matter of fact I'm in a damned awkward situation, and if any of you fellows can give me any advice how to deal with it I'd be grateful.'

'Let's have a drink and you tell us about it. With a K.C., a Home Office official and an eminent surgeon – if we can't tell you how to deal with a situation, nobody can.'

The K.C. got up and rang the bell for a waiter.

'It's about that damned boy of mine,' said Henry Garnet.

Drinks were ordered and brought. And this is the story that Henry Garnet told them.

The boy of whom he spoke was his only son. His name was Nicholas and of course he was called Nicky. He was eighteen. The Garnets had two daughters besides, one of sixteen and the other of twelve, but however unreasonable it seemed, for a father is generally supposed to like his daughters best, and though he did all he could not to show his preference, there was no doubt that the greater share of Henry Garnet's affection was given to his son. He was kind, in a chaffing, casual way, to his daughters, and gave them handsome presents on their birthdays and at Christmas; but he doted on Nicky. Nothing was too good for him. He thought the world of him. He could hardly take his eyes off him. You could not blame him, for Nicky was a son that any parent might have been proud of. He was six foot two, lithe but muscular, with broad shoulders and a slim waist, and he held himself gallantly erect; he had a charming head, well placed on the shoulders, with pale brown hair that waved slightly, blue eyes with long dark lashes under well-marked eyebrows, a full red mouth and a tanned, clean skin. When he smiled he showed very regular and very white teeth. He was not shy, but there was a modesty in his demeanour that was attractive. In social intercourse he was easy, polite and quietly gay. He was the offspring of nice, healthy, decent parents, he had been well brought up in a good home, he had been sent to a good school, and the general result was as engaging a specimen of young manhood as you were likely to find in a long time. You felt that he was as honest, open and virtuous as he looked. He had never given his parents a moment's uneasiness. As a child he was seldom ill and never naughty. As a boy he did everything that was expected of him. His school reports were excellent.

He was wonderfully popular, and he ended his career, with a creditable number of prizes, as head of the school and captain of the football team. But this was not all. At the age of fourteen Nicky had developed an unexpected gift for lawn tennis. This was a game that his father not only was fond of, but played very well, and when he discerned in the boy the promise of a tennis-player he fostered it. During the holidays he had him taught by the best professionals and by the time he was sixteen he had won a number of tournaments for boys of his age. He could beat his father so badly that only parental affection reconciled the older player to the poor show he put up. At eighteen Nicky went to Cambridge and Henry Garnet conceived the ambition that before he was through with the university he should play for it. Nicky had all the qualifications for becoming a great tennis-player. He was tall, he had a long reach, he was quick on his feet and his timing was perfect. He realized instinctively where the ball was coming and, seemingly without hurry, was there to take it. He had a powerful serve, with a nasty break that made it difficult to return, and his forehand drive, low, long and accurate, was deadly. He was not so good on the backhand and his volleying was wild, but all through the summer before he went to Cambridge Henry Garnet made him work on these points under the best teacher in England. At the back of his mind, though he did not even mention it to Nicky, he cherished a further ambition, to see his son play at Wimbledon, and who could tell, perhaps be chosen to represent his country in the Davis Cup. A great lump came into Henry Garnet's throat as he saw in fancy his son leap over the net to shake hands with the American champion whom he had just defeated, and walk off the court to the deafening plaudits of the multitude.

As an assiduous frequenter of Wimbledon Henry Garnet had a good many friends in the tennis world, and one evening he found himself at a City dinner sitting next to one of them, a Colonel Brabazon, and in due course began talking to him of Nicky and what chance there might be of his being chosen to play for his university during the following season.

'Why don't you let him go down to Monte Carlo and play in the spring tournament there?' said the Colonel suddenly.

'Oh, I don't think he's good enough for that. He's not nineteen yet, he only went up to Cambridge last October; he wouldn't stand a chance against all those cracks.'

'Of course, Austin and von Cramm and so on would knock spots off him, but he might snatch a game or two; and if he got up against some of the smaller fry there's no reason why he shouldn't win two or three matches. He's never been up against any of the first-rate players and it would be wonderful practice for him. He'd learn a lot more than he'll ever learn in the seaside tournaments you enter him for.'

'I wouldn't dream of it. I'm not going to let him leave Cambridge in the middle of a term. I've always impressed upon him that tennis is only a game and it mustn't interfere with work.'

Colonel Brabazon asked Garnet when the term ended.

'That's all right. He'd only have to cut about three days. Surely that could be arranged. You see, two of the men we were depending on have let us down, and we're in a hole. We want to send as good a team as we can. The Germans are sending their best players and so are the Americans.'

'Nothing doing, old boy. In the first place Nicky's not good enough, and secondly, I don't fancy the idea of sending a kid like that to Monte Carlo without anyone to look after him. If I could get away myself I might think of it, but that's out of the question.'

'I shall be there. I'm going as the non-playing captain of the English team. I'll keep an eye on him.'

'You'll be busy, and besides, it's not a responsibility I'd like to ask you to take. He's never been abroad in his life, and to tell you the truth, I shouldn't have a moment's peace all the time he was there.'

They left it at that and presently Henry Garnet went home. He was so flattered by Colonel Brabazon's suggestion that he could not help telling his wife.

'Fancy his thinking Nicky's as good as that. He told me he'd seen him play and his style was fine. He only wants more practice to get into the first flight. We shall see the kid playing in the semi-finals at Wimbledon yet, old girl.'

To his surprise Mrs Garnet was not so much opposed to the notion as he would have expected.

'After all the boy's eighteen. Nicky's never got into mischief yet and there's no reason to suppose he will now.'

'There's his work to be considered; don't forget that. I think it would be a very bad precedent to let him cut the end of term.'

'But what can three days matter? It seems a shame to rob him of a chance like that. I'm sure he'd jump at it if you asked him.'

'Well, I'm not going to. I haven't sent him to Cambridge just to play tennis. I know he's steady, but it's silly to put temptation in his way. He's much too young to go to Monte Carlo by himself.'

'You say he won't have a chance against these crack players, but you can't tell.'

Henry Garnet sighed a little. On the way home in the car it had struck him that Austin's health was uncertain and that von Cramm had his off-days. Supposing, just for the sake of argument, that Nicky had a bit of luck like that – then there would be no doubt that he would be chosen to play for Cambridge. But of course that was all nonsense.

'Nothing doing, my dear. I've made up my mind and I'm not going to change it.'

Mrs Garnet held her peace. But next day she wrote to Nicky, telling him what had happened, and suggested to him what she would do in his place if, wanting to go, he wished to get his father's consent. A day or two later Henry Garnet received a letter from his son. He was bubbling over with excitement. He had seen his tutor, who was a tennis-player himself, and the Provost of his college, who happened to know Colonel Brabazon, and no objection would be made to his leaving before the end of term; they both thought it an opportunity that shouldn't be missed. He didn't see what harm he could come to, and if only, just this once, his father would stretch a point, well, next term, he promised faithfully, he'd work like blazes. It was a very pretty letter. Mrs Garnet watched her husband read it at the breakfast table; she was undisturbed by the frown on his face. He threw it over to her.

'I don't know why you thought it necessary to tell Nicky something I told you in confidence. It's too bad of you. Now you've thoroughly unsettled him.'

'I'm sorry. I thought it would please him to know that Colonel Brabazon had such a high opinion of him. I don't see why one should only tell people the disagreeable things that are said about them. Of course I made it quite clear that there could be no question of his going.'

'You've put me in an odious position. If there's anything I hate it's for the boy to look upon me as a spoil-sport and a tyrant.'

'Oh, he'll never do that. He may think you are rather silly and unreasonable, but I'm sure he'll understand that it's only for his own good that you're being so unkind.'

'Christ,' said Henry Garnet.

His wife had a great inclination to laugh. She knew the battle was won. Dear, oh dear, how easy it was to get men to do what you wanted. For appearance sake Henry Garnet held out for forty-eight hours, but then he yielded, and a fortnight later Nicky came to London. He was to start for Monte Carlo next morning, and after dinner, when Mrs Garnet and her elder daughter had left them, Henry took the opportunity to give his son some good advice.

'I don't feel quite comfortable about letting you go off to a place like Monte Carlo at your age practically by yourself,' he finished. 'but there it is and I can only hope you'll be sensible. I don't want to play the heavy father, but there are three things especially that I want to warn you against: one is gambling, don't gamble; the second is money, don't lend anyone money; and the third is women, don't have anything to do with women. If you don't do any of those three things you can't come to much harm, so remember them well.'

'All right, father,' Nicky smiled.

'That's my last word to you. I know the world pretty well and believe me, my advice is sound.'

'I won't forget it. I promise you.'

'That's a good chap. Now let's go up and join the ladies.'

Nicky beat neither Austin nor von Cramm in the Monte Carlo

tournament, but he did not disgrace himself. He snatched an unexpected victory over a Spanish player and gave one of the Austrians a closer match than anyone had thought possible. In the mixed doubles he got into the semi-finals. His charm conquered everyone and he vastly enjoyed himself. It was generally allowed that he showed promise, and Colonel Brabazon told him that when he was a little older and had had more practice with first-class players he would be a credit to his father. The tournament came to an end and the day following he was to fly back to London. Anxious to play his best he had lived very carefully, smoking little and drinking nothing, and going to bed early; but on his last evening he thought he would like to see something of the life in Monte Carlo of which he had heard so much. An official dinner was given to the tennis-players and after dinner with the rest of them he went into the Sporting Club. It was the first time he had been there. Monte Carlo was very full and the rooms were crowded. Nicky had never before seen roulette played except in the pictures; in a maze he stopped at the first table he came to; chips of different sizes were scattered over the green cloth in what looked like a hopeless muddle; the croupier gave the wheel a sharp turn and with a flick threw in the little white ball. After what seemed an endless time the ball stopped and another croupier with a broad, indifferent gesture raked in the chips of those who had lost.

Presently Nicky wandered over to where they were playing *trente et quarante*, but he couldn't understand what it was all about and he thought it dull. He saw a crowd in another room and sauntered in. A big game of baccara was in progress and he was immediately conscious of the tension. The players were protected from the thronging bystanders by a brass rail; they sat round the table, nine on each side, with the dealer in the middle and the croupier facing him. Big money was changing hands. The dealer was a member of the Greek Syndicate. Nicky looked at his impassive face. His eyes were watchful, but his expression never changed whether he won or lost. It was a terrifying, strangely impressive sight. It gave Nicky, who had been thriftily brought up, a peculiar thrill to see someone risk a thousand pounds on the turn of a card and when he lost make a little joke and laugh. It was all terribly exciting. An acquaintance came up to him.

'Been doing any good?' he asked.

'I haven't been playing.'

'Wise of you. Rotten game. Come and have a drink.'

'All right.'

While they were having it Nicky told his friend that this was the first time he had ever been in the rooms.

'Oh, but you must have one little flutter before you go. It's idiotic to leave Monte without having tried your luck. After all it won't hurt you to lose a hundred francs or so.'

'I don't suppose it will, but my father wasn't any too keen on my coming at all and one of the three things he particularly advised me not to do was to gamble.'

But when Nicky left his companion he strolled back to one of the tables where they were playing roulette. He stood for a while looking at the losers' money being raked-in by the croupier and the money that was won paid out to the winners. It was impossible to deny that it was thrilling. His friend was right, it did seem silly to leave Monte without putting something on the table just once. It would be an experience, and at his age you had to have all the experience you could get. He reflected that he hadn't promised his father not to gamble, he'd promised him not to forget his advice. It wasn't quite the same, was it? He took a hundred-franc note out of his pocket and rather shyly put it on number eighteen. He chose it because that was his age. With a wildly beating heart he watched the wheel turn; the little white ball whizzed about like a small demon of mischief; the wheel went round more slowly, the little white ball hesitated, it seemed about to stop, it went on again; Nicky could hardly believe his eyes when it fell into number eighteen. A lot of chips were passed over to him and his hands trembled as he took them. It seemed to amount to a lot of money. He was so confused that he never thought of putting anything on the following round; in fact he had no intention of playing any more, once was enough; and he was surprised when eighteen again came up. There was only one chip on it.

'By George, you've won again,' said a man who was standing near to him.

'Me? I hadn't got anything on.'

'Yes, you had. Your original stake. They always leave it on unless you ask for it back. Didn't you know?'

Another packet of chips was handed over to him. Nicky's head reeled. He counted his gains: seven thousand francs. A queer sense of power seized him; he felt wonderfully clever. This was the easiest way of making money that he had ever heard of. His frank, charming face was wreathed in smiles. His bright eyes met those of a woman standing by his side. She smiled.

'You're in luck,' she said.

She spoke English, but with a foreign accent.

'I can hardly believe it. It's the first time I've ever played.'

'That explains it. Lend me a thousand francs, will you? I've lost everything I've got. I'll give it you back in half an hour.'

'All right.'

She took a large red chip from his pile and with a word of thanks disappeared. The man who had spoken to him before grunted.

'You'll never see that again.'

Nicky was dashed. His father had particularly advised him not to lend anyone money. What a silly thing to do! And to somebody he'd never seen in his life. But the fact was, he felt at that moment such love for the human race that it had never occurred to him to refuse. And that big red chip, it was almost impossible to realize that it had any value. Oh well, it didn't matter, he still had six thousand francs, he'd just try his luck once or twice more and if he didn't win he'd go home. He put a chip on sixteen, which was his elder sister's age, but it didn't come up; then on twelve, which was his younger sister's, and that didn't come up either; he tried various numbers at random, but without success. It was funny, he seemed to have lost his knack. He thought he would try just once more and then stop; he won. He had made up all his losses and had something left over. At the end of an hour, after various ups and downs, having experienced such thrills as he had never known in his life, he found himself with so many chips that they would hardly go in his pockets. He decided to go. He went to the changers' office and he gasped when twenty thousand-franc notes were spread out before him. He had never won so much money in his life. He put it in his pocket and was turning away when the woman to whom he had lent the thousand francs came up to him.

'I've been looking for you everywhere,' she said. 'I was afraid you'd gone. I was in a fever, I didn't know what you'd think of me. Here's your thousand francs and thank you so much for the loan.'

Nicky, blushing scarlet, stared at her with amazement. How he had misjudged her! His father had said, don't gamble; well, he had, and he'd made twenty thousand francs; and his father had said, don't lend anyone money; well he had, he'd lent quite a lot to a total stranger, and she'd returned it. The fact was that he wasn't nearly such a fool as his father thought: he'd had an instinct that he could lend her money with safety, and you see, his instinct was right. But he was so obviously taken aback that the little lady was forced to laugh.

'What is the matter with you?' she asked.

'To tell you the truth I never expected to see the money back.'

'What did you take me for? Did you think I was a – cocotte?'

Nicky reddened to the roots of his wavy hair.

'No, of course not.'

'Do I look like one?'

'Not a bit.'

She was dressed very quietly, in black, with a string of gold beads round her neck; her simple frock showed off a neat, slight figure; she had a pretty little face and a trim head. She was made up, but not excessively, and Nicky supposed that she was not more than three or four years older than himself. She gave him a friendly smile.

'My husband is in the administration in Morocco, and I've come to Monte Carlo for a few weeks because he thought I wanted a change.'

'I was just going,' said Nicky because he couldn't think of anything else to say.

'Already!'

'Well, I've got to get up early tomorrow. I'm going back to London by air.'

'Of course. The tournament ended today, didn't it? I saw you play, you know, two or three times.'

'Did you? I don't know why you should have noticed me.'

'You've got a beautiful style. And you looked very sweet in your shorts.'

Nicky was not an immodest youth, but it did cross his mind that perhaps she had borrowed that thousand francs in order to scrape acquaintance with him.

'Do you ever go to the Knickerbocker?' she asked.

'No. I never have.'

'Oh, but you mustn't leave Monte Carlo without having been there. Why don't you come and dance a little? To tell you the truth, I'm starving with hunger and I should adore some bacon and eggs.'

Nicky remembered his father's advice not to have anything to do with women, but this was different; you had only to look at the pretty little thing to know at once that she was perfectly respectable. Her husband was in what corresponded, he supposed, to the Civil Service. His father and mother had friends who were Civil Servants and they and their wives sometimes came to dinner. It was true that the wives were neither so young nor so pretty as this one, but she was just as ladylike as they were. And after winning twenty thousand francs he thought it wouldn't be a bad idea to have a little fun.

'I'd love to go with you,' he said. 'But you won't mind if I don't stay very long. I've left instructions at my hotel that I'm to be called at seven.'

'We'll leave as soon as ever you like.'

Nicky found it very pleasant at the Knickerbocker. He ate his bacon and eggs with appetite. They shared a bottle of champagne. They danced, and the little lady told him he danced beautifully. He knew he danced pretty well, and of course she was easy to dance with. As light as a feather. She laid her cheek against his and when their eyes met there was in hers a smile that made his heart go pit-a-pat. A coloured woman sang in a throaty, sensual voice. The floor was crowded.

'Have you ever been told that you're very good-looking?' she asked.

'I don't think so,' he laughed. 'Gosh,' he thought, 'I believe she's fallen for me.'

Nicky was not such a fool to be unaware that women often liked him, and when she made that remark he pressed her to him a little more closely. She closed her eyes and a faint sigh escaped her lips.

'I suppose it wouldn't be quite nice if I kissed you before all these people,' he said.

'What do you think they would take me for?'

It began to grow late and Nicky said that really he thought he ought to be going.

'I shall go too,' she said. 'Will you drop me at my hotel on your way?'

Nicky paid the bill. He was rather surprised at its amount, but with all that money he had in his pocket he could afford not to care, and they got into a taxi. She snuggled up to him and he kissed her. She seemed to like it.

'By Jove,' he thought, 'I wonder if there's anything doing.'

It was true that she was a married woman, but her husband was in Morocco, and it certainly did look as if she'd fallen for him. Good and proper. It was true also that his father had warned him to have nothing to do with women, but, he reflected again, he hadn't actually promised he wouldn't, he'd only promised not to forget his advice. Well, he hadn't; he was bearing it in mind that very minute. But circumstances alter cases. She was a sweet little thing; it seemed silly to miss the chance of an adventure when it was handed to you like that on a tray. When they reached the hotel he paid off the taxi.

'I'll walk home,' he said. 'The air will do me good after the stuffy atmosphere of that place.'

'Come up a moment,' she said. 'I'd like to show you the photo of my little boy.'

'Oh, have you got a little boy?' he exclaimed, a trifle dashed.

'Yes, a sweet little boy.'

He walked upstairs after her. He didn't in the least want to see the photograph of her little boy, but he thought it only civil to pretend he did. He was afraid he'd made a fool of himself; it occurred to him that she was taking him up to look at the photograph in order to show him in a nice way that he'd made a mistake. He'd told her he was eighteen.

'I suppose she thinks I'm just a kid.'

He began to wish he hadn't spent all that money on champagne at the night-club.

But she didn't show him the photograph of her little boy after all. They had no sooner got into her room than she turned to him, flung her arms round his neck, and kissed him full on the lips. He had never in all his life been kissed so passionately.

'Darling,' she said.

For a brief moment his father's advice once more crossed Nicky's mind and then he forgot it.

Nicky was a light sleeper and the least sound was apt to wake him. Two or three hours later he awoke and for a moment could not imagine where he was. The room was not quite dark, for the door of the bathroom was ajar, and the light in it had been left on. Suddenly he was conscious that someone was moving about the room. Then he remembered. He saw that it was his little friend, and he was on the point of speaking when something in the way she was behaving stopped him. She was walking very cautiously, as though she were afraid of waking him; she stopped once or twice and looked over at the bed. He wondered what she was after. He soon saw. She went over to the chair on which he had placed his clothes and once more looked in his direction. She waited for what seemed to him an interminable time. The silence was so intense that Nicky thought he could hear his own heart beating. Then, very slowly, very quietly, she took up his coat, slipped her hand into the inside pocket and drew out all those beautiful thousand-franc notes that Nicky had been so proud to win. She put the coat back and placed some other clothes on it so that it should look as though it had not been disturbed, then, with the bundle of notes in her hand, for an appreciable time stood once more stock-still. Nicky had repressed an instinctive impulse to jump up and grab her; it was partly surprise that had kept him quiet, partly the notion that he was in a strange hotel, in a foreign country, and if he made a row he didn't know what might happen. She looked at him. His eyes were partly closed and he was sure that she thought he was asleep. In the silence she could hardly fail to hear his regular breathing. When she had reassured herself that her movements had not disturbed him she stepped, with infinite caution, across the room. On a small table in the window a cineraria was growing in a pot. Nicky watched her now with his eyes wide open. The plant was evidently placed quite loosely in the pot, for taking it by the stalks she lifted it out; she put the banknotes in the bottom of the pot and replaced the plant. It was an excellent hiding-place. No one could have guessed that anything was concealed under that richly flowering plant. She pressed the earth down with her fingers and then, very slowly, taking care not to make the smallest noise, crept across the room, and slipped back into bed.

'Chéri,' she said, in a caressing voice.

Nicky breathed steadily, like a man immersed in deep sleep. The little lady turned over on her side and disposed herself to slumber. But though Nicky lay so still his thoughts worked busily. He was extremely indignant at the scene he had just witnessed, and to himself he spoke his thoughts with vigour.

'She's nothing but a damned tart. She and her dear little boy and her husband in Morocco. My eye! She's a rotten thief, that's what she is. Took me for a mug. If she thinks she's going to get away with anything like that, she's mistaken.'

He had already made up his mind what he was going to do with the money he had so cleverly won. He had long wanted a car of his own, and had thought it rather mean of his father not to have given him one. After all, a feller doesn't always want to drive about in the family bus. Well, he'd just teach the old man a lesson and buy one himself. For twenty thousand francs, two hundred pounds roughly, he could get a very decent second-hand car. He meant to get the money back, but just then he didn't know how. He didn't like the idea of kicking up a row, he was a stranger, in an hotel he knew nothing of; it might very well be that the beastly woman had friends there, he didn't mind facing anyone in a fair fight, but he'd look pretty foolish if someone pulled a gun on him. He reflected besides, very sensibly, that he had no proof the money was his. If it came to a showdown and she swore it was hers, he might very easily find himself hauled off to a police-station. He really didn't know what to do. Presently by her regular breathing he knew that the little lady was asleep. She must have fallen asleep with an easy mind, for she had done her job without a hitch. It infuriated Nicky that she should rest so peacefully while he lay awake worried to death. Suddenly an idea occurred to him. It was such a good one that it was only by the exercise of all his self-control that he prevented himself from jumping out of bed and carrying it out at once. Two could play at her game. She'd stolen his money; well, he'd steal it back again, and they'd be all square. He made up his mind to wait quite quietly until he was sure that deceitful woman was sound asleep. He waited for what seemed to him a very long time. She did not stir. Her breathing was as regular as a child's.

'Darling,' he said at last.

No answer. No movement. She was dead to the world. Very slowly, pausing after every movement, very silently, he slipped out of bed. He stood still for a while, looking at her to see whether he had disturbed her. Her breathing was as regular as before. During the time he was waiting he had taken note carefully of the furniture in the room so that in crossing it he should not knock against a chair or a table and make a noise. He took a couple of steps and waited, he took a couple of steps more; he was very light on his feet and made no sound as he walked; he took fully five minutes to get to the window, and here he waited again. He started, for the bed slightly creaked, but it was only because the sleeper turned in her sleep. He forced himself to wait till he had counted one hundred. She was sleeping like a log. With infinite care he seized the cineraria by the stalks and gently pulled it out of the pot; he put his other hand in, his heart beat nineteen to the dozen as his fingers touched the notes, his hand closed on them and he slowly drew them out. He replaced the plant and in his turn carefully pressed down the earth. While he was doing all this he had kept one eye on the form lying in the bed. It remained still. After another pause he crept softly to the chair on which his clothes were lying. He first put the bundle of notes in his coat pocket and then proceeded to dress. It took him a good quarter of an hour, because he could afford to make no sound. He had been wearing a soft shirt with his dinner jacket, and he congratulated himself on this, because it was easier to put on silently than a stiff one. He had difficulty in tying his tie without a looking-glass, but he very wisely reflected that it didn't really matter if it wasn't tied very well. His spirits were rising. The whole thing now began to seem rather a lark. At length he was completely dressed except for his shoes, which he took in his hand; he thought he would put them on when he got into the passage. Now he had to cross the room to get to the door. He reached it so quietly that he could not have disturbed the lightest sleeper. But the door had to be unlocked. He turned the key very slowly; it creaked.

'Who's that?'

The little woman suddenly sat up in bed. Nicky's heart jumped to his mouth. He made a great effort to keep his head.

'It's only me. It's six o'clock and I've got to go. I was trying not to wake you.'

'Oh, I forgot.'

She sank back on to the pillow.

'Now that you're awake I'll put on my shoes.'

He sat down on the edge of the bed and did this.

'Don't make a noise when you go out. The hotel people don't like it. Oh, I'm so sleepy.'

'You go right off to sleep again.'

'Kiss me before you go.' He bent down and kissed her. 'You're a sweet boy and a wonderful lover. *Bon voyage.*'

Nicky did not feel quite safe till he got out of the hotel. The dawn had broken. The sky was unclouded, and in the harbour the yachts and the fishing-boats lay motionless on the still water. On the quay fishermen were getting ready to start on their day's work. The streets were deserted. Nicky took a long breath of the sweet morning air. He felt alert and well. He also felt as pleased as Punch. With a swinging stride, his shoulders well thrown back, he walked up the hill and along the gardens in front of the Casino – the flowers in that clear light had a dewy brilliance that was delicious – till he came to his hotel. Here the day had already begun. In the hall porters with mufflers round their necks and berets on their heads were busy sweeping. Nicky went up to his room and had a hot bath. He lay in it and thought with satisfaction that he was not such a mug as some people might think. After his bath he did his exercises, dressed, packed and went down to breakfast. He had a grand appetite. No continental breakfast for him! He had grape-fruit, porridge, bacon and eggs, rolls fresh from the oven, so crisp and delicious they melted in your mouth, marmalade and three cups of coffee. Though feeling perfectly well before, he felt better after that. He lit the pipe he had recently learnt to smoke, paid his bill and stepped into the car that was waiting to take him to the aero-drome on the other side of Cannes. The road as far as Nice ran over the hills and below him was the blue sea and the coast-line. He couldn't help thinking it damned pretty. They passed through Nice, so gay and friendly in the early morning, and presently they came to a long stretch of straight road that ran by the sea. Nicky had paid his bill, not with the money that he had won the night before, but with the money his father had given him; he had changed a thousand francs to pay for supper at the Knickerbocker, but that deceitful little woman had returned him the thousand francs he had lent her, so that he still had twenty thousand-franc notes in his pocket. He thought he would like to have a look at them. He had so nearly lost them that they had a double value for him. He took them out of his hip-pocket into which for safety's sake he had stuffed them when he put on the suit he was travelling in, and counted them one by one. Something very strange had happened to them. Instead of there being twenty notes as there should have been there were twenty-six. He couldn't understand it at all. He counted them twice more. There was no doubt about it; somehow or other he had twenty-six thousand francs instead of the twenty he should have had. He couldn't make it out. He asked himself if it was possible that he had won more at the Sporting Club than he had realized. But no, that was out of the question; he distinctly remembered the man at the desk laying the notes out in four rows of five, and he had counted them himself. Suddenly the explanation occurred to him; when he had put his hand into the flower-pot, after taking out the cineraria, he had grabbed everything he felt there. The flower-pot was the little hussy's money-box and he had taken out not only his own money, but her savings as well. Nicky leant back in the car and burst into a roar of laughter. It was the funniest thing he had ever heard in his life. And when he thought of her going to the flower-pot some time later in the morning when she awoke, expecting to find the money she had so cleverly got away with, and finding, not only that it wasn't there, but that her own had gone too, he laughed more than ever. And so far as he was concerned there was nothing to do about it; he neither knew her name, nor the name of the hotel to which she had taken him. He couldn't return her money even if he wanted to.

'It serves her damned well right,' he said.

This then was the story that Henry Garnet told his friends over the bridge-table, for the night before, after dinner when his wife and daughter had left them to their port, Nicky had narrated it in full.

'And you know what infuriated me is that he's so damned pleased with himself. Talk of a cat swallowing a canary. And d'you know what he said to me when he'd finished? He looked at me with those innocent eyes of his and said: "You know, father, I can't help thinking there was something wrong with the advice you gave me. You said, don't gamble; well, I did, and I made a packet; you said, don't lend money; well, I did, and I got it back; and you said don't have anything to do with women; well, I did, and I made six thousand francs on the deal."'

It didn't make it any better for Henry Garnet that his three companions burst out laughing.

'It's all very well for you fellows to laugh, but you know, I'm in a damned awkward position. The boy looked up to me, he respected me, he took whatever I said as gospel truth, and now, I saw it in his eyes, he just looks on me as a drivelling old fool. It's no good my saying that one swallow doesn't make a summer;

he doesn't see that it was just a fluke, he thinks the whole thing was due to his own cleverness. It may ruin him.'

'You do look a bit of a damned fool, old man,' said one of the others. 'There's no denying that, is there?'

'I know I do, and I don't like it. It's so dashed unfair. Fate has no right to play one tricks like that. After all, you must admit that my advice was good.'

'Very good.'

'And the wretched boy ought to have burnt his fingers. Well, he hasn't. You're all men of the world, you tell me how I'm to deal with the situation now.'

But they none of them could.

'Well, Henry, if I were you, I wouldn't worry,' said the lawyer. 'My belief is that your boy's born lucky, and in the long run that's better than to be born clever or rich.'

P. G. Wodehouse

Goodbye to All Cats

As the club kitten sauntered into the smoking-room of the Drones Club and greeted those present with a friendly miauw, Freddie Widgeon, who had been sitting in a corner with his head between his hands, rose stiffly.

'I had supposed,' he said, in a cold, level voice, 'that this was a quiet retreat for gentlemen. As I perceive that it is a blasted Zoo, I will withdraw.'

And he left the room in a marked manner.

There was a good deal of surprise, not unmixed with consternation.

'What's the trouble?' asked an Egg, concerned. Such exhibitions of the naked emotions are rare at the Drones. 'Have they had a row?'

A Crumpet, always well-informed, shook his head.

'Freddie has had no personal breach with this particular kitten,' he said. 'It is simply that since that weekend at Matcham Scratchings he can't stand the sight of a cat.'

'Matcham what?'

'Scratchings. The ancestral home of Dahlia Prenderby in Oxfordshire.'

'I met Dahlia Prenderby once,' said the Egg. 'I thought she seemed a nice girl.'

'Freddie thought so, too. He loved her madly.'

'And lost her, of course?'

'Absolutely.'

'Do you know,' said a thoughtful Bean, 'I'll bet that if all the girls Freddie Widgeon has loved and lost were placed end to end – not that I suppose one could do it – they would reach half-way down Piccadilly.'

'Further than that,' said the Egg. 'Some of them were pretty tall. What beats me is why he ever bothers to love them. They always turn him down in the end. He might just as well never begin. Better, in fact, because in the time saved he could be reading some good book.'

'I think the trouble with Freddie,' said the Crumpet, 'is that he always gets off to a flying start. He's a good-looking sort of chap who dances well and can wiggle his ears, and the girl is dazzled for the moment, and this encourages him. From what he tells me, he appears to have gone very big with this Prenderby girl at the outset. So much so, indeed, that when she invited him down to Matcham Scratchings he had already bought his copy of *What Every Young Bridegroom Ought to Know.*'

'Rummy, these old country-house names,' mused the Bean. 'Why Scratchings, I wonder?'

'Freddie wondered, too, till he got to the place. Then he tells me he felt it was absolutely the *mot juste.* This girl Dahlia's family, you see, was one of those animal-loving families, and the house, he tells me, was just a frothing maelstrom of dumb chums. As far as the eye could reach, there were dogs scratching themselves and cats scratching the furniture. I believe, though he never met it socially, there was even a tame chimpanzee somewhere on the premises, no doubt scratching away as assiduously as the rest of them. You get these conditions here and there in the depths of the country, and this Matcham place was well away from the centre of things, being about six miles from the nearest station.'

It was at this station (said the Crumpet) that Dahlia Prenderby met Freddie in her two-seater, and on the way to the house there occurred a conversation which I consider significant – showing, as it does, the cordial relations existing between the young couple at that point in the proceedings. I mean, it was only later that the bitter awakening and all that sort of thing popped up.

'I do want you to be a success, Freddie,' said the girl, after talking a while of this and that. 'Some of the men I've asked down here have been such awful flops. The great thing is to make a good impression on Father.'

'I will,' said Freddie.

'He can be a little difficult at times.'

'Lead me to him,' said Freddie. 'That's all I ask. Lead me to him.'

'The trouble is, he doesn't much like young men.'

'He'll like me.'

'He will, will he?'

'Rather!'

'What makes you think that?'

'I'm a dashed fascinating chap.'

'Oh, you are?'

'Yes, I am.'

'You are, are you?'

'Rather!'

Upon which, she gave him a sort of push and he gave her a sort of push, and she giggled and he laughed like a paper bag bursting, and she gave him a kind of shove and he gave her a kind of shove, and she said 'You *are* a silly ass!' and he said 'What ho!' All of which shows you, I mean to say, the stage they had got to by this time. Nothing definitely settled, of course, but Love obviously beginning to burgeon in the girl's heart.

Well, naturally, Freddie gave a good deal of thought during the drive to this father of whom the girl had spoken so feelingly, and he resolved that he would not fail her. The way he would suck up to the old dad would be nobody's business. He proposed to exert upon him the full force of his magnetic personality, and looked forward to registering a very substantial hit.

Which being so, I need scarcely tell you, knowing Freddie as you do, that his first act on entering Sir Mortimer Prenderby's orbit was to make the scaliest kind of floater, hitting him on the back of the neck with a tortoiseshell cat not ten minutes after his arrival.

His train having been a bit late, there was no time on reaching the house for any stately receptions or any of that 'Welcome to

Meadowsweet Hall' stuff. The girl simply shot him up to his room and told him to dress like a streak, because dinner was in a quarter of an hour, and then buzzed off to don the soup and fish herself. And Freddie was just going well when, looking round for his shirt, which he had left on the bed, he saw a large tortoiseshell cat standing on it, kneading it with its paws.

Well, you know how a fellow feels about his shirt-front. For an instant, Freddie stood spellbound. Then with a hoarse cry he bounded forward, scooped up the animal, and carrying it out on to the balcony, flung it into the void. And an elderly gentleman, coming round the corner at this moment, received a direct hit on the back of his neck.

'Hell!' cried the elderly gentleman.

A head popped out of a window.

'Whatever is the matter, Mortimer?'

'It's raining cats.'

'Nonsense. It's a lovely evening,' said the head, and disappeared.

Freddie thought an apology would be in order.

'I say,' he said.

The old gentleman looked in every direction of the compass, and finally located Freddie on his balcony.

'I say,' said Freddie, 'I'm awfully sorry you got that nasty buffet. It was me.'

'It was not you. It was a cat.'

'I know. I threw the cat.'

'Why?'

'Well ...'

'Dam' fool.'

'I'm sorry,' said Freddie.

'Go to blazes,' said the old gentleman.

Freddie backed into the room, and the incident closed.

Freddie is a pretty slippy dresser, as a rule, but this episode had shaken him, and he not only lost a collar-stud but made a mess of the first two ties. The result was that the gong went while he was still in his shirt sleeves: and on emerging from his boudoir he was informed by a footman that the gang were already nuzzling their *bouillon* in the dining-room. He pushed straight on there, accordingly, and sank into a chair beside his hostess just in time to dead-heat with the final spoonful.

Awkward, of course, but he was feeling in pretty good form owing to the pleasantness of the thought that he was shoving his knees under the same board as the girl Dahlia: so, having nodded to his host, who was glaring at him from the head of the table, as much as to say that all would be explained in God's good time, he shot his cuffs and started to make sparkling conversation to Lady Prenderby.

'Charming place you have here, what?'

Lady Prenderby said that the local scenery was generally admired. She was one of those tall, rangy, Queen Elizabeth sort of women, with tight lips and cold, blanc-mange-y eyes. Freddie didn't like her looks much, but he was feeling, as I say, fairly fizzy, so he carried on with a bright zip.

'Pretty good hunting country, I should think.'

'I believe there is a good deal of hunting near here, yes.'

'I thought as much,' said Freddie. 'Ah, that's the stuff, is it not? A cracking gallop across good country with a jolly fine kill at the end of it, what, what? Hark for'ard, yoicks, tally-ho, I mean to say, and all that sort of thing.'

Lady Prenderby shivered austerely.

'I fear I cannot share your enthusiasm,' she said. 'I have the strongest possible objection to hunting. I have always set my face against it, as against all similar brutalizing blood-sports.'

This was a nasty jar for poor old Freddie, who had been relying on the topic to carry him nicely through at least a couple of courses. It silenced him for the nonce. And as he paused to collect his faculties, his host, who had now been glowering for six and a half minutes practically without cessation, put a hand in front of his mouth and addressed the girl Dahlia across the table. Freddie thinks he was under the impression that he was speaking in a guarded whisper, but, as a matter of fact, the words boomed through the air as if he had been a costermonger calling attention to his brussels sprouts.

'Dahlia!'

'Yes, Father?'

'Who's that ugly feller?'

'Hush!'

'What do you mean, hush? Who is he?'

'Mr Widgeon.'

'Mr Who?'

'Widgeon.'

'I wish you would articulate clearly and not mumble,' said Sir Mortimer fretfully. 'It sounds to me just like "Widgeon". Who asked him here?'

'I did.'

'Why?'

'He's a friend of mine.'

'Well, he looks a pretty frightful young slab of damnation to me. What I'd call a criminal face.'

'Hush!'

'Why do you keep saying "Hush"? Must be a lunatic, too. Throws cats at people.'

'Please, Father!'

'Don't say "Please, Father!" No sense in it. I tell you he does throw cats at people. He threw one at me. Half-witted, I'd call him – if that. Besides being the most offensive-looking young toad I've ever seen on the premises. How long's he staying?'

'Till Monday.'

'My God! And today's only Friday!' bellowed Sir Mortimer Prenderby.

It was an unpleasant situation for Freddie, of course, and I'm bound to admit he didn't carry it off particularly well. What he ought to have done, obviously, was to have plunged into an easy flow of small-talk: but all he could think of was to ask Lady Prenderby if she was fond of shooting. Lady Prenderby having replied that, owing to being deficient in the savage instincts and wanton blood-lust that went to make up a callous and cold-hearted murderess, she was not, he relapsed into silence with his lower jaw hanging down.

All in all, he wasn't so dashed sorry when dinner came to an end.

As he and Sir Mortimer were the only men at the table, most of the seats having been filled by a covey of mildewed females whom he had classified under the general heading of Aunts, it seemed to Freddie that the moment had now arrived when they would be able to get together once more, under happier conditions than those of their last meeting, and start to learn to appreciate one another's true worth. He looked forward to a cosy *tête-à-tête* over the port, in the course of which he would smooth over that cat incident and generally do all that lay within his power to revise the unfavourable opinion of him which the other must have formed.

But apparently Sir Mortimer had his own idea of the duties and obligations of a host. Instead of clustering round Freddie with decanters, he simply gave him a long, lingering look of distaste and shot out of the french window into the garden. A moment later, his head reappeared and he uttered the words: 'You and your dam' cats!' Then the night swallowed him again.

Freddie was a good deal perplexed. All this was new stuff to him. He had been in and out of a number of country-houses in his time, but this was the first occasion on which he had ever been left flat at the conclusion of the evening meal, and he wasn't quite sure how to handle the situation. He was still wondering when Sir Mortimer's head came into view again and its owner, after giving him another of those long, lingering looks, said: 'Cats, forsooth!' and disappeared once more.

Freddie was now definitely piqued. It was all very well, he felt, Dahlia Prenderby telling him to make himself solid with her father, but how can you make yourself solid with a fellow who doesn't stay put for a couple of consecutive seconds? If it was Sir Mortimer's intention to spend the remainder of the night flashing past like a merry-go-round, there seemed little hope of anything amounting to a genuine *rapprochement*. It was a relief to his feelings when there suddenly appeared from nowhere his old acquaintance the tortoiseshell cat. It seemed to offer to him a means of working off his spleen.

Taking from Lady Prenderby's plate, accordingly, the remains of a banana, he plugged the animal neatly at a range of two yards. It yowled and withdrew. And a moment later, there was Sir Mortimer again.

'Did you kick that cat?' said Sir Mortimer.

Freddie had half a mind to ask this old disease if he thought he was a man or a jack-in-the-box, but the breeding of the Widgeons restrained him.

'No,' he said, 'I did not kick that cat.'

'You must have done something to it to make it come charging out at forty miles an hour.'

'I merely offered the animal a piece of fruit.'

'Do it again and see what happens to you.'

'Lovely evening,' said Freddie, changing the subject.

'No, it's not, you silly ass!' said Sir Mortimer. Freddie rose. His nerve, I fancy, was a little shaken.

'I shall join the ladies,' he said with dignity.

'God help them!' replied Sir Mortimer Prenderby in a voice instinct with the deepest feeling, and vanished once more.

Freddie's mood, as he made for the drawing-room, was thoughtful. I don't say he has much sense, but he's got enough to know when he is and when he isn't going with a bang. Tonight, he realized, had been very far from going in such a manner. It was not, that is to say, as the Idol of Matcham Scratchings that he would enter the drawing-room, but rather as a young fellow who had made an unfortunate first impression and would have to do a lot of heavy ingratiating before he could regard himself as really popular in the home.

He must bustle about, he felt, and make up leeway. And, knowing that what counts with these old-style females who have lived in the country all their lives is the exhibition of those little politenesses and attentions which were all the go in Queen Victoria's time, his first action, on entering, was to make a dive for one of the aunts who seemed to be trying to find a place to put her coffee-cup.

'Permit me,' said Freddie, suave to the eyebrows.

And bounding forward with the feeling that this was the stuff to give them, he barged right into a cat.

'Oh, sorry,' he said, backing and bringing down his heel on another cat.

'I say, most frightfully sorry,' he said.

And, tottering to a chair, he sank heavily on to a third cat.

Well, he was up and about again in a jiffy, of course, but it was too late. There was the usual not-at-all-ing and don't-mention-it-ing, but he could read between the lines. Lady Prenderby's eyes had rested on his for only a brief instant, but it had been enough. His standing with her, he perceived, was now approximately what King Herod's would have been at an Israelite Mothers' Social Saturday Afternoon.

The girl Dahlia during these exchanges had been sitting on a sofa at the end of the room, turning the pages of a weekly paper, and the sight of her drew Freddie like a magnet. Her womanly sympathy was just what he felt he could do with at this juncture. Treading with infinite caution, he crossed to where she sat: and, having scanned the terrain narrowly for cats, sank down on the sofa at her side. And conceive his agony of spirit when he discovered that womanly sympathy had been turned off at the main. The girl was like a chunk of ice-cream with spikes all over it.

'Please do not trouble to explain,' she said coldly, in answer to his opening words. 'I quite understand that there are people who have this odd dislike of animals.'

'But dash it . . .' cried Freddie, waving his arm in a frenzied sort of way. 'Oh, I say, sorry,' he added, as his fist sloshed another of the menagerie in the short ribs.

Dahlia caught the animal as it flew through the air.

'I think perhaps you had better take Augustus, Mother,' she said. 'He seems to be annoying Mr Widgeon.'

'Quite,' said Lady Prenderby. 'He will be safer with me.'

'But, dash it . . .' bleated Freddie.

Dahlia Prenderby drew in her breath sharply.

'How true it is,' she said, 'that one never really knows a man till after one has seen him in one's own home.'

'What do you mean by that?'

'Oh, nothing,' said Dahlia Prenderby.

She rose and moved to the piano, where she proceeded to sing old Breton folk-songs in a distant manner, leaving Freddie to make out as best he could with a family album containing faded photographs with 'Aunt Emily bathing at Llandudno, 1893', and 'This is Cousin George at the fancy-dress ball' written under them.

And so the long, quiet, peaceful home evening wore on, till eventually Lady Prenderby mercifully blew the whistle and he was at liberty to sneak off to his bedroom.

You might have supposed that Freddie's thoughts, as he toddled upstairs with his candle, would have dwelt exclusively on the girl Dahlia. This, however, was not so. He did give her obvious shirtiness a certain measure of attention, of course, but what really filled his mind was the soothing reflection that at long last his path and that of the animal kingdom of Matcham Scratchings had now divided. He, so to speak, was taking the high road while they, as it were, would take the low road. For whatever might be the conditions prevailing in the dining-room, the drawing-room, and the rest of the house, his bedroom, he felt, must surely be a haven totally free from cats of all descriptions.

Remembering, however, that unfortunate episode before dinner, he went down on all fours and subjected the various nooks and crannies to a close examination. His eye could detect no cats. Relieved, he rose to his feet with a gay song on his lips: and he hadn't got much beyond the first couple of bars when a voice behind him suddenly started taking the bass: and, turning, he perceived on the bed a fine Alsatian dog.

Freddie looked at the dog. The dog looked at Freddie. The situation was one fraught with embarrassment. A glance at the animal was enough to convince him that it had got an entirely wrong angle on the position of affairs and was regarding him purely in the light of an intrusive stranger who had muscled in on its private sleeping quarters. Its manner was plainly resentful. It fixed Freddie with a cold, yellow eye and curled its upper lip slightly, the better to display a long, white tooth. It also twitched its nose and gave a *sotto voce* imitation of distant thunder.

Freddie did not know quite what avenue to explore. It was impossible to climb between the sheets with a thing like that on the counterpane. To spend the night in a chair, on the other hand, would have been foreign to his policy. He did what I consider the most statesmanlike thing by sidling out on to the balcony and squinting along the wall of the house to see if there wasn't a lighted window hard by, behind which might lurk somebody who would rally round with aid and comfort.

There was a lighted window only a short distance away, so he shoved his head out as far as it would stretch, and said:

'I say!'

There being no response, he repeated.

'I say!'

And, finally, to drive his point home, he added:

'I say! I say! I say!'

This time he got results. The head of Lady Prenderby suddenly protruded from the window.

'Who,' she enquired, 'is making that abominable noise?'

It was not precisely the attitude Freddie had hoped for, but he could take the rough with the smooth.

'It's me. Widgeon, Frederick.'

'Must you sing on your balcony, Mr Widgeon?'

'I wasn't singing. I was saying "I say".'

'What were you saying?'

'I say.'

'You say what?'

'I say I was saying "I say". Kind of a heart-cry, if you know what I mean. The fact is, there's a dog in my room.'

'What sort of dog?'

'A whacking great Alsatian.'

'Ah, that would be Wilhelm. Good night, Mr Widgeon.'

The window closed. Freddie let out a heart-stricken yip.

'But I say!'

The window reopened.

'Really, Mr Widgeon!'

'But what am I to do?'

'Do?'

'About this whacking great Alsatian!'

Lady Prenderby seemed to consider.

'No sweet biscuits,' she said. 'And when the maid brings you your tea in the morning please do not give him sugar. Simply a little milk in a saucer. He is on a diet. Good night, Mr Widgeon.'

Freddie was now pretty well nonplussed. No matter what his

hostess might say about this beastly dog being on a diet, he was convinced from its manner that its medical adviser had not forbidden it Widgeons, and once more he bent his brain to the task of ascertaining what to do next.

There were several possible methods of procedure. His balcony being not so very far from the ground, he could, if he pleased, jump down and pass a health-giving night in the nasturtium bed. Or he might curl up on the floor. Or he might get out of the room and doss downstairs somewhere.

This last scheme seemed about the best. The only obstacle in the way of its fulfilment was the fact that, when he started for the door, his room-mate would probably think he was a burglar about to loot silver of lonely country-house and pin him. Still, it had to be risked, and a moment later he might have been observed tiptoeing across the carpet with all the caution of a slack-wire artist who isn't any too sure he remembers the correct steps.

Well, it was a near thing. At the instant when he started, the dog seemed occupied with something that looked like a cushion on the bed. It was licking this object in a thoughtful way, and paid no attention to Freddie till he was half-way across No Man's Land. Then it suddenly did a sort of sitting high-jump in his direction, and two seconds later Freddie, with a draughty feeling about the seat of his trousers, was on top of the wardrobe, with the dog underneath looking up. He tells me that if he ever moved quicker in his life it was only on the occasion when, as a lad of fourteen, he was discovered by his uncle, Lord Bicester, smoking one of the latter's cigars in the library: and he rather thinks he must have clipped at least a fifth of a second off the record then set up.

It looked to him now as if his sleeping arrangements for the night had been settled for him. And the thought of having to roost on top of a wardrobe at the whim of a dog was pretty dashed offensive to his proud spirit, as you may well imagine. However, as you cannot reason with Alsatians, it seemed the only thing to be done: and he was trying to make himself as comfortable as a sharp piece of wood sticking into the fleshy part of his leg would permit, when there was a snuffling noise in the passage and through the door came an object which in the dim light he was at first not able to identify. It looked something like a pen-wiper and something like a piece of hearth-rug. A second and keener inspection revealed it as a Pekinese puppy.

The uncertainty which Freddie had felt as to the newcomer's status was shared, it appeared, by the Alsatian: for after raising its eyebrows in a puzzled manner it rose and advanced inquiringly. In a tentative way it put out a paw and rolled the intruder over. Then, advancing again, it lowered its nose and sniffed.

It was a course of action against which its best friend would have advised it. These Pekes are tough eggs, especially when, as in this case, female. They look the world in the eye, and are swift to resent familiarity. There was a sort of explosion, and the next moment the Alsatian was shooting out of the room with its tail between its legs, hotly pursued. Freddie could hear the noise of battle rolling away along the passage, and it was music to his ears. Something on these lines was precisely what that Alsatian had been asking for, and now it had got it.

Presently, the Peke returned, dashing the beads of perspiration from its forehead, and came and sat down under the wardrobe, wagging a stumpy tail. And Freddie, feeling that the All Clear had been blown and that he was now at liberty to descend, did so.

His first move was to shut the door, his second to fraternize with his preserver. Freddie is a chap who believes in giving credit where credit is due, and it seemed to him that this Peke had shown itself an ornament of its species. He spared no effort, accordingly, to entertain it. He lay down on the floor and let it lick his face two hundred and thirty-three times. He tickled it under the left ear, the right ear, and at the base of the tail, in the order named. He also scratched its stomach.

All these attentions the animal received with cordiality and marked gratification: and as it seemed still in pleasure-seeking mood and had plainly come to look upon him as the official Master of the Revels, Freddie, feeling that he could not disappoint it but must play the host no matter what the cost to himself, took off his tie and handed it over. He would not have done it for everybody, he says, but where this life-saving Peke was concerned the sky was the limit.

Well, the tie went like a breeze. It was a success from the start. The Peke chewed it and chased it and got entangled in it and dragged it about the room, and was just starting to shake it from side to side when an unfortunate thing happened. Misjudging its distance, it banged its head a nasty wallop against the leg of the bed.

There is nothing of the Red Indian at the stake about a puppy in circumstances like this. A moment later, Freddie's blood was chilled by a series of fearful shrieks that seemed to ring through the night like the dying cries of the party of the second part to a first-class murder. It amazed him that a mere Peke, and a juvenile Peke at that, should have been capable of producing such an uproar. He says that a Baronet, stabbed in the back with a paper-knife in his library, could not have made half such a row.

Eventually, the agony seemed to abate. Quite suddenly, as if nothing had happened, the Peke stopped yelling and with an amused smile started to play with the tie again. And at the same moment there was a sound of whispering outside, and then a knock at the door.

'Hallo?' said Freddie.

'It is I, sir. Biggleswade.'

'Who's Biggleswade?'

'The butler, sir.'

'What do you want?'

'Her ladyship wishes me to remove the dog which you are torturing.'

There was more whispering.

'Her ladyship also desires me to say that she will be reporting the affair in the morning to the Society for the Prevention of Cruelty to Animals.'

There was another spot of whispering.

'Her ladyship further instructs me to add that, should you prove recalcitrant, I am to strike you over the head with the poker.'

Well, you can't say this was pleasant for poor old Freddie,

and he didn't think so himself. He opened the door, to perceive, without, a group consisting of Lady Prenderby, her daughter Dahlia, a few assorted aunts, and the butler, with poker. And he says he met Dahlia's eyes and they went through him like a knife.

'Let me explain . . .' he began.

'Spare us the details,' said Lady Prenderby with a shiver. She scooped up the Peke and felt it for broken bones.

'But listen . . .'

'Good night, Mr Widgeon.'

The aunts said good night, too, and so did the butler. The girl Dahlia preserved a revolted silence.

'But, honestly, it was nothing, really. It banged its head against the bed . . .'

'What did he say?' asked one of the aunts, who was a little hard of hearing.

'He says he banged the poor creature's head against the bed,' said Lady Prenderby.

'Dreadful!' said the aunt.

'Hideous!' said a second aunt.

A third aunt opened up another line of thought. She said that with men like Freddie in the house, was anyone safe? She mooted the possibility of them all being murdered in their beds. And though Freddie offered to give her a written guarantee that he hadn't the slightest intention of going anywhere near her bed, the idea seemed to make a deep impression.

'Biggleswade,' said Lady Prenderby.

'M'lady?'

'You will remain in this passage for the remainder of the night with your poker.'

'Very good, m'lady.'

'Should this man attempt to leave his room, you will strike him smartly over the head.'

'Just so, m'lady.'

'But, listen . . .' said Freddie.

'Good night, Mr Widgeon.'

The mob scene broke up. Soon the passage was empty save for Biggleswade the butler, who had begun to pace up and down, halting every now and then to flick the air with his poker as if testing the lissomness of his wrist-muscles and satisfying himself that they were in a condition to ensure the right amount of follow-through.

The spectacle he presented was so unpleasant that Freddie withdrew into his room and shut the door. His bosom, as you may imagine, was surging with distressing emotions. That look which Dahlia Prenderby had given him had churned him up to no little extent. He realized that he had a lot of tense thinking to do, and to assist thought he sat down on the bed.

Or, rather, to be accurate, on the dead cat which was lying on the bed. It was this cat which the Alsatian had been licking just before the final breach in his relations with Freddie – the object, if you remember, which the latter had supposed to be a cushion.

He leaped up as if the corpse, instead of being cold, had been piping hot. He stared down, hoping against hope that the animal was merely in some sort of coma. But a glance told him that it had made the great change. He had never seen a deader cat. After life's fitful fever it slept well.

You wouldn't be far out in saying that poor old Freddie was now appalled. Already his reputation in this house was at zero, his name mud. On all sides he was looked upon as Widgeon the Amateur Vivisectionist. This final disaster could not but put the tin hat on it. Before he had had a faint hope that in the morning, when calmer moods would prevail, he might be able to explain that matter of the Peke. But who was going to listen to him if he were discovered with a dead cat on his person?

And then the thought came to him that it might be possible not to be discovered with it on his person. He had only to nip downstairs and deposit the remains in the drawing-room or somewhere and suspicion might not fall upon him. After all, in a super-catted house like this, cats must always be dying like flies all over the place. A housemaid would find the animal in the morning and report to G.H.Q. that the cat strength of the establishment had been reduced by one, and there would be a bit of tut-tutting and perhaps a silent tear or two, and then the whole thing would be forgotten.

The thought gave him new life. All briskness and efficiency, he picked up the body by the tail and was just about to dash out of the room when, with a silent groan, he remembered Biggleswade.

He peeped out. It might be that the butler, once the eye of authority had been removed, had departed to get the remainder of his beauty-sleep. But no. Service and Fidelity were evidently the watchwords at Matcham Scratchings. There the fellow was, still practising half-arm shots with the poker. Freddie closed the door.

And, as he did so, he suddenly thought of the window. There lay the solution. Here he had been fooling about with doors and thinking in terms of drawing-rooms, and all the while there was the balcony staring him in the face. All he had to do was to shoot the body out into the silent night, and let gardeners, not housemaids, discover it.

He hurried out. It was a moment for swift action. He raised his burden. He swung it to and fro, working up steam. Then he let it go, and from the dark garden there came suddenly the cry of a strong man in his anger.

'Who threw that cat?'

It was the voice of his host, Sir Mortimer Prenderby.

'Show me the man who threw that cat!' he thundered.

Windows flew up. Heads came out. Freddie sank to the floor of the balcony and rolled against the wall.

'Whatever is the matter, Mortimer?'

'Let me get at the man who hit me in the eye with a cat.'

'A cat?' Lady Prenderby's voice sounded perplexed. 'Are you sure?'

'Sure? What do you mean sure? Of course I'm sure. I was just dropping off to sleep in my hammock, when suddenly a great beastly cat came whizzing through the air and caught me properly in the eyeball. It's a nice thing. A man can't sleep in hammocks in his own garden without people pelting him with cats. I insist on the blood of the man who threw that cat.'

'Where did it come from?'

'Must have come from that balcony there.'

'Mr Widgeon's balcony,' said Lady Prenderby in an acid voice. 'As I might have guessed.'

Sir Mortimer uttered a cry.

'So might I have guessed! Widgeon, of course! That ugly feller. He's been throwing cats all the evening. I've got a nasty sore place on the back of my neck where he hit me with one before dinner. Somebody come and open the front door. I want my heavy cane, the one with the carved ivory handle. Or a horsewhip will do.'

'Wait, Mortimer,' said Lady Prenderby. 'Do nothing rash. The man is evidently a very dangerous lunatic. I will send Biggleswade to overpower him. He has the kitchen poker.'

Little (said the Crumpet) remains to be told. At two-fifteen that morning a sombre figure in dress clothes without a tie limped into the little railway station of Lower Smattering on the Wissel, some six miles from Matcham Scratchings. At three-forty-seven it departed London-wards on the up milk-train. It was Frederick Widgeon. He had a broken heart and blisters on both heels. And in that broken heart was that loathing for all cats of which you recently saw so signal a manifestation. I am revealing no secrets when I tell you that Freddie Widgeon is permanently through with cats. From now on, they cross his path at their peril.

Katherine Mansfield

Germans at Meat

Bread soup was placed upon the table. 'Ah,' said the Herr Rat, leaning upon the table as he peered into the tureen, 'that is what I need. My "magen" has not been in order for several days. Bread soup, and just the right consistency. I am a good cook myself' – he turned to me.

'How interesting,' I said, attempting to infuse just the right amount of enthusiasm into my voice.

'Oh yes – when one is not married it is necessary. As for me, I have had all I wanted from women without marriage.' He tucked his napkin into his collar and blew upon his soup as he spoke. 'Now at nine o'clock I make myself an English breakfast, but not much. Four slices of bread, two eggs, two slices of cold ham, one plate of soup, two cups of tea – that is nothing to you.'

He asserted the fact so vehemently that I had not the courage to refute it.

All eyes were suddenly turned upon me. I felt I was bearing the burden of the nation's preposterous breakfast – I who drank a cup of coffee while buttoning my blouse in the morning.

'Nothing at all,' cried Herr Hoffmann from Berlin. 'Ach, when I was in England in the morning I used to eat.'

He turned up his eyes and his moustache, wiping the soup drippings from his coat and waistcoat.

'Do they really eat so much?' asked Fraulein Stiegelauer. 'Soup and baker's bread and pig's flesh, and tea and coffee and stewed fruit, and honey and eggs, and cold fish and kidneys, and hot fish and liver? All the ladies eat, too, especially the ladies?'

'Certainly. I myself have noticed it, when I was living in a hotel in Leicester Square,' cried the Herr Rat. 'It was a good hotel, but they could not make tea – now –'

'Ah, that's one thing I *can* do,' said I, laughing brightly. 'I can make very good tea. The great secret is to warm the teapot.'

'Warm the teapot,' interrupted the Herr Rat, pushing away his soup plate. 'What do you warm the teapot for? Ha! ha! that's very good! One does not eat the teapot, I suppose?'

He fixed his cold blue eyes upon me with an expression which suggested a thousand premeditated invasions.

'So that is the great secret of your English tea? All you do is to warm the teapot.'

I wanted to say that was only the preliminary canter, but could not translate it, and so was silent.

The servant brought in veal, with sauerkraut and potatoes.

'I eat sauerkraut with great pleasure,' said the Traveller from North Germany, 'but now I have eaten so much of it that I cannot retain it. I am immediately forced to –'

'A beautiful day,' I cried, turning to Fraulein Stiegelauer. 'Did you get up early?'

'At five o'clock I walked for ten minutes in the wet grass. Again in bed. At half-past five I fell asleep, and woke at seven, when I made an "overbody" washing! Again in bed. At eight o'clock I had a cold-water poultice, and at half past eight I drank a cup of mint tea. At nine I drank some malt coffee, and began my "cure". Pass me the sauerkraut, please. You do not eat it?'

'No, thank you. I still find it a little strong.'

'Is it true,' asked the Widow, picking her teeth with a hairpin as she spoke, 'that you are a vegetarian?'

'Why, yes; I have not eaten meat for three years.'

'Im-possible! Have you any family?'

'No.'

'There now, you see, that's what you're coming to! Who ever heard of having children upon vegetables? It is not possible. But you never have large families in England now; I suppose you are too busy with your suffragetting. Now I have had nine children, and they are all alive, thank God. Fine, healthy babies – though after the first one was born I had to –'

'How *wonderful*!' I cried.

'Wonderful,' said the Widow contemptuously, replacing the hairpin in the knob which was balanced on the top of her head. 'Not at all! A friend of mine had four at the same time. Her husband was so pleased he gave a supper-party and had them placed on the table. Of course she was very proud.'

'Germany,' boomed the Traveller, biting round a potato which he had speared with his knife, 'is the home of the Family.'

Followed an appreciative silence.

The dishes were changed for beef, red currants and spinach. They wiped their forks upon black bread and started again.

'How long are you remaining here?' asked the Herr Rat.

'I do not know exactly. I must be back in London in September.'

'Of course you will visit München?'

'I am afraid I shall not have time. You see, it is important not to break into my "cure".'

'But you *must* go to München. You have not seen Germany if you have not been to München. All the Exhibitions, all the Art and Soul life of Germany are in München. There is the Wagner Festival in August, and Mozart and a Japanese collection of pictures – and there is the beer! You do not know what good beer is until you have been to München. Why, I see fine ladies every afternoon, but fine ladies, I tell you, drinking glasses so high.' He measured a good washstand pitcher in height, and I smiled. 'If I drink a great deal of München beer I sweat so,' said Herr Hoffmann. 'When I am here, in the fields or before my baths, I sweat, but I enjoy it; but in the town it is not at all the same thing.'

Prompted by the thought, he wiped his neck and face with his dinner napkin and carefully cleaned his ears.

A glass dish of stewed apricots was placed upon the table.

'Ah, fruit!' said Fraulein Stiegelauer, 'that is so necessary to health. The doctor told me this morning that the more fruit I could eat the better.'

She very obviously followed the advice.

Said the Traveller: 'I suppose you are frightened of an

invasion, too, eh? Oh, that's good. I've been reading all about your English play in a newspaper. Did you see it?'

'Yes.' I sat upright. 'I assure you we are not afraid.'

'Well, then, you ought to be,' said the Herr Rat. 'You have got no army at all – a few little boys with their veins full of nicotine poisoning.'

'Don't be afraid,' Herr Hoffmann said. 'We don't want England. If we did we would have had her long ago. We really do not want you.'

He waved his spoon airily, looking across at me as though I were a little child whom he would keep or dismiss as he pleased.

'We certainly do not want Germany,' I said.

'This morning I took a half bath. Then this afternoon I must take a knee bath and an arm bath,' volunteered the Herr Rat; 'then I do my exercises for an hour, and my work is over. A glass of wine and a couple of rolls with some sardines –'

They were handed cherry cake with whipped cream.

'What is your husband's favourite meat?' asked the Widow.

'I really do not know,' I answered.

'You really do not know? How long have you been married?'

'Three years.'

'But you cannot be in earnest! You would not have kept house as his wife for a week without knowing that fact.'

'I really never asked him; he is not at all particular about his food.'

A pause. They all looked at me, shaking their heads, their mouths full of cherry stones.

'No wonder there is a repetition in England of that dreadful state of things in Paris,' said the Widow, folding her dinner napkin. 'How can a woman expect to keep her husband if she does not know his favourite food after three years?'

'Mahlzeit!'

'Mahlzeit!'

I closed the door after me.

E. M. Delafield

from
The Provincial Lady in Wartime

September 23rd. – ... Spend large part of the day asking practically everybody I can think of, by telephone or letter, if they can suggest a war job for me.

Most of them reply that they are engaged in similar quest on their own account.

Go out into Trafalgar Square and see gigantic poster on Nelson's plinth asking me what form MY service is taking.

Other hoardings of London give equally prominent display to such announcements as that 300,000 Nurses are wanted, 41,000 Ambulance Drivers, and 500,000 Air-raid Wardens. Get into touch with Organizations requiring these numerous volunteers, and am told that queue five and a half miles long is already besieging their doors.

Ring up influential man at B.B.C. – name given me by Sir W. Frobisher as being dear old friend of his – and influential man tells me in tones of horror that they have a list of really *first-class* writers and speakers whom they can call upon at any moment – which, I gather, they have no intention of doing – and really couldn't possibly make any use of me whatever. At the same time, of course, I can always feel I'm Standing By.

I say Yes, indeed, and ring off.

Solitary ray of light comes from Serena Fiddlededee whom I hear in bathroom – on door of which she has pinned paper marked ENGAGED – at unnatural hour of 2 p.m. and who emerges in order to say that *until* I start work at the Ministry of Information, she thinks the Adelphi Canteen might be glad of occasional help, if voluntary, and given on night-shift.

Pass over reference to Ministry of Information and at once agree to go and offer assistance at Canteen. Serena declares herself delighted, and offers to introduce me there tonight.

Meanwhile, why not go and see Brigadier Pinflitton, said to be important person in A.R.P. circles? Serena knows him well, and will ring up and say that I am coming and that he will do well to make sure of my assistance before I am snapped up elsewhere.

I beg Serena to modify this last improbable adjuration, but admit that I should be glad of introduction to Brigadier P. if there is the slightest chance of his being able to tell me of something I can do. What does Serena think?

Serena thinks there's almost certain to be a fire-engine or something that I could drive, or perhaps I might decontaminate someone – which leads her on to an inquiry about my gas-mask. How, she wishes to know, do I get on inside it? Serena herself always feels as if she must faint after wearing it for two seconds. She thinks one ought to practise sitting in it in the evenings sometimes.

Rather unalluring picture is conjured up by this, but admit that Serena may be right, and I suggest supper together one evening, followed by sessions in our respective gas-masks.

We can, I say, listen to Sir Walford Davies.

Serena says That would be lovely, and offers to obtain black paper for windows of flat, and put it up for me with drawing-pins.

Meanwhile she will do what she can about Brigadier Pinflitton, but wiser to write than to ring up as he is deaf as a post.

September 25th. – No summons from Brigadier Pinflitton, the Ministry of Information, the B.B.C. or anybody else.

Letter from Felicity Fairmead inquiring if she could come and help me, as she is willing to do anything and is certain that I must be fearfully busy.

Reply-paid telegram from Rose asking if I know any influential person on the British Medical Council to whom she could apply for post.

Letter from dear Robin, expressing concern lest I should

be over-working, and anxiety to know exactly what form my exertions on behalf of the nation are taking ...

September 27th. – Day pursues usual routine, so unthinkable a month ago, now so familiar, and continually recalling early Novels of the Future by H. G. Wells – now definitely established as minor prophet. Have very often wondered why all prophecies so invariably of a disturbing nature, predicting unpleasant state of affairs all round. Prophets apparently quite insensible to any brighter aspects of the future.

Ring up five more influential friends between nine and twelve to ask if they know of any national work I can undertake. One proves to be on duty as L.C.C. ambulance driver – at which I am very angry and wonder how on earth she managed to get the job – two more reply that I am the tenth person at least to ask this and that they don't know of anything whatever for me, and the remaining two assure me that I must just *wait*, and in time I shall be told what to do.

Ask myself rhetorically whether it was for this that I left home?

Conscience officiously replies that I left home partly because I had no wish to spend the whole of the war in doing domestic work, partly because I felt too cut-off owing to distance between Devonshire and London, and partly from dim idea that London will be more central if I wish to reach Robin or Vicky in any emergency.

Meet Rose for luncheon. She says that she has offered her services to every hospital in London without success. The Hospitals, says Rose gloomily, are all fully staffed, and the beds are all empty, and nobody is allowed to go in however ill they are, and the medical staff goes to bed at ten o'clock every night and isn't called till eleven next morning because they haven't anything to do. The nurses, owing to similar inactivity, are all quarrelling amongst themselves and throwing the splints at one another's heads.

I express concern but no surprise, having heard much the same thing repeatedly in the course of the last three weeks. Tell Rose in return that I am fully expecting to be offered employment of great national importance by the Government at any moment. Can see by Rose's expression that she is not in the least taken in by this. She inquires rather sceptically if I have yet applied for work as voluntary helper on night-shift at Serena's canteen, and I reply with quiet dignity that I shall do so directly I can get anybody to attend to me.

Rose, at this, laughs heartily, and I feel strongly impelled to ask whether the war has made her hysterical – but restrain myself. We drink quantities of coffee, and Rose tells me what she thinks about the Balkans, Stalin's attitude, the chances of an air-raid over London within the week, and the probable duration of the war. In reply I give her my considered opinion regarding the impregnability or otherwise of the Siegfried Line, the neutrality of America, Hitler's intentions with regard to Rumania, and the effect of the petrol rationing on this country as a whole.

We then separate with mutual assurances of letting one another know if we Hear of Anything. In the meanwhile, says Rose rather doubtfully, do I remember the Blowfields? Sir Archibald Blowfield is something in the Ministry of Information, and it might be worth while ringing them up.

I do ring them up in the course of the afternoon, and Lady Blowfield – voice sounds melancholy over the telephone – replies that of course she remembers me well, we met at Valescure in the dear old days. Have never set foot in Valescure in my life, but allow this to pass, and explain that my services as lecturer, writer, or even shorthand typist, are entirely at the disposal of my country if only somebody will be good enough to utilise them.

Lady Blowfield emits a laugh – saddest sound I think I have ever heard – and replies that thousands and thousands of highly qualified applicants are waiting in a queue outside her husband's office. In *time*, no doubt, they will be needed, but at present there is Nothing, Nothing, Nothing! Unspeakably hollow effect of these last words sends my morale practically down to zero, but I rally and thank her very much. (What for?)

Have I tried the Land Army? inquires Lady Blowfield.

No, I haven't. If the plough, boots, smock and breeches are

indicated, something tells me that I should be of very little use to the Land Army.

Well, says Lady Blowfield with a heavy sigh, she's terribly, terribly sorry. There seems nothing for anybody to do, really, except wait for the bombs to rain down upon their heads.

Decline absolutely to subscribe to this view, and inquire after Sir Archibald.

Oh, Archibald is killing himself. Slowly but surely. He works eighteen hours a day, Sundays and all, and neither eats nor sleeps.

Then why, I urge, not let me come and help him, and set him free for an occasional meal at least. But to this Lady Blowfield replies that I don't understand at all. There will be work for us all eventually – provided we are not Wiped Out instantly – but for the moment we must *wait*. I inquire rather peevishly how long, and she returns that the war, whatever some people may say, is quite likely to go on for years and years. Archibald, personally, has estimated the probable duration at exactly twenty-two years and six months. Feel that if I listen to Lady Blowfield for another moment I shall probably shoot myself, and ring off.

Just as I am preparing to listen to the Budget announcement on the Six O'clock News, telephone rings and I feel convinced that I am to be sent for by someone at a moment's notice, to do something, somewhere, and dash to the receiver.

Call turns out to be from old friend Cissie Crabbe, asking if I can find her a war job. Am horrified at hearing myself replying that in time, no doubt, we shall all be needed, but for the moment there is nothing to do but *wait*.

Budget announcement follows and is all that one could have foreseen, and more. Evolve hasty scheme for learning to cook and turning home into a boarding-house after the war, as the only possible hope of remaining there at all.

September 28th. – Go through now habitual performance of pinning up brown paper over the windows and drawing curtains before departing to underworld. Night is as light as possible, and in any case only two minutes' walk.

Just as I arrive, Serena emerges in trousers, little suède jacket and tin hat, beneath which her eyes look positively gigantic. She tells me she is off duty for an hour, and suggests that we should go and drink coffee somewhere.

We creep along the street, feeling for edges of the pavement with our feet, and eventually reach a Lyons Corner House, entrance to which is superbly buttressed by mountainous stacks of sandbags with tiny little aperture dramatically marked 'In' and 'Out' on piece of unpainted wood. Serena points out that this makes it all look much more war-like than if 'In' and 'Out' had been printed in the ordinary way on cardboard.

She then takes off her tin hat, shows me her new gas-mask container – very elegant little vermilion affair with white spots, in waterproof – and utters to the effect that, for her part, she has worked it all out whilst Standing By and finds that her income tax will *definitely* be in excess of her income, which simplifies the whole thing. Ask if she minds, and Serena says No, not in the least, and orders coffee.

She tells me that ever since I last saw her she has been, as usual, sitting about in the underworld, but that this afternoon everybody was told to attend a lecture on the treatment of Shock. The first shock that Serena herself anticipates is the one we shall all experience when we get something to do. Tell her of my conversation over the telephone with Lady Blowfield and Serena says Pah! to the idea of a twenty-two-years war and informs me that she was taken out two days ago to have a drink by a very nice man in the Air Force, and he said Six months at the very outside – and he ought to know.

We talk about the Canteen – am definitely of opinion that I shall never willingly eat sausage-and-mashed again as long as I live – the income tax once more – the pronouncement of the cleaner of the Canteen that the chief trouble with Hitler is that he's such a *fidget* – and the balloon barrage, which, Serena assures me in the tone of one giving inside information, is all to come down in November. (When I indignantly ask why, she is unable to substantiate the statement in any way.) ...

Shortly afterwards Serena declares that she *must* go – positively *must*.

She then remains where she is for twenty minutes more, and when she does go, leaves her gas-mask behind her and we have to go back for it. The waiter who produces it congratulates Serena on having her name inside the case. Not a day, he says in an offhand manner, passes without half a dozen gas-masks being left behind by their owners and half of them have no name, and the other half just have 'Bert' or 'Mum' or 'Our Stanley', which, he says, doesn't take you anywhere at all.

He is thanked by Serena, whom I then escort to entrance of underworld, where she trails away swinging her tin helmet and assuring me that she will probably get the sack for being late if anybody sees her.

September 30th. – Am invited by Serena to have tea at her flat, Jewish refugees said to be spending day with relations at Bromley. Not, says Serena, that she wants to get rid of them – she likes them – but their absence does make more room in the flat.

On arrival it turns out that oldest of the refugees has changed his mind about Bromley and remained behind. He says he has a letter to write.

Serena introduces me – refugee speaks no English and I no German and we content ourselves with handshakes, bows, smiles and more handshakes. He looks patriarchal and dignified, sitting over electric fire in large great-coat.

Serena says he feels the cold. They all feel the cold. She can't bear to contemplate what it will be like for them when the cold really begins – which it hasn't done at all so far – and she has already piled upon their beds all the blankets she possesses. On going to buy others at large Store, she is told that all blankets have been, are being, and will be, bought by the government and that if by any extraordinary chance one or two *do* get through, they will cost five times more than ever before.

Beg her not to be taken in by this for one moment and quote case of Robert's aunt, elderly maiden lady living in Chester, who has, since outbreak of war, purchased set of silver dessert-knives, large chiming clock, bolt of white muslin, new rabbit-skin neck-tie and twenty-four lead pencils – none of which she required – solely because she has been told in shops that these will in future be unobtainable. Serena looks impressed and refugee and I shake hands once more.

Serena takes me to her sitting-room, squeezes past two colossal trunks in very small hall, which Serena explains as being luggage of her refugees. The rest of it is in the kitchen and under the beds, except largest trunk of all which couldn't be got beyond ground floor and has had to be left with hall porter.

Four O'clock News on wireless follows. Listeners once more informed of perfect unanimity on all points between French and English Governments. Make idle suggestion to Serena that it would be much more interesting if we were suddenly to be told that there had been several sharp divergences of opinion. And probably much truer too, says Serena cynically, and anyway, if they always agree so perfectly, why meet at all? She calls it waste of time and money.

Am rather scandalized at this, and say so, and Serena immediately declares that she didn't mean a word of it, and produces tea and admirable cakes made by Austrian refugee. Conversation takes the form – extraordinarily prevalent in all circles nowadays – of exchanging rather singular pieces of information, never obtained by direct means but always heard of through friends of friends.

Roughly tabulated, Serena's news is to following effect:

The whole of the B.B.C. is really functioning from a place in the Cotswolds, and Broadcasting House is full of nothing but sandbags.

A Home for Prostitutes has been evacuated from a danger zone outside London to Aldershot.

(At this I protest, and Serena admits that it was related by young naval officer who has reputation as a wit.)

A large number of war casualties have already reached London, having come up the Thames in barges, and are installed in blocks of empty flats by the river – but nobody knows they're there.

Hitler and Ribbentrop are no longer on speaking terms.

Hitler and Ribbentrop have made it up again.

The Russians are going to turn dog on the Nazis at any moment.

In return for all this, I am in a position to inform Serena:

That the War Office is going to Carnarvon Castle.

A letter has been received in London from a German living in Berlin, with a private message under the stamp saying that a revolution is expected to break out at any minute.

President Roosevelt has been flown over the Siegfried Line and flown back to Washington again, in the strictest secrecy.

The deb. at the canteen, on being offered a marshmallow out of a paper bag, has said: What *is* a marshmallow? (Probably related to a High Court Judge.)

The Russians are determined to assassinate Stalin at the first opportunity.

A woman fainted in the middle of Regent Street yesterday and two stretcher-bearers came to the rescue and put her on the stretcher, then dropped it and fractured both her arms. Serena assures me that in the event of her being injured in any air-raid she has quite decided to emulate Sir Philip Sidney and give everybody else precedence.

Talking of that, would it be a good idea to practise wearing our gas-masks?

Agree, though rather reluctantly, and we accordingly put them on and sit opposite one another in respective armchairs, exchanging sepulchral-sounding remarks from behind talc-and-rubber snouts.

Serena says she wishes to time herself, as she doesn't think she will be able to breathe for more than four minutes at the very most.

Explain that this is all nerves. Gas-masks may be rather warm – (am streaming from every pore) – and perhaps rather uncomfortable, and certainly unbecoming – but any sensible person can breathe inside them for hours.

Serena says I shall be sorry when she goes off into a dead faint.

The door opens suddenly and remaining Austrian refugees, returned early from Bromley, walk in and, at sight presented by Serena and myself, are startled nearly out of their senses and inquire in great agitation What is happening.

Remove gas-mask quickly – Serena hasn't fainted at all but is crimson in the face, and hair very untidy – and we all bow and shake hands.

Letter-writing refugee joins us – shakes hands again – and we talk agreeably round tea-table till the letter-motif recurs – they all say they have letters to write, and – presumably final – handshaking closes séance.

Just as I prepare to leave, Serena's bell rings and she says It's J. L. and I'm to wait, because she wants me to meet him.

J. L. turns out to be rather distinguished-looking man, face perfectly familiar to me from *Radio Times* and other periodicals as he is well-known writer and broadcaster. (Wish I hadn't been so obliging about gas-mask, as hair certainly more untidy than Serena's and have not had the sense to powder my nose.)

J. L. is civility itself and pretends to have heard of me often – am perfectly certain he hasn't – and even makes rather indefinite reference to my Work, which he qualifies as well known, but wisely gives conversation another turn immediately without committing himself further.

Serena produces sherry and inquires what J. L. is doing.

Well, J. L. is writing a book.

He is, as a matter of fact, going on with identical book – merely a novel – that he was writing before war began. It isn't that he *wants* to do it, or that he thinks anybody else wants him to do it. But he is over military age, and the fourteen different organizations to whom he has offered his services have replied, without exception, that they have far more people already than they know what to do with.

He adds pathetically that authors, no doubt, are very useless people.

Not more so than anybody else, Serena replies. Why can't they be used for propaganda?

J. L. and I – with one voice – assure her that every author in the United Kingdom has had exactly this idea, and has laid it before the Ministry of Information, and has been told in return to Stand By for the present.

In the case of Sir Hugh Walpole, to J. L.'s certain knowledge, a Form was returned on which he was required to state all particulars of his qualifications, where educated, and to which periodicals he has contributed, also names of any books he may ever have had published.

Serena inquires witheringly if they didn't want to know whether the books had been published at Sir H. W.'s own expense, and we all agree that if this is official reaction to Sir H.'s offer, the rest of us need not trouble to make any.

Try to console J. L. with assurance that there is to be a boom in books, as nobody will be able to do anything amusing in the evenings, what with black-out, petrol restrictions, and limitations of theatre and cinema openings, so they will have to fall back on reading.

Realize too late that this not very happily expressed.

J. L. says Yes indeed, and tells me that he finds poetry more helpful than anything else. The Elizabethans for choice. Don't I agree?

Reply at once that I am less familiar with the Elizabethan poets than I should like to be, and hope he may think this means that I know plenty of others. (Am quite unable to recall any poetry at all at the moment, except 'How they Brought the Good News from Ghent' and cannot imagine why in the world I should have thought of that.)

Ah, says J. L. very thoughtfully, there is a lot to be said for prose. He personally finds that the Greeks provide him with escapist literature. Plato.

Should not at all wish him to know that *The Fairchild Family* performs the same service for me – but remember with shame that E. M. Forster, in admirable wireless talk, has told us *not* to be ashamed of our taste in reading.

Should like to know if he would apply this to *The Fairchild Family* and can only hope that he would.

Refer to Dickens – compromise here between truth and desire to sound reasonably cultured – but J. L. looks distressed, says Ah yes – really? and changes conversation at once.

Can see that I have dished myself with him for good.

Talk about black-out – Serena alleges that anonymous friend

of hers goes out in the dark with extra layer of chalk-white powder on her nose, so as to be seen, and resembles Dong with the Luminous Nose.

J. L. not in the least amused and merely replies that there are little disks on sale, covered with luminous paint, or that pedestrians are now allowed electric torch if pointed downwards, and shrouded in tissue-paper. Serena makes fresh start, and inquires whether he doesn't know Sir Archibald and Lady Blowfield – acquaintances of mine.

He does know them – had hoped that Sir A. could offer him war work – but that neither here nor there. Lady Blowfield is a charming woman.

I say Yes, isn't she – which is quite contrary to my real opinion. Moreover, am only distressed at this lapse from truth because aware that Serena will recognize it as such. Spiritual and moral degradation well within sight, but cannot dwell on this now. (*Query*: Is it in any way true that war very often brings out the best in civil population? *Answer*: So far as I am concerned, Not at all.)

Suggestion from Serena that Sir Archibald and Lady Blowfield both take rather pessimistic view of international situation causes J. L. to state it as his considered opinion that no one, be he whom he may, *no one*, is in a position at this moment to predict with certainty what the Future may hold.

Do not like to point out to him that no one ever has been, and shortly afterwards J. L. departs, telling Serena that he will ring her up when he knows any more. (Any more what?)

October 1st. – Am at last introduced by Serena Fiddlededee to underworld Commandant. She is dark, rather good-looking young woman wearing out-size in slacks and leather jacket, using immensely long black cigarette-holder, and writing at wooden trestle-table piled with papers.

Serena – voice sunk to quite unnaturally timid murmur – explains that I am very anxious to make myself of use in any way whatever, while waiting to be summoned by Ministry of Information.

The Commandant – who has evidently heard this kind of

thing before – utters short incredulous ejaculation, in which I very nearly join, knowing even better than she does herself how thoroughly well justified it is.

Serena – voice meeker than ever – whispers that I can drive a car if necessary, and have passed my First Aid examination – (hope she isn't going to mention date of this achievement which would take us a long way back indeed) – and am also well used to Home Nursing. Moreover, I can write shorthand and use a typewriter.

Commandant goes on writing rapidly and utters without looking up for a moment – which I think highly offensive. Utterance is to the effect that there are no paid jobs going.

Oh, says Serena, sounding shocked, we never thought of anything like *that*. This is to be voluntary work, and anything in the world, and at any hour.

Commandant – still writing – strikes a bell sharply.

It has been said that the Canteen wants an extra hand, suggests Serena, now almost inaudible. She knows that I should be perfectly willing to work all through the night, or perhaps all day on Sundays, so as to relieve others. And, naturally, voluntary work. To this Commandant – gaze glued to her rapidly-moving pen – mutters something to the effect that voluntary work is all very well –

Have seldom met more un-endearing personality.

Bell is answered by charming-looking elderly lady wearing overall, and armlet badge inscribed *Messenger*, which seems to me unsuitable.

Commandant – tones very peremptory indeed – orders her to Bring the Canteen Time-Sheet. Grey-haired messenger flies away like the wind. Cannot possibly have gone more than five yards from the door before the bell is again struck, and on her reappearance Commandant says sharply that she has just asked for Canteen Time-Sheet. Why hasn't it come?

Obvious reply is that it hasn't come because only a pair of wings could have brought it in the time – but no one says this, and Messenger again departs and can be heard covering the ground at race-track speed.

Commandant continues to write – says Damn once, under

her breath, as though attacked by sudden doubt whether war will stop exactly as and when she has ordained – and drops cigarette ash all over the table.

Serena looks at me and profanely winks enormous eye.

Bell is once more banged – am prepared to wager it will be broken before week is out at this rate. It is this time answered by smart-looking person in blue trousers and singlet and admirable make-up. Looks about twenty-five, but has prematurely grey hair, and am conscious that this gives me distinct satisfaction.

(Not very commendable reaction.)

Am overcome with astonishment when she inquires of Commandant in brusque, official tones: Isn't it time you had some lunch, darling?

Commandant for the first time raises her eyes and answers No, darling, she can't possibly bother with lunch, but she wants a staff car instantly, to go out to Wimbledon for her. It's urgent.

Serena looks hopeful but remains modestly silent while Commandant and Darling rustle through quantities of lists and swear vigorously, saying that it's a most extraordinary thing, the Time-Sheets ought to be always available at a second's notice, and they never *are*.

Darling eventually turns to Serena, just as previous – and infinitely preferable – Messenger returns breathless, and asks curtly, Who is on the Staff Car? Serena indicates that she is herself scheduled for it, is asked why she didn't say so, and commanded to get car out instantly and dash to Wimbledon.

Am deeply impressed by this call to action, but disappointed when Commandant instructs her to go *straight* to No. 478 Mottisfont Road, Wimbledon, and ask for clean handkerchief, which commandant forgot to bring this morning.

She is to come *straight* back, as quickly as possible, *with* the handkerchief. Has she, adds Commandant suspiciously, quite understood?

Serena replies that she has. Tell myself that in her place I should reply No, it's all too complicated for me to grasp – but judging from lifelong experience, this is a complete fallacy and should in reality say nothing of the kind but merely wish, long afterwards, that I had.

Departure of Serena, in search, no doubt, of tin helmet and gas-mask, and am left, together with elderly Messenger, to be ignored by Commandant whilst she and Darling embark on earnest argument concerning Commandant's next meal, which turns out to be lunch, although time now five o'clock in the afternoon ...

Decide that if I am to be here indefinitely I may as well sit down, and do so.

Elderly Messenger gives me terrified, but I think admiring, look. Evidently this display of initiative quite unusual, and am, in fact, rather struck by it myself.

Darling [having dashed from the room] reappears with a tray. Black coffee has materialized and is flanked by large plate of scrambled eggs on toast, two rock-buns and a banana.

All are placed at Commandant's elbow and she wields a fork with one hand and continues to write with the other.

Have sudden impulse to quote to her historical anecdote of British Sovereign remarking to celebrated historian: Scribble, scribble, scribble, Mr Gibbon.

Do not, naturally, give way to it.

Darling asks me coldly If I want anything, and on my replying that I have offered my services to Canteen tells me to go *at once* to Mrs Peacock. Decide to assume that this means I am to be permitted to serve my country, if only with coffee and eggs, so depart, and Elderly Messenger creeps out with me.

I ask if she will be kind enough to take me to Mrs Peacock and she says Of course, and we proceed quietly – no rushing or dashing. (*Query:* Will not this dilatory spirit lose us the war? *Answer*: Undoubtedly, Nonsense!) Make note not to let myself be affected by aura of agitation surrounding Commandant and friend.

Messenger takes me past cars, ambulances, Rest-room, from which unholy din of feminine voices proceeds, and gives me information.

A Society Deb. is working in the Canteen. She is the only one in the whole place. A reporter came to interview her once and she was photographed kneeling on one knee beside an ambulance wheel, holding tools and things. Photograph published in several papers and underneath it was printed: Débutante Jennifer Jamfather Stands By on Home Front.

Reach Mrs Peacock, who is behind Canteen counter, sitting on a box, and looks kind but harassed.

She has a bad leg. Not a permanent bad leg but it gets in her way, and she will be glad of extra help.

Feel much encouraged by this. Nobody else has made faintest suggestion of being glad of extra help – on the contrary.

Raise my voice so as to be audible above gramophone ('Little Sir Echo') and wireless (... And so, bairns, we bid Goodbye to Bonnie Scotland) – roarings and bellowings of Darts Finals being played in a corner, and clatter of dishes from the kitchen – and announce that I am Come to Help – which I think sounds as if I were one of the Ministering Children Forty Years After.

Mrs Peacock, evidently too dejected even to summon up customary formula that there is nothing for me to do except Stand By as she is turning helpers away by the hundred every hour, smiles rather wanly and says I am very kind.

What, I inquire, can I do?

At the moment, nothing. (Can this be a recrudescence of Stand By theme?)

The five o'clock rush is over, and the seven o'clock rush hasn't begun. Mrs Peacock is taking the opportunity of sitting for a moment. She heroically makes rather half-hearted attempt at offering me half packing-case, which I at once decline, and ask about her leg.

Mrs P. displays it, swathed in bandages beneath her stocking, and tells me how her husband had two boxes of sand, shovel and bucket prepared for emergency use – (this evidently euphemism for incendiary bombs) – and gave full instructions to household as to use of them, demonstrating in back garden. Mrs P. herself took part in this, she adds impressively. I say Yes, yes, to encourage her, and she goes on. Telephone call then obliged her to leave the scene – interpolation here about nature of the call involving explanation as to young married niece – husband a sailor, dear little baby with beautiful big blue eyes – from whom call emanated.

Ninth pip-pip-pip compelled Mrs P. to ring off and, on

retracing her steps, she crossed first floor landing on which husband, without a word of warning, had meanwhile caused boxes of sand, shovel and bucket to be ranged, with a view to permanent instalment there. Mrs P. – not expecting any of them – unfortunately caught her foot in the shovel, crashed into the sand-boxes, and was cut to the bone by edge of the bucket.

She concludes by telling me that it really was a lesson. Am not clear of what nature, or to whom, but sympathize very much and say I shall hope to save her as much as possible.

Hope this proceeds from unmixed benevolence, but am inclined to think it is largely actuated by desire to establish myself definitely as canteen worker – in which it meets with success.

Return to Buckingham Street flat again coincides with exit of owner, who at once inquires whether I have ascertained whereabouts of nearest air-raid shelter.

Well, yes, I have in a way. That is to say, the A.R.P. establishment in Adelphi is within three minutes' walk, and I could go there. Owner returns severely that that is Not Good Enough. He must beg of me to take this question seriously, and pace the distance between bedroom and shelter and find out how long it would take to get there in the event of an emergency. Moreover, he declares there is a shelter nearer than the Adelphi, and proceeds to indicate it.

Undertake, reluctantly, to conduct a brief rehearsal of my own exodus under stimulus of air-raid alarm, and subsequently do so.

This takes the form of rather interesting little experiment in which I lay out warm clothes, heavy coat, *Our Mutual Friend* – Shakespeare much more impressive but cannot rise to it – small bottle of boiled sweets – sugar said to increase energy and restore impaired morale – and electric torch. Undress and get into bed, then sound imaginary tocsin, look at my watch, and leap up.

Dressing is accomplished without mishap and proceed downstairs and into street with *Our Mutual Friend*, boiled sweets and electric torch. Am shocked to find myself strongly inclined to run like a lamplighter, in spite of repeated instructions issued to the contrary. If this is the case when no raid at all is taking place, ask myself what it would be like with bombers overhead – and do not care to contemplate reply.

Streets seems very dark, and am twice in collision with other pedestrians. Reaction to this is merry laughter on both sides. (Effect of blackout on national hilarity quite excellent.)

Turn briskly down side street and up to entrance of air-raid shelter, which turns out to be locked. Masculine voice inquires where I think I am going, and I say, Is it the police? No, it is the Air-raid Warden. Explain entire situation; he commends my forethought and says that on the first sound of siren alarm He Will Be There. Assure him in return that in that case we shall meet, as I shall also Be There, with equal celerity, and we part – cannot say whether temporarily or for ever.

Wrist-watch, in pocket of coat, reveals that entire performance has occupied four and a half minutes only.

Am much impressed, and walk back reflecting on my own efficiency and wondering how best to ensure that it shall be appreciated by Robert, to whom I propose to write spirited account.

Return to flat reveals that I have left all the electric lights burning – though behind blue shades – and forgotten gas-mask, still lying in readiness on table.

Decide to put off writing account to Robert.

Undress and get into bed again, leaving clothes and other properties, ready as before – gas-mask in prominent position on shoes – but realize that if I have to go through whole performance all over again tonight, shall be very angry indeed.

October 2nd. – No alarm takes place. Wake at two o'clock and hear something which I think may be a warbling note from a siren – which we have been told to expect – but if so, warbler very poor and indeterminate performer, and come to the conclusion that it is not worth my attention and go to sleep again.

Post – now very late every day – does not arrive until after breakfast.

Short note from Robert informs me that all is well, he does not care about the way the Russians are behaving – (he never has) – his A.R.P. office has more volunteers than he knows what to do with – and young Cramp from the garage, who offered to learn method of dealing with unexploded bombs, has withdrawn after ten minutes' instruction on the grounds that he thinks it seems rather dangerous.

Robert hopes I am enjoying the black-out – which I think is satirical – and has not forwarded joint letter received from Robin as there is nothing much in it. (Could willingly strangle him for this.)

Vicky's letter, addressed to me, makes some amends, as she writes ecstatically about heavenly new dormitory, divine concert and utterly twee air-raid shelter newly constructed (towards which parents will no doubt be asked to contribute). Vicky's only complaint is to the effect that no air-raid has yet occurred, which is very dull.

Also receive immensely long and chatty letter from Aunt Blanche. Marigold and Margery are well, Doreen Fitzgerald and Cook have failed to reach identity of views regarding question of the children's supper but this has now been adjusted by Aunt Blanche and I am not to worry, and Robert seems quite all right, though not saying much.

Our Vicar's Wife has been to tea – worn to a thread and looking like death – but has declared that she is getting on splendidly and the evacuees are settling down, and a nephew of a friend of hers, in the Militia, has told his mother, who has written it to his aunt, who has passed it on to Our Vicar's Wife, that all Berlin is seething with discontent, and a revolution in Germany is scheduled for the first Monday in November.

Is this, asks Aunt Blanche rhetorically, what the Press calls Wishful Thinking?

She concludes with affectionate inquiries as to my well-being, begs me to go and see old Uncle A. when I have time, and is longing to hear what post I have been offered by the Ministry of Information. *P.S.*: what about the Sweep? Cook has been asking.

Have never yet either left home, or got back to it, without being told that Cook is asking about the Sweep.

Large proportion of mail consists of letters, full of eloquence, from tradespeople who say that they are now faced with a difficult situation which will, however, be improved on receipt of my esteemed cheque.

Irresistible conviction comes over me that my situation is even more difficult than theirs, and, moreover, no cheques are in the least likely to come and improve it.

Turn, in hopes of consolation, to remainder of mail and am confronted with Felicity Fairmead's writing – very spidery – on envelope, and typewritten letter within, which she has forgotten to sign. Tells me that she is using typewriter with a view to training for war work, and adds candidly that she can't help hoping war may be over before she finds it. This, says Felicity, is awful, she knows very well, but she can't help it. She is deeply ashamed of her utter uselessness, as she is doing nothing whatever except staying as Paying Guest in the country with delicate friend whose husband is in France, and who has three small children, also delicate, and one maid who isn't any use, so that Felicity and friend make the beds, look after the children, do most of the cooking and keep the garden in order. Both feel how wrong it is not to be doing real work for the country, and this has driven Felicity to the typewriter and friend to the knitting of socks and Balaclava helmets.

Felicity concludes with wistful supposition that *I* am doing something splendid.

Should be very sorry to enlighten her on this point, and shall feel constrained to leave letter unanswered until reality of my position corresponds rather more to Felicity's ideas.

Meanwhile, have serious thoughts of sending copies of her letter to numerous domestic helpers of my acquaintance who have seen fit to leave their posts at a moment's notice in order to seek more spectacular jobs elsewhere ...

Purchase overall for use in Canteen, debate the question of trousers and decide that I must be strong-minded enough to remain in customary clothing which is perfectly adequate to work behind the counter. Find myself almost immediately afterwards trying on very nice pair of navy-blue slacks, thinking that I look well in them and buying them.

Am prepared to take any bet that I shall wear them every time I go on duty.

As this is not to happen till nine o'clock tonight, determine to look up the Weatherbys, who might possibly be able to suggest whole-time National Service job – and old Uncle A. about whom Aunt Blanche evidently feels anxious.

Ring up Uncle A. – his housekeeper says he will be delighted to see me at tea-time – and also Mrs Weatherby, living in Chelsea, who invites me to lunch and says her husband, distinguished Civil Servant, will be in and would much like to meet me. Imagination instantly suggests that he has heard of me (in what connection, cannot possibly conceive), and, on learning that he is to be privileged to see me at his table, will at once realize that Civil Service would be the better for my assistance in some highly authoritative capacity.

Spend hours wondering what clothes would make me look most efficient, but am quite clear *not* slacks for the Civil Service. Finally decide on black coat and skirt, white blouse with frill of austere, *not* frilly, type, and cone-shaped black hat. Find that I look like inferior witch in third-rate pantomime in the latter, and take it off again. Only alternative is powder-blue with rainbow-like swathings, quite out of the question. Feel myself obliged to go out and buy small black hat, with brim like a jockey-cap and red edging. Have no idea whether this is in accordance with Civil Service tastes or not, but feel that I look nice in it.

Walk to Chelsea, and on looking into small mirror in handbag realize that I don't, after all. Can do nothing about it, and simply ask hall porter for Mrs Weatherby, and am taken up in lift to sixth-floor flat, very modern and austere, colouring entirely neutral and statuette – to me wholly revolting – of misshapen green cat occupying top of bookcase, dominating whole of the room.

Hostess comes in – cannot remember if we are on Christian-name terms or not, but inclined to think not and do not risk it – greets me very kindly and again repeats that her husband wishes to meet me.

(Civil Service appointment definitely in sight, and decide to offer Serena job as my private secretary.)

Discuss view of the river from window – Mrs Weatherby says

block of flats would be an excellent target from the air, at which we both laugh agreeably – extraordinary behaviour of the Ministry of Information, and delightful autumnal colouring in neighbourhood of Bovey Tracy, which Mrs Weatherby says she knows well.

Entrance of Mr Weatherby puts an end to this interchange, and we are introduced. Mr W. very tall and cadaverous, and has a beard, which makes me think of Agrippa.

He says that he has been wishing to meet me, but does not add why. Produces sherry and we talk about black-out, President Roosevelt – I say that his behaviour throughout entire crisis has been magnificent and moves me beyond measure – Mrs Weatherby agrees, but Agrippa seems surprised and I feel would like to contradict me but politeness forbids – and we pass on to cocker spaniels, do not know how or why.

Admirable parlourmaid – uniform, demeanour and manner all equally superior to those of Winnie, or even departed May – announces that Luncheon is served, madam, and just as I prepare to swallow remainder of sherry rapidly, pallid elderly gentleman crawls in, leaning on stick and awakening in me instant conviction that he is not long for this world.

Impression turns out to be not without foundation as it transpires that he is Agrippa's uncle, and has recently undergone major operation at London Nursing Home but was desired to leave it at five minutes' notice in order that bed should be available if and when required. Uncle asserts that he met this – as well he might – with protests but was unfortunately too feeble to enforce them and accordingly found himself, so he declares, on the pavement while still unable to stand. From this fearful plight he has been retrieved by Agrippa, and given hospitality of which he cannot speak gratefully enough.

Story concludes with examples of other, similar cases, of which we all seem to know several, and Mrs Weatherby's solemn assurance that all the beds of all the Hospitals and Nursing Homes in England are standing empty, and that no civilian person is to be allowed to be ill until the war is over.

Agrippa's uncle shakes his head, and looks worse than ever, and soon after he has pecked at chicken soufflé, waved away sweet omelette and turned his head from the sight of Camembert cheese, he is compelled by united efforts of the Weatherbys to drink a glass of excellent port and retire from the room.

They tell me how very ill he has been – can well believe it – and that there was another patient even more ill, in room next to his at Nursing Home, who was likewise desired to leave. She, however, defeated the authorities by dying before they had time to get her packing done.

Find myself exclaiming 'Well done!' in enthusiastic tone before I have time to stop myself, and am shocked. So, I think, are the Weatherbys – rightly.

Agrippa changes the conversation and asks my opinion about the value of the natural resources of Moravia. Fortunately answers his own question, at considerable length.

Cannot see that any of this, however interesting, is leading in the direction of war work for me.

On returning to drawing-room and superb coffee which recalls Cook's efforts at home rather sadly to my mind – I myself turn conversation forcibly into desired channel.

What an extraordinary thing it is, I say, that so many intelligent and experienced people are not, so far as one can tell, being utilised by the Government in any way!

Mrs Weatherby replies that she thinks most people who are *really* trained for anything worth while have found no difficulty whatever in getting jobs, and Agrippa declares that it is largely a question of Standing By, and will continue to be so for many months to come.

Does he, then, think that this will be a long war?

Agrippa, assuming expression of preternatural discretion, replies that he must not, naturally, commit himself. Government officials, nowadays, have to be exceedingly careful in what they say as I shall, he has no doubt, readily understand.

Mrs Weatherby strikes in to the effect that it is difficult to see how the war can be a very *short* one, and yet it seems unlikely to be a very *long* one.

I inquire whether she thinks it is going to be a middling one, and then feel I have spoken flippantly and that both disapprove of me.

Should like to leave at once, but custom and decency alike forbid as have only this moment finished coffee.

Ask whether anything has been heard of Pamela Pringle, known to all three of us, at which Agrippa's face lights up in the most extraordinary way and he exclaims that she is, poor dear, quite an invalid but as charming as ever.

Mrs Weatherby – face not lighting up at all but, on the contrary, resembling a thunder-cloud – explains that Pamela, since war started, has developed unspecified form of Heart and retired to large house near the New Forest where she lies on the sofa, in *eau-de-nil* velvet wrapper, and has all her friends down to stay in turns.

Her husband has a job with the Army and is said to be in Morocco, and she has dispatched the children to relations in America, saying that this is a terrible sacrifice, but done for their own sakes.

Can only reply, although I hope indulgently, that it all sounds to me exactly like dear Pamela. This comment more of a success with Mrs W. than with Agrippa, who stands up – looks as if he might touch the ceiling – and says that he must get back to work.

Have abandoned all serious hope of his offering me a post of national importance, or even of no importance at all, but put out timid feeler to the effect that he must be very busy just now.

Yes, yes, he is. He won't get back before eight o'clock tonight, if then. At one time it was eleven o'clock, but things are for the moment a little easier, though no doubt this is only temporary. (*Query*: Why is it that all those occupied in serving the country are completely overwhelmed by pressure of work but do not apparently dream of utilizing assistance pressed upon them by hundreds of willing helpers? *Answer* comes there none.)

Agrippa and I exchange unenthusiastic farewells, but he sticks to his guns to the last and says that he has always wanted to meet me. Does not, naturally, add whether the achievement of this ambition has proved disappointing or the reverse.

Linger on for a few moments in frail and unworthy hope that Mrs Weatherby may say something more, preferably scandalous, about Pamela Pringle, but she only refers, rather bleakly,

to Agrippa's uncle and his low state of health and asserts that
she does not know what the British Medical Association can be
thinking about.

Agree that I don't either – which is true not only now but at
all times – and take my leave. Tell her how much I have liked
seeing them both, and am conscious of departing from spirit of
truth in saying so, but cannot, obviously, inform her that the
only parts of the entertainment I have really enjoyed are her
excellent lunch and hearing about Pamela.

Go out in search of bus – all very few and far between now –
and contemplate visit to hairdresser's, but conscience officiously
points out that visits to hairdresser constitute an unnecessary
expense and could very well be replaced by ordinary shampoo
in bedroom basin at flat. Inner prompting – probably the Devil –
urges that Trade must be Kept Going and that it is my duty to
help on the commercial life of the nation.

Debate this earnestly, find that bus has passed the spot at
which I intended to get out, make undecided effort to stop it,
then change my mind and sit down again and am urged by
conductor to Make up My Mind. I shall have to move a lot
faster than that, he jocosely remarks, when them aeroplanes
are overhead. Much amusement is occasioned to passengers in
general, and we all part in high spirits.

Am much too early for Uncle A. and walk about the streets –
admire balloons which look perfectly entrancing – think about
income-tax, so rightly described as crushing, and decide not to
be crushed at all but readjust ideas about what constitutes
reasonable standard of living, and learn to cook for self and
family – and look at innumerable posters announcing contents
of evening papers.

Lowest level seems to me to be reached by one which features
exposé, doubtless apocryphal, of Hitler's sex life – but am not
pleased with another which inquires – idiotically – Why Not
Send Eden to Russia?

Could suggest hundreds of reasons why not, and none in
favour.

Remaining posters all display ingenious statements, implying
that tremendous advance has been made somewhere by Allies,

none of whom have suffered any casualties at all, with enormous losses to enemy.

Evolve magnificent piece of rhetoric, designed to make clear once and for all what does, and what does not, constitute good propaganda, and this takes me to Mansions in Kensington at the very top of which dwell Uncle A. and housekeeper, whose peculiar name is Mrs Mouse.

Sensation quite distinctly resembling small trickle of ice-cold water running down spine assails me, at the thought that rhetoric on propaganda will all be wasted, since no Government Department wishes for my assistance—but must banish this discouraging reflection and remind myself that at least I am to be allowed a few hours' work in Canteen.

Hall porter – old friend – is unfortunately inspired to greet me with expressions of surprise and disappointment that I am not in uniform. Most ladies are, nowadays, he says. His circle of acquaintances evidently more fortunate than mine. Reply that I have been trying to join something—but can see he doesn't believe it.

We go up very slowly and jerkily in aged Victorian lift – pitch dark and smells of horsehair – and porter informs me that nearly all the flats are empty, but he doubts whether 'Itler himself could move the old gentleman. Adds conversationally that, in his view, it is a *funny* war. Very funny indeed. He supposes we might say that it hasn't hardly begun yet, has it? Agree, though reluctantly, that we might.

Still, says the hall porter as lift comes to an abrupt stop, we couldn't very well have allowed '*im* to carry on as he was doing, could we, and will I please mind the step.

I do mind the step – which is about three feet higher than the landing – and ring Uncle A.'s bell.

Can distinctly see Mrs Mouse applying one eye to ground-glass panel at top of door before she opens it and welcomes my arrival. In reply to inquiry she tells me that Uncle A. is remarkably well and has been all along, and that you'd never give him seventy, let alone eighty-one. She adds philosophically that nothing isn't going to make him stir and she supposes, with hearty laughter, that he'll never be satisfied until he's had the both of them smothered in poison gas, set fire to, blown sky-high and buried under the whole of the buildings.

Point out that this is surely excessive and inquire whether they have a shelter in the basement. Oh yes, replies Mrs M., but she had the work of the world to get him down there when the early-morning alarm was given, at the very beginning of the war, as he refused to move until fully dressed and with his teeth in. The only thing that has disturbed him at all, she adds, is the thought that he is taking no active part in the war.

She then conducts me down familiar narrow passage carpeted in red, with chocolate-and-gilt wallpaper, and into rather musty but agreeable drawing-room crammed with large pieces of furniture, potted palm, family portraits in gilt frames, glass-fronted cupboards, china, books, hundreds of newspapers and old copies of *Blackwood's Magazine*, and grand piano on which nobody has played for about twenty-seven years.

Uncle A. rises alertly from mahogany knee-hole writing-table – very upright and distinguished-looking typical Diplomatic Service – (quite misleading, Uncle A. retired stock-broker) – and receives me most affectionately.

He tells me that I look tired – so I probably do, compared with Uncle A. himself – commands Mrs M. to bring tea, and wheels up an armchair for me in front of magnificent old-fashioned coal fire. Can only accept it gratefully and gaze in admiration at Uncle A.'s slim figure, abundant white hair and general appearance of jauntiness.

He inquires after Robert, the children and his sister – whom he refers to as poor dear old Blanche – (about fifteen years his junior) – and tells me that he has offered his services to the War Office and has had a very civil letter in acknowledgement, but they have not, as yet, actually found a niche for him. No doubt, however, of their doing so in time.

The Government is, in Uncle A.'s opinion, underrating the German strength, and as he himself knew Germany well in his student days at Heidelberg, he is writing a letter to *The Times* in order to make the position better understood.

He asks about evacuees – has heard all about them from Blanche – and tells me about his great-niece in Shropshire.

She is sitting in her manor-house waiting for seven evacuated children whom she has been told to expect; beds are already made, everything waiting, but children haven't turned up. I suggest that this is reminiscent of Snow White and seven little dwarfs, only no little dwarfs.

Uncle A. appears to be immeasurably amused and repeats at intervals: Snow White and no little dwarfs. Capital, capital!

Tea is brought in by Mrs M., and Uncle A. declines my offer of pouring out and does it himself, and plies me with hot scones, apricot jam and home-made ginger bread. All is the work of Mrs M. and I tell Uncle A. that she is a treasure, at which he looks rather surprised and says she's a good gel enough and does what she's told.

Can only remember, in awe-stricken silence, that Mrs M. has been in Uncle A.'s service for the past forty-six years.

Take my leave very soon afterwards and make a point of stating that I have presently to go on duty at A.R.P. Canteen, to which Uncle A. replies solicitously that I mustn't go over-doing it ...

1.30 a.m. – Return from Canteen after evening of activity which has given me agreeable illusion that I am now wholly indispensable to the Allies in the conduct of the war.

Canteen responsibilities, so far as I am concerned, involve much skipping about with orders, memorizing prices of different brands of cigarettes – which mostly have tiresome halfpenny tacked on to round sum, making calculation difficult – and fetching of fried eggs, rashers, sausages-and-mashed and Welsh rarebits from kitchen.

Mrs Peacock – leg still giving trouble – very kind, and fellow workers pleasant; old Mrs Winter-Gammon only to be seen in the distance, and Serena not at all.

Am much struck by continuous pandemonium of noise in Canteen, but become more accustomed to it every moment, and feel that air-raid warning, by comparison, would pass over my head quite unnoticed.

Richmal Crompton

William and the Young Man

William sat on the top of the bus, humming discordantly to himself. Whenever his eye fell upon a hatless head in the road below, he would take an acorn from his pocket and give careful aim. He did it absent-mindedly, almost mechanically. When an acorn fell on to the very top of the head (where he always aimed), he felt no joy or exultation, only the impersonal satisfaction of the artist who knows that his work is good. It was his usual way of beguiling the time on a bus journey. Only a completely bald head could rouse him to any real enthusiasm. His victims, rubbing their heads (an acorn can sting more than anyone who has not experienced it can realize) and glaring angrily about them, saw only a bus passing peacefully on its way, and, on the top, a small boy gazing wistfully into the distance.

Having reached the point of the road at which he meant to alight, William slid down the stairs using the hand rails only and not touching the steps with his feet (a point of honour this), and, before the conductor knew what he was about, had sprung from the bus on to the road, where he rolled over and over in the mud.

William was trying to learn to alight from a bus when it was going at full speed. His attempts showed more courage than science, as he always leapt free of it, both feet together in the attitude of one taking a 'long jump'. The results were, of course, painful, but William persisted in this method, with a rather pathetic trust in the precept 'Practice makes perfect'.

The driver of a motor car that was following the bus avoided his prostrate form by swerving wildly, then slowed down to bestow on him some picturesque home truths. William picked himself up, much cheered by the episode and by the addition of a few forceful terms to his vocabulary, and went on his way to the spot where he had arranged to meet Ginger, Douglas and Henry. He found them waiting for him.

'Crumbs!' said Ginger, eyeing his mud-covered form with interest, 'Wherever have you been?'

William, finding an unsuccessful descent from a bus too tame an adventure, invented another one in which a band of robbers had attacked him in the wood, and, after a spirited contest, had fled from him. None of them, of course, believed him, but William's adventures were always worth hearing. After listening with interest to his account (the robber chief's conversation was especially interesting, because William had enriched it with the gems dropped by the motorist) they turned to the real business of the day which was a Hare and Hounds race. It had been arranged that William was to be Hare and the others the Hounds. William had filled his pockets with torn paper, and the others had also brought contributions which they stuffed into his stockings and down his waistcoat.

'We're jolly well not goin' to have you sayin' you'd no more paper,' said Ginger.

'Mine's an ole Latin exercise book,' said Douglas, 'so that oughter be easy to see 'cause it's nearly all red ink.'

After partaking of refreshment in the shape of a bottle of liquorice water and a bagful of crusts of sandwiches that Henry had begged from the cook, who was making preparation for a tea party, they began the race.

William ran happily along the road, scattering his paper as he went. He was optimistic, and was convinced that the hounds had been misled by a detour he had made at the beginning of the race and were already miles away from him in the wrong direction. It came, therefore, as an unpleasant surprise, when he had been running about twenty minutes, to hear their voices quite close behind him. He stopped, panting, and looked around. A bend in the road hid them from view, and they could not have seen him yet. But the road was very long and very straight, and it was quite clear that before he reached the end of it they would have sighted him. There wasn't even a ditch, and on either side of the road was open country. Suddenly he noticed a lane on his left. It led between trees and grass, then curved quickly out of sight. William sped down it with energy suddenly renewed. It wasn't till he had sped down it for some distance and had put several bends of it between him and the main road, that he began to suspect that he was trespassing on someone's private property. It wasn't till he rounded a huge clump of rhododendron bushes and charged full tilt into an elegant party having tea on a terrace in front of a palatial mansion, that he fully realized what had happened. The lane had not been a lane. It had been the park entrance to one of the stately homes of England. It was too late to turn to flee, even if he had had sufficient breath and presence of mind. He stood there panting and gazing at the assembled party in horror. The horror with which William gazed at the assembled party, however, was as nothing to the horror with which the assembled party gazed at William, and their horror was on the whole the better justified. For William was not such a figure as one instinctively associates with the stately homes of England. His person and clothing still bore ample traces of his flying descent from the bus. His career as a hare had left visible marks upon him. He had lost his cap. His hair was an impenetrable jungle. Perspiration had mingled with the dust on his face and given him a wild and travel-stained appearance. He had moreover scratched one side of his face extensively in getting through a hedge. The party consisted of four elderly ladies of patrician appearance and one bored-looking young man. On the tea-table, William noticed, was such a chocolate cake as one seldom meets with outside one's dreams. A tall lady with an eagle nose, who was evidently the mistress of the stately home, rose and fixed William with an outraged eye.

'How *dare* you come trespassing in my garden like this, you naughty, dirty, little boy?' she said majestically. 'Do you know that I've a good mind to send for the police? Who's your father?'

Before William had time to answer (he was going to say that he was an orphan) the young man had leapt from his chair with a welcoming smile.

'By Jove, old chap,' he said, 'here you are at last! I've been expecting you all afternoon. This is a friend of mine, aunt, whom I asked to tea. You know that you very kindly said that any friend of mine would be welcome.'

The patrician-looking lady with the eagle nose blinked and swallowed. The young man was shaking William warmly by the hand, and drawing him down into an empty basket-chair near the table, where he continued to talk to him affectionately.

'A long walk from the station, isn't it, old chap? I'm sure you're hungry. Have some tea.'

Despite his odd behaviour the young man appeared to be a young man of sound enough sense. By 'tea' he meant chocolate cake. He did not offer William the insult of passing him the bread and butter. He passed him the chocolate cake and continued to pass it at very frequent intervals till no more was left. The ladies resumed their interrupted conversation, throwing occasional glances of dislike and dismay at William. So surprised had William been by his mysterious welcome, so utterly taken up by the heavenly flavour of the chocolate cake, that he completely forgot his function of hare till the last crumb of the chocolate cake had vanished. Then, just as he remembered it, the young man said, 'Like to have a look round the kitchen garden?' and William promptly forgot it again. The ladies' conversation died away into dumb horror, as they watched the form of William setting off to the kitchen garden with his new friend. William's stockings were working down, and small pieces of torn up papers were dropping from them, marking his trail, as though they continued to remember that he was a hare despite his own forgetfulness. His waistcoat, also, as if fortified by the chocolate cake, was remembering his duties for him, and dropping torn-up paper conscientiously across the velvet lawn.

'What – what an *extraordinary* child!' said one lady faintly.

'So – so *odd* that he should be Anthony's friend,' said another.

'Sometimes,' said Anthony's aunt impressively, 'sometimes I have serious doubts of Anthony's sanity.'

Meantime the young man had piloted William to the kitchen garden, and let him loose among the gooseberry bushes. The gooseberries were of the large, green, succulent kind, favoured by the stately homes of England, and the chocolate cake was already only a faint and distant memory. The young man was leaning negligently against the wall watching him.

'I fear,' he was saying, 'that I owe you an explanation and an apology. What is your name, by the way?'

'William,' said William shortly and indistinctly from the middle of a gooseberry bush.

'Well, William, I'll explain the situation as well as I can. You see I'm staying with my aunt. I stay with my aunt every summer. And I find her very trying. She preaches, William. She preaches all day and every day. She hardly stops even to take nourishment. She preaches on industry, and thrift and godliness and other similar subjects. The only reason why I haven't murdered her is because I'm not sure whether she's made her will yet. And I hatched a little plot with a friend of mine. She's always describing to me the type of man I should choose for my friend – a sort of blend of Little Lord Fauntleroy and Sir Charles Grandison – and she's often said that any friend of mine would be welcome here, so we hatched this little plot. He's quite inoffensive-looking naturally, but he can make himself up as the biggest bounder that ever came out of Creation. He's got a special suit for it fashioned in a check that you can hear ten miles away, and he's got a special bowler hat for it and rings and tiepin, and, with his nose reddened, he's the real, real thing. I told my aunt that a friend of mine might possibly be arriving for tea, and we'd arranged that he should don his bounder's outfit – red nose and all – and arrive. I was looking forward to it more than I've ever looked forward to anything in my life, when I got a letter from him this morning saying that he's down with flu and can't come. I was sitting at tea feeling as blue as the ocean waves, when suddenly I saw them all looking at someone with the very expressions with which I had dreamed of their looking at my friend. And so on the spur of the moment I claimed you as my friend. That is the whole story. You aren't offended, I hope?'

'Oh, no,' said William, but he spoke distantly. He could not help feeling that the rôle he played in the situation was not a heroic one.

'It has been an unqualified success,' went on the young man

in a propitiating manner as if anxious to dispel the coldness from William's manner. 'I have enjoyed the afternoon every bit as much as if my real friend had come, and I feel much indebted to you. Come over to this wall. There are some jolly fine nectarines on it.'

'Thanks awfully,' said William, his haughtiness melting.

The young man took him round the garden, pointing out the finest specialities, and, by the time they emerged from the last hothouse, William was conscious of a distinct sensation of internal congestion (a rare sensation for William) and of a feeling of unqualified cordiality towards the young man.

Wandering happily among the raspberry bushes, William saw that the young man was watching the ground with interest and became aware for the first time of the trail of paper that marked his track all round the kitchen garden, in and out of the hothouses, and finlly accompanied him to the raspberries. A largish piece of paper containing the words *Pax tenavit* (Douglas's rendering into Latin of 'He held his peace') heavily underlined in red ink, was in the act of floating gracefully to the ground from beneath his waistcoat.

'What on *earth* —' began the young man.

William looked about him in dismay. He felt grateful to the young man, and he had an uncomfortable suspicion that so far he had not presented himself to the young man in such a guise that the young man would remember him with that admiration and respect with which William liked to be remembered.

And now to appear as a hare who had not only broken the rules by invading private property, but had then proceeded to forget that it was a hare, would finally complete his humiliation.

Playing for time, he adopted his most mysterious expression.

'Huh!' he said. 'Yes, I've gotter take clues about with me so's people can find me if I'm missing. I go into some jolly dangerous places, I do.'

'Really?' said the young man with interest. 'Now let me guess what you are...' He frowned as if considering deeply, then his brow lightened, 'I *know*!' he said. 'You're a Scotland Yard man.'

William hadn't been quite sure what he was when he uttered

his cryptic remark, but, as soon as the young man said that he was a Scotland Yard man, he knew that he was one.

'Yes,' he said, modestly, 'but don't tell any one.'

'No, I won't,' said the young man, 'and it's a very strange thing, our meeting like this because I'm a famous international crook. I'll tell you some of my experiences and then you tell me some of yours.'

William had by this time reached the end of his redoubtable capacity for fruit eating, and they had made their way to two empty wheelbarrows, that stood side by side in a corner of the kitchen garden. The young man, unlike most grown-ups, knew how to make himself comfortable in a wheelbarrow. Reclining at ease in it and smoking a pipe, he told William a few of his adventures as a famous international crook. They included leaping from an aeroplane on to an express train, and swimming the Channel under water while police hunted for him in submarines on the surface. William listened enthralled, quite forgetting his rôle as a criminal investigator. So quickly did the time pass that he could hardly believe his ears when the young man said that it was time he went to dress for dinner.

'I've enjoyed your visit tremendously,' he said, 'and we must meet again soon, so that you can tell me a few of your adventures. I'm afraid I've monopolized the conversation.'

The young man escorted him to the gates. William was relieved to find the terrace empty. Evidently the guests had departed, and the eagle-nosed aunt had gone indoors. At the gate the young man shook hands with him cordially.

'Good-bye, old chap. Even if we have to meet in the course of our respective duties, I'm sure that we shall bear each other no ill-will.'

William walked to the old barn in a dream. His thwarted hounds were awaiting him, and set upon him furiously, but he soon calmed them, and in five minutes they were sitting round him listening intently, while he related to them the adventures of the famous international crook.

The next afternoon Mrs Brown sent William to the Vicarage with a note. William's mind was still full of the young man, and he was wondering whether it would be possible to meet him again today and hear a few more of his adventures. His surprise was great, therefore, when, on approaching the Vicarage, he saw the young man lightly shinning down a drainpipe from one of the upper windows and disappearing through the hedge of the back garden. William stood spellbound watching his retreating figure. Then he approached the Vicarage front door with his note. There was no reply to his knock. He went round to the back door. Again there was no reply. He knocked till he made the very saucepans in the Vicarage kitchen ring, and still there was no reply. It was quite obvious that the Vicarage was unoccupied. William walked home slowly and thoughtfully.

And the next day the Vicar, meeting William and his mother in the village, said:

'I'm feeling very much worried today, Mrs Brown. I've lost a really valuable miniature – an heirloom, in fact. I can't think what's happened to it. It was in its usual place in my study yesterday morning. I'm afraid – very much afraid – that it has been stolen.'

William walked on, his eyes nearly starting out of his head. In imagination he saw the young man (heavily masked) displaying the Vicar's miniature to his gang (also heavily masked) in an underground cellar. The young man had described the place so vividly to William that William felt he had actually seen it. It had secret underground passages leading into every station in London, so that the gang could escape at a moment's notice, and another leading into the middle of the Channel, so that they could when necessary swim across to France. It possessed also a maze, into which they lured those who discovered their hiding-place and from which it was impossible ever to escape. The room where the gang met had black hangings round the walls and a skull on the table at which they sat. Moreover the young man (he alone knew the secret) could switch on an electric current so that anyone entering the room while it was turned on fell dead on the threshold. So vivid in fact had been the young man's account that William was entirely out of conceit with his own Scotland Yard career (which seemed now intolerably dull) and the greatest aim of his life was to be allowed to join the young man's 'gang'. He supposed that he must wait until he had left school, but he would get the address of the gang's headquarters from the young man before he went away, so that he could join him immediately on leaving school.

Meeting the young man in the village street, he broached the subject. The young man was quite encouraging. He said, though, that he didn't take anyone under seventeen, and that even then William would have to work his way up from the bottom, beginning with small things like spoons and rings and gradually working up to the larger things. The young man said that he always did the big jobs – such as grandfather clocks and hall wardrobes – himself.

'But you *sometimes* do smaller things, don't you?' said William. He wanted the young man to know that he knew about the Vicar's miniature.

The young man assumed a mysterious expression and said, 'Ah-h-h!' and William was just going to tell him that he knew about the miniature, when the young man's aunt appeared suddenly at the bend of the road, and William, who knew that discretion was the better part of valour where aunts were concerned, muttered a hasty farewell and vanished.

He set off the next morning to find the young man and continue the conversation. He could not help making a detour by way of the Vicarage, however, because that pipe, down which he had seen the young man swarming so lightly, held now an irresistible glamour for him. He stood for a moment at the gate, and gazed at it with gaping eyes and mouth. While he was gazing, the front door opened, and out came the Vicar with a man whom William had never seen before. He was a tall man with a beard and piercing black eyes, and William knew at once that he was a Scotland Yard official whom the Vicar had summoned to clear up the mystery of the stolen miniature. The beard alone would have told him that even without the piercing eyes. Already William could see in imagination the scene in which this tall man stood confronting his friend and chief, tore off the beard with one hand, whipped a pistol out of his pocket with the other, and said, 'And now, Alias, I think our little account is settled.'

The young man had told William that, in common with many other famous criminals, he was called Alias.

The meeting made William vaguely uneasy. This man didn't look the kind of detective who is bamboozled by the criminal. Somehow he gave you the impression of being a better detective than the young man was a criminal, in spite of the skull and the black hangings. After all, it might be quite simple to cut off the electric current at the door, and, once this detective had got his men all round the place, guarding even the secret passage to the Channel, the gang wouldn't have much chance. Probably he'd got a plan of the maze in his pocket at the moment. William went home to lunch feeling very anxious. And at lunch Ethel said to his mother:

'Do you know who the man is who's staying at the Vicarage?'

And his mother said:

'Yes, dear. It's an old college friend of the Vicar's. He's a very distinguished literary man.'

And William's worst fears were confirmed. It was, of course, just what a detective who had come to stay at the Vicarage to clear up the mystery of the stolen miniature would naturally pretend to be. That and the beard gave him away as completely as if he openly wore his Scotland Yard badge.

William felt that not a moment was to be lost. The young man must be warned at once. He set off at a run to Maple Court where the young man's aunt lived (the young man had told William that she knew nothing of his secret career). At the gate he stopped, not quite sure how to proceed. He was not, of course, on the young man's aunt's visiting list. He was, in fact, if one may use the expression, on the reverse of her visiting list. He certainly could not walk up to her front door and demand to see her nephew. He decided to hang about the entrance gate unobtrusively in the hope of seeing him going in or out. It was impossible, however, for William to do anything unobtrusively, and an indignant gardener soon came down to stop him swinging on the gate. William stopped swinging and asked the gardener if the lady's nephew would be coming out that afternoon. The gardener recognized William with disgust as the 'young rap-scallion' who had been hanging about with Master Anthony in the kitchen garden last week, eating his best nectarines, and leaving a trail of dirty paper along his tidy path.

'No,' he said shortly, 'he's gone back to Town an' good riddance.'

William heaved a sigh of relief, said, 'Good riddance yourself,' gate-vaulted twice over the gate, then, avoiding a well-aimed box on the ears from the gardener, set off jauntily down the road. It was all right. He might have known it would be all right. Of course the young man had recognized the Scotland Yard official at a glance, just as William had done, and had lost no time in clearing off.

The next morning he met the Vicar and his friend in the road, and was seized with such a paroxysm of mirth at the thought of the futility of their search that it was impossible to conceal it. They stood and watched him with amazement as he went on down the road, his shoulders shaking helplessly.

'What an extraordinary boy,' said the Vicar's friend. 'Is he always like that?'

'He is a most peculiar child,' said the Vicar grimly.

'What was he laughing at?'

'I've no idea,' said the Vicar and added, 'I'm afraid he's inclined to be impertinent. I've noticed it on several occasions.'

For the next few days William gloated triumphantly over the situation – the sleuth tracking a victim who had long ago made good his escape. And then his exultation suddenly vanished. For the victim returned. He flew through the village driving a battered two-seater with a large suitcase beside him, and shot up the drive of Maple Court. William happened to be in the lane just outside. His eyes grew large with consternation. His mouth dropped open. He must have thought, of course, that the coast was clear and that the Scotland Yard man had gone. William must let him know at once. He mustn't stay one moment longer. Even now it might be too late. Even now – and just as William had got to that point in his thoughts, the bearded man with piercing eyes came round the bend in the lane, and accosted him curtly:

'Excuse me, my boy, can you tell me the way to Maple Court?'

He, too, must have seen the young man coming from the

station and he was on his way to arrest him. Only, by a miraculous chance, he wasn't sure of the way to the house, and, by a still more miraculous chance, it was William he asked. William felt that he held his friend's life in his hand, and must act promptly.

He assumed an ingratiating expression and said:

'Yes. You've come a bit out of the way. I'm going there myself, so I'll take you.'

'Thank you very much,' said the Scotland Yard man.

William concealed an exultant grin at the success of his ruse, and the two of them set off down the lane.

''Scuse me,' said William (he remembered that they were always very polite to each other in books till the final moment when they faced each other with revolvers); ''Scuse me, but what do you want to go to Maple Court for?'

'I'm giving a lecture there,' said the Scotland Yard man.

William had to bend down to pretend to pull his stockings up, to conceal his amusement at this. Jolly clever thing to say, of course, but they probably had special lessons at Scotland Yard in thinking of things to say like that. William had paused at a stile that led through a field up a hill.

'This is a short cut to it,' he said.

The bearded man followed him guilelessly.

When they had breasted the hill, and joined another main road, and walked for some distance along it, however, he said anxiously:

'I hope we aren't making any mistake. I was told that the place was quite near the Vicarage.'

'Well, they probably meant near compared with somewhere a long way off,' said William. 'We'll soon be there now.'

They walked on in silence for another half-mile. William was wondering what to do next. It had seemed a clever trick to divert the sleuth's course, but they could not continue to walk like this all night even though they were going away from Maple Court. At some point the sleuth would realise that he was walking in the wrong direction, and, even if he didn't, England was an island and sooner or later they must reach the sea, which would, of course, give the whole show away completely. They had reached now the outskirts of Marleigh, the next village to the one where William lived, and they were walking by a low wall that bordered the roadside.

'I think that Maple Court is jus' round this corner,' said William. 'Would you like to sit down on the wall a minute while I go an' see?'

The sleuth sat down willingly, mopping his brow.

'I simply can't understand it,' he said, 'they said most distinctly only a few yards.'

'Well, you see,' said William soothingly, 'people round here walk such a lot that it seems only a few yards to them.'

With that he left the sleuth and turned the corner into the village street of Marleigh. His intention was to slip down the hill again to Maple Court and warn the young man. He thought that it would take the sleuth some time to realize that he had been tricked, and then some more time to get down to Maple Court (the sleuth was not a good walker), and that altogether there should be ample time for the young man to make his escape.

William began to hurry through the village on his way to the other field path that led down the hill. But at the first house in the village street he stopped. A large room on the ground floor was lit up. In it he could see rows and rows of people sitting facing a small platform on which was a table and an empty chair. At the door stood a tall thin man, holding a watch in his hand and looking anxiously up and down the road. Seeing William at the gate he came down to him.

'Er – have you seen anyone coming up from the station, little boy?' he said. 'Our lecturer is half an hour late, and we're wondering what has happened to him.'

William gasped with delight. If he could get the sleuth in here as the lecturer, the inevitable complications and explanations would delay him still further.

'Yes,' he said, 'I did see a man comin' along the road. I'll go'n' fetch him, shall I?'

'Thank you, my boy. If he should be the lecturer, remind him that he'd arranged to address the Marleigh Temperance Society at 7 o'clock prompt. I'll go back to the audience. It's growing just a lee-tle restive.'

The tall thin man disappeared. William with great cunning and presence of mind arranged a hanging branch of a beech tree to hide the legend, The Chestnuts, on the open gate, then returned to the sleuth, who was still sitting on the wall and mopping his brow.

'It's just along here,' said William. The sleuth heaved a sigh of relief, and accompanied him through the gateway and up to the front door, where the tall thin man was standing to receive him.

'Delighted to see you, delighted to see you,' fluted the tall thin man nervously. 'Everyone is ready. Perhaps you'll step straight in here.'

The sleuth followed the tall thin man into the room. William could not resist lingering by the open window to see what turn events would take. The tall thin man led the sleuth up on to the platform and said:

'And now I won't take up any more valuable time, but will ask our friend to deliver his lecture to us at once.'

The sleuth stood up, took a sheaf of papers out of his pocket, and began without a moment's hesitation, 'Ladies and Gentlemen . . .'

William slipped away, chuckling to himself as he imagined the sensation of rage and baffled fury that the sleuth must be feeling. To be tricked into having to address a real audience as if he were a real lecturer. . . . But the episode gave William a wholesome respect for the methods of Scotland Yard. If you come out after your prey disguised as a lecturer, you even carried a lecture in your pocket so that in an emergency you could sustain the character. They were certainly foes worth fighting. They were, of course, his, William's, foes now. They would never forgive him for having saved their victim. They would know now that he was practically a member of the young man's gang. They would always keep an eye on him. William had pleasant visions of Scotland Yard men in various disguises following him to and from school, slipping along behind him under cover of the ditch or hedge. Perhaps when the young man knew what he had done he would let him join his gang at once without waiting till he left school. . .

He had reached the bottom of the hill now, and was running as fast as he could in the direction of Maple Court. There still wasn't a moment to be lost. The sleuth would probably make some excuse to stop lecturing when he'd done it for a few minutes, and then of course he would soon find his way back to Maple Court. The world was simply full of people ready to tell other people the way to places. . . .

At the gate of Maple Court stood the young man and the Vicar. The Vicar's being there made it rather awkward. Probably the Vicar knew by now that the young man had stolen his miniature, and was keeping an eye on him till the sleuth arrived. William must act very carefully.

'I simply can't think what's happened,' the Vicar was saying. 'He set off before me and I told him that it was only a few yards down the road. I can't think how he can possibly have missed it.'

Suddenly the young man caught sight of William.

'Hello!' he said. 'Here's my friend William. William, have you seen Mr Chance anywhere?'

'Mr Chance?' said William to gain time.

'Yes,' said the young man, 'John Chance. Surely even you have heard of John Chance?'

'No,' said William to gain more time.

'I should have thought that even you —' said the young man. 'Well, anyway, he's one of the most famous literary critics in England, and he's a college friend of the Vicar's, and a professor at the college that I honour with my presence, though he probably doesn't know me from Adam. Anyway the Vicar kindly arranged for him to address the Literary Society, of which my aunt is the President, on "The Drinking Songs of Britain", and he should have been here half an hour ago, and the Literary Society is getting tired of waiting.'

William looked from the Vicar to the young man and a horrible certainty together with a horrible doubt entered his head. The horrible certainty was a certainty that the sleuth was not a sleuth, and the horrible doubt was a doubt whether the young man was really a criminal.

'The question is, William,' said the Vicar irritably, 'have you seen Mr Chance?'

'Yes,' said William, 'I've just seen him in Marleigh.'

'*Marleigh?*' said the Vicar. 'How on earth did he get there?'

'I suppose he walked,' said William after a slight hesitation.

'Well, please take us to where you saw him,' said the Vicar.

William took them. The Vicar and the young man conversed amicably on the way. The Vicar was asking the young man about his studies and his college. It appeared that the young man lived a very full life at his college. He played rugger for his college and hockey for his University and rowed in his University boat. His account of his studies was vaguer and less enthusiastic. But there was something very convincing about it all, and the doubt in William's mind turned into a certainty. The young man was not a criminal. Such a life as he described would leave no time at all for criminal pursuits. He hadn't got a gang. He hadn't got an underground meeting-place, hung with black, with a skull on the table and with a secret passage to the Channel. Probably he wasn't even called Alias . . .

They had reached Marleigh now, and the Vicar had turned to William to say:

'Well, whereabouts was it you saw him?'

William pointed to The Chestnuts.

'I saw him going into that house.'

'How *extraordinary*!' said the Vicar. 'I do hope he hasn't lost his memory.'

The Vicar and the young man went up to the front door. It was open. They entered. William realized, of course, that this was the moment for flight, but William never could resist staying to see the end of an adventure. The young man and the Vicar had stopped at the door of the room where Mr Chance was lecturing. He was at that moment quoting the following lines:

> '*The peer I don't envy – I give him his bow,*
> *I scorn not the peasant, though never so low,*
> *But a club of good fellows like those that are here,*
> *And a bottle like this, are my glory and care.*'

His audience had at first been speechless with amazement, then restively indignant. This was the last straw. The tall thin man rose from the back of the room and said, 'This is an outrage, sir.'

Mr Chance raised his head from his papers in surprise.

'What is an outrage?' he demanded indignantly.

'Those words you have just quoted, and the whole of your lecture,' sputtered the tall thin man.

Mr Chance was evidently annoyed by this.

'Sir, you forget yourself,' he thundered.

'I do not forget myself,' squeaked the tall thin man; 'you are engaged to address the Temperance Society on the effects of Alcohol on the Liver and —'

'What do you mean, Sir?' said Mr Chance. 'I am not addressing any Temperance Society. I never have and I never will. I detest them. I am addressing the Helicon Literary Society on the Drinking Songs of Britain and —'

It was at this point that the Vicar interrupted. While he was in the middle of his explanation, a small rabbity man arrived in a state of great nervous agitation, explaining that he had got into the wrong train at Paddington, and hadn't been able to let them know, but had come on as quickly as possible. Someone kindly brought him a glass of soda-water to steady his nerves, and, taking the place just vacated by Mr Chance, he leapt headlong into the effects of Alcohol upon the Liver.

The Vicar and the young man had drawn the deposed and bewildered lecturer down to the gate, and there hasty explanations took place. At the end of the explanations they all looked round for William. But William was nowhere to be seen. William had decided that the moment had come for him to be in bed and asleep. In fact when the Vicar called at his home a few minutes later, after leaving Mr Chance and the young man at the gate of Maple Court, William was so soundly asleep that he resisted all his mother's attempts to awaken him.

But there had to be explanations, of course. They took place the next morning between William, William's father, the Vicar, and the young man. William defended himself with spirit.

'How could I *know*?' he demanded passionately. 'I'd seen him climbing down a drainpipe —'

'Yes, I did,' agreed the young man. 'I was passing the Village Hall, and the Vicar came out, and said that he'd left the list of Sunday School prize winners on his study table, and the place was locked up because his wife was in town and the maids out, and he'd forgotten to bring his keys. He'd got an unholy rabble of Sunday School prize winners in the Village Hall, and daren't leave them for a second, so I said I'd do my best. He told me his study window was open, so I took the short cut across the fields and made for that. That's true, isn't it?' he ended, turning to the Vicar.

'In essentials,' said the Vicar coldly. The Vicar hadn't liked having his Sunday School prize winners described as an 'unholy rabble'.

'And then you said a miniature had been stolen,' said William to the Vicar.

'I found I was mistaken,' said the Vicar testily. 'When I got home I found that the nail had come out of the wall and that the thing had fallen down behind the bookshelves. I'd completely forgotten till you mentioned it that I'd ever thought it had been stolen.'

'And you said —' went on William, turning accusingly to the young man.

'I know – I know,' said the young man. 'I'm afraid I let my imagination run away with me. I take the responsibility for the whole affair.'

William's father, however, refused to treat the young man as responsible for the whole affair (' 'Fraid of anyone his own size,' muttered William bitterly) and insisted on treating William as responsible for the whole affair. But the young man gave William a ten shilling note, and said that though he wasn't a criminal he'd always thought that it would be a very exciting career, and, if William still felt the same about it when he left school, they'd seriously consider the matter.

So that William did not really regret the incident.

Nor did Mr Chance.

On his return home he found an interviewer waiting to interview him. Mr Chance disliked being interviewed but he looked upon it as part of the day's work. In a bored and mournful fashion he gave his views upon the modern novel, the modern play, and modern poetry. In a bored and mournful fashion he gave the interviewer his candid opinion of his own work (it wasn't flattering so the interviewer toned it down). In a bored and mournful fashion he told the interviewer that he hadn't any hobbies and that he hated gardening. Then the interviewer brought out his final question.

'And what, Mr Chance,' he said, 'do you consider the greatest achievement of your life?'

The critic's bored and mournful manner vanished. He sat up, his eye gleamed, his lips curved into a proud smile.

'I consider that the greatest achievement of my life,' he said, 'is having delivered a lecture to the Marleigh Temperance Society on the Drinking Songs of Britain.'

Sylvia Townsend Warner

A Pair of Duelling Pistols

'Yes, I see. Take ye in one another's washing.'

Mr Edom had been trying to explain to Mrs Otter why, for professional reasons, he would rather show her duelling pistols to Mrs Vibart, the renowned expert on firearms, than buy them himself. In effect, he had succeeded; she had grasped the central truth. Whether she was aware of what she had grasped was another matter. He had not known Mrs Otter for all these years – of mingled solicitude and exasperated awe – without knowing that she grasped more readily than she attended.

The latest demonstration of Mrs Otter's powers was assembled on his desk: a folding rubber bath, venerably creased and sallow; an equally venerable gibus hat; a massive copy of Foxe's *Book of Martyrs*, five pickle forks, seven kettle holders, a Masonic apron, several flounces of black Maltese lace and a pair of duelling pistols in a rosewood case.

'I simply can't account for their having been in the attic for all these years, for I am constantly in the attic looking for things that might have got there; and you'd think I'd have enough enterprise to poke behind the cistern. But I can be positive they came from my first husband's aunt, who was the last of the Miss MacMahons. She was always buying things at bazaars, when she wasn't selling them. And when they got too much for her she used to send them on to us to be resold in Moses baskets.'

She disentangled a piece of newspaper from the flounces. 'Here you are. The *Northern Whig*. That proves it. She lived in Belfast and used to stand on a balcony saying, "To hell with the Pope!" In fact, that's how she died. Tonsillitis. Goodness, how cheap everything was in the twenties! You could have bought a whole steam laundry in working order for three hundred pounds.'

Mrs Otter fell silent, absorbed in the *Northern Whig*. Mr Collins, the assistant, seized a feather whisk and dusted a crystal chandelier, which jangled.

'So if you approve, Mrs Otter, I will write to Mrs Vibart immediately,' Mr Edom said.

'Mrs Vibart? Mrs Vibart? Oh yes, Mrs Vibart. I knew I'd heard the name; it struck me as sounding so villainous. Yes, do – if you're sure you won't be in any way the worse for it. And of course, love can hurry one into the most extraordinary surnames. I'm Otter. You're sure you don't want any of these other things?'

Mr Edom signified he did not. Mr Collins came forward to help Mrs Otter parcel up the bath, the hat, the apron, the *Martyrs*, the pickle forks, the lace, and the kettle holders. He produced a new sheet of wrapping paper, which crackled under his efficiency, and said repeatedly how glad he would be to take the parcel round that evening. It would be nothing to him. He enjoyed a walk after work. No doubt, thought Mr Edom, George was as anxious as he to be left in peace with the pistols. But he was overdoing his helpfulness. It sounded feverish.

'No, thank you. I can perfectly ... If you'll just open the ... Oh! You sweet pet! Mr Edom, there's such a nice buttony little cat on your doorstep. I think it wants to come in.'

Mr Collins, exclaiming 'Shoo!' and 'You're sure you can manage?' and again 'Shoo!,' farewelled Mrs Otter and fended off the cat. In his zeal, he shut himself out and stood on the pavement till he had seen the cat slip through a hole in the yard door. It was a close fit, but he knew she could do it. He had enlarged the hole himself, under the direction of Mrs Knowles the cleaner, who had appealed to him as a man to think what it was like not being able to call your measurements your own. The chorus of infant voices swelled in volume and intensity, then was hushed.

It was all Mrs Knowles' doing. These women, these females, had no sense of the befitting. They are at the mercy of their instincts. There were four kittens, and their voices grew louder daily.

He re-entered the Galleries. Mr Edom was hanging over the pistols. He called to Mr Collins to admire. 'These attics, George. These attics, these box-rooms. People simply don't know what's hidden away under their roofs.'

Mr Collins agreed. And while Mr Edom continued to fondle the pistols, lifting them from the maroon velvet cradles in which they lay so snugly, caressing their ivory butts, expatiating on the workmanship of their case, the exactitude of its hinges, and all in such perfect condition, Mr Collins looked at Mr Edom's trousers. It was profanation even to think of such trousers exposed to kittens who would cover them with hairs. Some dealers – a new school – wore corduroy trousers, knitted pullovers, neckerchiefs, an air of pastoral neglect. Such persons might very well allow cats in their show-rooms – some, in fact, did and made a feature of it. A Mrs Althea Budd boasted that she could sell any old saucer by leaving it on the floor with some milk in it, customers being the predatory race they are and always on the lookout for a chance to know better than you do. But Mr Edom's clothes, like his wares, were classical: his waistcoats a breath of the old order, his cravats seemly as collects appointed for Sundays after Trinity. Yet hidden away on this good man's premises was a tortoiseshell cat and four thriving kittens. For the moment, they were quiet, being satiated, but soon they would start their mewing again; and sooner or later Mr Edom must become aware of it. If that very bad cold he caught at old Parker's funeral had not left him slightly deaf, he would have heard them long before.

It was because of the very bad cold that Mr Collins was now the prey of a guilty secret. In Mr Edom's absence (his doctor had kept him at home for a week) Mrs Knowles became conversational.

'Have you seen our Moggie, Mr Collins?'

As she had cleaned the Galleries for over seven years and never broken as much as an item, Mrs Knowles felt herself part of the firm and used the proprietary first-person plural. He looked about him for a Moggie, supposing it was some local term, possibly for a tankard.

'It's ever such a pretty little cat. Taken quite a fancy to us. It's there in the yard every morning when I take out the rubbish. Rubs against me so grateful when I bring its drop of milk, and very partial to kippers. You come and have a look at it.'

It had been early impressed on Mr Collins that Mrs Knowles was above rubies and must not be crossed. He followed her into the yard, where the cat was reposing in a hamper of shavings. She looked plump. No doubt she caught mice.

Unfortunately, the fact that Mrs Knowles was entertaining a cat in Mr Edom's yard made less impression on Mr Collins than that she called it a Moggie and, when questioned, asked what else she should call it. As she mustn't be crossed, he left it at that. A Moggie. Perhaps it was a term for tortoiseshell cats, or for short-haired cats, or even for cats without attachments: Mrs Knowles asserted the cat in the yard had no home of its own, poor thing. Moggie. He consulted the Concise Oxford Dictionary on Mr Edom's desk. There was no 'Moggie' there. He went to the public library and sought the term in books about dialect and books about cats. That evening, he wrote a letter to *The Times*. There was a political crisis, and *The Times* printed his letter, a welcome sprig of ornamental parsley, on the leader page. It drew several answers. One directed him to '*mujer*', the Spanish for 'woman', corrupted to 'Moggie' by the gypsies; another derived it from the Grand Mogul, and said it was applied to Persian cats. Others were quite as ingenious. All the writers agreed in saying that the term 'Moggie' was reserved for she-cats.

He did not realize the force of this till Mrs Knowles asked him to enlarge the hole in the yard door. Even then, he glided onwards. Kittens, he knew, were drowned at birth. He would not like to drown a kitten himself, but no doubt Mrs Knowles was conversant with that sort of thing. For all that, he took pains not to be *tête-à-tête* with Mrs Knowles, hiding behind the buttresses of St John's Church or lurking in the tobacconist's till he had seen Mr Edom enter the Galleries. It was from behind

Mr Edom's back that she caught his eye as in a mantrap and held up four fingers.

When she went out with the rubbish he made a pretext of autumn leaves choking the gutters and followed her into the yard. There was Mrs Knowles with four doomed innocents squirming in her apron. They seemed very active for doomed innocents.

'She's been hiding them all this time,' said Mrs Knowles. 'The artful piece. Bless her heart!'

'But –'

'Two tabs, a black, and a ginger.'

The cat stood watching the apron, her embattled soul in her eyes. When the kittens were put down, she cleaned them imperiously. Then she rolled over on her side and gave suck.

'Did you ever see a prettier sight?' asked Mrs Knowles.

That was the worst of it. It was a pretty sight. He and Mrs Knowles, she grossly wallowing in the Life Force, he conscience-stricken at his murderous mind, compared very ill with it.

'What on earth are we to do now?'

Mrs Knowles went on simpering at the kittens.

'You must find homes for them!' he exclaimed. 'Good homes.'

'It's too soon for that, Mr Collins. But I'll look about. Blacks are lucky and gingers are always popular, but I don't know about the other two, the tabbies. If I could have got at them in time, I'd have drowned them. But I haven't the heart to do it now.'

She stooped and caressed the cat. Never before had Mr Collins felt such dislike for a woman as he now felt for Mrs Knowles. As he couldn't murder her, he walked away.

Mr Edom began to worry. George wasn't being his usual self. He was always fidgeting; he moved things about, he polished what was in no need of polishing, he knocked over the waste-paper basket, he even collided with the fine Victorian gong bought at the Tabley Manor sale. He developed a nervous cough. He talked at random. He read aloud from catalogues. He was incessantly industrious and perfectly amiable, yet gave

the impression that his mind was elsewhere. It occurred to Mr
Edom that George might be going a little deaf; he seemed to be
straining his ears all the time as though he heard imperfectly.
Perhaps it was love. In that case the loved one must be local,
for when Mr Edom suggested a few pick-me-up days at Brigh-
ton the suggestion was rejected as if he had spoken of a few days
in jail. Mr Edom said no more at the time, but privately decided
that whether George liked it or not and whether his malady was
in the heart or in the head he would be packed off for a change
of air as soon as Mrs Vibart had visited the Galleries.
Meanwhile, to take George's mind off his troubles, he talked
about Mrs Vibart.

Though the kittens' voices had grown ever louder and more
insistent and more difficult to drown; though their mother now
left them for longer and longer intervals and came to sun herself
on the Galleries doorstep; though a day was bound to come
when the kittens followed her through the pop-hole and sat
there with her, a bait for public compassion, which might ignore
one cat but certainly wouldn't fail to notice five, Mr Collins,
intermittently surfacing from his distraction, realized that Mrs
Vibart was indeed somebody, and that with a mind at leisure
from itself he would have very much looked forward to seeing
her.

If she had been a Hester Bateman teapot, Mr Edom could
not have esteemed her more highly. She was, he related, self-
made – the daughter of a county family who had married a
hunting man. The hunting man had a collection of swordsticks.
Mrs Vibart, by the process of familiarity, distinguished that
many of them were fakes. When he died from an accident in the
hunting field, she kept one Andrea Ferrara as a souvenir, sold
the rest, and turned her attention to firearms. She frequented
auctions, where, from time to time, she bought a mixed lot. The
Ring was accustomed to ladies buying a mixed lot for the sake
of a preserving pan, say, or a garden hose; it was a good six years
before the professionals noticed that most of the constituents of
the mixed lots knocked down to Mrs Vibart presently appeared
at auctions elsewhere. By the time they had discovered what she
was up to and begun to hound her, she had outwitted them so

successfully that she could afford to outbid them. She was brilliantly lucky, single-minded, the unquestioned authority in her field; it was believed that she had bequeathed her private collection to Girton College, Cambridge.

Mr Collins had never seen Mr Edom in a state so nearly approaching excitement. It could not be snobbery in so cool a man, so it must be veneration. Ambition did not come into it. 'There's nothing in the Galleries she'd look at,' he said with pride. 'It'll be the pistols or nothing.' Mr Collins thought of cups and lips and of how his dear employer might be disgraced in the very moment of his triumph. In dreams he saw Moggie ripping Mrs Vibart's stockings and kittens in molt swarming all over Mr Edom. With greater urgency he besought Mrs Knowles to find homes for them. And Mr Edom wondered if it would not have been better to insist on that seaside holiday. He particularly wanted George to make a good impression and it didn't seem at all likely that he would.

The day of Mrs Vibart's visit came. Mr Edom had on his best waistcoat. He was calm. The case of duelling pistols lay on his desk – the opening would come later. Mrs Vibart was driving from Old Windsor (she scorned London) and would arrive at eleven-thirty. She would be on the dot, said Mr Edom with the confidence of a votary.

At eleven-twenty-five Mrs Dudley, a lady who occasionally wanted to buy something quaint, undulated into the Galleries. Her mien was condescending, her voice assertively kindly. 'I understand you have some kittens to dispose of, Mr Edom. May I have a look at them?'

'Kittens?' said Mr Edom, 'Kittens?' His manner was unruffled, his face serene. 'Kittens.' On this third repetition he changed the accentuation of the word and seemed to be musing on kittens in general.

'I think I can put my hand on some,' panted Mr Collins.

'Thank you, George.'

But the words were lost on Mr Collins, who had rushed out of the Galleries. It was the two tabby kittens he came back with.

'Tabbies,' remarked Mrs Dudley censoriously.

'These are the true old English tabbies,' said Mr Collins,

surpassing himself as he hoped never to have to surpass himself
again, for it was a dreadful sensation. 'It is rare to find them
nowadays, especially with such regular markings and with the
butterfly pattern so clear on the back.'

'Oh. Well, I must admit I don't know much about cats. But
if you want a home for one of them –'

'Ten and sixpence,' said Mr Edom.

'Ten and sixpence? But I don't want both of them, I just
want a plain ordinary cat to keep down mice.'

'Each,' said Mr Edom.

'Two guineas,' said a clear voice from the doorway.

Looking round, Mrs Dudley saw a tall, grey-haired woman
who seemed to her very plainly dressed, and instantly took a
strong dislike to her. 'Twenty-five shillings for that one!' she
exclaimed, and remained with her mouth open, appalled at the
words which fury had wrenched from it.

'Five guineas for the pair,' said Mrs Vibart.

'Never, never in all my life...'

Unable to specify further, Mrs Dudley left the Galleries, nearly
falling over the cat, who had come round to see what was
happening.

'Fun while it lasted,' said Mrs Vibart. 'Mr Edom, you must
allow me to congratulate you on your assistant. I thought he
did admirably. It isn't everybody who knows about the butterfly
pattern.'

'I got it out of a book,' mumbled Mr Collins.

'The right way to begin,' said she, 'unless one's a cat and
doesn't need book learning. If you can let me have a good deep
hamper, with plenty of clean straw, I'll take them back with me.
They're fine kittens. I'm delighted to have found them. One
should always buy kittens in pairs. They keep each other warm
and don't pine.'

Followed by the cat, Mr Collins went off to pack the kittens.
Mrs Vibart turned to Mr Edom. 'Now for the pistols.' When
he opened the case, she said, 'Ah!'

Robert Graves

Period Piece

It was one July in the reign of Edward the Good, *alias* Edward
the Peacemaker, and I went for the long weekend to Castle
Balch – fine place in Oxfordshire – my cousin Tom's roost.
Tom was a bit of a collector, not that I ever held that against
Tom, and Eva must take the principal blame, if any: meaning
that the people she invited for house-parties were excessively
what the Yankees call (or called) 'high-toned' – artist-fellows,
M.P.s, celebrities of all sorts, not easy to compete against. On
this particular occasion, Eva had flung her net wide and made
a stupendous haul. To wit: Nixon-Blake, R. A., who had painted
the picture of the year – do they have pictures of the year
nowadays? It's years since I visited Burlington House – and
Ratface Dingleby, who had taken his twenty-foot *Ruby* round
the Horn that same February. Saw his obituary in *The Times* a
couple of years ago: lived to ninety, not born to be drowned.
And, what the devil was his name? the elephant-hunter who
won the V.C. in the Transvaal? – Captain Scrymgeour, of
course! He got killed under Younghusband in Tibet a year or
two later. And Charlie Batta, the actor-manager. None of whom
I could count as cronies. *Homines novi*, in point of fact. Fortunately, Mungo Montserrat was there; my year at Eton. And
Doris, his spouse, a bit stuffy, but a good sort: another cousin
of mine. I teem with cousins.

   This being described as a tennis week-end, we had all brought
our flannels and rackets, prepared to emulate the Doherty brothers, then all the go. Both Castle Balch courts played admirably – gardener a magician with turf – but being July, of course it
rained and rained ceaselessly from Friday afternoon to Monday
afternoon and the tournament was literally washed out. We

enjoyed pretty good sport none the less – Tom had a squash court for fellows like Mungo and me who were too energetic to content themselves with baccarat and billiards. And Charlie Batta sent to Town for some pretty actresses who happened to be seasonally unemployed, or unemployable. Furthermore, Eva invented a lot of very humorous wheezes, as the current slang was, to embarrass us – some of them pretty close to the knuckle. But no tennis tournament took place; though a beautiful silver rose-bowl was waiting on the smoking-room mantelpiece to reward the winner.

Forgot to mention the Bishop of Bangalore, who had been invited in error. The fun never started until he had turned in, but fortunately the bish loved his pillow even more than his neighbour. On Monday evening then, about 12.15 a.m. in mellow lamp light, don't you know, when the ladies had retired to their rest and the Bishop had joined them – no allegation intended – Tom spoke up and said forthrightly: 'Gentlemen, I'm as deeply grieved by this tennis fiasco as you are, and I don't want that jerry knocking around the Castle for ever afterwards to remind me of it. Tell you what: I'll present same to the fellow who supplies the best answer to a question that Eva was too modest to propound with her own lips: "What were the most thrilling moments of your life?"'

We all drew numbers out of the Bishop's fascinatingly laced top hat, and spun our yarns in the order assigned by fate. Apart from Mungo and me, every personage present was a born raconteur. I assure you: to hear Charlie Batta, who tee'd off, tell us how he played *Hamlet* in dumb show to a cellarful of Corsican bandits who were holding him for ransom, and how, waiving the three thousand sov.s at which he had been priced, they afterwards escorted him in triumph to Ajaccio, firing *feux-de-joie* all the way in tribute to his art – that was worth a gross of silver bowls. And doughty Scrymgeour on safari in German East, when he bagged the hippo and the rhino with a right and left; my word, Scrymgeour held us! Next, the R. A. (told you his name, forgotten it again – had a small red imperial, eyes like ginger-ale, and claimed to have re-introduced the yellow hunting waistcoat, though that was an inexactitude). He

recorded an encounter with a gypsy girl in a forest near Buda-
pest – the exact physical type he had envisaged for his picture
The Sorceress – whom he persuaded with coins and Hunnish
endearments to pose in the nude; after which he painted those
Junoesque curves and contours, those delicate flesh tints – and
so forth, don't you know – with ecstatic inspiration and anatomic
exactitude, careless though her jealous lover had by this time
entered the grotto and was covering him with an inlaid fowling
piece. At last the murder weapon clattered to the ground and
he heard a strangled voice exclaim: 'Gorgio, I cannot shoot you.
I bow before your genius! Keep the girl – leave me the picture –
go!'

Finally poor old Mungo, who had drawn No. 13, was pre-
vailed upon to take the floor. My heart went out to him, me
having made a damned mess of my own effort. These were
Mungo's exact words: 'Gentlemen, I'm a simple chappy, never
had any exciting adventures like you chappies. Sorry. However.
If you want to know. The most thrilling moments of my life
were when I married Doris – you all know Doris – and, well,
when she and I ... (pause) ... They still are, in fact.'

Mungo brought the house down. Tom thrust the rose-bowl
into his unwilling hands, treated him to the stiffest whisky and
soda on which I have ever clapped eyes, and sent him crookedly
upstairs to the bedroom; where Doris was being kept awake,
not by the sounds of revelry from the smoke-room, but by the
frightful snores of the Bishop next door.

'What *have* you got there, Mungo?' she asked crossly.

'Rose-bowl,' Mungo mumbled. 'Tom offered it to the chappy
who could best answer Eva's question about the most thrilling
moments in his life. They all told such capital stories that, when
it was my turn, I got into a mortal funk. But we had drawn lots
from the Bishop's hat, and this inspired me. I said: "When
Doris and I kneel side by side in church giving thanks to Heaven
for all the blessings that have been showered on us." And they
gave me the prize!'

'How *could* you, Mungo! You know that was a dreadful lie.
Oh, now I feel so ashamed! It's not as though prayers and
Church are anything to joke about.' She enlarged on this aspect

of the case for quite a while, and Mungo resignedly hung his head. Whisky always made him melancholy; I can't say why.

The next morning the party broke up: one and all were catching the 10.45 express to Town. Doris Montserrat noticed a lot of admiring or curious glances flung in her direction, and conscience pricked. She stood on the hall staircase and made a startling little speech.

'Gentlemen, I'm afraid that Mungo won the rose-bowl on false pretences last night. He has only done ... what he said he did ... three times. The first time was before we married; I made him. The second was when we married; he could hardly have avoided it. The third was after we married, and then he fell asleep in the middle ...'

Elizabeth Bowen

The Cheery Soul

On arriving, I first met the aunt of whom they had told me, the aunt who had not yet got over being turned out of Italy. She sat resentfully by the fire, or rather the fireplace, and did not look up when I came in. The acrid smell that curled through the drawing-room could be traced to a grate full of sizzling fir cones that must have been brought in damp. From the mantelpiece one lamp, with its shade tilted, shed light on the parting of the aunt's hair. It could not be said that the room was cheerful: the high, curtained bow windows made draughty caves; the armchairs and sofas, pushed back against the wall, wore the air of being renounced for ever. Only a row of discreet greeting-cards (few with pictures) along the top of a bureau betrayed the presence of Christmas. There was no holly, and no pieces of string.

I coughed and said: 'I feel I should introduce myself,' and followed this up by giving the aunt my name, which she received with apathy. When she did stir, it was to look at the parcel that I coquettishly twirled from its loop of string. 'They're not giving presents, this year,' she said in alarm. 'If I were you, I should put that back in my room.'

'It's just – my rations.'

'In that case,' she remarked, 'I really don't know what you had better do.' Turning away from me she picked up a small bent poker, and with this began to interfere with the fir cones, of which several, steaming, bounced from the grate. 'A good wood stove,' she said, 'would make all the difference. At Sienna, though they say it is cold in winter, we never had troubles of this kind.'

'How would it be,' I said, 'if I sat down?' I pulled a chair a little on to the hearthrug, if only for the idea of the thing. 'I gather our hosts are out. I wonder where they have gone to?'

'Really, I couldn't tell you.'

'My behaviour,' I said, 'has been shockingly free-and-easy. Having pulled the bell three times, waited, had a go at the knocker . . .'

' . . . I heard,' she said, slightly bowing her head.

'I gave *that* up, tried the door, found it unlocked, so just marched in.'

'Have you come about something?' she said with renewed alarm.

'Well, actually, I fear that I've come to stay. They have been so very kind as to . . .'

' . . . Oh, I remember – someone *was* coming.' She looked at me rather closely. 'Have you been here before?'

'Never. So this is delightful,' I said firmly. 'I am billeted where I work' (I named the industrial town, twelve miles off, that was these days in a ferment of war production), 'my land-lady craves my room for these next two days for her daughter, who is on leave, and, on top of this, to be frank, I'm a bit old-fashioned: Christmas alone in a strange town didn't appeal to me. So you can see how I sprang at . . .'

'Yes, I can see,' she said. With the tongs, she replaced the cones that had fallen out of the fire. 'At Orvieto,' she said, 'the stoves were so satisfactory that one felt no ill effects from the tiled floors.'

As I could think of nothing to add to this, I joined her in listening attentively to the hall clock. My entry into the drawing-room having been tentative, I had not made so bold as to close the door behind me, so a further coldness now seeped through from the hall. Except for the clock – whose loud tick was reluctant – there was not another sound to be heard: the very silence seemed to produce echoes. The Rangerton-Karneys' absence from their own house was becoming, virtually, osten-tatious. 'I understand,' I said, 'that they are tremendously busy. Practically never not on the go.'

'They expect to have a finger in every pie.'

Their aunt's ingratitude shocked me. She must be (as they

had hinted) in a difficult state. They had always spoken with the most marked forbearance of her enforced return to them out of Italy. In England, they said, she had no other roof but theirs, and they were constantly wounded (their friends told me) by her saying she would have preferred internment in Italy.

In common with all my fellow-workers at — , I had a high regard for the Rangerton-Karneys, an admiration tempered, perhaps, with awe. Their energy in the promotion of every war effort was only matched by the austerity of their personal lives. They appeared to have given up almost everything. That they never sat down could be seen from their drawing-room chairs. As 'local people' of the most solid kind they were on terms with the bigwigs of every department, the key minds of our small but now rather important town. Completely discreet, they were palpably 'in the know'.

Their house in the Midlands, in which I now so incredibly found myself, was largish, built of the local stone, *circa* 1860 I should say from its style. It was not very far from a railway junction, and at a still less distance from a canal. I had evaded the strictures on Christmas travel by making the twelve-mile journey by bicycle – indeed, the suggestion that I should do this played a prominent part in their invitation. So I bicycled over. My little things for the two nights were contained in one of those useful American-cloth suitcases, strapped to my back-wheel carrier, while my parcel of rations could be slung, I found, from my handlebar. The bumping of this parcel on my right knee as I pedalled was a major embarrassment. To cap this, the misty damp of the afternoon had caused me to set off in a mackintosh. At the best of times I am not an expert cyclist. The grateful absence of hills (all this country is very flat) was cancelled out by the greasiness of the roads, and army traffic often made me dismount – it is always well to be on the safe side. Now and then, cows or horses loomed up abruptly to peer at me over the reeking hedgerows. The few anonymous villages I passed through all appeared, in the falling dusk, to be very much the same: their inhabitants wore an air of war-time discretion, so I did not dare risk snubs by asking how far I had come. My pocket map, however, proved less unhelpful when I

found that I had been reading it upside down. When, about half
way, I turned on my lamp, I watched mist curdle under its
wobbling ray. My spectacles dimmed steadily; my hands
numbed inside my knitted gloves (the only Christmas present
I had received so far) and the mist condensed on my muffler
in fine drops.

I own that I had sustained myself through this journey on
thoughts of the cheery welcome ahead. The Rangerton-Karneys'
invitation, delivered by word of mouth only three days ago, had
been totally unexpected, as well as gratifying. I had had no
reason to think they had taken notice of me. We had met rarely,
when I reported to the committees on which they sat. That the
brother and two sisters (so much alike that people took them
for triplets) had attracted *my* wistful notice, I need not say. But
not only was my position a quite obscure one; I am not generally
sought out; I make few new friends. None of my colleagues had
been to the Rangerton-Karneys' house: there was an idea that
they had given up guests. As the news of their invitation to me
spread (and I cannot say I did much to stop it spreading) I rose
rapidly in everyone's estimation.

In fact, their thought had been remarkably kind. Can you
wonder that I felt myself favoured? I was soon, now, to see their
erstwhile committee faces wreathed with seasonable and genial
smiles. I never was one to doubt that people unbend at home.
Perhaps a little feverish from my cycling, I pictured blazing
hearths through holly-garlanded doors.

Owing to this indulgence in foolish fancy, my real arrival
rather deflated me.

'I suppose they went out after tea?' I said to the aunt.

'After lunch, I think,' she replied. 'There was no tea.' She
picked up her book, which was about Mantegna, and went on
reading, pitched rather tensely forward to catch the light of the
dim-bulbed lamp. I hesitated, then rose up, saying that perhaps
I had better deliver my rations to the cook. 'If you can,' she
said, turning over a page.

The whirr of the clock preparing to strike seven made me
jump. The hall had funny acoustics – so much so that I strode
across the wide breaches from rug to rug rather than hear my

step on the stone flags. Draught and dark coming down a shaft announced the presence of stairs. I saw what little I saw by the flame of a night-light, palpitating under a blue glass inverted shade. The hall and the staircase windows were not blacked out yet. (Back in the drawing-room, I could only imagine, the aunt must have so far bestirred herself as to draw the curtains.)

The kitchen was my objective – as I had said to the aunt. I pushed at a promising baize door: it immediately opened upon a vibration of heat and rich, heartening smells. At these, the complexion of everything changed once more. If my spirits, just lately, had not been very high, this was no doubt due to the fact that I had lunched on a sandwich, then had not dared leave my bicycle to look for a cup of tea. I was in no mood to reproach the Rangerton-Karneys for this Christmas break in their well-known austere routine.

But, in view of this, the kitchen was a surprise. Warm, and spiced with excellent smells, it was in the dark completely but for the crimson glow from between the bars of the range. A good deal puzzled, I switched the light on – the black-out, here, had been punctiliously done.

The glare made me jump. The cook must have found, for her own use, a quadruple-power electric bulb. This now fairly blazed down on the vast scrubbed white wood table, scored and scarred by decades of the violent chopping of meat. I looked about – to be staggered by what I did not see. Neither on range, table, nor outsize dresser were there signs of the preparation of any meal. Not a plate, not a spoon, not a canister showed any signs of action. The heat-vibrating top of the range was bare; all the pots and pans were up above, clean and cold, in their places along the rack. I went so far as to open the oven door – a roasting smell came out, but there was nothing inside. A tap drip-drop-dripped on an upturned bowl in the sink – but nobody had been peeling potatoes there.

I put my rations down on the table and was, dumbfounded, preparing to turn away, when a white paper on the white wood caught my eye. This paper, in an inexpert line of block-printing, bore the somewhat unnecessary statement: I AM NOT HERE. To this was added, in brackets: 'Look in the fish kettle.' Though this be no affair of mine, could I fail to follow it up? Was this some new demonstration of haybox cookery; was I to find our dinner snugly concealed? I identified the fish kettle, a large tin object (about the size, I should say, of an infant's bath) that stood on a stool halfway between the sink and range. It wore a tight-fitting lid, which came off with a sort of plop: the sound in itself had an ominous hollowness. Inside, I found, again, only a piece of paper. This said: 'Mr. & the 2 Misses Rangerton-Karney can boil their heads. This holds 3.'

I felt that the least I could do for my hosts the Rangerton-Karneys was to suppress this unkind joke, so badly out of accord with the Christmas spirit. I *could* have dropped the paper straight into the kitchen fire, but on second thoughts I went back to consult the aunt. I found her so very deep in Mantegna as to be oblivious of the passage of time. She clearly did not like being interrupted. I said: 'Can you tell me if your nephew and nieces had any kind of contretemps with their cook today?'

She replied: 'I make a point of not asking questions.'

'Oh, so do I,' I replied, 'in the normal way. But I fear . . .'

'You fear what?'

'She's gone,' I said. 'Leaving this . . .'

The aunt looked at the paper, then said: 'How curious.' She added: 'Of course, she has gone: that happened a year ago. She must have left several messages, I suppose. I remember that Etta found one in the mincing machine, saying to tell them to mince their gizzards. Etta seemed very much put out. That was *last* Christmas Eve, I remember – dear me, what a coincidence . . . So you found this, did you?' she said, re-reading the paper with less repugnance than I should have wished to see. 'I expect, if you went on poking about the kitchen . . .'

Annoyed, I said tartly: 'A reprehensible cook!'

'No worse than other English cooks,' she replied. 'They all declare they have never heard of a *pasta*, and that oil in cookery makes one repeat. But I always found her cheerful and kind. And of course I miss her – Etta's been cooking since.' (This was the elder Miss Rangerton-Karney.)

'But look,' I said, 'I was led to *this* dreadful message, by another one, on the table. *That* can't have been there a year.'

'I suppose not,' the aunt said, showing indifference. She picked up her book and inclined again to the lamp.

I said: 'You don't think some other servant . .'

She looked at me like a fish.

'They *have* no other servants. Oh no: not since the cook . . .' Her voice trailed away. 'Well, it's all very odd, I'm sure.'

'It's worse than odd, my dear lady: there won't be any dinner.'

She shocked me by emitting a kind of giggle. She said 'Unless they *do* boil their heads.'

The idea that the Rangerton-Karneys might be out on a cook-hunt rationalized this perplexing evening for me. I am always more comfortable when I can tell myself that people are, after all, behaving accountably. The Rangerton-Karneys always acted in trio. The idea that one of them should stay at home to receive me while the other two went ploughing round the dark country would, at this crisis, never present itself. The Rangerton-Karneys' three sets of thoughts and feelings always appeared to join at the one root: one might say that they had a composite character. One thing, I could reflect, about misadventures is that they make for talk and often end in a laugh. I tried in vain to picture the Rangerton-Karneys laughing – for that was a thing I had never seen.

But if Etta is now resigned to doing the cooking . . .? I thought better not to puzzle the thing out.

Screening my electric torch with my fingers past the uncurtained windows, I went upstairs to look for what might be my room. In my other hand I carried my little case – to tell the truth, I was anxious to change my socks. Embarking on a long passage, with doors ajar, I discreetly projected my torch into a number of rooms. All were cold; some were palpably slept in, others dismantled. I located the resting-places of Etta, Max and Paulina by the odour of tar soap, shoe-leather and boiled woollen underclothes that announced their presences in so many committee rooms. At an unintimate distance along the passage, the glint of my torch on Florentine bric-à-brac suggested the headquarters of the aunt. I did at last succeed, by elimination, in finding the spare room prepared for me. They had put me just across the way from their aunt. My torch and my touch revealed a made-up bed, draped in a glacial white starched quilt, two fringed towels straddling the water-jug, and virgin white mats to receive my brushes and comb. I successively bumped my knee (the knee still sore from the parcel) on two upright chairs. Yes, this must be the room for me. Oddly enough, it was much less cold than the others – but I did not think of that at the time. Having done what was necessary to the window, I lit up, to consider my new domain.

Somebody had been lying on my bed. When I rest during the day, I always remove the quilt, but whoever it was had neglected to do this. A deep trough, with a map of creases, appeared. The creases, however, did not extend far. Whoever it was had lain here in a contented stupor.

I worried – Etta might blame me. To distract my thoughts, I opened my little case and went to put my things on the dressing-table. The mirror was tilted upwards under the light, and something was written on it in soap: DEARIE, DON'T MIND ME. I at once went to the washstand, where the soap could be verified – it was a used cake, one corner blunted by writing. On my way back, I kicked over a black bottle, which, so placed on the floor as to be in easy reach from the bed, now gaily and noisily bowled away. It was empty – I had to admit that its contents, breathed out again, gave that decided character to my room.

The aunt was to be heard, pattering up the stairs. Was this belated hostess-ship on her part? She came into view of my door, carrying the night-light from the hall table. Giving me a modest, affronted look she said: 'I thought I'd tidy my hair.'

'The cook has been lying on my bed.'

'That would have been very possible, I'm afraid. She was often a little – if you know what I mean. But, she left last Christmas.'

'She's written something.'

'I don't see what one can do,' the aunt said, turning into her room. For my part, I dipped a towel into the jug and reluctantly tried to rub out the cook's message, but this only left a blur all over the glass. I applied to this the drier end of the towel. Oddly enough (perhaps) I felt fortified: this occult good feeling was,

somehow, warming. The cook was supplying that touch of
nature I had missed since crossing the Rangerton-Karneys'
threshold. Thus, when I stepped back for another look at the
mirror, I was barely surprised to find that a sprig of mistletoe
had been twisted around the cord of the hanging electric light.

My disreputable psychic pleasure was to be interrupted.
Downstairs, in the caves of the house, the front door bell jangled,
then jangled again. This was followed by an interlude with the
knocker: an imperious rat-a-tat-tat. I called across to the aunt:
'Ought one of us to go down? It might be a telegram.'

'I don't think so – why?'

We heard the glass door of the porch (the door through which
I had made my so different entry) being rattled open; we heard
the hall traversed by footsteps with the weight of authority. In
response to a mighty '*Anyone there*?' I defied the aunt's judgement and went hurrying down. Coming on a policeman outlined
in the drawing-room door, my first thought was that this must
be about the black-out. I edged in, silent, just behind the
policeman: he looked about him suspiciously, then saw me.
'And who might you be?' he said. The bringing out of his
notebook gave me stage fright during my first and other replies.
I explained that the Rangerton-Karneys had asked me to come
and stay.

'Oh, they did?' he said. 'Well, that is a laugh. Seen much of
them?'

'Not so far.'

'Well, you won't.' I asked why: he ignored my question, asked
for all my particulars, quizzed my identity card. 'I shall check
up on all this,' he said heavily. 'So they asked you for Christmas,
did they? And just *when*, may I ask, was this invitation issued?'

'Well, er – three days ago.'

This made me quite popular. He said: 'Much as I thought.
Attempt to cover their tracks and divert suspicion. I daresay
you blew off all round about them having asked you here?'

'I may have mentioned it to one or two friends.'

He looked pleased again and said: 'Just what they reckoned
on. Not a soul was to guess they had planned to bolt. As for
you – *you're* a cool hand, I must say. Just walked in, found the

place empty and dossed down. Never once strike you there was anything fishy?'

'A good deal struck me,' I replied austerely. 'I took it, however, that my host and his sisters had been unexpectedly called out – perhaps to look for a cook.'

'Ah, cook,' he said. 'Now what brought that to your mind?'

'Her whereabouts seemed uncertain, if you know what I mean.'

Whereupon, he whipped over several leaves of his notebook. 'The last cook employed here,' he said, 'was in residence here four days, departing last Christmas Eve, December 24th, 194–. We have evidence that she stated locally that she was unable to tolerate certain goings-on. She specified interference in her department, undue advantage taken of the rationing system, mental cruelty to an elderly female refugee ...'

I interposed: 'That would certainly be the aunt.'

' ... and failure to observe Christmas in the appropriate manner. On this last point she expressed herself violently. She further adduced (though with less violence of feeling) that her three employers were "dirty spies, with their noses in everything". Subsequently, she withdrew this last remark; her words were, "I do not wish to make trouble, as I know how to make trouble in a way of my own." However, certain remarks she had let drop have been since followed up, and proved useful in our inquiries. Unhappily, we cannot check up on them, as the deceased met her end shortly after leaving this house.'

'The *deceased*?' I cried, with a sinking heart.

'Proceeding through the hall door and down the approach or avenue, in an almost total state of intoxication, she was heard singing "God rest you merry, gentlemen, let nothing you dismay". She also shouted: "Me for an English Christmas!" Accosting several pedestrians, she informed them that in her opinion times were not what they were. She spoke with emotion (being intoxicated) of turkey, mince pies, ham, plum pudding, etc. She was last seen hurrying in the direction of the canal, saying she must get brandy to make her sauce. She was last heard in the vicinity of the canal. The body was recovered from the canal on Boxing Day, December 26th, 194–.'

'But what,' I said, 'has happened to the Rangerton-Karneys?'

'Now, now!' said the policeman, shaking his finger sternly. 'You *may* hear as much as is good for you, one day – or you may not. Did you ever hear of the Safety of the Realm? I don't mind telling you one thing – you're lucky. You might have landed yourself in a nasty mess.'

'But, good heavens – the *Rangerton-Karneys*! They know everyone.'

'Ah,' he said, 'but it's that kind you have to watch.' Heavy with this reflection, his eye travelled over the hearthrug. He stooped with a creak and picked up the aunt's book. 'Wop name,' he said, 'propaganda: sticks out a mile. Now, don't you cut off anywhere, while I am now proceeding to search the house.'

'Cut off?' I nearly said. 'What do you take me for?' Alone, I sat down in the aunt's chair and dropped a few more fir cones into the extinct fire.

Stella Gibbons

Christmas at Cold Comfort Farm

It was Christmas Eve. Dusk, a filthy mantle, lay over Sussex when the Reverend Silas Hearsay, Vicar of Howling, set out to pay his yearly visit to Cold Comfort Farm. Earlier in the afternoon he had feared he would not be Guided to go there, but then he had seen a crate of British Port-type wine go past the Vicarage on the grocer's boy's bicycle, and it could only be going, by that road, to the farmhouse. Shortly afterwards he was Guided to go, and set out upon his bicycle.

The Starkadders, of Cold Comfort Farm, had never got the hang of Christmas, somehow, and on Boxing Day there was always a run on the Howling Pharmacy for lint, bandages, and boracic powder. So the Vicar was going up there, as he did every year, to show them the ropes a bit. (It must be explained that these events took place some years before the civilizing hand of Flora Poste had softened and reformed the Farm and its rude inhabitants.)

After removing two large heaps of tussocks which blocked the lane leading to the Farm and thereby releasing a flood of muddy, icy water over his ankles, the Vicar wheeled his machine on towards the farmhouse, reflecting that those tussocks had never fallen there from the dung-cart of Nature. It was clear that someone did not want him to come to the place. He pushed his bicycle savagely up the hill, muttering.

The farmhouse was in silence and darkness. He pulled the ancient hell-bell (once used to warn excommunicated persons to stay away from Divine Service) hanging outside the front door, and waited.

For a goodish bit nothing happened. Suddenly a window far

above his head was flung open and a voice wailed into the twilight –

'No! No! No!'

And the window slammed shut again.

'You're making a mistake, I'm sure,' shouted the Vicar, peering up into the webby thongs of the darkness. 'It's me. The Rev. Silas Hearsay.'

There was a pause. Then –

'Beant you postman?' asked the voice, rather embarrassed.

'No, no, of course not; come, come!' laughed the Vicar, grinding his teeth.

'I be comin',' retorted the voice. 'Thought it were postman after his Christmas Box.' The window slammed again. After a very long time indeed the door suddenly opened and there stood Adam Lambsbreath, oldest of the farm servants, peering up at the Reverend Hearsay by the light of a lonely rushdip (so called because you dipped it in grease and rushed to wherever you were going before it went out).

'Is anyone at home? May I enter?' enquired the Vicar, entering, and staring scornfully round the desolate kitchen, at the dead blue ashes in the grate, the thick dust on hanch and beam, the feathers blowing about like fun everywhere. Yet even here there were signs of Christmas, for a withered branch of holly stood in a shapeless vessel on the table. And Adam himself ... there was something even more peculiar than usual about him.

'Are you ailing, man?' asked the Vicar irritably, kicking a chair out of the way and perching himself on the edge of the table.

'Nay, Rev., I be niver better,' piped the old man. '*The older the berry, The more it makes merry.*'

'Then why,' thundered the Vicar, sliding off the table and walking on tiptoe towards Adam with his arms held at full length above his head, 'are you wearing three of Mrs Starkadder's red shawls?'

Adam stood his ground.

'I mun have a red courtepy, master. Can't be Santa Claus wi'out a red courtepy,' he said. 'Iverybody knows that. Ay, the hand o' Fate lies heavy on us all, Christmas and all the year round alike, but I thought I'd bedight meself as Santa Claus, so I did, just to please me little Elfine. And this night at midnight I be goin' around fillin' the stockin's, if I'm spared.'

The Vicar laughed contemptuously.

'So that were why I took three o' Mrs Starkadder's red shawls,' concluded Adam.

'I suppose you have never thought of God in terms of Energy? No, it is too much to expect.' The Reverend Hearsay re-seated himself on the table and glanced at his watch. 'Where in Energy's name *is* everybody? I have to be at the Assembly Rooms to read a paper on *The Future of the Father Fixation* at eight, and I've got to feed first. If nobody's coming, I'd rather go.'

'Won't ee have a dram o' swede wine first?' a deep voice asked, and a tall woman stepped over the threshold, followed by a little girl of twelve or so with yellow hair and clear, beautiful features. Judith Starkadder dropped her hat on the floor and leant against the table, staring listlessly at the Vicar.

'No swede wine, I thank you,' snapped the Reverend Hearsay. He glanced keenly round the kitchen in search of the British Port-type, but there was no sign of it. 'I came up to discuss an article with you and yours. An article in *Home Anthropology*.'

' 'Twere good of ee, Reverend,' she said tiredly.

'It is called *Christmas: From Religious Festival to Shopping Orgy*. Puts the case for Peace and Good Will very sensibly. Both good for trade. What more can you want?'

'Nothing,' she said, leaning her head on her hand.

'But I see,' the Vicar went on furiously, in a low tone and glaring at Adam, 'that here, as everywhere else, the usual childish wish-fantasies are in possession. Stars, shepherds, mangers, stockings, fir-trees, puddings ... Energy help you all! I wish you good night, and a prosperous Christmas.'

He stamped out of the kitchen, and slammed the door after him with such violence that he brought a slate down on his back tyre and cut it open, and he had to walk home, arriving there too late for supper before setting out for Godmere.

After he had gone, Judith stared into the fire without speaking, and Adam busied himself with scraping the mould from a jar of mincemeat and picking some things which had fallen into it out of a large crock of pudding which he had made yesterday.

Elfine, meanwhile, was slowly opening a small brown paper parcel which she had been nursing, and at last revealed a small and mean-looking doll dressed in a sleazy silk dress and one under-garment that did not take off. This she gently nursed, talking to it in a low, sweet voice.

'Who gave you that, child?' asked her mother idly.

'I told you, mother. Uncle Micah and Aunt Rennett and Aunt Prue and Uncle Harkaway and Uncle Ezra.'

'Treasure it. You will not get many such.'

'I know, mother; I do. I love her very much, dear, dear Caroline,' and Elfine gently put a kiss on the doll's face.

'Now, missus, have ee got the Year's Luck? Can't make puddens wi'out the Year's Luck,' said Adam, shuffling forward.

'It's somewhere here. I forget –'

She turned her shabby handbag upside down, and there fell out on the table the following objects:

A small coffin-nail.

A menthol cone.

Three bad sixpences.

A doll's cracked looking-glass.

A small roll of sticking-plaster.

Adam collected these objects and ranged them by the pudding basin.

'Ay, them's all there,' he muttered. 'Him as gets the sticking-plaster'll break a limb; the menthol cone means as you'll be blind wi' headache, the bad coins means as you'll lose all yer money, and him as gets the coffin-nail will die afore the New Year. The mirror's seven years' bad luck for someone. Aie! In ye go, curse ye!' and he tossed the objects into the pudding, where they were not easily nor long distinguishable from the main mass.

'Want a stir, missus? Come, Elfine, my popelot, stir long, stir firm, your meat to earn,' and he handed her the butt of an old rifle, once used by Fig Starkadder in the Gordon Riots.

Judith turned from the pudding with what is commonly described as a gesture of loathing, but Elfine took the rifle butt and stirred the mixture once or twice.

'Ay, now tes all mixed,' said the old man, nodding with satisfaction. 'Tomorrer we'll boil un fer a good hour, and un'll be done.'

'Will an hour be enough?' said Elfine. 'Mrs Hawk-Monitor up at Hautcouture Hall boils hers for eight hours, ... and another four on Christmas Day.'

'How do ee know?' demanded Adam. 'Have ee been runnin' wi' that young goosepick Mus' Richard again?'

'You shut up. He's awfully decent.'

'Tisn't decent to run wi' a young popelot all over the downs in all weathers.'

'Well, it isn't any of your business, so shut up.'

After an offended pause, Adams said:

'Well, niver fret about puddens. None of 'em here has iver tasted any puddens but mine, and they won't know no different.'

At midnight, when the farmhouse was in darkness save for the faint flame of a nightlight burning steadily beside the bed of Harkaway, who was afraid of bears, a dim shape might have been seen moving stealthily along the corridor from bedroom to bedroom. It wore three red shawls pinned over its torn nightshirt and carried over its shoulder a nosebag (the property of Viper the gelding), distended with parcels. It was Adam, bent on putting into the stockings of the Starkadders the presents which he had made or bought with his savings. The presents were chiefly swedes, beetroots, mangel-wurzels and turnips, decorated with coloured ribbons and strips of silver paper from tea packets.

'Ay,' muttered the old man, as he opened the door of the room where Meriam, the hired girl, was sleeping over the Christmas week. 'An apple for each will make 'em retch, a couple o' nuts will warm their wits.'

The next instant he stepped back in astonishment. There was a light in the room and there, sitting bolt upright in bed beside her slumbering daughter, was Mrs Beetle.

Mrs Beetle looked steadily at Adam, for a minute or two. Then she observed:

'Some 'opes.'

'Nay, niver say that, soul,' protested Adam, moving to the bedrail where hung a very fully fashioned salmon-pink silk stocking with ladders all down it. "Tisn't so. Ee do know well that I looks on the maidy as me own child.'

Mrs Beetle gave a short laugh and adjusted a curler. 'You better not let Agony 'ear you, 'intin' I dunno wot,' said Mrs Beetle. "Urry up and put yer rubbish in there, I want me sleep out; I got to be up at cock-wake ter-morrer.'

Adam put a swede, an apple and a small pot in the stocking and was tip-toeing away when Mrs Beetle, raising her head from the pillow, inquired:

'Wot's that you've give 'er?'

'Eye-shadow,' whispered Adam hoarsely, turning at the door.

'*Wot?*' hissed Mrs Beetle, inclining her head in an effort to hear. "Ave you gorn crackers?'

'Eye-shadow. To put on the maidy's eyes. 'Twill give that touch o' glamour as be irresistible; it do say so on pot.'

'Get out of 'ere, you old trouble-maker! Don't she 'ave enough bother resistin' as it is, and then you go and give 'er ... 'ere, wait till I –' and Mrs Beetle was looking around for something to throw as Adam hastily retreated.

'And I'll lay you ain't got no present fer me, ter make matters worse,' she called after him.

Silently he placed a bright new tin of beetle-killer on the washstand and shuffled away.

His experiences in the apartments of the other Starkadders were no more fortunate, for Seth was busy with a friend and was so furious at being interrupted that he threw his riding-boots at the old man, Luke and Mark had locked their door and could be heard inside roaring with laughter at Adam's discomfiture, and Amos was praying, and did not even get up off his knees or open his eyes as he discharged at Adam the goat-pistol which he kept ever by his bed. And everybody else had such enormous holes in their stockings that the small presents Adam put in them fell through on to the floor along with the big ones, and when the Starkadders got up in the morning and rushed round to the foot of the bed to see what Santa had brought, they stubbed their toes on the turnips and swedes and walked on the smaller presents and smashed them to smith-ereens.

So what with one thing and another everybody was in an even worse temper than usual when the family assembled round the long table in the kitchen for the Christmas dinner about half-past two the next afternoon. They would all have sooner been in some place else, but Mrs Ada Doom (Grandmother Doom, known as Grummer) insisted on them all being there, and as they did not want her to go mad and bring disgrace on the House of Starkadder, there they had to be.

One by one they came in, the men from the fields with soil on their boots, the women fresh from hennery and duck filch with eggs in their bosoms that they gave to Mrs Beetle who was just making the custard. Everybody had to work as usual on Christmas Day, and no one had troubled to put on anything handsomer than their usual workaday clouts stained with mud and plough-oil. Only Elfine wore a cherry-red jersey over her dark skirt and had pinned a spray of holly on herself. An aunt, a distant aunt named Mrs Poste, who lived in London, had unexpectedly sent her the pretty jersey. Prue and Letty had stuck sixpenny artificial posies in their hair, but they only looked wild and queer.

At last all were seated and waiting for Ada Doom.

'Come, come, mun we stick here like jennets i' the trave?' demanded Micah at last. 'Amos, Reuben, do ee carve the turkey. If so be as we wait much longer, 'twill be shent, and the sausages, too.'

Even as he spoke, heavy footsteps were heard approaching the head of the stairs, and everybody at once rose to their feet and looked towards the door.

The low-ceilinged room was already half in dusk, for it was a cold, still Christmas Day, without much light in the grey sky, and the only other illumination came from the dull fire, half-buried under a tass of damp kindling.

Adam gave a last touch to the pile of presents, wrapped in hay and tied with bast, which he had put round the foot of the withered thorn-branch that was the traditional Starkadder Christmas-tree, hastily rearranged one of the tufts of sheep's-wool that decorated its branches, straightened the raven's skeleton that adorned its highest branch in place of a fairy-doll or star, and shuffled into his place just as Mrs Doom reached the foot of the stairs, leaning on her daughter Judith's arm. Mrs Doom struck at him with her stick in passing as she went slowly to the head of the table.

'Well, well. What are we waiting for? Are you all mishooden?' she demanded impatiently as she seated herself. 'Are you all here? All? Answer me!' banging her stick.

'Ay, Grummer,' rose the low, dreary drone from all sides of the table. 'We be all here.'

'Where's Seth?' demanded the old woman, peering sharply on either side of the long row.

'Gone out,' said Harkaway briefly, shifting a straw in his mouth.

'What for?' demanded Mrs Doom.

There was an ominous silence.

'He said he was going to fetch something, Grandmother,' at last said Elfine.

'Ay. Well, well, no matter, so long as he comes soon. Amos, carve the bird. Ay, would it were a vulture, 'twere more fitting! Reuben, fling these dogs the fare my bounty provides. Sausages ... pah! Mince-pies ... what a black-bitter mockery it all is! Every almond, every raisin, is wrung from the dry, dying soil and paid for with sparse greasy notes grudged alike by bank and buyer. Come, Ezra, pass the ginger wine! Be gay, spawn! Laugh, stuff yourselves, gorge and forget, you rat-heaps! Rot you all!' and she fell back in her chair, gasping and keeping one eye on the British Port-type that was now coming up the table.

'Tes one of her bad days,' said Judith tonelessly. 'Amos, will you pull a cracker wi' me? We were lovers ... once.'

'Hush, woman.' He shrank back from the proffered treat. 'Tempt me not wi' motters and paper caps. Hell is paved wi' such.' Judith smiled bitterly and fell silent.

Reuben, meanwhile, had seen to it that Elfine got the best bit off the turkey (which is not saying much) and had filled her glass with Port-type wine and well-water.

The turkey gave out before it got to Letty, Prue, Susan,

Phoebe, Jane and Rennett, who were huddled together at the foot of the table, and they were making do with brussels-sprouts as hard as bullets drenched with weak gravy, and home-brewed braket. There was silence in the kitchen except for the sough of swallowing, the sudden suck of drinking.

'WHERE IS SETH?' suddenly screamed Mrs Doom, flinging down her turkey-leg and glaring round.

Silence fell; everyone moved uneasily, not daring to speak in case they provoked an outburst. But at that moment the cheerful, if unpleasant, noise of a motor-cycle was heard outside, and in another moment it stopped at the kitchen door. All eyes were turned in that direction, and in another moment in came Seth.

'Well, Grummer! Happen you thought I was lost!' he cried impudently, peeling off his boots and flinging them at Meriam, the hired girl, who cowered by the fire gnawing a sausage skin.

Mrs Doom silently pointed to his empty seat with the turkey-leg, and he sat down.

'She hev had an outhees. Ay, 'twas terrible,' reproved Judith in a low tone as Seth seated himself beside her.

'Niver mind, I ha' something here as will make her chirk like a mellet,' he retorted, and held up a large brown paper parcel. 'I ha' been to the Post Office to get it.'

'Ah, gie it me! Aie, my lost pleasurings! Tes none I get, nowadays; gie it me now!' cried the old woman eagerly.

'Nay, Grummer. Ee must wait till pudden time,' and the young man fell on his turkey ravenously.

When everyone had finished, the women cleared away and poured the pudding into a large dusty dish, which they bore to the table and set before Judith.

'Amos? Pudding?' she asked listlessly. 'In a glass or on a plate?'

'On plate, on plate, woman,' he said feverishly, bending forward with a fierce glitter in his eyes. 'Tes easier to see the Year's Luck so.'

A stir of excitement now went through the company, for everybody looked forward to seeing everybody else drawing illluck from the symbols concealed in the pudding. A fierce, attentive silence fell. It was broken by a wail from Reuben –

'The coin – the coin! Wala wa!' and he broke into deep, heavy sobs. He was saving up to buy a tractor, and the coin meant, of course, that he would lose all his money during the year.

'Never mind, Reuben, dear,' whispered Elfine, slipping an arm round his neck. 'You can have the penny father gave me.'

Shrieks from Letty and Prue now announced that they had received the menthol cone and the sticking-plaster, and a low mutter of approval greeted the discovery by Amos of the broken mirror.

Now there was only the coffin-nail, and a ghoulish silence fell on everybody as they dripped pudding from their spoons in a feverish hunt for it; Ezra was running his through a tea-strainer.

But no one seemed to have got it.

'Who has the coffin-nail? Speak, you draf-saks!' at last demanded Mrs Doom.

'Not I.' 'Nay.' 'Niver sight nor snitch of it,' chorussed everybody.

'Adam!' Mrs Doom turned to the old man. 'Did you put the coffin-nail into the pudding?'

'Ay, mistress, that I did – didn't I, Mis' Judith, didn't I, Elfine, my liddle lovesight?'

'He speaks truth for once, mother.'

'Yes, he did, Grandmother. I saw him.'

'*Then where is it?*' Mrs Doom's voice was low and terrible and her gaze moved slowly down the table, first on one side and then on the other, in search of signs of guilt, while everyone cowered over their plates.

Everyone, that is, except Mrs Beetle, who continued to eat a sandwich that she had taken out of a cellophane wrapper, with every appearance of enjoyment.

'Carrie Beetle!' shouted Mrs Doom.

'I'm 'ere,' said Mrs Beetle.

'Did you take the coffin-nail out of the pudding?'

'Yes, I did.' Mrs Beetle leisurely finished the last crumb of sandwich and wiped her mouth with a clean handkerchief. 'And will again, if I'm spared till next year.'

'You ... you ... you ...' choked Mrs Doom, rising in her chair and beating the air with her clenched fists. 'For two hundred years ... Starkadders ... coffin-nails in puddings ... and now ... you ... dare ...'

'Well, I 'ad enough of it las' year,' retorted Mrs Beetle. 'That pore old soul Earnest Dolour got it, as well you may remember—'

'That's right. Cousin Earnest,' nodded Mark Dolour. 'Got a job workin' on the oil-field down Henfield way. Good money, too.'

'Thanks to me, if he 'as,' retorted Mrs Beetle. 'If I 'adn't put it up to you, Mark Dolour, you'd 'ave let 'im die. All of you was 'angin' over the pore old soul waitin' for 'im to 'and in 'is dinner pail, and Micah (wot's old enough to know better, 'eaven only knows) askin' 'im could 'e 'ave 'is wrist-watch if anything was to 'appen to 'im ... it fair got me down. So I says to Mark, why don't yer go down and 'ave a word with Mr Earthdribble the undertaker in Howling and get 'im to tell Earnest it weren't a proper coffin-nail at all, it were a throw-out, so it didn't count. The bother we 'ad! Shall I ever fergit it! Never again, I says to meself. So this year there ain't no coffin-nail. I fished it out o' the pudden meself. Parss the water, please.'

'Where is it?' whispered Mrs Doom, terribly. 'Where is this year's nail, woman?'

'Down the –' Mrs Beetle checked herself, and coughed, 'down the well,' concluded Mrs Beetle firmly.

'Niver fret, Grummer, I'll get it up fer ee! Me and the water voles, we can dive far and deep!' and Urk rushed from the room laughing wildly.

'There ain't no need,' called Mrs Beetle after him. 'But anything to keep you an' yer rubbishy water voles out of mischief!' And Mrs Beetle went into a cackle of laughter, alternately slapping her knee and Caraway's arm, and muttering, 'Oh, cor, wait till I tell Agony! "Dive far and deep." Oh, cor!' After a minute's uneasy silence –

'Grummer.' Seth bent winningly towards the old woman, the large brown paper parcel in his hand. 'Will you see your present now?'

'Aye, boy, aye. Let me see it. You're the only one that has thought of me, the only one.'

Seth was undoing the parcel, and now revealed a large book, handsomely bound in red leather with gilt lettering.

'There, Grummer. 'Tis the year's numbers o' *The Milk Producers' Weekly Bulletin and Cowkeepers' Guide*. I collected un for ee, and had un bound. Art pleased?'

'Ay. 'Tis handsome enough. A graceful thought,' muttered the old lady, turning the pages. Most of them were pretty battered, owing to her habit of rolling up the paper and hitting anyone with it who happened to be within reach. ''Tis better so. 'Tis heavier. Now I can *throw* it.'

The Starkadders so seldom saw a clean and handsome object at the farmhouse (for Seth was only handsome) that they now crept round, fascinated, to examine the book with murmurs of awe. Among them came Adam, but no sooner had he bent over the book than he recoiled from it with a piercing scream.

'Aie! . . . aie! aie!'

'What's the matter, dotard?' screamed Mrs Doom, jabbing at him with the volume. 'Speak, you kaynard!'

'Tes calf! Tes bound in calf! And tes our Pointless's calf, as she had last Lammastide, as was sold at Godmere to Farmer Lust!' cried Adam, falling to the floor. At the same instant, Luke hit Micah in the stomach, Harkaway pushed Ezra into the fire, Mrs Doom flung the bound volume of *The Milk Producers' Weekly Bulletin and Cowkeepers' Guide* at the struggling mass, and the Christmas dinner collapsed into indescribable confusion.

In the midst of the uproar, Elfine, who had climbed on to the table, glanced up at the window as though seeking help, and saw a laughing face looking at her, and a hand in a yellow string glove beckoning with a riding-crop. Swiftly she darted down from the table and across the room, and out through the half-open door, slamming it after her.

Dick Hawk-Monitor, a sturdy boy astride a handsome pony, was out in the yard.

'Hallo!' she gasped. 'Oh, Dick, I am glad to see you!'

'I thought you never would see me – what on earth's the matter in there?' he asked curiously.

'Oh, never mind them, they're always like that. Dick, do tell me, what presents did you have?'

'Oh, a rifle, and a new saddle, and a fiver – lots of things. Look here, Elfine, you mustn't mind, but I brought you –'

He bent over the pony's neck and held out a sandwich box, daintily filled with slices of turkey, a piece of pudding, a tiny mince-pie and a crystallized apricot.

'Thought your dinner mightn't be very –' he ended gruffly.

'Oh, Dick, it's lovely! Darling little . . . what is it?'

'Apricot. Crystallized fruit. Look here, let's go up to the usual place, shall we? – and I'll watch you eat it.'

'But you must have some, too.'

'Man! I'm stoked up to the brim now! But I dare say I could manage a bit more. Here, you catch hold of Rob Roy, and he'll help you up the hill.'

He touched the pony with his heels and it trotted on towards the snow-streaked Downs, Elfine's yellow hair flying out like a shower of primroses under the grey sky of winter.

Evelyn Waugh

Basil Seal Rides Again

TO MRS IAN FLEMING

Dear Ann

In this senile attempt to recapture the manner of my youth I have resurrected characters from earlier stories which, if you ever read them, you will have forgotten.

Basil Seal was the hero of *Black Mischief* (1932) and *Put Out More Flags* (1942). Through my ineptitude the colour of his eyes changed during the intervening decade. At the end of the latter book he considered marriage with the newly widowed, very rich Angela Lyne who had long been his mistress. Ambrose Silk, an aesthete, also appeared in that book. Peter, Lord Pastmaster, first appeared as Peter Beste-Chetwynde in *Decline and Fall* (1928). His mother, later Lady Metroland, appeared there and in *Vile Bodies* (1930). Alaistair Digby-Vane-Trumpington was Lady Metroland's lover in 1928 and Sonia's husband in 1942.

Albright is new: an attempt to extract something from the rum modern world of which you afford me occasional glimpses in your hospitable house.

I should have liked to drop the title in favour of what I have here used as subtitle, but it was suggested that this might smack of sharp practice to readers who saw the story in the *Sunday Telegraph* and *Esquire* and might be led to expect something new.

Ever your affec. coz.

E. W.

Combe Florey
December 1962

I

'Yes.'

'What d'you mean: "Yes"?'

'I didn't hear what you said.'

'I said he made off with all my shirts.'

'It's not that I'm the least deaf. It's simply that I can't concentrate when a lot of fellows are making a row.'

'There's a row now.'

'Some sort of speech.'

'And a lot of fellows saying: "Shush".'

'Exactly. I can't concentrate. What did you say?'

'This fellow made off with all my shirts.'

'Fellow making the speech?'

'No, no. Quite another fellow – called Albright.'

'I don't think so. I heard he was dead.'

'This one isn't. You can't say he stole them exactly. My daughter gave them to him.'

'All?'

'Practically all. I had a few in London and there were a few at the wash. Couldn't believe it when my man told me. Went through all the drawers myself. Nothing there.'

'Bloody thing to happen. *My* daughter wouldn't do a thing like that.'

Protests from neighbouring diners rose in volume.

'They can't want to hear this speech. It's the most awful rot.'

'We seem to be getting unpopular.'

'Don't know who all these fellows are. Never saw anyone before except old Ambrose. Thought I ought to turn out and support him.'

Peter Pastmaster and Basil Seal seldom attended public banquets. They sat at the end of a long table under chandeliers and pier-glasses, looking, for all the traditional brightness of the hotel, too bright and too private for their surroundings. Peter was a year or two the younger but he, like Basil, had scorned to order his life with a view of longevity or spurious youth. They were two stout, rubicund, richly dressed old buffers who might have passed as exact contemporaries.

The frowning faces that were turned towards them were of all ages from those of a moribund Celtic bard to the cross adolescent critic's for whose dinner Mr Bentley, the organizer, was paying. Mr Bentley had, as he expressed it, cast his net wide. There were politicians and publicists there, dons and cultural attachés, Fulbright scholars, representatives of the Pen Club, editors; Mr Bentley, homesick for the *belle époque* of the American slump, when in England the worlds of art and fashion and action harmoniously mingled, had solicited the attendance of a few of the early friends of the guest of honour and Peter and Basil, meeting casually a few weeks before, had decided to go together. They were celebrating the almost coincident events of Ambrose Silk's sixtieth birthday and his investiture with the Order of Merit.

Ambrose, white-haired, pallid, emaciated, sat between Dr Parsnip, Professor of Dramatic Poetry at Minneapolis, and Dr Pimpernell, Professor of Poetic Drama at St Paul. These distinguished expatriates had flown to London for the occasion. It was not the sort of party at which decorations are worn but as Ambrose delicately inclined in deprecation of the honeyed words that dripped around him, no one could doubt his effortless distinction. It was Parsnip who was now on his feet attempting to make himself heard.

'I hear the cry of "silence",' he said with sharp spontaneity. His voice had assumed something of the accent of his place of exile but his diction was orthodox – august even; he had quite discarded the patiently acquired proletarian colloquialisms of thirty years earlier. 'It is apt, for, surely, the object of our homage tonight is epitomized in that golden word. The voice which once clearly spoke the message of what I for one, and many of us here, will always regard as the most glorious decade of English letters, the nineteen-thirties,' (growls of dissent from the youthful critic) 'that voice tardily perhaps, but at long last so illustriously honoured by official recognition, has been silent for a quarter of a century. Silent in Ireland, silent in Tangier, in Tel Aviv and Ischia and Portugal, now silent in his native

London, our guest of honour has stood for us as a stern rebuke, a recall to artistic reticence and integrity. The books roll out from the presses, none by Ambrose Silk. Not for Ambrose Silk the rostrum, the television screen; for him the enigmatic and monumental silence of genius . . .'

'I've got to pee,' said Basil.

'I always want to nowadays.'

'Come on then.'

Slowly and stiffly they left the hotel dining-room.

As they stood side by side in the lavatory Basil said: 'I'm glad Ambrose has got a gong. D'you think the fellow making the speech was pulling his leg?'

'Must have been. Stands to reason.'

'You were going to tell me something about some shirts.'

'I did tell you.'

'What was the name of the chap who got them?'

'Albright.'

'Yes, I remember; a fellow called Clarence Albright. Rather an awful chap. Got himself killed in the war.'

'No one that I knew got killed in the war except Alastair Trumpington.'

'And Cedric Lyne.'

'Yes, there was Cedric.'

'And Freddy Sothill.'

'I never really considered I knew him,' said Basil.

'This Albright married someone – Molly Meadows, perhaps?'

'*I* married Molly Meadows.'

'So you did. I was there. Well, someone like that. One of those girls who were going round at the time – John Flintshire's sister, Sally perhaps. I expect your Albright is her son.'

'He doesn't look like anyone's son.'

'People always are,' said Basil, 'sons or daughters of people.'

This truism had a secondary, antiquated and, to Peter, an obvious meaning, which was significant of the extent by which Basil had changed from *enfant terrible* to 'old Pobble', the name by which he was known to his daughter's friends.

The change had been rapid. In 1939 Basil's mother, his sister, Barbara Sothill, and his mistress, Angela Lyne, had seen the war as the opportunity for his redemption. His embattled country, they supposed, would find honourable use for those deplorable energies which had so often brought him almost into the shadows of prison. At the worst he would fill a soldier's grave; at the best he would emerge as a second Lawrence of Arabia. His fate was otherwise.

Early in his military career, he lamed himself, blowing away the toes of one foot while demonstrating to his commando section a method of his own device for demolishing railway bridges, and was discharged from the army. From this disaster was derived at a later date the sobriquet 'Pobble'. Then, hobbling from his hospital bed to the registry office, he married the widowed Angela Lyne. Hers was one of those few, huge, astutely dispersed fortunes which neither international calamities nor local experiments with socialism could seriously diminish. Basil accepted wealth as he accepted the loss of his toes. He forgot he had ever walked without a stick and a limp, had ever been lean and active, had ever been put to desperate shifts for quite small sums. If he ever recalled that decade of adventure it was as something remote and unrelated to man's estate, like an end-of-term shortness of pocket money at school.

For the rest of the war and for the first drab years of peace he had appeared on the national register as 'farmer'; that is to say, he lived in the country in ease and plenty. Two dead men, Freddy Sothill and Cedric Lyne, had left ample cellars. Basil drained them. He had once expressed the wish to become one of the 'hard-faced men who had done well out of the war'. Basil's face, once very hard, softened and rounded. His scar became almost invisible in rosy suffusion. None of his few clothes, he found, now buttoned comfortably and when, in that time of European scarcity, he and Angela went to New York, where such things could then still be procured by the well-informed, he bought suits and shirts and shoes by the dozen and a whole treasury of watches, tie-pins, cuff-links and chains so that on his return, having scrupulously declared them and paid full duty at the customs – a thing he had never in his life done before – he remarked of his elder brother, who, after a tediously successful diplomatic career spent in gold-lace or starched linen, allowed himself in retirement (and reduced circumstances), some laxity in dress: 'Poor Tony goes about looking like a scarecrow.'

Life in the country palled when food rationing ceased. Angela made over the house they had called 'Cedric's Folly' and its grottoes to her son Nigel on his twenty-first birthday, and took a large, unobtrusive house in Hill Street. She had other places to live, a panelled seventeenth-century apartment in Paris, a villa on Cap Ferrat, a beach and bungalow quite lately acquired in Bermuda, a little palace in Venice which she had once bought for Cedric Lyne but never visited in his lifetime – and among them they moved with their daughter Barbara. Basil settled into the orderly round of the rich. He became a creature of habit and of set opinions. In London, finding Bratt's and Bellamy's disturbingly raffish, he joined that sombre club in Pall Mall that had been the scene of so many painful interviews with his self-appointed guardian, Sir Joseph Mannering, and there often sat in the chair which had belonged prescriptively to Sir Joseph and, as Sir Joseph had done, pronounced his verdict on the day's news to any who would listen.

Basil turned, crossed to the looking-glasses and straightened his tie. He brushed up the copious grey hair. He looked at himself with the blue eyes which had seen so much and now saw only the round, rosy face in which they were set, the fine clothes of English make which had replaced the American improvisations, the starched shirt which he was almost alone in wearing, the black pearl studs, the button-hole.

A week or two ago he had had a disconcerting experience in this very hotel. It was a place he had frequented all his life, particularly in the latter years, and he was on cordial terms with the man who took the men's hats in a den by the Piccadilly entrance. Basil was never given a numbered ticket and assumed he was known by name. Then a day came when he sat longer than usual over luncheon and found the man off duty. Lifting the counter he had penetrated to the rows of pegs and retrieved his bowler and umbrella. In the ribbon of the hat he found a label, put there for identification. It bore the single pencilled word 'Florid'. He had told his daughter, Barbara, who said: 'I wouldn't have you any different. Don't for heaven's sake go taking one of those cures. You'd go mad.'

Basil was not a vain man; neither in rags nor in riches had he cared much about the impression he made. But the epithet recurred to him now as he surveyed himself in the glass.

'Would you say Ambrose was "florid", Peter?'

'Not a word I use.'

'It simply means flowery.'

'Well, I suppose he is.'

'Not fat and red?'

'Not Ambrose.'

'Exactly.'

'I've been called "florid".'

'You're fat and red.'

'So are you.'

'Yes, why not? Almost everyone is.'

'Except Ambrose.'

'Well, he's a pansy. I expect he takes trouble.'

'We don't.'

'Why the hell should we?'

'We don't.'

'Exactly.'

The two old friends had exhausted the subject.

Basil said: 'About those shirts. How did your girl ever meet a fellow like that?'

'At Oxford. She insisted on going up to read History. She picked up some awfully rum friends.'

'I suppose there were girls there in my time. We never met them.'

'Nor in mine.'

'Stands to reason the sort of fellow who takes up with under-graduettes has something wrong with him.'

'Albright certainly has.'

'What does he look like?'

'I've never set an eye. My daughter asked him to King's Thursday when I was abroad. She found he had no shirts and she gave him mine.'

'Was he hard up?'

'So she said.'

'Clarence Albright never had any money. Sally can't have brought him much.'

'There may be no connexion.'

'Must be. Two fellows without money both called Albright. Stands to reason they're the same fellow.'

Peter looked at his watch.

'Half past eleven. I don't feel like going back to hear those speeches. We showed up. Ambrose must have been pleased.'

'He was. But he can't expect us to listen to all that rot.'

'What did he mean about Ambrose's "silence"? Never knew a fellow who talked so much.'

'All a lot of rot. Where to now?'

'Come to think of it, my mother lives upstairs. We might see if she's at home.'

They rose to the floor where Margot Metroland had lived ever since the destruction of Pastmaster House. The door on the corridor was not locked. As they stood in the little vestibule loud, low-bred voices came to them.

'She seems to have a party.'

Peter opened the door of the sitting-room. It was in darkness save for the ghastly light of a television set. Margot crouched over it, her old taut face livid in the reflection.

'Can we come in?'

'Who are you? What d'you want? I can't see you.'

Peter turned on the light at the door.

'Don't do that. Oh, it's you Peter. And Basil.'

'We've been dining downstairs.'

'Well, I'm sorry; I'm busy, as you can see. Turn the light out and come and sit down if you want to, but don't disturb me.'

'We'd better go.'

'Yes. Come and see me when I'm not so busy.'

Outside Peter said: 'She's always looking at that thing nowadays. It's a great pleasure to her.'

'Where to now?'

'I thought of dropping in at Bellamy's.'

'I'll go home. I left Angela on her own. Barbara's at a party of Robin Trumpington's.'

'Well, good night.'

'I say, those places where they starve you – you know what I mean – do they do any good?'

'Molly swears by one.'

'She's not fat and red.'

'No. She goes to those starving places.'

'Well, good night.'

Peter turned east, Basil north, into the mild, misty October night. The streets at this hour were empty. Basil stumped across Piccadilly and up through Mayfair, where Angela's house was almost the sole survivor of the private houses of his youth. How many doors had been closed against him then that were now open to all comers as shops and offices!

The lights were on. He left his hat and coat on a marble table and began the ascent to the drawing-room floor, pausing on the half-landing to recuperate.

'Oh, Pobble, you toeless wonder. You always turn up just when you're wanted.'

Florid he might be, but there were compensations. It was not thus that Basil had often been greeted in limber youth. Two arms embraced his neck and drew him down, an agile figure inclined over the protuberance of his starched shirt, a cheek was pressed to his and teeth tenderly nibbled the lobe of his ear.

'Babs, I thought you were at a party. Why on earth are you dressed like that?'

His daughter wore very tight very short trousers, slippers and a thin jersey. He disengaged himself and slapped her loudly on the behind.

'Sadist. It's that sort of party. It's a "happening".'

'You speak in riddles, child.'

'It's a new sort of party the Americans have invented. Nothing is arranged beforehand. Things just happen. Tonight they cut off a girl's clothes with nail scissors and then painted her green. She had a mask on so I don't know who it was. She might just be someone hired. Then what happened was Robin ran out of drink so we've all gone scouring for it. Mummy's in bed and doesn't know where old Nudge keeps the key and we can't wake him up.'

'You and your mother have been into Nudge's bedroom?'

'Me and Charles. He's the chap I'm scouring with. He's downstairs now trying to pick the lock. I think Nudge must be sedated, he just rolled over snoring when we shook him.'

At the foot of the staircase a door led to the servants' quarters. It opened and someone very strange appeared with an armful of bottles. Basil saw below him a slender youth, perhaps a man of twenty-one, who had a mop of dishevelled black hair and a meagre black fringe of beard and whiskers; formidable, contemptuous blue eyes above grey pouches; a proud, rather childish mouth. He wore a pleated white silk shirt, open at the neck, flannel trousers, a green cummerbund and sandals. The appearance, though grotesque, was not specifically plebeian and when he spoke his tone was pure and true without a taint of accent.

'The lock was easy,' he said, 'but I can't find anything except wine. Where d'you keep the whisky?'

'Heavens, I don't know,' said Barbara.

'Good evening,' said Basil.

'Oh, good evening. Where do you keep the whisky?'

'Is it a fancy dress party?' Basil asked.

'Not particularly,' said the young man.

'What have you got there?'

'Champagne of some kind. I didn't notice the label.'

'He's got the Cliquot rosé,' said Basil.

'How clever of him,' said Barbara.

'It will probably do,' said the young man. 'Though most people prefer whisky.'

Basil attempted to speak but found no words.

Barbara quoted:

' "His Aunt Jobiska made him drink

Lavender water tinged with pink,

For the world in general knows

There's nothing so good for a Pobble's toes." Come along, Charles, I think we've got all we're going to get here. I sense a grudging hospitality.'

She skipped downstairs, waved from the hall and was out of the front door, while Basil still stood dumbfounded.

At length, even more laboriously than he was wont, he continued upward. Angela was in bed reading.

'You're home early.'

'Peter was there. No one else I knew except old Ambrose. Some booby made a speech. So I came away.'

'Very wise.'

Basil stood before Angela's long looking-glass. He could see her behind him. She put on her spectacles and picked up her book.

'Angela, I don't drink much nowadays, do I?'

'Not as much as you used.'

'Or eat?'

'More.'

'But you'd say I led a temperate life?'

'Yes, on the whole.'

'It's just age,' said Basil. 'And dammit, I'm not sixty yet.'

'What's worrying you, darling?'

'It's when I meet young men. A choking feeling – as if I was going to have an apoplectic seizure. I once saw a fellow in a seizure, must have been about the age I am now – the Lieutenant-Colonel of the Bombardiers. It was a most unpleasant spectacle. I've been feeling lately something like that might strike me any day. I believe I ought to take a cure.'

'I'll come too.'

'Will you really, Angela? You are a saint.'

'Might as well be there as anywhere. They're supposed to be good for insomnia too. The servants would like a holiday. They've been wearing awfully overworked expressions lately.'

'No sense taking Babs. We could send her to Malfrey.'

'Yes.'

'Angela, I saw the most awful looking fellow tonight with a sort of beard – here, in the house, a friend of Babs. She called him "Charles".'

'Yes, he's someone new.'

'What's his name?'

'I did hear. It sounded like a pack of fox hounds I once went out with. I know – Albrighton.'

'Albright,' cried Basil, the invisible noose tightening. 'Albright, by God.'

Angela looked at him with real concern. 'You know,' she said, 'you really do look rather rum. I think we'd better go to one of those starving places at once.'

And then what had seemed a death-rattle turned into a laugh. 'It was one of Peter's shirts,' he said, unintelligibly to Angela.

2

It may one day occur to a pioneer of therapeutics that most of those who are willing to pay fifty pounds a week to be deprived of food and wine, seek only suffering and that they could be cheaply accommodated in rat-ridden dungeons. At present the profits of the many thriving institutions which cater for the ascetic are depleted by the maintenance of neat lawns and shrubberies and, inside, of the furniture of a private house and apparatus resembling that of a hospital.

Basil and Angela could not immediately secure rooms at the sanatorium recommended by Molly Pastmaster. There was a waiting list of people suffering from every variety of infirmity. Finally they frankly outbid rival sufferers. A man whose obesity threatened the collapse of his ankles, and a woman raging with hallucinations were informed that their bookings were defective, and on a warm afternoon Basil and Angela drove down to take possession of their rooms.

There was a resident physician at this most accommodating house. He interviewed each patient on arrival and ostensibly considered individual needs.

He saw Angela first. Basil sat stolidly in an outer room, his hands on the head of his cane, gazing blankly before him. When at length he was admitted, he stated his needs. The doctor did not attempt any physical investigation. It was a plain case.

'To refrain from technical language you complain of speechlessness, a sense of heat and strangulation, dizziness and sub-sequent trembling?' said this man of science.

'I feel I'm going to burst,' said Basil.

'Exactly. And these symptoms only occur when you meet young men?'

'Hairy young men especially.'

'Ah.'

'*Young puppies.*'

'And with puppies too? That is very significant. How do you react to kittens?'

'I mean the young men are puppies.'

'Ah. And are you fond of puppies, Mr Seal?'

'Reasonably.'

'Ah.' The man of science studied the paper on his desk. 'Have you always been conscious of this preference for your own sex?'

'I'm not conscious of it now.'

'You are fifty-eight years and ten months. That is often a crucial age, one of change, when repressed and unsuspected inclinations emerge and take control. I should strongly recommend your putting yourself under a psychoanalyst. We do not give treatment of that kind here.'

'I just want to be cured of feeling I'm going to burst.'

'I've no doubt our régime will relieve the symptoms. You will not find many young men here to disturb you. Our patients are mostly mature women. There is a markedly virile young physical training instructor. His hair is quite short but you had better keep away from the gym. Ah, I see from your paper that you are handicapped by war-wounds. I will take out all physical exercise from your timetable and substitute extra periods of manipulation by one of the female staff. Here is your diet sheet. You will notice that for the first forty-eight hours you are restricted to turnip juice. At the end of that period you embark on the carrots. At the end of the fortnight, if all goes well, we will have you on raw eggs and barley. Don't hesitate to come and see me again if you have any problem to discuss.'

The sleeping quarters of male and female inmates were sep-arated by the length of the house. Basil found Angela in the drawing-room. They compared their diet sheets.

'Rum that it should be exactly the same treatment for insomnia and apoplexy.'

'That booby thought I was a pansy.'

'It takes a medical man to find out a thing like that. All these years and I never knew. They're always right, you know. So that's why you're always going to that odd club.'

'This is no time for humour. This is going to be a very grim fortnight.'

'Not for me,' said Angela. 'I came well provisioned. I'm only here to keep you company. And there's a Mrs Somebody next door to me who I used to know. She's got a private cache of all the sleeping-pills in the world. I've made great friends with her already. *I* shall be all right.'

On the third day of his ordeal, the worst according to *habitués* of the establishment, there came a telephone call from Barbara.

'Pobble, I want to go back to London. I'm bored.'

'Bored with Aunt Barbara?'

'Not with *her*, with *here*.'

'You stay where you're put, chattel.'

'No. *Please*, I want to go home.'

'Your home is where I am. You can't come here.'

'No. I want to go to London.'

'You can't. I sent the servants away for a fortnight.'

'Most of my friends live without servants.'

'You've sunk into a very low world, Babs.'

'Don't be such an ass. Sonia Trumpington hasn't any servants.'

'Well, she won't want you.'

'Pobble, you sound awfully feeble.'

'Who wouldn't who's only had one carrot in the last three days.'

'Oh, you are brave.'

'Yes.'

'How's mummy?'

'Your mother is not keeping the régime as strictly as I am.'

'I bet she isn't. Anyway, please, can I go back to London?'

'No.'
'You mean "No"?'
'Yes.'
'Fiend.'

Basil had gone hungry before. From time to time in his varied youth, in desert, tundra, glacier and jungle, in garrets and cellars, he had briefly endured extremities of privation. Now in the periods of repose and solitude, after the steam bath and the smarting deluge of the showers, after the long thumping and twisting by the huge masseuse, when the chintz curtains were drawn in his bedroom and he lay towel-wrapped and supine gazing at the pattern of the ceiling paper, familiar, forgotten pangs spoke to him of his past achievements.

He defined his condition to Angela after the first week of the régime. 'I'm not rejuvenated or invigorated. I'm etherealized.'
'You look like a ghost.'
'Exactly. I've lost sixteen pounds three ounces.'
'You're overdoing it. No one else keeps these absurd rules. We aren't expected to. It's like the *rien ne va plus* at roulette. Mrs What's-her-name has found a black market in the gym kept by the sergeant-instructor. We ate a grouse pie this morning.'

They were in the well-kept grounds. A chime of bells announced that the brief recreation was over. Basil tottered back to his masseuse.

Later, light-headed and limp, he lay down and stared once more at the ceiling paper.

As a convicted felon might in long vigils search his history for the first trespass that had brought him to his present state, Basil examined his conscience. Fasting, he knew, was in all religious systems the introduction to self-knowledge. Where had he first played false to his destiny? After the conception of Barbara; after her birth. She, in some way, was at the root of it. Though he had not begun to dote on her until she was eight years old, he had from the first been aware of his own paternity. In 1947, when she was a year old, he and Angela had gone to New York and California. That enterprise, in those days, was nefarious. Elaborate laws restricted the use of foreign currencies and these they had defied, drawing freely on undisclosed assets. But on his return he had made a full declaration to the customs. It was no immediate business of theirs to inquire into the sources of his laden trunks. In a mood of arrogance he had displayed everything and paid without demur. There lay the fount and origin of the deviation into rectitude that had disfigured him in recent years. As though waking after a night's drunkenness – an experience common enough in his youth – and confusedly articulating the disjointed memories of outrage and absurdity, he ruefully contemplated the change he had wrought in himself. His voice was not the same instrument as of old. He had first assumed it as a conscious imposture; it had become habitual to him; the antiquated, worldly-wise moralities which, using that voice, he had found himself obliged to utter, had become his settled opinions. It had begun as nursery clowning for the diversion of Barbara; a parody of Sir Joseph Mannering; darling, crusty old Pobble performing the part expected of him; and now the parody had become the *persona*.

His meditation was interrupted by the telephone. 'Will you take a call from Mrs Sothill?'

'Babs.'

'Basil. I just wondered how you were getting on.'

'They're very pleased with me.'

'Thin?'

'Skinny. And concerned with my soul.'

'Chump. Listen. I'm concerned with Barbara's soul.'

'What's she been up to?'

'I think she's in love.'

'Rot.'

'Well, she's moping.'

'I expect she misses me.'

'When she isn't moping she's telephoning or writing letters.'

'Not to me.'

'Exactly. There's someone in London.'

'Robin Trumpington?'

'She doesn't confide.'

'Can't you listen in on the telephone?'

'I've tried that, of course. It's certainly a man she's talking to. I can't really understand their language but it sounds very affectionate. You won't like it awfully if she runs off, will you?'

'She'd never think of such a thing. Don't put ideas into the child's head, for God's sake. Give her a dose of castor oil.'

'*I* don't mind, if *you* don't. I just thought I should warn.'

'Tell her I'll soon be back.'

'She knows that.'

'Well, keep her under lock and key until I get out.'

Basil reported the conversation to Angela. 'Barbara says Barbara's in love.'

'Which Barbara?'

'Mine. Ours.'

'Well, it's quite normal at her age. Who with?'

'Robin Trumpington, I suppose.'

'He'd be quite suitable.'

'For heaven's sake, Angie, she's only a child.'

'I fell in love at her age.'

'And a nice mess that turned out. It's someone after my money.'

'*My* money.'

'I've always regarded it as mine. I shan't let her have a penny. Not till I'm dead anyway.'

'You look half dead now.'

'I've never felt better. You simply haven't got used to my new appearance.'

'You're very shaky.'

'"Disembodied" is the word. Perhaps I need a drink. In fact I know I do. This whole business of Babs has come as a shock – at a most unsuitable time. I might go and see the booby doctor.'

And, later, he set off along the corridor which led to the administrative office. He set off but had hardly hobbled six short paces when his newly sharpened conscience stabbed him. Was this the etherealized, the reborn, Basil slinking off like a schoolboy to seek the permission of a booby doctor for a simple adult indulgence? He turned aside and made for the gym.

There he found two large ladies in bathing-dresses sitting astride a low horse. They swallowed hastily and brushed crumbs from their lips. A rubbery young man in vest and shorts addressed him sternly: 'One moment, sir. You can't come in here without an appointment.'

'My visit is unprofessional,' said Basil. 'I want a word with you.'

The young man looked doubtful. Basil drew his note case from his pocket and tapped it on the knob of his cane.

'Well, ladies, I think that finishes the work-out for this morning. We're getting along very nicely. We mustn't expect immediate results you know. Same routine tomorrow.' He replaced the lid on a small enamelled bin. The ladies looked hungrily at it but went in peace.

'Whisky,' said Basil.

'Whisky? Why, I couldn't give you such a thing even if I had it. It would be as much as my job's worth.'

'I should think it is precisely what your job *is* worth.'

'I don't quite follow, sir.'

'My wife had grouse pie this morning.'

He was a cheeky young man much admired in his own milieu for his bounce. He was not abashed. A horrible smirk of complicity passed over his face. 'It wasn't really grouse,' he said. 'Just a stale liver pâté the grocer had. They get so famished here they don't care what they're eating, the poor creatures.'

'Don't talk about my wife in those terms,' said Basil, adding: 'I shall know what I'm drinking, at a pound a snort.'

'I haven't any whisky, honest. There may be a drop of brandy in the first-aid cupboard.'

'Let's look at it.'

It was of a reputable brand. Basil took two snorts. He gasped. Tears came to his eyes. He felt for support on the wall-bars beside him. For a moment he feared nausea. Then a great warmth and elation were kindled inside him. This was youth indeed; childhood no less. Thus he had been exalted in his first furtive swigging in his father's pantry. He had drunk as much brandy as this twice a day, most days of his adult life, after a variety of preliminary potations and had felt merely a slight heaviness. Now in his etheralized condition he was, as it were, raised from the earth, held aloft and then lightly deposited; a mystical experience as though on Ganges bank or a spur of the Himalayas.

There was a mat near his feet, thick, padded, bed-like. Here he subsided and lay in ecstasy; quite outside his body, high and happy, his spirit soared; he shut his eyes.

'You can't stay here, sir. I've got to lock up.'

'Don't worry,' said Basil. 'I'm not here.'

The gymnast was very strong; it was a light task to hoist Basil on one of the trollies which in various sizes were part of the equipment of the sanatorium, and thus recumbent, dazed but not totally insensible, smoothly propelled up the main corridor, he was met by the presiding doctor.

'What have you there, sergeant?'

'Couldn't say at all. Never saw the gentleman before.'

'It looks like Mr Seal. Where did you find him?'

'He just walked into the gym, sir, looking rather queer and suddenly he passed out.'

'Gave you a queer look? Yes.'

'He rolls through the air with the greatest of ease, that daring young man on the flying trapeze,' Basil chanted with some faint semblance of tune in his voice.

'Been overdoing it a bit, sir, I wouldn't wonder.'

'You might be right, sergeant. You had better leave him now. The female staff can take over. Ah. Sister Gamage, Mr Seal needs help in getting to his room. I think the régime has proved too strenuous for him. You may administer an ounce of brandy. I will come and examine him later.'

But when he repaired to Basil's room he found his patient deeply sleeping.

He stood by the bed, gazing at his patient. There was an expression of peculiar innocence on the shrunken face. But the physician knew better.

'I will see him in the morning,' he said and then went to instruct his secretary to inform the previous applicants that two vacancies had unexpectedly occurred.

3

'The sack, the push, the boot. I've got to be out of the place in an hour.'

'Oh Basil, that *is* like old times, isn't it?'

'Only deep psychoanalysis can help me, he says, and in my present condition I am a danger to his institution.'

'Where shall we go? Hill Street's locked up. There won't be anyone there until Monday.'

'The odd thing is I have no hangover.'

'Still ethereal?'

'Precisely. I suppose it means an hotel.'

'You might telephone to Barbara and tell her to join us. She said she was keen to leave.'

But when Angela telephoned to her sister-in-law, she heard: 'But isn't Barbara with you in London? She told me yesterday you'd sent for her. She went up by the afternoon train.'

'D'you think she can have gone to that young man?'

'I bet she has.'

'Ought I to tell Basil?'

'Keep it quiet.'

'I consider it very selfish of her. Basil isn't at all in good shape. He'll have a fit if he finds out. He had a sort of fit yesterday.'

'Poor Basil. He may never know.'

Basil and Angela settled their enormous bill. Their car was brought round to the front. The chauffeur drove, Angela sat beside Basil who huddled beside her occasionally crooning ill-remembered snatches of 'the daring young man on the flying trapeze'. As they approached London they met all the outgoing Friday traffic. Their own way was clear. At the hotel Basil went straight to bed – 'I don't feel I shall ever want another bath as long as I live,' he said – and Angela ordered a light meal for him of oysters and stout. By dusk he had rallied enough to smoke a cigar.

Next morning he was up early and spoke of going to his club.

'That dingy one?'

'Heavens no, Bellamy's. But I don't suppose there'll be many chaps there on a Saturday morning.'

There was no one. The barman shook him up an egg with port and brandy. Then, with the intention of collecting some books, he took a taxi to Hill Street. It was not yet eleven o'clock. He let himself into what should have been the empty and silent house. Music came from the room on the ground floor where small parties congregated before luncheon and dinner. It was a dark room, hung with tapestry and furnished with Bühl. There he found his daughter, dressed in pyjamas and one of her mother's fur coats, seated on the floor with her face caressing a transistor radio. Behind her in the fire-place large lumps of coal lay on the ashes of the sticks and paper which had failed to kindle them.

'Darling Pobble, never more welcome. I didn't expect you till Monday and I should have been dead by then. I can't make out how the central heating works. I thought the whole point of it was it just turned on and didn't need a man. Can't get the fire to burn. And don't start: "Babs, what are you doing here?" I'm freezing, that's what.'

'Turn that damn thing off.'

In the silence Barbara regarded her father more intently. 'Darling, what have they been doing to you? You aren't yourself at all. You're tottering. Not my fine stout Pobble at all. Sit down at once. Poor Pobble, all shrunk like a mummy. Beasts!'

Basil sat and Barbara wriggled round until her chin rested on his knees. 'Famine baby,' she said. Star-sapphire eyes in the child-like face under black touselled hair gazed deep into star-sapphire eyes sunk in empty pouches. 'Belsen atrocity,' she added fondly. 'Wraith. Skeleton-man. Dear dug-up corpse.'

'Enough of this flattery. Explain yourself.'

'I told you I was bored. You know what Malfrey's like as well as I do. Oh the hell of the National Trust. It's not so bad in the summer with the charabancs. Now it's only French art experts – half a dozen a week, and all the rooms still full of oilcloth promenades and rope barriers and Aunt Barbara in the flat over the stables and those ridiculous Sothills in the bachelors' wing and the height of excitement a pheasant shoot with lunch in the hut and then nothing to eat except pheasant and . . . Well, I registered a formal complaint, didn't I?, but you were too busy starving to pay any attention, and if your only, adored daughter's happiness doesn't count for more than senile vanity . . .' she paused, exhausted.

'There's more to it than that.'

'There is *something* else.'

'What?'

'Now, Pobble, you have to take this calmly. For your own good, not for mine. I'm used to violence, God knows. If you had been poor the police would have been after you for the way you've knocked me about all these years. I can take it; but you, Pobble, you are at an age when it might be dangerous. So keep quite calm and I'll tell you. I'm engaged to be married.'

It was not a shock; it was not a surprise. It was what Basil had expected. 'Rot,' he said.

'I happen to be in love. You must know what that means. You must have been in love once – with mummy or someone.'

'Rot. And dammit, Babs, don't blub. If you think you're old enough to be in love, you're old enough not to blub.'

'That's a silly thing to say. It's being in love makes me blub. You don't realize. Apart from being perfect and frightfully funny he's an artistic genius and everyone's after him and I'm jolly lucky to have got him and you'll love him too once you know him if only you won't be stuck-up and we got engaged on the telephone so I came up and he was out for all I know someone else *has* got him and I almost died of cold and now you come in looking more like a vampire than a papa and start saying "rot".'

She pressed her face on his thigh and wept.

After a time Basil said: 'What makes you think Robin paints?'

'Robin? Robin Trumpington? You don't imagine I'm engaged to *Robin*, do you? He's got a girl of his own he's mad about. You don't know much about what goes on, do you, Pobble? If it's only Robin you object to, everything's all right.'

'Well, who the hell do you think you are engaged to?'

'Charles, of course.'

'Charles à Court. Never heard of him.'

'Don't pretend to be deaf. You know perfectly well who I mean. You met him here the other evening only I don't think you really took him in.'

'*Albright*,' said Basil. It was evidence of the beneficial effect of the sanatorium that he did not turn purple in the face, did not gobble. He merely asked quietly: 'Have you been to bed with this man?'

'Not to *bed*.'

'Have you slept with him?'

'Oh, no *sleep*.'

'You know what I mean. Have you had sexual intercourse with him?'

'Well, perhaps; not in bed; on the floor and wide awake; you *might* call it intercourse, I suppose.'

'Come clean, Babs. Are you a virgin?'

'It's not a thing any girl likes having said about her, but I think I am.'

'*Think?*'

'Well, I suppose so. Yes, really. But we can soon change all that. Charles is set on marriage, bless him. He says it's easier to get married to girls if they're virgins. I can't think why. I don't mean a big wedding. Charles is very unsocial and he's an orphan, no father, no mother, and his relations don't like him, so we'll just be married quietly in a day or two and then I thought if you and mummy don't want it we might go to the house in Bermuda. We shan't be any trouble to you at all, really. If you want to go to Bermuda, we'll settle for Venice, but Charles says that's a bit square and getting cold in November, so Bermuda will really be better.'

'Has it occurred to either of you that you need my permission to marry?'

'Now don't get legal, Pobble. You know I love you far too much ever to do anything you wouldn't like.'

'You'd better get dressed and go round to your mother at Claridges.'

'Can't get dressed. No hot water.'

'Have a bath there. I had better see this young man.'

'He's coming here at twelve.'

'I'll wait for him.'

'You'll freeze.'

'Get up and get out.'

There followed one of those scuffles that persisted between father and daughter even in her eighteenth year which ended in her propulsion, yelping.

Basil sat and waited. The bell could not be heard in the ante-room. He sat in the window and watched the doorstep, saw a taxi draw up and Barbara enter it still in pyjamas and fur coat carrying a small case. Later he saw his enemy strolling confidently from Berkeley Square. Basil opened the door.

'You did not expect to see me?'

'No, but I'm very glad to. We've a lot to discuss.'

They went together to the ante-room. The young man was less bizarre in costume than on their previous meeting but his hair was as copious and his beard proclaimed his chosen, deleterious status. They surveyed one another in silence. Then Basil said: 'Lord Pastmaster's shirts are too big for you.'

It was a weak opening.

'It's not a thing I should have brought up if you hadn't,' said Albright, 'but *all* your clothes look too big for *you*.'

Basil covered his defeat by lighting a cigar.

'Barbara tells me you've been to that sanatorium in Kent,' continued the young man easily; 'there's a new place, you know, much better, in Sussex.'

Basil was conscious of quickening recognition. Some faint, odious inkling of kinship; had he not once, in years far gone by, known someone who had spoken in this way to his elders? He drew deeply on his cigar and studied Albright. The eyes, the whole face seemed remotely familiar; the reflection of a reflection seen long ago in shaving-mirrors.

'Barbara tells me you have proposed marriage to her.'

'Well, *she* actually popped the question. I was glad to accept.'

'You are Clarence Albright's son?'

'Yes, did you know him? I barely did. I hear he was rather awful. If you want to be genealogical, I have an uncle who is a duke. But I barely know him either.'

'And you are a painter?'

'Did Barbara tell you that?'

'She said you were an artistic genius.'

'She's a loyal little thing. She must mean my music.'

'You compose?'

'I improvise sometimes. I play the guitar.'

'Professionally?'

'Sometimes – in coffee bars, you know.'

'I do not know, I'm afraid. And you make a living by it?'

'Not what *you* would call a living.'

'May I ask, then, how you propose to support my daughter?'

'Oh, that doesn't come into it. It's the other way round. I'm doing what you did, marrying money. Now I know what's in your mind. "Buy him off," you think. I assure you that won't work. Barbara is infatuated with me and, if it's not egotistical to mention it, I am with her. I'm sure you won't want one of those "Gretna Green Romances" and press photographers following you about. Besides, Barbara doesn't want to be a nuisance to you. She's a loyal girl, as we've already remarked. The whole thing can be settled calmly. Think of the taxes your wife will save by a good solid marriage settlement. It will make no appreciable difference to your own allowance.'

And still Basil sat steady, unmoved by any tremor of that volcanic senility which a fortnight ago would have exploded in scalding, blinding showers. He was doing badly in this first encounter, which he had too lightly provoked. He must take thought and plan. He was not at the height of his powers. He had been prostrate yesterday. Today he was finding his strength. Tomorrow experience would conquer. This was a worthy antagonist and he felt something of the exultation which a brave of the sixteenth century might have felt when in a brawl he suddenly recognized in the clash of blades a worthy swordsman.

'Barbara's mother has the best financial advice,' he said.

'By the way, where is Barbara? She arranged to meet me here.'

'She's having a bath in Claridges.'

'I ought to go over and see her. I'm taking her out to lunch. You couldn't lend me a fiver, could you?'

'Yes,' said Basil. 'Certainly.'

If Albright had known him better he would have taken alarm at this urbanity. All he thought was: 'Old crusty's a much softer job than anyone told me.' And Basil thought: 'I hope he spends it all on luncheon. That bank-note is all he will ever get. He deserved better.'

4

Sonia Trumpington had never remarried. She shared a flat with her son Robin but saw little of him. Mostly she spent her day alone with her needlework and in correspondence connected with one or two charitable organizations with which, in age, she had become involved. She was sewing when Basil sought her out after luncheon (oysters again, two dozen this time with a pint of champagne – his strength waxed hourly) and she continued to stitch at the framed grospoint while he confided his problem to her.

'Yes. I've met Charles Albright. He's rather a friend of Robin's.'

'Then perhaps you can tell me what Barbara sees in him.'

'Why, *you*, of course,' said Sonia. 'Haven't you noticed? He's the dead spit – looks, character, manner, everything.'

'Looks? Character? Manner? Sonia, you're raving.'

'Oh, not as you are now, not even after your cure. Don't you remember at all what you were like at his age?'

'But he's a monster.'

'So were you, darling. Have you quite forgotten? It's all as clear as clear to me. You Seals are so incestuous. Why do you suppose you got keen on Barbara? Because she's just like Barbara Sothill. Why is Barbara keen on Charles? Because he's *you*.'

Basil considered this proposition with his newly re-sharpened wits.

'That beard.'

'I've seen you with a beard.'

'That was after I came back from the Arctic and I never played the guitar in my life,' he said.

'Does Charles play the guitar? First I've heard of it. He does all sorts of things – just as you did.'

'I wish you wouldn't keep bringing me into it.'

'Have you quite forgotten what you were like? Have a look at some of my old albums.'

Like most of her generation Sonia had in youth filled large volumes with press-cuttings and photographs of herself and her friends. They lay now in a shabby heap in a corner of the room.

'That's Peter's twenty-firster at King's Thursday. First time I met you, I think. Certainly the first time I met Alastair. He was Margot's boy-friend then, remember? She was jolly glad to be rid of him ... That's my marriage. I bet you were there.' She turned the pages from the posed groups of bride, bridegroom and bridesmaids to the snapshots taken at the gates of St Margaret's. 'Yes, here you are.'

'No beard. Perfectly properly dressed.'

'Yes, there are more incriminating ones later. Look at that ... and that.'

They opened successive volumes. Basil appeared often.

'I don't think any of them very good likenesses,' said Basil stiffly. 'I'd just come back from the Spanish front there – of course I look a bit untidy.'

'It's not clothes we're talking about. Look at your expression.'

'Light in my eyes,' said Basil.

'1937. That's another party at King's Thursday.'

'What a ghastly thing facetious photographs are. What on earth am I doing with that girl?'

'Throwing her in the lake. I remember the incident now. I took the photograph.'

'Who?'

'I've no idea. Perhaps it says on the back. Just "Basil and Betty". She must have been much younger than us, not our kind at all. I've got an idea she was the daughter of some duke or other. The Stayles – that's who she was.'

Basil studied the picture and shuddered. 'What can have induced me to behave like that?'

'Youthful high spirits.'

'I was thirty-four, God help me. She's very plain.'

'I'll tell you who she is – was. Charles Albright's mother. That's an odd coincidence if you like. Let's look her up and make sure.'

She found a *Peerage* and read: 'Here we are. Fifth daughter of the late duke. Elizabeth Ermyntrude Alexandra, for whom H.R.H. The Duke of Connaught stood sponsor. Born 1920. Married 1940 Clarence Albright, killed in action 1943. Leaving issue. Died 1956. I remember hearing about it – cancer, very young. That's Charles, that issue.'

Basil gazed long at the photograph. The girl was plump and, it seemed, wriggling; annoyed rather than amused by the horseplay. 'How one forgets. I suppose she was quite a friend of mine once.'

'No, no. She was just someone Margot produced for Peter.'

Basil's imagination, once so fertile of mischief, lately so dormant, began now, in his hour of need, to quicken and stir.

'That photograph has given me an idea.'

'Basil, you've got that old villainous look. What are you up to?'

'Just an idea.'

'You're not going to throw Barbara into the Serpentine.'

'Something not unlike it,' he said.

'Let us go and sit by the Serpentine,' said Basil to his daughter that afternoon.

'Won't it be rather cold?'

'It will be quiet. Wrap up well. I have to talk to you seriously.'

'Good temper?'

'Never better.'

'Why not talk here?'

'Your mother may come in. What I have to say doesn't concern her.'

'It's about me and Charles, I bet.'

'Certainly.'

'Not a scolding?'

'Far from it. Warm fatherly sympathy.'

'It's worth being frozen for that.'

They did not speak in the car. Basil sent it away, saying they would find their own way back. At that chilly teatime, with the leaves dry and falling, there was no difficulty in finding an empty seat. The light was soft; it was one of the days when London seems like Dublin.

'Charles said he'd talked to you. He wasn't sure you loved him.'

'I love him.'

'Oh, *Pobble*.'

'He did not play the guitar but I recognized his genius.'

'Oh, Pobble, what are you up to?'

'Just what Sonia asked.' Basil leaned his chin on the knob of his cane. 'You know, Babs, that all I want is your happiness.'

'This doesn't sound at all like you. You've got some sly scheme.'

'Far from it. You must never tell him or your mother what I am about to say. Charles's parents are dead so they are not affected. I knew his mother very well; perhaps he doesn't know how well. People often wondered why she married Albright. It was a blitz marriage, you know, while he was on leave and there were air raids every night. It was when I was first out of hospital, before I married your mother.'

'Darling Pobble, it's very cold here and I don't quite see what all this past history has to do with me and Charles.'

'It began,' said Basil inexorably, 'when – what was her name? – Betty was younger than you are now. I threw her into the lake at King's Thursday.'

'What began?'

'Betty's passion for me. Funny what excites a young girl – with you a guitar, with Betty a ducking.'

'Well, I think that's rather romantic. It sort of brings you and Charles closer.'

'Very close indeed. It was more than romantic. She was too young at the beginning – just a girlish crush. I thought she would get over it. Then, when I was wounded, she took to visiting me every day in hospital and the first day I came out – you won't be able to understand the sort of exhilaration a man feels at a time like that, or the appeal lameness has for some women, or the sense of general irresponsibility we all had during the blitz – I'm not trying to excuse myself. I was not the first man. She had grown up since the splash in the lake. It only lasted a week. Strictly perhaps I should have married her, but I was less strict in those days. I married your mother instead. You can't complain about that. If I hadn't, you wouldn't exist. Betty had to look elsewhere and fortunately that ass Albright turned up in the nick. Yes, Charles is your brother, so how could I help loving him?'

Soundlessly Barbara rose from the seat and sped through the twilight, stumbled on her stiletto heels across the sand of the Row, disappeared behind the statuary through Edinburgh Gate. Basil at his own pace followed. He stopped a taxi, kept it waiting at the curb while he searched Bellamy's vainly for a friendly face, drank another eggnog at the bar, went on towards Claridges.

'What on earth's happened to Barbara?' Angela asked. 'She came in with a face of tragedy, didn't speak and now she's locked herself in your bedroom.'

'I think she's had a row with that fellow she was keen on. What was his name? Albright. A good thing really, a likeable fellow but not at all suitable. I daresay Babs needs a change of scene. Angie, if it suits you, I think we might all three of us go to Bermuda tomorrow.'

'Can we get tickets?'

'I have them already. I stopped at the travel office on my way from Sonia's. I don't imagine Babs will want much dinner tonight. She's best left alone at the moment. I feel I could manage a square meal. We might have it downstairs.'

Frank O'Connor

The Drunkard

It was a terrible blow to Father when Mr Dooley on the terrace died. Mr Dooley was a commercial traveller with two sons in the Dominicans and a car of his own, so socially he was miles ahead of us, but he had no false pride. Mr Dooley was an intellectual, and, like all intellectuals, the thing he loved best was conversation, and in his own limited way Father was a well-read man and could appreciate an intelligent talker. Mr Dooley was remarkably intelligent. Between business acquaintances and clerical contacts, there was very little he didn't know about what went on in town, and evening after evening he crossed the road to our gate to explain to Father the news behind the news. He had a low, palavering voice and a knowing smile, and Father would listen in astonishment, giving him a conversational lead now and again, and then stump triumphantly in to Mother with his face aglow and ask: 'Do you know what Mr Dooley is after telling me?' Ever since, when somebody has given me some bit of information off the record I have found myself on the point of asking: 'Was it Mr Dooley told you that?'

Till I actually saw him laid out in his brown shroud with the rosary beads entwined between his waxy fingers I did not take the report of his death seriously. Even then I felt there must be a catch and that some summer evening Mr Dooley must reappear at our gate to give us the low-down on the next world. But Father was very upset, partly because Mr Dooley was about one age with himself, a thing that always gives a distinctly personal turn to another man's demise; partly because now he would have no one to tell him what dirty work was behind the latest scene at the Corporation. You could count on your fingers the number of men in Blarney Lane who read the papers as Mr

Dooley did, and none of these would have overlooked the fact that Father was only a labouring man. Even Sullivan, the carpenter, a mere nobody, thought he was a cut above Father. It was certainly a solemn event.

'Half past two to the Curragh,' Father said meditatively, putting down the paper.

'But you're not thinking of going to the funeral?' Mother asked in alarm.

''Twould be expected,' Father said, scenting opposition. 'I wouldn't give it to say to them.'

'I think,' said Mother with suppressed emotion, 'it will be as much as anyone will expect if you go to the chapel with him.'

('Going to the chapel,' of course, was one thing, because the body was removed after work, but going to a funeral meant the loss of a half-day's pay.)

'The people hardly know us,' she added.

'God between us and all harm,' Father replied with dignity, 'we'd be glad if it was our own turn.'

To give Father his due, he was always ready to lose a half day for the sake of an old neighbour. It wasn't so much that he liked funerals as that he was a conscientious man who did as he would be done by; and nothing could have consoled him so much for the prospect of his own death as the assurance of a worthy funeral. And, to give Mother her due, it wasn't the half-day's pay she begrudged, badly as we could afford it.

Drink, you see, was Father's great weakness. He could keep steady for months, even for years, at a stretch, and while he did he was as good as gold. He was first up in the morning and brought the mother a cup of tea in bed, stayed at home in the evenings and read the paper; saved money and bought himself a new blue serge suit and bowler hat. He laughed at the folly of men who, week in week out, left their hard-earned money with the publicans; and sometimes, to pass an idle hour, he took pencil and paper and calculated precisely how much he saved each week through being a teetotaller. Being a natural optimist he sometimes continued this calculation through the whole span of his prospective existence and the total was breathtaking. He would die worth hundreds.

If I had only known it, this was a bad sign; a sign he was becoming stuffed up with spiritual pride and imagining himself better than his neighbours. Sooner or later, the spiritual pride grew till it called for some form of celebration. Then he took a drink – not whisky, of course; nothing like that – just a glass of some harmless drink like lager beer. That was the end of Father. By the time he had taken the first he already realized that he had made a fool of himself, took a second to forget it and a third to forget that he couldn't forget, and at last came home reeling drunk. From this on it was 'The Drunkard's Progress', as in the moral prints. Next day he stayed in from work with a sick head while Mother went off to make his excuses at the works, and inside a fortnight he was poor and savage and despondent again. Once he began he drank steadily through everything down to the kitchen clock. Mother and I knew all the phases and dreaded all the dangers. Funerals were one.

'I have to go to Dunphy's to do a half-day's work,' said Mother in distress. 'Who's to look after Larry?'

'I'll look after Larry,' Father said graciously. 'The little walk will do him good.'

There was no more to be said, though we all knew I didn't need anyone to look after me, and that I could quite well have stayed at home and looked after Sonny, but I was being attached to the party to act as a brake on Father. As a brake I had never achieved anything, but Mother still had great faith in me.

Next day, when I got home from school, Father was there before me and made a cup of tea for both of us. He was very good at tea, but too heavy in the hand for anything else; the way he cut bread was shocking. Afterwards, we went down the hill to the church, Father wearing his best blue serge and a bowler cocked to one side of his head with the least suggestion of the masher. To his great joy he discovered Peter Crowley among the mourners. Peter was another danger signal, as I knew well from certain experiences after Mass on Sunday morning: a mean man, as Mother said, who only went to funerals for the free drinks he could get at them. It turned out that he hadn't even known Mr Dooley! But Father had a sort of contemptuous regard for him as one of the foolish people who wasted their good money in public-houses when they could be saving it. Very little of his own money Peter Crowley wasted!

It was an excellent funeral from Father's point of view. He had it all well studied before we set off after the hearse in the afternoon sunlight.

'Five carriages!' he exclaimed. 'Five carriages and sixteen covered cars! There's one alderman, two councillors and 'tis unknown how many priests. I didn't see a funeral like this from the road since Willie Mack, the publican, died.'

'Ah, he was well liked,' said Crowley in his husky voice.

'My goodness, don't I know that?' snapped Father. 'Wasn't the man my best friend? Two nights before he died – only two nights – he was over telling me the goings-on about the housing contract. Them fellows in the Corporation are night and day robbers. But even I never imagined he was as well connected as that.'

Father was stepping out like a boy, pleased with everything: the other mourners, and the fine houses along Sunday's Well. I knew the danger signals were there in full force: a sunny day, a fine funeral and a distinguished company of clerics and public men were bringing out all the natural vanity and flightiness of Father's character. It was with something like genuine pleasure that he saw his old friend lowered into the grave; with the sense of having performed a duty and the pleasant awareness that however much he would miss poor Mr Dooley in the long summer evenings, it was he and not poor Mr Dooley who would do the missing.

'We'll be making tracks before they break up,' he whispered to Crowley as the gravediggers tossed in the first shovelfuls of clay, and away he went, hopping like a goat from grassy hump to hump. The drivers, who were probably in the same state as himself, though without months of abstinence to put an edge on it, looked up hopefully.

'Are they nearly finished, Mick?' bawled one.

'All over now bar the last prayers,' trumpeted Father in the tone of one who brings news of great rejoicing.

The carriages passed us in a lather of dust several hundred yards from the public-house, and Father, whose feet gave him trouble in hot weather, quickened his pace, looking nervously over his shoulder for any sign of the main body of mourners crossing the hill. In a crowd like that a man might be kept waiting.

When we did reach the pub the carriages were drawn up outside, and solemn men in black ties were cautiously bringing out consolation to mysterious females whose hands reached out modestly from behind the drawn blinds of the coaches. Inside the pub there were only the drivers and a couple of shawly women. I felt if I was to act as a brake at all, this was the time, so I pulled Father by the coattails.

'Dadda, can't we go home now?' I asked.

'Two minutes now,' he said, beaming affectionately. 'Just a bottle of lemonade and we'll go home.'

This was a bribe, and I knew it, but I was always a child of weak character. Father ordered lemonade and two pints. I was thirsty and swallowed my drink at once. But that wasn't Father's way. He had long months of abstinence behind him and an eternity of pleasure before. He took out his pipe, blew through it, filled it, and then lit it with loud pops, his eyes bulging above it. After that he deliberately turned his back on the pint, leaned one elbow on the counter in the attitude of a man who did not know there was a pint behind him, and deliberately brushed the tobacco from his palms. He had settled down for the evening. He was steadily working through all the important funerals he had ever attended. The carriages departed and the minor mourners drifted in till the pub was half full.

'Dadda,' I said, pulling his coat again, 'can't we go home now?'

'Ah, your mother won't be in for a long time yet,' he said benevolently enough. 'Run out in the road and play, can't you?'

It struck me as very cool, the way grown-ups assumed that you could play all by yourself on a strange road. I began to get bored as I had so often been bored before. I knew Father was quite capable of lingering there till nightfall. I knew I might have to bring him home, blind drunk, down Blarney Lane, with all the old women at their doors, saying: 'Mick Delaney is on it again.' I knew that my mother would be half crazy with anxiety;

that next day Father wouldn't go out to work; and before the end of the week she would be running down to the pawn with the clock under her shawl. I could never get over the lonesomeness of the kitchen without a clock.

I was still thirsty. I found if I stood on tiptoe I could just reach Father's glass, and the idea occurred to me that it would be interesting to know what the contents were like. He had his back to it and wouldn't notice. I took down the glass and sipped cautiously. It was a terrible disappointment. I was astonished that he could even drink such stuff. It looked as if he had never tried lemonade.

I should have advised him about lemonade but he was holding forth himself in great style. I heard him say that bands were a great addition to a funeral. He put his arms in the position of someone holding a rifle in reverse and hummed a few bars of Chopin's Funeral March. Crowley nodded reverently. I took a longer drink and began to see that porter might have its advantages. I felt pleasantly elevated and philosophic. Father hummed a few bars of the Dead March in *Saul*. It was a nice pub and a very fine funeral, and I felt sure that poor Mr Dooley in Heaven must be highly gratified. At the same time I thought they might have given him a band. As Father said, bands were a great addition.

But the wonderful thing about porter was the way it made you stand aside, or rather float aloft like a cherub rolling on a cloud, and watch yourself with your legs crossed, leaning against a bar counter, not worrying about trifles, but thinking deep, serious, grown-up thoughts about life and death. Looking at yourself like that, you couldn't help thinking after a while how funny you looked, and suddenly you got embarrassed and wanted to giggle. But by the time I had finished the pint, that phase too had passed; I found it hard to put back the glass, the counter seemed to have grown so high. Melancholia was supervening again.

'Well,' Father said reverently, reaching behind him for his drink, 'God rest the poor man's soul, wherever he is!' He stopped, looked first at the glass, and then at the people round him. 'Hello,' he said in a fairly good-humoured tone, as if he were just prepared to consider it a joke, even if it was in bad taste, 'who was at this?'

There was silence for a moment while the publican and the old women looked first at Father and then at his glass.

'There was no one at it, my good man,' one of the women said with an offended air. 'Is it robbers you think we are?'

'Ah, there's no one here would do a thing like that, Mick,' said the publican in a shocked tone.

'Well, someone did it,' said Father, his smile beginning to wear off.

'If they did, they were them that were nearer it,' said the woman darkly, giving me a dirty look; and at the same moment the truth began to dawn on Father. I suppose I must have looked a bit starry-eyed. He bent and shook me.

'Are you all right, Larry?' he asked in alarm.

Peter Crowley looked down at me and grinned.

'Could you beat that?' he exclaimed in a husky voice.

I could, and without difficulty. I started to get sick. Father jumped back in holy terror that I might spoil his good suit, and hastily opened the back door.

'Run! run! run!' he shouted.

I saw the sunlit wall outside with the ivy overhanging it, and ran. The intention was good but the performance was exaggerated, because I lurched right into the wall, hurting it badly, as it seemed to me. Being always very polite, I said 'Pardon' before the second bout came on me. Father, still concerned for his suit, came up behind and cautiously held me while I got sick.

'That's a good boy!' he said encouragingly. 'You'll be grand when you get that up.'

Before, I was not grand! Grand was the last thing I was. I gave one unmerciful wail out of me as he steered me back to the pub and put me sitting on the bench near the shawlies. They drew themselves up with an offended air, still sore at the suggestion that they had drunk his pint.

'God help us!' moaned one, looking pityingly at me, 'isn't it the likes of them would be fathers?'

'Mick,' said the publican in alarm, spraying sawdust on my

tracks, 'that child isn't supposed to be in here at all. You'd better take him home quick in case a bobby would see him.'

'Merciful God!' whimpered Father, raising his eyes to heaven and clapping his hands silently as he only did when distraught, 'what misfortune was on me? Or what will his mother say? ... If women might stop at home and look after their children themselves!' he added in a snarl for the benefit of the shawlies. 'Are them carriages all gone, Bill?'

'The carriages are finished long ago, Mick,' replied the publican.

'I'll take him home,' Father said despairingly ... 'I'll never bring you out again,' he threatened me. 'Here,' he added, giving me the clean handkerchief from his breast pocket, 'put that over your eye.'

The blood on the handkerchief was the first indication I got that I was cut, and instantly my temple began to throb and I set up another howl.

'Whisht, whisht, whisht!' Father said testily, steering me out the door. 'One'd think you were killed. That's nothing. We'll wash it when we get home.'

'Steady now, old scout!' Crowley said, taking the other side of me. 'You'll be all right in a minute.'

I never met two men who knew less about the effects of drink. The first breath of fresh air and the warmth of the sun made me groggier than ever and I pitched and rolled between wind and tide till Father started to whimper again.

'God Almighty, and the whole road out! What misfortune was on me didn't stop at my work! Can't you walk straight?'

I couldn't. I saw plain enough that, coaxed by the sunlight, every woman old and young in Blarney Lane was leaning over her half-door or sitting on her doorstep. They all stopped gabbling to gape at the strange spectacle of two sober, middle-aged men bringing home a drunken small boy with a cut over his eye. Father, torn between the shamefast desire to get me home as quick as he could, and the neighbourly need to explain that it wasn't his fault, finally halted outside Mrs Roche's. There was a gang of old women outside a door at the opposite side of the road. I didn't like the look of them from the first. They

seemed altogether too interested in me. I leaned against the wall
of Mrs Roche's cottage with my hands in my trousers pockets,
thinking mournfully of poor Mr Dooley in his cold grave on
the Curragh, who would never walk down the road again, and,
with great feeling, I began to sing a favorite song of Father's.

> *Though lost to Mononia and cold in the grave*
> *He returns to Kincora no more.*

'Wisha, the poor child!' Mrs Roche said. 'Haven't he a lovely
voice, God bless him!'

That was what I thought myself, so I was the more surprised
when Father said 'Whisht!' and raised a threatening finger at
me. He didn't seem to realize the appropriateness of the song,
so I sang louder than ever.

'Whisht, I tell you!' he snapped, and then tried to work up a
smile for Mrs Roche's benefit. 'We're nearly home now. I'll
carry you the rest of the way.'

But, drunk and all as I was, I knew better than to be carried
home ignominiously like that.

'Now,' I said severely, 'can't you leave me alone? I can walk
all right. 'Tis only my head. All I want is a rest.'

'But you can rest at home in bed,' he said viciously, trying to
pick me up, and I knew by the flush on his face that he was very
vexed.

'Ah, Jasus,' I said crossly, 'what do I want to go home for?
Why the hell can't you leave me alone?'

For some reason the gang of old women at the other side of
the road thought this very funny. They nearly split their sides
over it. A gassy fury began to expand in me at the thought
that a fellow couldn't have a drop taken without the whole
neighbourhood coming out to make game of him.

'Who are ye laughing at?' I shouted, clenching my fists at
them. 'I'll make ye laugh at the other side of yeer faces if ye
don't let me pass.'

They seemed to think this funnier still; I had never seen such
ill-mannered people.

'Go away, ye bloody bitches!' I said.

'Whisht, whisht, whisht, I tell you!' snarled Father,

abandoning all pretence of amusement and dragging me along behind him by the hand. I was maddened by the women's shrieks of laughter. I was maddened by Father's bullying. I tried to dig in my heels but he was too powerful for me, and I could only see the women by looking back over my shoulder.

'Take care or I'll come back and show ye!' I shouted. 'I'll teach ye to let decent people pass. Fitter for ye to stop at home and wash yeer dirty faces.'

' 'Twill be all over the road,' whimpered Father. 'Never again, never again, not if I lived to be a thousand!'

To this day I don't know whether he was forswearing me or the drink. By way of a song suitable to my heroic mood I bawled 'The Boys of Wexford', as he dragged me on home. Crowley, knowing he was not safe, made off and Father undressed me and put me to bed. I couldn't sleep because of the whirling in my head. It was very unpleasant, and I got sick again. Father came in with a wet cloth and mopped up after me. I lay in a fever, listening to him chopping sticks to start a fire. After that I heard him lay the table.

Suddenly the front door banged open and Mother stormed in with Sonny in her arms, not her usual gentle, timid self, but a wild, raging woman. It was clear that she had heard it all from the neighbours.

'Mick Delaney,' she cried hysterically, 'what did you do to my son?'

'Whisht, woman, whisht, whisht!' he hissed, dancing from one foot to the other. 'Do you want the whole road to hear?'

'Ah,' she said with a horrifying laugh, 'the road knows all about it by this time. The road knows the way you filled your unfortunate innocent child with drink to make sport for you and that other rotten, filthy brute.'

'But I gave him no drink,' he shouted, aghast at the horrifying interpretation the neighbours had chosen to give his misfortune. 'He took it while my back was turned. What the hell do you think I am?'

'Ah,' she replied bitterly, 'everyone knows what you are now. God forgive you, wasting our hard-earned few ha'pence on drink, and bringing up your child to be a drunken corner-boy like yourself.'

Then she swept into the bedroom and threw herself on her knees by the bed. She moaned when she saw the gash over my eye. In the kitchen Sonny set up a loud bawl on his own, and a moment later Father appeared in the bedroom door with his cap over his eyes, wearing an expression of the most intense self-pity.

'That's a nice way to talk to me after all I went through,' he whined. 'That's a nice accusation, that I was drinking. Not one drop of drink crossed my lips the whole day. How could it when he drank it all? I'm the one that ought to be pitied, with my day ruined on me, and I after being made a show for the whole road.'

But next morning, when he got up and went out quietly to work with his dinner-basket, Mother threw herself on me in the bed and kissed me. It seemed it was all my doing, and I was being given a holiday till my eye got better.

'My brave little man!' she said with her eyes shining. 'It was God did it you were there. You were his guardian angel.'

Graham Greene

A Shocking Accident

I

Jerome was called into his housemaster's room in the break
between the second and the third class on a Thursday morning.
He had no fear of trouble, for he was a warden – the name that
the proprietor and headmaster of a rather expensive preparatory
school had chosen to give to approved, reliable boys in the lower
forms (from a warden one became a guardian and finally before
leaving, it was hoped for Marlborough or Rugby, a crusader).
The housemaster, Mr Wordsworth, sat behind his desk with an
appearance of perplexity and apprehension. Jerome had the odd
impression when he entered that he was a cause of fear.

'Sit down, Jerome,' Mr Wordsworth said. 'All going well
with the trigonometry?'

'Yes, sir.'

'I've had a telephone call, Jerome. From your aunt. I'm afraid
I have bad news for you.'

'Yes, sir?'

'Your father has had an accident.'

'Oh.'

Mr Wordsworth looked at him with some surprise. 'A serious
accident.'

'Yes, sir?'

Jerome worshipped his father: the verb is exact. As man re-
creates God, so Jerome re-created his father – from a restless
widowed author into a mysterious adventurer who travelled in
far places – Nice, Beirut, Majorca, even the Canaries. The time
had arrived about his eighth birthday when Jerome believed
that his father either 'ran guns' or was a member of the British

Secret Service. Now it occurred to him that his father might have been wounded in 'a hail of machine-gun bullets'.

Mr Wordsworth played with the ruler on his desk. He seemed at a loss how to continue. He said, 'You know your father was in Naples?'

'Yes, sir.'

'Your aunt heard from the hospital today.'

'Oh.'

Mr Wordsworth said with desperation, 'It was a street accident.'

'Yes, sir?' It seemed quite likely to Jerome that they would call it a street accident. The police of course had fired first; his father would not take human life except as a last resort.

'I'm afraid your father was very seriously hurt indeed.'

'Oh.'

'In fact, Jerome, he died yesterday. Quite without pain.'

'Did they shoot him through the heart?'

'I beg your pardon. What did you say, Jerome?'

'Did they shoot him through the heart?'

'Nobody shot him, Jerome. A pig fell on him.' An inexplicable convulsion took place in the nerves of Mr Wordsworth's face; it really loooked for a moment as though he were going to laugh. He closed his eyes, composed his features and said rapidly as though it were necessary to expel the story as rapidly as possible. 'Your father was walking along a street in Naples when a pig fell on him. A shocking accident. Apparently in the poorer quarters of Naples they keep pigs on their balconies. This one was on the fifth floor. It had grown too fat. The balcony broke. The pig fell on your father.'

Mr Wordsworth left his desk rapidly and went to the window, turning his back on Jerome. He shook a little with emotion.

Jerome said, 'What happened to the pig?'

2

This was not callousness on the part of Jerome, as it was inter-
preted by Mr Wordsworth to his colleagues (he even discussed
with them whether, perhaps, Jerome was yet fitted to be a
warden). Jerome was only attempting to visualize the strange
scene to get the details right. Nor was Jerome a boy who cried;
he was a boy who brooded, and it never occurred to him at his
preparatory school that the circumstances of his father's death
were comic – they were still part of the mystery of life. It was
later, in his first term at his public school, when he told the
story to his best friend, that he began to realize how it affected
others. Naturally after that disclosure he was known, rather
unreasonably, as Pig.

Unfortunately his aunt had no sense of humour. There was
an enlarged snapshot of his father on the piano; a large sad man
in an unsuitable dark suit posed in Capri with an umbrella (to
guard him against sunstroke), the Faraglione rocks forming the
background. By the age of sixteen Jerome was well aware that
the portrait looked more like the author of *Sunshine and Shade*
and *Rambles in the Balearics* than an agent of the Secret Service.
All the same he loved the memory of his father: he still possessed
an album fitted with picture-postcards (the stamps had been
soaked off long ago for his other collection), and it pained him
when his aunt embarked with strangers on the story of his
father's death.

'A shocking accident,' she would begin, and the stranger
would compose his or her features into the correct shape for
interest and commiseration. Both reactions, of course, were
false, but it was terrible for Jerome to see how suddenly, midway
in her rambling discourse, the interest would become genuine.
'I can't think how such things can be allowed in a civilized
country,' his aunt would say. 'I suppose one has to regard Italy
as civilized. One is prepared for all kinds of things abroad, of
course, and my brother was a great traveller. He always carried
a water-filter with him. It was far less expensive, you know,
than buying all those bottles of mineral water. My brother

always said that his filter paid for his dinner wine. You can see from that what a careful man he was, but who could possibly have expected when he was walking along the Via Dottore Manuele Panucci on his way to the Hydrographic Museum that a pig would fall on him?' That was the moment when the interest became genuine.

Jerome's father had not been a very distinguished writer, but the time always seems to come, after an author's death, when somebody thinks it worth his while to write a letter to the *Times Literary Supplement* announcing the preparation of a biography and asking to see any letters or documents or receive any anecdotes from friends of the dead man. Most of the biographies, of course, never appear – one wonders whether the whole thing may not be an obscure form of blackmail and whether many a potential writer of a biography or thesis finds the means in this way to finish his education at Kansas or Nottingham. Jerome, however, as a chartered accountant, lived far from the literary world. He did not realize how small the menace really was, or that the danger period for someone of his father's obscurity had long passed. Sometimes he rehearsed the method of recounting his father's death so as to reduce the comic element to its smallest dimensions – it would be of no use to refuse information, for in that case the biographer would undoubtedly visit his aunt, who was living to a great old age with no sign of flagging.

It seemed to Jerome that there were two possible methods – the first led gently up to the accident, so that by the time it was described the listener was so well prepared that the death came really as an anti-climax. The chief danger of laughter in such a story was always surprise. When he rehearsed this method Jerome began boringly enough.

'You know Naples and those high tenement buildings? Somebody once told me that the Neapolitan always feels at home in New York just as the man from Turin feels at home in London because the river runs in much the same way in both cities. Where was I? Oh, yes. Naples, of course. You'd be surprised in the poorer quarters what things they keep on the balconies of those sky-scraping tenements – not washing, you know, or bedding, but things like livestock, chickens or even pigs. Of course the pigs get no exercise whatever and fatten all the quicker.' He could imagine how his hearer's eyes would have glazed by this time. 'I've no idea, have you, how heavy a pig can be, but these old buildings are all badly in need of repair. A balcony on the fifth floor gave way under one of those pigs. It struck the third floor balcony on its way down and sort of ricochetted into the street. My father was on the way to the Hydrographic Museum when the pig hit him. Coming from that height and that angle it broke his neck.' This was really a masterly attempt to make an intrinsically interesting subject boring.

The other method Jerome rehearsed had the virtue of brevity.

'My father was killed by a pig.'

'Really? In India?'

'No, in Italy.'

'How interesting. I never realized there was pig-sticking in Italy. Was your father keen on polo?'

In course of time, neither too early nor too late, rather as though, in his capacity as a chartered accountant, Jerome had studied the statistics and taken the average, he became engaged to be married: to a pleasant fresh-faced girl of twenty-five whose father was a doctor in Pinner. Her name was Sally, her favourite author was still Hugh Walpole, and she had adored babies ever since she had been given a doll at the age of five which moved its eyes and made water. Their relationship was contented rather than exciting, as became the love-affair of a chartered accountant; it would never have done if it had interfered with the figures.

One thought worried Jerome, however. Now that within a year he might himself become a father, his love for the dead man increased; he realized what affection had gone into the picture-postcards. He felt a longing to protect his memory, and uncertain whether this quiet love of his would survive if Sally were so insensitive as to laugh when she heard the story of his father's death. Inevitably she would hear it when Jerome brought her to dinner with his aunt. Several times he tried to tell her himself, as she was naturally anxious to know all she could that concerned him.

'You were very small when your father died?'

'Just nine.'

'Poor little boy,' she said.

'I was at school. They broke the news to me.'

'Did you take it very hard?'

'I can't remember.'

'You never told me how it happened.'

'It was very sudden. A street accident.'

'You'll never drive fast, will you, Jemmy?' (She had begun to call him 'Jemmy'.) It was too late then to try the second method – the one he thought of as the pig-sticking one.

They were going to marry quietly in a registry-office and have their honeymoon at Torquay. He avoided taking her to see his aunt until a week before the wedding, but then the night came and he could not have told himself whether his apprehension was more for his father's memory or the security of his own love.

The moment came all too soon. 'Is that Jemmy's father?' Sally asked, picking up the portrait of the man with the umbrella.

'Yes, dear. How did you guess?'

'He has Jemmy's eyes and brow, hasn't he?'

'Has Jerome lent you his books?'

'No.'

'I will give you a set for your wedding. He wrote so tenderly about his travels. My own favourite is *Nooks and Crannies*. He would have had a great future. It made that shocking accident all the worse.'

'Yes?'

Jerome longed to leave the room and not see that loved face crinkle with irresistible amusement.

'I had so many letters from his readers after the pig fell on him.' She had never been so abrupt before.

And then the miracle happened. Sally did not laugh. Sally sat with open eyes of horror while his aunt told her the story, and at the end, 'How horrible,' Sally said. 'It makes you think, doesn't it? Happening like that. Out of a clear sky.'

Jerome's heart sang with joy. It was as though she had appeased his fear for ever. In the taxi going home he kissed her with more passion than he had ever shown and she returned it. There were babies in her pale blue pupils, babies that rolled their eyes and made water.

'A week today,' Jerome said, and she squeezed his hand. 'Penny for your thoughts, my darling.'

'I was wondering,' Sally said, 'what happened to the poor pig?'

'They almost certainly had it for dinner,' Jerome said happily and kissed the dear child again.

H. E. Bates

Silas the Good

In a life of ninety-five years, my Uncle Silas found time to try most things, and there was a time when he became a grave-digger.

The churchyard at Solbrook stands a long way outside the village on a little mound of bare land above the river valley.

And there, dressed in a blue shirt and mulatto brown corduroys and a belt that resembled more than anything a length of machine shafting, my Uncle Silas used to dig perhaps a grave a month.

He would work all day there at the blue-brown clay without seeing a soul, with no one for company except crows, the pewits crying over the valley or the robin picking the worms out of the thrown-up earth. Squat, misshapen, wickedly ugly, he looked something like a gargoyle that had dropped off the roof of the little church, something like a brown dwarf who had lived too long after his time and might go on living and digging the graves of others for ever.

He was digging a grave there one day on the south side of the churchyard on a sweet, sultry day in May, the grass already long and deep, with strong golden cowslips rising everywhere among the mounds and the gravestones, and bluebells hanging like dark smoke under the creamy waterfalls of hawthorn bloom.

By noon he was fairly well down with the grave, and had fixed his boards to the sides. The spring had been very dry and cold, but now, in the shelter of the grave, in the strong sun, it seemed like midsummer. It was so good that Silas sat in the bottom of the grave and had his dinner, eating his bread and mutton off the thumb, and washing it down with the cold tea he always carried in a beer-bottle. After eating, he began to feel drowsy, and finally he went to sleep there, at the bottom of the grave, with his wet, ugly mouth drooping open and the beer-bottle in one hand and resting on his knee.

He had been asleep for a quarter of an hour or twenty minutes when he woke up and saw someone standing at the top of the grave, looking down at him. At first he thought it was a woman. Then he saw his mistake. It was a female.

He was too stupefied and surprised to say anything, and the female stood looming down at him, very angry at something, poking holes in the grass with a large umbrella. She was very pale, updrawn and skinny, with a face, as Silas described it, like a turnip lantern with the candle out. She seemed to have size nine boots on and from under her thick black skirt Silas caught a glimpse of an amazing knickerbocker leg, baggy, brown in colour, and about the size of an airship.

He had no time to take another look before she was at him. She waved her umbrella and cawed at him like a crow, attacking him for indolence and irreverence, blasphemy and ignorance.

She wagged her head and stamped one of her feet, and every time she did so the amazing brown bloomer seemed to slip a little farther down her leg, until Silas felt it would slip off altogether. Finally, she demanded, scraggy neck craning down at him, what did he mean by boozing down there, on holy ground, in a place that should be sacred for the dead?

Now at the best of times it was difficult for my Uncle Silas, with ripe, red lips, one eye bloodshot and bleary, and a nose like a crusty strawberry, not to look like a drunken sailor. But there was only one thing that he drank when he was working, and that was cold tea. It was true that it was always cold tea with whisky in it, but the basis remained, more or less, cold tea.

Silas let the female lecture him for almost five minutes, and then he raised his panama hat and said, 'Good afternoon, ma'am. Ain't the cowslips out nice?'

'Not content with desecrating holy ground,' she said, 'you're intoxicated, too!'

'No, ma'am,' he said, 'I wish I was.'

'Beer!' she said. 'Couldn't you leave the beer alone in here, of all places?'

Silas held up the beer-bottle. 'Ma'am,' he said, 'what's in here wouldn't harm a fly. It wouldn't harm you.'

'It is responsible for the ruin of thousands of homes all over England!' she said.

'Cold tea,' Silas said.

Giving a little sort of snort she stamped her foot and the bloomer-leg jerked down a little lower. 'Cold tea!'

'Yes, ma'am. Cold tea.' Silas unscrewed the bottle and held it up to her. 'Go on, ma'am, try it. Try it if you don't believe me.'

'Thank you. Not out of that bottle.'

'All right. I got a cup,' Silas said. He looked in his dinner basket and found an enamel cup. He filled it with tea and held it up to her. 'Go on, ma'am, try it. Try it. It won't hurt you.'

'Well!' she said, and she reached down for the cup. She took it and touched her thin bony lips to it. 'Well, it's certainly some sort of tea.'

'Just ordinary tea, ma'am,' Silas said. 'Made this morning. You ain't drinking it. Take a good drink.'

She took a real drink then, washing it round her mouth.

'Refreshin', ain't it?' Silas said.

'Yes,' she said, 'it's very refreshing.'

'Drink it up,' he said. 'Have a drop more. I bet you've walked a tidy step?'

'Yes,' she said, 'I'm afraid I have. All the way from Bedford. Rather farther than I thought. I'm not so young as I used to be.'

'Pah!' Silas said. 'Young? You look twenty.' He took his coat and spread it on the new earth above the grave. 'Sit down and rest yourself, ma'am. Sit down and look at the cowslips.'

Rather to his surprise, she sat down. She took another drink of the tea and said, 'I think I'll unpin my hat.' She took off her hat and held it in her lap.

'Young?' Silas said. 'Ma'am, you're just a chicken. Wait till you're as old as me and then you can begin to talk. I can remember the Crimea!'

'Indeed?' she said. 'You must have had a full and varied life.'

'Yes, ma'am.'

She smiled thinly, for the first time. 'I am sorry I spoke as I did. It upset me to think of anyone drinking in this place.'

'That's all right, ma'am,' Silas said. 'That's all right. I ain't touched a drop for years. Used to, ma'am. Bin a regular sinner.'

Old Silas reached up to her with the bottle and said, 'Have some more, ma'am,' and she held down the cup and filled it up again. 'Thank you,' she said. She looked quite pleasant now, softened by the tea and the smell of cowslips and the sun on her bare head. The bloomer-leg had disappeared and somehow she stopped looking like a female and became a woman.

'But you've reformed now?' she said.

'Yes, ma'am,' Silas said, with a slight shake of his head, as though he were a man in genuine sorrow. 'Yes, ma'am. I've reformed.'

'It was a long fight?'

'A long fight, ma'am? I should say it was, ma'am. A devil of a long fight.' He raised his panama hat a little. 'Beg pardon, ma'am. That's another thing I'm fighting against. The language.'

'And the drink,' she said, 'how far back does that go?'

'Well, ma'am,' Silas said, settling back in the grave, where he had been sitting all that time, 'I was born in the hungry 'forties. Bad times, ma'am, very bad times. We was fed on barley pap, ma'am, if you ever heard talk of barley pap. And the water was bad, too, ma'am. Very bad. Outbreaks of smallpox and typhoid and all that. So we had beer, ma'am. Everybody had beer. The babies had beer. So you see, ma'am,' Silas said, 'I've been fighting against it for eighty years and more. All my puff.'

'And now you've conquered it?'

'Yes, ma'am,' said my Uncle Silas, who had drunk more in eighty years than would keep a water-mill turning, 'I've conquered it.' He held up the beer-bottle. 'Nothing but cold tea. You'll have some more cold tea, ma'am, won't you?'

'It's very kind of you,' she said.

So Silas poured out another cup of the cold tea and she sat on the graveside and sipped it in the sunshine, becoming all the time more and more human.

'And no wonder,' as Silas would say to me afterwards, 'seeing it was still the winter ration we were drinking. You see, I had a summer ration with only a nip of whisky in it, and then I had a winter ration wi' pretty nigh a mugful in it. The weather had been cold up to that day and I hadn't bothered to knock the winter ration off.'

They sat there for about another half an hour, drinking the cold tea, and during that time there was nothing she did not hear about my Uncle Silas's life: not only how he had reformed on the beer and was trying to reform on the language but he had long since reformed on the ladies and the horses and doubtful stories and the lying and everything else that a man can reform on.

Indeed, as he finally climbed up out of the grave to shake hands with her and say good afternoon, she must have got the impression that he was a kind of ascetic lay brother.

Except that her face was very flushed, she walked away with much the same dignity as she had come. There was only one thing that spoiled it. The amazing bloomer-leg had come down again, and Silas could not resist it.

'Excuse me, ma'am,' he called after her, 'but you're liable to lose your knickerbockers.'

She turned and gave a dignified smile and then a quick, saucy kind of hitch to her skirt, and the bloomer-leg went up, as Silas himself said, as sharp as a blind in a shop-window.

That was the last he ever saw of her. But that afternoon, on the 2.45 up-train out of Solbrook, there was a woman with a large umbrella in one hand and a bunch of cowslips in the other. In the warm, crowded carriage there was a smell of something stronger than cold tea, and it was clear to everyone that one of her garments was not in its proper place. She appeared to be a little excited, and to everybody's embarrassment she talked a great deal.

Her subject was someone she had met that afternoon.

'A good man,' she told them. 'A good man.'

The Lull

I

There was a bar in this fire-station. On the bar was a case of beer. A fireman was taking bottles from this case, placing the full bottles on to shelves. He was alone.

Another came in. This one was minus his tunic. He wore a check shirt. The barman began to take him off, without looking up from what he was doing.

'You – you – you fool,' the barman said. The way he spoke you would have thought one or the other stuttered.

'Ten Woodbines, thank you.'

'Ten,' the barman said.

A bell in the cash register. Then silence. These two men stood in silence.

'Cigarette?'

'No, not just yet, thanks all the same, Gerald. I don't smoke such a lot these days.'

'Not like you used to, eh?'

What lay behind this last remark was that Gerald, the man in the check shirt, was echoing an opinion widely held in the station, that this barman often put his sticky fingers, which were of the same length, into the till. But it was said without malice. The barman let it pass. He knew the personnel expected to be robbed, within reason. He lifted another full case on to the bar. After a pause, he said:

'They don't get any lighter. Is there anything on tonight?'

He asked this pleasantly, to get his own back. He was referring to the fact that Gerald, because he did odd jobs carpentering for the officer in charge, was excused the tactical exercises held every evening to keep the men out of bed.

'Not that I know of,' the other replied. His tone of voice was to show, elaborately, that he did not care.

'We want another blitz,' remarked the barman.

'We do,' he was answered.

Neither of these firemen stuttered.

'I saw old Sambo today.'

The other did not move.

'Why d'you wear that bloody shirt?' the first man went on. He kept his eyes on the bottles he arranged. 'Has your Mrs got such a number that she can't put your dusters to the proper use? Because we could do with one or two at 'ome. Yes,' he broke off, 'I seen Sam.'

'That fellow with a squint.'

'That's right. Sam Race.'

A short silence.

'You know the last time I seen him?' the barman went on.

'On a working party?' This was a reference to the fact that, because he pleaded he had to check his stock, the barman was excused fatigues.

'On a working party! No! Along Burdett Road the night of that bad blitz.'

'Really?'

'I've not seen 'im since the night Willy Tennant got down under the pump, when old Ted Fowler moved up one. It was surprising it didn't break his leg.'

'The wheel went right over?' the man in the shirt asked, as though inquiring whether the blackbird had got the worm.

'You're telling me. I was there. Yes, from that day until this morning I didn't set eyes on Sam. That's a strange thing, come to look at it.'

They stood, in silence again, leaning each side of the bar. They pondered at the linoleum which covered the counter.

'Sure you couldn't do with a drink?' the barman asked at last.

'Quite sure, thanks.'

At this a third fireman came in.

'Well, brother?'

That is to say the barman and the third fireman were both members of the Fire Brigades Union.

'I'll 'ave one of them small light ales, Joe, please. Will you try one?'

'No, thanks all the same. Been out on short leave?' He called it 'leaf'.

'Yes, I 'ad a drop of short.'

A bell in the cash register.

'I was just tellin' Gerald,' the man went on, 'I seen Sam Race as I was on me way round to the brewer's this morning.'

'Wally Race you mean, Joe.'

'No, Wally Race is the brother.'

'Wally Race 'as no brother,' the third man stuck to his guns.

'What'll you bet me, Gus?'

'Wally Race 'as no brother. 'E's lived at 'ome ever since I can remember. With 'is mother and 'er old man. No, he's an only child, Wally Race is.'

'Come on, Gus, what'll you bet?'

'I wouldn't want to take your money, Joe.'

'What if you do, that's my business! It's my money, ain't it? Come on now, just for a lark, how much?'

'What, on three fourteen and six a week?'

'Some of you chaps just won't 'ave a go. Forgotten what it's like I suppose.'

The barman pretended disgust. He lifted two empty cases down. He began to polish glasses when Gerald, in his check shirt, turned all at once, and hurried out of the room.

'What's 'e making now?' the third man asked.

'Bedside table. Bloody marvellous the work he turns out. You can't see 'is joins, only with a magnifying glass.'

'Yes. The Boy Marvel.'

Silence yet again. Then a fourth man entered.

'Quite busy, thank you, this evenin',' the barman remarked in greeting. He meant it. 'Bloody awful quiet it is in behind this bar sometimes. What can I do for you, brother?'

'Wallop,' the fourth man demanded.

'Now then, Ted, you know there ain't none. We can do you light ale, in quarts or 'alf pints, ditto brown ale, or a nice bottle of Guinness.'

'What, at eightpence 'alfpenny. Not likely.'

They looked at each other, amiably.

'What's become of the Bar Committee?' the fourth man inquired.

'What's become of it?' the barman Joe echoed. 'It's still in existence.'

'Then it's time it 'eld another meeting.'

'These small lights aren't bad, Ted,' the third man said.

'I don't want none o' that. I like it all right, but those lights don't like me. Too gassy.'

'All right then, mate, but make up your mind.' Having said this, the barman began to polish glasses again.

''Ow much a week, now, is this job you've got behind that bar worth to you?' the fourth man went on.

The barman ignored it. Instead he remarked:

'I seen Sam Race this morning.'

'Well, I think I'll risk a brown, Joe. Out of the large bottle.'

'Pronto. Yes, 'e looked very queer, did old Sambo.'

'Sam who?'

'Sam Race. Why, you must remember him, Ted.'

'Wally Race you mean.'

'No, Sam.'

'What station?'

''E's moved,' the barman replied, nonplussed for the instant. 'I disremember where exactly,' he went on rather lamely. This attracted the third man's attention, who asked:

'What station was 'e at?'

The barman pulled himself together. He knew what to say to this.

'Where d'you think, Gus? Up Goldington Road, at 4U of course, with Matty Franks.' He was improvising.

'With 'oo?' the fourth man objected.

'Old Matty Franks,' the barman answered irritably.

A bell in the cash register. A pause.

'Never 'eard of 'im,' the fourth man announced. 'Good 'ealth,' he said.

'God bless,' the third fireman replied.

'Never heard of Matty Franks?' the barman went on. 'The

rottenest old bastard in the Service. Up Goldington Road just past the Ploughshare?'

The two men looked at the barman, ruminating. The fourth man was about to object he was not acquainted with a pub of that name up the road when they all heard a sad cry of 'Come and get it', from below, from the messroom.

'Already?' the fourth man asked aloud. He gulped his down. He left.

The third fireman finished his half pint, and went.

The moment he was alone the barman poured himself out a light from one of the quart bottles.

A bell did not ring in the cash register. Joe had his drinks on the house, when no one was looking.

Silence. He let a lonely belch. He pondered the linoleum which covered the counter.

After five minutes, a kitchen orderly for the day brought the barman up his supper.

'Fred,' the barman said, 'it's getting very slow in this bloody dump.'

'You're telling me,' Fred replied.

'I've 'ad Gus and Ted on about Sam Race.'

''Oo?'

'Sam Race.'

'I don't seem to recollect a Sam Race, Joe.'

'No, nor there ain't never been. There's only the one Wally Race, who squints something 'orrible. Yet they wouldn't 'ave a bet on it. Not one o' them. What a game, eh?'

'You've said it,' Fred replied, uninterested. He went out.

The barman began to eat his supper.

2

Another evening. The same bar. Five or six firemen sat around. Two were without a drink. A fifth man held the floor.

'Yes,' he said, 'a great big woman, my aunt was, twenty-two stone she weighed. And a real wicked old lady. My dad wouldn't allow us kids to have nothing to do with 'er. I'll tell you what she did once. It was a Sunday morning, on the way to church.'

'On the way to church?' another fireman asked.

'Yes, yes, mate, that sort are churchgoers, very often. I'll never forget. Just as she came up on a sheep she put her umbrella right into it. "Err," she said, "you horrid thing." Went right in, the point did.'

No one accepted this. He realized it. He had to go on.

'Terrible she was. Used to kill cats for the enjoyment. She was well hated. D'you know the manner she used to dispatch 'em? By strangilation.'

'Strangled them, eh?' another asked.

'Yes, mate. She put a cord round the neck with a slip knot. Then she'd pass the end through the keyhole. She took the key out first of course. Then she'd take a turn round her body with the free end. To finish up she just leaned on that door. With all her weight it didn't take more'n a minute.'

'How d'you mean, a turn round 'er body?'

'Well, she'd entice the cat in first, see. After that she'd put a slip knot round its neck,' and this fifth fireman went on into an involved description of the method favoured by his aunt. No one was wiser at the end. In the pause which followed two of the others started a quiet argument between each other as to the performance of a particular towing vehicle.

The fifth man began his last attempt.

'She was hated, real hated she was in the country thereabouts,' he told them. 'My dad always said she'd come unstuck at the finish. And so she did. It was remarkable the way it come about.'

'What was that then, Charley?' someone asked, from politeness.

'The way she died, mate. It was to do with a duck for her supper. Eighty-six years old she was. She couldn't manage to wring this duck's neck. So she got out the old chopper, held the bird down on the block and plonk, the 'ead was gone. Well, this head, it can't 'ave fallen in the basket. When she bent down to pick up the 'ead, she let the carcass fall. And it fell right side up, right side up that bloody carcass fell, on its bloody feet and all. And did it run! Well she must 'ave taken fright. She must

'ave started runnin', with the duck 'ard after. She run out into
the garden. The blood from the stump left a trail behind. It
followed 'er every turn, that decapitated duck did. Until in the
finish she fell down. Dead as mutton she was. 'Eart failure.
She'd took fright. But credit it or not, that duck landed on
her arse as she lay there, stretched out. That's where my first
cousin, the nephew, came on 'em both. Cold as a stone, she was
already.'

'Damn that for a bloody tale, Charley.'

'You don't believe me, ah? Well, I tell you, it's the bloody
truth. It's the nerves or something. You'll see the same with
chickens that's had their heads cut off. If it's done sudden they'll
run around.'

'Not that distance.'

'I'm sayin' to you, this 'appened just like I told you, Joe. All
right, disbelieve me then.'

A game of darts was suggested. All joined in.

3

But it was noticeable that, whenever a stranger came into the
bar, these firemen, who had not been on a blitz for eighteen
months, would start talking back to what they had seen of the
attack on London in 1940. They were seeking to justify the
waiting life they lived at present, without fires.

A stranger did not have to join in, his presence alone was
enough to stimulate them who felt they no longer had their lives
now that they were living again, if life in a fire-station can be
called living.

These men were passing through a period which may be
compared with the experience of changing fast trains. A traveller
on the crowded platform cannot be said to command his destiny,
who stands, agape, waiting for the next express. It is signalled,
he knows that it will be packed, it is down the line. The unseen
approach keeps him, as it were, suspended, that is no more than
breathing, but more than ready to describe the way he has

arrived to a man he does not know, waiting in the same disquiet, at his shoulder.

4

It was an evening session in this bar. They had all had a few beers. The stranger, posted to this station for the night because it was short of riders, stayed bored, expressionless, without a hope of comfort. They were sitting back against the walls, in a rectangle. A silence fell. Then the sixth man began. He asked:

'Joe, remember the night we were called to Jacob's Place?'

'I'll likely never forget that, mate.'

'Nor me.'

Silence. But everyone listened.

'What was that, then?' a seventh man inquired.

'They called us on to number five Jacob's Place,' he began again, consciously dramatic.

'Number seventeen, Alfred,' the barman said.

'You may be right at that,' the sixth man answered, unwilling to argue because he wanted to get on with his story. 'It's of no consequence,' he added, already beginning to be put out, 'the point is some geezer in the street tells us there's a job in the roof, so of course Joe here an' me gets crackin'. The rest of the crew set in to a hydrant, while the two of us run upstairs with the stirrup pump in case we can put it out easy. It turns out to be one of them houses where there's just a caretaker, like, an' all the furniture is covered with sheets be'ind locked doors. Ghostly. You know the kind, a smashing place, but 'aunted. There must've been fifteen or sixteen rooms. Well there's a lot of cold smoke choking us on the top floor, but we find the old trap-door to the roof all right. It was quite a pleasure to get out in the air again, it certainly was, wasn't it, Joe?'

'It was that,' Joe said back.

'We begin taking a few tiles off,' he went on, 'and we find a place where it's a bit 'ot, but we still 'aven't come on the seat of the fire, we're rummagin' about, like, on top of that bloody roof when all of a sudden there's a bloody blubbering noise up in the sky over'ead, yes, like a dog bloody 'owling in a bass voice, and coming down out of the moon though we couldn't see nothink. Was I scared. I thinks to meself it's another bloody secret weapon. I called out to you, didn't I, mate?'

'You may 'ave done, Alf. I was too busy tryin' to get down out of it.'

'Yes, we had a bit of a scramble. Joe 'ere was nearest, so he goes down first. Well, there was no point in that "after you" stunt, was there? Yes, and as I was coming last down through the trap-door, I looks up, and I sees what had put the wind up me to such an extent. Know what it was?'

Everyone in the room, bar the stranger, could have told him. They had heard this story often. And the stranger was not interested.

Alfred answered himself.

'A bloody barrage balloon,' he said. 'The shrapnel had got at it. The blubbering noise is occasioned by the fabric rubbin' together as it comes down, or the gas escapin' out of the envelope, one or the other. I couldn't rightly say. But it didn't half put the wind up me.'

'And me,' said Joe.

Silence fell again. Each man drank sparingly of his beer. Knowing the story had not been a success because it had been told before, Alfred tried to get some response from the stranger.

'What station are you from?' he asked.

This man awoke with a start from a doze of misery. He replied obliquely, saying:

'I'm a C.O. you know.'

'A conchie? Well, why not,' Alfred generously said.

'I've never been out on a job,' the stranger answered. 'And I don't know if I should put out fires,' he went on, desperate, 'I don't rightly know if I ought.'

A heavier silence followed.

5

Hyde Park on Sunday. It was hot. A fireman in mufti and a young girl were, of an afternoon, by that part of the Serpentine in which fishing is allowed. They had put themselves back from dazzling water, on deck chairs.

A girl of eighteen went slowly by, dressed in pink, a careful inexpensive outfit, one of thousands off a hook. From her deck chair the other said, rapid and sly:

'La petite marquise Osine est toute belle.'

He had been admiring the calves and tender ankles that girl dragged through thin, olive green grass. He laughed. He was caught out. He turned to his companion.

'Henry,' she went on, bilingual, speaking only a little less fast, 'surely you remember?'

He was sleepy. He shook his head. She recited, quick and low:

> 'Oui, certes, il est doux,
> Le roman d'un premier amant. L'âmes'essaie,
> C'est un jeune coureur à la premier haie.
> C'est si mignard qu'on croit à peine que c'est mal.
> Quelque chose d'étonnamment matutinal.'

He said, 'Yes.' He did not turn away again. He admired her nose, which had caught his eye, as it always did.

'Verlaine?' he asked.

She wondered what he was looking at so particularly about her.

'D'you think my hair's too long?'

'No, I don't,' he replied, 'it's lovely. That was Verlaine, wasn't it?'

She thought, of course he's the one who likes my nose.

'You know you're the worst read man I've ever met.'

'Worse than Archie Small?'

'No, not quite. I like Archie because he's not read anything at all. That's probably why he dances so well.'

What lay behind the remark was that this man Henry could

not dance. Before he had time to take it up she began again, lying back in the chair, looking at him with half-closed eyes, almost in a sing-song,

> *'Ses cheveux, noir tas sauvage où*
> *Scintille un barbare bijou,*
> *La font reine et la font fantoche.'*

She was worried about whether her hair was right.

'Ah,' he said. He stretched. She was wearing an olive green bow of velvet on it.

She shut her eyes, gated them with eyelashes. It was very hot. After a pause she went on, thinking of his youngest sister, her friend.

> *'La femme pense à quelque ancienne compagne,*
> *Laquelle a tout, voiture et maison de campagne,*
> *Tandis que les enfants, leurs poings dans leurs yeux clos,*
> *Ronflant sur leur assiette, imitent des sanglots.'*

'Me, with you, I suppose,' he remarked. 'Go on,' he said. He shut his eyes. 'I'm enjoying this.'

She wondered that he could see himself as a child with her, when he was old enough to be her father.

Both were sleepy from a good lunch. After a while she added slowly, in a low voice:

> *'Bien que parfois nous sentions*
> *Battre nos cœurs sous nos mantes*
> *A des pensers clandestins,*
> *En nous sachant les amantes*
> *Futures des libertins.'*

'Henry,' she said, when there had been another silence. 'You don't know where that comes from, do you?'

He did not open his eyes. 'Verlaine,' he said. He was smiling.

'Yes,' she answered, and shut her eyes. 'It's called "La chanson des Ingénues".'

> *'Nous sommes les Ingénues*
> *Aux bandeaux plats, à l'œil bleu,*
> *Qui vivons, presque inconnues,*
> *Dans les romans qu'on lit peu.'*

'How sweet,' he said, rather dry. At that moment the sirens sounded. Everybody looked up. It was cloudlessly bare and blue.

'Goodness,' she remarked, without conviction and not moving. 'How worried Mummy will be about me.' They sat on. They did not close their eyes again. It was awkward.

Then he suggested they might go to a film, saying it was waste to spend a leave day in the park. She jumped at it. They hurried off, arm in arm, to the USA.

6

The ninth fireman said:

'A 'ornet? No, I can't recollect that I ever met with a 'ornet. But crows now. I remember the first time I seen a crow, to really notice, like. Yus. I was out on the allotment. On the previous leave day I'd put me beansticks in just lovely. But this mornin' when I comes to see how the beans was shapin' there's not a bloody bean stick stood in the bloody soil. They was by far too 'eavy for 'em. I couldn't make it out at first. But just as I'm bendin' to 'ave a look, there's a bloody great bloody black thing that comes swoop at me out of the sky. I thought it was the blitz all over again for a minute. So then I puts me 'and up and 'as a peep. There was seven of the buggers in the oak tree there at the bottom, where the road goes along by our allotments. An' can't they 'alf 'oller. Kraa, kraa. A chap come with a gun and killed three. Bloody great things they was. The rest never came back. No, we never seen them no more.'

7

Two firemen were walking back to the station from the factory in which they made shell caps for the two hours during which they were allowed short leave, every second day.

The tenth man said to the eleventh:

'I'm browned off, Wal, completely.'

The eleventh answered:

'You're not the only one.'

'Wal, d'you think there'll ever be another blitz?'

'Well, mate, if he doesn't put one on soon we shall all be crackers.'

'You're telling me.'

'And they are going insane, in every station every day. Have you heard about the patrol man over at 18.Y.?'

'What was that, Wal?'

'Well it seems that the officer in charge finds something to take him out of his office, and as he comes out he sees no one on guard on the gate. So he looks around, and still he can't spot the patrol man. Till something tells him to look up. And there is the chap that should have been on the gate, sitting across the peak of the roof, hauling on a long line (120 feet of rope) he has between his hands. So he calls to 'im, sarcastic, "'Ow are you gettin' on there?" And this is the answer he gets: "I've saved five."'

'No.'

'It's as true as I'm here. So this officer in charge he climbs as far as he can get inside the building, till he comes to a window across from where his patrol man is sitting. He's one of those fat bastards, and he's a bit out of breath with the climb, you understand. He doesn't know what to make of it. So he calls out:

' "You've saved five, 'ave you?"

' "Yessir. And I'm about done up."

' ""Ang on there, then, and I'll be with yer," the officer in charge sings out to him.

' "You can't," is the answer he gets. "I'm surrounded." Surrounded by fire he meant. In the finish they had to call out the turntable ladders to bring him down. To anyone not acquainted with this job it seems hardly possible, do it?'

'They'll be bringing the plain van any day for me,' the tenth man replied. They walked on, silent.

The passers-by despised them in this uniform that, two years ago, was good in any pub for a drink from a stranger.

Samuel Beckett

Fingal

The last girl he went with, before a memorable fit of laughing incapacitated him from gallantry for some time, was pretty, hot and witty, in that order. So one fine Spring morning he brought her out into the country, to the Hill of Feltrim in the country. They turned east off the road from Dublin to Malahide short of the Castle woods and soon it came into view, not much more than a burrow, the ruin of a mill on the top, choked lairs of furze and brambles passim on its gentle slopes. It was a landmark for miles around on account of the high ruin. The Hill of the Wolves.

They had not been very long on the top before he began to feel a very sad animal indeed. But she was to all appearance in high spirits, enjoying the warm sun and the prospect.

'The Dublin mountains' she said 'don't they look lovely, so dreamy.'

Now Belacqua was looking intently in the opposite direction, across the estuary.

'It's the east wind' he said.

She began to admire this and that, the ridge of Lambay Island, rising out of the brown woods of the Castle, Ireland's Eye like a shark, and the ridiculous little hills far away to the north, what were they?

'The Naul' said Belacqua. 'Is it possible you didn't know the Naul?' This in the shocked tone of the travelled spinster: 'You don't say you were in Milan (to rime with villain) and never saw the Cena?' 'Can it be possible that you passed through Chambery and never called on Mme de Warens?'

'Fingal dull!' he said. 'Winnie you astonish me.'

They considered Fingal for a time together in silence. Its coast eaten away with creeks and marshes, tesserae of small fields, patches of wood springing up like a weed, the line of hills too low to close the view.

'When it's a magic land' he sighed 'like Saône-et-Loire.'

'That means nothing to me' said Winnie.

'Oh yes' he said, 'bons vins et Lamartine, a champaign land for the sad and serious, not a bloody little toy Kindergarten like Wicklow.'

You make great play with your short stay abroad, thought Winnie.

'You and your sad and serious' she said. 'Will you never come off it?'

'Well' he said 'I'll give you Alphonse.'

She replied that he could keep him. Things were beginning to blow up nasty.

'What's that on your face?' she said sharply.

'Impetigo' said Belacqua. He had felt it coming with a terrible itch in the night and in the morning it was there. Soon it would be a scab.

'And you kiss me' she exclaimed 'with that on your face.'

'I forgot' he said. 'I get so excited you know.'

She spittled on her handkerchief and wiped her mouth. Belacqua lay humbly beside her, expecting her to get up and leave him. But instead she said:

'What is it anyway? What does it come from?'

'Dirt' said Belacqua, 'you see it on slum children.'

A long awkward silence followed these words.

'Don't pick it darling' she said unexpectedly at last, 'you'll only make it worse.'

This came to Belacqua like a drink of water to drink in a dungeon. Her goodwill must have meant something to him. He returned to Fingal to cover his confusion.

'I often come to this hill' he said 'to have a view of Fingal, and each time I see it more as a back-land, a land of sanctuary, a land that you don't have to dress up to, that you can walk on in a lounge suit, smoking a cigar.' What a geyser, she thought. 'And where much has been suffered in secret, especially by women.'

'This is all a dream' she said. 'I see nothing but three acres and cows. You can't have Cincinnatus without a furrow.'

Now it was she who was sulky and he who was happy.

'Oh Winnie' he made a vague clutch at her sincerities, for she was all anyway on the grass, 'you look very Roman this minute.'

'He loves me' she said, in earnest jest.

'Only pout' he begged, 'be Roman, and we'll go on across the estuary.'

'And then ... ?'

And then! Winnie take thought!

'I see' he said 'you take thought. Shall we execute a contract?'

'No need' she said.

He was wax in her hands, she twisted him this way and that. But now their moods were in accordance, things were somehow very pleasant all of a sudden. She gazed long at the area of contention and he willed her not to speak, to remain there with her grave face, a quiet *puella* in a blurred world. But she spoke (who shall silence them, at last?), saying that she saw nothing but the grey fields of serfs and the ramparts of ex-favourites. Saw! They were all the same when it came to the pinch – clods. If she closed her eyes she might see something. He would drop the subject, he would not try to communicate Fingal, he would lock it up in his mind. So much the better.

'Look' he pointed.

She looked, blinking for the focus.

'The big red building' he said 'across the water, with the towers.'

At last she thought she saw what he meant.

'Far away' she said 'with the round tower?'

'Do you know what that is' he said 'because my heart's right there.'

Well, she thought, you lay your cards on the table.

'No' she said, 'it looks like a bread factory to me.'

'The Portrane Lunatic Asylum' he said.

'Oh' she said 'I know a doctor there.'

Thus, she having a friend, he his heart, in Portrane, they agreed to make for there.

They followed the estuary all the way round, admiring the theories of swans and the coots, over the dunes and past the

Martello tower, so that they came on Portrane from the south and the sea instead of like a vehicle by the railway bridge and the horrible red chapel of Donabate. The place was as full of towers as Dun Laoghaire of steeples: two Martello, the red ones of the asylum, a watertower and the round. Trespassing unawares, for the notice-board was further on towards the coastguard station, they climbed the rising ground to this latter. They followed the grass margin of a ploughed field till they came to where a bicycle was lying, half hidden in the rank grass. Belacqua, who could on no account resist a bicycle, thought what an extraordinary place to come across one. The owner was out in the field, scarifying the dry furrows with a fork.

'Is this right for the tower?' cried Belacqua.

The man turned his head.

'Can we get up to the tower?' cried Belacqua.

The man straightened up and pointed.

'Fire ahead' he said.

'Over the wall?' cried Belacqua. There was no need for him to shout. A conversational tone would have been heard across the quiet field. But he was so anxious to make himself clear, so he dreaded the thought of having to repeat himself, that he not merely raised his voice, but put on a flat accent that astonished Winnie.

'Don't be an eejit' she said, 'if it's straight on it's over the wall.'

But the man seemed pleased that the wall had been mentioned, or perhaps he was just glad of an opportunity to leave his work, for he dropped his fork and came lumbering over to where they were standing. There was nothing at all noteworthy about his appearance. He said that their way lay straight ahead, yes, over the wall, and then the tower was on top of the field, or else they could go back till they came to the road and go along it till they came to the Banks and follow up the Banks. The Banks? Was this fellow one of the more harmless lunatics? Belacqua asked was the tower an old one, as though it required a Dr Petrie to see that it was not. The man said it had been built for relief in the year of the Famine, so he had heard, by a Mrs Somebody whose name he misremembered in honour of her husband.

'Well Winnie' said Belacqua, 'over the wall or follow up the Banks?'

'There's a rare view of Lambay from the top' said the man.

Winnie was in favour of the wall, she thought that it would be more direct now that they had come so far. The man began to work this out. Belacqua had no one but himself to blame if they never got away from this machine.

'But I would like to see the Banks' he said.

'If we went on now' said Winnie 'now that we have come so far, and followed the Banks down, how would that be?'

They agreed, Belacqua and the man, that it needed a woman to think these things out. Suddenly there was a tie between them.

The tower began well; that was the funeral meats. But from the door up it was all relief and no honour; that was the marriage tables.

They had not been long on the top before Belacqua was a sad animal again. They sat on the grass with their faces to the sea and the asylum was all below and behind them.

'Right enough' said Winnie 'I never saw Lambay look so close.'

Belacqua could see the man scraping away at his furrow and felt a sudden longing to be down there in the clay, lending a hand. He checked the explanation of this that was beginning and looked at the soft chord of yellow on the slope, gorse and ragwort juxtaposed.

'The lovely ruins' said Winnie 'there on the left, covered with ivy.' Of a church and, two small fields further on, a square bawnless tower.

'That' said Belacqua 'is where I have sursum corda.'

'Then hadn't we better be getting on' said Winnie, quick as lightning.

'This absurd tower' he said, now that he had been told, 'is before the asylum, and they are before the tower.' He didn't say! 'The crenels on the wall I find as moving . . .'

Now the loonies poured out into the sun, the better behaved

left to their own devices, the others in herds in charge of warders. The whistle blew and the herd stopped; again, and it proceeded.

'As moving' he said 'and moving in the same way, as the colour of the brick in the old mill at Feltrim.'

Who shall silence them, at last?

'It's pinked' continued Belacqua, 'and as a little fat overfed boy I sat on the floor with a hammer and a pinking-iron, scalloping the edge of a red cloth.'

'What ails you?' asked Winnie.

He had allowed himself to get run down, but he scoffed at the idea of a sequitur from his body to his mind.

'I must be getting old and tired' he said 'when I find the nature outside men compensating for the nature inside me, like Jean-Jacques sprawling in a bed of saxifrages.'

'Appearing to compensate' she said. She was not sure what she meant by this, but it sounded well.

'And then' he said 'I want very much to be back in the caul, on my back in the dark for ever.'

'A short ever' she said 'and working day and night.'

The beastly punctilio of women.

'Damn it' he said 'you know what I mean. No shaving or haggling or cold or hugger-mugger, no' – he cast about for a term of ample connotation – 'no night-sweats.'

Below in the playground on their right some of the milder patients were kicking a football. Others were lounging about, alone and in knots, taking their ease in the sun. The head of one appeared over the wall, the cheek on the hands. Another, he must have been a very tame one, came half-way up the slope, disappeared into a hollow, emerged after a moment and went back the way he had come. Another, his back turned to them, stood fumbling at the wall that divided the grounds of the asylum from the field where they were. One of the gangs was walking round and round the playground. Below on the other hand a long line of workmen's dwellings, in the gardens children playing and crying. Abstract the asylum and there was little left of Portrane but ruins.

Winnie remarked that the lunatics seemed very sane and well-behaved to her. Belacqua agreed, but he thought that the head over the wall told a tale. Landscapes were of interest to Belacqua only in so far as they furnished him with a pretext for a long face.

Suddenly the owner of the bicycle was running towards them up the hill, grasping the fork. He came barging over the wall, through the chord of yellow and pounding along the crest of the slope. Belacqua rose feebly to his feet. This maniac, with the strength of ten men at least, who should withstand him? He would beat him into a puddle with his fork and violate Winnie. But he bore away as he drew near, for a moment they could hear his panting, and plunged on over the shoulder of the rise. Gathering speed on the down grade, he darted through the gate in the wall and disappeared round a corner of the building. Belacqua looked at Winnie, whom he found staring down at where the man had as it were gone to ground, and then away at the distant point where he had watched him scraping his furrows and been envious. The nickel of the bike sparkled in the sun.

The next thing was Winnie waving and halloing. Belacqua turned and saw a man walking smartly towards them up the slope from the asylum.

'Dr Sholto' said Winnie.

Dr Sholto was some years younger than Belacqua, a pale dark man with a brow. He was delighted – how would he say? – at so unexpected a pleasure, honoured he was sure to make the acquaintance of any friend of Miss Coates. Now they would do him the favour to adjourn . . .? This meant drink. But Belacqua, having other fish to fry, sighed and improvised a long courteous statement to the effect that there was a point in connection with the church which he was most anxious to check at first hand, so that if he might accept on behalf of Miss Coates, who was surely tired after her long walk from Malahide . . .

'Malahide!' ejaculated Dr Sholto.

. . . and be himself excused, they could all three meet at the main entrance of the asylum in, say, an hour. How would that be? Dr Sholto demurred politely. Winnie thought hard and said nothing.

'I'll go down by the Banks' said Belacqua agreeably 'and follow the road round. Au revoir.'

They stood for a moment watching him depart. When he ventured to look back they were gone. He changed his course and came to where the bicycle lay in the grass. It was a fine light machine, with red tyres and wooden rims. He ran down the margin to the road and it bounded alongside under his hand. He mounted and they flew down the hill and round the corner till they came at length to the stile that led into the field where the church was. The machine was a treat to ride, on his right hand the sea was foaming among the rocks, the sands ahead were another yellow again, beyond them in the distance the cottages of Rush were bright white, Belacqua's sadness fell from him like a shift. He carried the bicycle into the field and laid it down on the grass. He hastened on foot, without so much as a glance at the church, across the fields, over a wall and a ditch, and stood before the poor wooden door of the tower. The locked appearance of this did not deter him. He gave it a kick, it swung open and he went in.

Meantime Dr Sholto, in his pleasantly appointed sanctum, improved the occasion with Miss Winifred Coates. Thus they were all met together in Portrane, Winnie, Belacqua, his heart and Dr Sholto, and paired off to the satisfaction of all parties. Surely it is in such little adjustments that the benevolence of the First Cause appears beyond dispute. Winnie kept her eye on the time and arrived punctually with her friend at the main entrance. There was no sign of her other friend.

'Late' said Winnie 'as usual.'

In respect of Belacqua Sholto felt nothing but rancour.

'Pah' he said, 'he'll be sandpapering a tomb.'

A stout block of an old man in shirt sleeves and slippers was leaning against the wall of the field. Winnie still sees, as vividly as when they met her anxious gaze for the first time, his great purple face and white moustaches. Had he seen a stranger about, a pale fat man in a black leather coat.

'No miss' he said.

'Well' said Winnie, settling herself on the wall, to Sholto, 'I suppose he's about somewhere.'

A land of sanctuary, he had said, where much had been suffered secretly. Yes, the last ditch.

'You stay here' said Sholto, madness and evil in his heart, 'and I'll take a look in the church.'

The old man had been showing signs of excitement.

'Is it an escape?' he inquired hopefully.

'No no' said Winnie, 'just a friend.'

But he was off, he was unsluiced.

'I was born on Lambay' he said, by way of opening to an endless story of a recapture in which he had distinguished himself, 'and I've worked here man and boy.'

'In that case' said Winnie 'maybe you can tell me what the ruins are.'

'That's the church' he said, pointing to the near one, it had just absorbed Sholto, 'and that' pointing to the far one, ''s the tower.'

'Yes' said Winnie 'but what tower, what was it?'

'The best I know' he said 'is some Lady Something had it.'

This was news indeed.

'Then before that again' it all came back to him with a rush 'you might have heard tell of Dane Swift, he kep a' – he checked the word and then let it come regardless – 'he kep a motte in it.'

'A moth?' exclaimed Winnie.

'A motte' he said 'of the name of Stella.'

Winnie stared out across the grey field. No sign of Sholto, nor of Belacqua, only this puce mass up against her and a tale of a motte and a star. What was a motte?

'You mean' she said 'that he lived there with a woman?'

'He kep her there' said the old man, he had read it in an old Telegraph and he would adhere to it, 'and came down from Dublin.'

Little fat Presto, he would set out early in the morning, fresh and fasting, and walk like camomile.

Sholto appeared on the stile in the crenellated wall, waving blankly. Winnie began to feel that she had made a mess of it.

'God knows' she said to Sholto when he came up 'where he is.'

'You can't hang around here all night' he said. 'Let me drive you home, I have to go up to Dublin anyhow.'

'I can't leave him' wailed Winnie.

'But he's not here, damn it' said Sholto, 'if he was he'd be here.'

The old man, who knew his Sholto, stepped into the breach with a tender of his services: he would keep his eyes open.

'Now' said Sholto, 'he can't expect you to wait here for ever.'

A young man on a bicycle came slowly round the corner from the Donabate direction, saluted the group and was turning into the drive of the asylum.

'Tom' cried Sholto.

Tom dismounted. Sholto gave a brief satirical description of Belacqua's person.

'You didn't see that on the road' he said 'did you?'

'I passed the felly of it on a bike' said Tom, pleased to be of use, 'at Ross's gate, going like flames.'

'On a BIKE!' cried Winnie. 'But he hadn't a bike.'

'Tom' said Sholto 'get out the car, look sharp now and run her down here.'

'But it can't have been him' Winnie was furious for several reasons, 'I tell you he had no bike.'

'Whoever it is' said Sholto, master of the situation, 'we'll pass him before he gets to the main road.'

But Sholto had underestimated the speed of his man, who was safe in Taylor's public-house in Swords, drinking and laughing in a way that Mr Taylor did not like, before they were well on their way.

J. I. M. Stewart

Teddy Lester's Schooldays

Harold Amroth was an immensely distinguished man with few close friends. Into becoming so distinguished he had been obliged to put more effort than many, since he came of humble people and had left school at fourteen. Numerous captains of industry and the like are proud of having done this, and have enjoyed a wide circle of acquaintance as well. But Amroth was a scientist. It might be better to say a savant, since he inhabited regions where, as the poet says, 'Physic of Metaphysic begs defence', and one may see (if one is clever enough oneself) 'Mystery to Mathematics fly'. To attain this empyrean he'd had further to travel than any man ever had to reach a board room, and the effort had perhaps a little confined him in the sphere of personal relations. He was on record, however, as a tolerably successful family man. Now a widower, he had two married sons who didn't much bother about him, two reasonably attentive married daughters, and a number of almost grown-up grand-children. The grandchildren were also becoming rather elusive – except, indeed, for a grandson, Robin Amroth, an under-graduate in his second year at Oxford. Robin was a boy much given to conscientious behaviour, with family duty well up on his list.

Latterly Amroth had turned into something of a recluse, living in a remote manor house, Danvers Place, which had been the property of his wife, who had been a woman of considerable independent fortune. This seclusion on the part of a man of intellectual eminence, willing from time to time to pronounce upon a wide range of public issues, attracted comment from those who were aware of it. On the one hand it enhanced the authority with which he spoke when he did speak. But on the other it prompted some to suppose that there must be something a bit odd, something increasingly eccentric, about old Harold Amroth.

It was a woman of almost his own age, Patricia Lawless, who perhaps knew him best, and who yet sometimes felt that she didn't know a great deal. She had been his secretary for many years: the sort of secretary whose father turns out to have been an Air Vice-Marshal or an Admiral. This, and a native strength of character, and also certain special circumstances of her employment, had combined to establish her in a significant position within the Amroth household. Mrs Amroth had been an invalid of the Victorian sort, seldom leaving her sofa, and Amroth himself had very little aptitude for the practical affairs of life. So it came to be understood that Miss Lawless ran things. Eventually she found, without particularly desiring it, that whenever authority had to be exerted it was she who was expected to do so – even if it came to rebuking her employer's butler or sacking his wife's housekeeper. And it was an authority that extended itself to some extent over two younger generations of Amroths. The hazards of this were obvious, but Miss Lawless was an intelligent woman and managed very well – so well, indeed, that she had come to be tolerantly regarded (but also a little feared) as a kind of honorary aunt and great aunt respectively by the children and grandchildren of the senior Amroths.

When Mrs Amroth died Miss Lawless saw that there must be a change. She was herself by this time a woman of some means, and she could have continued to run things at Danvers without suffering the imputation of eagerness to become Harold Amroth's second wife. She distrusted, however, the open-ended commitment she saw ahead of her if she stayed put – and felt, too, that it would be to Harold's advantage as a widower if he had to bestir himself and stand on his own feet. As for the children, they had long ago scattered and gone their own ways. The grandchildren were either at universities or, like Robin at that time, near the end of their schooldays; even in the holidays they seldom came to Danvers now. So, after a decent interval, Miss Lawless resigned her employment, took herself off to London, and addressed herself to various sorts of social endeavour in the city's East End. Naturally, the break was by no means entire. She was like the retired senior member of a firm who still figures as a 'consultant' on its letter-head, and who is in fact sometimes called in on sticky occasions. Miss Lawless frequently ran down to Danvers for the weekend, and in fact enjoyed an open invitation to turn up without notice at any time. She no longer kept an eye comprehensively on household affairs; they had to take their chance with a capable housekeeper. But she did keep an eye on Harold.

There was no particular reason why these visits should have become less frequent as time went on. Harold always received her cordially. His housekeeper, Mrs Duckett, who now felt the domestic economy of Danvers to be wholly within her own control, was well disposed to Miss Lawless and frequently asked her advice. But Miss Lawless did find herself turning up less often, all the same. Her concern was with Harold's health – his health and spirits – and she judged that the state of the case here could be better assessed at, say, six-weekly than fortnightly intervals. Moreover Harold was becoming yet more reclusive in various ways, so she may have begun to feel, almost unconsciously, that her visits were, after all, in some degree felt as intrusive.

It was certainly true that Harold was less and less tolerant of any effect of a crush of people around him. He had persuaded Mrs Duckett to part with a couple of maids, and had himself pensioned off his gardener and dismissed his under-gardener in furtherance of an arrangement whereby a firm of 'garden contractors' descended on Danvers at set intervals with what Miss Lawless judged to be devastating effect. And these were quite clearly not measures of economy. Harold had long ago blotted money out of his capacious mind, and it was simply not possible for him to turn mean. What he could conceivably turn into was a recluse of a positively pathological kind. There had already been a 'feature' about him in a popular paper in which he had been termed 'the hermit of Danvers'.

That Harold Amroth should thus appear in that particular sort of public print was a significant index of the position he had achieved. His work as a physicist would have been incomprehensible to anybody without a highly specialized training, but as a publicist of a dignified sort he increasingly enjoyed a national reputation. His secret here (if it may be spoken of in that way) was perhaps to have projected this image of himself very sparingly yet over a great many years. This, the cynical were inclined to say, is the best way to build up a kind of charismatic aura around oneself in the regard of the many-headed vulgar.

In terms of mere social *mores* he had been a very assimilative 'new man'. Even without the marriage he had made and the style of life it had brought him he would almost certainly have taken on, circumspectly and unobtrusively, the behaviour and assumptions of an upper class. Miss Lawless (who had been born there) sometimes wondered whether in this progress a good deal of hidden strain had been involved, and that he might be an easier person had he remained a simpler one. He had never done anything to conceal his origins – announcing firmly in reference books, for example, that his education had been at 'Dudley Road Elementary School' in a Midland town. But he might fairly have been called reticent, and Miss Lawless had certainly never heard him talk about Dudley Road. She asked herself whether Harold keenly felt himself to have missed in boyhood and youth experiences not to be enjoyed at a later age.

This was all rather speculative. More certain was the strain that had been involved simply in such a scientific career as Amroth's. At times he had worked himself beyond the point of exhaustion, and it was known that at one period, not long before his marriage, he had actually suffered a severe nervous breakdown. About this, very decidedly, he never talked. And there had been another occasion – much later on, and when Miss Lawless was already in his employment – when he had disappeared abruptly to America for almost four months: ostensibly on a research project of such military significance that nothing whatever could be uttered about it. Miss Lawless had suspected at the time that this mysterious episode masked the onset and running its course of another nervous disturbance. As Harold aged, therefore, she had good reason to keep that periodic watch not only over his physical health but also over what could be observed of his nervous tone.

It had for some years been Miss Lawless's habit to spend a month in Italy during the spring, and it so happened one year that she went off on her holiday when she had not been down to Danvers for some weeks. On her return from Urbino a visit was much overdue, and some immediate thought of it was already in her head when she was rung up by Robin Amroth. Robin, who was a very diffident youth, was profuse in apologies. But he was worried about something. Could he come and explain?

Miss Lawless was accustomed to lending a hand in the fixes Amroth grandchildren got into from time to time. Robin was her favourite. He was a worrying type, never sulky but regularly with a frown of perplexity on his brow. He was clever, as nearly the whole lot were, but he also owned a sensibility unknown to any of the others. He was slim and sandy and freckled, and he always came back to your recollection as good-looking, although in fact he was not particularly so. Miss Lawless used to tell herself that she was as near being in love with Robin Amroth as made no matter.

She was fairly sure what the trouble would be. Robin was about to take some examination – she believed in English Literature – which ran to what Oxford called 'Classified Honours' or something of the kind. It wouldn't be rational in Robin to say that he hadn't an earthly chance of a First. But he was going to own to a despairing feeling that he was bound *just* to miss one. Miss Lawless, although she had an intelligent woman's sense of the absurdity of such things, would sympathize with Robin and hearten him as she could. To intimate the degree of her concern she at once asked him to lunch with her in a restaurant, and chose rather an expensive one into the bargain.

There proved to be an element of miscalculation in this – or, rather, an unknown factor which threw the plan a little awry. Since their last meeting Robin had discovered the duty of being a vegetarian. Indeed, he had become a vegan, and that seemed to mean that he could eat virtually nothing at all. There was a menu the size of a large table-napkin, and Robin (who probably regarded such an object as rather vulgar, anyway) studied it for long and in despair. He clearly hated the thought of embarrassing his hostess, and at the mere thought of it was distinguishably flushing beneath his freckles. He was unflinching in his adherence to principle, all the same. Eventually an admissible salad was compounded for him and a submissive waiter brought him a glass of water.

Miss Lawless, who was of course not embarrassed, tried not to be amused either – and then discerned that Robin himself was aware of the fun. There was no doubt whatever that he was a most attractive boy. Miss Lawless was encouraged to take the bull by the horns at once and ask him about the progress of his work.

'Oh, I suppose it's going to be all right on the day, Lawful.' (The Amroth children all called her that.) Robin spoke as if the matter hadn't been on his mind. 'At least, they say it is, and I suppose they know their business. Only you do regularly hear of tutors being vastly indignant because they feel a pupil has been unjustly done by. So it must be the fact that their judgement is sometimes astray. It's a highly subjective business, when you come to think of it, and not a thing to worry about all that.' Producing this surprising and gratifying evidence of enhanced maturity, Robin gave a sudden shy smile. 'I say! Did you think that's what I was going to be on about?'

'Yes, Robin, I did. Is the salad all right?'

'Oh, yes, lovely. Only I must just —'

Robin fell silent, absorbed in a delicate manual operation. Very improperly, some almost microscopic creeping thing had been left to harbour in his modest refection. Now he coaxed it tenderly on to a fragment of lettuce leaf, stood up, glanced round the restaurant, spotted an elaborate arrangement of ferns and flowers in a window, and promptly carried this fellow-creature to sanctuary there. He returned, sat down composedly, started to say something and thought better of it, put in a little time nibbling a radish, and then abruptly spoke up.

'It's that I'm rather worried about Grandad,' he said. 'Have you seen him lately, Lawful?'

'No – not since some time before I left for Italy. I've been thinking about going down to Danvers one weekend soon.'

'I wish you would. I don't think he's very well.'

'Then of course I'll go down at once.' Miss Lawless glanced curiously at Robin, aware of some discomposure in him distinct from any simple anxiety about his grandfather's health. 'Did he complain at all? Or say anything about seeing Dr Ferris?'

'No, nothing like that. He asked me to lunch with him at Danvers last Sunday, you see, and I drove over from Oxford. He's rather intimidating in a way, being so immensely what he is.' Robin, perhaps more than his brothers and sisters, was aware of Harold Amroth's standing in the intellectual world. 'But he has always been very decent to me, and tremendously interesting as well. So I always look forward to his invitations.'

'Yes?' It seemed to Miss Lawless that Robin was a little shying away from what he had to say. 'You saw at once that he wasn't well?'

'Well, yes – but the whole set-up at Danvers seemed to have gone a bit to pieces. You know that he has got rid of everybody except Mrs Duckett and some half-witted girl from the village?'

'*Everybody?*'

'Yes, indeed. It gave the place a curiously empty and isolated feel – even, you know, although one never used to see all that of the maids and so on. And even Mrs Duckett had gone off for her fortnight's holiday. So Grandad and I just picnicked. That was all right, of course. But I had a feeling that he'd asked me over on impulse, or out of some odd curiosity —'

'Curiosity, Robin?' Miss Lawless was perplexed.

'I'll come to that.' Robin was somehow growing increasingly uncomfortable. 'I thought he was rather regretting bothering with me – but only because he didn't want to be bothering with anybody. He looks haggard, and rather yellow, and at first he was gloomy in a way I'd never seen him before. But later he perked up a little and talked quite a lot. Asking me questions, mostly. Only, you see, there was something queer about them. Have you ever heard, Lawful, that there are illnesses – grave organic diseases, really – that produce drastic character changes?'

'I believe there are – although I've never come across anything of the kind. Are you really saying that something of the sort is happening to your grandfather, Robin?'

'Perhaps I'm exaggerating.' It was clear that Robin was striving to be of a fair mind. 'He just asked me a lot of questions about school. He asked me whether I was ever caned.'

It was Miss Lawless's impulse to say, 'And were you?' The question would never have come into her head, but struck her as fair enough and not without interest. She instantly saw, however, that this wouldn't at all do. Robin was deeply upset.

'Perhaps,' she said seriously, 'he's taking up the subject of corporal punishment in schools. He may be going to write something about it.'

'It didn't feel like that. He wanted to know a lot about just how it was done. It was rather indecent, really.'

'I see.' Miss Lawless thought that she understood fairly well this over-sensitive youth's feeling of a wounded privacy. But it didn't, she felt, necessarily come to very much. In tête-à-tête with his grandson Harold had betrayed an indecorous interest in one of the milder forms of flagellation, not yet fallen wholly into disuse in these islands. It was unfortunate, and he had chosen the wrong boy. It might even betoken the emergence in Harold of a streak of senescence. But Robin mustn't be let inflate it in this fashion. 'I can understand its being awkward,' she said, 'a distinguished old man rather fingering over such a subject, if that was how it was. But I don't think it really important, Robin, not as the question of his physical health is important. I'll go down to Danvers in the next few days – and see Dr Ferris, among other things.'

Robin finished his salad in silence. He was evidently considering whether it was incumbent upon him to say more. And he decided it was.

'I know it sounds trivial in itself,' he said. 'And I know I'm too easily made jumpy by such things. But I wouldn't have called you in, so to speak, if I hadn't a queer sense that there's something more – something hidden in Grandad, or hidden *by*

Grandad – that may bob up to his discredit later on. It's just a hunch, and impossible to make sound sensible. But I have it, and I've felt I have to tell you so – because I know, Lawful, all the strength you've been to our family for a long time.' Robin fell silent again, as if once more wondering whether here was enough. And again it was not. 'It's that increasing solitude that chiefly worries me. Sending his whole household away, and being in that great place alone. "Solitude is the surest nurse of all prurient passions." It was somebody else who distrusted solitude who said that. Samuel Johnson.'

Miss Lawless was silent in her turn. She wasn't at all diverted by Robin's producing this scrap of undergraduate erudition. She had a duty – there wasn't a doubt of it – to take seriously the misgivings of this serious and intelligent boy.

She judged it prudent, however, to give twenty-four hours to considering the implications of what had been disclosed to her, and this period she passed in the normal pursuit of her affairs. She put in a substantial spell in a Citizens' Advice Bureau, and then did some shopping. This took her finally to the admirable establishment in Soho of a certain Mme Cadec, where she bought a set of six earthenware *cocottes*. She then walked to a bus stop on her way home. There was no bus, nor any queue waiting for one, and she took a short turn up and down the street. In the course of this her eye was caught by a large notice saying SEX SHOP.

Miss Lawless held no strong feminist persuasions. She did not believe that Robin Amroth was a male chauvinist pig in the making. She was unoffended when letters arrived for her bearing the prefix *Miss* rather than the modish *Ms*. But she did feel that there was no sort of behaviour which ought to be judged more unbecoming in a woman than a man. She therefore paused before the shop-window and informed herself, in a general way, of the kind of wares that were on sale within. What she saw first was a book called *The History of the Rod*; it had a pictorial cover on which a man, tied up and stripped to the waist, but well-groomed and evidently composed nevertheless, was awaiting correction by a policeman in shirt-sleeves and a helmet, who exhibited the same appearance of placid well-being as his victim. The second book bore the more spirited title *The Lure of the Lash*, and portrayed simply a cat-o'-nine-tails brandished in air by an invisible hand.

Miss Lawless, whom her recent lunch had rendered a little sensitive to such things, turned away at once. She did, however, glance through the open door of the shop as she went by. There was a rack of what she knew to be called 'girlie books', and from the covers of these magazines one could deduce that the currently fashionable pose for naked ladies was bottom up or bottom out. In these it might have been said that the flagellation theme – or at least the spanking theme – was just round the corner. But mainly the shop was given over to real books of a sort; there were shelves with row upon row of them. All – Miss Lawless conjectured – would be 'soft' porn; at the back of the establishment there would be kept the 'hard' stuff for reliable and more demanding customers. Considering briefly these commonplace sordid facts, Miss Lawless was at the same time aware of an entirely puzzling sensation. It lingered with her only for a moment, but this was long enough for her to recognize it as something like the *déjà-vu* phenomenon. She doubted whether she had ever peered into a 'sex shop' before. But of course that was beside the point. The essence of *déjà vu* is that the memory is a false one; the subject is treating as a recollection what he is in fact simultaneously perceiving for the first time. That was it. Nevertheless the experience continued obscurely to baffle and trouble her as she sat on the top deck of her bus.

She drove down to Danvers Place on the following evening, without ringing up Harold to announce her arrival. This was entirely in order. Her right to impromptu descents on the house had for long been a recognized thing, and Mrs Duckett always kept her old room ready for her. It was true that Mrs Duckett was probably still on holiday, and that Harold's solitude would be entire. ('The surest nurse of all prurient passions', she repeated to herself a shade uneasily. Dr Johnson had probably been right, as he was more often than not.) She didn't, of course, want to give an effect of pouncing on Harold; of catching him red-handed, so to speak, in an increasingly injudicious mode of life. An element of surprise might be revealing, all the same.

Dusk was falling as she drove the last few miles through empty downland. She had always thought it curious that so isolated a dwelling was to be found within little more than an hour's run from London. For a time she had supposed that the ancient house had perhaps been built as a hunting-lodge, surrounded only by woodland which had long since vanished away. But this, she had soon discovered, was not so. In the eighteenth century there had been several hamlets on the small estate, the ruins of which could still be surveyed by the curious. Some large drift in rural economy had brought about the change, and in the same period Danvers had passed into the hands of the sort of people from whom Harold's wife had come: nabobs and city merchants intent on establishing themselves as landed people in a moderate way. To the all-but original manor house – a rambling structure of timber posts, rails and struts interspersed with dark red brick – little that was immediately obvious had ever been added. Danvers Place was a house of acknowledged architectural and artistic importance in its own particular flight, and Harold had always been concerned to keep it as it should be kept. Or at least he had been this till recently. Skirting the topiary garden, and noticing the uncertain shapes now silhouetted against the afterglow in the western sky, Miss Lawless again had misgivings about those garden contractors.

She now had a more immediate misgiving as well. With even Mrs Duckett away, Harold might have grown tired of fending for himself and have taken himself off too. But it wasn't likely, for she had an impression that he now hardly ever left home. And when she drove into the old stable yard it was to see, sure enough, his lumbering antique Daimler in its customary place behind unclosed doors. She brought her own small Fiat to a halt, got out, and removed her suitcase. From where she stood the house appeared to be in total darkness, and the effect of solitude and vacancy thus rendered was enhanced by a silence which had descended on the scene like a curtain as soon as she had switched off her engine. She had arrived at Danvers at dusk or in darkness often enough, and frequently in these latter years when there had been no great stir of life around the place. But now she would have been glad to hear an owl scream or the crickets cry. Very obscurely, she even felt a sinister significance in the fact that she had arrived at Danvers totally unobserved: that even her having left town for the weekend was unknown to anyone in the world. She was not a nervous woman, and she was able to take, as it were, a dispassionate glance at the uneasiness invading her. As there was nothing perceptible to sense that could perturb other than a fanciful person, she was constrained to the view that something mildly telepathic was at work, and that within Danvers she was about to come upon a state of affairs decidedly out of joint. And as she walked round to the front of the house there strangely came back to her that moment in Soho in which she had glanced through the door of a shop and had been unaccountably surprised – for that was it – by what was on view there. It was surprising now to have thus inconsequently arrived at a better definition of her response to that surely trivial occasion. But almost at once all this vanished from her mind. She had rounded the side of the house, and there was a familiar patch of warm red light falling on part of the terrace in front of it.

Almost in the moment that she rang a bell the front door opened and Harold Amroth stood framed in it before her.

'My dear Patricia,' he said, 'how nice. What a good surprise.' And instantly her suitcase was in his hand, for he had the alert punctiliousness in such matters of a man who has come to them rather late. 'I'm all alone. We'll have a great deal of fun.' His voice was reassuring, and so even was the faint jocularity of what he had said. When the cat's away the mice will play – and so will children or lovers. Mrs Duckett was presumably the cat.

'I'm going to be a terrible nuisance, Harold,' Miss Lawless said. 'I've even arrived hungry.' As she spoke she stepped indoors and half-turned, so that for the first time she saw Harold in a clear light. She was filled with an instant dismay. It had been almost stupid in Robin, when reporting on his grandfather, to highlight that unfortunate turn in a conversation at the expense of what was so plain to see. Harold Amroth was a sick man.

'Better and better,' Harold said – swiftly, as if he detected what had been revealed to her. 'I'll just nip up with your gear to your room, and while you tidy I'll forage around. There's a cold duck, I know, and there's bread and a Stilton, and no end of Bordeaux: Lynch-Bages '66. I came on a whole case of it only the other day.'

Miss Lawless made some cheerful reply. Harold in his time had learnt all about being a good host. She knew that Chateau Lynch-Bages 1966 was rather grand for their occasion, and that therefore Harold carried off his proposed production of it gaily. She realized too – a tiny thing – that he believed, whether accurately or not, that it was more correct by some old-fashioned standard to say 'Bordeaux' than 'claret'. And she knew that – although there is little to be said for the concept of endearing foible – her affection for Harold was based upon her awareness of such small vulnerabilities carried through life by the boy from Dudley Road. But at least it wasn't a condescending affection. For Harold Amroth she owned, in a last analysis, more of respect than of any other sentiment. She was close to Robin in this; in holding in very high regard indeed the place Harold had won for himself not only in science but in the intellectual and moral life of the community.

'We'll eat here by the fire,' Harold said a little later. 'Perhaps it's a mild spring night outside, Patricia, but it's devilish cold in here. Danvers, if you ask me, was built by Aeolus for himself and all his progeny. Curly little winds scampering all over the house. I never feel warm in it now. I expect I'll keep this fire going until July.'

They were in the great hall – it deserved to be called that – of Danvers Place: a large panelled chamber with an open timber roof centred on a lantern which was not quite rainproof or even quite bird-proof either. It had always been a joke of Harold's that it was so uncomfortable as to be virtually uninhabitable, but in spite of this he spent a good part of the day in it. It was here, certainly, that he had expected the social life of the household to take place. For himself he reserved, at one end of the house, a room of almost equal size to house a notable library; and in the attics a region even more guarded and secluded which was called the workshop. A substantial area of the house, known in Victorian times as the nursery wing, had been turned into a small museum of the history of science. A couple of public schools in the neighbourhood were invited to send over a group of boys from time to time, and Harold would himself show them round. Afterwards he would give them an excellent tea in the great hall, during which he would tease them with questions like 'Which is it most important to be: literate or numerate?' And to whichever answer was first uttered with confidence he would rejoin, 'Quite right – absolutely right,' and carry round the plate of doughnuts or meringues. The boys, who all knew in advance about this prescriptive courtesy, were invariably delighted by it.

As she ate her duck and drank her claret Miss Lawless recalled one or two of these occasions with amusement. But not for long. She found it difficult to remove her mind from the disturbing fact that Harold looked so ill. The subject must be brought into the open; she would be failing in her duty if she shied away from that and received no assurance that he was under proper medical care. But she resolved to defer this until the meal was over, and she cast about for a topic that could be treated with some lightness of air.

'Harold, dear,' she asked, 'have you been inventing anything lately?'

This question referred to something not quite to be classed, perhaps, as endearing foible. It had always amused Harold to invent things; and it was to this hobby, indeed, that the attic workshop was understood to owe its being. When wearing this hat Harold did his best to be the mad scientist of the popular imagination as immortalized by Heath Robinson. In fact he had come up from time to time with unassuming gadgets of simple domestic utility – but also (it was rumoured) with certain suggestions for engines of war quite in the Leonardo class. He himself never spoke of this activity except as a joke or harmless eccentricity.

'Well, now,' he said at once, 'take the business of uncorking a bottle – like this one – it's not at all bad, is it? – that we're discussing now. Think of a chap – a bit of an invalid, perhaps – who wants a drink, but mustn't venture on much muscular effort. What is he to do? Somebody has already shown him how to inject a gas through the cork and simply force it out that way. But no civilized man wants to gas his wine, and moreover there's always a risk of exploding the bottle. Of course you could have a power-driven corkscrew, with an additional device for applying the required leverage to the lip of the bottle. But it would be hard to cut out all vibration that way, and one doesn't want – does one? – to apply vibro-massage to poor old Lynch-Bages.'

'Of course not,' Miss Lawless said. She was not quite at ease before this elaborate jocosity. She wondered whether there had been a hint of self-reference in that business of an invalid who must avoid muscular effort.

'So what we need is the magnetic cork. It has a cone-shaped ferrous insert, point upwards, near its base. After that you take a low-powered electro-magnet to it, and there you are.'

Miss Lawless didn't even pretend to be much amused by this nonsense, although to some extent she had invited it. She felt something defensive about such talk, as if Harold were resolved to stave off honest and equal communication with a flow of badinage. That *was* male chauvinism. So she changed her mind and spoke up with gravity at once.

'Harold, you won't mind my saying that you don't look too well. Is there anything wrong with the works?'

'Not seriously, I hope.' Miss Lawless was relieved to see that Harold was at least not offended. 'The fact is I had a fall a couple of months ago, and it shook me a little.'

'What sort of fall?'

'A thoroughly stupid one, I'm afraid. I was scrambling over a dry-stone wall when I tumbled and brought chunks of the confounded thing down on top of me. It was very absurd. But I was quite badly bruised.'

'But that's healed now?'

'Lord, yes! Only Ferris talks a certain amount of rot about possible sequelae. Wandering blood-clots, it seems. The human heart doesn't exactly welcome them as visitors, you know.'

'I do know. But that's simply a threat of possible disaster in the future. It oughtn't too much to affect your present health – or even spirits. There's nothing else?'

'My dear, the machine wears out. It's a very great puzzle. Here we are, sitting in the middle of it and feeling much as before. But inexorably it's wearing out, running down. As for my spirits, they're not perhaps too good either, and I'm sorry if you detect something factitious in my chirpiness. But my meditations are of time, you see. Time that has transfigured me.'

This apposite quotation from an Irish poet might have come from Robin Amroth, and it turned Miss Lawless's mind in his direction.

'I saw Robin the other day,' she said. 'He was so pleased that you asked him to lunch. But I think he too was aware of you as being a little below par.'

'He would be.' Now, for the first time, Harold seemed a shade uneasy. 'Robin is a highly intelligent boy – and perceptive, as well – which isn't the same thing. I hope he'll go far.'

'He's almost disablingly sensitive, in a way. I'll tell you rather a comical thing.' Miss Lawless had suddenly resolved to risk something. 'He was quite upset because you asked him whether he'd ever been caned at school.'

'He was, indeed.' Harold said this quietly, but something in his tone made Miss Lawless instantly repent of her rashness. 'Having that experience – or missing it, for that matter – is a boy's own business. Isn't that it?'

'Yes, I think so – something like that, Harold. With a boy like Robin, at least.'

'What I was after, you see, was one of those silly inventor jokes. I thought it would amuse him. We'd been talking about all that.' Harold had now become agitated. He was actually looking at Miss Lawless warily, as if calculating what it would be prudent to confess. 'It had just come into my head as a ludicrous phantasy; an adjustable whacking-machine, you might say. Set a dial, and it delivers a precise measure of what is required. No scope for too much zeal, or for favouritism coming into play.'

'You didn't go on to say all this to Robin?'

'I remember a primitive device of the sort in a comic when I was a boy.' Harold looked broodingly at Miss Lawless, and then started as if her question had only just reached him. 'Of course not. I did at least see my mistake. And I've worried about it ever since.'

Miss Lawless didn't feel that Harold's explanation of that small failure in tact with his grandson much improved matters, any more than did his statement that it was still much in his head. She was displeased with herself for having introduced the topic, and indisposed to hear any more about it.

'Go on with your wine, Harold, while I clear up a little,' she said, getting to her feet. They were sitting, as Harold had proposed, at a small table drawn up near the fireplace of the great hall. There was a big fire on the hearth, and every now and then Harold would reach forward and toss another log on it – carelessly, so that the sparks flew around in an alarming fashion.

'No, no – do sit down.' Harold seemed disturbed. 'We have so much to talk about, Patricia. Sue Sarten will do the chores in the morning. She comes on a bicycle at eight o'clock and tidies round. An invaluable girl. Dumb, of course.'

'Dumb – a bit thick, you mean?'

'No, no – Sue's probably rather clever. But really dumb. It's a wonderful dispensation. And she's never here for more than a couple of hours.'

'It sounds most inadequate. When does Mrs Duckett get back?'

'Mrs Duckett?' As Harold repeated the name he again looked oddly wary. 'She doesn't, as a matter of fact. I changed my mind, and have written to tell her I'm fixing her up with a pension.'

'You mean to be entirely alone, even when there's that possibility – if it's only a small possibility – of falling suddenly ill?'

'I'll be all right, my dear. Or probably I shall. It won't much matter if I'm not.'

Miss Lawless had asked her question with more composure than she felt. It may be repeated that she was not a nervous woman, and she was certainly one capable of decisive action in a crisis – much as her forebears had been at the Battle of Jutland and in similar situations. But she did now have a strong sense that the situation at Danvers Place was getting out of control – and that moreover it had a hinterland, at present obscure to her, from which there loomed and threatened just that sort of discreditable disclosure of which Robin had confessed himself apprehensive. There would come a moment – she was sure of this – when Harold, who was much more sick and depressed than the tone of his talk acknowledged, would require a firm hand extended to him – or even some curtain, some smoke-screen, dropped between him and an inquisitive world.

'I suppose I've said something morbid,' Harold was saying. 'And mock-Stoical, and so on. If it be now, 'tis not to come. But I honestly don't know, Patricia, that I'm afraid of death. Are you?'

'From time to time, yes.' Miss Lawless didn't know quite what to make of this turn in Harold's talk. 'So what *are* you afraid of?'

'Pain, in the first place. That's obvious. But next after that, I think, being seen for silly.'

'Being *what*?'

'Being detected as at all sharing in the pervasive absurdity of the universe. It's immodest, I suppose, to think to escape from that. But I'd like to do it, all the same.' Harold laughed softly. It was the first time he had laughed that night. 'Do you know, Patricia, I think we'd better go to bed? Ferris's orders, so far as I'm concerned. And I actually obey them – which doesn't say much for that noble facing of the dark. Is there anything you require? I shoved tea things, and so on, in your room.'

'Thank you very much. A book, perhaps. Do you mind if I find one in the library? You remember how I used to do that.'

'Go right ahead when you want to. And you remember how the light switches go.' Harold was on his feet, and giving a perfunctory kick at a straying log on the hearth. It was evidently his intention to be the first to go upstairs. And he did now look tired as well as ill. Miss Lawless suspected that her unheralded descent upon Danvers had imposed upon him some additional stress that he didn't care to admit. It was all the more incumbent upon her that she should take firm action if it were required.

The library at Danvers Place was a surprising room, chiefly because it was quite out of keeping with the rest of the house. Towards the close of the eighteenth century the then owner, having decided that he ought to possess something in the classical taste, had gone right to the top and called in Robert Adam for the job. The existing apartment was unpromising, being not long enough to sustain the appearance of a gallery and not quite broad enough to look like a well-proportioned room. By playing tricks with a coffered ceiling, and with the spacing of certain *trompe-l'œil* pilasters appearing to protrude beyond the rows of books they punctuated, Adam had successfully masked this infelicity, but at the expense of risking the impression that there was something not quite genuine about the total spectacle. Were the books, like the pilasters, just painted on? It was, of course, far from being so. Indeed, even where doors lurked concealed behind an apparently uninterrupted array of volumes, the volumes were real volumes, and an entire section of them could be made to pivot on what must have been uncommonly strong hinges.

At its further end, which closed upon a structure apsidal in form, the books on view had the character of those commonly to be found in a country-house library; they had probably 'come with the property' when Harold Amroth – or his wife – had bought it forty years before. But of course the greater part of the room was given over to Amroth's own books – and it would have been hard to tell, moving from bay to bay, whether one was in the working-library of a scientist or a scholar. The learning of the British Academy weighed down one set of shelves and the labours of the Royal Society another. There was also a good deal of what used to be called polite literature. It was polite literature that Miss Lawless entered the library in search of.

Miss Lawless was not very fond of the library. Although it was not totally forbidden territory as was the attic 'workshop', it had been the custom of the household to enter it very seldom, since its owner did a good deal of his reading and writing there. Miss Lawless had always felt this to be slightly absurd; Harold ought to have had a more modest sanctum for treatment of this knock-on-the-door order. But she may also have been sensitive to the architect's sophisticated juggling, with its faint suggestion of things being other than they seemed. Certainly some such generalized feeling was lurking in her mind tonight.

Harold still bought books in considerable numbers. There was a long shelf where recent accessions were prescriptively ranged for a time, and this space was almost fully occupied now. Miss Lawless crossed the room and studied it. Many of the volumes belonged to past centuries; they had come from antiquarian booksellers and concerned for the most part early discoveries and speculations in physics and astronomy; no doubt they were destined for that choice little museum of the history of science. But there were recent works too, and these tended to be philosophical or sociological, although they included a scattering of theology as well. Miss Lawless, searching for something lighter, had a look at several novels and popular biographies in turn. None of them much attracted her, and she told herself that she would probably not find it easy at the moment to fix her mind on reading at all. She had better go straight to bed, resigning herself to a certain amount of worrying about Harold before sleep came to her rescue.

There were a few more new books, however, on Harold's desk, and she went over to examine them. They turned out to be a more or less coherent group, each concerned either with some major Christian mystic or with some aspect of Neo-Platonic philosophy. It was an edifying little exhibition, and no doubt meant that Harold had consented to write an extended review of the volumes for some appropriate journal. She had better not, therefore, disturb these books – nor at present, indeed, did she feel quite up to that sort of thing. But as she was turning away from the big desk she happened to notice at one end of it the catalogue of a second-hand bookseller, open at its first page. She glanced at this quite idly, and read:

PART ONE

Curiosa and Erotica

1. ARETINO, Pietro (1492–1556): *Académie des Dames*, The 'licentious' dialogues. Includes the sonnets which became the subject of the cel-

ebrated indelicate drawings by Giulio Romano (mentioned by Shake-speare in *Winter's Tale*, V. ii)...

2. BRETONNE, Nicolas Restif de la (1734–1806): *Monsieur Nicolas* (16 vols., 1794–1797). (Restif, inordinately vain and of extremely relaxed morals, was not undeservedly nicknamed the 'Rousseau of the gutter')...

3. CLELAND, John (1709–1789): *Memoirs of a Woman of Pleasure*. The rare 8vo. edition, without place or date, which alone contains the episode of the heroine's witnessing a homosexual encounter. *Vide* Ashbee's *Catena Librorum Tacendorum*...

Miss Lawless turned over a couple of pages of the bulky catalogue in a kind of dire fascination. She had never had such a thing in her hands before, and she was astounded by this proliferation of often extremely expensive indecent books. But then she looked no further. Abandoning all thought of the solace of reading, she turned out the lights in the library, attended to the fire-guard which Harold had neglected in the great hall, and went up to bed.

Very unexpectedly, she went to sleep almost at once. Predictably, on the other hand, she woke up in the small hours. For a moment she felt a strong impression that some disturbance in the house had been responsible, even that she had heard a cry, and a thud as of a heavy object falling. This, however, vanished abruptly from her consciousness – and for the strangest of reasons. It had been succeeded by an equally momentary but extremely vivid visual phenomenon. The sensation was not that of recovering the tail-end of a dream, although there was something dream-like in what had fleetingly appeared as if flowing before her. In fact she knew perfectly well, even in the instant of seeing it, that here was that trick of projecting a creation of the mind seemingly into outer space which most characteristically occurs upon the fringes of sleep. What she had thus glimpsed was an open door, revealing within shelf upon shelf of books. And the books surprised her. It was something different that ought to have been there. Miss Lawless had to confront this only for a second. Then illumination came to her.

*

Nobody had ever disturbed Harold Amroth in his workshop, or indeed entered it upon any occasion. When Harold was closeted in it, busy with his inventions, he had to be contacted on a house-telephone, should some emergency require his attention. Miss Lawless, although she had actually lived at Danvers Place for considerable periods of time, had in fact ascended to the attic floor on only two or three occasions. It was one of these occasions that she was recalling now. The house-telephone was out of order, and an important visitor from abroad had unexpectedly presented himself. Miss Lawless had thought it best to give Harold this news in person, and had gone upstairs and knocked at the workshop door. Harold had opened it at once, emerged, and closed it behind him. They had then gone downstairs together. But Miss Lawless had made the puzzling observation that the workshop had no appearance of a workshop at all, being simply a small study lined with books. Later she explained the puzzle to herself – or explained it away – quite easily. The topography of those attic regions was vague to her, and the room she had glimpsed must simply communicate with another, or others, beyond it. The inventions must be fabricated there. So eventually the small odd occasion had passed from her recollection. It had lurked somewhere in her mind, nevertheless – and not without linking itself, surely, with other and obscure apprehensions which she couldn't bring to consciousness at all. There could be no other accounting for her curious experience in Soho.

Yet wasn't what was hinting itself to her nonsense? Of course the glimpsed attic book-room was indeed only the first of several interconnecting chambers, and merely contained a large collection of books of a technical character. And might it not be possible to verify this fact now? No sooner had these questions formed themselves than Miss Lawless had sprung out of bed, thrust her feet into slippers, wrapped her dressing-gown around her, and was ready to put matters to the test. She had a small electric torch in her bag, and Harold's room was remote from her own. Unless he was himself roaming the house at this unlikely hour there was no risk of an embarrassing encounter.

Nevertheless she was doing something covert, clandestine.

Intermittently through centuries, she supposed, people had prowled Danvers in the dead of night: pilfering servants, guilty lovers, insomniacs, somnambulists, men and women haunted by sin, crazed with grief. This invisible army was around her as she climbed the final staircase. She had to tell herself that here was no time to be fanciful. It was something quite simple that she had to discover. Yet it proved to be not altogether easy. She hesitated to turn on any lights, and the beam of her torch was scarcely a sufficient guide in these almost unknown surroundings. For some moments she doubted whether she could be sure of the right corridor, of the right door at the end of it. Then, suddenly, the door was in front of her. She recalled it clearly, even down to the small detail that it was fitted with both a Yale and a mortise lock. Almost certainly there was no other interior door in Danvers Place so provided. But there was nothing sinister in that. Harold's hobby, his labours as an inventor, no doubt required a certain security. Miss Lawless put out a hand, and found the door locked. That too was only as it should be.

But this door *was* at the end of its corridor! It simply faced directly down it. The corridor itself had doors on one side and windows on the other – this wing of the house being an exceptionally narrow one, and in fact nothing but a single row of rooms each of modest size. And at the end was this crucial room, which would be slightly larger simply because incorporating the breadth of the corridor. All this was entirely precise, and negatived that vague notion of intercommunicating attic chambers. But Miss Lawless was thorough. She entered every other room on the corridor, and found all of them empty. She opened a window upon a faint moonlight, which showed her that the architecture of the wing was as she now perfectly well knew it must be. Her nocturnal investigation was concluded.

Miss Lawless returned to her room, and her first sensation when she had got into bed again was of simple relief. It had been the sense of mystery and uncertainty that was alarming, and now she commanded the dimensions of the situation she felt more composed. 'Trivial' was the word she tried to hold on

to. Harold – the family Harold and the public Harold – was, as
most of us are, companioned by a hidden self; and his particular
hidden self involved a hidden collection of books. Every now
and then he repaired to that upper chamber and refreshed
himself by reading Aretino and heaven knew what else. It was
the 'what else' that Miss Lawless now found still worrying
her, after all. She remembered what she had glimpsed in the
catalogue downstairs: the existence of scores, of hundreds of
dirty books – *Librorum Tacendorum*, unfit to be talked about.
And there they had been in that Soho shop: pornographic books,
sadistic books, kinky books galore!

Moreover didn't people who succumbed to such tastes frequently acquire not only indecent books but indecent objects as
well? Miss Lawless seemed to recall a small shopkeeper's wife
turning up at her Advice Bureau among whose numerous dis-
tresses was the fact that her husband spent a lot of money in
this way. Miss Lawless had made a note, *Buys sexual engines*,
by way of recording this consultation.

She was far from wanting to feel deeply shocked by what she
had discovered. It must simply be viewed, she told herself, as
presenting a practical problem. And the problem, crudely put,
was simply that of Harold's posthumous reputation. For here
was a man of the highest intellectual distinction who happened
also to enjoy a large measure of popular interest and acclaim.
He was a very sick man, now living in almost total solitude in
this great house: 'the hermit of Danvers' according to that cheap
public print. On this level he would be quickly forgotten, but
for a short time his career and death would be 'news'. From
that 'news' it was most unlikely that the existence of the small
private library in the attics would escape. People would turn up
at Danvers to make inventories for probate – that sort of thing –
and in some pub or other the intriguing discovery would be
discreetly leaked for reward. Here was the problem, and it was
an urgent one. Miss Lawless felt little doubt that Dr Ferris,
were he apprised of the facts, would undoubtedly agree that it
was so.

She must have it out with Harold in the morning. Without
hint of moral dispproval, or even of moral discomfort, she must

represent to him the propriety – if only for his children's and grandchildren's sake – of so arranging his affairs as to quit this world with a decent regard to conventional modes of conduct. There need be no immediate bonfire. Harold need merely instruct his solicitors that upon his death his former secretary Miss Lawless was to be given immediate access to the 'workshop' and permitted to dispose of its contents at her discretion. It mightn't be strictly legal. But in the circumstances no respectable family solicitor would think twice about that.

Miss Lawless was so satisfied with this view of the matter that again she went to sleep almost at once. She woke up for good, however, a couple of hours later, and discovered that it was six o'clock. Having decided to make her early-morning tea, she found that Harold had provided everything except the tea itself: the small silver caddy on her bedside table was empty. But at least she knew just how to replenish it, and once more – this time in the pale light of dawn – she donned her dressing-gown and left her room. Arrived at the head of the main staircase, a Jacobean feature heavy with dry blackened oak, she glanced along a corridor running through another wing of the house. Something was humped on the floor near the end of it, and for a moment she thought it must be a big shaggy dog. Then she remembered the sounds which had merely touched the fringe of her consciousness on her first waking up. She ran. It was Harold. He was lying in his pyjamas just outside his open bedroom door. Having been a VAD in the war, Miss Lawless was not long in doubt about the state of the case. Harold was dead. That wandering visitor had reached his heart.

Not unnaturally, this sad discovery for a time drove all nonsense about the attic book-room out of Miss Lawless's head. Her first duty must be to ring up Dr Ferris. It was her only duty, for that matter, apart from then at once communicating with Harold's children. For this was a household in which her standing was no longer other than that of a guest.

She went to the telephone, and her finger was on the dial before quite a new feeling stayed her hand. It was a feeling – not to be resisted although surely irrational – of horror and revulsion before the situation in which she had involved herself. She, and she alone, stood between Harold and disgrace. And not even disgrace in any robust and tragic sense. Harold was going to be 'seen for silly', just as he had feared. A silly senile old man, lurking among smutty books! Was there anything she could do – and do swiftly? Within a couple of hours the dumb girl, Sue Sarten, would arrive on her bicycle, and it was only by simulating an improbable ignorance that she could defer summoning Ferris even until then. Thereafter she would have no authority whatever. She could only hasten to report to the first of Harold's two sons whom she could locate the imminent scandal to prevent which some measure must be instantly put in hand.

But Miss Lawless took a poor view of those two inattentive middle-aged men. They might well prove unreliable, and they would certainly be insensitive. Even if the thing remained a family secret Robin would inevitably be told about it. Eventually, in fact, all sorts of people would be told. Cronies in clubs! The thought was intolerable. But it was Robin who really counted – who really and truly alone counted with Miss Lawless. Had there been no Robin Amroth the plan she now carried out would probably not so much as have occurred to her.

It was a perfectly simple plan, depending on the fact that, just as she had arrived at Danvers totally unknown to the world on the previous evening, so – with any luck – could she depart early this morning. She might be ten miles on her road before she so much as encountered another vehicle. And she had never really liked Danvers Place – or rather she had never liked it for Harold. Harold as a member of what the reference books called the Landed Gentry had never been quite right. The Master's Lodging of some Cambridge college would have better become him, and probably left him a less lonely man in the end.

She got the dead man into his bed again, and made other prudent dispositions. What was going to happen would no doubt be investigated after a fashion by expert persons, but she was not much impressed by that. Harold's known carelessness about that big fire downstairs was an important point, and so was the fact that an ancient tinder-dry half-timbered dwelling such as this one would behave like a torch within minutes. As for the indecent books in the attic, there would certainly have been no detailed insurance of them, and a few surviving volumes in a charred condition would attract no interest whatever. The fire must, of course, start in the great hall. It was fortunate that she always carried a spare tin of petrol under the bonnet of the Fiat.

Yes, it was perfectly simple. And, sure enough, it all went like clockwork. Harold Amroth's was a noble funeral pyre.

Unexpectedly when it happened – although she must at one time have been given notice of the fact – Miss Lawless found that she had been named as one of the dead man's executors. She had often assisted his sons in one way or another. But, although she was so plainly a person of breeding and cultivation, they had never (unlike Robin and some of the other grandchildren) thought of her as more than a useful secretary and faithful Girl Friday. So she was saddled with various small chores which she didn't at all resent. Her appointment in Harold's will kept her in the picture. And this meant that she would be in a position to act forcibly were there any attempt to do down Robin.

Nothing of the sort in fact occurred. Robin turned out to have been Harold's favourite grandson, and in a discreet way he did a little better out of the carve-up than did anybody else. So Miss Lawless's job proved to be not much more than settling bills and attending to communications which arrived from here and there in ignorance of their proposed recipient's decease. There weren't many of these latter. Harold Amroth's death – apparently of a heart-attack precipitated by his waking up to find himself in the middle of a hideous conflagration – had been widely publicized, so there were not many people who didn't know about it.

There was a small bill from the bookseller – and the bookseller's name, being slightly unusual, was one which Miss Lawless remembered. 'Ciprian Cartlidge' had appeared on that fateful catalogue on Harold's desk in the library at Danvers. The bill was for the supply of a book called *Teddy Lester's Schooldays*, which was described as 'fine'. Miss Lawless concluded that *Teddy Lester's Schooldays* was a novel, and that 'fine' described the condition of the physical object rather than the literary quality of the work. But the bill somehow made her uneasy. She decided to call on Mr Cartlidge and discharge the debt in person.

Mr Cartlidge (or 'the pornographer', as Miss Lawless thought of him) proved to be silver-haired and softly spoken. He showed no surprise that his establishment should thus be visited by an elderly gentlewoman. Nor, so far as its appearance went, was there any reason why he should do so. His shop was not at all like the one in Soho. What its window displayed, upon a background of dull purple velvet, was a couple of ancient maps of Berkshire and a folio volume open upon an aquatint of Windsor Castle.

'Lord Amroth,' Miss Lawless began briskly, 'died, as you may know, early in May.' (Harold had been a Life Peer – a condition which Miss Lawless, true to her own order, regarded as mildly absurd, and would thus invoke only upon formal occasions.) 'I have called to pay this bill myself, as a quick means of determining whether there is any further outstanding account with you. It is desirable that everything of the kind should be settled as soon as possible.'

'Quite so, quite so. And it is Miss Lawless, is it not?' The pornographer appeared remarkably well-informed. 'May I say, madam, that your brother, General Lawless, is one of my most valued customers?' Mr Cartlidge paused fractionally on this possibly disturbing intelligence. 'A keen lepidopterist indeed is the General.'

'A lepidopterist?' There was really no need for Miss Lawless to repeat the word. As a boy Gerald had put in much time collecting butterflies, and he had maintained this interest in a learned way throughout a long career in the Indian Army.

'Yes, indeed. The lepidoptera, Miss Lawless, are one of our specialities. Nowadays, you know, an antiquarian bookseller must specialize. I regret the fact, but there it is.' Mr Cartlidge spread out resigned hands a little too near to Miss Lawless's nose. 'Lord Amroth, however, was not much interested in the lepidoptera.'

'Definitely not,' Miss Lawless said coldly.

'But he was among the most loyal – if I may venture to express it that way – of our Part Three customers.'

'Of your what, Mr Cartlidge?'

'I speak in terms of our regular catalogues, madam. Part One is *Curiosa and Erotica*. A steady line, that – although, I fear, censurable in some regards. Part Two is *Insectivora and Lepidoptera*. And Part Three is *Juvenilia*. We use the word a little loosely, perhaps. Not as betokening the early writing of eminent authors, but rather literature primarily intended for younger readers. But only primarily, mark you. A great many mature persons maintain that interest.'

'Including Lord Amroth?' Miss Lawless heard herself ask. 'And hence *Teddy Lester's Schooldays?*'

'Certainly. And I have little doubt, Miss Lawless, that his lordship's collection of boys' fiction was the best in the country. And largely acquired through ourselves, I'm proud to say. All the early stuff – Gunby Hadath, Desmond Coke and so on – and then complete runs of both the *Gem* and the *Magnet*. St Jim's and Greyfriars, you know. Harry Wharton and Tom Merry and Billy Bunter. You may have heard of him, madam.'

'I remember Bessie Bunter,' Miss Lawless said drily.

'Ah, yes – in the *Schoolgirl*, that is. But I don't think his lordship ever collected the girls' papers. They haven't quite the same appeal, I'd say. Bloaters toasted by the study fire, and a breathless hush in the close that night. Nostalgic reading, in a way. I don't doubt his lordship was an Eton College boy. I'm glad we found *Teddy Lester's Schooldays* for him before it was too late. Good clean exciting stuff, all the Teddy Lester books.'

'Would you say that they contain a good deal about corporal punishment?'

'It crops up, of course.' Mr Cartlidge appeared unsurprised by this question. 'A good licking now and then is part of the dear old rough-and-tumble – eh? But I'd say there isn't much of it in the Teddy Lesters. I can only remember the weak prefect – Pole, I think he's called – who has to be shown by an old hand how to give six with full effect to a bully. A matter of the right flick of the wrist, it was.'

'Thank you.' Miss Lawless had now heard enough, or more than enough. But there was one further question she had to ask. 'You are quite sure, Mr Cartlidge, that nothing further is owing to you? For instance, Lord Amroth never bought books from Part One of your catalogues?'

'Definitely not.' If Mr Cartlidge detected that these two queries failed to hitch on to one another at all closely, he again gave no sign. It was detectable, nevertheless, that he was far from being at sea. 'His lordship,' he amplified, 'took no interest whatever in all that sort of thing. Recollections of early childhood – eh? Or, at least, of later childhood. You will recall, Miss Lawless, the poet Gray's beautiful *Ode On a Distant Prospect of Eton College*? Such fond memories were undoubtedly his lordship's, and I am happy to think that my firm was able to play its part in quickening them.'

'Lord Amroth,' Miss Lawless said, 'was educated at Dudley Road Elementary School.'

Having delivered herself of this, Miss Lawless paid her money for *Teddy Lester's Schooldays*, and bade Mr Cartlidge good morning.

Not unnaturally, it was slowly and thoughtfully that she made her way back to her dwelling. There had undoubtedly been an element of misapprehension in the affair. But would not Harold, after all, have very decidedly been seen for 'silly' if it had transpired that he was hung up on the *Magnet* and the *Gem* and the innumerable progeny of *Tom Brown*, and *St Winifred's*, and *Stalky & Co*? It had been as innocent as filling a series of attics with Hornby trains, but it would make an awkward final page in a biography. And Miss Lawless, as has been recorded, had never cared for Danvers Place, anyway. There was really nothing to regret. She made a note, however, that when she next invited Robin Amroth to lunch with her it ought to be at a good vegetarian restaurant.

Flann O'Brien

The Martyr's Crown

Mr Toole and Mr O'Hickey walked down the street together in the morning.

Mr Toole had a peculiarity. He had the habit, when accompanied by another person, of saluting total strangers; but only if these strangers were of important air and costly raiment. He meant thus to make it known that he had friends in high places, and that he himself, though poor, was a person of quality fallen on evil days through some undisclosed sacrifice made in the interest of immutable principle early in life. Most of the strangers, startled out of their private thoughts, stammered a salutation in return. And Mr Toole was shrewd. He stopped at that. He said no more to his companion, but by some little private gesture, a chuckle, a shake of the head, a smothered imprecation, he nearly always extracted the one question most melodious to his ear: *'Who was that?'*

Mr Toole was shabby, and so was Mr O'Hickey, but Mr O'Hickey had a neat and careful shabbiness. He was an older and a wiser man, and was well up to Mr Toole's tricks. Mr Toole at his best, he thought, was better than a play. And he now knew that Mr Toole was appraising the street with beady eye.

'Gorawars!' Mr Toole said suddenly.

We are off, Mr O'Hickey thought.

'Do you see this hop-off-my-thumb with the stick and the hat?' Mr Toole said.

Mr O'Hickey did. A young man of surpassing elegance was approaching; tall, fair, darkly dressed; even at fifty yards his hauteur seemed to chill Mr O'Hickey's part of the street.

'Ten to one he cuts me dead,' Mr Toole said. 'This is

one of the most extraordinary pieces of work in the whole world.'

Mr O'Hickey braced himself for a more than ordinary impact. The adversaries neared each other.

'*How are we at all, Sean a chara?*' Mr Toole called out.

The young man's control was superb. There was no glare, no glance of scorn, no sign at all. He was gone, but had left in his wake so complete an impression of his contempt that even Mr Toole paled momentarily. The experience frightened Mr O'Hickey.

'Who ... who was *that?*' he asked at last.

'I knew the mother well,' Mr Toole said musingly. 'The woman was a saint.' Then he was silent.

Mr O'Hickey thought: There is nothing for it but bribery – again. He led the way into the public house and ordered two bottles of stout.

'As you know,' Mr Toole began, 'I was Bart Conlon's right-hand man. We were through 'twenty and 'twenty-one together. Bart, of course, went the other way in 'twenty-two.'

Mr O'Hickey nodded and said nothing. He knew that Mr Toole had never rendered military service to his country.

'In any case,' Mr Toole continued, 'there was a certain day early in 'twenty-one and orders came through that there was to be a raid on the Sinn Fein office above in Harcourt Street. There happened to be a certain gawskogue of a cattle-jobber from the County Meath had an office on the other side of the street. And he was well in with a certain character by the name of Mick Collins. I think you get me drift?'

'I do,' Mr O'Hickey said.

'There was six of us,' Mr Toole said, 'with meself and Bart Conlon in charge. Me man the cattle-jobber gets an urgent call to be out of his office accidentally on purpose at four o'clock, and at half-four the six of us is parked inside there with two machine-guns, the rifles and a class of a homemade bomb that Bart used to make in his own kitchen. The military arrived in two lurries on the other side of the street at five o'clock. That was the hour in the order that came. I believe that man Mick Collins had lads working for him over in the War Office across in London. He was a great stickler for the British being punctual on the dot.'

'He was a wonderful organizer,' Mr O'Hickey said.

'Well, we stood with our backs to the far wall and let them have it through the open window and them getting down offa the lurries. Sacred godfathers! I never seen such murder in me life. Your men didn't know where it was coming from, and a lot of them wasn't worried very much when it was all over, because there was no heads left on some of them. Bart then gives the order for retreat down the back stairs; in no time we're in the lane, and five minutes more the six of us upstairs in Martin Fulham's pub in Camden Street. Poor Martin is dead since.'

'I knew that man well,' Mr O'Hickey remarked.

'Certainly you knew him well,' Mr Toole said, warmly. 'The six of us was marked men, of course. In any case, fresh orders come at six o'clock. All hands was to proceed in military formation, singly, by different routes to the house of a great skin in the Cumann na mBan, a widow be the name of Clougherty that lived on the south side. We were all to lie low, do you understand, till there was fresh orders to come out and fight again. Sacred wars, they were very rough days them days; will I ever forget Mrs Clougherty! She was certainly a marvellous figure of a woman. I never seen a woman like her to bake bread.'

Mr O'Hickey looked up.

'Was she,' he said, 'was she . . . all right?'

'She was certainly nothing of the sort,' Mr Toole said loudly and sharply. 'By God, we were all thinking of other things in them days. Here was this unfortunate woman in a three-storey house on her own, with some quare fellow in the middle flat, herself on the ground floor, and six blood-thirsty pultogues hiding above on the top floor, every man-jack ready to shoot his way out if there was trouble. We got feeds there I never seen before or since, and the *Independent* every morning. Outrage in Harcourt Street. The armed men then decamped and made good their escape. I'm damn bloody sure we made good our escape. There was one snag. We couldn't budge out. No exercise at all – and that means only one thing . . .'

'Constipation?' Mr O'Hickey suggested.

'The very man,' said Mr Toole.

Mr O'Hickey shook his head.

'We were there a week. Smoking and playing cards, but when nine o'clock struck, Mrs Clougherty come up, and, Protestant, Catholic or Jewman, all hands had to go down on the knees. A very good ... strict ... woman, if you understand me, a true daughter of Ireland. And now I'll tell you a damn good one. About five o'clock one evening I heard a noise below and peeped out of the window. Sanctified and holy godfathers!'

'What was it – the noise?' Mr O'Hickey asked.

'What do you think, only two lurries packed with military, with my nabs of an officer hopping out and running up the steps to hammer at the door, and all the Tommies sitting back with their guns at the ready. Trapped! That's a nice word – *trapped!* If there was ever rats in a cage, it was me unfortunate brave men from the battle of Harcourt Street. God!'

'They had you at what we call a disadvantage,' Mr O'Hickey conceded.

'She was in the room herself with the teapot. She had a big silver satteen blouse on her; I can see it yet. She turned on us and gave us all one look that said: *Shut up, ye nervous lousers.* Then she foostered about a bit at the glass and walks out of the room with bang-bang-bang to shake the house going on downstairs. And I seen a thing ...'

'What?' asked Mr O'Hickey.

'She was a fine – now you'll understand me, Mr O'Hickey,' Mr Toole said carefully; 'I seen her fingers on the buttons of the satteen, if you follow me, and she leaving the room.'

Mr O'Hickey, discreet, nodded thoughtfully.

'I listened at the stairs. Jakers I never got such a drop in me life. She clatters down and flings open the halldoor. This young pup is outside, and asks – awsks – in the law-de-daw voice, "Is there any men in this house?" The answer took me to the fair altogether. She puts on the guttiest voice I ever heard outside Moore Street and says, "Sairtintly not at this hour of the night; I wish to God there was. Sure, how could the poor unfortunate women get on without them, officer?" Well lookat. I nearly fell down the stairs on top of the two of them. The next thing I hear is, "Madam this and madam that," and "Sorry to disturb and I beg your pardon," "I trust this and I trust that," and then the whispering starts, and at the wind-up the halldoor is closed and into the room off the hall with the pair of them. This young bucko out of the Borderers in a room off the hall with a headquarters captain of the Cumann na mBan! *Give us two more stouts there, Mick!'*

'That is a very queer one, as the man said,' Mr O'Hickey said.

'I went back to the room and sat down. Bart had his gun out, and we were all looking at one another. After ten minutes we heard another noise.'

Mr Toole poured out his stout with unnecessary care.

'It was the noise of the lurries driving away,' he said at last. 'She'd saved our lives, and when she come up a while later she said "We'll go to bed a bit earlier tonight, boys; kneel down all." That was Mrs Clougherty the saint.'

Mr O'Hickey, also careful, was working at his own bottle, his wise head bent at the task.

'What I meant to ask you was this,' Mr O'Hickey said, 'that's an extraordinary affair altogether, but what has that to do with that stuck-up young man we met in the street, the lad with all the airs?'

'Do you not see it, man?' Mr Toole said, in surprise. 'For seven hundred years, thousands – no, I'll make it millions – of Irish men and women have died for Ireland. We never rared jibbers; they were glad to do it, and will again. But that young man was *born* for Ireland. There was never anybody else like him. Why wouldn't he be proud?'

'The Lord save us!' Mr O'Hickey cried.

'A saint I called her,' Mr Toole said, hotly. 'What am I talking about – she's a martyr and wears the martyr's crown today!'

William Sansom

Time Gents, Please

'Meet you under the Clock, old boy?'

'Meet you under the Clock!'

These were the words those two exchanged before they took their pleasures; they referred to that great Clock that hangs above the platforms at Victoria, grimy old trystwatch dear to denizens of the Surreyed South as is the Strand to citizens returned from Empires in the East. The Strand still topical for tropic chaps, the Clock still ticking tryst for Farquhar's and for Urquhart's cricket caps.

Those were their names, and cricketing their pleasure. Cricket, and junketing with Old Boys; in between times, once or twice a year an evening out – cheers, chaps! – upon the beer. The two lived thus by Fixtures. Not young, not middle-aged, adrift in their tiresome thirties, born of old parents, taught by older masters, *they* were fixtures too – time for them had not much moved along, fixtures they lived by Fixtures. Yet to turn a penny, all the older ways aslump, each had had to join a job of up-and-coming kind. Thus you might hear the fellows say, vaguely but with meaning: 'Farquhar's in a radio way, Urquhart's in Dry Cleaning.'

'Meet you under the Clock, old boy?'

'Meet you under the Clock!'

Click the two receivers went! And each would glance up at the smaller clock in each's little office – Friday the day, the next day Saturday Off – as if to urge along the weary hours. Then Farquhar'd sigh and sell a superhet, and Urquhart miles away would shrink a blouse. 'Fabriolize your shrunks,' he'd later say: and Farquhar'd make a megacycle pay.

But come the Saturday you'd see them grey of bag, of buttoned blazer blue, pork-pie greenly set aloft, brown of each shining shoe – you'd see them gruff a timely greeting, on time and under Time, watches shot from cuff comparing times with Time above. 'Time for a quick one?' 'No time like the present.' Each with a small green ticket wet in hand would wet each whistle – then the train, the drowsing day of cricket.

Sometimes, and those *were* times, two Fixtures came at once! Magpies versus Wandsworth First – and after that, a dinner for the Old Oakhampton Boys! A willow, then an Oak – Hamptonians all! They'd carry in their batlong bags black clothes as well as white, and puffing up from victory to Victoria, dash down the stairway of the Gents to slam a penny door and change their pants. But on the way, before they slipped the lock: 'Meet you under the Clock, old boy?' 'Meet you under the Clock.' Then wrestle there alone with ties, with butterflies and other flies, raising a well-cocked eyebrow at graffiti, much of it lost forever – more's the pity.

Later out they'd brisk – two Magpies, lean and tanned, to meet beneath the Clock and then repair with forty other Oakers up the stairs of tilish gilt Pagoni's, where – how beautiful the stagly ones! – they'd pool their first-rate stories of a secondary school. Later the Older Boys would start on Ypres; they'd beg their pardon, catch them with their Caen. The old 'uns then would shed their tears for Better 'Oles and Armentiers: easy the riposte to that, Tons of Flak and Bags of Frat. The school song sung, the handshakes done, they'd split a cab to the Clock (eyes on the cabby's clock the while) and then with a great gruff goodnight smile make off to their sleepy beds. Farquhar and Urquhart, sleepy-heads, off to their sleepy beds.

'Meet you under the Clock, old boy?'
   'Meet you under the Clock.'
   Thus their life they whiled away as Farquhar went his radio way while Urquhart drily cleaned. Urquhart wrote out little cards: 'May we have your shirt, sir?' Farquhar'd sell A.I. T.Vs. – A.C.–D.C. 'they're a cert, sir.' 'Fires shaped like electric fans, fans like electric fires!' 'Renovated, cleaned and spotted, worn or torn wear, we're the Dyers!' 'Buy our brand-new Telewhizz,

bright with visual hiccup! Buy my fluorescent lamp, my little plastic pick-up!' 'De Luxe, de Luxe! There are no flukes! Give *us* your dirty garment! The pleasure's ours, the risk is yours, if it's ruined there's no harm meant!'

Time went by and life was fairly sweet. Though there was bitterness in work, they turned each year a better penny; though they decried the passing of the older ways, in themselves they stayed the course, they stayed the same, they stayed, they played and stayed.

But Fate is not so easily appeased. Fate is never very pleased to leave such uneventful lives alone. It was a day indeed of Double Event, a day of batting and of Old Boy's bat, when Fate took a die and deftly cast – Farquhar and Urquhart saw the first Event, they never saw the last.

'Meet you under the Clock, old boy?'

'Meet you under the Clock!'

'Time for a swift one?' 'One for the road?' 'No time like the nonce!' That was all right, all right so far – sucking their cigs in the train they felt, all is as right as rain. But neither knew what the Hon. Sec. knew, the man who fixed the Fixtures, *he'd* been to the pictures, and on the screen in the news he'd seen a Ladies' Team! *Ladies!* How ridiculous! Just as a joke he'd arranged a match, the Ladies were too willing, but knowing the boys would never believe, he'd kept the matter up his sleeve – the whole thing should be killing!

When Farquhar saw his first white skirt he nearly toppled over, Urquhart tore at a chunk of field and filled his mouth with clover. Can it be true? Is it a dream? Pinch me! Pinch *me*! A Ladies' Team! Blazers and blouses, stockings and skirts! The principle, sir, it's *that* that hurts! 'Things aren't what they were,' they groaned. But soon the Ladies taught 'em that things aren't what you wear at all – the girls went in to slaughter 'em.

Brawned as bloody Amazons! Baleful as Bacchantes! Thrills and chills and spills and frills – the flashing of their panties! Bails to the right of them, balls to the left – slogging for sixes and sevens! Body line! Filthy swine! Got 'er! You rotter! Never were two elevens ever more ruseful, accuseful, abuseful ... Howzat? And howzis – here's one for your trousis! And here, where it hurts, is one for your skirts ... Cricket that day lost its greenswardly chastity! Weep for the willow on that very nasty day!

Farquhar and Urquhart gave many a shudder – this wasn't cricket, this was blue murder! Oh for their weekday workaday days; there they could show their mettle – how sweet a process Drifix was, how dear an electric kettle! Both for the first time ever known longed to be far from the bowling. 'Mine was a clean game, though it be dry.' 'A console, how consoling.' Meanwhile the weary day wore on, the odds got worse and ever worse, chilled to the score those boys became, and Fate prepared her huge black hearse...

Weary the day! O for stumps to be drawn! But the Ladies were batting and drawing it fine. Magpies were one-eighty-seven all out, the Ladies a hundred and eighty for nine! Urquhart was irked, and Farquhar felt – Hark! Cheers from the crowd! A boundary for four ! Now three to be even – but the girls gave them more ... Maud Winterthorpe batting, and tough as a navvy, slogged a sixer right over the roof of the pavvy! The Magpies were beaten, the gentlemen done, the maidens were over, the Ladies had won!

'Meet you under the Clock, old boy?'

'Meet you under the Clock.'

Beaten and bruised, 'We are not amused!' Victoria heard them swear. And Farquhar and Urquhart went down the stair to change in their cupboards bare. Down the cool stair of the Gentlemen's, half the gentlemen they were.

And under the Clock they met again, shaking their sorry heads, all dressed up in their black and white for their Dinner, their drinks, their beds. But never that night did they reach their beds, never their sleepy beds.

'Terrible day,' they sorrily said as they stood beneath the Clock. 'Never again will I be the same' – as they stood beneath the Clock. 'Times are too fast for us, times aren't the same.' 'Are we too slow, old boy? Are *we* to blame?'

Time *was* too fast for them, Time moved at speed, Time moved too fast for them that night indeed. Under the Clock they encountered their Hell – for that was the night the great Clock fell.

It fell from its grimy great big top, it fell for a forty-five-foot drop, it fell like a sword Damoclean on top of Farquhar and Urquhart – and Time had a Stop.

'Meet you under the Clock, old boy?'
'Meet you under the Clock.'

But now all that was over; never more would those our heroes stand beneath the Clock. That clock was fallen, they were fallen too. Fate struck a crushing blow – yet She was not unbending, this story has a faintly happy ending. Neither was killed. None got the *coup de grâce*. Farquhar was clocked by the Minute hand, Urq in the back with the Face. Bloody but not unbowed the head, they both spent a year in a hospital bed.

The Ladies, not Hades, again enter here – for each of them married a nurse. For the rest of their lives they played with their wives – and none of them's much the worse.

Julian Maclaren Ross

Funny Things Happen

I. THE SPY WHO WAS A CHARACTER
FROM CONRAD

Funny things are always happening to me.

For example, no sooner was I discharged from the army than I got mistaken for a spy. Nearly got arrested, too.

I was staying with a friend in the country. Call him Peter. What he does is quite important, but he was not doing it then. He was on leave from the Ministry. I was on leave too. My twenty-eight days hadn't expired. As a reaction from three years of khaki and clean fatigue I'd bought myself a crimson corduroy coat. It was this coat that got me into trouble – that and my beard. I'd grown a beard as well. It doesn't take me long to grow a beard. It was getting along nicely. I'd already started trimming the point.

Anyhow, we were in the local one night, it was a Saturday and pretty full up, and there were a couple of blokes in a corner staring at us hard. I thought they were just staring at my beard, so I didn't take much notice. Then one of them got up and came over to me.

'Can I see your identity card, please?' he said.

'You can't,' I said. 'I haven't got one.'

'You hear that, Joe?' he said, turning to the other man who'd come up behind him. 'He hasn't got one.'

The other one nodded and rubbed his hands, looking pleased. 'Got any papers at all?' he asked me.

'Yes,' I said, 'discharge papers.'

'Let's see them,' the first one said.

'You go to hell,' I said. 'Why should I show them to *you*?'

'We're police officers,' the second said. 'C.I.D.'

'Show me your warrant card then,' I said.

People had started to turn round and look at us. This seemed to make both the men uncomfortable. The second one said in a low voice: 'This is a confidential matter. We're on special duty.'

The first one, however, raised his voice. 'Hell, Joe,' he said, 'why kid-glove him? He's our man all right. Look at the coat. Corduroy, ain't it?'

'There's the beard, though,' the other said. 'They didn't tell us nothing 'bout a beard.'

'Maybe false,' the first said. 'Stuck on.'

'If you pull it to see I shall certainly sock you,' I told him.

The second looked serious. 'Offering violence,' he said. 'Police officer. Execution of his duty.'

Peter had been getting drinks at the bar. He now came up with a pint in each hand and said: 'What's the row?'

'Do you know this man, sir?' the second said. Peter hasn't a beard: hence the Sir. He was smoking a pipe, too. He said: 'Of course I do. Friend of mine.'

'Is his name MacWhirr?'

'It is not,' Peter said.

'MacWhirr's dead,' I said. 'He died with Joseph Conrad.'

The first man got excited again at that. 'Hear that, Joe?' he said. 'Comrade! A communist!'

'Conrad, not Comrade,' I said. 'Wrote books.'

'MacWhirr was one of his characters,' Peter said.

'Can't be the same bloke,' the second man said.

The first said: 'Books! You read books?'

'I write them too,' I said.

Everybody in the pub had gathered round by this time.

Peter said sharply: 'Time you told us what all this is about. Here are my papers if you want to see them.' He got out his Ministry card. The second man started to apologize at sight of this. He backed away, grabbing his pal by the arm and muttering: 'Mistake, sir. No offence.'

Before we knew what was happening, they were on their way out. Peter said: 'Just a moment!' Too late: the door had banged behind them.

We didn't follow; we went back to our drinking. But a few minutes later I felt a dig in the ribs. A hoarse voice whispered: 'Your name MacWhirr, guv'nor?'

I whipped round, almost upsetting my beer. A sort of tramp stood beside me. Three days' growth on his chin, a jacket that came down past his knees and a bowler without a brim.

'Who the heck are you?' I said.

'Police officer,' he said. 'Special duty.'

Both Peter and I became very angry at this. We asked him for his warrant card. Out it came at once. He looked over our papers with his brimless bowler pushed back. 'Thank you, gentlemen,' he said, 'all in order,' handing them to us and bowing, 'sorry to've bothered you.'

'But look here,' Peter said, 'we've just been questioned by police officers. Two men.'

'Don't know anything about 'em,' he said. 'Probably spies.'

'Why should they be spies?'

'Man we're after's a spy,' he said. 'MacWhirr. Takes photographs. Makes sketches. All got up like a nartist, see? Corduroys. That's how we come to make the error; they didn't give us no description.'

'Well, I'm damned,' Peter said. 'Have a drink.'

'Not on duty, thanking you, sir,' and he shuffled out.

We didn't see any more detectives that evening, but later on in the week Peter and I were out for a walk and there, in the valley below us, was a man in a green corduroy suit, sitting on a stool sketching.

'My God,' I said, 'look! MacWhirr!'

'How d'you know it is?' Peter said. He's by nature cautious. We argued for some time. I was all for going down and asking him, but Peter said one couldn't go up to a total stranger and say 'Are you a spy?' just like that. Besides, he might be armed.

So in the end Peter stayed behind to watch he didn't escape and I went for the local Home Guard unit. But when I got there all I found was a corporal soaking his feet in a bath of hot water, and he'd never heard of MacWhirr. 'Oo?' he said.

'MacWhirr,' I said. 'The well-known spy!'

'Don't know nothing about him,' he said.

'Where're your officers?' I said.

'Captain's playing badminton,' he said. 'Can't disturb *him*.'

'Listen,' I said. 'If you don't take action you're aiding and abetting the escape of a spy. *And you know what they do to spies, don't you?*'

That shook him. 'All right, all right,' he said, and lifted his feet out of the bath. It took him some time to get his boots on and there was a further delay while the captain was dragged from the Badminton Club. Finally, however, the whole section fixed bayonets and went charging off. They wanted to arrest Peter at first. Two of them were already poking their points into his stomach when I came up. The rest were rushing down the slope at the man in the corduroy suit, who gave a wild yell and sprang up, knocking over his sketching stool as he saw them.

'Look out, men!' the captain shouted. 'He may have a gun on him!'

Alas, he hadn't. He wasn't MacWhirr at all. Some quite well-known artist taking a holiday in the country. And didn't he raise cain. Threatened libel and God knows what. We'd the devil of a job to smooth him down. Most unreasonable. As we told him, we were simply doing our duty as citizens. It was his own fault; wearing corduroys and so on, of course he got into trouble. He'd only himself to blame.

2. CALL A POLICEMAN

I can tell you another story about police and coats. This time the police were uniformed and the coat was a teddy bear one. I was wearing it because it's the sort of overcoat film-magnates are supposed to wear, and I'd just gone into the film business myself. I wasn't a magnate of course, not yet: the coat was perhaps a bit premature. But still.

A man in a Soho pub offered to buy this coat off me for fifty quid.

'Fact,' he said. 'Fifty nicker. Ready cash.'

I looked him over. He didn't look as though he had fifty pence.

'Sorry,' I said. 'It's not for sale.'

'On the dot,' he said. 'Give it you now. Ten minutes time.'

'Nothing doing,' I said.

He turned round to his pals. 'Listen boys,' he said, 'I just offered this geezer fifty nicker for his coat, half a hundred, and what d'you think? The basket won't sell out.'

The Boys looked grave. 'That's a fair offer, pal,' one of them said. 'Be wise to take it.'

'Your own good,' another said.

'No soap,' I said. 'Not selling.'

I turned to go out. I'd had enough of that pub. The beer was bad, too.

One of the Boys barred my way. 'Now be reasonable,' he said. I picked up a glass. The potman, a nervous type, called out: 'Please, gents, please.' I put my back against the counter.

'Ah, let the ignorant basket go,' a man with a Cockney accent said. He had on a kilt.

'Don't know what's good for him,' the man who'd made the offer said. He spat on the floor.

I walked through the Boys to the door. 'Be seeing you,' a voice said.

'Not if I can help it,' I called back.

Outside it was pitch-black and pouring with rain. I turned into a pub in the next street. Old Frank was leaning on the counter with what looked like a whisky in front of him. 'What you having?' he asked me.

'A Scotch,' I said.

'No Scotch, only Irish,' the landlord said.

'Do you take me for Liam O'Flaherty?' I said. 'I'll have a Scotch ale.'

'Bloody Nationalist,' Frank said.

'Cheers,' I said.

The door opened and the fellow who'd offered me fifty nicker came in.

'This bloke's pinched my coat!' he bawled, pointing at me.

'Don't talk rot,' I said. 'I've had this coat seven years.'

'You took it off the peg in the other pub and walked out bold as brass.' He caught hold of my lapels.

'Fetch a policeman then,' I said.

'I don't need no coppers,' he bawled. 'You give me back my coat.'

In no time we were surrounded. A woman with feathers in her hat joined in on both sides. 'Squabbling over fur coats when me boys is out fighting in Africa,' she said.

'Frank,' I said, 'fetch a policeman.'

'Sure,' Frank said and dived through the door. He was glad to get out.

The fellow who said I'd stolen the coat made to follow, loosing his hold. I in my turn detained him firmly. 'Let me go,' he said, 'you big bullying bastard.'

'Oh, no,' I said. 'You stay here and wait for the police.'

He stopped struggling and whispered: 'Give me a quid and we'll say no more about it.'

'You give me fifty quid,' I countered, 'or I'll hand you over to the coppers.'

The woman with the feather hat screamed: 'Blackmail,' and aimed a blow at me with her umbrella. She hit the other man instead. A free-for-all started. I suddenly tired of the whole business and made a dash for the door.

A shout went up of 'Stop thief!' I turned left in the street and then right. The rain pelted down. One pair of running feet followed me, but I was gaining. 'Taxi!' I roared.

And there, miraculously, was a taxi! 'Where to, sir?' the driver said, slowing down.'

'Guilford street,' I said. But a hand caught the belt of my coat as I was climbing in. It was that man again. I hit him and knocked him into the gutter. Alas, when I turned again, the tail-light of the taxi was vanishing in the black-out.

The man was starting to scramble up again. There was nothing for it, much as I dislike violence. I knocked him down and sat on his head. 'Police!' I shouted. 'Police!'

The man shouted Help, but his voice was a bit stifled. He was trying to bite the seat of my pants.

It was a damn silly situation, when you come to think of it: sitting on a man in Soho, with rain gradually soaking me to the skin. A drunk American soldier staggered up. Several more people gathered round.

'This man's tried to pinch my coat,' I explained.

'But he hasn't a coat,' someone said, flashing on a torch.

'That's just it,' I said.

Then suddenly I heard Frank's voice. 'Round here somewhere, constable,' he was saying. Heaven knows where he managed to find a policeman that time of night, but he'd done it all right.

'Here!' I shouted. 'Help! Police!'

The policeman turned-on his bull's-eye lantern. 'Now then, now then,' he said. The crowd melted away. I stood up. The man I'd been sitting on stood up, too. Both of us began shouting accusations at each other.

'Now then, now then,' the policeman said. 'Who's charging who?'

I started to explain. Frank shouted suddenly: 'Stop him!' We all turned. The man was in full flight, running down a side-street. The policeman at once gave chase. Frank and I were left. 'Come on,' I said, 'let's go to the tube.'

'Righto,' Frank said.

So we walked off arm-in-arm.

There's a sequel to this, though. When I got home I found my wallet had been pinched. About ten quid in it, too.

I tell you, it doesn't pay to get mixed up with the police.

Angus Wilson

Crazy Crowd

Jennie leaned forward and touched him on the knee. 'What are you thinking about, darling?' she asked. 'I was thinking about Tuesday' Peter said. 'It was nice, wasn't it?' said Jennie, and for a moment the memory of being in bed with him filled her so completely that she lay back with her eyes closed and her lips slightly apart. This greatly excited Peter and he felt the presence of the old gentleman in the opposite corner of the carriage as an intolerable intrusion. A moment later she was staring at him, her large dark eyes with their long lashes dwelling on him with that sincere, courageous look that made him worship her so completely. 'All the same, Peter, I wish you didn't have to say Tuesday in that special voice.' 'What should I have said?' he asked nervously 'I should have thought you could have said "I was thinking how nice it was when we were in bed together" or something like that.' Peter laughed 'I see what you mean' he said. 'I wonder if you do.' 'I think so. You prefer to call a spade a spade.' 'No, I don't' said Jennie. 'Spades have nothing to do with it' she lit a cigarette with an abrupt, angry gesture. 'There's nothing shocking about it. No unpleasant facts to be faced. It's just that I don't like covering over something rather good and pleasant with all that stickiness, that hestitating and making it sacred with a special kind of hushed voice. I think that kind of thing clogs up the works.' 'Yes' said Peter 'Perhaps it does. But isn't it just a convention? Does it mean any more?' 'I think so' said Jennie 'I think it does.' She put on her amber-rimmed glasses and took out her Hugo's Italian Course. Peter felt completely sick; he must make it all right with her now or there would be one of those angry silences that he could not bear. 'I do understand what you mean' he said 'I just didn't get it for a moment that was all.' Jennie wrinkled up her nose at him and pressed his hand softly. 'Never mind, silly' she said and smiled, but she went back to her Italian grammar.

Peter longed to say something more, to make sure that everything was all right, but he remembered what Jennie had said to him about wasting time trying to undo things that were done. As he looked at her peering so solemnly at the book in front of her and making notes on a piece of paper from time to time, he felt once more how privileged he was to have won her love. She was so clear-sighted, so firm in her judgements, so tenacious in her application. Here she was learning Italian, and learning it competently, not just playing at it, and all because she intended a visit to Italy some time next year. They had almost quarrelled about it some weeks ago when she had refused to go to Studio One to see the Raimu film because she had her next lesson to prepare. 'Aren't you being rather goody-goody about all this?' he had said, but she had shown him immediately how false was his perspective. 'No, darling, it's not a question of being good, it's just a matter of thinking ahead a little, being sensible even if it means being a bore sometimes. If I went to Italy without having read something of their literature and without being able to speak adequately I should feel such a fraud.' 'You mean because you would be having something on easy terms that others could appreciate more.' 'No, no' she had cried 'damn all that about others, that's just sentimentality. No, I'm thinking of myself, of my own integrity. Peter, surely you can see that one must have some clear picture of one's life in front of one. You can't just grab at pleasure like a greedy schoolboy, Raimu this evening because I want it, no Italian because I don't. The whole thing would be such an impossible mess.' Then she had leaned over the back of his chair and stroked his hair. 'Listen to me' she had said 'talking to you like this, you who have done so much with your life even at twenty-seven, fighting that dismal Baptist background, winning scholarships, getting a First, being an officer in His Majesty's Navy and now being an A.P. at the Ministry and a jolly good A.P. too. That's really the trouble, you've read everything, you know all the languages, I don't. Be patient with me, darling, be patient with my ignorance.' She had paused for a moment, frowning, then she had added 'Not that I think you should ever stop learning. The trouble is, you know, that you've got swallowed up by the Ministry. Town planning is a wonderful thing but it isn't enough for someone like you, you need something creative in your leisure time too.'

Of course he realized that she was right, he had fallen into the habit of thinking that he could rest on his laurels. There had been so much activity in the past few years, constant examinations, adapting himself to new situations, new strata of society, first Cambridge, then the Navy, and now the Ministry and life in London, he had begun to think that he could rest for a bit and just have fun, provided he did his job properly. But Jennie had seen through that. It wasn't as if she could not have fun too when she wanted it, and in a far more abandoned, less inhibited way than he could ever manage, but she had a sense of balance, had not been thrown out of gear by the war. And so he had promised to resume his University research work on the Pléiade.

Peter opened the new book on Du Bellay and read a few pages, but somehow with Jennie sitting opposite he could not concentrate and he began to stare out of the window. Already the train was moving through the flats of Cambridgeshire: an even yellow surface of grass after the summer's heat, cut by the crisscross of streams with their thick rushes and pollarded willows; only occasionally did the eye find a focal point – the hard black and white of some Frisians pasturing, the rusty symmetry of a Georgian mansion, the golden billowing of a copse in the September wind, and – marks of creeping urbanization – the wire fences and outhouses of the smallholdings with their shining white geese and goats. It seemed strange to think that Jennie's home which she had painted in such warm, happy, even, if the word had not been debased, cosy colours should lie among such plain, almost deadening landscape. But as Peter gazed longer he began to feel that there was a dependability, an honest good sense about these levels that was much what he admired so in her, and perhaps as she had built that brilliant, gay attractive nature upon plain and good foundation, so the Cockshotts had created their home alive, bright, happy-go-lucky, 'crazy', Jennie had often described it, upon this sensible land.

He tried to picture her family from the many things she had said about them. His own home background was so different that he found it difficult to follow her warm, impulsive description of her childhood. Respect for parents, he understood, and acceptance of the recognized forms and ceremonies or else rebellion from them, but he had been far too busy winning scholarships and passing examinations to attempt the intimate undertones, the almost emotional companionship of which Jennie spoke, nor would his parents, with their austere conceptions of filial obedience tempered only by their ambitions for his future, have understood or encouraged such overtures. He felt greatly drawn to the easy familiarity that she had described, yet much afraid that her family would not like him.

It was clear that the only course was to maintain a friendly silence and trust to Jennie to interpret as she had done so often in London. Her affection for her father was deep and he imagined it was reciprocated. Indeed the wealthy barrister who had retired from the law so early sounded a most attractive gentle creature, with his love of the country, his local antiquarianism and his great artistic integrity which had caused him to publish so little, to polish and polish as he aimed at perfection. A survival, of course, but a lovable and amusing person; Peter's only fear was that he would fail to grasp the many leisured-class hypotheses by which Mr Cockshott obviously lived, but there again Jennie had explained so much.

Her stepmother, Nan, remained more vague. Some children, certainly, would have resented the intrusion of an American woman into their home, but Jennie and her brother had apparently completely accepted Nan, though there were clearly things in her that Jennie felt difficult to assimilate, for she often said laughingly that her stepmother had on such and such an occasion been 'rather pathetically Yankee'. Thinking of the garrulous, over-earnest American academical women he had known, Peter had thought this an unpleasant condemnation; but his acquaintance was very limited, and Jennie had explained that Southerners were quite different 'awfully English really, only with an extra chic for which any English girl would sell her all.' Peter thought that perhaps Nan might be a little alarming, but obviously very worthwhile.

Then there was Jennie's brother Hamish who had been her companion in all those strange, happy fantasy games of her childhood. She had explained carefully that he was not an intellectual, but that he was very learned in country lore and had read all sorts of out-of-the way books on subjects that interested him. Jennie admired him because he had hammered out ideas for himself in so many different spheres – had his own philosophy of life and his own views on art and politics. Some of these views sounded strangely crazy to Peter, and perhaps a bit cocksure, but still he was only twenty-two and as Jennie had pointed out views didn't matter when one was young, what really counted was thinking for oneself. It would be necessary to go very easy with a fellow like that, Peter reflected, thinking of his own obstinate defiance of heterodox ideas at that age; it had been mostly due to shyness he remembered. And lastly there was Flopsy, who was some sort of cousin, though he could never unravel the exact relationship. She was certainly somebody outside his former experience, not that he was unused to the presence of elderly unmarried female relations in the homes of family friends, but their activities were always confined to household matters, women's gossip, or good works. This Flopsy was a much more positive character, for not only did she run the household, and with such a happy-go-lucky family she must be kept very busy, but she appeared also to be the confidante of all their troubles. The extent to which even someone so self-reliant as Jennie depended upon her advice was amazing, but she was obviously a rare sort of person. He felt that he already knew and liked her from the many stories he had heard of her downright tongue, her great common sense and her sudden frivolities, he only hoped that he would not fall too much below her idea of the ideal suitor, but at least he felt that so shrewd and honest a woman would see through his awkwardness to his deep love for Jennie. Anyhow, he decided, if anything went wrong it would only be his own fault, for it was really a privilege to be meeting such unusual people who

were yet so simple and warm hearted, above all it was a great
privilege to be meeting Jennie's family.

As she stepped from the carriage on to the little country
platform Jennie looked back for a moment at her lover. 'Frightened, darling?' she asked and as Peter nodded assent 'There's
no earthly need' she said, 'I'm pretty certain you'll approve of
them and I know they'll love you. Anyhow anyone who fails to
make the grade will have to reckon with me. So you've been
warned' she ended with mock severity. A sudden gust of wind
blew from behind her as she stood on the platform, causing her
to hold tightly to the little red straw hat perched precariously
on her head, blowing the thick, dark wavy hair in strands on
which the sun played, moulding her cherry and white flowered
dress to her slender figure, underlining the beauty of her long,
well-shaped legs. It gave a moment's desire to Peter that made
him fear the discomfort of the weekend, doubt his ability to
keep their mutual bond that parental feelings were to be
respected, love-making forsworn.

But desire could not endure, already they had been claimed
by Nan. 'Honey' she cried in her soft Southern drawl, throwing
her arms around Jennie's neck 'Honey, it's good to see you. I
know it's only a week, but it's seemed like an age.' 'Darling
Nan' cried Jennie, and her embrace was almost that of a little
girl, as she kicked her feet up behind her. 'Darling Nan, this is
Peter. Peter, this is Nan.' The sunburnt, florid face, with its
upturned, freckled nose turned to Peter, the blue eyes gazed
steadily at him, then Nan broke into a broad, good-natured
smile, the wide, loose mouth parting to reveal even, white teeth.
She gave Peter's hand a hearty shake 'My! this is a good
moment' she said. 'A very good moment.' Then she turned
again to Jennie, and holding her at arm's length. 'You look
awfully pale, dear' she said 'I hate to think of you up there in
those dreadful smoky streets, and it's been so lovely here. We
have the most beautiful autumns here, Peter.' 'They're the same
as autumns anywhere else, darling' said Jennie. 'That they're
not' said Nan 'Everything's kind of special round here. You just
wait till you see our trees, Peter, great splendid red and gold
creatures. I better warn you I shan't like you at all if you don't

fall in love with our countryside. But I know you will, you're no townsman, not with those powerful shoulders. I like your Peter,' she said to Jennie. 'There you are, darling, she likes you.' 'Well, for heaven's sake, look at that' cried Nan 'Hamish hasn't moved out of the car' and she pointed at a tall, dark-haired young man whose legs seemed to fill the back of the grey car towards which they were advancing.

It gave Peter a shock to see Jennie's eyes staring from a man's face. He felt the moment had come to be positive. 'Hullo, Hamish' he said with what he hoped was a friendly smile, but the young man ignored him. 'That's a revolting dress' he said to Jennie, in a mumble that came from behind his pipe. 'Not so revolting as a green tie and a blue shirt' said his sister. 'Really, darling, you need me here to take your colour sense in hand.' 'Parkinson's wife been took again, and it's a mercy she come through, what with being her eighth and born with a hump like a camel' said Hamish. 'Never' said Jennie 'and her such a good woman. What be they callin' "the littl'un?"' 'They don't give 'er no name' said Hamish 'for fear she be bewitched.' ''Appen it'll be so' said Jennie.

'For heavens's sake, you two' said Nan 'What will Peter think of you? Aren't they the craziest pair? Look at poor Peter standing there wondering what sort of place he's come to.' Peter endeavoured to explain that he understood them to be imitating rustics, but Nan would not allow him to comprehend. 'My dear, there's no need to hide it from me. I know exactly what you're thinking "What ever made me come down to this crazy place among these crazy people?" And so they are – the crazy Cockshotts. My dear' she called to Jennie in the back of the car 'it's going to be the most terrible picnic, I've just not thought a thing about what to eat or what to drink, so heaven knows what you'll find, children.' 'Never mind, darling,' called Jennie 'the Lord will provide.' 'He'd better' said Nan 'or I'll never go to that awful old church again.'

To Peter sitting in front with her it seemed that Nan never ceased speaking for the whole nine miles of their drive to the house. He could not help feeling that in her garrulity she was much like other American women, but he felt sure that he was missing some quality through his own obtuseness. He found it easy enough to answer her innumerable questions for a murmur of assent was all she required; her sudden changes, however, from talk about the village and rationing or praise of the countryside to a more intimate note confused him greatly. 'I do hope you're going to like us' she said, fixing him with her honest blue eyes, to the great detriment of her driving 'because I know we're going to like you very, very much.'

As a background to Nan's slow drawl he could hear a constant conversation in varying degrees of rustic accent, coming from the back of the car, sometimes giving place to giggles from Jennie and great guffaws from Hamish, sometimes to horseplay in which wrestling and hair-pulling were followed by shrieks of laughter. Only twice did the two conversations merge. 'Jennie' called Nan once 'You never told me Peter was a beautiful young man. He's beautiful.' 'Nan, Nan, don't say it. You'll make him conceited' said Jennie. 'I can't help it' said Nan 'If I see anything beautiful, whether it's trees or flowers or a lovely physique I just have to say so.' 'He's certainly better than Jennie's last young man' said Hamish 'the one with spavins and a cauliflower ear. Peter's ears appear to be of the normal size.' 'We pride ourselves on our ears in my family' said Peter, trying to join in the fun, but Hamish was intent on his own act. 'Then there was the young dental mechanic, a charming fellow, indeed brilliant as dental mechanics go, but unfortunately he smelt. You don't smell, do you?' he called to Peter. 'Don't be rude, Hamish' said Jennie, and Nan chimed in with 'Now Hamish you're just being horrible and coarse.' 'Ah, I forgot' said Hamish 'the susceptibilities of the great bourgeoisie, no reference must ever be made to the effects of the humours of the human body upon the olfactory nerves. Peter, I apologize.'

Luckily Peter was not called upon to reply, for Nan directed his attention to a Queen Anne house. 'My! what a shame' she said 'the Piggotts are from home. I know you'd just adore the Piggotts. They're the most wonderful, old English family. They've lived in that lovely old house for generations, but to meet them they're the simplest folk imaginable. Why! old Sir Charles looks just like a dear old farmer . . .' and she continued happily to discourse on the necessary interdependence of good breeding and simplicity, occasionally adding remarks to the effect that having roots deep in the countryside was what really mattered. Suddenly she paused and shouting over her shoulder to Jennie she called 'My dear the most awful thing! I quite forgot to tell you we've all got to go to the Bogush-Smiths to tea.' 'Oh, Nan, no!' cried Jennie 'not the Bogus-S's.' 'We always call them the Bogus-Smiths' said Nan by way of explanation 'they're a terrible vulgar family that comes from Heaven knows where. They've got the most lovely old place, a darling eighteenth-century dower house but they've just ruined it. They've made it all olde-worlde, of course they just haven't got any taste. Don't you agree, Peter, that vulgarity is the most dreadful of the Deadly Sins?' Peter murmured assent. 'I knew you would' said Nan 'I wish you could see Mrs Bogush-Smith gardening in all her rings. I just hate to see hands in a garden when they don't really belong to the soil. The awful thing is, Jennie' she added 'that everything grows there. I suppose' she ended with a sigh 'people just have green fingers or they haven't.' 'The Bogus-S's have *money*' said Hamish 'and a sense of the power of money, that's what I like about them. If the people who really belong to the land are effete and weak and humane, then let those who have money and are prepared to use it ruthlessly take over. I can respect the Bogus-Smiths' vulgarity, it's strong. When I'm with them it's gloves off. Mr Bogus-S. sweats his workmen and Mrs Bogus-S. her servants but they've got what they want. I like going there, it's a clash of wills, my power against theirs.' 'Hamish is crazy on Power' said Nan explaining again. 'Very well, darling you shall go and Peter and Jennie can stay at home. The Brashers will be there.' 'Oh, hell' said Hamish, and Jennie roaring with laughter began to chant.

> '*In their own eyes the Brashers*
> *Are all of them dashers*
> *The Boys are all Mashers*
> *And the girls are all smashers.*'

A chorus in which Hamish joined with a deafening roar, and even Nan hummed the tune. 'The Brashers shall serve my will and that of the Bogus-Smiths' said Hamish 'They shall be our helots.' 'Thus spake Zarathustra' said Jennie with mock gravity. Hamish began to pull her hat off, and had they not turned into the drive at that moment there would have been another wrestling bout.

They approached a long grey early Victorian house with a veranda and a row of elegant French windows with olive green shutters. 'Now isn't it just the ugliest house you've ever seen?' asked Nan. Peter thought it had great charm and said so. 'Well, yes' said Nan 'the children love it and I suppose it is quaint. But think if it was one of those lovely old red brick Queen Anne farmhouses.' A bent old man in a straw hat was tending a chrysanthemum bed, Jennie began to shout excitedly through the window. 'Mr Porpentine, darling Mr Porpentine' she cried. 'What a curious name' said Peter, whose mind had indeed begun to wander under the impact of Nan's chatter. 'Oh, Peter, darling, really' said Jennie. 'It isn't his real name, it's because he's so prickly, you know "the fretful porpentine". Only of course he isn't really prickly, he's an old darling.' Further explanations were cut short by their arrival at the front porch. Nan led the way into a long, high-ceilinged room, into which the sunlight was streaming through the long windows. 'This is the sitting room' said Nan 'it's in the most terrible mess. But at least it *is* human, it's lived in.' And lived in it clearly was – to an unfamiliar visitor like Peter the room appeared like a chart of some crowded group of islands, deep armchairs and sofas in a faded flowered cretonne stood but a few feet from each other, and where the bewildered navigator might hope to pass between them there was always some table or stool to bar his way. Movement was made the more dangerous because some breakable object was balanced precariously on every available flat surface. There were used plates and unused plates, half finished dishes of sandwiches, half empty cups of coffee, ashtrays standing days deep in cigarette ends; even the family photographs on the mantelpiece seemed to be pushing half finished glasses of beer over the edge. It was impossible to sit down, for the chairs and sofas were filled with books, sewing, workboxes, unfolded newspapers, and in one case a tabby cat and two pairs of pliers.

When at last some spaces were cleared the chair springs groaned and creaked beneath the weight of their sitters. Peter sank into a chair of which the springs were broken, hitting the calves of his legs against an unsuspected wooden edge. It was clear that the chairs and sofas were each the favourite of some member of the family, had indeed been over long lived in.

'My dears' said Nan 'I'm ashamed' and she waved her hand towards a plate of unfinished veal and ham pie that was placed on the 'poof'. 'Suicide Sal's away and we've been picnicking.' 'Oh I'm so disappointed' cried Jennie 'I had so wanted Peter to see Suicide Sal.' 'My dear, she's had another accident.' ''Tis Jim Tomlin 'ave got 'er into trouble this time' said Hamish. 'They do say she be minded to throw 'erself in pond.' 'Oh! Hamish don't be so dreadful' said Nan and she began to repeat the story of her servant problems that Peter had heard in the car.

Suddenly the door opened and a little birdlike elderly woman in a neat grey skirt and coat seemed almost to hop into the room. She had a face of faded prettiness with kitten eyes, but at this moment her lips were compressed, her forehead wrinkled, and she was pushing back a wisp of grey hair with a worried gesture. 'Oh Nan there you are at last' she said 'I just can't get that lemon meringue pie of yours right. The oven won't come down and I'm sure the wretched thing will burn.' 'Flopsy' cried Jennie and 'How's my canary bird?' said Flopsy as they embraced. 'Flopsy this is Peter.' 'How do you do?' said Flopsy. 'You're taller than I expected and thinner. That young man of yours needs feeding, Jennie. Well. Peter or no Peter he won't get any dinner tonight if we don't look after that pie. Come on Nan.' 'Happy darling?' asked Jennie. Peter was too exhausted to do more than smile, but alone with her he felt he could do so sincerely. 'Good' she said, then 'Where can Daddy be?' she asked and began to call 'Dads, Dads, where are you?'

Mr Cockshott was a much smaller man than Peter had expected. Despite his bald head fringed with grey and his grey toothbrush moustache he had a boyish, almost Puckish expression which made him seem younger than his fifty-seven years. He wore an old, shapeless tweed suit with bulging pockets and a neat grey foulard bow tie. 'Jennie, darling, you're looking very pretty' he said, kissing her on the forehead, as she sat on the sofa, running his hand over her hair. 'Dads' said Jennie 'darling Dads. This is Peter.' 'So you're the brave man who's had the temerity to take on this little wretch' said Mr Cockshott. 'It doesn't require much courage' said Peter 'the regard is so great.' 'Good, good' said Mr Cockshott absently 'How are things at the Ministry? Humming, I suppose.' It was the first question about himself that anyone had asked Peter and he was about to answer when Mr Cockshott went on. 'Of course they are. I never yet heard of a Government Office where things were *not* humming. Though what they're humming about is rather a different question, eh? Well, you'll find things very quiet down here. Not but what there's not been a deal of trouble about Abbot Gladwin's yearly returns. These mortmain tenures are liable to cause a rumpus you know' he said turning to Jennie. 'It's not like simple scutage where the return is a plain per capitem. Between you and me the abbot's had a lot of trouble with his *own* tenants. I'm by no means sure that Dame Alice hasn't suppressed a pig or two and as for Richard the Smith, frankly the man's a liar.' 'Darling don't mystify Peter. He's talking about his old twelfth century, Peter. Have you had a reply from the Record Office yet, darling?' 'Yes,' said Mr Cockshott 'Most unsatisfactory. Of course it was a turbulent century, Barrett' he said to Peter 'and the turbulence was not without repercussions even in our remote part of the world. For instance I've been able to relate the impact of Richard Coeur de Lion's ransom directly to ...' But there he was interrupted by the return of Nan. 'For heaven's sake, Gordon' she said 'just look at you. You dreadful, disreputable creature. I appeal to you Peter, doesn't he look just like the wrong end of a salvage campaign? I just can't imagine what that starchy Mrs Brasher will say if she sees you.' 'If Mrs Brasher does see me, and considering her myopic tendencies I consider that very unlikely, she will undoubtedly, as the current phrase goes, fall for me.' 'May be, dear, may be' said Nan 'but nevertheless your trousers are going to get a patch in them. Flopsy' she called 'Flopsy, bring a needle and help sew up Gordon's pants.' 'Poor Dads!'

said Jennie 'aren't you shockingly bullied? Cross my heart, spit on my finger' she added, 'I'll never treat my man like this virago' and she pressed Nan's elbow tenderly. Peter smiled uneasily and uncrossed his legs. But Mr Cockshott was purring as a buzz of feminine interest surrounded him. 'I'll tell you a secret, Barrett' he said 'Women are like touchy Collie dogs, they need humouring.' Peter was about to reply in what he felt to be a suitable man to man vein, when he was startled by finding a large bodkin thrust into his left hand. 'Hold that' said Flopsy 'and don't sit gaping.' The kindness that lay behind her gruff voice was almost unbearable. 'You'll have to learn to be useful if you want to earn your bread and butter in this house. No drones here.' 'Oh for crying out loud' said Nan 'Flopsy you're scaring the poor boy into fits.' 'Peter's not frightened, are you darling?' said Jennie. 'Why it didn't take him any time to see how much Flopsy's bark meant.' Peter laughed and tried to smile at Flopsy. 'I shan't eat you up, young man' she said. But Mr Cockshott was growing restive, his face took on an expression of caricatured thoughtfulness and he bit on his pipe. 'Of course, I might appear with no trousers at all' he said. 'Aesthetically I should be perfectly justified, for I still have a very fine leg. Hygienically – well the weather is very warm and trousers are an undesirable encumbrance. Socially I make my own laws. I have only one hestitation and that is in the moral sphere. I have no doubt at all that the sight of my splendid limbs would cause Mrs Brasher to become discontented with her own spouse's spindly shanks; and whilst I have the greatest contempt for that horsetoothed, henpecked gentleman, I have also the highest respect for the institution of marriage. No, I must remain a martyr to the cause of public morality.' A chorus of laughter greeted this sally and Nan declared he was impossible, whilst Jennie dared him to carry out his threats. 'Oh, Dads, do' she cried 'I'd so adore to see Mrs Brasher's face. Go on, I dare you', but Dads just shook his head. 'Flopsy shall make me a kilt in the long winter evenings' he declared. 'I'll make you a bag to put your head in if you don't stand still while I'm patching you' said Flopsy, laughing. 'Heathenish woman, how right they were to give you that outlandish name.' 'It's not an outlandish name' said Jennie 'Flopsy's a lovely name. It comes from the Flopsy Bunnies in *Peter Rabbit*.' 'It does not' said Hamish, entering the room. 'It is taken from the immortal English Surrealist Edward Lear and his Mopsikon-Flopsikon bear.' After what seemed to Peter an age the family were ready to depart, he would not have dared to confess to Jennie his relief as he heard the car disappear down the drive.

Despite all Nan's apologies that the evening meal was just a picnic, Peter decided that they lived very well; with the combined produce of the garden, neighbouring farms, and American relations it was clear that austerity had not seriously touched them. Sweet corn and tunny fish was followed by roast chicken, and the meal ended with open apple tart and lemon meringue pie. Everybody ate very heartily, whilst deploring the hard times in which they lived. To Mr Cockshott no regime could be called civilized that compelled a discriminating palate to take beer rather than wine with dinner. Hamish was unable to see what else could result from a sentimental system designed to level down. Flopsy suspected that to get decent food it would soon be necessary to descend the mines, where she had no doubt that caviare and foie gras were being consumed hourly. Nan adored the farmhouse simplicity of it all and had always wanted to live on such wholesome fare, but she deplored the disappearance of the old English hospitality which scarcity compelled. Jennie with one eye on Peter remained silent, but in face of such unaccustomed plenty Peter was in no critical mood. Indeed as he sat in an armchair with a cup of Nan's excellent American coffee and a glass of cointreau unearthed by Mr Cockshott from his treasure house, he did not even feel alarmed that he had been left alone with Hamish.

For a time there was silence as Hamish looked at the evening paper gloomily, then quite suddenly he said 'Well, we've reached the final point of fantasy. Vitiate the minds or what pass for the minds of the people with education, teach them to read and write, feed their imaginations with sexual and criminal fantasies known as films, and then starve them in order to pay for these delightful erotic celluloids. Circenses without panem it seems.' 'Yes' said Peter 'it's pretty bad. I don't suppose anyone would be the worse for the disappearance of a lot of the films we get from America. But you tend to forget perhaps the routine nature of so many jobs today, people need recreation and some emotional outlet.' 'I don't accept industrialization as an excuse for anything' said Hamish. 'We made the machines, we can get rid of them. People seem to forget that our wills are still free. As to recreation, that died out with village life. I don't know quite what you mean by emotional outlet, judging by most films I take it you refer to sexual intercourse, there I'm oldfashioned enough to believe that marriage for the purposes of procreation is still quite an intelligent answer. But if you mean the need for something not purely material, some exercise of the sense of awe, you people killed that when you killed churchgoing.' Peter laughed and denied that he was responsible for the decline in Church congregations. '*Do* you go to church?' said Hamish. 'No' said Peter 'I suppose I incline to agnosticism in religion.' 'You incline to agnosticism' said Hamish scornfully 'which means I suppose that you prefer to believe the latest miracle performed by some B.Sc. London to the authority of 2,000 years.' 'I don't think the divergence of science and religion is quite the issue nowadays' said Peter as calmly as he could manage 'After all so many modern physicists are by no means hostile to religious belief.' 'Very kind of them I'm sure' said Hamish 'In any case I was not talking about what the B.B.C. calls "belief in God", that is not a thing for discussion really. I was talking of churchgoing. The greatest dereliction of duty in an irresponsible age is the failure of the educated and propertied classes to set an example by attending their parish churches.' 'You would hardly advocate attendance at church by non-believers.' 'My dear fellow' said Hamish 'all this talk about belief or non-belief is rather crude. A Roman gentleman might privately be a Stoic or an Epicurean but that didn't prevent him from performing his duty to his country by sacrificing to the Gods. We have privileges and we must act accordingly by setting an example to our inferiors.' 'I think' said Peter angrily 'that that view is crazy as well as unchristian.' 'Yes' said Hamish 'so does the *Sunday Express*. I think that the only dignified approach to the modern world *is* to be classed as crazy.' Further acrimony was prevented by the appearance of Mr Cockshott with some papers and Hamish retired.

'Where has Jennie gone?' asked Peter rather restively. 'In these unhallowed times' said Mr Cockshott 'even the fairest of women have to partake in the household duties, in short the women of the house are assisting cook with the washing up.' 'But can't I help?' asked Peter. 'Good Heavens, my dear boy. No. Let us retain some of the privileges of our sex. Jennie tells me you have a taste for literature, so I've brought you a few occasional writings of mine for a little light bedside reading.' Peter took the offerings with a sincere interest. 'I should very much like to read them' he said. 'Thank you' said Mr Cockshott 'thank you. I project a longer work – a history of North Cambridgeshire which will be at once, I hope, a scholarly account of the changing institutions and a work of literary value and entertainment describing the social scene with its quaint everyday characters and customs. Unfortunately my position as a J.P. and a local landlord, though only of course on a small scale, leaves me less time for writing than I should like. In any case I am not one who is content with information without style. That's why I'm afraid I quarrel with our good neighbours the Cambridge Fellows. I find most of their painstaking researches quite unreadable, but then I'm neither a pedagogue nor a pedant. On the other hand, though I believe that imagination must infuse the pages of history if they are to live, I could not write what is known as the popular historical biography. I have too much sense of accuracy and too little interest in the seamy side of the past to do that, nor have I the requisite standard of vulgarity in my writing. In fact I'm rather a fish out of water, a fact that is always brought home to me when I attend the meetings of historical or antiquarian societies.' It seemed to Peter that Mr Cockshott talked for hours about the various quarrels he had engaged in with eminent historians and authors, he began to feel more and more drowsy and the desire to be with Jennie, to touch and feel her became stronger and stronger. At last the door was opened and Nan appeared. 'Oh! Gordon' she said 'look at poor Peter he's so tired and white. You want to go to bed, don't you?' 'I am rather tired after the journey'

said Peter, but he hastened to add 'It's all been awfully interesting and I'm very much looking forward to reading these
articles.'

As he walked along the corridor to his room he passed an
open door of another bedroom. Inside two figures were locked
in each other's arms. He went quickly and, he hoped, silently
past. He told himself that he had always known how tremendously fond Jennie was of her brother, but all the same the
droop of her body and the force of Hamish's embrace troubled
him much that night.

Peter sat in a deck chair after breakfast the next morning
attempting to read Mr Cockshott's account of the Black Death
in Little Fromling, but he could not attend to the essay. He felt
tired and irritable, for he had slept poorly. He found himself
wondering where Jennie had gone, she had slipped away after
breakfast to make the beds, promising to join him in a few
minutes, and now nearly an hour had passed. He decided to go
and look for her. He found Mr Cockshott in the morning room
writing letters. 'Do you know where Jennie is?' he asked. 'Ah
where indeed?' said Mr Cockshott. 'That's what I'm always
asking when she's here at the weekends. I never seem to see
anything of her. We're all a bit jealous over Jennie. But her
independence is part of her charm. She will be free, she won't
be monopolized.' 'I had no intention of monopolizing her. I
just wanted to talk to her that's all.' 'My dear boy I quite
understand your feelings and it's very naughty of her to have
left her guest like this. But we're rather a crazy family, lacking
in the conventions, or rather perhaps I should say we make our
own.' Peter decided to seek her elsewhere. He went upstairs to
his bedroom, there he found Flopsy making the bed. 'You can't
come up to your room now' said Flopsy. 'The chambermaid's
at work.' 'I was looking for Jennie.' 'Well you mustn't look like
an angry dog, you'll never hold Jennie that way. You like her a
lot, don't you?' 'I'm very fond of Jennie' said Peter 'very fond
indeed.' 'Good Heavens I should hope so and more. Any man
in his senses would be head over heels about Jennie. But there'
she added 'I'm partial.' But she obviously did not think so. 'If
it's any satisfaction to you' said Peter savagely 'I'm in love with

Jennie and that's why I want to see her.' 'Good for you' said Flopsy. 'But don't bite my head off. We Cockshotts are a crazy crowd, you know, you can't drive us. Well, now be off. I must make this bed.' Peter wandered out into the garden where he found Nan in an old waterproof and a battered felt hat making a bonfire. 'Have you seen Jennie?' he asked. 'Oh Peter' she said 'Has she left you on your own? No! that's too bad. But there you are that's the Cockshotts all over, they're completely crazy.' 'Don't you find it rather a strain?' asked Peter. 'Maybe at first I did a little, but they're so natural and simple I love that way of living' for a moment she looked away from him. 'They do ask rather a lot from people' she said, and her voice sounded for the first time sincere. A moment later her blue eyes were looking at him with that frank, open stare which he was beginning to mistrust. 'It's not that really, it's just that they ask a lot of life. You see they're big people and big people are often kind of strange to understand.' She laid her hand on Peter's arm 'Go see if she's in the Tree House' she said. 'It's a kind of funny old place she and Hamish made when they were kids and they still love it. It's down at the end of the garden by the little wood.'

Jennie and Hamish were sitting on a wooden platform up in an elm tree when Peter found them. They were practising tying knots in a piece of rope. Peter's anger must have shown itself for Jennie called out 'Welcome, darling, welcome to the Tree House. You ought to make three salaams before you're allowed in, but we'll let you off this time, won't we Hamish?' 'Certainly' said Hamish, who also appeared anxious to placate Peter. 'I thought you went to Church on Sunday mornings' said Peter. 'Everything must give way to the hospitality due to friends' said Hamish with a charming smile. 'There was no need to have stayed away for me.' 'Now, Peter,' said Jennie 'that's rude after Hamish has been so nice.' 'We ought to saw some logs' said Hamish 'Would you like to give a hand?' 'Oh yes do let's' said Jennie 'You and Peter can take the double saw, and I'll do the small branches.'

Peter did not find it very easy to keep up to Hamish's pace, he got very hot and out of breath, the sawdust kept flying in his face and the teeth of the saw stuck suddenly in the knots of wood so that they were both violently jolted. 'I say' said Hamish 'I don't think you're very good at this. Perhaps we'd better stop.' 'No' said Jennie who was angry at Peter's inefficiency 'Certainly not, it does Peter good to do things he's not good at.' Peter immediately let go off his end of the saw so that it swung sharply round almost cutting off Hamish's arm. 'Bloody Hell' said Hamish, but Peter took no notice, he strode rapidly away down the path through the little copse. Jennie ran after him. 'Good Heavens, Peter' she called 'Whatever is the matter? Don't be such an idiot. Just because I said it was good for you to go on sawing and so it would have been.' 'It's a great deal more than that' said Peter tensely 'as you'd see if you weren't blind with love of your family.' 'Darling, what has upset you? Surely you aren't annoyed with Hamish, why he's only a child.' 'I'm well aware of that' said Peter 'a vain, spoilt child to be petted and fussed one minute and bullied and ordered about the next. And your father's just as bad. Well I don't want a lot of women petting and bullying me, not Nan, nor your beloved Flopsy, no nor even you.' 'Peter you're crazy.' 'Good God! I'm only trying to live up to your family. I've had it ever since I arrived "The Crazy Cockshotts" and bloody proud of it. I've had it from you and your father, from Flopsy and from Nan, wretched woman she ought to know all about it, and I've had it from your Fascist brother. You're all a damned sight too crazy for me to live up to.' Jennie was getting quite out of breath, trying to keep up with Peter's increasing pace. Suddenly she flung herself down in the thick bracken at the side of the path. 'Stop! Peter, stop!' she called. Peter stood still over her and she stretched out her hand to him, pulling him down on top of her. Her mouth pressed tightly to his, and her hands stroked his hair, his arms, his back, soothing and caressing him. Gradually his anger died from him and the tension relaxed as in his turn he held her to him.

Dylan Thomas

Where Tawe Flows

Mr Humphries, Mr Roberts, and young Mr Thomas knocked on the front door of Mr Emlyn Evans's small villa, 'Lavengro', punctually at nine o'clock in the evening. They waited, hidden behind a veronica bush, while Mr Evans shuffled in carpet slippers up the passage from the back room and had trouble with the bolts.

Mr Humphries was a school teacher, a tall, fair man with a stammer, who had written an unsuccessful novel.

Mr Roberts, a cheerful, disreputable man of middle age, was a collector for an insurance company; they called him in the trade a body-snatcher, and he was known among his friends as Burke and Hare, the Welsh Nationalist. He had once held a high position in a brewery office.

Young Mr Thomas was at the moment without employment, but it was understood that he would soon be leaving for London to make a career in Chelsea as a free-lance journalist; he was penniless, and hoped, in a vague way, to live on women.

When Mr Evans opened the door and shone his torch down the narrow drive, lighting up the garage and hen-run but missing altogether the whispering bush, the three friends bounded out and cried in threatening voices: 'We're Ogpu men, let us in!'

'We're looking for seditious literature,' said Mr Humphries with difficulty, raising his hand in a salute.

'Heil, Saunders Lewis! and we know where to find it,' said Mr Roberts.

Mr Evans turned off his torch. 'Come in out of the night air, boys, and have a drop of something. It's only parsnip wine,' he added.

They removed their hats and coats, piled them on the end of the banister, spoke softly for fear of waking up the twins, George and Celia, and followed Mr Evans into his den.

'Where's the trouble and strife, Mr Evans?' said Mr Roberts in a cockney accent. He warmed his hands in front of the fire and regarded with a smile of surprise, though he visited the house every Friday, the neat rows of books, the ornate roll-top desk that made the parlour into a study, the shining grandfather clock, the photographs of children staring stiffly at a dickybird, the still, delicious home-made wine, that had such an effect, in an old beer bottle, the sleeping tom on the frayed rug. 'At home with the *bourgeoisie*.'

He was himself a homeless bachelor with a past, much in debt, and nothing gave him more pleasure than to envy his friends their wives and comforts and to speak of them intimately and disparagingly.

'In the kitchen,' said Mr Evans, handing out glasses.

'A woman's only place,' said Mr Roberts heartily, 'with one exception.'

Mr Humphries and Mr Thomas arranged the chairs round the fire, and all four sat down, close and confidential and with full glasses in their hands. None of them spoke for a time. They gave one another sly looks, sipped and sighed, lit the cigarettes that Mr Evans produced from a draughts box, and once Mr Humphries glanced at the grandfather clock and winked and put his finger to his lips. Then, as the visitors grew warm and the wine worked and they forgot the bitter night outside, Mr Evans said, with a little shudder of forbidden delight: 'The wife will be going to bed in half an hour. Then we can start the good work. Have you all got yours with you?'

'And the tools,' said Mr Roberts, smacking his side pocket.

'What's the word until then?' said young Mr Thomas.

Mr Humphries winked again. 'Mum!'

'I've been waiting for tonight to come round like I used to wait for Saturdays when I was a boy,' said Mr Evans, 'I got a penny then. And it all went to gob-stoppers and jelly-babies, too.'

He was a traveller in rubber, rubber toys and syringes and

bath mats. Sometimes Mr Roberts called him the poor man's friend to make him blush. 'No! no! no!' he would say, 'you can look at my samples, there's nothing like that there.' He was a Socialist.

'I used to buy a packet of Cinderellas with my penny,' said Mr Roberts, 'and smoke them in the slaughter-house. The sweetest little smoke in the world. You don't see them now.'

'Do you remember old Jim, the caretaker, in the slaughter-house?' asked Mr Evans.

'He was after my time; I'm no chicken, like you boys.'

'You're not old, Mr Roberts, think of G.B.S.'

'No clean Shavianism for me, I'm an unrepentant eater of birds and beasts,' said Mr Roberts.

'Do you eat flowers, too?'

'Oh! oh! you literary men, don't you talk above my head now. I'm only a poor old resurrectionist on the knocker.'

'He'd put his hand down in the guts-box and bring you out a rat with its neck broken clean as a match for the price of a glass of beer.'

'And it was beer then.'

'Shop! shop!' Mr Humphries beat on the table with his glass. 'You mustn't waste stories, we'll need them all,' he said. 'Have you got the abattoir anecdote down in your memory book, Mr Thomas?'

'I'll remember it.'

'Don't forget, you can only talk at random now,' said Mr Humphries.

'OK, Roderick!' Mr Thomas said quickly.

Mr Roberts put his hands over his ears. 'The conversation is getting esoteric,' he said. 'Excuse my French! Mr Evans, have you such a thing as a rook rifle? I want to scare the highbrows off. Did I ever tell you the time I lectured to the John O' London's Society on "The Utility of Uselessness"? That was a poser. I talked about Jack London all the time, and when they said at the end that it wasn't a lecture about what I said it was going to be, I said, "Well, it was useless lecturing about that, wasn't it?" and they hadn't a word to say. Mrs Dr Davies was in the front row, you remember her? She gave that first lecture on W. J. Locke and got spooned in the middle. Remember her talking about the "Bevagged Loveabond," Mr Humphries?'

'Shop! shop!' said Mr Humphries, groaning, 'keep it until after.'

'More parsnip!'

'It goes down the throat like silk, Mr Evans.'

'Like baby's milk.'

'Say when, Mr Roberts.'

'A word of four syllables denoting a period of time. Thank you! I read that on a matchbox.'

'Why don't they have serials on matchboxes? You'd buy the shop up to see what Daphne did next,' Mr Humphries said.

He stopped and looked round in embarrassment at the faces of his friends. Daphne was the name of the grass widow in Manselton for whom Mr Roberts had lost both his reputation and his position in the brewery. He had been in the habit of delivering bottles to her house, free of charge, and he had bought her a cocktail cabinet and given her a hundred pounds and his mother's rings. In return, she held large parties and never invited him. Only Mr Thomas had noticed the name, and he was saying: 'No, Mr Humphries, on toilet rolls would be best.'

'When I was in London,' Mr Roberts said, 'I stayed with a couple called Armitage in Palmer's Green. He made curtains and blinds. They used to leave each other messages on the toilet paper every single day.'

'If you want to make a Venetian blind,' said Mr Evans, 'stick him in the eye with a hatpin.' He felt, always, a little left out of his evenings at home, and he was waiting for Mrs Evans to come in, disapprovingly, from the kitchen.

'I've often had to use, "Dear Tom, don't forget the Watkinses are coming to tea," or, "To Peggy, from Tom, in remembrance." Mr Armitage was a Mosleyite.'

'Thugs!' said Mr Humphries.

'Seriously, what are we going to do about this uniformication of the individual?' Mr Evans asked. Maud was in the kitchen still; he heard her beating the plates.

'Answering your question with another,' said Mr Roberts, putting one hand on Mr Evans's knee, 'what individuality is there left? The mass-age produces the mass-man. The machine produces the robot.'

'As its slave,' Mr Humphries articulated clearly, 'not, mark you, as its master.'

'There you have it. There it is. Tyrannic dominance by a sparking plug, Mr Humphries, and it's flesh and blood that always pays.'

'Any empty glasses?'

Mr Roberts turned his glass upside down. 'That used to mean, "I'll take on the best man in the room in a bout of fisticuffs," in Llanelly. But seriously, as Mr Evans says, the old-fashioned individualist is a square peg now in a round hole.'

'What a hole!' said Mr Thomas.

'Take our national – what did Onlooker say last week? – our national misleaders.'

'You take them, Mr Roberts, we've got rats already,' Mr Evans said with a nervous laugh. The kitchen was silent. Maud was ready.

'Onlooker is a *nom de plume* for Basil Gorse-Williams,' said Mr Humphries. 'Did anyone know that?'

'*Nom de guerre*. Did you see his article on Ramsay Mac? " A sheep in wolf's clothing."'

'Know him!' Mr Roberts said scornfully, 'I've been sick on him.'

Mrs Evans heard the last remark as she came into the room. She was a thin woman with bitter lines, tired hands, the ruins of fine brown eyes, and a superior nose. An unshockable woman, she had once listened to Mr Roberts's description of his haemorrhoids for over an hour on a New Year's Eve and had allowed him, without protest, to call them the grapes of wrath. When sober, Mr Roberts addressed her as 'ma'am' and kept the talk to weather and colds. He sprang to his feet and offered her his chair.

'No, thank you, Mr Roberts,' she said in a clear, hard voice, 'I'm going to bed at once. The cold disagrees with me.'

Go to bed, plain Maud, thought young Mr Thomas. 'Will you have a little warm, Mrs Evans, before you retire?' he said.

She shook her head, gave the friends a thin smile, and said

to Mr Evans: 'Put the world right before you come to bed.'

'Good night, Mrs Evans.'

'It won't be after midnight this time, Maud, I promise. I'll put Sambo out in the back.'

'Good night, ma'am.'

Sleep right, hoity.

'I won't disturb you gentlemen any more,' she said. 'What's left of the parsnip wine for Christmas is in the boot cupboard, Emlyn. Don't let it waste. Good night.'

Mr Evans raised his eyebrows and whistled. 'Whew! boys.' He pretended to fan his face with his tie. Then his hand stopped still in the air. 'She was used to a big house,' he said, 'with servants.'

Mr Roberts brought out pencils and fountain pens from his side pocket. 'Where's the priceless MS? Tempus is fugiting.'

Mr Humphries and Mr Thomas put notebooks on their knees, took a pencil each, and watched Mr Evans open the door of the grandfather clock. Beneath the swinging weights was a heap of papers tied up in a blue bow. These Mr Evans placed on the desk.

'I call order,' said Mr Roberts. 'Let's see where we were. Have you got the minutes, Mr Thomas?'

'"*Where Tawe flows*,"' said Mr Thomas, '"a Novel of Provincial Life. Chapter One: a cross-section description of the town, Dockland, Slums, Suburbia, etc." We finished that. The title decided upon was: Chapter One, "The Public Town". Chapter Two is to be called "The Private Lives", and Mr Humphries has proposed the following: "Each of the collaborators take one character from each social sphere or stratum of the town and introduce him to the readers with a brief history of his life up to the point at which we commence the story, i.e. the winter of this very year. These introductions of the characters, hereafter to be regarded as the principal protagonists, and their biographical chronicles, shall constitute the second chapter." Any questions, gentlemen?'

Mr Humphries agreed with all he had said. His character was a sensitive schoolmaster of advanced opinions, who was misjudged and badly treated.

'No questions,' said Mr Evans. He was in charge of Suburbia. He rustled his notes and waited to begin.

'I haven't written anything yet,' Mr Roberts said, 'it's all in my head.' He had chosen the Slums.

'Personally,' said Mr Thomas, 'I haven't made up my mind whether to have a barmaid or a harlot.'

'What about a barmaid who's a harlot too?' Mr Roberts suggested. 'Or perhaps we could have a couple of characters each? I'd like to do an alderman. And a gold-digger.'

'Who had a word for them, Mr Humphries?' said Mr Thomas. 'The Greeks.'

Mr Roberts nudged Mr Evans and whispered: 'I just thought of an opening sentence for my bit. Listen, Emlyn. "On the rickety table in the corner of the crowded, dilapidated room, a stranger might have seen, by the light of the flickering candle in the gin-bottle, a broken cup, full of sick or custard."'

'Be serious, Ted,' said Mr Evans, laughing. 'You wrote that sentence down.'

'No, I swear, it came to me just like that!' He flicked his fingers. 'And who's been reading my notes?'

'Have you put anything on paper yourself, Mr Thomas?'

'Not yet, Mr Evans.' He had been writing, that week, the story of a cat who jumped over a woman the moment she died and turned her into a vampire. He had reached the part of the story where the woman was an undead children's governess, but he could not think how to fit it into the novel.

'There's no need, is there,' he asked, 'for us to avoid the fantastic altogether?'

'Wait a bit! wait a bit!' said Mr Humphries, 'let's get our realism straight. Mr Thomas will be making all the characters Blue Birds before we know where we are. One thing at a time. Has anyone got the history of his character ready?' He had his biography in his hand, written in red ink. The writing was scholarly and neat and small.

'I think my character is ready to take the stage,' said Mr Evans. 'But I haven't written it out. I'll have to refer to the notes and make the rest up out of my head. It's a very silly story.'

'Well, you must begin, of course,' said Mr Humphries with disappointment.

'Everybody's biography is silly,' Mr Roberts said. 'My own would make a cat laugh.'

Mr Humphries said: 'I must disagree there. The life of that mythical common denominator, the man in the street, is dull as ditch-water, Mr Roberts. Capitalist society has made him a mere bundle of repressions and useless habits under that symbol of middle-class divinity, the bowler.' He looked quickly away from the notes in the palm of his hand. 'The ceaseless toil for bread and butter, the ogres of unemployment, the pettifogging gods of gentility, the hollow lies of the marriage bed. Marriage,' he said, dropping his ash on the carpet, 'legal monogamous prostitution.'

'Whoa! whoa! there he goes!'

'Mr Humphries is on his hobby-horse again.'

'I'm afraid,' said Mr Evans, 'that I lack our friend's extensive vocabulary. Have pity on a poor amateur. You're shaming my little story before I begin.'

'I still think the life of the ordinary man is most extraordinary,' Mr Roberts said, 'take my own ...'

'As the secretary,' said Mr Thomas, 'I vote we take Mr Evans's story. We must try to get *Tawe* finished for the spring list.'

'My *Tomorrow and Tomorrow* was published in the summer in a heat wave,' Mr Humphries said.

Mr Evans coughed, looked into the fire, and began.

'Her name is Mary,' he said, 'but that's not her name really. I'm calling her that because she is a real woman and we don't want any libel. She lives in a house called "Bellevue", but that's not the proper name, of course. A villa by any other name, Mr Humphries. I chose her for my character because her life story is a little tragedy, but it's not without its touches of humour either. It's almost Russian. Mary – Mary Morgan now but she was Mary Phillips before she married and that comes later, that's the anti-climax – wasn't a suburbanite from birth, she didn't live under the shadow of the bowler, like you and me. Or like me, anyway. I was born in "The Poplars" and now I'm in "Lavengro". From bowler to bowler, though I must say, apropos of Mr Humphries's diatribe, and I'm the first to admire his point of view, that the everyday man's just as interesting a character study as the neurotic poets of Bloomsbury.'

'Remind me to shake your hand,' said Mr Roberts.

'You've been reading the Sunday papers,' said Mr Humphries accusingly.

'You two argue the toss later on,' Mr Thomas said. ' "Is the Ordinary Man a Mouse?" Now, what about Mary?'

'Mary Phillips,' continued Mr Evans, ' – and any more interruptions from the intelligentsia and I'll get Mr Roberts to tell you the story of his operations, no pardons granted – lived on a big farm in Carmarthenshire, I'm not going to tell you exactly where, and her father was a widower. He had any amount of what counts and he drank like a fish, but he was always a gentleman with it. Now, now! forget the class war, I could see it smouldering. He came of a very good, solid family, but he raised his elbow, that's all there is to it.'

Mr Roberts said: 'Huntin', fishin', and boozin'.'

'No, he wasn't quite county and he wasn't a *nouveau riche* either. No Philippstein about him, though I'm not an anti-Semite. You've only got to think of Einstein and Freud. There are bad Christians, too. He was just what I'm telling you, if you'd only let me, a man of good old farming stock who'd made his pile and now he was spending it.'

'Liquidating it.'

'He'd only got one child, and that was Mary, and she was so prim and proper she couldn't bear to see him the worse for drink. Every night he came home, and he was always the worse, she'd shut herself in her bedroom and hear him rolling about the house and calling for her and breaking the china sometimes. But only sometimes, and he wouldn't have hurt a hair on her head. She was about eighteen and a fine-looking girl, not a film star, mind, not Mr Roberts's type at all, and perhaps she had an Oedipus complex, but she hated her father and she was ashamed of him.'

'What's my type, Mr Evans?'

'Don't pretend not to know, Mr Roberts. Mr Evans means the sort you can take home and show her your stamp collection.'

'I will have hush,' said Mr Thomas.

"Ave 'ush, is the phrase,' Mr Roberts said. 'Mr Thomas, you're afraid we'll think you're patronizing the lower classes if you drop your aspirates.'

'No nasturtiums, Mr Roberts,' said Mr Humphries.

'Mary Phillips fell in love with a young man whom I shall call Marcus David,' Mr Evans went on, still staring at the fire, avoiding his friends' eyes, and speaking to the burning pictures, 'and she told her father: "Father, Marcus and I want to be engaged. I'm bringing him home one night for supper, and you must promise me that you'll be sober."

'He said, "I'm always sober!" but he wasn't sober when he said it, and after a time he promised.

' "If you break your word, I'll never forgive you," Mary said to him.

'Marcus was a wealthy farmer's son from another district, a bit of a Valentino in a bucolic way, if you can imagine that. She invited him to supper, and he came, very handsome, with larded hair. The servants were out. Mr Phillips had gone to a mart that morning and hadn't returned. She answered the door herself. It was a winter's evening.

'Picture the scene. A prim, well-bred country girl, full of fixations and phobias, proud as a duchess, and blushing like a dairy-maid, opening the door to her beloved and seeing him standing there on the pitch-black threshold, shy and handsome. This is from my notes.

'Her future hung on that evening as on a thread. "Come in," she insisted. They didn't kiss, but she wanted him to bow and print his lips on her hand. She took him over the house, which had been specially cleaned and polished, and showed him the case with Swansea china in it. There wasn't a portrait gallery, so she showed him the snaps of her mother in the hall and the photograph of her father, tall and young and sober, in the suit he hunted otters in. And all the time she was proudly parading their possessions, attempting to prove to Marcus, whose father was a J.P., that her background was prosperous enough for her to be his bride, she was waiting fearfully the entrance of her father.

' "O God," she was praying, when they sat down to a cold supper, "that my father will arrive presentable." Call her a snob, if you will, but remember that the life of country gentry, or near gentry, was bound and dictated by the antiquated totems and fetishes of possession. Over supper she told him her family tree and hoped the supper was to his taste. It should have been a hot supper, but she didn't want him to see the servants who were old and dirty. Her father wouldn't change them because they'd always been with him, and there you see the Toryism of this particular society rampant. To cut a long story short (this is only the gist, Mr Thomas), they were half-way through supper, and their conversation was becoming more intimate, and she had almost forgotten her father, when the front door burst open and Mr Phillips staggered into the passage, drunk as a judge. The dining-room door was ajar and they could see him plainly. I will not try to describe Mary's kaleidoscopic emotions as her father rocked and mumbled in a thick voice in the passage. He was a big man – I forgot to tell you – six foot and eighteen stone.

' "Quick! quick! under the table!" she whispered urgently, and she pulled Marcus by the hand and they crouched under the table. What bewilderment Marcus experienced we shall never know.

'Mr Phillips came in and saw nobody and sat down at the table and finished all the supper. He licked both plates clean, and under the table they heard him swearing and guzzling. Every time Marcus fidgeted, Mary said: "Shhh!"

'When there was nothing left to eat, Mr Phillips wandered out of the room. They saw his legs. Then, somehow, he climbed upstairs, saying words that made Mary shudder under the table, words of four syllables.'

'Give us three guesses,' said Mr Roberts.

'And she heard him go into his bedroom. She and Marcus crept out of hiding and sat down in front of their empty plates.

' "I don't know how to apologize, Mr David," she said, and she was nearly crying.

' "There's nothing the matter," he said, he was an amenable young man by all accounts, "he's only been to the mart at Carmarthen. I don't like t.t.s myself."

' "Drink makes men sodden beasts," she said.

'He said she had nothing to worry about and that he didn't mind, and she offered him fruit.

' "What will you think of us, Mr David? I've never seen him like that before."

'The little adventure brought them closer together, and soon they were smiling at one another and her wounded pride was almost healed again, but suddenly Mr Phillips opened his bedroom door and charged downstairs, eighteen stone of him, shaking the house.

' "Go away!" she cried softly to Marcus, "please go away before he comes in!"

'There wasn't time. Mr Phillips stood in the passage in the nude.

'She dragged Marcus under the table again, and she covered her eyes not to see her father. She could hear him fumbling in the hall-stand for an umbrella, and she knew what he was going to do. He was going outside to obey a call of nature. "O God," she prayed, "let him find an umbrella and go out. Not in the passage! Not in the passage!" They heard him shout for his umbrella. She uncovered her eyes and saw him pulling the front door down. He tore it off its hinges and held it flat above him and tottered out into the dark.

' "Hurry! please hurry!" she said. "Leave me now, Mr David." She drove him out from under the table.

' "Please, please go now," she said, "we'll never meet again. Leave me to my shame." She began to cry, and he ran out of the house. And she stayed under the table all night.'

'Is that all?' said Mr Roberts. 'A very moving incident, Emlyn. How did you come by it?'

'How can it be all?' said Mr Humphries. 'It doesn't explain how Mary Phillips reached "Bellevue". We've left her under a table in Carmarthenshire.'

'I think Marcus is a fellow to be despised,' Mr Thomas said. 'I'd never leave a girl like that, would you, Mr Humphries?'

'Under a table, too. That's the bit I like. That's a position. Perspectives were different,' said Mr Roberts, 'in those days. That narrow puritanism is a spent force. Imagine Mrs Evans under the table. And what happened afterwards? Did the girl die of cramp?'

Mr Evans turned from the fire to reprove him. 'Be as flippant as you will, but the fact remains that an incident like that has a lasting effect on a proud, sensitive girl like Mary. I'm not defending her sensitivity, the whole basis of her pride is outmoded. The social system, Mr Roberts, is not in the box. I'm telling you an incident that occurred. Its social implications are outside our concern.'

'I'm put in my place, Mr Evans.'

'What happened to Mary then?'

'Don't vex him, Mr Thomas, he'll bite your head off.'

Mr Evans went out for more parsnip wine, and, returning, said:

'What happened next? Oh! Mary left her father, of course. She said she'd never forgive him, and she didn't, so she went to live with her uncle in Cardiganshire, a Dr Emyr Lloyd. He was a J.P. too, and rolling in it, about seventy-five – now, remember the age – with a big practice and influential friends. One of his oldest friends was John William Hughes – that's not his name – the London draper, who had a country house near his. Remember what the great Caradoc Evans says? The Cardies always go back to Wales to die when they've rooked the cockneys and made a packet.

'And the only son, Henry William Hughes, who was a nicely educated young man, fell in love with Mary as soon as he saw her and she forgot Marcus and her shame under the table and she fell in love with him. Now don't look disappointed before I begin, this isn't a love story. But they decided to get married, and John William Hughes gave his consent because Mary's uncle was one of the most respected men in the country and her father had money and it would come to her when he died and he was doing his best.

'They were to be married quietly in London. Everything was arranged. Mr Phillips wasn't invited. Mary had her trousseau.

Dr Lloyd was to give her away. Beatrice and Betti William Hughes were bridesmaids. Mary went up to London with Beatrice and Betti and stayed with a cousin, and Henry William Hughes stayed in the flat above his father's shop, and the day before the wedding Dr Lloyd arrived from the country, saw Mary for tea, and had dinner with John William Hughes. I wonder who paid for it, too. Then Dr Lloyd retired to his hotel. I'm giving you these trivial details so that you can see how orderly and ordinary everything was. There the actors were, safe and sure.

'Next day, just before the ceremony was to begin, Mary and her cousin, whose name and character are extraneous, and the two sisters, they were both plain and thirty, waited impatiently for Dr Lloyd to call on them. The minutes passed by, Mary was crying, the sisters were sulking, the cousin was getting in everybody's way, but the doctor didn't come. The cousin telephoned the doctor's hotel, but she was told he hadn't spent the night there. Yes, the clerk in the hotel said, he knew the doctor was going to a wedding. No, his bed hadn't been slept in. The clerk suggested that perhaps he was waiting at the church.

'The taxi was ticking away, and that worried Beatrice and Betti, and at last the sisters and the cousin and Mary drove together to the church. A crowd had gathered outside. The cousin poked her head out of the taxi window and asked a policeman to call a churchwarden, and the warden said that Dr Lloyd wasn't there and the groom and the best man were waiting. You can imagine Mary Phillips's feelings when she saw a commotion at the church door and a policeman leading her father out. Mr Phillips had got his pockets full of bottles, and how he ever got into the church in the first place no one knew.'

'That's the last straw,' said Mr Roberts.

'Beatrice and Betti said to her: "Don't cry, Mary, the policeman's taking him away. Look! he's fallen in the gutter! There's a splash! Don't take on, it'll be all over soon. You'll be Mrs Henry William Hughes." They were doing their best.

'"You can marry without Dr Lloyd," the cousin told her,

and she brightened through her tears – anybody would be crying – and at that moment another policeman – '

'Another!' said Mr Roberts.

' – made his way through the crowd and walked up to the door of the church and sent a message inside. John William Hughes and Henry William Hughes and the best man came out, and they all talked to the policeman, waving their arms and pointing to the taxi with Mary and the bridesmaids and the cousin in it.

'John William Hughes ran down the path to the taxi and shouted through the window: "Dr Lloyd is dead! We'll have to cancel the wedding."

'Henry William Hughes followed him and opened the taxi door and said: "You must drive home, Mary. We've got to go to the police station."

' "And the mortuary," his father said.

'So the taxi drove the bride-to-be home, and the sisters cried worse than she did all the way.'

'That's a sad end,' said Mr Roberts with appreciation. He poured himself another drink.

'It isn't really the end,' Mr Evans said, 'because the wedding wasn't just cancelled. It never came off.'

'But why?' asked Mr Humphries, who had followed the story with a grave expression, even when Mr Phillips fell in the gutter. 'Why should the doctor's death stop everything? She could get someone else to give her away. I'd have done it myself.'

'It wasn't the doctor's death, but where and how he died,' said Mr Evans. 'He died in bed in a bed-sitting-room in the arms of a certain lady. A woman of the town.'

'Kiss me!' Mr Roberts said. 'Seventy-five years old. I'm glad you asked us to remember his age, Mr Evans.'

'But how did Mary Phillips come to live in "Bellevue"? You haven't told us that,' Mr Thomas said.

'The William Hugheses wouldn't have the niece of a man who died in those circumstances – '

'However complimentary to his manhood,' Mr Humphries said, stammering.

' – marry into their family, so she went back to live with her father and he reformed at once – oh! she had a temper, those days – and one day she met a traveller in grain and pigs' food and she married him out of spite. They came to live in "Bellevue", and when Mr Phillips died he left his money to the chapel, so Mary got nothing after all.'

'Nor her husband either. What did you say he travelled in?' asked Mr Roberts.

'Grain and pigs' food.'

After that, Mr Humphries read his biography, which was long and sad and detailed and in good prose; and Mr Roberts told a story about the slums, which could not be included in the book.

Then Mr Evans looked at his watch. 'It's midnight. I promised Maud not after midnight. Where's the cat? I've got to put him out; he tears the cushions. Not that I mind. Sambo! Sambo!'

'There he is, Mr Evans, under the table.'

'Like poor Mary,' said Mr Roberts.

Mr Humphries, Mr Roberts, and young Mr Thomas collected their hats and coats from the banister.

'Do you know what time it is, Emlyn?' Mrs Evans called from upstairs.

Mr Roberts opened the door and hurried out.

'I'm coming now, Maud, I'm just saying good night. Good night,' Mr Evans said in a loud voice. 'Next Friday, nine sharp,' he whispered. 'I'll polish my story up. We'll finish the second chapter and get going on the third. Good night, comrades.'

'Emlyn! Emlyn!' called Mrs Evans.

'Good night, Mary,' said Mr Roberts to the closed door.

The three friends walked down the drive.

Muriel Spark

The First Year of My Life

I was born on the first day of the second month of the last year
of the First World War, a Friday. Testimony abounds that
during the first year of my life I never smiled. I was known as
the baby whom nothing and no one could make smile. Everyone
who knew me then has told me so. They tried very hard, singing
and bouncing me up and down, jumping around, pulling faces.
Many times I was told this later by my family and their friends;
but, anyway, I knew it at the time.

You will shortly be hearing of that new school of psychology,
or maybe you have heard of it already, which, after long and
far-adventuring research and experiment, has established that
all of the young of the human species are born omniscient.
Babies, in their waking hours, know everything that is going on
everywhere in the world; they can tune in to any conversation
they choose, switch on to any scene. We have all experienced
this power. It is only after the first year that it was brainwashed
out of us; for it is demanded of us by our immediate environment
that we grow to be of use to it in a practical way. Gradually,
our know-all brain-cells are blacked out, although traces remain
in some individuals in the form of E.S.P., and in the adults of
some primitive tribes.

It is not a new theory. Poets and philosophers, as usual, have
been there first. But scientific proof is now ready and to hand.
Perhaps the final touches are being put to the new manifesto in
some cell at Harvard University. Any day now it will be given
to the world, and the world will be convinced.

Let me therefore get my word in first, because I feel pretty
sure, now, about the authenticity of my remembrance of things
past. My autobiography, as I very well perceived at the time,

started in the very worst year that the world had ever seen so far. Apart from being born bedridden and toothless, unable to raise myself on the pillow or utter anything but farmyard squawks or police-siren wails, my bladder and my bowels totally out of control, I was further depressed by the curious behaviour of the two-legged mammals around me. There were those black-dressed people, females of the species to which I appeared to belong, saying they had lost their sons. I slept a great deal. Let them go and find their sons. It was like the special pin for my nappies which my mother or some other hoverer dedicated to my care was always losing. These careless women in black lost their husbands and their brothers. Then they came to visit my mother and clucked and crowed over my cradle. I was not amused.

'Babies never really smile till they're three months old,' said my mother. 'They're not *supposed* to smile till they're three months old.'

My brother, aged six, marched up and down with a toy rifle over his shoulder:

> *The Grand old Duke of York*
> *He had ten thousand men;*
> *He marched them up to the top of the hill*
> *And he marched them down again.*
>
> *And when they were up, they were up.*
> *And when they down, they were down.*
> *And when they were neither down nor up*
> *They were neither up nor down.*

'Just listen to him!'
'Look at him with his rifle!'
I was about ten days old when Russia stopped fighting. I tuned in to the Czar, a prisoner, with the rest of his family, since evidently the country had put him off his throne and there had been a revolution not long before I was born. Everyone was talking about it. I tuned into the Czar. 'Nothing would ever induce me to sign the treaty of Brest-Litovsk,' he said to his wife. Anyway, nobody had asked him to.

At this point I was sleeping twenty hours a day to get my

strength up. And from what I discerned in the other four hours of the day I knew I was going to need it. The Western Front on my frequency was sheer blood, mud, dismembered bodies, blistering crashes, hectic flashes of light in the night skies, explosions, total terror. Since it was plain I had been born into a bad moment in the history of the world, the future bothered me, unable as I was to raise my head from the pillow and as yet only twenty inches long. 'I truly wish I were a fox or a bird,' D. H. Lawrence was writing to somebody. Dreary old creeping Jesus. I fell asleep.

Red sheets of flame shot across the sky. It was 21 March, the fiftieth day of my life, and the German Spring Offensive had started before my morning feed. Infinite slaughter. I scowled at the scene, and made an effort to kick out. But the attempt was feeble. Furious, and impatient for some strength, I wailed for my feed. After which I stopped wailing but continued to scowl.

> *The grand old Duke of York*
> *He had ten thousand men . . .*

They rocked the cradle. I never heard a sillier song. Over in Berlin and Vienna the people were starving, freezing, striking, rioting and yelling in the streets. In London everyone was bustling to work and muttering that it was time the whole damn business was over.

The big people around me bared their teeth; that meant a smile, it meant they were pleased or amused. They spoke of ration cards for meat and sugar and butter.

'Where will it all end?'

I went to sleep. I woke and tuned in to Bernard Shaw who was telling someone to shut up. I switched over to Joseph Conrad who, strangely enough, was saying precisely the same thing. I still didn't think it worth a smile, although it was expected of me any day now. I got on to Turkey. Women draped in black huddled and chattered in their harems; yak-yak-yak. This was boring, so I came back to home base.

In and out came and went the women in British black. My mother's brother, dressed in his uniform, came coughing. He had been poison-gassed in the trenches. '*Tout le monde à la bataille!*' declaimed Marshal Foch, the old swine. He was now Commander-in-Chief of the Allied Forces. My uncle coughed from deep within his lungs, never to recover but destined to return to the Front. His brass buttons gleamed in the firelight. I weighed twelve pounds by now; I stretched and kicked for exercise, seeing that I had a lifetime before me, coping with this crowd. I took six feeds a day and kept most of them down by the time the *Vindictive* was sunk in Ostend harbour, on which day I kicked with special vigour in my bath.

In France the conscripted soldiers leapfrogged over the dead on the advance and littered the fields with limbs and hands, or drowned in the mud. The strongest men on all fronts were dead before I was born. Now the sentries used bodies for barricades and the fighting men were unhealthy from the start. I checked my toes and my fingers, knowing I was going to need them. *The Playboy of the Western World* was playing at the Court Theatre in London, but occasionally I beamed over to the House of Commons, which made me drop off gently to sleep. Generally, I preferred the Western Front where one got the true state of affairs. It was essential to know the worst, blood and explosions and all, for one had to be prepared, as the boy scouts said. Virginia Woolf yawned and reached for her diary. Really, I preferred the Western Front.

In the fifth month of my life I could raise my head from my pillow and hold it up. I could grasp the objects that were held out to me. Some of these things rattled and squawked. I gnawed on them to get my teeth started. 'She hasn't smiled yet?' said the dreary old aunties. My mother, on the defensive, said I was probably one of those late smilers. On my wavelength Pablo Picasso was getting married and early in that month of July the Silver Wedding of King George V and Queen Mary was celebrated in joyous pomp at St Paul's Cathedral. They drove through the streets of London with their children. Twenty-five years of domestic happiness. A lot of fuss and ceremonial handing over of swords went on at the Guildhall where the King and Queen received a cheque for £53,000 to dispose of for charity as they thought fit. *Tout le monde à la bataille!*

Income tax in England had reached six shillings in the pound. Everyone was talking about the Silver Wedding; yak-yak-yak, and ten days later the Czar and his family, now in Siberia, were invited to descend to a little room in the basement. Crack, crack, went the guns; screams and blood all over the place, and that was the end of the Romanoffs. I flexed my muscles. 'A fine healthy baby,' said the doctor; which gave me much satisfaction.

Tout le monde à la bataille! That included my gassed uncle. My health had improved to the point where I was able to crawl in my playpen. Bertrand Russell was still cheerily in prison for writing something seditious about pacifism. Tuning in as usual to the Front Lines it looked as if the Germans were winning all the battles yet losing the war. And so it was. The upper-income people were upset about the income tax at six shillings to the pound. But all women over thirty got the vote. 'It seems a long time to wait,' said one of my drab old aunts, aged twenty-two. The speeches in the House of Commons always sent me to sleep which was why I missed, at the actual time, a certain oration by Mr Asquith following the armistice on 11 November. Mr Asquith was a greatly esteemed former prime minister later to be an Earl, and had been ousted by Mr Lloyd George. I clearly heard Asquith, in private, refer to Lloyd George as 'that damned Welsh goat'.

The armistice was signed and I was awake for that. I pulled myself on to my feet with the aid of the bars of my cot. My teeth were coming through very nicely in my opinion, and well worth all the trouble I was put to in bringing them forth. I weighed twenty pounds. On all the world's fighting fronts the men killed in action or dead of wounds numbered 8,538,315 and the warriors wounded and maimed were 21,219,452. With these figures in mind I sat up in my high chair and banged my spoon on the table. One of my mother's black-draped friends recited:

> *I have a rendezvous with Death*
> *At some disputed barricade,*
> *When spring comes back with rustling shade*
> *And apple blossoms fill the air –*
> *I have a rendezvous with Death.*

Most of the poets, they said, had been killed. The poetry made them dab their eyes with clean white handkerchiefs.

Next February on my first birthday, there was a birthday-cake with one candle. Lots of children and their elders. The war had been over two months and twenty-one days. 'Why doesn't she smile?' My brother was to blow out the candle. The elders were talking about the war and the political situation. Lloyd George and Asquith. Asquith and Lloyd George. I remembered recently having switched on to Mr Asquith at a private party where he had been drinking a lot. He was playing cards and when he came to cut the cards he tried to cut a large box of matches by mistake. On another occasion I had seen him putting his arm around a lady's shoulder in a Daimler motor car, and generally behaving towards her in a very friendly fashion. Strangely enough she said, 'If you don't stop this nonsense immediately I'll order the chauffeur to stop and I'll get out.' Mr Asquith replied, 'And pray, what reason will you give?' Well anyway it was my feeding time.

The guests arrived for my birthday. It was so sad, said one of the black widows, so sad about Wilfred Owen who was killed so late in the war, and she quoted from a poem of his:

> *What passing bells for these who die as cattle?*
> *Only the monstrous anger of the guns.*

The children were squealing and toddling around. One was sick and another wet the floor and stood with his legs apart gaping at the puddle. All was mopped up. I banged my spoon on the table of my high chair.

> *But I've a rendezvous with Death*
> *At midnight in some flaming town;*
> *When spring trips north again this year,*
> *And I to my pledged word am true,*
> *I shall not fail that rendezvous.*

More parents and children arrived. One stout man who was warming his behind at the fire, said, 'I always think those words of Asquith's after the armistice were so apt . . .'

They brought the cake close to my high chair for me to see, with the candle shining and flickering above the pink icing. 'A pity she never smiles.'

'She'll smile in time,' my mother said, obviously upset.

'What Asquith told the House of Commons just after the war,' said that stout gentleman with his backside to the fire, '– so apt, what Asquith said. He said that the war has cleansed and purged the world, by God! I recall his actual words: "All things have become new. In this great cleansing and purging it has been the privilege of our country to play her part..."'

That did it. I broke into a decided smile and everyone noticed it, convinced that it was provoked by the fact that my brother had blown out the candle on the cake. 'She smiled!' my mother exclaimed. And everyone was clucking away about how I was smiling. For good measure I crowed like a demented raven. 'My baby's smiling!' said my mother.

'It was the candle on her cake,' they said.

The cake be damned. Since that time I have grown to smile quite naturally, like any other healthy and house-trained person, but when I really mean a smile, deeply felt from the core, then to all intents and purposes it comes in response to the words uttered in the House of Commons after the First World War by the distinguished, the immaculately dressed and the late Mr Asquith.

Benedict Kiely

Eton Crop

I had an uncle once, a man of three score years and three, and when my reason's dawn began he'd take me on his knee, and often talk, whole winter nights, things that seemed strange to me. He was a man of gloomy mood and few his converse sought. But, it was said, in solitude his conscience with him wrought and, there, before his mental eye some hideous vision brought...

Here and now I see him in my mental eye. He is in evening dress. He is always in evening dress. Tails. White bow. Silver watchchain. He raises his right hand. He raises it higher. He puts the back of his right hand to his right temple and extends and stiffens his fingers. The hideous vision may at this moment be catching up on him.

The night the big boxer swung at the man who taunted him and missed and, quite by accident, grazed Belinda's beautiful right cheek, established the Eton Crop forever for me as a special sort of hairstyle. Say Eton Crop to anyone under thirty or, perhaps, under forty today and they'll think you mean a sort of a horse-whip in use at a famous public-school, or a haircut administered there as a discipline, something like a crewcut. Or a bit of Swinburnian diversion.

Belinda, though, is part of another story. And Anna belongs to Eugene who was simple and honest and brave, proved to be brave, moreover, in a bloody battle that shook the world. But Maruna of the songs and the elocutions, Maruna of the silken thigh and the disabled electric kettle, Maruna belongs to me. Or the memory of Maruna.

What the man who taunted the big boxer said was: You're

better at the dancing than you are at the boxing. What else are you good at?

So the big boxer swung and, being a little boozed and, possibly, also intoxicated by his company, missed and grazed Belinda, and she was in the house for a fortnight until the shiner faded and she could step forth to tell the town her side of the story. She said that he was a perfect gentleman and that she would dance with him again any time he asked her. There were so many girls in the town who envied her even that glancing blow. She said that it would be something to tell her grand-children about. That was Belinda for you. She was a girl who always looked ahead.

The big boxer was on tour from one town to the next, not boxing, not dancing except for recreation, but singing from the stage. About the dear little town in the old County Down and about his little grey home in the West, and the hills of Donegal, and the tumbledown shack in Athlone. And kindred matters. But that was the only time he ever came our way.

There was not one in all the house who did not fear his, my uncle's frown, save I, a little careless child who gambolled up and down. And often peeped into his room and plucked him by the gown.

No, he is not in a gown now. He is still in evening dress. His head is raised. There is a pained expression on his face. The pain must be in his chest. For the tips of the fingers of both hands are sensitively feeling his breastbone.

For I was an orphan and alone, my father was his brother. And all their lives I knew that they had fondly loved each other. And in my uncle's room there hung the picture of my mother.

My uncle's right hand is pressed strongly against his forehead. He has taken a step forward, leading with the left foot.

There was a curtain over it (that picture of my mother), 'twas in a darkened place, and few, or none, had ever looked upon my mother's face. Or seen her pale, expressive smile of melancholy grace.

One night I do remember well . . .

But hold on a moment, I hear you ask me, who is this uncle

and what is he doing in here with Belinda and the big boxer, and Anna and Eugene and Maruna whom we have not yet met. Later, later, as the sailor said.

Eugene was in love with Anna and kept, not her picture, but a picture of Ginger Rogers pinned underneath the lid of his desk in the last but one year of secondary school. Ginger Rogers for the one time, that I know of, in her lovely life was a proxy or a stand-in. He could not keep Anna pinned underneath the lid of his desk. And for two compelling reasons: she went to the secondary school in the Loreto Convent over the hill and on the other side of the parochial house; and her uncle was a parish priest in a mountainy village ten miles away. If her picture were to be discovered in Eugene's desk, and recognized, life might never be the same again for Anna in the convent or Anna in the village. But Ginger Rogers was just Ginger Rogers, and loved by a lot of people and did not have, as far as any of us knew, an uncle anywhere a parish priest.

Eugene loved long and deeply. No doubt at all about that. Somewhere in the Pennine Chain, or in the Lake District, or somewhere, there's an Inn at the tiptop of a high pass. In the visitors' book a fellow who had cycled or walked up all that way wrote, long ago, that if the girl he loved lived up there he would worship and cherish her, ever and ever, but climb up to visit her, never no never. That wasn't Eugene. At weekends, and all through the holidays, he cycled, or walked and wheeled the bike, five miles up steep roads, free-wheeled five miles down, then, having refreshed his love, pushed or walked up again five miles and, by God's mercy who made the world that way, was enabled to free-wheel home the rest of the road. He gave it up in the end and went to the wars which he may have found easier going. Anyway she was a flirt of a girl even if her uncle was a parish priest and she, an orphan, lived in the parochial house: and she styled her hair in the Eton Crop. As did Belinda. And Maruna. That and some other matters they had in common. Eugene's sister, Pauline, who was marvellous, had her hair in pigtails for a while but she switched to the Eton Crop and was even more marvellous. Eton Crop was the way to be. It was a style that went with youth and beauty and of necessity, you might say, with a well-shaped head. The only comparable thing today might be a sort of Pageboy style, if that's what you call it. Except that Pageboy has a tame, even servile connotation while the Eton Crop had about it the suggestion of daring, you might almost say: Fast. If the word was any longer comprehensible. We have so accelerated. And it also seems to me, conscious as I am of *tempora mutantur et nos mutamur in illis*, and all the rest of it, that the Crop was easier on the eye, male and sexist, than the coloured contemporary Papuan.

One night I do remember well. As I said. Or somebody said.

My uncle is still in evening dress. He has raised his right arm just as if he were a policeman on point duty. Stopped the whole street with one wave of his hand. His left arm is extended, rigid, pointing downwards to the ground at an angle of about thirty degrees.

One night I do remember well, the wind was howling high. And through the ancient corridors it sounded drearily. I sat and read in that old hall. My uncle sat close by.

I read, but little understood, the words upon that book. For with a sidelong glance I marked my uncle's fearful look. And saw how all his quivering frame in strong convulsions shook.

A silent terror o'er me stole, a strange, unusual dread. His lips were white as bone, his eyes sunk far down in his head. He gazed on me, but 'twas the gaze of the unconscious dead.

Then suddenly he turned him round and drew aside the veil which hung before my mother's face. Perchance, my eyes might fail.

Gesture: Be careful not to allow the hands to move apart before the word, face, is uttered. The words in italic indicate where the hands may begin to come together. A slight startled movement is appropriate at: Perchance, my eyes might fail.

And indeed and indeed. I quite agree.

But ne'er before that face to me had seemed so ghastly pale.

— Come hither, boy, my uncle said.

I started at the sound. 'Twas choked and stifled in his throat and hardly utterance found.

— Come hither, boy.

Then fearfully he cast his eyes around.

My uncle is sitting down. But on an ordinary kitchen chair, which is odd in that old hall, my uncle's room. The choking is getting the better of him. Again he raises his right arm. Touches his right temple with the back of his right hand. Extends his left leg to a painful rigidity. Leans back in the chair. Will he topple over? But no, by a miracle of cantilevership he is still in the saddle, and still talking.

That lady was thy mother once. Thou wert her only child . . .

Maruna had a pert, birdlike face, a style most attractive to me at that time. She was a very senior girl, all of nineteen, and was not compelled, when off parade and out of the convent-grounds, to wear school uniform. No more than was Belinda, who had left school for two years and was as far away from me and my contemporaries as Uranus, or Venus, from the earth. But Maruna was still within reach, or sight, or desire, and because she could wear real clothes was an inspiriting vision of things to come. Out there somewhere was the World and Ginger Rogers and Life. Maruna was the symbol. She also sang like an angel. She sang at school concerts. She sang in the choir in the village she came from. One Christmas morning, it was said, people travelled miles to hear her *Adeste*. She sang at parochial concerts in the village and in the town. She sang at concerts all over the place. And she recited. That was what first brought us together: recitation. And at the same concert in the town hall. She was asking the townspeople about what was he doing, the Great God, Pan, down in the reeds by the river.

As for me: I was telling them, in the words of Patrick Pearse, that the beauty of the world hath made me sad, this beauty that will pass, that sometimes my heart hath shaken with great joy to see a leaping squirrel in a tree or a red ladybird upon a stalk.

At that time I had never seen a squirrel, brown or grey, except in Bostock and Wombell's travelling menagerie, and thought a ladybird was a bird.

Not a word of the whole thing did I believe. And the hell was frightened out of me. My first public appearance. She was two years older than me and as confident as Gracie Fields and had appeared on every stage within a forty-mile radius and she was as lovely as the doves in the grounds of the parish church. She was on the bill before me and for some reason, unknown to God or man or woman, she kissed me in the darkness of the wings before she stepped into the radiance and the applause. Afterwards she told me that the kiss was to give me confidence. But I doubt if it did. Even in the dark she was as daunting as Cleopatra. Then she was out there before the world and not a bother on her, and there was I, Caliban in the Stygian shades of gloom.

Now there were dirty-minded fellows who went to school with me who had their own notions about what he was doing, the Great God, Pan, down in the reeds by the river: and who were nasty enough to imply that it was nothing for a decent girl to be asking about, or miming on the stage, or anywhere else ...

That lady was thy mother once, thou wert her only child.

Well, once is enough to be anybody's mother.

My uncle is still balancing perilously on that kitchen chair, his right hand raised high but both feet firmly planted. Pray God he shall not fall.

— Oh boy, I've seen her when she looked on thee and smiled. She smiled upon thy father, boy. 'Twas that which drove me wild.

He may topple.

It must be remembered it is an old man who speaks.

— He was my brother but his form was fairer far than mine. I grudged not that. He was the prop of our ancestral line ...

Lansdowne Road and Twickenham and all that. Prop? The line?

... and manly beauty was of him a token and a sign.

— Boy, I had loved her too. Nay more. 'Twas I that loved her first. For months, for years, the golden thoughts within my soul I nursed. He came. He conquered. They were wed. My airblown bubble burst.

He is still in evening dress. He is still on that chair. But his hands are raised to heaven or the roof.

— Then on my mind a shadow fell and evil hopes grew rife. The damning thought struck in my heart and cut me like a knife: that she, whom all my days I loved, should be another's wife.

— I left my home. I left the land. I crossed the stormy sea. In vain, in vain, wher'er I turned my memory went with me . . .

But my uncle has not gone anywhere. He is still before my eyes. He is leaning sideways on that chair, perhaps to indicate the rolling motion of a ship at sea.

And he is still in evening dress.

Can you hazard a guess now as to what was he doing, the Great God, Pan, down in the reeds by the river? He was spreading ruin and scattering ban, and breaking the golden lilies afloat with the dragonfly, and splashing and paddling with hooves of a goat.

She stamped on the stage. Her dainty feet were transformed. She was a marvel as a mimic.

He was tearing out a reed was the Great God, Pan, from the deep cool bed of the river.

Gently, coaxingly she drew it out from the footlights. It was clearly visible.

He was high on the shore was the Great God, Pan, whittling away what leaves the reed had: and from her sleeveless sleeve, or from somewhere sacredly invisible, she had produced a short, shining knife.

He was drawing out the pith of a reed like the heart of a man, and my heart most painfully followed her fingers. He was notching holes was the Great God, Pan, and dropping his mouth to a hole in the reed and blowing in power by the river, and the sun on the hill forgot to die, and the lilies revived, and the dragonfly came back to dream on the river: and the whole town thundered its appreciation and there was I in the darkness paralysed with love or something for that wonder of a girl, and with fear of the ordeal before me.

For when she had disposed of the Great God, Pan, there was nothing or nobody could save me from having to stand out there in the blinding brightness to grapple with Patrick Pearse and the melancholy beauty of the world. If she had not kissed me again, somewhere in the region of the back of the neck, and gently propelled me forward, I'd never have made it: and then there I was, stiff as a post, raising my right arm and then lowering it for the leaping squirrel and the red ladybird, raising my left arm, lowering it, like a bloody railway signal, for little rabbits in a field at evening lit by a slanting sun. The bit about children with bare feet upon the sands of some ebbed sea or playing on the streets of little towns in Connacht, I actually liked and believed in. That, my elder brother said, was the only bit in which I did not sound totally lugubrious, and all honour to the glorious dead and Patrick Pearse. But from the streets of the little towns the road wound downhill all the way and when the poet said that, between one thing and another, he had gone upon his way sorrowful, everybody believed me.

Yet I had a few friends at the back of the hall who contrived to set a cheer going.

On the chaste and protective stairs between the two dressing rooms, one male, one female, she kissed me once, she kissed me twice. And didn't give a damn if the world was watching. As some of it was. She said I was good for a beginner and not to worry, that I could be heard all over the hall. She allowed me to walk hand-in-hand with her to the place where her relatives were waiting to drive her home.

So there sits my uncle, pursued by his memory and roaming the wide world, but still in evening dress, still balanced precariously on that creaking chair. Although I cannot hear it, I know that it must creak.

— My whole existence, he says, night and day in memory seemed to be. I came again, I found them here . . .

The strain of all this is proving too much for him. His mouth is agape. He raises both hands as if somebody were pointing a pistol at him.

— Thou'rt like thy father, boy . . .

Well, why not, nuncle?

His rhyming for the moment has tripped over its feet. Thou'rt, for God sake. Did anybody ever say: Thou'rt?

— Thou'rt like thy father, boy. They doated on that pale face.

Whose pale face?

— I've seen them kiss and toy. I've seen her locked in his strong arms, wrapt in delirious joy.

He simply should not have been peeping.

The tone of his voice now is vindictive to begin with, weakening to the mildly sarcastic. His hands are clenched for a moment and allowed to rest on his knees.

— By heaven it was a fearful sight to see my brother now and mark the placid calm which sat forever on his brow, which seemed in bitter scorn to say: I am more loved than thou.

— He disappeared. Draw nearer, child. He died. No one knew how. The murdered body ne'er was found. The tale is hushed up now. But there was one who rightly guessed the hand that struck the blow. It drove her mad – yet not his death, no, not his death alone, for she had clung to hope when all knew well that there was none.

He is up, with a half-jump, on his feet.

— No, boy, it was a sight she saw that froze her into stone.

My uncle makes a long pause in his speaking. He looks fearfully around as if seeking to discover the cause of my, evidently growing, alarm, by following the direction of my glances. Then he's off again:

— I am thy uncle, child, why stare so fearfully aghast?

But, nuncle, why not?

— The arras waves, he says, but know'st thou not 'tis nothing but the blast. I, too, have had my fears like these, but such vain fears are past.

But not the rheumatics from sitting in the draughts.

— I'll show you what thy mother saw...

Now we're for it.

Eugene really must have been in love with Anna or he never would have cycled over all those mountains. Yet when the impulse, whatever it was, ended, he forgot about it very rapidly. Or so it appeared to us. One night I asked him about it. We were playing football in the dark. That may seem an odd caper to be at. But let me explain. Since Eugene's father was an officer in the British army we had easy access, day or night, to the great river-surrounded halfmoon of playing fields below the greystone barracks. Except to the hockey-pitch which was a sort of sanctuary. The smoothness of it was a wonder to behold and it felt like silk to the finger, or to the bare feet when on summer nights a few of us would sneak out there, bootless, to play football with a ball painted white. That was away before 1939 and the world was easy. No warning bugles were blown, no rallentandos unloosed over our heads. That was the first white football we ever saw. Footballs in those days were mostly brown.

When, under the protection of darkness, I asked Eugene if he were still in love with Anna, he said he supposed he was but that you couldn't be sure about those things. It took me years to realize that what he meant was that he couldn't be sure about Anna. As for Maruna and myself. Well, I felt her leg once, also in the dark or the half-dark of one of the town's two cinemas. Felt rather her stocking, and that was the height of it. And had a notion for a long time afterwards, and without reasoning about it, that women, or their thighs, were, like the grass on the hockey-pitch, made of silk. Which is not so.

Thomas Moore, now that I think of it, felt the foot of Pauline Bonaparte. Left or right we are not told, but it was then reputed to be the daintiest or something foot in Europe. How did anybody contrive to work that one out? A foot-judging beauty parade? Sponsored by whom? And who felt all the feet?

Did the big boxer, I wonder, remember Belinda for any length of time. Insofar as we knew he had felt only her right cheek and that, and so to speak, only in passing.

— I'll show you what thy mother saw, my uncle repeats.

His tone is hesitating and fearful.

He says: I feel 'twill ease my breast. And this wild tempest-laden night suits with my purpose best.

He raises his arms as if he were about to take off. But instead he goes down on one knee.

— Come hither! Thou hast often sought to open this old chest. It has a secret spring. The touch is known to me alone.

Try as I may, I can see no chest. But my uncle is moving his hands back and forwards over something that clearly isn't there.

— Slowly, he says, the lid is raised and now what see you that you groan so heavily. That Thing . . .

He heavily emphasizes and repeats those two words.

— That Thing is but a bare-ribbed skeleton . . .

He has thrown his hat (metaphorical) at rhyme and/or what the poet called rhythmical animation.

— A sudden crash. The lid fell down. Three strides he backward gave.

He, or the voice of One Invisible, is telling me what is happening, what he is doing. But no crash do I hear. Nor has he stepped backward. He is again standing up but his feet are quite steady in the one place. This you may feel, and I must admit, is most confusing and it also now seems that my uncle is about to throw a fit.

— Oh God, he cries, it is my brother's self returning from the grave. His clutch of lead is on my throat. Will no one help or save.

He clutches his own throat. He collapses backwards on to that unshakable cane-chair.

Sometime during the summer that followed Pan's invention of the flute and the lamentations of Patrick Pearse on the sadness and transiency of beauty, Maruna came into town one Saturday and in her hand, naked and unashamed, an electric kettle that wouldn't work. It was early days then for electric kettles. Real specialists and diagnosticians in their elemental ailments may have been few. How many elements anyway, in an electric kettle when it is alive and well? Air? Fire? Water? And Earth, if you consider the metal as earth, the bowels of the earth?

We were good friends, but just friends, by that time, Maruna and myself. So I carried the kettle and was proud to, and proud to be seen walking with her. She carried a cord shopping-bag with a handbag in it and, as I recall, three thin books. We walked the town from place to place, hardware stores, building-yards, and one motor-garage, and nowhere found a man to mend the kettle. Until we met Alec who was wise beyond his generation and who had first suggested playing football in the dark, preferably in mixed doubles which we never did achieve: and who told us that Ernie Murdoch, the photographer, could fix electric kettles.

— And he can fix more than electric kettles.

— What else can he fix, Maruna asked.

She seemed a little nervous of Alec. He had a grey, level glance and a well-chiselled, handsome face and a name with the girls, of all sorts.

— Your kettle-carrier, he said, will tell you. The slave of the kettle. Ali Baba.

But the kettle-carrier pretended ignorance, or innocence, and we left Alec smiling and Ernie fixed the kettle: and afterwards Maruna and myself went to the pictures. How could I tell her that Ernie sold rubber goods and allied products, down in the reeds by the river? She might not have known what they were about. Explication at the time would have been beyond me.

Ali Baba and the forty thieves were hard at it in one of the two cinemas. But after that gibe about the slave of the kettle I preferred the other palace. It had Virginia Bruce and John Boles and Douglas Montgomery, and others, and the Swiss Alps and balconies and flowers, and everybody singing that I've told every little star just how sweet I think you are, why haven't I told you. I've told the ripples in the brook, made my heart an open book . . .

She sang with them. She was a bird.

And down in the reeds by the river I once, just once and only for a moment, touched her silken thigh. That was as far as I ever got or perhaps, then, had the courage to try to go. There be mysteries. No golden lilies were trampled on. It was an innocent sort of a world.

Anyway, that was the end of it. She went one way and I went another, not with conscious deliberation, just went. Early days can be like that.

— Will no one help or save?

No one does.

This you may be glad to hear is positively my uncle's last

appearance on this or any other stage. It might even seem that he has no more to say. That third person unseen, unknown, sums up for the unfortunate man who murdered his brother and locked him in a box, and drove his sister-in-law to lunacy.

— That night they laid him on his bed in raving madness tossed. He gnashed his teeth and with wild oaths blasphemed the Holy Ghost.

On the page before me the man in evening dress raises his right hand, bows his head reverently to atone for the blasphemy, and places his left hand round about where his heart may be presumed to beat.

— And ere the light of morning broke, a sinner's soul was lost.

And here and now, as I turn the last page in this little book, the man in evening dress covers his face with his hands. The instructions or directions in the text that accompanies the verse and the illustrations say that the eyes may be raised at the beginning of this passage and that the attitude given in the accompanying illustration must not be adopted until the final word, and that the reciter may then stand with his face covered for a few seconds, and with great effect.

Then beside that, and in the margin of the page, and in small neat birdlike script, someone has long ago written: Bring electric kettle to town. See musical picture with John Boles and Virginia Bruce.

So this curious little book is all that is left to me of Maruna and her singing and reciting, and of football in the dark and of Eugene who came to be a hero, and of Anna from over the mountains, and Belinda and the big boxer, and Pauline who was marvellous. Was it one of the three thin books that I saw in Maruna's shopping-bag on the day of the electric kettle? Did that gesticulating uncle go round and round the town with us and even into the studio of Ernie Murdoch who had power over life and electric kettles? Did he crouch in the dark when I touched silk and heard Virginia Bruce sing and Maruna sing with her: Friends ask me am I in love, I always answer yes...

As for the book. I open it again, for the hundredth time since, the day before yesterday, it came into my possession. A young man stopped me on a road in Donnybrook and handed it to me. He said: You knew my mother. She talked a lot about you. She said to me once that if ever I ran across you I was to pass this little book on to you.

And later, when we had talked for a while: She died a year ago. Singing to the end.

Humming the other day I was, about I've told every little star when a young person said to me that I knew the latest. And genuinely meant it. For a haunting song may return but a lost beauty never. Yet I can seldom look at or use an electric kettle without remembering Maruna. Away back in those days I wrote a poem to her: or about her, for I never had the nerve to show it to her. Here it is. It looks better in prose as most poems would nowadays. It was jampacked with extravagant statements. As that: On a dew-drenched April morning, the sky-assaulting lark, with his rising paean of gladness, to which mortal ears must hark, did never sing so sweetly nor ever praise so meetly as her voice, with full throat vibrant on the starless scented dark.

And wilder still: Never from the lofty steeple did the swinging bells chime down with a note so soul-exalting o'er the morning-misted town, as her voice in trilling rushes, from her lips the soft sound gushes on the air that heaves and dances like a bed of wind-stirred down...

Wonderwoman. Up and away.

There was a third verse, pointing a moral.

Sed satis.

Here followeth an exact description of the book.

Five inches by seven. Forty-seven pages, approx.

Cloth, now very much off-white, with green binding. One of a series of Illustrated Recitations by R. C. Buchanan: *The Uncle* by Henry Glassford Bell. Elocution taught by the aid of photography.

That is: Mr Bell wrote the horrendous poem and Mr Buchanan illustrated it with thirty-six photographic reproductions of a man in evening dress elocuting like bedamned. And added an appendix telling you how you also could elocute that poem.

There was even a special edition of the poem, with musical background by Sir Julius Benedict and for the especial benefit of Sir Henry Irving when he felt the need to elocute.

How carefully and how often, I wonder, had Maruna studied that book? What secret life did she lead that I knew nothing about? To think that the movements of her body should have been monitored by Henry Glassford Bell who wrote that woeful poem, and by R. C. Buchanan who worked out the gestures, he said, to foster the love of elocution which, he said, was pre-eminently the art whose principles require to be imparted by oral demonstration. That's what the man said. Kissing in the dark wings, kissing on the stairway. Even then, said R. C. Buchanan, this instruction demands ceaseless repetition before it begins to bear fruit.

Should I have simply kissed back? Not felt in the dark for the smoothness of a silk stocking, while everyone suddenly burst out singing about I've told every little star?

But why did the sailor say: Later, later.

Please.

Kingsley Amis

Moral Fibre

'Hallo,' I said. 'Who are you?' I said it to a child of about three who was pottering about on the half landing between the ground floor of the house, where some people called Davies lived, and the first floor, where I and my wife and children lived. The child now before me was not one of mine. He looked old-fashioned in some way, probably because instead of ordinary children's clothes he wore scaled-down versions of grown-up clothes, including miniature black lace-up boots. His eyes were alarmed or vacant, their roundness repeated in the rim of the amber-coloured dummy he was sucking. As I approached he ran incompetently away up the further flight. I'd tried to speak heartily to him, but most likely had only sounded accusing. Accusing was how I often felt in those days, especially after a morning duty in the Library Reference Room, being talked to most of the way by my colleague, Ieuan Jenkins, and about his wife's headaches too.

I mounted in my turn and entered the kitchen, where my own wife, called Jean, was straining some potatoes into the wash-hand basin that did, but only just did, as a sink. 'Hallo, darling,' she said. 'How were the borrowers this morning, then?'

'They were readers this morning, not borrowers,' I said, kidding her.

'Aw, same thing.'

'Yes, that's right. They were as usual, I'm sorry to say. Who was that extraordinary child I saw on the stairs?'

'Ssshh ... Must have been one of Betty's. She had to bring them with her.' Jean pointed towards the sitting-room, where clicks and thumps suggesting domestic work could be heard.

'Betty's?' I whispered. 'What's going on?'

'She's just finishing up in there. Betty Arnulfsen. You remember, the girl Mair Webster was going to fix us up with. You know.'

'Oh, the delinquent. I'd forgotten all about it.'

'She's coming to lunch.'

'Betty Arnulfsen?'

'No, Mair, dull.'

'Oh, Christ.'

'Now, don't be nasty, John. She's been very kind to us. Just because she's a bit boring, that doesn't mean she ...'

'*Just* because. A *bit* boring. If it were only that. The woman's a menace, a threat to Western values. Terrifying to think of her being a social worker. All that awful knowing-best stuff, being quite sure what's good for people and not standing any nonsense and making them knuckle under and going round saying how she fully appreciates the seriousness and importance of her job, as if that made it all right. They bloody well ought to come and ask me before they let anybody be a social worker.'

'Then there wouldn't be any. You can take these plates in. She'll be here any minute.'

It was all most interesting, and in a way that things that happened to me hardly ever were. Mair Webster, who knew us because her husband was a senior colleague of mine on the staff of the Aberdarcy (Central) Public Library, had brought off what must have seemed to her a smart double coup by providing, as the twice-a-week domestic help we craved, one of the fallen women with whom her municipal duties brought her into contact. It had turned out that the woman in question wasn't really fallen, just rather inadmissibly inclined from the perpendicular. She'd had an illegitimate child or two and had recently or some time ago neglected or abandoned it or them – Mair had a gift of unmemorability normally reserved for far less emphatic characters – but that was all over now and the girl was taking proper care of her young, encouraged by her newly acquired husband, a Norwegian merchant seaman and a 'pretty good type' according to Mair, who went on about it as if she'd masterminded the whole thing. Perhaps she had. Anyway, meeting Betty Arnulfsen was bound to be edifying, however imperfectly fallen she might be.

In the sitting-room, which doubled as dining-room and lunching-room when people like Mair were about, a smallish dark girl of nineteen or twenty was rearranging rugs and pushing chairs back into position. At my entry the child I'd seen earlier tottered behind the tall boxlike couch, where another of the same size was already lurking. Of this supplementary child I could make out nothing for certain, apart from a frizzy but sparse head of ginger hair. The girl had looked up at me and then quickly and shyly away again.

'Good morning,' I said, in the sort of tone officials visiting things are fond of and good at. I seemed not to have chosen this tone. It wasn't my day for tones.

'Morning, Mr Lewis,' she muttered, going on with her work. 'Miserable old weather.'

This notification, although accurate enough as far as it went, drew no reply. I fussed round the gate-leg table for a bit, fiddling with plates and cutlery and stealthily watching Betty Arnulfsen. Her straight black hair was ribboned in place by what looked like the belt of an old floral-pattern dress. In her plain skirt and jumper and with her meek expression she had the air of an underpaid shopgirl or bullied supply teacher. She wore no make-up. Altogether she wasn't my idea of a delinquent, but then few people are my idea of anything.

There was a ring at the front-door bell, a favourite barking-trigger of the dog that lived downstairs. On my wife's orders I went and let in Mair Webster, whose speed off the verbal mark proved to be at its famed best. By the time we reached the kitchen I already had a sound general grasp of the events of her morning. These included a bawling-out of the Assistant Child Care Officer down at the Town Hall, and a longer, fiercer, more categorical bawling-out of the foster-mother of one of 'her' babies. 'Is Betty here?' she added without pause. 'Hallo, Jean dear, sorry I'm late, been dreadfully pushed this morning, everybody screaming for help. How's Betty getting on? Where is she? I just want to have a word with her a minute.'

I was close enough behind Mair to see the children returning to defensive positions behind the couch and Betty looking harried. It was my first view of her in full face and I thought her quite pretty, but pale and washed out. I also noticed that the ginger-haired child was sucking a dummy similar to that of its fellow.

'Ah, good morning, Betty,' Mair said bluffly. 'How are you getting on? Do you like working for Mrs Lewis?'

'Aw, all right.'

Mair's lion-like face took on the aspect of the king of beasts trying to outstare its tamer. 'I think you know my name, don't you, Betty? It's polite to use it, you know.'

At this I went out into the kitchen again, but not quickly enough to avoid hearing Betty saying, 'Sorry, Mrs Webster,' and, as I shut the door behind me, Mair saying, 'That's more like it, isn't it, Betty?'

'What's the matter with you?' Jean asked me.

I stopped stage-whispering obscenities and spoke some instead, using them to point or fill out a report of the recent exchange. In a moment the sitting-room door was reopened, catching me in mid-scatologism, and Mair's voice asked my wife to come in 'a minute'. At the ensuing conference, I was told later, Betty's willingness, industry and general efficiency as a domestic help were probed and a favourable account of them given. Meanwhile I put to myself the question whether the removal of all social workers, preferably by execution squads, wouldn't do everyone a power of good. You had to do something about ill-treated, etc., children all right, but you could see to that without behaving like a sort of revivalist military policeman.

The meeting next door broke up. Betty and her children were hurried out of the place, the former carrying a tattered parcel my wife had furtively thrust into her hands. I found out after-wards that among other things it contained a tweed skirt of Jean's I particularly liked her in and my own favourite socks. This was charity run riot.

At lunch, Mair said efficiently: 'The trouble with girls like that is that they've got no moral fibre.'

'How do you mean?' I asked.

'I mean this, John. They've no will of their own, you see.

They just drift. Line of least resistance all the time. Now Betty didn't really want to abandon those twins of hers – she was quite a good mother to them, apparently, when she was living with her parents and going out to work at this café. Then she went to a dance and met this dirty swine of a crane driver and he persuaded her to go and live with him – he's got a wife and child himself, a real beauty, he is – and he wouldn't take the twins, so she just went off and left them and let her parents look after them. Then the swine went off with another woman and Betty's father wouldn't have her back in the house. Said he'd forgiven her once when she had the twins when she was sixteen and he wasn't going to forgive her again. He's strong chapel, you see, believes in sinners being cast into the outer darkness, you know the kind of thing. It's a tragic story, isn't it?'

'Yes,' I said, and went on to talk about the conflict between generations, I think it was. Mair's technique when others ventured beyond a couple of sentences was to start nodding, stepping up the tempo as long as they continued. When her face was practically juddering with nods I gave in.

'Well,' she went on in a satisfied tone, 'going back to where I was just now, Betty's father got into such a rage with her that he threw the twins out as well, and she got her job back at the café, which wasn't really a good thing because it's not a very desirable place, but at least it meant that there was some money coming in, but she couldn't take the twins to work with her, so she parked them with the woman she was renting her room from. Then she, the woman, went out for the evening one time when she was working late, Betty I mean, and the twins were left unattended and they ran out into the street and wandered about and a policeman found them and that's how we got brought into it. They were in a dreadful state, poor little dabs, half in rags and – quite filthy. I had the devil's own job stopping them being taken into care, I can tell you. You see, while Betty was with her parents in a decent home she looked after them all right, but on her own, with bad examples all round her, she just let things slide. No moral fibre there, I'm afraid. Well, I fixed her up at the day nursery – didn't know there were such things, she said, but I told her she'd just been too lazy to inquire – and after that things jogged along until this Norwegian came into the café for a cup of tea and saw Betty and Bob's your uncle.'

'Hasn't the Norwegian got to go back to Norway ever?' Jean asked, her eyes on the forkful of fish that had been oscillating for some minutes between Mair's plate and her mouth.

'He's going over for a few weeks soon, he says. He's got a job at a chandler's in Ogmore Street – it's run by Norwegians, like a lot of them. Decent people. They've been married six weeks now, him and Betty, and he's very fond of the twins and keeps her up to the mark about them, and of course I give her a good pep talk every so often.'

'Of course,' I said.

'One job I had to do was take her out of that café. Lot of undesirables hang round the place, you know. A girl like Betty, quite pretty and none too bright, she'd have been just their meat. It's something to have kept her out of their clutches. Oh, yes, I'm quite proud of myself in a way.'

One Sunday afternoon a couple of months later I was dozing in front of the fire – Jean had taken the kids out for a walk with a pal of hers and the pal's kids – when the doorbell rang. Wondering if the caller mightn't at last be some beautiful borrower come to avow her love, I hurried downstairs. The person on the door-step was certainly a woman and probably on the right side of thirty, but she wasn't beautiful. Nor – I'd have taken any odds – was she a borrower, not with that transparent mac, that vehement eye shadow, that squall of scent. 'Good afternoon,' I said.

The woman smiled, fluttering her Prussian-blue eyelids. 'You remember me, don't you, Mr Lewis? Betty Arnulfsen.'

I felt my own eyes dilate. 'Why, of course,' I said genially. 'How are you, Betty? Do come in.'

'Aw, all right, thank you. Thanks.'

'Haven't seen you for a long time.' Not for several weeks, in fact. She'd turned up three more times to do our chores and then that had suddenly been that. Application to Mair Webster had produced an evasive answer – an extreme and, as I now saw it, suspicious rarity.

'I was just passing by, see, so I thought I'd drop in and see how you was all getting along, like.'

'Good. It's very nice to see you again. Well, what have you been doing with yourself?'

It could have been more delicately put, for somebody, whether herself or not, had plainly been doing a good deal with Betty one way and another. As we stood confronted by the sitting-room fire I saw that her hair, which had been of a squaw-like sleekness, now looked like some kind of petrified black froth, and that her face was puffy underneath the yellowish coating of make-up. At the same time she'd altogether lost her hounded look: she seemed sure of herself, even full of fun. She wore a tight lilac costume with purple stripes on it and carried a long-handled umbrella that had elaborate designs on the plastic.

'Aw, I been doing lots of things,' she said in answer to my question. 'Having a bit of a good time for a change. Soon got brassed off with that old cow Webster telling me what I must do and what I mustn't do. I been keeping out of her way, going to live my own life for a change, see? I got a bit of money now. Here, have a fag.'

'No, thanks, I don't smoke.'

'Go on, it'll do you good, man.'

'No, honestly, I never do.'

'I can tell you're one of the careful ones.' She laughed quite a bit at this stroke, giving me a chance to notice the purplish inner portions of her lips where the lipstick had worn away or not reached. With a kind of indulgent contempt, she went on: 'And how you been keeping? Still working down that old library?'

'Oh, yes, I feel I ought to give them a hand occasionally.'

'Don't you get brassed off with it now and then?'

'Yes, I do, but I keep going. Can't afford to weaken.'

'That's the boy. Got to keep the dough coming in, haven't you?'

'Well, it helps, you know.'

'What you pulling in down there? Never mind, don't suppose you want to say. What you get up to after work?'

'Nothing out of the ordinary.'

'What you do, then, when you goes out for a night? Where do you go?'

'Oh, just here and there. I sometimes have a few along at the corner, at the General Picton.'

'I expect you got your own mates.' Her cigarette had gone out and she relit it. She wasn't really at home with it: smoking was something she was still in the process of taking up. After spitting out a shred of tobacco, she said: 'Never go round the pubs in Ogmore Street, do you?'

'Not as a rule, no.'

(Ogmore Street leads into the docks, and on these and associated grounds is usually steered well clear of during the hours of darkness by persons of refinement and discrimination.)

'We gets up to some games down Ogmore Street. We haves the time of our bloody lives, we do.'

'I bet you do.'

'Yeah,' she said with great conviction. 'Jean gone out, have she?'

'Just taken the kids for a breath of fresh air. I don't suppose she'll be long.'

'Ah. They all right, the kids?'

'Pretty fair. What are you up to yourself these days?'

She gave a great yell of laughter. 'That's a question, that is. What don't I bloody get up to? What am I up to, eh? That's a good one.' Then her manner grew seriously informative. 'I got in with the business girls now, see?'

'Oh, really?' A momentary vision of Betty drinking morning coffee at the Kardomah with a group of secretaries and short-hand typists was briefly presented to me, before being penetrated by her true meaning. 'Er ... good fun?'

'It's all right, you know. Got its points, like. See what I got here.' She opened her handbag, a shiny plastic affair in a pink pastel shade, and, after I'd sat there wondering for a moment or two, drew out a roll of crumpled pound notes bound with an elastic band. 'Take you a long time to pull in this much down the library, wouldn't it?'

'Oh, no doubt about that.'

'We goes with the boys round the docks and the sailors when

they comes off the ships. They're the best. They wants a bit of fun and they don't care what they pays for it. They got plenty of dough, see? They goes on the bloody binge down there. Lots of Norgies we gets. I like the Norgies.'

'Oh, yes, your husband's one, isn't he?'

This second deviation from the path of true tact was as little heeded as the first. 'That's right. He've gone back to Norway now.'

'For good?'

'No, don't think so. Father's in trouble or something. Reckon he'll fetch up again some time.'

'How are the twins?' The domestic note, once struck, might be a handy one to prolong. What was the time? Where was Jean? Would she bring her red-faced English oh-I-say-darling pal back with her? Why not?

'They're OK. I got someone looking after them OK. These Norgies are dead funny though. Makes me die. The Welsh boys, now, they likes me with my vest on, don't want it no other way, but the Norgies don't care for that, they wants everything off, and they don't like it outside, they always goes home with you for it. They likes to take their time, like. You know Joe Leyshon?'

'I've heard of him. Used to be in the fight game, didn't he?'

'He runs a lot of the girls down Ogmore Street, but I won't let him run me. He wants to run me, but I don't like him. Some of his mates is dead funny, though. We broke into a shop the other night over Cwmharan way. Didn't get anything much, few fags and things, but we had a laugh. Mad buggers, they are. We goes down the Albany mostly. You know the Albany? It's all right. You ought to come down there one night and have a couple of drinks and a bit of fun. What about it? I'm going down there tonight.'

'Well, I don't want to come barging in.'

'Go on, I'd show you around, you wouldn't come to no harm, I promise you. They're all right there, really. I'd see you had a good time. You could tell Jean you was out with your mates, see?'

'It's very kind of you, Betty, but honestly I don't think I

could. I'm pretty well fixed up here, you know what I mean, and so I don't ...'

'I tell you one thing, John.'

'What's that?'

'You're afraid to go with me.'

So many factors amalgamated to put this beyond serious dispute that reply was difficult. 'Oh, I wouldn't say that,' I said after a moment, trying to ram jocoseness into tone and manner. 'No, I wouldn't say that at all.'

Betty evidently saw through this. She said: 'You are. You're afraid.'

'It isn't that exactly. It's just that I try to stick to my wife as far as possible,' I told her, certain that I sounded like some ferret-faced Christian lance-corporal in a barrack-room discussion.

'Yeah, I know, you'd fold up if you hadn't got her there to cling on to. You hangs around all the bloody time.' Contempt had returned to her voice, edged this time with bitterness, but she showed none of either when she went on to add: 'You're a good boy.'

'I wouldn't say – I don't know. Betty, you mustn't mind me saying this, but isn't it rather risky to go round breaking into places with these pals of yours? Aren't you afraid of getting caught?'

'Aw, short life and a merry one's what I say. It's worth it for a bit of excitement. Don't get much chance of a thrill these days, eh?'

'Well, it's up to you, but you don't want to get – you know – sent down, do you? The twins wouldn't have ...'

'Don't preach, now. I gets brassed off with bloody preaching.'

'I'm sorry, I didn't mean to sound like that.'

'Okay.' She smiled.

In the succeeding silence a door boomed shut below. The slapping gait of my daughter Eira became audible, overlaid and in part obscured by the characteristic bellowing squeal of her younger brother. Both sounds began to ascend the stairs.

'Jean back, eh?' Betty got to her feet. 'I better be going.'

'Oh, don't go, stay and have a cup of tea with us.'

'I better not.'

Eira ran into the room, stopping short when she saw Betty and then moving towards the fire by a circuitous route, hugging the wall and the couch. 'Put my coat off,' she said to me distantly.

'Hallo,' Betty said with an elaborate rising inflection. 'Hallo. And whose little girl are you? Let auntie take your coat off, then. Come on, flower. That's right. Had a lovely run, have you? Did you see any bunnies? How you've grown. And you're bold as ever, I declare. Yes, you are. You're bold, very very bold. Yes, you are. You're very very brazen by there.'

Jean came in with the baby. 'Well, hallo, Betty,' she said, grinning. 'Nice to see you. Christ, shut up, can't you?' This last was addressed to the baby, who seemed almost, but not quite, worn out with mortal pain.

'Sorry I couldn't come along that Tuesday like we said, Mrs Lewis, but the twins was poorly and I couldn't fix it to let you know.'

'That's all right, Betty. I'll put the kettle on.'

'Let me take the baby for you.'

'Oh, thanks a lot. John, you might have kept the fire up.'

'Sorry, dear.' I picked up the coal scuttle, which was one of the obliquely-truncated-cone type. It proved to weigh less than it should, less than a coal scuttle with any coal in it could. I could hardly remember ever having made up the fire without encountering, at the very outset, a light coal scuttle.

During a long, foul-mouthed ardour in the coal cupboard under the stairs, I thought first how funny it was that a fallen woman – really fallen now, right smack over full length – should talk to a child in just the same style as the perpendicularly upright went in for. But then presumably there were parts of the fallen that were bound to remain unfallen, quite important parts too. This brought up the whole mystery of prostituted existence: not what happened to your womanhood or your springs of emotion or your chances of getting clued up on the splendours and miseries of the flesh – screw all that – but what it was like to be a prostitute during the times when you weren't actually behaving like one, when you were in mufti: on a bus, cooking the baked beans, doing the ironing, going shopping, chatting to a neighbour, buying the Christmas presents. It must be like going round ordinarily and all the time you were a spy or a parson or a leading authority on Rilke, things which you surely often forgot about being. Anyway, to judge by the representative upstairs, being a prostitute was something you could be done a power of good by, and without having to be horrible first, either. As regards not having to get horrible later on, that too could no doubt be arranged, especially if you could keep out of the way of the various sets of men in white coats who, according to report, tended to close in on you after a few years in the game. That was a nasty prospect all right, and resembled many a kindred nastiness thought up by the Godhead in seeming a disproportionate penalty for rather obscure offences. Still, that minor cavil about the grand design had been answered long ago, hadn't it? Yes, more answers than one had been offered.

A little coal, too little to be worth expelling, had entered my shoe. I bore the scuttle upstairs to find Jean and Eira in the kitchen and Betty still holding the baby. Her demeanour had quietened and she was more like the Betty I had first met when she said: 'You won't tell Jean all what I been saying, will you?'

'Of course I won't.'

'And you won't tell that old Webster I been up?'

'Christ, no. What do you think I am?'

'She's a cow.'

'Oh, she's a cow all right.'

Betty nodded slowly, frowning, half-heartedly jogging the baby on her knee. Then she said: 'She's a real cow.'

This refinement upon the original concept made me laugh. Betty joined in. We laughed together for some time, so that Eira came in from the kitchen to see what the joke was.

'I don't mind telling you I was very depressed about that girl at one time,' Mair Webster said. 'Quite frankly I thought we might be going to lose her. It upset me a good deal, one way and another. Once her husband was out of the way for a couple of months, as soon as his back was turned she just took the line of least resistance. Her old cronies at the café, you see, she took up with them again, and got things fixed up with another of them there with minding each other's children while the other was off after the men, turn and turn about and sharing the same flat, or couple of rooms rather, the most sordid den you could possibly imagine, I'm not exaggerating, I promise you. Well, I soon got Betty and the twins out of that hell hole and fixed them up in a decent place, good enough for the time being, anyway, until Arnulfsen got back from Norway. They've quite a nice little flat now – well, you'll be able to judge, John. It's nothing very grand, of course, but it's a darned sight better than what people like that are used to. Oh, thank you, Jean dear.'

'Everything looks pretty bright then, doesn't it?' my wife asked, pouring coffee. 'Troubles seem to be over.' Her manner showed a relief that I guessed to be partly personal. The strain of not telling Mair about Betty's earlier visit hadn't been lightly borne.

'I don't think I should say that exactly,' Mair said. 'Arnulfsen's forgiven her all right, and she's trying to make a go of it, quite seriously, I can tell. But they keep being bothered by the crowd she used to be in with before, girls who used to be in the same gang looking her up, and once they even had a lascar trying to force his way in; wanted to renew old acquaintance and got her address from the café, I suppose. There've been one or two things like that. And then some of the neighbours have got to hear about Betty's past and they keep teasing her about it, call out in the street after her. Chapel spirit gone sour, you see. It makes Arnulfsen pretty wild.'

While Jean expressed her indignation, I was wondering fairly hard how I was going to 'be able to judge' the Arnulfsens' flat. Was I in some way committed to a tea party there, or what? An answer couldn't be long delayed, for Mair was draining her cup and rising. 'Come along,' she said. 'We've not got too much time.'

'Time for what, Mair? I'm sorry . . .'

She threw me a momentary leonine glare before dipping to pick up her handbag. When she spoke, it was with an incredulity to which those accustomed to plan for others must often be subject. Since what she had lined up for me was necessitated both by logic and by natural law, how could I conceivably not know what it was? 'But surely you're coming along to Betty's with me? I'm only popping in to see how she is. Then I can drop you at the library by two-fifteen. Cheerio, Jean dear. Thank you for a lovely lunch. We must fix up a coffee date for next week. I'll give John a ring, if I can manage to pick a time when he's at the seat of custom.'

Wiggling her eyebrows at me to enjoin silence, Jean went into a vivacious speech which lasted more or less until I was sitting in Mair's car next to its owner. Opened envelopes, typed lists, printed forms lay about us as at some perfunctory demonstration of bureaucracy at work. Jean continued her facial ballet until we left.

I knew Mair was going to tell me some more, or possibly run over a few familiar but essential points, about what being a social worker was like. She enjoyed getting me on my own and doing this because, it appeared, I was a man and, as such, easy to talk to. Sometimes her husband came into these conversations, but not often, and when he did it was likely to be as a feature of her exposition of what being married to a social worker's husband was like. I hoped we were going to get the practical today; some of Mair's case histories were of great anthropological interest, and those that weren't were still a lot better than the theoretical.

We got the theoretical, but crossed with the autobiographical, which helped a bit. What had first attracted her to the idea of social work? Ah, there were many answers to this conundrum, every one of them demanding careful or at any rate lengthy consideration. Mair had taken a course in psychology, so she knew all about the power impulse and its tendency to be present in those who made a living out of good works. Several of her colleagues were prone to this affliction, and she had even detected it in herself before now. That was where psychological training was so useful: you knew how to examine your own motives and to guard against unworthy ones. With that out of the way, she felt safe in asserting that it was the duty of the mature and responsible elements of the community to do what they could for their less gifted fellows. At one time the more conscientious kind of squire had stood in a similar relation to his tenants, the right-minded employer to his workmen and their families, but the rise of oligopoly (Mair kept up with Labour Party research pamphlets) had put paid to all that. One of the many all-important tasks of our society was the training of specialists for functions which at one time had been discharged as by-products of other functions. A case very much in point here was provided by the constantly expanding duties of – well, Mair recognized the term *social workers*, but for her own part she preferred (having once attended a Social Science Summer School in Cardiff) to think of herself and her associates as *technicians in paternalism*.

When she brought that one out I had the infrequent experience of seeing her face express only a limited satisfaction with what she'd said. We penetrated farther into an uncongenial district. Then Mair added: 'Actually, John, I'm not altogether happy about that label.'

'You're not?'

'No, I'm not. It's a scientific term, of course, and so it's quite accurate in a way, but like all scientific terms it's incomplete, it doesn't really say enough, doesn't go far enough, leaves out a lot. It leaves out the thing that keeps us all going, sees us over the rough patches and stops us losing faith, which is the one thing we can't afford to do in our job. It's – well, I can't think of any better name for it than ... idealism. You can laugh if you like —' she turned her profile far enough round to assure me that any such laughter had better remain internal – 'but that's what it is. Just a simple, old-fashioned urge to do good, not in a chapel way, naturally, but scientifically, because we know what we're doing, but that's the basis of the whole thing, no point in beating about the bush. I know that sort of talk makes you feel uncomfortable, but I believe in —'

Before she could mention calling a spade a spade, a mode of nomenclature she often recommended, I told her that that wasn't quite it, and went on: 'This isn't aimed at you, Mair, but I think doing good to people's rather a risky thing. You can lay up a lot of trouble, for yourself as well as the people who're being done good to. And it's so hard to be sure that the good you're trying to do really is good, the best thing for that person, and the justification of the whole business is a bit —'

'I'm in favour of taking risks. There's far too much playing safe these days, it's ruining the country, all this stick-in-the-mud attitude. I believe in taking off my coat and getting on with the job.'

'But, Mair, these are risks that involve other people. You're deciding what's best for them and then doing it, just like that. You don't give them a chance to —'

'If you'd done as much social work as I have, John, perhaps you'd have some idea of how many people there are in this world who are constitutionally incapable of knowing what's best for them. They're like children. You wouldn't let Eira be the judge of what was best for her, would you? You wouldn't let her put her hand in the fire to see if it was hot, would you?'

'No, of course not, but children aren't —'

'I know you think social work's something terribly complicated and difficult. Well, believe me, ninety or ninety-five per cent of the time it couldn't be simpler, at least making the right decision couldn't: getting it carried out is something else again, of course, but the actual decision's a piece of cake, because you're dealing with complete fools or complete swine or both. You'd think the same after a month in my job, I know you would.'

'I hope not.'

'Honestly, John, if people in general thought like you there wouldn't be any progress at all.'

'No, there wouldn't, would there?'

At this fundamental point Mair steered the car to the kerb and stopped it, not, it transpired, in order to fight me but because we'd arrived. Facing us when we got out was a meagre row of shops: a newsagent's with a lot of advertisements written on postcards, a barber-cum-tobacconist, an outfitter's whose window stock alone would have outfitted a hundred middle-aged ladies in wool from head to foot, and a place that had no doubt once been a shop in the full sense but was now white-washed to above eye level. This last establishment had to one side of it a door, recently painted a British Railways brown, and a bell which Mair rang. Then she took me by the arm and drew me a yard or two along the pavement.

I said: 'What's this in aid of, then?' in what was supposed to be a bantering tone. Actually I was only half noticing; my mind was busy trying to decide what Mair's 'you'd think the same after a month in the job' thing had reminded me of.

'You don't want to be in front of the front door of a house like this when they open it.'

'Oh?' That was it: the veteran colonial administrator to the just-out-from-England colonial administrator. *We're all a bit pro-wog when we first get out here, my boy; it's only natural. Soon wears off, though, you'll find.* 'Why not?'

'Well, the door opening makes the draught rush through the house, and the draught carries the bugs with it. You don't want them to land on you.'

'You mean really bugs?' She had my full attention now.

'You don't want them to land on you.'

'Hallo, Mrs Webster, don't often see you up this way.'

'Oh, good afternoon, Emrys, how are you?' Mair turned animatedly towards the new arrival, a young police constable with a long, pale nose. 'Wife all right?'

'Well, no, she hasn't been too grand, actually. They had her back in for three days' observation the week before last, and the doctor said —' His voice became indistinguishable, chiefly because he was lowering its pitch, but also because he was removing its source in the direction of the shop that had committed itself so whole-heartedly to the woollen garment. Mair retreated with him, nodding a fair amount. I was still feeling impressed by her bit of know-how about the bugs. Real front-line stuff, that.

'Yes, who's here, please?' This came from the now open front door, at which a small red-haired, red-faced man was standing.

'My name's Lewis.'

'I don't know you. What you want here?'

I looked along the pavement to where Mair, nodding faster, was standing with her back to me. It must have had all the appearance of a furtive, sidelong, up-to-no-good look. Like a fool, I said: 'I'm a friend of your wife's.' As I said this, I smiled.

'Get out of here,' the red-haired man bawled. He wore a red shirt. 'Get out, you bastard.'

'Look, it's all right, there's no need to —'

'Get out quick, you bastard.' For the first time he saw Mair and the policeman, who were now approaching. 'Mrs Webster, hallo. And you, officer. Take away this bastard.'

'Now calm down, Bent, nothing to get excited about. Mr Lewis is with me. He and his wife have been very kind to Betty. He's come along with me to see how you all are. He's a friend of mine.'

'Sorry, Mrs Webster. Sorry, sir, very sorry.'

'That's all right, Bent, Mr Lewis doesn't mind. He knows you didn't mean anything. You just forget it. Now, can we come in?'

'Please, yes, come in.'

'Bye-bye, Emrys, give Maureen my love. Tell her I'll pop in to see her in a day or two. And don't you worry. She's a good strong girl and with the better weather coming she'll soon pull round, I guarantee.'

'Thank you very much, Mrs Webster. Goodbye now.'

Before he turned away I caught a glimpse of Emrys's face and was startled to see on it an expression of relief and gratitude, quite as if he'd just received an important reassurance of some kind. I followed Mair across the threshold, frowning and shaking my head at life's endless enigma.

Bugs or no bugs, the house revealed itself to me as not too bad. There were loose and cracked floorboards, but none missing, and no damp; the kitchen we penetrated to was dark all right, but it smelt no worse than stale; through its open door I could see a scullery with a row of clean cups hanging above the sink and a dishcloth spread over the taps to dry. One of the twins came into view in that quarter, took in the sight of visitors and doubled away again.

'Good afternoon, Betty,' Mair was saying in her hospital-rounds manner. 'My goodness, you have done well, haven't you? You really ought to be congratulated. You have made the place look nice.'

She went on like that while I glanced round the place. It did look nice enough as far as it went, but that wasn't at all far. Most noticeably, there was an absence of the unnecessary things, the ornaments, the photographs and pictures, the postcards on the mantelpiece that every home accumulates. It was as if the moving men had just dumped the furniture down, leaving the small stuff to be unpacked later, only in this case there was nothing to unpack. Curtains perhaps fell into the category of the unnecessary, even, with a small single window like this one, of the excessive. They were of Betty's favourite lilac shade, and ranks of mauve personages, with sword and fan, periwig and towering hair-do, were doing a minuet on them. At this sight I felt pity stirring. Get back, you brute, I said internally, giving it a mental kick on the snout. Then I felt angry with a whole lot of people, but without much prospect of working out just who.

Mair was nearing her peroration. I looked covertly at Betty. Although no longer tarted up, she hadn't recovered the quiet, youthful air she'd had when I first saw her. She wore a grey cardigan which seemed designed to accentuate the roundness of her shoulders. The circles under her eyes weren't the temporary kind. She was staring up at Mair with the sarcastic patience of someone listening to a shaky alibi. Bent Arnulfsen, after standing about uneasily for a time, went out into the scullery and I heard water plunging into a kettle. Still talking, the old moral commando moved to follow him. 'I just want to have a word with Bent a minute,' she said, and shut the door behind her.

'Well, how are things?' I asked.

Betty glanced at me without friendliness, then away. 'OK,' she muttered, picking at a hole in the cover of her chair.

'Your husband seems a nice chap.'

'What you know about it, eh?'

'I'm only going on how he struck me.'

'Aw, he's OK, I suppose. He's a good boy.'

'There's a lot to be said for good boys.'

'Suppose so.'

'You seem to have settled down here nicely.'

'Yeah.'

'Jean and the children asked to be remembered to you, by the way.'

To shrug both her shoulders would have meant heaving herself up from the chair back, so she made do with just shrugging the uppermost one. It was clear to me that there was nothing left of the cordiality of our last meeting, and no wonder. A man who had seen her when she was free was the last kind of person on earth who should have been allowed to see her now she was tamed. And in any contact not made on terms of equality the speech of one party or the other will fall almost inevitably into the accents and idioms of patronage, as I'd just heard my own speech doing. Severity is actually more respectful. But that wouldn't do here. Would anything? I said: 'Do you ever miss the old life?'

'What you want to know for? What's it got to do with you?'

'Nothing. I was only asking.'

'Well, don't ask, see? Mind your own bloody business, see? What you want to come here for anyway?'

'I'm sorry, Betty. I just came to see how you were getting on.'

'Like old Webster, eh? Well I don't like people coming along to see how I'm getting on, see? I gets brassed off with it, see?'

As she got up from her chair to make her point more forcibly, the scullery door opened and Mair came back into the room. My sense of relief filled me with shame. Triumph swept over Betty's face at being about to do what she must have wanted to do for quite a time.

'Your husband certainly thinks the world of you, Betty,' Mair led off. 'He's been telling me —'

'Get out, you old cow,' Betty shouted, blinking fast. 'I doesn't want you here, see? I got enough to put up with with the bloody neighbours hanging over the fence and staring in the bloody windows and them buggers upstairs complaining. I got enough without you poking your bloody nose in, see? Just you piss off quick and leave me alone.'

'Please, my dear, be quiet.' Bent Arnulfsen had reappeared in the scullery doorway. In one hand he held a brown enamel teapot, in the other the hand of one of the twins. 'Mrs Webster is kind. And this gentleman.'

'You keep out of this, man. Go on, Webster, what you waiting for? I said get out, didn't I? Who do you think you are, that's what I'd like to know – poking your bloody nose in everywhere and telling every bugger what to do. You're beyond, you are, Webster. Bloody beyond. And as for you —' At the moment when Betty, who was now crying, turned to me, Mair looked at her wristwatch with a quick movement. 'Who asked you to come snooping in, that's what I'd like to know,' Betty started to say to me, but Mair cut in.

'I'm afraid we shan't be able to manage that cup of tea, Bent,' she said interestedly; 'I'd no idea the time was getting along like this. I must take Mr Lewis off to his place of work or I shall get into trouble. I'll be in next week as usual and I'm sure things will have settled down by then. Goodbye, Betty; don't upset yourself, there's a good girl. Goodbye, Bent.'

With another look at me, full of accusation, Betty blundered out into the scullery and banged the door. Later I thought how cruel it was that she'd been met by bland preoccupation instead of the distress or anger she'd longed to provoke, that her brave show of defiance must have seemed to her to have misfired. But at the time I only wanted to get out before she came back.

Brushing aside Bent Arnulfsen's halting apologies, Mair led me away. 'Astonishing how predictable these girls are,' she said as we drove off. 'I'd seen that little lot coming for some time. You usually get it sooner or later and afterwards you often find you get on better than you did before. Sort of clears the air in a way. Next week she'll be falling over herself and holding on to my hand and going on about "Oh, Mrs Webster, how could I have said what I did, what a pig I was to you, Mrs Webster, and you so kind", and not being able to do enough for me. Not that that phase lasts very long, either. No, there's no doubt about it, if you look for thanks in this job you're wasting your time and letting yourself in for a big disappointment. The approval of your conscience is all the reward you ever get.'

'Seen this?' my wife asked later in the same year.

I took the local paper from her and read that Elizabeth Grace Arnulfsen (19) had been sentenced to two months' imprisonment for helping to burgle a café in Harrieston. (The two men who'd been with her got longer sentences.) Mrs Mair Webster, it was further reported, had spoken of her belief that Elizabeth Arnulfsen was weak willed rather than vicious and had been led astray by undesirable companions. She said this out of her thorough knowledge of the girl's character, and had been thanked for saying it.

'Well, I hope Mair's satisfied,' I said, throwing the paper down.

'Don't be silly, you know she'll be very cut up. She's always done her best for Betty.'

'Her worst, you mean.'

'Don't talk so soft.'

'Betty only burgled that place to get her own back.'

'What, on Mair?'

'Yes, I should say it was chiefly on Mair. Not on society or any of that crap. As a method of not being the kind of person Mair wanted her to be.'

'Mm. Sounds more like just high spirits to me. And according to what you told me Betty'd been breaking into places quite a time back.'

'Not until Mair'd started licking her into shape.'

'You're exaggerating the whole thing, John. What should have happened according to you, anyway? Betty going on being a tart?'

'Why not?'

'What about the twins and this Bent bloke?'

'Yes. No, she shouldn't have gone on being a tart, or couldn't or something. Pity in a way, though. She was enjoying herself.'

'You don't know anything about it. I'm going to make supper.'

'I know how not to deal with people like Betty. Shall I give you a hand?'

'No, you make the cocoa after. How do you stop people being tarts? How would you do it if it was you?'

'Always assuming I thought I ought to try. It's all a mess. It all needs going into.'

'Who's going to go into it? You and Mair?'

'No, just me. What about that supper?'

I could picture Mair doing what she'd have called helping Betty through the ordeal, going to see her in prison, meeting her when she got out and at once settling down again to the by now surely hopeless task of inducing her to lead a normal life with her husband and children. And what would friend Lewis be up to while all this was going on? Getting boozed with his mates, having fantasies about some new beautiful borrower, binding about his extra evening duties in the summer and explaining to his wife that you couldn't have good social workers, because the only kind of chap who'd make a good one was also the kind of chap who'd refuse to be one. Of the two of us, it had to be admitted that on the face of it Mair had a claim to be considered the less disreputable character, up there in the firing line while cowards flinched and traitors sneered.

Once you got off the face of it, though, and got on to what Mair was actually doing up there in the firing line, the picture changed a bit, just as things like the Labour Party looked better from some way away than close to. This was a timely reflection, because I'd been almost starting to admire Mair rather, and admiring someone you think is horrible is horrible. It was true enough that you had to have social workers, in the same way that you had to have prison warders, local government officials, policemen, military policemen, nurses, parsons, scientists, mental-hospital attendants, politicians and – for the time being anyway, God forgive us all – hangmen. That didn't mean that you had to feel friendly disposed towards any such person, bar the odd nurse perhaps, and then only on what you might call extrinsic grounds.

Actually, of course, it wasn't Mair I ought to have been cogitating about. Mair, with her creed of take-off-your-coat-and-get-on-with-it (and never mind what 'it' is), could be run out of town at any stage, if possible after being bound and gagged and forced to listen to a no-holds barred denunciation of her by Betty. What if anything should or could be done about

Betty, and who if anyone should or could do it and how – that
was the real stuff. I was sorry to think how impossible it was
for me to turn up at the gaol on the big day, holding a bunch
of flowers and a new plastic umbrella.

Gwyn Thomas

An Ample Wish

Dear Mr Saltzmann, Dear Mr Broccoli,

I hear you are looking for a new James Bond and you suggest a younger man. I think this is a mistake. You need an older man and I think I fill the bill. I am sixty-six. I am still an effective lover and a pretty handy tenor with an extraordinary ear. If ever you should get James Bond to sing, and it's about time he did, for a change, I'm your man. Women singers have always seemed to admire me for the last forty years, and that's a long time in a place like Belmont.

I notice that you want a man who walks well. You say he should move like Robert Mitchum, Gary Cooper, Clark Gable. I haven't actually seen these men. I only went to the cinema when I was on the rota of voluntary ushers at the Welfare Hall. And when I had that job I was too busy sticking tickets on my little wire spear and warning people about canoodling and gambling, and so on.

There was a lot of gambling in that cinema. If the picture was dull, groups of voters would out with torches and cards and start gaming. I don't know whether the darkness did anything to lower their moral standards of honesty, but these gamblers were always fighting and accusing each other of cheating. So I never saw any of the actors you mention, Gable and the others, and I have no idea of what was so special in the way they walked.

I think I walk all right. I live on a hill riddled with ruts and pot-holes. I have grown very agile over the years dodging these traps. Even when I go spinning in the dark I'm up like a flash. I think this would come in useful for me when I have to fling myself flat at the approach of bullets.

I am also a good dancer, although as Bond the agent I would

probably have to learn a few new steps. When I was younger I was a good dancer of the slinky type. I was too slinky for some people. Around here they favour a dull, decorous shuffle. In 1925 I came near an award at the Tango Contest at the Arcadia Ballroom in Belmont. Alderman Brinley Beynon still says that he would have tipped me for the premier trophy, a crimson rose bowl, if there had not been so strong a dash of the dago in my style.

I was chauffeur to the mayors of Belmont for five years. I was sacked for driving too fast and putting the mayors on edge, especially Alderman Beynon who was the one who sacked me. I gave Alderman Beynon a rough drive. I had had a mixture of cherry brandy and drambuie in the Liberal Club. I mention this to show that my taste in drinks is not common. I touched eighty miles per hour that afternoon. People on the pavements could hear his teeth and chain rattling.

A few days later he apologized for sacking me and offered me the job back. But I had fixed myself up with a job as chauffeur at the steel works. The mayor was in drink. He confessed to me that he had made love to various women with whom I had associated, and he said that these women still spoke of me with ardour and wanted to see me again.

At sixty-six I am still active on this front, like a well-trained setter on the track of any bit of crumble. That's why I think you need an older man for Bond. It would give people something to live up to. It would encourage them to see a pensioner as lithe and active as a man bulging with youth. Last summer I won the walking race for the over-sixties in the steel-works sports. I'm so thin I had more trouble with the elastic of my shorts than with my competitors.

I think that I should mention that I tend to walk in a rather low-slung sort of way. I asked Alderman Beynon if he thought this would spoil my chances as a successor to Sean Connery. He said no, like a shot. He said there could be advantages in appearing to be sitting down when you are actually standing up. Deceiving people is what secret agents are all about. He says I have a natural gift for duplicity, very double-faced and loose in my traffic with the truth. I'm the man he'd send to tackle any tricky negotiations on behalf of the Council, he says. As soon as I started to talk they'd need flood-lighting to see the point.

So you see my qualities. Ardour, cunning, speed. And you don't need to worry about my speaking voice. I have a strong, clear voice. I can switch from a shout of command to a murmur of love in however short a time you may fancy. I had a lot of brothers and sisters who resented my superior ways and enjoyed being truly vulgar themselves. They tried to shout me down. To counter this I had to develop an amazing volume and flexibility.

In 1919 I gained the Silver Daffodil award given to the best reciter at the Belmont Semi-National Eisteddfod by Councillor Gilbert Beynon, father of the alderman and himself a reciter on whose rounded style I was prone to model my own. The two poems I recited in that victory year of 1919 were 'The Shooting of Dan MacGrew' and 'A Drunkard's Remorse'. The latter was so terrifying in its truth and horror all concert organizers told me to drop it and repeat MacGrew.

In my thirties I had a phase as an open-air evangelist. My missionary area was a corner of the Belmont market square. It did me no harm although it might have foxed a few of the faithful. My homemade pulpit was a large, hollow contraption with an acoustic that made decisions on sound-level tricky. Passages in my appeal meant to cajole and persuade came out like the roar of cannon. People took me for a clown. They laughed at me. A mocking flock and that acoustic did for my mission.

Oh, and there was that chap who had a stall next to my position. It was a canvas stall with two big, smoky naphtha flares. They nearly choked me. A lot of people thought I was peddling a new faith that gave coughing its true place in the human riddle. The stall-holder's name was Glossop. He sold gew-gaws such as painted tea-mugs that leaked and cigarette lighters with fireproof wicks and brittle flints that wore out the thumb.

Glossop had a sharp, knowing face and when it was caught in the glare of those naphtha lamps he had a diabolical look that caused people to buy just to keep on the right side of bad luck. Glossop taught me a lot of quick-fire banter meant to ginger up the slower clients. I also practised his diabolical look and I think those two things would fit very well into the glib cynical things that Bond is always coming out with.

Glossop was a powerful amorist. He paid his women with those painted tea-mugs and many local kitchens are still full of them because Glossop was busy. He brought me along rapidly in this same field. He lifted me clear over the hurdles of my long-standing chastity and turned me into one of the zone's most pervasive rakes. Alderman Beynon says that Glossop would have been in a position to give the best possible extra-mural course in lechery, and he envies me the experience of having been Glossop's apprentice.

Glossop also gave me recipes for potent restoratives. I never know weariness. Glossop got the secret of these tonics from his grandfather, a herbalist and magician. His mixtures have been known to make old rugs levitate and embrace. Last September, in a mixed works outing to Bourton-on-the-Water I was still doling out great helpings of affection at a quarter to midnight. It was a field day. Bond would have had his chips by tea-time. If you make me Bond and let me show my true scope he and I will bring a new sunlight into the prospects of the aged.

I'm afraid I've never had much to do with guns. This is a place dead set against anything abrupt, especially bangs. Guns are not liked. I didn't serve in the war. I had a job in security at the steel works. Keeping an eye on things, but unarmed. The Germans would have given their right jackboot to get their hands on a vital industrial unit like that. So I can claim to have been one of the men who, although ununiformed, kept this prize away from the enemy.

But I have a neighbour, Mr Cleghorn, who has a collection of guns. I didn't know about this until a few weeks ago. He always had a bright look about him, as if he had something interesting and important on his mind. I thought it was just greed or a late passion. It was these guns. It is a good collection. It ranges from a frail-looking gun, which, says Cleghorn, belonged to the only highwayman ever to practise around here. The first time I tried it it fell apart. The highwayman probably had the same sort of luck. You can't ask people to stand and deliver in the right threatening tone if you are looking for bits of your gun.

Mr Cleghorn also has a Biretta which Mr Bond has been known to use. Mr Cleghorn was giving me a bit of drill with it last Monday. It was on top of the mountain. If we practised down in the town they'd have whipped us inside before the echoes died away. I saw a woman on our way up to the practice pitch. I fancied her and wished to make her mine.

Mr Cleghorn, a bit of a dry stick, noticed this and told me he did not favour lust. I couldn't explain to him that I had my eye on a role that mingled marksmanship, spying and wooing. His attitude disturbed me. On my first shot my hand shook. Quite without intending to, I shot him. Not much, just a graze, and he's just as patient and gentle as ever. Next Monday, he says, we'll go through the whole collection, starting with the flintlock, and by the time you want to see me I'll be the master of any weapon you want to put in my hand. Knowing that you'll bear me in mind . . .

George MacDonald Fraser

Monsoon Selection Board

Our coal-bunker is old, and it stands beneath an ivy hedge, so that when I go to it in wet weather, I catch the combined smells of damp earth and decaying vegetation. And I can close my eyes and be thousands of miles away, up to my middle in a monsoon ditch in India, with my face pressed against the tall slats of a bamboo fence, and Martin-Duggan standing on my shoulders, swearing at me while the rain pelts down and soaks us. And all around there is mud, and mud, and more mud, until I quit dreaming and come back to the mundane business of getting a shovelful of coal for the sitting-room fire.

It is twenty years and more since I was in India. My battalion was down on the Sittang Bend, trying to stop the remnants of the Japanese Army escaping eastwards out of Burma – why we had to do this no one really understood, because the consensus of opinion was that the sooner Jap escaped the better, and good luck to him. Anyway, the war was nearly over, and one lance-corporal more or less on the battalion strength didn't make much difference, so they sent me out of the line to see if a War Office Selection Board would adjudge me fit to be commissioned.

I flew out and presented myself to the board, bush-hat on head, beard on chin, kukri on hip, all in sweaty jungle green and as tough as a buttered muffin. Frankly, I had few hopes of being passed. I had been to a board once before, back in England, and had fallen foul of a psychiatrist, a mean-looking little man who bit his nails and asked me if I had an adventurous spirit. (War Office Selection Boards were always asking questions like that.) Of course, I told him I was as adventurous as all get-out, and he helped himself to another piece of nail and said cunningly:

'Then why don't you sign on to sail on a Norwegian whaler?'

This, in the middle of the war, mark you, to a conscript. So, thinking he was being funny, I replied with equal cunning that I didn't speak Norwegian, ha-ha. He just loved that; anyway, I didn't pass.

So I flew out of Burma without illusions. This particular board had a tough reputation; last time, the rumour went, they had passed only three candidates out of thirty. I looked round at my fellow applicants, most of whom had at least three stripes and seemed to be full of confidence, initiative, leadership, and flannel – qualities that Selection Boards lap up like gravy – and decided that whoever was successful this time it wasn't going to be me. There were two other Fourteenth Army infantrymen, Martin-Duggan and Hayhurst, and the three of us, being rabble, naturally drifted together.

I should explain about Selection Boards. They lasted about three days, during which time the candidates were put through a series of written and practical tests, and the Board officers just watched and made notes. Then there were interviews and discussions, and all the time you were being assessed and graded, and at the finish you were told whether you were in or out. If in, you went to an Officer Cadet Training Unit where they trained you for six months and then gave you your commission; if out, back to your unit.

But the thing that was universally agreed was that there was no known way of ensuring success before a Selection Board. There were no standard right answers to their questions, because their methods were all supposed to be deeply psychological. The general view throughout the Army was that they weren't fit to select bus conductors, let alone officers, but that is by the way.

One of the most unpleasant features of a Selection Board was that you were on test literally all the time. At meal times, for instance, there was an examining officer at each table of about six candidates, so we all drank our soup with exaggerated care, offered each other the salt with ponderous politeness, and talked on a plane so lofty that by comparison a conversation in the Athenaeum Club would have sounded like an argument in a gin-mill. And all the time our examiner, a smooth, beady gentleman, kept an eye on us and weighed us up while pretending to be a boon companion.

It wasn't too easy for him, for at our second meal I displayed such zeal in offering him a bottle of sauce that I put it in his lap. I saw my chances fading from that moment, and by the time we fell in outside for our first practical test my nerves were in rags.

It was one of those idiotic problems where six of you are given a log, representing a big gun-barrrel, and have to get it across a river with the aid of a few ropes and poles. No one is put in command; you just have to cooperate, and the examiners hover around to see who displays most initiative, leadership, ingenuity, and what-have-you. The result is that everyone starts in at once telling the rest what to do. I had been there before, so I let them argue and tried to impress the Board by being practical. I cleverly tied a rope round the log, and barked a sharp command to Martin-Duggan and Hayhurst. They tugged on the rope and the whole damned thing went into the river. At this there was a deadly silence broken only by the audible scribbling of the examiners, and then the three of us sheepishly climbed down the bank to begin salvage operations.

This set the tone of our whole performance in the tests. Given a bell tent to erect we reduced it to a wreck of cord and canvas inside three minutes; ordered to carry from Point A to Point B an ammunition box which was too heavy for one man and which yet did not provide purchase for two, we dropped it in a ditch and upbraided each other in sulphurous terms, every word of which the examiners recorded carefully. Asked to swing across a small ravine on a rope, we betrayed symptoms of physical fear, and Hayhurst fell and hurt his ankle. Taking all in all, we showed ourselves lacking in initiative, deficient in moral fibre, prone to recrimination, and generally un-officer-like.

So it went on. We were interviewed by the psychiatrist who asked Hayhurst whether he smoked. Hayhurst said no – he had actually given it up a few days before – and then noticed that the psychiatrist's eyes were fixed on his right index finger, which was still stained yellow with nicotine. My own interview was, I like to think, slightly less of a triumph from the psychiatrist's point of view. He asked me if I had an adventurous spirit, and I quickly said yes, so much so that my only regret about being in the Army was that it prevented me from signing on to sail on a Norwegian whaler.

If, at this point, he had said: 'Oh, do you speak Norwegian, then?' he would have had me over a barrel. But instead he fell back on the Selection Board classic, which is: 'Why do you want to be an officer?'

The honest answer, of course, is to say, like Israel Hands, 'Because I want their pickles and wines and that,' and to add that you are sick of being shoved around like low-life, and want to lord it over your fellow-man for a change. But honest answer never won fair psychiatrist yet, so I assumed my thoughtful, stuffed look, and said earnestly that I simply wanted to serve the army in my most useful capacity, and I felt, honestly, sir, that I could do the job. The pay was a lot better, too, but I kept that thought to myself.

He pursed up and nodded, and then said: 'I see you want to be commissioned in the—Highlanders. They're a pretty tough bunch, you know. Think you can handle a platoon of them?'

I gave him my straight-between-the-eyes look which, coupled with my twisted smile, tells people that I'm a lobo wolf from Kelvinside and it's my night to howl. Just for good measure I added a confident, grating laugh, and he asked with sudden concern if I was going to be sick. I quickly reassured him, but he kept eyeing me askance and presently he dismissed me. As I went out he was scribbling like crazy.

Then there were written tests, in one of which we had to record our instant reactions to various words flashed on a blackboard. With me there was not one reaction in each case, but three. The first was just a mental numbness, the second was the reaction which I imagined the examiners would regard as normal, and the third (which naturally was what I finished up writing down) was the reaction which I was sure would be regarded as abnormal to a degree. Some people are like this: they are compelled to touch naked electric wiring and throw themselves down from heights. Some perverse streak makes them seek out the wrong answers.

Thus, given the word 'board', I knew perfectly well that the safe answer would be 'plank' (unless you chose to think that 'board' meant 'Selection Board', in which case you would write down 'justice', 'mercy', or 'wisdom'). But with the death wish in full control I had to write down 'stiff'.

Similarly, reason told me to react to 'cloud', 'father', and 'sex' by writing down 'rain', 'W. G. Grace', and 'birds and bees'. So of course I put down 'cuckoo', 'Captain Hook', and 'Grable'. To make matters worse I then scored 'Grable' out in a panic and wrote 'Freud', and then changed my mind again, scoring out 'Freud' and substituting 'Lamour'. Heavy breathing at my elbow at this point attracted my attention, and there was one of the examiners, peeking at my paper with his eyes bugging. By this time I was falling behind in my reactions, and was in such a frenzied state that when they eventually flashed 'Freud' on the board I think my response was 'Father Grable'. That must have made them think.

They then showed us pictures, and we had to write a story about each one. The first picture showed a wretch with an expression of petrified horror on his face, clinging to a rope. Well, that was fairly obviously a candidate escaping from a Selection Board and discovering that his flight was being observed by a team of examiners taking copious notes. Then there was a picture of a character with a face straight out of Edgar Allan Poe, being apprehended by a policeman. (Easy: the miscreant was the former principal of a Selection Board, cashiered for drunkenness and embezzlement, and forced to beg his bread in the gutter, being arrested for vagrancy by a copper who turned out to be a failed candidate.)

But the one that put years on all the many hundreds of candidates who must have regarded it with uninspired misery was of an angelic little boy sitting staring soulfully at a violin. There are men all over the world today who will remember that picture when Rembrandt's 'Night Watch' is forgotten. As art it was probably execrable, and as a mental stimulant it was the original lead balloon. Just the sight of that smug, curly-headed little Bubbles filled you with a sense of gloom. One Indian candidate was so affected by it that he began to weep; Hayhurst, after much mental anguish, produced the idea that it was one of Fagin's apprentices gloating over his first haul; my own thought was that the picture represented the infant Stradivarius coming to the conclusion that given a well-organized sweatshop there was probably money in it.

Only Martin-Duggan dealt with the thing at length; the picture stirred something in his poetic Irish soul. The little boy, he recorded for the benefit of the examiners, was undoubtedly the son of a famous concert violinist. His daddy had been called up to the forces during the war, and the little boy was left at home, gazing sadly at the violin which his father would have no opportunity of playing until the war was over. The little boy was terribly upset about this, the thought of his father's wonderful music being silenced; he felt sure his daddy would pine away through being deprived of his violin-playing. Let the little boy take heart, said Martin-Duggan; he needn't worry, because if his daddy played his cards right he would get himself promoted to the post of quarter-master, and then he would be able to fiddle as much as he liked.

Martin-Duggan was terribly pleased with this effort; the poor sap didn't seem to understand that in military circles a joke is only as funny as the rank of its author is exalted, and Martin-Duggan's rank couldn't have been lower.

Of course, by the time the written tests were over, the three of us were quite certain that we were done for. Our showing had probably been about as bad as it could be, we thought, and our approach to the final ordeal of the Selection Board, on the third afternoon, was casual, not to say resigned. This was a trip over the assault course – a military obstacle race in which you tear across country, climb walls, swing on ropes, crawl through tunnels, and jump off ramps. The climax is usually something pretty horrid, and in this case it consisted of a monsoon ditch four feet deep in water, at the end of which was a huge bamboo fence up which you had to climb in three-man teams, helping each other and showing initiative, intelligence, cheerfulness, and other officer-like qualities, if possible.

We were the last three over, and as we waded up the ditch, encouraging each other with military cries, the rain was lashing down something awful. There was a covered shelter overlooking the ditch, and it was crammed with examiners – all writing away as they observed the floundering candidates – as well as the top brass of the board. All the other candidates had successfully scaled the fence, and were standing dripping with mud and water, waiting to see how we came on.

Our performance, viewed from the bank, must have been something to see. I stood up to my waist in water against the fence, and Martin-Duggan climbed on my shoulders, and Hayhurst climbed on his, and I collapsed, and we all went under. We did this about five or six times, and the gallery hooted with mirth. Martin-Duggan, who was a proud, sensitive soul, got mad, and swore at me and kicked me, and Hayhurst made a tremendous effort and got on to the top of the fence. He pulled Martin-Duggan up, and the pair of them tried to pull me up, too, but I wasn't having any. I was rooted up to my middle in the sludge, and there I was going to stay, although I made it look as though I was trying like hell to get up.

They tugged and strained and swore, and eventually Martin-Duggan slipped and came down with a monumental splash, and Hayhurst climbed down as well. The spectators by this time were in hysterics, and when we had made three or four more futile efforts – during which I never emerged from the water once – the officer commanding the board leaned forward and said:

'Don't you chaps think you'd better call it a day?'

I don't know what Martin-Duggan, a mud-soaked spectre, was going to reply, but I beat him to it. Some heaven-sent inspiration struck me, because I said, in the most soapy, sycophantic, Eric-or-Little-by-Little voice I have ever used in my life:

'Thank you, sir, we'd prefer to finish the course.'

It must have sounded impressive, for the C.O. stood back, almost humbly, and motioned us to continue. So we did, floundering on with tremendous zeal and getting nowhere, until we were almost too weary to stand and so mud-spattered that we were hardly recognizable as human beings. And the C.O., bless him, leaned forward again, and I'll swear there was a catch in his voice as he said:

'Right, that's enough. Well tried. And even if you didn't finish it, there's one thing I'd like to say. I admire guts.' And all the examiners, writing for dear life, made muted murmurs of assent.

What they and the C.O. didn't know was that my trousers had come off while we were still wading up the ditch, and that was why I had never budged out of the water and why we had never got up the fence. A good deal I had endured, but I was not going to appear soaked and in my shirt-tail before all the board and candidates, not for anything. And as we waded back down the ditch and out of sight round the bend, I told Martin-Duggan and Hayhurst so.

And we passed, I suppose because we showed grit, determination, endurance, and all the rest of it. Although with Selection Boards you never could tell. Only the three of us know that what got us through was the loss of my pants, and military history has been made out of stranger things than that.

William Trevor

Raymond Bamber and Mrs Fitch

For fifteen years, ever since he was twenty-seven, Raymond Bamber had attended the Tamberleys' autumn cocktail party. It was a function to which the Tamberleys inclined to invite their acquaintances rather than their friends, so that every year the faces changed a bit: no one except Raymond had been going along to the house in Eaton Square for as long as fifteen years. Raymond, the Tamberleys felt, was a special case, for they had known him since he was a boy, having been close friends of his father's.

Raymond was a tall man, six foot two inches, with spectacles and a small moustache. He was neat in all he did, and he lived what he himself referred to as a tidy life.

'I come here every year,' said Raymond at the Tamberleys', to a woman he had not met before, a woman who was tall too, with a white lean face and lips that were noticeably scarlet. 'It is an occasion for me almost, like Christmas or Easter. To some extent, I guide my life by the Tamberleys' autumn party, remembering on each occasion what has happened in the year gone by.'

'My name is Mrs Fitch,' said the woman, poking a hand out for a drink. 'Is that vermouth and gin?' she enquired of the Tamberleys' Maltese maid, and the maid agreed that it was. 'Good,' said Mrs Fitch.

'Raymond, Raymond,' cried the voice of Mrs Tamberley as Mrs Tamberley materialized suddenly beside them. 'How's Nanny Wilkinson?'

'She died,' murmured Raymond.

'Of course she did,' exclaimed Mrs Tamberley. 'How silly of me!'

'Oh no –'

'You put that sweet notice in *The Times*. His old nurse,' explained Mrs Tamberley to Mrs Fitch. 'Poor Nanny Wilkinson,' she said, and smiled and bustled off.

'What was all that?' asked Mrs Fitch.

'It's one of the things that happened to me during the year. The other was –'

'What's your name, anyway?' the woman interrupted. 'I don't think I ever caught it.'

Raymond told her his name. He saw that she was wearing a black dress with touches of white on it. Her shoulders were bare and bony; she had, Raymond said to himself, an aquiline face.

'The other thing was that an uncle died and left me a business in his will. That happened, actually, before the death of Nanny Wilkinson and to tell you the truth, Mrs Fitch, I just didn't know what to do. "What could I do with a business?" I said to myself. So I made my way to Streatham where the old lady lived. "Run a business, Raymond? You couldn't run a bath," she said.' Raymond laughed, and Mrs Fitch smiled frostily, looking about her for another drink. 'It rankled, that, as you may imagine. Why couldn't I run a business? I thought. And then, less than a week later, I heard that she had died in Streatham. I went to her funeral, and discovered that she'd left me a prayer-book in her will. All that happened in the last year. You see, Mrs Fitch?'

Mrs Fitch, her eyes on her husband, who was talking to a woman in yellow in a distant corner of the room, said vaguely:

'What about the business?'

'I sold the business. I live alone, Mrs Fitch, in a flat in Bayswater; I'm forty-two. I'm telling you that simply because I felt that I could never manage anything like taking on a business so suddenly. That's what I thought when I had considered the matter carefully. No good being emotional, I said to myself.'

'No,' said Mrs Fitch. She watched the woman move quite close to her husband and engage him in speech that had all the air of confidential talk. The woman wasn't young, Mrs Fitch noticed, but had succeeded in giving the impression of youth. She was probably forty-four, she reckoned; she looked thirty.

So Mrs Tamberley had seen the notice in *The Times*, Raymond thought. He had worded it simply and had stated in a straightforward manner the service that Nanny Wilkinson had given over the years to his family. He had felt it her due, a notice in *The Times*, and there was of course only he who might do it. He remembered her sitting regally in his nursery teaching him his tidiness. Orderliness was the most important thing in life, she said, after a belief in the Almighty.

'Get me a drink, dear,' said Mrs Fitch suddenly, holding out an empty glass and causing Raymond to notice that this woman was consuming the Tamberleys' liquor at a faster rate than he.

'Gin and vermouth,' ordered Mrs Fitch. 'Dry,' she added. 'Not that red stuff.'

Raymond smiled and took her glass while Mrs Fitch observed that her husband was listening with rapt care to what the woman in yellow was saying to him. In the taxi-cab on the way to the Tamberleys', he had remarked as usual that he was fatigued after his day's work. 'An early night,' he had suggested. And now he was listening carefully to a female: he wouldn't leave this party for another two hours at least.

'It was quite a blow to me,' said Raymond, handing Mrs Fitch a glass of gin and vermouth, 'hearing that she was dead. Having known her, you see, all my life –'

'Who's dead now?' asked Mrs Fitch, still watching her husband.

'Sorry,' said Raymond. 'How silly of me! No, I meant, you see, this old lady whom I had known as Nanny Wilkinson. I was saying it was a blow to me when she died, although of course I didn't see much of her these last few years. But the memories are there, if you see what I mean; and you cannot of course erase them.'

'No,' said Mrs Fitch.

'I was a particularly tall child, with my spectacles of course, and a longish upper lip. "When you're a big man," I remember her saying to me, "you'll have to grow a little moustache to cover up all that lip." And I declare, Mrs Fitch, I did.'

'I never had a nanny,' said Mrs Fitch.

'"He'll be a tennis-player," people used to say – because of my height, you see. But in fact I turned out to be not much good on a tennis court.'

Mrs Fitch nodded. Raymond began to say something else, but Mrs Fitch, her eyes still fixed upon her husband, interrupted him. She said:

'Interesting about your uncle's business.'

'I think I was right. I've thought of it often since, of sitting down in an office and ordering people to do this and that, instead of remaining quietly in my flat in Bayswater. I do all my own cooking, actually, and cleaning and washing up. Well, you can't get people, you know. I couldn't even get a simple char, Mrs Fitch, not for love nor money. Of course it's easy having no coal fires to cope with: the flat is all-electric, which is what, really, I prefer.'

Raymond laughed nervously, having observed that Mrs Fitch was, for the first time since their conversation had commenced, observing him closely. She was looking into his face, at his nose and his moustache and his spectacles. Her eyes passed up to his forehead and down the line of his right cheek, down his neck until they arrived at Raymond's Adam's apple. He continued to speak to her, telling of the manner in which his flat in Bayswater was furnished, how he had visited the Sanderson showrooms in Berners Street to select materials for chair-covers and curtains. 'She made them for me,' said Raymond. 'She was almost ninety then.'

'What's that?' said Mrs Fitch. 'Your nurse made them?'

'I measured up for her and wrote everything down just as she had directed. Then I travelled out to Streatham with my scrap of paper.'

'On a bicycle.'

Raymond shook his head. He thought it odd of Mrs Fitch to suggest, for no logical reason, that he had cycled from Bayswater to Streatham. 'On a bus actually,' he explained. He paused, and then added: 'I could have had them made professionally, of course, but I preferred the other. I thought it would give her an interest, you see.'

'Instead of which it killed her.'

'No, no. No, you've got it confused. It was in 1964 that she made the curtains and the covers for me. As I was saying, she died only a matter of months ago.'

Raymond noticed that Mrs Fitch had ceased her perusal of his features and was again looking vacantly into the distance. He was glad that she had ceased to examine him because had she continued he would have felt obliged to move away from her, being a person who was embarrassed by such intent attention. He said, to make it quite clear about the covers and the curtains:

'She died in fact of pneumonia.'

'Stop,' said Mrs Fitch to the Tamberleys' Maltese maid who happened to be passing with a tray of drinks. She lifted a glass to her lips and consumed its contents while reaching out a hand for another. She repeated the procedure, drinking two glasses of the Tamberleys' liquor in a gulping way and retaining a third in her left hand.

'Nobody tells the truth,' said Mrs Fitch after all that. 'We come to these parties and everything's a sham.'

'What?' said Raymond.

'You know what I mean.'

Raymond laughed, thinking that Mrs Fitch was making some kind of joke. 'Of course,' he said, and laughed again, a noise that was more of a cough.

'You told me you were forty-two,' said Mrs Fitch. 'I in fact am fifty-one, and have been taken for sixty-five.'

Raymond thought he would move away from this woman in a moment. He had a feeling she might be drunk. She had listened pleasantly enough while he told her a thing or two about himself, yet here she was now speaking most peculiarly. He smiled at her and heard her say:

'Look over there, Mr Bamber. That man with the woman in yellow is my husband. We were born in the same year and in the same month, January 1915. Yet he could be in his thirties. That's what he's up to now; pretending the thirties with the female he's talking to. He's praying I'll not approach and give the game away. D'you see, Mr Bamber?'

'That's Mrs Anstey,' said Raymond. 'I've met her here before. The lady in yellow.'

'My husband has eternal youth,' said Mrs Fitch. She took a mouthful of her drink and reached out a hand to pick a fresh one from a passing tray. 'It's hard to bear.'

'You don't look fifty-one,' said Raymond. 'Not at all.'

'Are you mocking me?' cried Mrs Fitch. 'I do not look fifty-one. I've told you so: I've been taken for sixty-five.'

'I didn't mean that. I meant –'

'You were telling a lie, as well you know. My husband is telling lies too. He's all sweetness to that woman, yet it isn't his nature. My husband cares nothing for people, except when they're of use to him. Why do you think, Mr Bamber, he goes to cocktail parties?'

'Well –'

'So that he may make arrangements with other women. He desires their flesh and tells them so by looking at it.'

Raymond looked serious, frowning, thinking that that was expected of him.

'We look ridiculous together, my husband and I. Yet once we were a handsome couple. I am like an old crow while all he has is laughter lines about his eyes. It's an obsession with me.'

Raymond pursed his lips, sighing slightly.

'He's after women in this room,' said Mrs Fitch, eyeing her husband again.

'Oh, no, now –'

'Why not? How can you know better than I, Mr Bamber? I have had plenty of time to think about this matter. Why shouldn't he want to graze where the grass grows greener, or appears to grow greener? That Anstey woman is a walking confidence trick.'

'I think,' said Raymond, 'that I had best be moving on. I have friends to talk to.' He made a motion to go, but Mrs Fitch grasped part of his jacket in her right hand.

'What I say is true,' she said. 'He is practically a maniac. He has propositioned women in this very room before this. I've heard him at it.'

'I'm sure –'

'When I was a raving beauty he looked at me with his gleaming eye. Now he gleams for all the others. I'll tell you something, Mr Bamber.' Mrs Fitch paused. Raymond noticed that her eyes were staring over his shoulder, as though she had no interest in him beyond his being a person to talk at. 'I've gone down on my bended knees, Mr Bamber, in order to have this situation cleared up: I've prayed that that man might look again with tenderness on his elderly wife. But God has gone on,' said Mrs Fitch bitterly, 'in His mysterious way, not bothering Himself.'

Raymond did not reply to these observations. He said instead that he hadn't liked to mention it before but was Mrs Fitch aware that she was clutching in her right hand part of his clothes?

'He shall get to know your Anstey woman,' said Mrs Fitch. 'He shall come to know that her father was a bear-like man with a generous heart and that her mother, still alive in Guildford, is difficult to get on with. My husband shall come to know all the details about your Anstey woman: the plaster chipping in her bathroom, the way she cooks an egg. He shall know what her handbags look like, and how their clasps work – while I continue to wither away in the house we share.'

Raymond asked Mrs Fitch if she knew the Griegons, who were, he said, most pleasant people. He added that the Griegons were present tonight and that, in fact, he would like to introduce them to her.

'You are trying to avoid the truth. What have the Griegons to recommend them that we should move in their direction and end this conversation? Don't you see the situation, Mr Bamber? I am a woman who is obsessed because of the state of her marriage, how I have aged while he has not. I am obsessed by the fact that he is now incapable of love or tenderness. I have failed to keep all that alive because I lost my beauty. There are lines on my body too, Mr Bamber: I would show you if we were somewhere else.'

Raymond protested again, and felt tired of protesting. But

Mrs Fitch, hearing him speak and thinking that he was not yet clear in his mind about the situation, supplied him with further details about her marriage and the manner in which, at cocktail parties, her husband made arrangements for the seduction of younger women, or women who on the face of it seemed younger. 'Obsessions are a disease,' said Mrs Fitch, drinking deeply from her glass.

Raymond explained then that he knew nothing whatsoever about marriage difficulties, to which Mrs Fitch replied that she was only telling him the truth. 'I do not for a moment imagine,' she said, 'that you are an angel come from God, Mr Bamber, in order to settle the unfortunateness. I didn't mean to imply that when I said I had prayed. Did you think I thought you were a messenger?' Mrs Fitch, still holding Raymond's jacket and glancing still at her husband and the woman in yellow, laughed shrilly. Raymond said:

'People are looking at us, the way you are pulling at my clothes. I'm a shy man –'

'Tell me about yourself. You know about me by now: how everything that once seemed rosy has worked out miserably.'

'Oh, come now,' said Raymond, causing Mrs Fitch to repeat her laughter and to call out for a further drink. The Tamberleys' maid hastened towards her. 'Now then,' said Mrs Fitch. 'Tell me.'

'What can I tell you?' asked Raymond.

'I drink a lot these days,' said Mrs Fitch, 'to help matters along. Cheers, Mr Bamber.'

'Actually I've told you quite a bit, you know. One thing and another –'

'You told me nothing except some nonsense about an old creature in Streatham. Who wants to hear that, for Christ's sake? Or is it relevant?'

'Well, I mean, it's true, Mrs Fitch. Relevant to what?'

'I remember you, believe it or not, in this very room on this same occasion last year. "Who's that man?" I said to the Tamberley woman and she replied that you were a bore. You were invited, year by year, so the woman said, because of some friendship between the Tamberleys and your father. In the distant past.'

'Look here,' said Raymond, glancing about him and noting to his relief that no one appeared to have heard what Mrs Fitch in her cups had said.

'What's the matter?' demanded Mrs Fitch. Her eyes were again upon her husband and Mrs Anstey. She saw them laugh together and felt her unhappiness being added to as though it were a commodity within her body. 'Oh yes,' she said to Raymond, attempting to pass a bit of the unhappiness on. 'A grinding bore. Those were the words of Mrs Tamberley.'

Raymond shook his head. 'I've known Mrs Tamberley since I was a child,' he said.

'So the woman said. You were invited because of the old friendship: the Tamberleys and your father. I cannot tell a lie, Mr Bamber: she said you were a pathetic case. She said you hadn't learned how to grow up. I dare say you're a pervert.'

'My God!'

'I'm sorry I cannot tell lies,' said Mrs Fitch, and Raymond felt her grip tighten on his jacket. 'It's something that happens to you when you've been through what I've been through. That man up to his tricks with women while the beauty drains from my face. What's it like, d'you think?'

'I don't know,' said Raymond. 'How on earth could I know? Mrs Fitch, let's get one thing clear: I am not a pervert.'

'Not? Are you sure? They may think you are, you know,' said Mrs Fitch, glancing again at her husband. 'Mrs Tamberley has probably suggested that very thing to everyone in this room. Crueller, though, I would have thought, to say you were a grinding bore.'

'I am not a pervert –'

'I can see them sniggering over that all right. Unmentionable happenings between yourself and others. Elderly newspaper-vendors –'

'Stop!' cried Raymond. 'For God's sake, woman –'

'You're not a Jew, are you?'

Raymond did not reply. He stood beside Mrs Fitch, thinking that the woman appeared to be both drunk and not of her right mind. He did not wish to create a scene in the Tamberleys' drawing-room, and yet he recognized that by the look of her she intended to hold on to his jacket for the remainder of the evening. If he attempted to pull it away from her, she would not let go: she did not, somehow, seem to be the kind of woman who would. She wouldn't mind a scene at all.

'Why,' said Mrs Fitch, 'did you all of a sudden begin to tell me about that woman in Streatham, Mr Bamber, and the details about your chair-covers and curtains? Why did you tell me about your uncle dying and trying to leave you a business and your feeling that in your perverted condition you were unfit to run a business?'

Raymond's hands began to shake. He could feel an extra tug on his jacket, as though Mrs Fitch was now insisting that he stand closer to her. He pressed his teeth together, grinding his molars one upon another, and then opened his mouth and felt his teeth and his lips quivering. He knew that his voice would sound strange when he spoke. He said:

'You are being extremely offensive to me, Mrs Fitch. You are a woman who is a total stranger to me, yet you have seen fit to drive me into a corner at a cocktail party and hold me here by force. I must insist that you let go my jacket and allow me to walk away.'

'What about me, Mr Bamber? What about my husband and your Anstey woman? Already they are immoral on a narrow bed somewhere; in a fifth-class hotel near King's Cross station.'

'Your husband is still in this room, Mrs Fitch. As well you know. What your husband does is not my business.'

'Your business is your flat in Bayswater, is it? And curtains and covers from the Sanderson showrooms in Berners Street. Your world is people dying and leaving you stuff in wills – money and prayer-books and valuable jewellery that you wear when you dress yourself up in nurse's uniform.'

'I must ask you to stop, Mrs Fitch.'

'I could let you have a few pairs of old stockings if they interest you. Or garments of my husband's.'

Mrs Fitch saw Raymond close his eyes. She watched the flesh on his face redden further and watched it twitch in answer to a pulse that throbbed in his neck. There was sweat on his forehead. Her husband, a moment before, had reached out a hand and placed it briefly on the female's arm.

'So your nanny was a guide to you,' said Mrs Fitch. 'You hung on all her words, I dare say?'

Raymond did not reply. He turned his head away, trying to control the twitching in his face. The sweat poured freely now. Eventually he said, quietly and with the suspicion of a stammer:

'She was a good woman. She was kind in every way.'

'She taught you neatness.'

Raymond was aware, as Mrs Fitch spoke that sentence, that she had moved appreciably closer to him. He could feel her knee pressing against his. He felt a second knee, and felt next that his leg had been cleverly caught by her, between her own legs.

'Look here,' said Raymond.

'Yes?'

'Mrs Fitch, what are you trying to do?'

Mrs Fitch increased the pressure of her knees. Her right hand moved into Raymond's jacket pocket. 'I am a little the worse for wear,' she said, 'but I can still tell the truth.'

'You are embarrassing me.'

'What are your perversions? Tell me, Mr Bamber.'

'I have no perversions of any kind. I live a normal life.'

'Shall I come to you with a pram? I'm an unhappy woman, Mr Bamber. I'll wear black woollen stockings. I'll show you those lines on my body.'

'Please,' said Raymond, thinking he would cry in a moment.

Already people were glancing at Mrs Fitch's legs gripping his so strongly. Her white face and her scarlet lips were close to his eyes. He could see the lines on her cheeks, but he turned his glance away from them in case she mentioned again the lines on her body. She is a mad, drunken nymphomaniac, said Raymond to himself, and thought that never in all his life had anything so upsetting happened to him.

'Embrace me,' said Mrs Fitch.

'Please, I beg you,' said Raymond.

'You are a homosexual. A queer. I had forgotten that.'

'I'm not a homosexual,' shouted Raymond, aware that his voice was piercingly shrill. Heads turned and he felt the eyes of the Tamberleys' guests. He had been heard to cry that he was not a homosexual, and people had wished to see for themselves.

'Excuse me,' said a voice. 'I'm sorry about this.'

Raymond turned his head and saw Mrs Fitch's husband standing behind him. 'Come along now, Adelaide,' said Mrs Fitch's husband. 'I'm sorry,' he said again to Raymond. 'I didn't realise she'd had a tankful before she got here.'

'I've been telling him the truth,' said Mrs Fitch. 'We've exchanged life-stories.'

Raymond felt her legs slip away, and he felt her hand withdraw itself from the pocket of his jacket. He nodded in a worldly way at her husband and said in a low voice that he understood how it was.

'He's a most understanding chap,' said Mrs Fitch. 'He has a dead woman in Streatham.'

'Come along now,' ordered her husband in a rough voice, and Raymond saw that the man's hand gripped her arm in a stern manner.

'I was telling that man the truth,' said Mrs Fitch again, seeming to be all of a sudden in an ever greater state of inebriation. Very slowly she said: 'I was telling him what I am and what you are, and what the Tamberleys think about him. It has been home-truths corner here, for the woman with an elderly face and for the chap who likes to dress himself out as a children's nurse and go with women in chauffeur's garb. Actually, my dear, he's a homosexual.'

'Come along now,' said Mrs Fitch's husband. 'I'm truly sorry,' he added to Raymond. 'It's a problem.'

Raymond saw that it was all being conducted in a most civilized manner. Nobody shouted in the Tamberleys' drawing-room, nobody noticed the three of them talking quite quietly in a corner. The Maltese maid in fact, not guessing for a moment that anything was amiss, came up with her tray of drinks and before anyone could prevent it, Mrs Fitch had lifted one to her lips. '*In vino veritas*,' she remarked.

Raymond felt his body cooling down. His shirt was damp

with sweat, and he realized that he was panting slightly and he wondered how long that had been going on. He watched Mrs Fitch being aided through the room by her husband. No wonder, he thought, the man had been a little severe with her, if she put up a performance like that very often; no wonder he treated her like an infant. She was little more than an infant, Raymond considered, saying the first thing that came into her head, and going on about sex. He saw her lean form briefly again, through an opening in the crowded room, and he realized without knowing it that he had craned his neck for a last glimpse. She saw him too, as she smiled and bowed at Mrs Tamberley, appearing to be sober and collected. She shook her head at him, deploring him or suggesting, even, that he had been the one who had misbehaved. Her husband raised a hand in the air, thanking Raymond for his understanding.

Raymond edged his way through all the people and went to find a bathroom. He washed his face, taking his spectacles off and placing them beside a piece of lime-green soap. He was thinking that her husband was probably just like any other man at a cocktail party. How could the husband help it, Raymond thought, if he had not aged and if other women found him pleasant to talk to? Did she expect him to have all his hair plucked out and have an expert come to line his face?

Leaning against the wall of the bathroom, Raymond thought about Mrs Fitch. He thought at first that she was a fantastic woman given to fantastic statements, and then he embroidered on the thought and saw her as being more subtle than that. 'By heavens!' said Raymond aloud to himself. She was a woman, he saw, who was pathetic in what she did, transferring the truth about herself to other people. She it was, he guessed, who was the grinding bore, so well known for the fact that she had come to hear the opinion herself and in her unbalanced way sought to pretend that others were bores in order to push the thing away from her. She was probably even, he thought, a little perverted the way in which she had behaved with her knees, and sought to imbue others with this characteristic too, so that she, for the moment, might feel rid of it: Mrs Fitch was clearly a case for a psychiatrist. She had said that her husband was a maniac where women were concerned; she had said that he had taken Mrs Anstey to a bed in King's Cross when Mrs Anstey was standing only yards away, in front of her eyes. *In vino veritas*, she had said, for no reason at all.

One morning, Raymond imagined, poor Mr Fitch had woken up to find his wife gabbling in that utterly crazy manner about her age and her hair and the lines on her body. Probably the woman was a nuisance with people who came to the door, the deliverers of coal and groceries, the milkman and the postman. He imagined the Express Dairy on the telephone to Mrs Fitch's husband, complaining that the entire milkround was daily being disorganized because of the antics of Mrs Fitch, who was a bore with everyone.

It accounted for everything, Raymond thought, the simple fact that the woman was a psychological case. He closed his eyes and sighed with relief, and remembered then that he had read in newspapers about women like Mrs Fitch. He opened his eyes again and looked at himself in the mirror of the Tamberleys' smallest bathroom. He touched his neat moustache with his fingers and smiled at himself to ascertain that his teeth were not carrying a piece of cocktail food. 'You have a tea-leaf on your tooth,' said the voice of Nanny Wilkinson, and Raymond smiled, remembering her.

Raymond returned to the party and stood alone watching the people talking and laughing. His eyes passed from face to face, many of which were familiar to him. He looked for the Griegons with whom last year he had spent quite some time, interesting them in a small sideboard that he had just had french polished, having been left the sideboard in the will of a godmother. The man, a Mr French amusingly enough, had come to Raymond's flat to do the job there in the evenings, having explained that he had no real facilities or premises, being a postman during the day. 'Not that he wasn't an expert polisher,' Raymond had said. 'He did a most beautiful job. I heard of him through Mrs Adams who lives in the flat below. I thought it was reasonable, you know: seven guineas plus expenses. The sideboard came up wonderfully.'

'Hullo,' said Raymond to the Griegons.

'How d'you do?' said Mrs Griegon, a pleasant, smiling woman, not at all like Mrs Fitch. Her husband nodded at Raymond, and turned to a man who was talking busily.

'Our name is Griegon,' said Mrs Griegon. 'This is my husband, and this is Dr Oath.'

'I know,' said Raymond, surprised that Mrs Griegon should say who she was since they had all met so pleasantly a year ago. 'How do you do, Dr Oath?' he said, stretching out a hand.

'Yes,' said Dr Oath, shaking the hand rapidly while continuing his conversation.

Mrs Griegon said: 'You haven't told us your name.'

Raymond, puzzled and looking puzzled, said that his name was Raymond Bamber. 'But surely you remember our nice talk last year?' he said. 'I recall it all distinctly: I was telling you about Mr French who came to polish a sideboard, and how he charged only seven guineas.'

'Most reasonable,' said Mrs Griegon. '*Most* reasonable.'

'We stood over there,' explained Raymond, pointing. 'You and I and Mr Griegon. I remember I gave you my address and telephone number in case if you were ever in Bayswater you might like to pop in to see the sideboard. You said to your husband at the time, Mrs Griegon, that you had one or two pieces that could do with stripping down and polishing, and Mr French, who'll travel anywhere in the evenings and being, as you say, so reasonable –'

'Of course,' cried Mrs Griegon. 'Of course I remember you perfectly, and I'm sure Archie does too.' She looked at her husband, but her husband was listening carefully to Dr Oath.

Raymond smiled. 'It looks even better now that the initial shine has gone. I'm terribly pleased with it.' As he spoke, he saw the figure of Mrs Fitch's husband entering the room. He watched him glance about and saw him smile at someone he'd seen. Following the direction of this smile, Raymond saw Mrs Anstey smiling back at Mrs Fitch's husband, who at once made his way to her side.

'French polishing's an art,' said Mrs Griegon.

What on earth, Raymond wondered, was the man doing back at the Tamberleys' party? And where was Mrs Fitch? Nervously, Raymond glanced about the crowded room, looking for the black and white dress and the lean aquiline features of the woman who had tormented him. But although, among all the brightly-coloured garments that the women wore, there were a few that were black and white, none of them contained Mrs Fitch. 'We come to these parties and everything's a sham,' her voice seemed to say, close to him. 'Nobody tells the truth.' The voice came to him in just the same way as Nanny Wilkinson's had a quarter of an hour ago, when she'd been telling him that he had a tea-leaf on his tooth.

'Such jolly parties,' said Mrs Griegon. 'The Tamberleys are wonderful.'

'Do you know a woman called Mrs Fitch?' said Raymond. 'She was here tonight.'

'Mrs Fitch!' exclaimed Mrs Griegon with a laugh.

'D'you know her?'

'She's married to that man there,' said Mrs Griegon. She pointed at Mr Fitch and sniffed.

'Yes,' said Raymond. 'He's talking to Mrs Anstey.'

He was about to add that Mr Fitch was probably of a social inclination. He was thinking already that Mr Fitch probably had a perfectly sound reason for returning to the Tamberleys'. Probably he lived quite near and having seen his wife home had decided to return in order to say goodbye properly to his hosts. Mrs Anstey, Raymond had suddenly thought, was for all he knew Mr Fitch's sister: in her mentally depressed condition it would have been quite like Mrs Fitch to pretend that the woman in yellow was no relation whatsoever, to have invented a fantasy that was greater even than it appeared to be.

'He's always up to that kind of carry-on,' said Mrs Griegon. 'The man's famous for it.'

'Sorry?' said Raymond.

'Fitch. With women.'

'Oh but surely –'

'Really,' said Mrs Griegon.

'I was talking to Mrs Fitch earlier on and she persisted in

speaking about her husband. Well, I felt she was going on rather. Exaggerating, you know. A bit of a bore.'

'He has said things to me, Mr Bamber, that would turn your stomach.'

'She has a funny way with her, Mrs Fitch has. She too said the oddest things –'

'She has a reputation,' said Mrs Griegon, 'for getting drunk and coming out with awkward truths. I've heard it said.'

'Not the truth,' Raymond corrected. 'She says things about herself, you see, and pretends she's talking about another person.'

'What?' said Mrs Griegon.

'Like maybe, you see, she was saying that she herself is a bore the way she goes on – well, Mrs Fitch wouldn't say it just like that. What Mrs Fitch would do is pretend some other person is the bore, the person she might be talking to. D'you see? She would transfer all her own qualities to the person she's talking to.'

Mrs Griegon raised her thin eyebrows and inclined her head. She said that what Raymond was saying sounded most interesting.

'An example is,' said Raymond, 'that Mrs Fitch might find herself unsteady on her feet through drink. Instead of saying that she was unsteady she'd say that you, Mrs Griegon, were the unsteady one. There's a name for it, actually. A medical name.'

'Medical?' said Mrs Griegon.

Glancing across the room, Raymond saw that Mr Fitch's right hand gripped Mrs Anstey's elbow. Mr Fitch murmured in her ear and together the two left the room. Raymond saw them wave at Mrs Tamberley, implying thanks with the gesture, implying that they had enjoyed themselves.

'I can't think what it is now,' said Raymond to Mrs Griegon, 'when people transfer the truth about themselves to others. It's some name beginning with an R, I think.'

'How nice of you,' said Mrs Tamberley, gushing up, 'to put that notice in *The Times*.' She turned to Mrs Griegon and said that, as Raymond had probably told her, a lifelong friend of his, old Nanny Wilkinson, had died a few months ago. 'Every year,' said Mrs Tamberley, 'Raymond told us all how she was bearing up. But now, alas, she's died.'

'Indeed,' said Mrs Griegon, and smiled and moved away.

Without any bidding there arrived in Raymond's mind a picture of Mrs Fitch sitting alone in her house, refilling a glass from a bottle of Gordon's gin. '*In vino veritas*,' said Mrs Fitch, and began to weep.

'I was telling Mrs Griegon that I'd been chatting with Mrs Fitch,' said Raymond, and then he remembered that Mrs Tamberley had very briefly joined in that chat. 'I found her strange,' he added.

'Married to that man,' cried Mrs Tamberley. 'He drove her to it.'

'Her condition?' said Raymond, nodding.

'She ladles it into herself,' said Mrs Tamberley, 'and then tells you what she thinks of you. It can be disconcerting.'

'She really says anything that comes into her head,' said Raymond, and gave a light laugh.

'Not actually,' said Mrs Tamberley. 'She tells the truth.'

'Well, no, you see –'

'You haven't a drink,' cried Mrs Tamberley in alarm, and moved at speed towards her Maltese maid to direct the girl's attention to Raymond's empty glass.

Again the image of Mrs Fitch arrived in Raymond's mind. She sat as before, alone in a room, while her husband made off with a woman in yellow. She drank some gin.

'Sherry, sir?' said the Maltese maid, and Raymond smiled and thanked her, and then, in an eccentric way and entirely on an impulse, he said in a low voice:

'Do you know a woman called Mrs Fitch?'

The girl said that that Mrs Fitch had been at the party earlier in the evening, and reminded Raymond that he had in fact been talking to her.

'She had a peculiar way with her,' explained Raymond. 'I just wondered if ever you had talked to her, or had listened to what she herself had to say.' But the Maltese maid shook her head, appearing not to understand.

'Mrs Fitch's a shocker,' said a voice behind Raymond's back, and added: 'That poor man.'

There was a crackle of laughter as a response, and Raymond, sipping his sherry, turned about and moved towards the group that had caused it. The person who had spoken was a small man with shiny grey hair. 'I'm Raymond Bamber,' said Raymond, smiling at him. 'By the sound of things, you saw my predicament earlier on.' He laughed, imitating the laughter that had come from the group. 'Extremely awkward.'

'She gets tight,' said the small man. 'She's liable to tell a home truth or two.' He began to laugh again. '*In vino veritas*,' he said.

Raymond looked at the people and opened his mouth to say that it wasn't quite so simple, the malaise of Mrs Fitch. 'It's all within her,' he wished to say. 'Everything she says is part of Mrs Fitch, since she's unhappy in a marriage and has lost her beauty.' But Raymond checked that speech, uttering in fact not a word of it. The people looked expectantly at him, and after a long pause the small man said:

'Mrs Fitch can be most embarrassing.'

Raymond heard the people laugh again with the same sharpness and saw their teeth for a moment harshly bared and noted that their eyes were like polished ice. They would not understand, he thought, the facts about Mrs Fitch, any more than Mrs Griegon had seemed to understand, or Mrs Tamberley. It surprised Raymond, and saddened him, that neither Mrs Griegon nor Mrs Tamberley had cared to accept the truth about the woman. It was, he told himself, something of a revelation that Mrs Griegon, who had seemed so pleasant the year before, and Mrs Tamberley, whom he had known almost all his life, should turn out to be no better than this group of hard-eyed people. Raymond murmured and walked away, still thinking of Mrs Griegon and Mrs Tamberley. He imagined them laughing with their husbands over Mrs Fitch, repeating that she was a bore and a drunk. Laughter was apparently the thing, a commodity that reflected the shallowness of minds too lazy to establish correctly the facts about people. And they were minds, as had been proved to Raymond, that didn't even bother to survey properly the simple explanations of eccentric conduct – as though even that constituted too much trouble.

Soon afterwards, Raymond left the party and walked through the autumn evening, considering everything. The air was cool on his face as he strode towards Bayswater, thinking that as he continued to live his quiet life Mrs Fitch would be attending parties that were similar to the Tamberleys', and she'd be telling the people she met there that they were grinding bores. The people might be offended, Raymond thought, if they didn't pause to think about it, if they didn't understand that everything was confused in poor Mrs Fitch's mind. And it would serve them right, he reflected, to be offended – a just reward for allowing their minds to become lazy and untidy in this modern manner. 'Orderliness,' said the voice of Nanny Wilkinson, and Raymond paused and smiled, and then walked on.

John Morrow

Walk Tall, If You Dare

I got on very well with my father until one summer's morning not long after my twelfth birthday. A shadow fell across his face. Mine. And we were standing up ... 'Will you for God's sake git outa my light,' he growled, five-fut-three in hobnails; 'the way you're goin' you'll outgrow yer strength. Look at ye – like a hern' between the eyes!'

At fourteen I was five foot, eight inches tall – most of it head – and he swore I was losing control of my limbs. 'I dunno where you git it from. All my side were normal people,' he moaned, glaring at Mother (four-fut-eleven).

When I left school I wanted to join the Royal Navy Boy Service and be a gunner just like Daddy (in 1930 he still hadn't fully recovered his hearing, lost in a broadside at Jutland). 'You – a gunner!' he sneered. 'There'd be no room for the bloody gun in the turret,' and went on to tell harrowing stories about hysterical six-foot sailors leaving their brains smeared on the lintels of low hatchways. About this time too he began to point out that the builders of backstreet terrace houses had not envisaged anyone growing over, say, five-fut-seven. I was sixteen (five-fut-ten) when he kicked me clean out of bed one night. (We had only two bedrooms and I had a seventeen-year-old sister. Social Workers had not been invented then.) After that I slept at Granny's house two doors up.

At eighteen I reached my zenith: five foot, eleven and seven-eighths inches in bare feet according to the official police scale in Queen Street Barracks. The chum who accompanied me that day clocked in at only five foot nine, one inch below the police regulation minimum. If his Father had been a Peeler they would have allowed him the inch – Uncles rated a half-inch – but as he had neither, the only thing for it was the rack. He went straight home and threw out his mattress, replacing it with two-by-four planks; for six months he slept on his back with weights attached to his ankles and wrists; at every available waking moment he hung upside down from a horizontal bar which he had mounted in his bedroom; and at the end of the six months he walked cannily down to Queen Street one morning and passed the scale at exactly five foot ten. (He is now a five foot, eight inch sergeant with twenty-five years service and the Queen's Police Medal for bravery during the Shankill Road riots in 1971. A photograph in the *Police Gazette* of the time shows him, revolver in hand, allegedly giving a pep talk to a line of battle-caparisoned Peelers. 'Sergeant Malachy O'Hare,' says the caption, 'rallies his men for a charge on the Shankill.' His actual words at that moment, he told me later, were: 'The first one of youse bastards calls me Malachy up here I'll blow his fucking head off.')

I think the sergeant who measured Malachy and me that morning must have been on commission for new recruits. He insisted on accompanying me home in order to get my parents' consent, which would enable him to get me on the next draft to Enniskillen Depot. Father wouldn't hear tell of it. 'You'll be stuck out in the arsehole of Fermanagh for life,' he howled, after the sergeant had left with his tail between his legs. 'That's why we get all the country yauckles down here. I'd give you one year out in them bogs an' you'd be a gibberin' wino. They all are.'

I should have known better. In Father's black and white book all Peelers were alcoholic, debt-ridden skivvy-hunters, all C of I clergymen failed medical students, all doctors 'Quacks', all dentists sadistic ether-sniffers and all officers idiot sons. Later on there was a prospect of my becoming apprenticed to a plumber. 'A bloody honey-diver!' was Father's reaction. 'A turd-navigator! No son of mine'll ever –' etc . . .

Since leaving the Navy he had laboured on and off in Harland and Wolff's brass moulding shop; hot, heavy, poisonous work. During one of his 'off' periods he was sent by the Buroo to a spell job in a linen warehouse. 'Now there's the life,' he would say nostalgically ever after: 'clean hands an' a dry back. A gentleman's job.'

So it was to his satisfaction that I ended up in the linen trade – which, he had neglected to tell me, was just one step better than the Buroo. Luckily it was just then going into the post-war slump from which it was never to recover. Immediately I finished my apprenticeship I became redundant and flew almost at once to 'that refuge', as Paddy Kavanagh has it, 'of poor scholars and spoiled Priests': the insurance business.

Until then, contrary to Father's prognostications, I had not found any great disadvantage in being over five-fut-five. There had been a time in my late teens when I kept a wary eye on adjacent midgets, half expecting a head-on assault on my private parts at any minute, the method used by Father to bring down a gigantic Marine in Portsmouth in 1916 and described graphically by him many times during my stretching years. ('The bigger they are, the harder they fall.') But the midget threat receded as I filled out to those proportions remarked on by Granny thus: 'Uniform or not, son, you're one of God's Peelers.' On my first day in the insurance business I discovered what she meant . . .

The agency allotted to me was in that part of the city which a tourist brochure might describe as 'colourful', meaning a den of thieves, dodgers and dalein'-men. My initial entrance into one notorious street, I learnt later, caused no less than three householders to exit over their backyard walls. That first week the almost universal reaction to my hearty knock was a pair of apprehensive eyes round the door jamb – until I stated my business. 'Christ! You put the heart crosswise in me! It's all right, Jimmy; it's only the insurance fella.' On my second morning a pot full of piss dropped from a bedroom window missed me by inches.

In time, of course, everyone got to know who and what I was; but the experiences of that first week had unnerved me slightly. What was to prevent some transient ruffian from making a snap judgement on sight and having something more deadly than a quart of stale piss to hand? I decided that the less I looked like a Peeler the better. In those days – the middle fifties – Peelers still favoured the shaved neck; I let my hair grow over my collar (that I might run up against someone with a pathological hatred of actors or socialist solicitors was an outside chance I had to take). Plainclothes Peelers and detectives wore hairy tweed jackets, checked shirts and flannels; I affected a line in chunky polo-necks, golf jackets and pastel-shaded corduroys. I even managed, agonizingly, to squeeze my feet into size ten instead of ten-and-a-half – but mostly, when it was dry, I wore sandals.

Now anyone who remembers the sartorial mores of the Fifties will have realized that I was running into another kind of trouble: in my eagerness not to look like the hunter I was beginning to resemble the prey – and a fairly exotic species at that. I first became aware of this one day when I took short in Great Victoria Street and nipped into the GNR station for a quick pump. I had just taken stance at the Gothic urinal of my choice when a voice from the next 'Deluge' said: 'Do you come here often?' He must have been six-fut-three, had a shaved neck and wore a hairy tweed, flannels and brown boots. In place of the checked shirt he sported the black bib and collar of a Protestant clergyman. His ploughworn face contorted into something like a knowing wink ... Shocked speechless, I nicked and hurried away. At the lavatory entrance a small man with wavy hair and a pink corduroy jacket sidled up alongside and murmured: 'Watch out for the vicar, dear – Vice Squad.'

It caused me to tone down my future ensembles, though I never totally reverted to normal business gear. You see, I had become clothes conscious for the first time in my life – and anyway, the swinging Sixties were soon upon us and the entire male population under forty (including the Vice Squad) went all hirsute and casual.

In 1965 I was promoted to Audit Inspector and left my old area to tour the country doing quarterly audits. In 1969 I was working in the Ardoyne area of Belfast, accompanying the local agent on his rounds and checking the books. Politically, it was a touchy time. On the Saturday morning one of our calls was at the house of a very pious Catholic family. We had to pick our way through an obstacle course of holy statuary to reach the living room where the family was assembled: Mother and

Father, two teenaged daughters and a son. I remember pretending to admire a coloured photograph of a coffined child on the wall (one of six studies) while the agent got on with his business. Then one of the daughters, looking up at me quizzically, said: 'You remind me of somebody.'

For this I had a stock riposte: 'Just think of all the handsome lads you know' – which I now trotted out.

'I know,' she cried, clapping hands delightedly: 'the Big Fella.'

Mick Collins was my first thought. Flattered, I was about to make some deprecatory remark when the son looked up from *The United Irishman* and asked:

'Who?'

'Ian Paisley,' came the chilling reply; 'the spittin' image. Could be his brother.'

The very next day I started growing the beard. I let it run rampant and in three months time was having stomach trouble because, the doctor said, I was eating more hair than food and was suffering from a complaint hitherto found only in the cat family. The agents complained that I was frightening their clients' children. The manager ultimated that I either trim or come off the road. I refused and took up a less lucrative position in the claims office. (They use me as a 'threatening presence' in the interview room when they are settling a motor claim. I either stand still and glower silently out of my bush, or pace back and forth issuing the odd low growl at strategic points in the dialogue, depending on the character strength of the injured party. After an hour or two of that most people are glad to admit that their deceased vehicle had been nowhere near the first-class category in *Glass's Guide*.)

But then time, particularly springtime, heals ... One day last spring, having been turned out of our temporary offices because of a bomb scare, I took myself for a dander around the sunlit city centre. The beard steamed and itched in the mild heat – some limbs of the lower undergrowth, the doctor said, showed signs of turning back on themselves, threatening to penetrate my windpipe in time. I thought longingly of tingling soap and an open razor. On the Queen's Bridge I gazed out over black

water to the inviting slopes of the Cave Hill and contemplated
the old life on the open road: the fishing gear in the boot; pints
consumed in cool empty taverns in the morning ... A bomb
went off nearby and I wondered if it was the office again, our
fourth in six years. After all, what had I to lose?

I had myself almost convinced when, having just passed
Musgrave Street Police Barracks heading for the security gate
at Ann Street, I heard this voice behind me: a woman's voice,
raised. Looking back, I saw two women, one trying to restrain
the other. The one being restrained appeared to be pointing in
my direction, shouting something. She was middleaged, stout,
and was obviously not-all-there, full of wine, or both. Her face
was like a blood pudding, her hair awry, and as I watched she
suddenly broke free from her keeper and charged towards me,
screeching. Terrified, I took to my heels across Victoria Street
to the security gate. There were two queues. Looking straight
ahead, I could hear the thunder of the mad lady's feet coming
up behind me. Her friend caught her just in time and dragged
her into the women's queue. Now I could hear the import of
her howls ... 'Oh well may ye run ... An' don't think because
yer done up like Andy Gump I don't know ye. I seen ye comin'
outa bloody Belsen back there. You're the huer that pulled the
toenails outa our Kevvie, y'bloody SS man ye...' and more,
and worse.

The queues looked at her and me with no great interest,
shuffling steadily towards the searchers. A blue haired lady with
a face like those seen under red-white-and-blue umbrellas on
the Twelfth morning glared round and said: 'Bloody ridiccullus!'
in a loud voice. I had nearly reached the searchers now. A soldier
on duty moved down to where the mad lady was struggling with
her minder and mouthing dire threats. 'Shut yer mouth, y'dirty
clart,' said the blue-haired lady. She and I reached the searchers
at the same moment. I looked back and saw the soldier engaged
in earnest conversation with madwoman and minder, both of
whom were pointing at me. The blue-haired lady met my eye
and winked. 'Niver mind, constable,' she said solicitously; 'just
you pull all the toenails you've a mind to and more power to
yer elbow.' Breaking from the searcher's grip I went like a

hare up Ann Street, through Cornmarket into High Street and thanked God that the office was still there.

And that's where I am still, the office, browbeating clients. On exceptionally wet days I take a lunchtime stroll inside the security area. You'll know me if you see me: the hairy fellow in dark glasses, probably wearing something like a knee-length suede kaftan and tangerine bell-bottomed cords. I shall also be carrying a white stick and have – the ultimate deterrent, I hope – a club foot.

I'd give anything to be a clean-shaven midget like Daddy.

The Night Watchman's Occurrence Book

November 21. 10.30 p.m. C. A. Cavander takes over duty at C—Hotel all corrected. *Cesar Alwyn Cavander*

7 a.m. C. A. Cavander hand over duty to Mr Vignales at C—Hotel no report. *Cesar Alwyn Cavander*

November 22. 10.30 p.m. C. A. Cavander take over duty at C—Hotel no report. *Cesar Alwyn Cavander*

7 a.m. C. A. Cavander hand over duty to Mr Vignales at C—Hotel all corrected. *Cesar Alwyn Cavander*

This is the third occasion on which I have found C. A. Cavander, Night Watchman, asleep on duty. Last night, at 12.45 a.m., I found him sound asleep in a rocking chair in the hotel lounge. Night Watchman Cavander has therefore been dismissed.

Night Watchman Hillyard: This book is to be known in future as 'The Night Watchman's Occurrence Book'. In it I shall expect to find a detailed account of everything that happens in the hotel tonight. Be warned by the example of ex-Night Watchman Cavander. *W. A. G. Inskip, Manager*

Mr Manager, remarks noted. You have no worry where I am concern sir. *Charles Ethelbert Hillyard, Night Watchman*

November 23. 11 p.m. Night Watchman Hillyard take over duty at C— Hotel with one torch light 2 fridge keys and room keys 1, 3, 6, 10 and 13. Also 25 cartoons Carib Beer and 7 cartoons

Heineken and 2 cartoons American cigarettes. Beer cartoons intact Bar intact all corrected no report. *Charles Ethelbert Hillyard*

7 a.m. Night Watchman Hillyard hand over duty to Mr Vignales at C— Hotel with one torch light 2 fridge keys and room keys, 1, 3, 6, 10 and 13. 32 cartoons beer. Bar intact all corrected no report. *Charles Ethelbert Hillyard*

Night Watchman Hillyard: Mr Wills complained bitterly to me this morning that last night he was denied entry to the bar by you. I wonder if you know exactly what the purpose of this hotel is. In future all hotel guests are to be allowed entry to the bar at whatever time they choose. It is your duty simply to note what they take. This is one reason why the hotel provides a certain number of beer cartons (please note the spelling of this word). *W. A. G. Inskip*

Mr Manager, remarks noted. I sorry I didnt get the chance to take some education sir. *Chas. Ethelbert Hillyard*

November 24. 11 p.m. N. W. Hillyard take over duty with one Torch, 1 Bar Key, 2 Fridge Keys, 32 cartons Beer, all intact. 12 Midnight Bar close and Barman left leaving Mr Wills and others in Bar, and they left at 1 a.m. Mr Wills took 16 Carib Beer, Mr Wilson 8, Mr Percy 8. At 2 a.m. Mr Wills come back in the bar and take 4 Carib and some bread, he cut his hand trying to cut the bread, so please don't worry about the stains on the carpet sir. At 6 a.m. Mr Wills come back for some soda water. It didn't have any so he take a ginger beer instead. Sir you see it is my intention to do this job good sir, I can't see how Night Watchman Cavander could fall asleep on this job sir. *Chas. Ethelbert Hillyard*

You always seem sure of the time, and guests appear to be in the habit of entering the bar on the hour. You will kindly note the exact time. The clock from the kitchen is left on the window near the switches. You can use this clock but you MUST replace it every morning before you go off duty. *W. A. G. Inskip*

Noted. *Chas. Ethelbert Hillyard*

November 25. Midnight Bar close and 12.23 a.m. Barman left leaving Mr Wills and others in Bar. Mr Owen take 5 bottles Carib, Mr Wilson 6 Bottles Heineken, Mr Wills 18 Carib and they left at 2.52 a.m. Nothing unusual. Mr Wills was helpless, I don't see how anybody could drink so much, eighteen one man alone, this work enough to turn anybody Seventh Day Adventist, and another man come in the bar, I dont know his name, I hear they call him Paul, he assist me because the others couldn't do much, and we take Mr Wills up to his room and take off his boots and slack his other clothes and then we left. Don't know sir if they did take more while I was away, nothing was mark on the Pepsi Cola board, but they was drinking still, it look as if they come back and take some more, but with Mr Wills I want some extra assistance sir.

Mr Manager, the clock break I find it break when I come back from Mr Wills room sir. It stop 3.19 sir. *Chas. E. Hillyard*

More than 2 lbs of veal were removed from the Fridge last night, and a cake that was left in the press was cut. It is your duty, Night Watchman Hillyard, to keep an eye on these things. I ought to warn you that I have also asked the Police to check on all employees leaving the hotel, to prevent such occurrences in the future. *W. A. G. Inskip*

Mr Manager, I don't know why people so anxious to blame servants sir. About the cake, the press lock at night and I dont have the key sir, everything safe where I am concern sir. *Chas. Hillyard*

November 26. Midnight Bar close and Barman left. Mr Wills didn't come, I hear he at the American base tonight, all quiet, nothing unusual.

Mr Manager, I request one thing. Please inform the Barman to let me know sir when there is a female guest in the hotel sir. *C. E. Hillyard*

This morning I received a report from a guest that there were screams in the hotel during the night. You wrote All Quiet. Kindly explain in writing. *W. A. G. Inskip*.
Write Explanation here:

EXPLANATION. Not long after midnight the telephone ring and a woman ask for Mr Jimminez. I try to tell her where he was but she say she cant hear properly. Fifteen minutes later she came in a car, she was looking vex and sleepy, and I went up to call him. The door was not lock, I went in and touch his foot and call him very soft, and he jump up and begin to shout. When he come to himself he said he had Night Mere, and then he come down and went away with the woman, was not necessary to mention.

Mr Manager, I request you again, please inform the Barman to let me know sir when there is a female guest in the hotel. *C. Hillyard*

November 27. 1 a.m. Bar close, Mr Wills and a American 19 Carib and 2.30 a.m. a Police come and ask for Mr Wills, he say the American report that he was robbed of $200.00¢, he was last drinking at C— with Mr Wills and others. Mr Wills and the Police ask to open the Bar to search it, I told them I cannot open the Bar for you like that, the Police must come with the Manager. Then the American say it was only joke he was joking, and they try to get the Police to laugh, but the Police looking the way I feeling. Then laughing Mr Wills left in a garage car as he couldn't drive himself and the American was waiting outside and they both fall down as they was getting in the car, and Mr Wills saying any time you want a overdraft you just come to my bank kiddo. The Police left walking by himself. *C. Hillyard*

Night Watchman Hillyard: 'Was not necessary to mention'!! You are not to decide what is necessary to mention in this night watchman's occurrence book. Since when have you become sole owner of the hotel as to determine what is necessary to mention? If the guest did not mention it I would never have known that there were screams in the hotel during the night. Also will you kindly tell me who Mr Jimminez is? And what rooms he occupied or occupies? And by what right? You have been told by me personally that the names of all hotel guests are on the slate next to the light switches. If you find Mr Jimminez's name on this slate, or could give me some information about him, I will be most warmly obliged to you. The lady you ask about is Mrs Roscoe,

Room 12, as you very well know. It is your duty to see that guests are not pestered by unauthorized callers. You should give no information about guests to such people, and I would be glad if in future you could direct such callers straight to me. *W. A. G. Inskip*

Sir was what I ask you two times, I dont know what sort of work I take up, I always believe that nightwatchman work is a quiet work and I dont like meddling in white people business, but the gentleman occupy Room 12 also, was there that I went up to call him, I didn't think it necessary to mention because was none of my business sir. *C.E.H.*

November 28. 12 Midnight Bar close and Barman left at 12.20 a.m. leaving Mr Wills and others, and they all left at 1.25 a.m. Mr Wills 8 Carib, Mr Wilson 12, Mr Percy 8, and the man they call Paul 12. Mrs Roscoe join the gentlemen at 12.33 a.m., four gins, everybody calling her Minnie from Trinidad, and then they start singing that song, and some others. Nothing unusual. Afterwards there were mild singing and guitar music in Room 12. A man come in and ask to use the phone at 2.17 a.m. and while he was using it about 7 men come in and wanted to beat him up, so he put down the phone and they all ran away. At 3 a.m. I notice the padlock not on the press, I look inside, no cake, but the padlock was not put on in the first place sir. Mr Wills come down again at 6 a.m. to look for his sweet, he look in the Fridge and did not see any. He took a piece of pineapple. A plate was covered in the Fridge, but it didn't have anything in it. Mr Wills put it out, the cat jump on it and it fall down and break. The garage bulb not burning. *C.E.H.*

You will please sign your name at the bottom of your report. You are in the habit of writing Nothing Unusual. Please take note and think before making such a statement. I want to know what is meant by nothing unusual. I gather, not from you, needless to say, that the police have fallen into the habit of visiting the hotel at night. I would be most grateful to you if you could find the time to note the times of these visits. *W.A.G. Inskip*

Sir, nothing unusual means everything usual. I dont know, nothing I writing you liking. I don't know what sort of work

this night watchman work getting to be, since when people have
to start getting Cambridge certificate to get night watchman
job, I ain't educated and because of this everybody think they
could insult me. *Charles Ethelbert Hillyard*

November 29. Midnight Bar close and 12.15 Barman left leaving
Mr Wills and Mrs Roscoe and others in the Bar. Mr Wills and
Mrs Roscoe left at 12.30 a.m. leaving Mr Wilson and the man
they call Paul, and they all left at 1.00 a.m. Twenty minutes to
2 Mr Wills and party return and left again at 5 to 3. At 3.45 Mr
Wills return and take bread and milk and olives and cherries,
he ask for nutmeg too, I said we had none, he drink 2 Carib,
and left ten minutes later. He also collect Mrs Roscoe bag. All
the drinks, except the 2 Carib, was taken by the man they call
Paul. I don't know sir I don't like this sort of work, you better
hire a night barman. At 5.30 Mrs Roscoe and the man they call
Paul come back to the bar, they was having a quarrel, Mr Paul
saying you make me sick, Mrs Roscoe saying I feel sick, and
then she vomit all over the floor, shouting I didn't want that
damned milk. I was cleaning up when Mr Wills come down to
ask for soda water, we got to lay in more soda for Mr Wills but
I need extra assistance with Mr Wills Paul and party sir.

The police come at 2, 3.48 and 4.52. They sit down in the
bar a long time. Firearms discharge 2 times in the back yard.
Detective making inquiries. I don't know sir, I thinking it would
be better for me to go back to some other sort of job. At 3 I
hear somebody shout Thief, and I see a man running out of the
back, and Mr London, Room 9, say he miss 80 cents and a pack
of cigarettes which was on his dressing case. I don't know when
the people in this place does sleep. *Chas. Ethelbert Hillyard*

Night Watchman Hillyard: A lot more than 80 cents was stolen. Several
rooms were in fact entered during the night, including my own. You
are employed to prevent such things occurring. Your interest in the
morals of our guests seems to be distracting your attention from your
duties. Save your preaching for your roadside prayer meetings. Mr
Pick, Room 7, reports that in spite of the most pressing and repeated
requests, you did not awaken him at 5. He has missed his plane to
British Guiana as a result. No newspapers were delivered to the rooms

this morning. I am again notifying you that papers must be handed personally to Doorman Vignales. And the messenger's bicycle, which I must remind you is the property of the hotel, has been damaged. What do you *do* at nights? *W. A. G. Inskip*

Please don't ask me sir.

Relating to the damaged bicycle: I left the bicycle the same place where I meet it, nothing took place so as to damage it. I always take care of all property sir. I dont know how you could think I have time to go out for bicycle rides. About the papers, sir, the police and them read it and leave them in such a state that I didn't think it would be nice to give them to guests. I wake up Mr Pick, room 7, at 4.50 a.m. 5 a.m. 5.15 a.m. and 5.30. He told me to keep off, he would not get up, and one time he pelt a box of matches at me, matches scatter all over the place I always do everything to the best of my ability sir. But God is my Witness I never find a night watchman work like this, so much writing I dont have time to do anything else, I dont have four hands and six eyes and I want this extra assistance with Mr Wills and party sir. I am a poor man and you could abuse me, but you must not abuse my religion sir because the good Lord sees All and will have His revenge sir, I don't know what sort of work and trouble I land myself in, all I want is a little quiet night work and all I getting is abuse. *Chas. E. Hillyard*

November 30. 12.25 a.m. Bar close and Barman left 1.00 a.m. leaving Mr Wills and party in Bar. Mr Wills take 12 Carib Mr Wilson 6, Mr Percy 14. Mrs Roscoe five gins. At 1.30 a.m. Mrs Roscoe left and there were a little singing and mild guitar playing in Room 12. Nothing unusual. The police came at 1.35 and sit down in the bar for a time, not drinking, not talking, not doing anything except watching. At 1.45 the man they call Paul come in with Mr McPherson of the SS Naparoni, they was both falling down and laughing whenever anything break and the man they call Paul say Fireworks about to begin tell Minnie Malcolm coming the ship just dock. Mr Wills and party scatter leaving one or two bottles half empty and then the man they call Paul tell me to go up to Room 12 and tell Minnie Roscoe that Malcolm coming. I don't know how people could behave so the thing enough to make anybody turn priest. I notice the padlock on the bar door break off it hanging on only by a little piece of wood. And when I went up to Room 12 and tell Mrs Roscoe that Malcolm coming the ship just dock the woman get sober straight away like she dont want to hear no more guitar music and she asking me where to hide where to go. I dont know, I feel the day of reckoning is at hand, but she not listening to what I saying, she busy straightening up the room one minute packing the next, and then she run out into the corridor and before I could stop she run straight down the back stairs to the annexe. And then 5 past 2, still in the corridor, I see a big man running up to me and he sober as a judge and he mad as a drunkard and he asking me where she is where she is. I ask whether he is a authorized caller, he say you don't give me any of that crap now, where she is, where she is. So remembering about the last time and Mr Jimminez I direct him to the manager office in the annexe. He hear a little scuffling inside Mr Inskip room and I make out Mr Inskip sleepy voice and Mrs Roscoe voice and the red man run inside and all I hearing for the next five minutes is bam bam bodow bodow bow and this woman screaming. I dont know what sort of work this night watchman getting I want something quiet like the police. In time things quiet down and the red man drag Mrs Roscoe out of the annexe and they take a taxi, and the Police sitting down quiet in the bar. Then Mr Percy and the others come back one by one to the bar and they talking quiet and they not drinking and they left 3 a.m. 3.15 Mr Wills return and take one whisky and 2 Carib. He asked for pineapple or some sweet fruit but it had nothing.

6 a.m. Mr Wills came in the bar looking for soda but it aint have none. We have to get some soda for Mr Wills sir.

6.30 a.m. the papers come and I deliver them to Doorman Vignales at 7 a.m. *Chas. Hillyard*

Mr Hillyard: In view of the unfortunate illness of Mr Inskip, I am temporarily in charge of the hotel. I trust you will continue to make your nightly reports, but I would be glad if you could keep your entries as brief as possible. *Robt. Magnus, Acting Manager*

December 1. 10.30 p.m. C. E. Hillyard take over duty at C— Hotel all corrected 12 Midnight Bar close 2 a.m. Mr Wills 2 Carib, 1 bread 6 a.m. Mr Wills 1 soda 7 a.m. Night Watchman Hillyard hand over duty to Mr Vignales with one torch light 2 Fridge keys and Room keys 1, 3, 6 and 12. Bar intact all corrected no report. *C.E.H.*

Iain Crichton-Smith

Mr Heine

It was ten o'clock at night and Mr Bingham was talking to the mirror. He said 'Ladies and gentlemen', and then stopped, clearing his throat, before beginning again, 'Headmaster and colleagues, it is now forty years since I first entered the teaching profession – Will that do as a start, dear?'

'It will do well as a start, dear,' said his wife Lorna.

'Do you think I should perhaps put in a few jokes,' said her husband anxiously. 'When Mr Currie retired, his speech was well received because he had a number of jokes in it. My speech will be delivered in one of the rooms of the Domestic Science Department where they will have tea and scones prepared. It will be after class hours.'

'A few jokes would be acceptable,' said his wife, 'but I think that the general tone should be serious.'

Mr Bingham squared his shoulders, preparing to address the mirror again, but at that moment the doorbell rang.

'Who can that be at this time of night?' he said irritably.

'I don't know, dear. Shall I answer it?'

'If you would, dear.'

His wife carefully laid down her knitting and went to the door. Mr Bingham heard a murmur of voices and after a while his wife came back into the living room with a man of perhaps forty-five or so who had a pale rather haunted face, but who seemed eager and enthusiastic and slightly jaunty.

'You won't know me,' he said to Mr Bingham. 'My name is Heine. I am in advertising. I compose little jingles such as the following:

> *When your dog is feeling depressed*
> *Give him Dalton's. It's the best.*

I used to be in your class in 1944–5. I heard you were retiring
so I came along to offer you my felicitations.'

'Oh?' said Mr Bingham turning away from the mirror regret-
fully.

'Isn't that nice of Mr Heine?' said his wife.

'Won't you sit down?' she said and Mr Heine sat down,
carefully pulling up his trouser legs so that he wouldn't crease
them.

'My landlady of course has seen you about the town,' he
said to Mr Bingham. 'For a long time she thought you were a
farmer. It shows one how frail fame is. I think it is because of
your red healthy face. I told her you had been my English
teacher for a year. Now I am in advertising. One of my best
rhymes is:

> *Dalton's Dogfood makes your collie*
> *Obedient and rather jolly.*

You taught me Tennyson and Pope. I remember both rather
well.'

'The fact,' said Mr Bingham, 'that I don't remember you
says nothing against you personally. Thousands of pupils have
passed through my hands. Some of them come to speak to me
now and again. Isn't that right, dear?'

'Yes,' said Mrs Bingham, 'that happens quite regularly.'

'Perhaps you could make a cup of coffee, dear,' said Mr
Bingham and when his wife rose and went into the kitchen, Mr
Heine leaned forward eagerly.

'I remember that you had a son,' he said. 'Where is he
now?'

'He is in educational administration,' said Mr Bingham
proudly. 'He has done well.'

'When I was in your class,' said Mr Heine, 'I was eleven or
twelve years old. There was a group of boys who used to make
fun of me. I don't know whether I have told you but I am a
Jew. One of the boys was called Colin. He was taller than me,
and fair-haired.'

'You are not trying to insinuate that it was my son,' said Mr
Bingham angrily. 'His name was Colin but he would never do

such a thing. He would never use physical violence against anyone.'

'Well,' said Mr Heine affably, 'it was a long time ago, and in any case

> *The past is past and for the present*
> *It may be equally unpleasant.*

Colin was the ringleader, and he had blue eyes. In those days I had a lisp which sometimes returns in moments of nervousness. Ah, there is Mrs Bingham with the coffee. Thank you, Madam.'

'Mr Heine says that when he was in school he used to be terrorized by a boy called Colin who was fair-haired,' said Mr Bingham to his wife.

'It is true,' said Mr Heine, 'but as I have said it was a long time ago and best forgotten about. I was small and defenceless and I wore glasses. I think, Mrs Bingham, that you yourself taught in the school in those days.'

'Sugar?' said Mrs Bingham. 'Yes. As it was during the war years and most of the men were away I taught Latin. My husband was deferred.'

'*Amo, amas, amat*,' said Mr Heine. 'I remember I was in your class as well.

'I was not a memorable child,' he added, stirring his coffee reflectively, 'so you probably won't remember me either. But I do remember the strong rhymes of Pope which have greatly influenced me. And so, Mr Bingham, when I heard you were retiring I came along as quickly as my legs would carry me, without tarrying. I am sure that you chose the right profession. I myself have chosen the right profession. You, sir, though you did not know it at the time placed me in that profession.'

Mr Bingham glanced proudly at his wife.

'I remember the particular incident very well,' said Mr Heine. 'You must remember that I was a lonely little boy and not good at games.

> *Keeping wicket was not cricket.*
> *Bat and ball were not for me suitable at all.*

And then again I was being set upon by older boys and given a drubbing every morning in the boiler room before classes commenced. The boiler room was very hot. I had a little talent in those days, not much certainly, but a small poetic talent. I wrote verses which in the general course of things I kept secret. Thus it happened one afternoon that I brought them along to show you, Mr Bingham. I don't know whether you will remember the little incident, sir.'

'No,' said Mr Bingham, 'I can't say that I do.'

'I admired you, sir, as a man who was very enthusiastic about poetry, especially Tennyson. That is why I showed you my poems. I remember that afternoon well. It was raining heavily and the room was indeed so gloomy that you asked one of the boys to switch on the lights. You said, "Let's have some light on the subject, Hughes." I can remember Hughes quite clearly, as indeed I can remember your quips and jokes. In any case Hughes switched on the lights and it was a grey day, not in May but in December, an ember of the done sun in the sky. You read one of my poems. As I say, I can't remember it now but it was not in rhyme. "Now I will show you the difference between good poetry and bad poetry," you said, comparing my little effort with Tennyson's work, which was mostly in rhyme. When I left the room I was surrounded by a pack of boys led by blue-eyed fair-haired Colin. The moral of this story is that I went into advertising and therefore into rhyme. It was a revelation to me.

> *A revelation straight from God*
> *That I should rhyme as I was taught.*

So you can see, sir, that you are responsible for the career in which I have flourished.'

'I don't believe it, sir,' said Mr Bingham furiously.

'Don't believe what, sir?'

'That that ever happened. I can't remember it.'

'It was Mrs Gross my landlady who saw the relevant passage about you in the paper. I must go immediately, I told her. You thought he was a farmer but I knew differently. That man does not know the influence he has had on his scholars. That is why I came,' he said simply.

'Tell me, sir,' he added, 'is your son married now?'

'Colin?'

'The same, sir.'

'Yes, he's married. Why do you wish to know?'

'For no reason, sir. Ah, I see a photograph on the mantelpiece. In colour. It is a photograph of the bridegroom and the bride.

> *How should we not hail the blooming bride*
> *With her good husband at her side?*

What is more calculated to stabilize a man than marriage? Alas I never married myself. I think I never had the confidence for such a beautiful institution. May I ask the name of the fortunate lady?'

'Her name is Norah,' said Mrs Bingham sharply. 'Norah Mason.'

'Well, well,' said Mr Heine enthusiastically. 'Norah, eh? We all remember Norah, don't we? She was a lady of free charm and great beauty. But I must not go on. All those unseemly pranks of childhood which we should consign to the dustbins of the past. Norah Mason, eh?' and he smiled brightly. 'I am so happy that your son married Norah.'

'Look here,' said Mr Bingham, raising his voice.

'I hope that my felicitations, congratulations, will be in order for them too, I sincerely hope so, sir. Tell me, did your son Colin have a scar on his brow which he received as a result of having been hit on the head by a cricket ball?'

'And what if he had?' said Mr Binham.

'Merely the sign of recognition, sir, as in the Greek tragedies. My breath in these days came in short pants, sir, and I was near-sighted. I deserved all that I got. And now sir, forgetful of all that, let me say that my real purpose in coming here was to give you a small monetary gift which would come particularly from myself and not from the generality. My salary is a very comfortable one. I thought of something in the region of ... Oh look at the time. It is nearly half-past eleven at night.

> *At eleven o'clock at night*
> *The shades come out and then they fight.*

I was, as I say, thinking of something in the order of ...'

'Get out, sir,' said Mr Bingham angrily. 'Get out, sir, with your insinuations. I do not wish to hear any more.'

'I beg your pardon,' said Mr Heine in a wounded voice.

'I said "Get out, sir." It is nearly midnight. Get out.'

Mr Heine rose to his feet. 'If that is the way you feel, sir. I only wished to bring my felicitations.'

'We do not want your felicitations,' said Mr Bingham. 'We have enough of them from others.'

'Then I wish you both goodnight and you particularly, Mr Bingham, as you leave the profession you have adorned for so long.'

'GET OUT, sir,' Mr Bingham shouted, the veins standing out on his forehead.

Mr Heine walked slowly to the door, seemed to wish to stop and say something else, but then changed his mind and the two left in the room heard the door being shut.

'I think we should both go to bed, dear,' said Mr Bingham, panting heavily.

'Of course, dear,' said his wife. She locked the door and said, 'Will you put the lights out or shall I?'

'You may put them out, dear,' said Mr Bingham. When the lights had been switched off they stood for a while in the darkness, listening to the little noises of the night from which Mr Heine had so abruptly and outrageously come.

'I can't remember him. I don't believe he was in the school at all,' said Mrs Bingham decisively.

'You are right, dear,' said Mr Bingham, who could make out the outline of his wife in the half-darkness. 'You are quite right, dear.'

'I have a good memory and I should know,' said Mrs Bingham as they lay side by side in the bed. Mr Bingham heard the cry of the owl, throatily soft, and turned over and was soon fast asleep. His wife listened to his snoring, staring sightlessly at the objects and furniture of the bedroom which she had gathered with such persistence and passion over the years.

Fay Weldon

Horrors of the Road

Miss Jacobs, I don't believe in psychotherapy. I really do think
it's a lot of nonsense. Now it's taken me considerable nerve to
say that – I'm a rather mild person and hate to be thought rude.
I just wouldn't want to be here under false pretences: it wouldn't
be fair to you, would it?

But Piers wants me to come and see you, so of course I will.
He's waiting outside in your pretty drawing-room: I said he
should go, and come back when the session was up: that I'd be
perfectly all right but he likes to be at hand in case anything
happens. Just sometimes I do fall forward, out of my chair – so
far I haven't hurt myself. Once it was face-first into a feather
sofa; the second was trickier – I was with Martin – he's my little
grandchild, you know, David's boy, the only one so far – at the
sandpit in the park and I just pitched forward into the sand.
Someone sent for an ambulance but it wasn't really necessary –
I was perfectly all right, instantly. Well, except for this one big
permanent fact that my legs don't work.

I'm a great mystery to the doctors. Piers has taken me everywhere – Paris, New York, Tokyo – but the verdict seems to be
the same: it's all in my head. It is a hysterical paralysis. I find
this humiliating: as if I'd done it on purpose just to be a nuisance.
I'm the last person in the world to be a nuisance!

Did you see Piers? Isn't he handsome? He's in his mid-fifties,
you know, but so good-looking. Of course he has an amazing
brain – well, the whole world knows that – and I think that
helps to keep people looking young. I have a degree in

Economics myself – unusual for a housewife of my age – but of course I stayed home to devote myself to Piers and the children. I think, on the whole, women should do that. Don't you? Why don't you answer my questions? Isn't that what you're supposed to do? Explain me to myself? No?

I must explain myself to myself! Oh.

Behind every great man stands a woman. I believe that. Piers is a Nobel Prize winner. Would he have done it without me? I expect so. He just wouldn't have had me, would he, or the four children? They're all doing very well. Piers was away quite a lot when the children were young – he's a particle physicist, as I'm sure you know. He had to be away. They don't keep cyclotrons in suitably domestic places, and the money had to be earned somehow. But we all always had these holidays together, in France. How we loved France. How well we knew it. Piers would drive; I'd navigate; the four children piled in the back! Of course these days we fly. There's just Piers and me. It's glamorous and exciting, and people know who he is so the service is good. Waiters don't mind so much ... Mind what? ... I thought you weren't supposed to ask questions. I was talking about holidays, in the past, long ago. Well, not so long ago. We went on till the youngest was fifteen; Brutus that is, and he's only twenty now. Can it be only five years?

I miss those summer dockside scenes: the cars lined up at dusk or dawn waiting for the ferry home: sunburned families, careless and exhausted after weeks in the sun. By careless I don't mean without care – just without caring any more. They'll sleep all night in their cars to be first in the queue for the ferry, and not worry about it; on the journey out they'd have gone berserk. Brown faces and brittle blonde hair and grubby children; and the roof-racks with the tents and the water cans and the boxes of wine and strings of garlic. Volvos and Cortinas and Volkswagen vans. Of course our cars never looked smart: we even started out once with a new one, but by the time we came back it was dented and bumped and battered. French drivers are so dreadful, aren't they; and their road signs are impossible.

How did the paralysis start? It was completely unexpected. There were no warning signs – no numbness, no dizziness, nothing like that. It was our thirtieth wedding anniversary. To celebrate we were going to do a tour of France in Piers' new MG. It can do 110 mph, you know, but Piers doesn't often go at more than fifty-five – that's the speed limit in the States, you know, and he says they know what they're doing – it's the best speed for maximum safety – but he likes to have cars that can go fast. To get out of trouble in an emergency, Piers says. We were going on the Weymouth/Cherbourg route – I'm usually happier with Dover/Calais – the sea journey's shorter for one thing, and somehow the longer the journey through England the more likely Piers is to forget to drive on the right once we're in France. I've noticed it. But I don't argue about things like that. Piers knows what he's doing – I never backseat drive. I'm his wife, he's my husband. We love each other.

So we were setting out for Weymouth, the bags were packed, the individual route maps from the AA in the glove compartment – they'd arrived on time, for once. (I'd taken a Valium in good time – my heart tends to beat rather fast, almost to the point of palpitations, when I'm navigating.) I was wearing a practical non-crease dress – you know what long journeys are like – you always end up a little stained. Piers loves melons and likes me to feed him wedges as we drive along – and you know how ripe a ripe French melon can be. Piers will spend hours choosing one from a market stall. He'll test every single one on display – you know, sniffing and pressing the ends for just the right degree of tenderness – until he's found one that's absolutely perfect. Sometimes, before he's satisfied, he'll go through the fruit boxes at the back of the stall as well. The French like you to be particular, Piers says. They'll despise you if you accept just anything. And then, of course, if the melon's not to go over the top, they have to be eaten quite quickly – in the car as often as not...

Anyway, as I was saying, I was about to step into the car when my legs just kind of folded and I sank down on to the pavement, and that was six months ago, and I haven't walked since. No, no palpitations since either. I can't remember if I had palpitations before I was married – I've been married for ever!

And there was no holiday. Just me paralysed. No tour of France. Beautiful France. I adore the Loire and the châteaux, don't you? The children loved the West Coast: those stretches of piny woods and the long, long beaches and the great Atlantic rollers – but after the middle of August the winds change and everything gets dusty and somehow grizzly. When the children were small we camped, but every year the sites got more formal and more crowded and more full of *frites* and Piers didn't like that. He enjoyed what he called 'wilderness camping'. In the camping guides which describe the sites there's always an area section – that is, the area allowed for each tent. Point five of a hectare is crowded: two hectares perfectly possible. Piers liked ten hectares, which meant a hillside somewhere and no television room for the children or *frites* stall – and that meant more work for me, not that I grudged it: a change of venue for cooking – such lovely portable calor gas stoves we had: you could do a three-course meal on just two burners if you were clever, if the wind wasn't too high – is as good as a rest from cooking. It was just that the children preferred the crowded sites, and I did sometimes think they were better for the children's French. An English sparrow and a French sparrow sing pretty much the same song. But there you are, Piers loved the wilderness. He'd always measure the actual hectarage available for our tent, and if it didn't coincide with what was in the book would take it up with the relevant authorities. I remember it once ending up with people having to move their tents at ten in the evening to make proper room for ours – we'd driven three hundred miles that day and Brutus was only two. That wasn't Piers' fault: it was the camp proprietor's. Piers merely knocked him up to point out that our site wasn't the dimension it ought to be, and he over-reacted quite dreadfully. I was glad to get away from that site in the morning, I can tell you. It really wasn't Piers' fault; just one of those things. I'm glad it was only a stop-over. The other campers just watched us go, in complete silence. It was weird. And Fanny cried all the way to Poitiers.

Such a tearful little thing, Fanny. Piers liked to have a picnic lunch at about three o'clock – the French roads clear at mid-day while everyone goes off to gorge themselves on lunch, so you can make really good time wherever you're going. Sometimes I did wonder where it was we *were* going to, or *why* we had to make such time, but on the other hand those wonderful white empty B roads, poplar-lined, at a steady 55 mph ... anyway, we'd buy our lunch at mid-day – wine and pâté and long French bread and orangina for the children, and then at three start looking for a nice place to picnic. Nothing's harder! If the place is right, the traffic's wrong. Someone's on your tail hooting – how those French drivers do hoot – they can see the GB plates – they know it means the driver's bound to forget and go round roundabouts the wrong way – and before you know it the ideal site is passed. The ideal site has a view, no snakes, some sun and some shade, and I like to feel the car's right off the road – especially if it's a Route Nationale – though Piers doesn't worry too much. Once actually some idiot did drive right into it – he didn't brake in time – but as Piers had left our car in gear, and not put on the handbrake or anything silly, it just shot forward and not much damage was done. How is it that other cars always look so smooth and somehow new? I suppose their owners must just keep them in garages all the time having the bumps knocked out and re-sprays – well, fools and their money are often parted, as Piers keeps saying.

What was I talking about? Stopping for lunch. Sometimes it would be 4.30 before we found somewhere really nice, and by four you could always rely on Fanny to start crying. I'd give her water from the Pschitt bottle – how the children giggled – Pschitt – every year a ritual, lovely giggle – and break off bread from the loaf for her, but still she grizzled: and Daddy would stop and start and stare over hedges and go a little way down lanes and find them impossible and back out onto the main road, and the children would fall silent, except for Fanny. Aren't French drivers rude? Had you noticed? I'd look sideways at a passing car and the driver would be staring at us, screwing his thumb into his head, or pretending to slit his throat with his finger – and always these honks and hoots, and once someone pulled in and forced us to stop and tried to drag poor Piers out of the car, goodness knows why. Just general Gallic over-excitement, I suppose. Piers is a wonderfully safe driver. I do think he sometimes inconveniences other cars the way he stops at intersections – you know how muddling their road signs are, especially on city ring roads, and how they seem to be telling you to go right or left when actually they mean straight on. And Piers is a scientist – he likes to be sure he's doing the right thing. I have the maps; I do my best: I memorize whole areas of the country, so I will know when passing through, say, Limoges, on the way from Périgueux to Issoudun, and have to make lightning decisions – Piers seems to speed up in towns. No! Not the Tulle road, not the Clermont road, not the Montluçon but the Châteauroux road. Only the Châteauroux road isn't marked! Help! What's its number? Dear God, it's the N20! We'll die! The N147 to Bellac then, and cut through on the B roads to Argenton, La Châtre ... So look for the Poitiers sign. Bellac's on the road to Poitiers –

So he stops, if he's not convinced I'm right, and takes the map himself and studies it before going on. Which meant, in later years, finding his magnifying glass. He hates spectacles! And you know what those overhead traffic lights are like in small country towns, impossible to see, so no one takes any notice of them! Goodness knows how French drivers survive at all. We had one or two nasty misses through no fault of our own every holiday; I did in the end feel happier if I took Valium. But I never liked Piers to know I was taking it – it seemed a kind of statement of lack of faith – which is simply untrue. Look at the way he carried me in, cradled me in his arms, laid me on this sofa! I trust him implicitly. I am his wife. He is my husband.

What was I saying? Fanny grizzling. She took off to New Zealand as soon as she'd finished her college course. A long way away. Almost as far as she could get, I find myself saying, I don't know why. I know she loves us and we certainly love her. She writes frequently. David's a racing car driver. Piers and I are very upset about this. Such a dangerous occupation. Those cars get up to 200 mph – and Piers did so hate speed. Angela's doing psychiatric nursing. They say she has a real gift for it.

I remember once I said to Piers – we were on the ring road round Angers – turn left here, meaning the T-junction we were approaching – but he swung straight left across the other carriageway, spying a little side road there – empty because all the traffic was round the corner, held up by the lights, ready to surge foward. He realized what he'd done, and stopped, leaving us broadside across the main road. 'Reverse!' I shrieked, breaking my rule about no backseat driving, and he did, and we were just out of the way when the expected wall of traffic bore down. 'You should have said second left,' he said, 'that was very nearly a multiple pile-up!' You can't be too careful in France. They're mad drivers, as everyone knows. And with the children in the car too –

But it was all such fun. Piers always knew how to get the best out of waiters and chefs. He'd go right through the menu with the waiter, asking him to explain each dish. If the waiter couldn't do it – and it's amazing how many waiters can't – he would send for the chef and ask him. It did get a little embarrassing sometimes, if the restaurant was very busy, but as Piers said, the French understand food and really appreciate it if you do too. I can make up my mind in a flash what I want to eat: Piers takes ages. As I say, he hates to get things wrong. We'd usually be last to leave any restaurant we ate in, but Piers doesn't believe in hurrying. As he says, a) it's bad for the digestion and b) they don't mind: they're glad to see us appreciating what they have to offer. So many people don't. French waiters are such a rude breed, don't you think? They always seem to have kind of glassy eyes. Goodness knows what they're like if you're *not* appreciating what they have to offer!

And then wine. Piers believes in sending wine back as well as food. Standards have to be maintained. He doesn't believe in serving red wines chilled in the modern fashion, no matter how new they are. And that a bottle of wine under eight francs is as worth discussing as one at thirty francs. He's always very polite: just sends for the wine waiter to discuss the matter, but of course he doesn't speak French, so difficulties sometimes arise. Acrimony almost. And this kind of funny silence while we leave.

And always when we paid the bill before leaving our hotel, Piers would check and re-check every item. He's got rather short-sighted over the years: he has to use a magnifying glass. The children and I would sit waiting in the car for up to an hour while they discussed the cost of hot water and what a reasonable profit was, and why it being a fête holiday should make a difference. I do sometimes think, I admit, that Piers has a love/hate relationship with France. He loves the country; he won't go holidaying in Italy or Spain, only France – and yet, you know, those *Dégustation-Libres* that have sprung up all over the place – 'free disgustings', as the children call them – where you taste the wine before choosing? Piers goes in, tastes everything, and if he likes nothing – which is quite often – buys nothing. That, after all, is what they are offering. *Free* wine-tasting. He likes me to go in with him, to taste with him, so that we can compare notes, and I watch the enthusiasm dying in the proprietor's eyes, as he is asked to fetch first this, then that, then the other down from the top shelf, and Piers sips and raises his eyebrows and shakes his head, and then hostility dawns in the shopkeeper's eye, and then boredom, and then I almost think something which borders on derision – and I must tell you, Miss Jacobs, I don't like it, and in the end, whenever we passed a *Dégustation-Libre* and I saw the glint in his eye, and his foot went on the brake – he never looked in his mirror – there was no point, since it was always adjusted to show the car roof – I'd take another Valium – because I think otherwise I would scream, I couldn't help myself. It wasn't that I didn't love and trust and admire Piers, it was the look in the French eye –

Why don't I scream? What are you after? Abreaction? I know the terms – my daughter Angela's a psychiatric nurse, as I told you, and doing very well. You think I was finally traumatized at the last *Dégustation*? And that's why I can't walk? You'd like to believe that, wouldn't you? I expect you're a feminist – I notice you're wearing a trouser suit – and like to think everything in this world is the man's fault. You want me to scream out tension and rage and terror and horror? I won't! I tell you, France is a joyous place and we all loved those holidays and had some wonderful meals and some knock-out wines, thanks to Piers, and as for his driving, we're all alive, aren't we? Piers, me, David, Angela, Fanny, Brutus. All alive! That must prove something. It's just I don't seem able to walk, and if you would be so kind as to call Piers, he will shift me from your sofa to the chair and wheel me home. Talking will get us nowhere. I do love my husband.

Michael Frayn

Through the Wilderness

It is nice now that all you boys have got cars of your own (*said Mother*). You know how much it means to me when the three of you drive down to see me like this, and we can all have a good old chatter together.

JOHN: That's right, Mother. So, as I was saying, Howard, I came down today through Wroxtead and Sudstow.

HOWARD: Really? I always come out through Dorris Hill and West Hatcham.

RALPH: I find I tend to turn off at the traffic lights in Manor Park Road myself and follow the 43 bus route through to the White Hart at Broylesden.

MOTHER: Ralph always was the adventurous one.

JOHN: Last time I tried forking right just past the police station in Broylesden High Street. I wasn't very impressed with it as a route, though.

HOWARD: Weren't you? That's interesting. I've occasionally tried cutting through the Broylesden Heath Estate. Then you can either go along Mottram Road South or Creese End Broadway. I think it's handy to have the choice.

RALPH: Of course, much the prettiest way for my money is to carry on into Hangmore and go down past the pickles factory in Sunnydeep Lane.

MOTHER: Your father and I once saw Lloyd George going down Sunnydeep Lane in a *wheelbarrow* ...

HOWARD: Did you, Mother? I'm not very keen on the Sunnydeep Lane way personally. I'm a great believer in turning up Hangmore Hill and going round by the pre-fabs on the Common.

RALPH: Yes, yes, there's something to be said for that, too.

What was the traffic like in Sudstow, then, John?

JOHN: Getting a bit sticky.

HOWARD: Yes, it was getting a bit sticky in Broylesden. How was it in Dorris Hill, Ralph?

RALPH: Sticky, pretty sticky.

MOTHER: The traffic's terrible round here now. There was a most frightful accident yesterday just outside when ...

HOWARD: Oh, you're bound to get them in traffic like this. Bound to.

RALPH: Where did you strike the traffic in Sudstow, then, John?

JOHN: At the lights by the railway bridge. Do you know where I mean?

RALPH: Just by that dance hall where they had the trouble?

JOHN: No, no. Next to the neon sign advertising mattresses.

HOWARD: Oh, you mean by the caravan depot? Just past Acme Motors?

JOHN: Acme Motors? You're getting mixed up with Heaslam Road, Surley.

HOWARD: I'm pretty sure I'm not, you know.

JOHN: I think you are, you know.

HOWARD: I don't think I am, you know.

JOHN: Anyway, that's where I struck the traffic.

RALPH: I had a strange experience the other day.

JOHN: Oh, really?

RALPH: I turned left at the lights in Broylesden High Street and cut down round the back of Coalpit Road. Thought I'd come out by the Wemblemore Palais. But what do you think happened? I came out by a new parade of shops, and I thought, hello, this must be Old Hangmore. Then I passed an Odeon –

JOHN: An Odeon? In Old Hangmore?

RALPH: – and I thought, that's strange, there's no Odeon in Old Hangmore. Do you know where I was? In *New* Hangmore!

HOWARD: Getting lost in New Hangmore's nothing. I got lost last week in Upsome!

JOHN: I went off somewhere into the blue only yesterday not a hundred yards from Sunnydeep Lane!

MOTHER: I remember I once got lost in the most curious circumstances in Singapore...

RALPH: Anybody could get lost in Singapore, Mother.

JOHN: To become personal for a moment, Howard, how's your car?

HOWARD: Not so bad, thanks, not so bad. And yours?

JOHN: Not so bad, you know. How's yours, Ralph?

RALPH: Oh, not so bad, not so bad at all.

MOTHER: I had another of my turns last week.

HOWARD: We're talking about cars, Mother, CARS.

MOTHER: Oh, I'm sorry.

JOHN: To change the subject a bit – you know where Linden Green Lane comes out, just by Upsome Quadrant?

HOWARD: Where Tunstall Road joins the Crescent there?

RALPH: Just by the Nervous Diseases Hospital?

JOHN: That's right. Where the new roundabout's being built.

HOWARD: Almost opposite a truss shop with a giant model of a rupture belt outside?

RALPH: Just before you get to the bus station?

HOWARD: By the zebra crossing there?

JOHN: That's right. Well, I had a puncture there on Friday.

RALPH: Well, then, I suppose we ought to think about getting back.

HOWARD: I thought I might turn off by the paint factory on the by-pass this time and give the Apex roundabout a miss.

JOHN: Have either of you tried taking that side road at Tillotsons' Corner?

RALPH: There's a lot to be said for both ways. A lot to be said.

MOTHER: I'll go and make the tea while you discuss it, then. I know you've got more important things to do than sit here listening to an old woman like me chattering away all afternoon.

Beryl Bainbridge

People for Lunch

'We simply must,' said Margaret.

'Do we have to?' asked Richard.

'No,' said Margaret, 'but we will. We've been to them eight weekends on the trot. It looks awful.'

Thinking about it, Richard supposed she was right. Every Sunday throughout May and June they had motored down to Tunbridge Wells, arriving in time for lunch. They had left again at six o'clock, after Dora and Charles had made them a cup of Earl Grey tea. Apart from an obligatory inspection of the kiddies' new bicycles or skateboards, or being forced to listen to some long feeble jokes told by young Sarah, the hours spent in Dora's well-appointed house had been pleasant and restful. 'I don't think they expect to be asked back,' said Richard.

'They're not like that.'

'Not *expect*,' agreed Margaret. 'But I think we should.'

Dora and Charles were asked for the following Sunday. Richard and Charles had gone to university together, been articled together, and now worked for the same firm of lawyers, in the litigation department. 'Jolly nice of you,' said Charles, when he heard. 'We're looking foward to it.'

It had been a little tricky suggesting to Dora that she leave the children behind. 'They'll be so bored here,' explained Margaret, when speaking to her on the phone. 'As you know we've only a backyard. There's no sun after eleven o'clock in the morning. And Malcolm won't be here.' She didn't feel too awkward about it because after all Dora had a marvellous woman who lived in, and Dora herself was frightfully keen once the penny had dropped.

'How did you put it?' asked Richard worriedly. 'I hope you didn't imply we . . .'

'Don't be silly,' said Margaret crossly. 'You know me. I was the soul of tact.'

Two unfortunate events occurred on the morning of the luncheon party. The sky, which earlier had been clear and blue, filled with clouds, and Malcolm, who had promised faithfully he was going out, changed his mind. He said there was a programme he wanted to watch on TV at one o'clock.

'You can't,' wailed Margaret. 'We'll be sitting down for lunch.'

'I'm watching,' said Malcolm. He switched on the set and lay full-length on the wicker couch from Thailand, flicking cigarette ash on to the pine floor.

'Can't watch the telly, old chap,' said Richard bravely. ' 'Fraid not. We've people coming.'

'Piss off,' said Malcolm.

At midday Richard suggested Malcolm come with him to the pub to buy the beer. 'I'm not shifting,' said Malcolm. 'I don't want to miss my programme.'

While Richard was away, the clouds lifted and the sun shone. Margaret looked out of the window at the square of paving stones set with shrubs and bordered by a neat privet hedge. Although only seventeen, Malcolm was extremely tenacious of purpose. He would spend the entire lunch hour jumping up and switching on the telly after Richard had turned it off. The only slight chance of stopping him lay in hitting him over the head, and then there'd be a punch-up and it would undoubtedly spoil the atmosphere. She began to carry chairs through to the front door; if it were not for the privet hedge, they would be sitting practically on the pavement, but it couldn't be helped.

'What the hell are you doing?' asked Richard, when he returned with the drink.

'It's your fault,' cried Margaret shrilly. 'You shouldn't have boxed the television in. I'm not entertaining guests with that damn thing blazing away.' After several harsh words Richard strode into the house and began to manhandle the table into the hall.

'I will not ask you to help,' he called to Malcolm. 'I will not point out that your unreasonable behaviour is the cause of all this upheaval.' He swore as the table, wedged in the narrow passage, crushed his fingers against the jamb of the door.

'Stop muttering,' shouted Malcolm. 'If you've got anything to say, say it to my face.'

The table, once settled on flagstones, sloped only partially at one end. Covered with a tablecloth, a vase of roses placed in the centre, the effect was charming. 'I think it's better than indoors,' said Margaret. 'I really do.'

'I could have a heart attack,' said Richard. '– We both could – and that boy would trample over us to change channels.'

'Sssh!' said Margaret. 'Don't upset yourself.'

Dora and Charles arrived promptly at 12.30. The moment they stepped out of the car the sun went behind a cloud.

'It's a little informal,' said Margaret gaily, 'but we thought you'd prefer to sit outside.'

'Rather,' said Charles, gazing at the row of bins behind the upright chairs. Richard kissed Dora and Margaret kissed Charles; the merest brush of lips against stubble and powder. 'I'm afraid I haven't shaved,' said Richard.

'Good God,' cried Charles, who had performed this ritual at 7.30. 'Who the hell shaves on Sunday?'

They went into the front room and had a drop of sherry, standing in a group at the window and eyeing the table outside as if it were a new car that had just been delivered.

'Lovely roses,' said Charles.

'Home-grown?' asked Dora. They had to shout to be heard above the noise of the television.

'No,' said Margaret. 'We do have roses in the backyard, but the slightest hint of wind and they fall apart.'

'I know the feeling,' said Dora, who could be very dry on occasion.

They all laughed, particularly Dora.

'Belt up,' said Malcolm.

They trooped in and out, carrying the salad bowl and the condiments, the glasses for the wine.

'This is fun,' said Charles, stumbling over a geranium pot

and kicking a milk bottle down the steps. He insisted on fetching the dustpan and brush. Malcolm was eating an orange and spitting pips at the skirting board.

'You're doing "O" levels, I suppose,' said Charles. 'Or is it "A"s?'

'You what?' said Malcolm.

'Any idea what you want to do?' asked Charles, leaning on the handle of the brush.

'Nope,' said Malcolm.

'Plenty of time,' said Charles. He went outside and confided to Richard. 'Nice boy you've got there. Quiet but deep.'

'Possibly,' said Richard uneasily.

It was an enjoyable lunch. Margaret was a good cook and Richard refilled the glasses even before they were empty. It was quite secluded behind the hedge, until closing time. Then a stream of satisfied customers from the pub round the corner began to straggle past the house.

'What's so good about this area of London,' said Richard, after hastily dispatching a caught-short Irishman who had lurched through the privet unbuttoning his flies, 'is that it's not sickeningly middle-class.'

'Absolutely,' agreed Charles, listening to the splattering of water on the pavement behind his chair.

Margaret was lacking spoons for the pudding. 'Please, Charles,' she appealed, touching him briefly on the shoulder.

He ran inside the house glad to be of service. He looked in the drawers and on the draining board.

After a moment Margaret too came indoors. There was no sign of Malcolm. 'Have you found them?' she shouted.

'Stop it,' said Charles.

'They're right in front of your eyes,' she bellowed.

'For God's sake,' he whispered. 'They'll see us.'

He backed away down the room. It was infuriating, he thought, the knack women had of behaving wantonly at the wrong moments. Had they been alone in some private place, depend upon it, Margaret would have been full of excuses and evasions. In all the twelve years he had known her, there had never been a private place. He had wanted there to be, but he hadn't liked to plan it. God knows, life was sordid enough as it was. He didn't know how old Richard stood it – his wife giving off signals the way she did. The amount of lipstick Margaret wore, the tints in her hair, the way everything wobbled when she moved. Dora was utterly different. You could tell just by looking at her that she wasn't continually thinking about men.

'Where's Malcolm?' asked Margaret.

'I've no idea,' he said. He found he was being manoeuvred between a wall cupboard and the cooker. He had never known her so determined. He glanced desperately at the window. All he could see was the back of his wife's head. 'All right, you little bitch,' he said hoarsely. The word excited him dreadfully. It was so offensive. He never called Dora a bitch, not unless they were arguing. 'You've asked for it,' he said. Eyes closed and breathing heavily, he held out his arms. Margaret, looking over her shoulder, was in time to see Richard rising from his chair. He waved. She fled soundlessly from the room.

Dora quite enjoyed being in the front yard. It was handy being so near the dustbins. When the weather was good they often lunched on the lawn in Tunbridge Wells, but there the grass was like a carpet to Charles and he grew livid if so much as a crumb fell to the ground.

'Where's Malcolm gone?' asked Margaret. Richard told her he was in the basement, probably listening to records. Actually he had seen Malcolm sloping off down the street a quarter of an hour before, but he didn't want to worry her. Lately, Malcolm had taken to going out for hours at a stretch and coming home in an elated condition. They both knew it was due to pot-smoking, or worse. In a sense it was a relief to them that he had at last found something which interested him.

'Do you know,' said Charles. 'I do wonder if we're doing the right thing, burying the children down in the country.'

'Oh, come on,' scoffed Margaret. 'All that space and fresh air ... not to mention their ponies.'

'I know exactly what he means,' said Dora. 'They're very protected. When I think of Malcolm at Sarah's age, he was streets ahead of her.'

'Was he?' said Richard.

'Well, he was so assured,' Dora explained. 'Handing round the wine, joining in the conversation. I always remember that time we came for dinner with Bernard and Elsa, and Malcolm hid under the table.'

'I remember that,' said Charles thoughtfully. 'He crapped.' There was a moment's startled silence. 'It was your word,' Charles said hastily, looking at Richard. 'I remember clearly. I said to you, I think Malcolm's had a little accident, and you said to me, Oh dear, he's done a crap. I thought it was marvellous of you. I really did.'

'Really he did,' said Dora.

'I wonder what happened to Elsa,' said Margaret. When they had finished their coffee, Richard fetched a tray and began to gather the dishes together. It had grown chilly.

'Leave those,' said Margaret, shivering.

Dora put on her old cardigan. It hung shapelessly from her neck to her thigh. Peering through the hedge she caught sight of the camellia in next door's garden. 'Isn't it a beauty,' she enthused, waving her woolly arms in excitement.

'I'll show it to you,' offered Richard. 'They won't mind you taking a dekko. They're a nice couple. He's something of a character. He wears Osh-Coshes.'

'Charles,' said Dora. 'Please ring Mrs Antrim. Just to check if the kiddies are all right.'

Obediently Charles went into the house. He was followed by Margaret.

The telephone was on a shelf outside the bathroom door. He couldn't remember the code number. 'Doesn't he remember his little codey-wodey number?' said Margaret, who had been drinking quite heavily.

'Be careful,' he protested. 'The front door's open.'

'They've gone next door to look at the flowers,' she said.

'They might pop back at any moment.'

'Well, come in here then.' And with brute force she pushed him from the phone towards the bathroom.

It was quite flattering in a way, the urgent manner in which she propelled him through the door. He wished her teeth would stop chattering; she was making the devil of a noise. Feeling a bit of an ass, he sat on the edge of the bath while she stood over him and rumpled his hair.

'Steady on,' he said. 'I haven't a comb on me.'

'Kiss me,' she urged. 'Kiss me.'

'Look here,' he said, wrenching her fingers out of his ears. 'This is neither the time nor the place. I can't relax in this kind of situation.'

'Oh, shut up,' she said, and shoved him quite viciously so that he lost his balance and lay half in and half out of the bath. At that instant she thought she heard someone coming up the hall.

'Christ,' she moaned, dropping to one knee and peering through the keyhole. There was no one there. 'Listen,' she told Charles, who was struggling to get out of the bath. 'If they come back, I'll go and you stay here. You can come out later.'

'What if Richard wants to use the lavatory?' he asked worriedly. Margaret said if that happened, he must nip down the steps into the yard and hide in the basement until the coast was clear.

'But what about Malcolm?' asked Charles. 'Malcolm's down there.' Margaret assured him Malcolm would be in the front room of the basement. Even if he did see Charles it wouldn't make much difference – Malcolm hardly said one articulate word from one week to the next.

'If you're sure,' breathed Charles. Half-heartedly he embraced her. He didn't quite know how far he should go. He felt a bit out of his depth. 'Are we ... is it ... should we?' he murmured.

'Play it by ear,' Margaret said mysteriously.

Charles was just unbuttoning his blazer when they both heard footsteps outside. In a flash Margaret was through the bathroom door and closing it behind her. He heard her calling. 'Cooee, I'm here.' Panic-stricken, he undid the bolt of the back door and crept on to the small veranda. Beneath him lay the yard, overgrown with weeds and littered with rose petals. A rambler, diseased and moulting, clung ferociously to the brick wall. Trembling, he descended the steps and inched his way towards the basement door. He stepped into Richard's study, gloomy as the black hole of Calcutta and bare of furniture save for a desk and a chair. Margaret had been right. Malcolm was in the front room playing records. Charles recognized some of the tunes from *Chorus Line*. He wasn't over-fond of modern music but he couldn't help being impressed by the kind of enjoyment Malcolm seemed to be experiencing. There were distinct sighs and moans coming from beyond the wall. He eased himself into Richard's chair and waited for Margaret to send some sort of signal. The amount of paperwork Richard brought home was staggering. No wonder poor old Margaret behaved badly. Of course she didn't have any hobbies or attend evening classes. She wasn't like Dora, who was out several nights a week at French circles and history groups. He supposed things were different in the country. For some reason he felt terribly sleepy – probably nerves at being in such an absurd situation. He began to shake with weak and silent laughter and, when it was over, fell into a peaceful doze.

He was awakened by a shower of spoons clattering on to the flagstones outside the window. The record in the next room had been turned off. Cautiously he advanced into the yard and peered upwards. Someone was standing at the kitchen window. Adopting what he hoped was a casual stride, he walked to the back wall and inspected the rambling rose. 'Green-fly,' he shouted knowledgeably, looking up at the window. 'Riddled with green-fly.' It was Margaret's face at the window. She beckoned him to come upstairs.

When he came down the hall, Richard was standing at the front door with Dora. He turned and looked at Charles with disgust.

'I've been pottering about in the garden,' stammered Charles. He thought he might faint.

'Isn't it sickening,' said Richard. 'Someone's pinched the table.'

Charles stood on the top step and looked distressed. 'Where are the dishes?' he said, at last. 'And the glasses?'

'Gone,' cried Margaret shrilly. 'Every damn thing.' She put the kettle on to boil while Richard phoned the police. When

Richard came back, Charles offered to jump in the car and drive in all directions. 'They can't have got far,' he said.

'He's already driven round the block umpteen times,' snapped Margaret.

Just as the tea was being poured out Malcolm strolled in and helped himself to the cup intended for Dora. He leaned against the draining board, stirring his tea with the end of a biro.

'Where have you been?' asked Margaret. 'You've been out for hours.'

'The park,' said Malcolm.

'Use a spoon,' ordered Richard. Shrugging his shoulders, Malcolm ferreted in the kitchen drawer. 'There ain't no spoons,' he said. His father ran up and down stairs, looking to see if his camera had gone or his cufflinks, or the silver snuff box left him by his uncle.

Charles and Dora couldn't stay for the arrival of the police. Charles said he hoped they'd understand but he didn't want to risk running into heavy traffic. Driving home to Tunbridge Wells, he told Dora he thought it had been a bit silly of Margaret to put the table in the front yard. 'I'm the last person in the world,' he said, 'to laugh at other people's misfortunes, particularly Richard's, but it struck me as affected, you know. Damned affected. I was right up against a dust-bin. Come to think of it, it was bloody insulting.'

'Why?' asked Dora.

'Well, I think she was probably poking fun at us. You know, lunch on the lawn ... that sort of thing.'

'Rubbish,' said Dora. 'She's just starved of sunshine.'

Charles felt awful. It was sheer worry that made him speak so spitefully of his friends. As soon as Malcolm had mentioned he had spent the afternoon in the park, he had realized how mistaken he himself had been about the noises in the basement. While he had sat at Richard's desk, the thieves had obviously been in the next room. He felt almost an accomplice. And those damned spoons lying in the yard – the police would think the thieves had dropped them. He could never tell Richard about it. Richard would be bound to ask what the hell he'd been doing in the basement. Even if it didn't occur to him for one moment that he'd been after old Margaret, he'd still think it odd of him to have been snooping around his desk. Nor, thought Charles sadly, could he confide in old Dora.

She was leaning trustingly against his shoulder, tired after her pleasant day, humming the theme song from *Chorus Line*.

Michael Foley

Dympna

At that time I was a young officer stationed in the town of L—,
in the province of S—. I was a youth of some twenty or so years
and had I known what I know now I suppose it would have
worked out very differently. Sometimes, after a meal and a good
wine, my behaviour seems silly and squalid, like some wretched
little milliner in heat. At other times the old magic returns . . .

L— had once been a fashionable watering place but by the
time of these events, was a refuge for the senile and diseased. I
was billeted with one such old couple, who fed me on watery
soup and indifferent stew. After dinner I partook of my
recreation, a stroll around the somnolent squares and crumbling
exhausted terraces.

And yet I was happy enough. The days passed in routine
duties, the nights in roamings and imaginings. What does a
young lieutenant need, apart from his uniform and his horse?

Then one evening I wandered far from the main square and
came upon a brightly lit eating place – the San Remo Fish
Restaurant. I went straight in, only to discover a den of the
lowest sort. It was as I was on the point of leaving that I saw
Dympna.

How could I have failed to do so? Not even the wretched
uniform could conceal the svelte grace of her body. And her
face – the incandescent lips, the small pointed rodent's teeth,
the soft filmy grey eyes beneath lashes like mourning veils, eyes
lit now and then by a spark of silver like a sliver of moonlight
on a somnolent canal. All at once I was certain. I knew that the
intrigues, the deceits, the insinuations – all the obstalcles the
world invents to delay the inevitable happiness of those who
belong to each other – all these would vanish like insubstantial

shadows from the moment we exchanged our first words. And yet I was chary of these first words, like an artist who fears to violate the shimmering grandeur of his vision.

I ordered a meal, engaging the other waitress, a revolting stunted creature. Afterwards I sent her off with a message for Dympna. In a moment she was scuttling back.

'She says you've a face like a badger's arse turned inside out and white-washed.'

'But this is preposterous!'

'She says you're mental. She says you're not wise.'

I left at once, my soul seething in tumultuous eruption. But I was not discouraged. This was surely some charming coquetry for I could not see her other than dizzy with desire, kindling me with her strange eyes, inflaming me with her pale hands. On the following night I was back in the San Remo and attracted her attention boldly.

'Dympna,' I began, 'Dympna, let us not linger on the banal ceremonies in which so much of life's precious time is lost.'

'Dear God, you need your head looked at.' And she was gone – gone the sulphurous eyes and the ravening despoiling mouth. I understood that she could drain one's marrow, granulate the lungs, demolish the loins. As she passed I caught her arm wildly – but she shook herself free.

'Dear you're not a bit nice, ye can go off people ye know.'

Once more I had to leave. And on returning for the third night in succession I discovered that she was not even there. Her friend said it was her night off.

'She says you've two chances, a dog's and none. She says you're a real nancy boy dressed like yon.'

'But . . . but this is my uniform.' And as I rose to leave I heard a wicked hiss I seemed to recognize, 'Dirty body. Scabby head. Gravy ring,' and then the friend unmistakeably, 'God forgive ye and pardon ye, Dympna Doherty.'

After this I attempted to avoid the San Remo. It was useless. Each night was spent pacing my room, like a caged beast to whom the night air bears the scents and odours of the jungle. During the day my nerves were in revolt, crying out against the petty sufferings they were subjected to every minute – a slamming door, a rasp of boots, a harsh parade ground bellow. Then again there were whole hours when I was so far from being sensitive that, if the barracks were burning down, I could not move.

At last I gave in and returned. As I pushed through the San Remo door I heard a voice I knew.

'Hi dreamboat.' I turned.

'Not you, shipwreck.' It was Dympna, her grey eyes more mysterious than ever, rebellious and melancholy, at once reminiscent of graveyard and banqueting hall. Then she was gone again, carrying egg and chips, and I realized the futility of meeting in such a place.

It would have to be above the San Remo, where she had a little room. Here she would be lithe, feline, frenzied, her carnal appetites excessive and bizarre. Her desire would be cold, hard, implacable. I would experience the strange sensation of fire swathed in blocks of ice. We would be swallowed up in a sea of those languid pleasures that unite the spirit with the mysterious flesh. With shudders and caresses we would exhaust the violence of our desire and each become the heart-throb of the other's being. Awestruck I would return to my room and lie there broken, helpless, my brain whirring undone in my skull.

But a very different scene met my eyes. She herself was in bed naked – and the bed was the evidence of her treachery. A selection of tawdry gifts, nylon stockings, cheap scent, a music box grinding out some popular melody. On the floor was a crumpled American serviceman's uniform and in the middle of the floor was the American himself, clad only in jockey shorts and a gold watch.

'Know where I can catch a cab?' he inquired. And still Dympna remained sardonic and aloof.

'Is your face hurting?' she asked.

'Wha ...? What ...?'

'Because the way you're standing there you'd think you were simple.'

The American guffawed and at once I was upon him, forcing him to the ground, feeling the neck snap in my hands like rotten wood. Dympna cried out in panic but her frantic entreaties grew faint and finally died on the tingling silence. Only then did I realize what had happened. My career, my life – all in ruins! But a fiendish cunning seized me and it was the work of a moment to arrange the two as though they had heedlessly strangled each other at the vertiginous climax of their passion. I left the San Remo for the last time and that same night arranged for a transfer far from L—.

Many times have I thought of returning – but something has always prevented me. Perhaps I cherish her lingering ghost and do not wish to subject it to the squares and terraces of L— and to the odours and squalor of the San Remo Fish Restaurant.

Ah Dympna, Dympna – my pale lady of pleasure, my despair!

James Kelman

Renee

I had landed in a position of some authority offering scope for advancement. A storekeeper. I kept records of food for the stores of food I had authority of. The Foodstore was a fairly large smallroom. I had no assistants. Those in superior positions held little or no authority over me. I was belonging to the few able to match figures on paper with objects on shelves and was left alone to get on with it.

Members of the kitchenstaff came to obtain grub and it was down to me to check they were due this grub. If so I marked it all in a wee notebook I kept hidden in a concealed spot. The chap I succeeded was at that moment serving a bit of time as an effect of his failure to conceal said notebook. He left the fucker lying around for any mug to find. And eventually someone pulled a stroke with cases of strong drink, and this predecessor of mine wound up taking the blame.

The kitchenstaff consisted of females most of whom were Portuguese but though I found them really desirable they seemed to regard Scotchmen with disfavour. And the rest of the British for that matter. They spoke very little English. I could manage La Muchacha Hermosa in their own language but it got me nowhere. Alongside them worked a pair of girls from somewhere on the southeastern tip of England, one in particular I was disposed towards. The other was not bad. I had to carry on the chat with both however because generally speaking this always transpires in such circumstances viz when you are on your tod and have nobody to help out in 4somes. Obviously I had no desire to escort both on a night out. But neither did I wish to ask one lest the other was hurt. What a mug! Never mind. It could have gone on for ages but for the intervention of the Portuguese. At long last they successfully conveyed to me that a certain girl from the southeastern tip of England wouldnt take it amiss if I was to dive in with the head down. Joan was her name; she seemed surprised when I asked her out but she was pleased. We walked down to the local pictures after work. The Odeon. People considered it a dump but I didnt; it showed two full-length feature films while the flash joints up west were charging a fortune for the privilege of seeing one.

My relations with the other girl declined palpably which was a bit of a pity because I quite liked her. She began visiting the Foodstore only when absolutely necessary. Then soon after this Joan was becoming irritated all the time. To some extent I couldnt blame her. My financial situation was hopeless and the very ideas of equality and going dutch were anathema to her. The upshot was the Odeon three weeks running. She hated it. That last conversation was totally ridiculous, me standing about humming and hawing and trying to assume a woebegone countenance. She said nothing but her face inflamed, she was quite passionate in some ways. The bloody Odeon again, she muttered and set off marching down the Gray's Inn Road.

I strode after her. But not too quickly because I was having to figure out a speech. By the time I had counted through the last of my coins and paid for the two tickets she was through in the foyer at the end of the sweeties' queue. She paid a fortune for chocolate but the thought of assisting me with the tickets never crossed her mind. And neither did the thought of walking off and leaving me – anything was better than spending the night indoors back at the female hostel where she stayed with her pal.

I waited for her to stick the sweeties and so on into her handbag then paused as she stepped past me and into the hall, where I handed the tickets to the aged usherette who was also from Scotland and occasionally gave me a cheery smile.

It was supposed to be hazardous for single women alone in the Odeon but to me that was extremely doubtful, perhaps if they'd had a halfbottle of rum sticking out their coat pockets. I never saw any bother. Just sometimes it was less than straightforward distinguishing the soundtrack from the racket caused by a few dozen snoring dossers. By the time we reached the seats the speech was forgotten about and we settled down to watch the movie. Later I slipped my arm about her shoulders and that was that, and we nestled in for a cuddle. On the road home afterwards we continued on past the local pub, straight to the female hostel. We stood in at the entrance out from the worst of the wind. There was no chance of her smuggling me inside. The place was very strict about that. Men were not wanted at all costs. She had hinted once or twice about my getting her into my own quarters. But it was not possible. In fact – well, the rumour circulating amongst the kitchenstaff at that precise moment concerned myself; they were saying I used the Foodstore as a sort of home-from-home to the extent that I actually slept in it. It was the main joke and I helped it along, telling them I was having a coloured television installed, plus a four-poster bed and a small portable bar, the usual sort of nonsense. The truth of the matter is that I *was* sleeping in the place; but nobody knew for sure and none had the authority to enter the Foodstore unless I was with them, this last being a new condition of the post because of the plight of my predecessor. Two keys only existed: one was held by myself while the other was kept in the office of the security staff. That was in case of emergencies. But I reckoned that with me being there on the premises most of the time there would be very little scope for 'emergencies'. I had overheard a couple of those in superior positions refer to the plight of my predecessor as an 'emergency'. The idea of becoming one myself was not appealing. But as long as the Foodstore remained under my control I had grounds for optimism; for the first time in a long while I was beginning to feel confident about the future. Even so, just occasionally, I could suddenly become inveighed by a sense of panic and if outside of the Foodstore I had to rush straight back to ensure everything was OK, that I hadnt forgotten to lock the bloody door. That Saturday night I started getting fidgety with Joan.

It was getting on for midnight according to her watch and I had visions of folk stealing in and filling swagbags full of grub and strong drink. And also there was an underlying suspicion that all was not well between Joan and myself, a sort of coldness, even a slight impatience. Eventually I asked her if anything was up but she said there wasnt then told me she had been invited to a good party the following night and would it be OK if she went. Of course it was OK. I quite fancied going myself. Good parties are uncommon. Especially in London. Things have a habit of going badly. I told Joan that but she said it would probably be all right, it was taking place in the home of the big brother of a former boyfriend. That sounds great, I said.

What d'you mean jock? she said.

Nothing.

Joan was good at kidding on she didnt notice things, my sarcasm was one of them. And five minutes later I was striding back down the road and sneaking in past the security office and down the long dark corridors to the Foodstore.

I didnt see her the next day but she sent a note via one of the Portuguese women, just to say she would meet me at the lounge door of the local pub at 8 that evening. It was after 9 when she arrived and I was into my third pint. She apologized. She was looking really great as well and there was a perfume she had on that was something special. Then too the material of her dress; I touched the side of her arm and there seemed to be a kind of heat radiated from it. Or else the Guinness was stronger than usual. And I kept having to stop myself from touching the nape of her neck. I noticed the landlord of the pub glancing at me in a surreptitious fashion as if fearing I might do something that would embarrass us all.

Joan kept looking at her watch until I swallowed down the last of the beer and collected my tobacco tin and matches. It was cold and blowy, and nobody was about. Nor were there any buses in view. It was as well to start walking. Joan wasnt too pleased; each time a taxi passed she made a show of looking to see if it was for hire. Eventually we reached Chancery Lane tube station.

As it transpired the party was not too bad at all, plenty of food and stuff. Joan's pal was there too but she seemed to be ignoring us. I lost sight of her amid the people who were bustling about dancing and the rest of it. Joan as well, eventually I lost sight of her. I went into a wee side room next to the kitchen, opened a can of beer and sat on a dining chair. A fellow came in who was involved with another of the girls from the hostel; he supported Charlton Athletic and we spoke about football for a time, then women. His girlfriend was older than him and it was causing problems with her parents or her roommates or something. His voice grated on me and it was as if he was just kidding on he was a Londoner. He kept on yapping. I began to wonder if maybe it was a plot of some sort to detain me.

Shortly before midnight a girl told me to go along to the end bedroom on the first floor. Joan was there. She nodded me inside but bypassed me, shutting the door behind me; and there was her pal, Renee was her name, she was sitting on the edge of the bed crying her eyes out. I took my tin out to roll a smoke then put it away again. She knew I was there. I stepped across and touched her shoulder. OK? I said.

She shook the hand off. She had stopped crying but was trembling a little. I rolled a smoke now and offered her it but she didnt smoke. She dried her nose with a tissue. I laid my hand on her arm and asked if she was feeling any better. When she didnt answer I said: Will I tell Joan to come in?

No, she replied. She sniffed and dried her nose again. I stood smoking while she continued to sit there staring at the floor.

Do you want me to leave? I said.

Yes.

Joan had gone. Downstairs in the main dancing room I found her doing a slow one with this monkey dressed in a cravat and strange trousers. Over she came, she was frowning. Jock, she said, how's Renee? is she all right?

I think so. What was up with her?

She paused a moment then shrugged briefly, glanced away from me. Look jock, she said, I better finish the dance with David.

Oh good. Ask him if he's selling that cravat.

It wouldnt suit you, she muttered, and off she went. A loud dancing record started and other people got up on to the floor. I returned to the wee side room. The Charlton Athletic supporter was sitting on the floor with another guy; they both watched me enter. That was enough. Cheerio, I said.

It was time to get back to the Foodstore. I went into the kitchen first though and lifted a handful of cocktail sausages, wrapped them in a napkin and stuck them into my pocket and also as well a halfbottle of gin. Out in the hall I bumped into a couple at the foot of the stairs. I asked them if Renee was still in the end bedroom but they didn't seem to understand what I said.

Closing the front door after me I waited a moment in the porch, then I opened the gin and swigged a mouthful. It was really fucking horrible and didnt even taste like gin. I set off walking. Along the street and round from Basset Road I saw Renee away about fifty yards off, standing at an empty taxi rank. A man approached her and looked as if he was trying to chat her up. She stood stiffly, gazing directly to the front. He stepped towards her and she said something to him. Hey Renee! I shouted. Hey ... I trotted along the road and the man walked smartly off in the opposite direction.

Renee was frowning, and she looked at me. He thought I was a prostitute, she said, he asked me how much I charged ... She turned and stared after him but he had vanished.

Dont worry, I said, that kind of thing happens all the time. London. You waiting for a taxi?

Yes. She stepped back the way and continued speaking without looking at me. I shouldnt've come. I had a headache most of the day. I just shouldnt've come. I wasnt going to. I changed my mind at the last minute.

It was rubbish anyway, I said. Looked as if it was going to be good at the start and then it wasnt.

She nodded. Where's Joan?

Joan ... I shrugged. I pressed the lid of the tobacco tin but put it back on and brought out the gin instead. She didnt want any of it. She rubbed her forehead. If you've got a sore head, I said, this night air'll clear it. Eh, come on we'll walk for a bit.

She continued to stand there.

It's quite a nice night.

Jock, I just want to go home.

I know, but just ... a lot of queeries hang about here you know – we'll probably pick up a taxi quite soon. Eh? hey ... I brought out the cocktail sausages, unwrapped the napkin, passed her a couple. Then we carried on, eating as we walked. I began telling her about some sort of nonsense connected to the Foodstore to which she made no comment though she was quite interested. Then she started talking about her life, just general stuff to do with her family back home in this south-eastern tip of England which is apparently very green. Joan was her best pal and they had come up from there together. This was their first job and they were supposed to be sticking it out till something better turned up. Meantime they were supposed to be saving for this great flat they planned on acquiring. Has it got all mod cons? I said.

Pardon?

I shook my head but when she saw me smiling she started smiling as well. And she added, Sometimes you're funny jock.

I am not always sure about women, about what exactly is going on with them. This was just such an occasion. But I knew it was OK to put my arm round her shoulders. She continued talking about the hostel then about the kitchen and the Portuguese women whom she liked working beside because they were always having a laugh. And then I knew about the blunder I had committed; it was Renee I was supposed to have asked out back at the beginning, not Joan. It was basic and simple and everything was explained. I was glad she wasnt looking straight at my face.

A taxi trundled past. We were walking quite the thing though and scarcely noticed till it was out of earshot. Beyond Marble Arch the wind had died and it was not a bad night considering it was still only March. We had the full length of Oxford Street ahead of us but it was fine, and the shop windows were there to be looked into. I took Renee's hand and she smiled as if she had just remembered something funny; it had nothing to do with me.

When we arrived at the hostel she didnt want to go in. We moved into the space to the side of the entrance and started kissing immediately. And the way her eyes had closed as she turned her face to meet me, a harmony. I asked if it was definitely out of the question to smuggle me inside.

Honestly jock.

Are you sure?

There's just no way.

I was breathing her perfume, the point behind her ear. She had her coat open and my jacket was open, our arms round each other's waist. I had been hard since stepping into the space, and Renee was not backing away from it. We continued kissing. She definitely did not want to go in and up to her room, and it was because of Joan. She'll be there in the morning, said Renee, and I wont bear to look at her. Not now.

That was that. I opened my tin and rolled a cigarette. She was waiting for me to make things happen. Eventually I said, Listen Renee, the trouble with the place I stay in, it's 8 bloody beds to a room and that I mean you cant even get leaving a suitcase because somebody'll knock it. No kidding.

She pulled away to look at me properly. I brought out the gin, offered her a swig, took one myself when she declined. There was an all-night snackbar across at the Square and I asked if she fancied a cup of coffee. She shrugged. The two of us came out on to the pavement, walked for a couple of minutes together without speaking. Then we had our arms round each other again and we walked that way that the bodies link, the thighs fast together, the feet keeping pace and so on. At last I said, Right: how would you like to find out where I really stay?

I didnt look at her. But when she made no answer I did, and I could see she was trying not to smile. What's up? I asked.

Oh jock!

What?

She shook her head, lips tightly shut; but not able to stop smiling now.

I dont stay in the Foodstore if that's what you're thinking.

Yes you do.

What?

You do jock.

Naw I dont.

Oh well then I'm looking forward to meeting your landlord! And she laughed aloud.

I chipped away the cigarette and had another swig of gin, gestured with it to her but she shook her head. You're wrong, I said.

Am I!

Well you're no, but you are.

Oh, I see. Renee shook her head: All the kitchenstaff know!

They dont.

Jock, they do.

They fucking dont! I'll tell you something, it was me started the rumour in the first place.

You?

Aye, of course.

But the Portuguese women all laugh about it jock.

Aye OK, but it's like a double bluff; when it comes right down to it they dont really believe it.

Joan does.

Joan . . .

It was her that told me.

Oh christ. I took out my tin and rolled another fag immediately. Look, I said, Renee I mean the only reason I do it's because of the thieving that goes on in there. You cant turn your back. Christ, you know what like it is!

She didnt answer.

As far as I'm concerned I'm only going to stay there till I make sure I'm no going to get fucking set up – cause that's what they're trying to fucking do, and I'm no kidding.

There's no need to swear about it.

Sorry.

Anyhow, you dont have to worry.

What?

About who knows; it's only the kitchenstaff, and they wont say anything.

How do you know?

They wont.

What a life!

Jock, don't worry.

I wonder how the hell they found out.

Renee chuckled. Maybe you were snoring!

She seemed to take it for granted I could smuggle the two of us inside with the greatest of ease, and showed not the slightest interest in how it was to be accomplished. I led her round into the narrow, enclosed alley at the back of the building and told her to wait at a special spot. She smiled and kissed my nose. Renee, I said, you're actually crazy, do you know that?

Not as crazy as you. She raised her eyebrows.

It was never easy getting inside the building at night and that was another reason why I didnt go out very often. The security man on nightshift was from Yorkshire and me and him got on quite well together. Usually the way I managed things was to chap the window of his office and go in for a cup of tea and a chat. He assumed I was just stopping off on my road home and when I said good night he paid no further attention, never for one moment even dreaming I would be sneaking back beneath the window and along the corridor to the rear staircase. Tonight he kept me yapping for more than twenty minutes. I left him seated at his desk, twiddling the tuner of his transistor radio; he spent most of the night trying for a clear sound on the BBC World Service.

*

She stepped forwards from the shadows when I appeared at the window. We were both shivering with nervousness and it made it the more awkward when she clambered up and over the sill. I snibbed the window afterwards. That was the sort of thing Yorky would have discovered routinely. We went quickly along and down to the basement, and along to where the Foodstore was situated beyond the kitchen and coldrooms. Once inside I locked the door and stood there with my eyes shut and breathing very harshly.

All right? she said.

Aye.

She smiled, still shivering. Can you put on a light?

No, too risky. Sometimes I use a candle ... I crossed the narrow floor and opened the shutters; the light from the globes at either end of the alley was barely sufficient to see each other by. I opened them more fully.

God, she said, it cant be very nice staying here.

Well, it's only temporary remember ... I brought out the rags and sacking from the teachests, fixed us a place to sit down comfortably. It was always a warm place too. She unbuttoned her coat. I opened the halfbottle and this time she took a small mouthful of the gin. We leaned our backs against the wall and sighed simultaneously, and grinned at each other. This is actually crazy, I said.

She chuckled.

Perishable items? I said.

Pardon?

I've got milk stout and diabetic lager and butter and cheese and stale rolls, plus honey and some cakes from yesterday morning. Interested?

No thanks.

More gin?

She shook her head in a significant way and we smiled at each other again, before moving closely in together.

The daylight through the window. I blinked my eyes open. My right arm seemed to be not there any longer, Renee was lying on it, facing into the wall. I was hard. I turned on to my side and moved to rub against her; soon she was awake.

When eventually I was on top and moving to enter her she stared in horror beyond my head, and then she screamed. Through the window and across the alley up in the ground-floor window a crowd of female faces, all gesticulating and laughing. The Portuguese women. I grabbed at the sacking to try and cover the two of us. Renee had her head to the side, shielding her face in below my chest. Oh jock, she was crying. Oh jock.

Dont worry, dont worry.

How long've they been watching!

It's all right, dont worry.

Oh jock, oh jock . . .

Dont worry.

Shut the shutters, please.

I did as she asked without putting on my clothes first. I quite enjoyed the exhibitionist experience of it. Renee dressed without speaking. I tried to talk her into coming down to Kings Cross for a coffee so we could discuss things but she shook her head and mumbled a negative. She was absolutely depressed. I put my hands on her shoulders and gazed into her eyes, hoping we would manage to exchange a smile but there was nothing coming from her. It had just turned 7 a.m. I'm going to go home, she said. She lifted her bag and waited for me to unlock the door, and she left saying, Bye jock.

It was time for me to leave as well. This had been a warning. I gathered the chattels immediately and filled a plastic bag with perishables. I got my all-important notebook from its concealed spot, just in case of future emergencies, and left, leaving the key in the lock.

Julian Barnes

The Stowaway

They put the behemoths in the hold along with the rhinos, the
hippos and the elephants. It was a sensible decision to use them
as ballast; but you can imagine the stench. And there was no
one to muck out. The men were overburdened with the feeding
rota, and their women, who beneath those leaping fire-tongues
of scent no doubt reeked as badly as we did, were far too delicate.
So if any mucking-out was to happen, we had to do it ourselves.
Every few months they would winch back the thick hatch on
the aft deck and let the cleaner-birds in. Well, first they had to
let the smell out (and there weren't too many volunteers for
winch-work); then six or eight of the less fastidious birds would
flutter cautiously around the hatch for a minute or so before
diving in. I can't remember what they were all called – indeed,
one of those pairs no longer exists – but you know the sort I
mean. You've seen hippos with their mouths open and bright
little birds pecking away between their teeth like distraught
dental hygienists? Picture that on a larger, messier scale. I am
hardly squeamish, but even I used to shudder at the scene below
decks: a row of squinting monsters being manicured in a sewer.

There was strict discipline on the Ark: that's the first point
to make. It wasn't like those nursery versions in painted wood
which you might have played with as a child – all happy couples
peering merrily over the rail from the comfort of their well-
scrubbed stalls. Don't imagine some Mediterranean cruise on
which we played languorous roulette and everyone dressed for
dinner; on the Ark only the penguins wore tailcoats. Remember:
this was a long and dangerous voyage – dangerous even though
some of the rules had been fixed in advance. Remember too that
we had the whole of the animal kingdom on board: would you

have put the cheetahs within springing distance of the antelope? A certain level of security was inevitable, and we accepted double-peg locks, stall inspections, a nightly curfew. But regrettably there were also punishments and isolation cells. Someone at the very top became obsessed with information gathering; and certain of the travellers agreed to act as stool pigeons. I'm sorry to report that ratting to the authorities was at times widespread. It wasn't a nature reserve, that Ark of ours; at times it was more like a prison ship.

Now, I realize that accounts differ. Your species has its much repeated version, which still charms even sceptics; while the animals have a compendium of sentimental myths. But they're not going to rock the boat, are they? Not when they've been treated as heroes, not when it's become a matter of pride that each and every one of them can proudly trace its family tree straight back to the Ark. They were chosen, they endured, they survived: it's normal for them to gloss over the awkward episodes, to have convenient lapses of memory. But I am not constrained in that way. I was never chosen. In fact, like several other species, I was specifically not chosen. I was a stowaway; I too survived; I escaped (getting off was no easier than getting on); and I have flourished. I am a little set apart from the rest of animal society, which still has its nostalgic reunions: there is even a Sealegs Club for species which never once felt queasy. When I recall the Voyage, I feel no sense of obligation; gratitude puts no smear of Vaseline on the lens. My account you can trust.

You presumably grasped that the 'Ark' was more than just a single ship? It was the name we gave to the whole flotilla (you could hardly expect to cram the entire animal kingdom into something a mere three hundred cubits long). It rained for forty days and forty nights? Well, naturally it didn't – that would have been no more than a routine English summer. No, it rained for about a year and a half, by my reckoning. And the waters were upon the earth for a hundred and fifty days? Bump that up to about four years. And so on. Your species has always been hopeless about dates. I put it down to your quaint obsession with multiples of seven.

In the beginning, the Ark consisted of eight vessels: Noah's galleon, which towed the stores ship, then four slightly smaller boats, each captained by one of Noah's sons, and behind them, at a safe distance (the family being superstitious about illness), the hospital ship. The eighth vessel provided a brief mystery: a darting little sloop with filigree decorations in sandalwood all along the stern, it steered a course sycophantically close to that of Ham's ark. If you got to leeward you would sometimes be teased with strange perfumes; occasionally, at night, when the tempest slackened, you could hear jaunty music and shrill laughter – surprising noises to us, because we had assumed that all the wives of all the sons of Noah were safely ensconced on their own ships. However, this scented, laughing boat was not robust: it went down in a sudden squall, and Ham was pensive for several weeks thereafter.

The stores ship was the next to be lost, on a starless night when the wind had dropped and the lookouts were drowsy. In the morning all that trailed behind Noah's flagship was a length of fat hawser which had been gnawed through by something with sharp incisors and an ability to cling to wet ropes. There were serious recriminations about that, I can tell you; indeed, this may have been the first occasion on which a species disappeared overboard. Not long afterwards the hospital ship was lost. There were murmurings that the two events were connected, that Ham's wife – who was a little short on serenity – had decided to revenge herself upon the animals. Apparently her lifetime output of embroidered blankets had gone down with the stores ship. But nothing was ever proved.

Still, the worst disaster by far was the loss of Varadi. You're familiar with Ham and Shem and the other one, whose name began with a J; but you don't know about Varadi, do you? He was the youngest and strongest of Noah's sons; which didn't, of course, make him the most popular within the family. He also had a sense of humour – or at least he laughed a lot, which is usually proof enough for your species. Yes, Varadi was always cheerful. He could be seen strutting the quarterdeck with a parrot on each shoulder; he would slap the quadrupeds affectionately on the rump, which they'd acknowledge with an appreciative bellow; and it was said that this ark was run on much less tyrannical lines than the others. But there you are: one morning we awoke to find that Varadi's ship had vanished from the horizon, taking with it one fifth of the animal kingdom. You would, I think, have enjoyed the simurgh, with its silver head and peacock's tail; but the bird that nested in the Tree of Knowledge was no more proof against the waves than the brindled vole. Varadi's elder brothers blamed poor navigation; they said Varadi had spent far too much time fraternizing with the beasts; they even hinted that God might have been punishing him for some obscure offence committed when he was a child of eighty-five. But whatever the truth behind Varadi's disappearance, it was a severe loss to your species. His genes would have helped you a great deal.

As far as we were concerned the whole business of the Voyage began when we were invited to report to a certain place by a certain time. That was the first we heard of the scheme. We didn't know anything of the political background. God's wrath with his own creation was news to us; we just got caught up in it willy-nilly. *We* weren't in any way to blame (you don't really believe that story about the serpent, do you? – it was just Adam's black propaganda), and yet the consequences for us were equally severe: every species wiped out except for a single breeding pair, and that couple consigned to the high seas under the charge of an old rogue with a drink problem who was already into his seventh century of life.

So the word went out; but characteristically they didn't tell us the truth. Did you imagine that in the vicinity of Noah's palace (oh, he wasn't poor, that Noah) there dwelt a convenient example of every species on earth? Come, come. No, they were obliged to advertise, and then select the best pair that presented itself. Since they didn't want to cause a universal panic, they announced a competition for twosomes – a sort of beauty contest cum brains trust cum Darby-and-Joan event – and told contestants to present themselves at Noah's gate by a certain month. You can imagine the problems. For a start, not everyone has a competitive nature, so perhaps only the grabbiest turned up. Animals who weren't smart enough to read between the lines felt they simply didn't need to win a luxury cruise for two, all expenses paid, thank you very much. Nor had Noah and his staff allowed for the fact that some species hibernate at a given time of year; let alone the more obvious fact that certain animals travel more slowly than others. There was a particularly relaxed sloth, for instance – an exquisite creature, I can vouch for it personally – which had scarcely got down to the foot of its tree before it was wiped out in the great wash of God's vengeance. What do you call that – natural selection? I'd call it professional incompetence.

The arrangements, frankly, were a shambles. Noah got behind with the building of the arks (it didn't help when the craftsmen realized there weren't enough berths for them to be taken along as well); with the result that insufficient attention was given to choosing the animals. The first normally presentable pair that came along was given the nod – this appeared to be the system; there was certainly no more than the scantiest examination of pedigree. And of course, while they *said* they'd take two of each species, when it came down to it ... Some creatures were simply Not Wanted On Voyage. That was the case with us; that's why we had to stow away. And any number of beasts, with a perfectly good legal argument for being a separate species, had their claims dismissed. No, we've got two of you already, they were told. Well, what difference do a few extra rings round the tail make, or those bushy tufts down your backbone? We've got *you*. Sorry.

There were splendid animals that arrived without a mate and had to be left behind; there were families which refused to be separated from their offspring and chose to die together; there were medical inspections, often of a brutally intrusive nature; and all night long the air outside Noah's stockade was heavy with the wailings of the rejected. Can you imagine the atmosphere when the news finally got out as to why we'd been asked to submit to this charade of a competition? There was much jealousy and bad behaviour, as you can imagine. Some of the nobler species simply padded away into the forest, declining to survive on the insulting terms offered them by God and Noah, preferring extinction and the waves. Harsh and envious words were spoken about fish; the amphibians began to look distinctly smug; birds practised staying in the air as long as possible. Certain types of monkey were occasionally seen trying to construct crude rafts of their own. One week there was a mysterious outbreak of food poisoning in the Compound of the Chosen, and for some of the less robust species the selection process had to start all over again.

There were times when Noah and his sons got quite hysterical. That doesn't tally with your account of things? You've always been led to believe that Noah was sage, righteous and God-fearing, and I've already described him as a hysterical rogue with a drink problem? The two views aren't entirely incompatible. Put it this way: Noah was pretty bad, but *you should have seen the others*. It came as little surprise to us that God decided to wipe the slate clean; the only puzzle was that he chose to preserve anything at all of this species whose creation did not reflect particularly well on its creator.

At times Noah was nearly on the edge. The Ark was behind schedule, the craftsmen had to be whipped, hundreds of terrified animals were bivouacking near his palace, and nobody knew when the rains were coming. God wouldn't even give him a date for that. Every morning we looked at the clouds: would it be a westerly wind that brought the rain as usual, or would God send his special downpour from a rare direction? And as the weather slowly thickened, the possibilities of revolt grew. Some of the rejected wanted to commandeer the Ark and save themselves, others wanted to destroy it altogether. Animals of a speculative bent began to propound rival selection principles, based on beast size or utility rather than mere number; but Noah loftily refused to negotiate. He was a man who had his little theories, and he didn't want anyone else's.

As the flotilla neared completion it had to be guarded round the clock. There were many attempts to stow away. A craftsman was discovered one day trying to hollow out a priest's hole among the lower timbers of the stores ship. And there were some pathetic sights: a young elk strung from the rail of Shem's ark; birds dive-bombing the protective netting; and so on. Stowaways, when detected, were immediately put to death; but these public spectacles were never enough to deter the desperate. Our species, I am proud to report, got on board without either bribery or violence; but then we are not as detectable as a young elk. How did we manage it? We had a parent with foresight. While Noah and his sons were roughly frisking the animals as they came up the gangway, running coarse hands through suspiciously shaggy fleeces and carrying out some of the earliest and most unhygienic prostate examinations, we were already well past their gaze and safely in our bunks. One of the ship's carpenters carried us to safety, little knowing what he did.

For two days the wind blew from all directions simultaneously; and then it began to rain. Water sluiced down from a bilious sky to purge the wicked world. Big drops exploded on the deck like pigeons' eggs. The selected representatives of each species were moved from the Compound of the Chosen to their allotted ark: the scene resembled some obligatory mass wedding. Then they screwed down the hatches and we all started getting used to the dark, the confinement and the stench. Not that we cared much about this at first: we were too exhilarated by our survival. The rain fell and fell, occasionally shifting to hail and rattling on the timbers. Sometimes we could hear the crack of thunder from outside, and often the lamentations of the abandoned beasts. After a while these cries grew less frequent: we knew that the waters had begun to rise.

Eventually came the day we had been longing for. At first we thought it might be some crazed assault by the last remaining pachyderms, trying to force their way into the Ark, or at least knock it over. But no: it was the boat shifting sideways as the water began to lift it from the cradle. That was the high point of the Voyage, if you ask me; that was when fraternity among the beasts and gratitude towards man flowed like the wine at Noah's table. Afterwards ... but perhaps the animals had been naïve to trust Noah and his God in the first place.

Even before the waters rose there had been grounds for unease. I know your species tends to look down on our world, considering it brutal, cannibalistic and deceitful (though you might acknowledge the argument that this makes us closer to you rather than more distant). But among us there had always been, from the beginning, a sense of equality. Oh, to be sure, we ate one another, and so on; the weaker species knew all too well what to expect if they crossed the path of something that was both bigger and hungry. But we merely recognized this as being the way of things. The fact that one animal was capable of killing another did not make the first animal superior to the second; merely more dangerous. Perhaps this is a concept difficult for you to grasp, but there was a mutual respect amongst us. Eating another animal was not grounds for despising it; and being eaten did not instill in the victim – or the victim's family – any exaggerated admiration for the dining species.

Noah – or Noah's God – changed all that. If you had a Fall, so did we. But we were pushed. It was when the selections were being made for the Compound of the Chosen that we first noticed it. All this stuff about two of everything was true (and you could see it made a certain basic sense); but it wasn't the end of the matter. In the Compound we began to notice that some species had been whittled down not to a couple but to seven (again, this obsession with sevens). At first we thought the extra five might be travelling reserves in case the original pair fell sick. But then it slowly began to emerge. Noah – or Noah's God – had decreed that there were two classes of beast: the clean and the unclean. Clean animals got into the Ark by sevens; the unclean by twos.

There was, as you can imagine, deep resentment at the divisiveness of God's animal policy. Indeed, at first even the clean animals themselves were embarrassed by the whole thing; they knew they'd done little to deserve such special patronage. Though being 'clean', as they rapidly realized, was a mixed blessing. Being 'clean' meant that they could be eaten. Seven animals were welcome on board, but five were destined for the galley. It was a curious form of honour that was being done them. But at least it meant they got the most comfortable quarters available until the day of their ritual slaughter.

I could occasionally find the situation funny, and give vent to the outcast's laugh. However, among the species who took themselves seriously there arose all sorts of complicated jealousies. The pig did not mind, being of a socially unambitious nature; but some of the other animals regarded the notion of uncleanliness as a personal slight. And it must be said that the system – at least, the system as Noah understood it – made very little sense. What was so special about cloven-footed ruminants, one asked oneself? Why should the camel and the rabbit be given second-class status? Why should a division be introduced between fish that had scales and fish that did not? The swan, the pelican, the heron, the hoopoe: are those not some of the finest species? Yet they were not awarded the badge of cleanliness. Why round on the mouse and the lizard – which had enough problems already, you might think – and undermine their self-confidence further? If only we could have seen some glimpse of logic behind it all; if only Noah had explained it better. But all he did was blindly obey. Noah, as you will have been told many times, was a very God-fearing man; and given the nature of God, that was probably the safest line to take. Yet if you could have heard the weeping of the shellfish, the grave and puzzled complaint of the lobster, if you could have seen the mournful shame of the stork, you would have understood that things would never be the same again amongst us.

And then there was another little difficulty. By some unhappy chance, our species had managed to smuggle seven members on board. Not only were we stowaways (which some resented), not only were we unclean (which some had already begun to despise), but we had also mocked those clean and legal species by mimicking their sacred number. We quickly decided to lie about how many of us there were – and we never appeared together in the same place. We discovered which parts of the ship were welcoming to us, and which we should avoid.

So you can see that it was an unhappy convoy from the beginning. Some of us were grieving for those we had been forced to leave behind; others were resentful about their status; others again, though notionally favoured by the title of cleanness, were rightly apprehensive about the oven. And on top of it all, there was Noah and his family.

I don't know how best to break this to you, but Noah was not a nice man. I realize this idea is embarrassing, since you are all descended from him; still, there it is. He was a monster, a puffed-up patriarch who spent half his day grovelling to his God and the other half taking it out on us. He had a gopher-wood stave with which ... well, some of the animals carry the stripes to this day. It's amazing what fear can do. I'm told that among your species a severe shock may cause the hair to turn white in a matter of hours; on the Ark the effects of fear were even more dramatic. There was a pair of lizards, for instance, who at the mere sound of Noah's gopher-wood sandals advancing down the companion-way would actually change colour. I saw it myself: their skin would abandon its natural hue and blend with the background. Noah would pause as he passed their stall, wondering briefly why it was empty, then stroll on; and as his footsteps faded the terrified lizards would slowly revert to their normal colour. Down the post-Ark years this has apparently proved a useful trick; but it all began as a chronic reaction to 'the Admiral'.

With the reindeer it was more complicated. They were always nervous, but it wasn't just fear of Noah, it was something deeper. You know how some of us animals have powers of foresight? Even *you* have managed to notice that, after millennia of exposure to our habits. 'Oh, look,' you say, 'the cows are sitting down in the field, that means it's going to rain.' Well, of course it's all much subtler than you can possibly imagine, and the point of it certainly isn't to act as a cheap weather-vane for human beings. Anyway ... the reindeer were troubled with something deeper than Noah-angst, stranger than storm-nerves; something ... long-term. They sweated up in their stalls, they whinnied neurotically in spells of oppressive heat; they kicked out at the gopher-wood partitions when there was no obvious danger – no subsequently proven danger, either – and when Noah had been, for him, positively restrained in his behaviour. But the reindeer sensed something. And it was something beyond what we then knew. As if they were saying, You think this is the worst? Don't count on it. Still, whatever it was, even the reindeer couldn't be specific about it. Something distant, major ... long-term.

The rest of us, understandably enough, were far more concerned about the short term. Sick animals, for instance, were always ruthlessly dealt with. This was not a hospital ship, we were constantly informed by the authorities; there was to be no disease, and no malingering. Which hardly seemed just or realistic. But you knew better than to report yourself ill. A little bit of mange and you were over the side before you could stick your tongue out for inspection. And then what do you think happened to your better half? What good is fifty per cent of a breeding pair? Noah was hardly the sentimentalist who would urge the grieving partner to live out its natural span.

Put it another way: what the hell do you think Noah and his family ate in the Ark? They ate *us*, of course. I mean, if you look around the animal kingdom nowadays, you don't think this is all there ever was, do you? A lot of beasts looking more or less the same, and then a gap and another lot of beasts looking more or less the same? I know you've got some theory to make sense of it all – something about relationship to the environment and inherited skills or whatever – but there's a much simpler explanation for the puzzling leaps in the spectrum of creation. One fifth of the earth's species went down with Varadi; and as for the rest that are missing, Noah's crowd ate them. They did. There was a pair of Arctic plovers, for instance – very pretty birds. When they came on board they were a mottled bluey-brown in plumage. A few months later they started to moult. This was quite normal. As their summer feathers departed, their winter coat of pure white began to show through. Of course we weren't in Arctic latitudes, so this was technically unnecessary; still, you can't stop Nature, can you? Nor could you stop Noah. As soon as he saw the plovers turning white, he decided that they were sickening, and in tender consideration for the rest of the ship's health he had them boiled with a little seaweed on the side. He was an ignorant man in many respects, and certainly no ornithologist. We got up a petition and explained certain things to him about moulting and what-have-you. Eventually he seemed to take it in. But that was the Arctic plover gone.

Of course, it didn't stop there. As far as Noah and his family were concerned, we were just a floating cafeteria. Clean and unclean came alike to them on the Ark; lunch first, then piety, that was the rule. And you can't imagine what richness of wildlife Noah deprived you of. Or rather, you can, because that's precisely what you do: you imagine it. All those mythical beasts your poets dreamed up in former centuries: you assume, don't you, that they were either knowingly invented, or else they were alarmist descriptions of animals half-glimpsed in the forest after too good a hunting lunch? I'm afraid the explanation's more simple: Noah and his tribe scoffed them. At the start of the Voyage, as I said, there was a pair of behemoths in our hold. I didn't get much of a look at them myself, but I'm told they were impressive beasts. Yet Ham, Shem or the one whose name began with J apparently proposed at the family council that if you had the elephant and the hippopotamus, you could get by without the behemoth; and besides – the argument combined practicality with principle – two such large carcases would keep the Noah family going for months.

Of course, it didn't work out like that. After a few weeks there were compaints about getting behemoth for dinner every night, and so – merely for a change of diet – some other species was sacrificed. There were guilty nods from time to time in the direction of domestic economy, but I can tell you this: there was a lot of salted behemoth left over at the end of the journey.

The salamander went the same way. The real salamander, I mean, not the unremarkable animal you still call by the same name; our salamander lived in fire. That was a one-off beast and no mistake; yet Ham or Shem or the other one kept pointing out that on a wooden ship the risk was simply too great, and so both the salamanders and the twin fires that housed them had to go. The carbuncle went as well, all because of some ridiculous story Ham's wife had heard about it having a precious jewel inside its skull. She was always a dressy one, that Ham's wife. So they took one of the carbuncles and chopped its head off; split the skull and found nothing at all. Maybe the jewel is only found in the female's head, Ham's wife suggested. So they opened up the other one as well, with the same negative result.

I put this next suggestion to you rather tentatively; I feel I have to voice it, though. At times we suspected a kind of system behind the killing that went on. Certainly there was more extermination than was strictly necessary for nutritional purposes –

far more. And at the same time some of the species that were killed had very little eating on them. What's more, the gulls would occasionally report that they had seen carcases tossed from the stern with perfectly good meat thick on the bone. We began to suspect that Noah and his tribe had it in for certain animals simply for being what they were. The basilisk, for instance, went overboard very early. Now, of course it wasn't very pleasant to look at, but I feel it my duty to record that there was very little eating underneath those scales, and that the bird certainly wasn't sick at the time.

In fact, when we came to look back on it after the event, we began to discern a pattern, and the pattern began with the basilisk. You've never seen one, of course. But if I describe a four-legged cock with a serpent's tail, say that it had a very nasty look in its eye and laid a misshapen egg which it then employed a toad to hatch, you'll understand that this was not the most alluring beast on the Ark. Still, it had its rights like everyone else, didn't it? After the basilisk it was the griffon's turn; after the griffon, the sphinx; after the sphinx, the hippo-griff. You thought they were all gaudy fantasies, perhaps? Not a bit of it. And do you see what they had in common? They were all cross-breeds. We think it was Shem – though it could well have been Noah himself – who had this thing about the purity of the species. Cock-eyed, of course; and as we used to say to one another, you only had to look at Noah and his wife, or at their three sons and their three wives, to realize what a genetically messy lot the human race would turn out to be. So why should they start getting fastidious about cross-breeds?

Still, it was the unicorn that was the most distressing. That business depressed us for months. Of course, there were the usual sordid rumours – that Ham's wife had been putting its horn to ignoble use – and the usual posthumous smear campaign by the authorities about the beast's character; but this only sickened us the more. The unavoidable fact is that Noah was jealous. We all looked up to the unicorn, and he couldn't stand it. Noah – what point is there in not telling you the truth? – was bad-tempered, smelly, unreliable, envious and cowardly. He wasn't even a good sailor: when the seas were high he would retire to his cabin, throw himself down on his gopher-wood bed and leave it only to vomit out his stomach into his gopher-wood wash-basin; you could smell the effluvia a deck away. Whereas the unicorn was strong, honest, fearless, impeccably groomed, and a mariner who never knew a moment's queasiness. Once, in a gale, Ham's wife lost her footing near the rail and was about to go overboard. The unicorn – who had deck privileges as a result of popular lobbying – galloped across and stuck his horn through her trailing cloak, pinning it to the deck. Fine thanks he got for his valour; the Noahs had him casseroled one Embarkation Sunday. I can vouch for that. I spoke personally to the carrier-hawk who delivered a warm pot to Shem's ark.

You don't have to believe me, of course; but what do your own archives say? Take the story of Noah's nakedness – you remember? It happened after the Landing. Noah, not surprisingly, was even more pleased with himself than before – he'd saved the human race, he'd ensured the success of his dynasty, he'd been given a formal covenant by God – and he decided to take things easy in the last three hundred and fifty years of his life. He founded a village (which you call Arghuri) on the lower slopes of the mountain, and spent his days dreaming up new decorations and honours for himself: Holy Knight of the Tempest, Grand Commander of the Squalls, and so on. Your sacred text informs you that on his estate he planted a vineyard. Ha! Even the least subtle mind can decode that particular euphemism: he was drunk all the time. One night, after a particularly hard session, he'd just finished undressing when he collapsed on the bedroom floor – not an unusual occurrence. Ham and his brothers happened to be passing his 'tent' (they still used the old sentimental desert word to describe their palaces) and called in to check that their alcoholic father hadn't done himself any harm. Ham went into the bedroom and ... well, a naked man of six hundred and fifty odd years lying in a drunken stupor is not a pretty sight. Ham did the decent, the filial thing: he got his brothers to cover their father up. As a sign of respect – though even at that time the custom was passing out of use – Shem and the one beginning with J entered their father's chamber backwards, and managed to get him into bed without letting their gaze fall on those organs of generation which mysteriously incite your species to shame. A pious and honourable deed all round, you might think. And how did Noah react when he awoke with one of those knifing new-wine hangovers? He cursed the son who had found him and decreed that all Ham's children should become servants to the family of the two brothers who had entered his room arse-first. Where is the sense in that? I can guess your explanation: his sense of judgement was affected by drink, and we should offer pity not censure. Well, maybe. But I would just mention this: *we* knew him on the Ark.

He was a large man, Noah – about the size of a gorilla, although there the resemblance ends. The flotilla's captain – he promoted himself to Admiral halfway through the Voyage – was an ugly old thing, both graceless in movement and indifferent to personal hygiene. He didn't even have the skill to grow his own hair except around his face; for the rest of his covering he relied on the skins of other species. Put him side by side with the gorilla and you will easily discern the superior creation: the one with graceful movement, superior strength and an instinct for delousing. On the Ark we puzzled ceaselessly at the riddle of how God came to choose man as His protégé ahead of the more obvious candidates. He would have found most other species a lot more loyal. If He'd plumped for the gorilla, I doubt there'd have been half so much disobedience – probably no need to have had the Flood in the first place.

And the smell of the fellow ... Wet fur growing on a species which takes pride in grooming is one thing; but a dank, salt-encrusted pelt hanging ungroomed from the neck of a negligent species to whom it doesn't belong is quite another matter. Even when the calmer times came, old Noah didn't seem to dry out (I am reporting what the birds said, and the birds could be trusted). He carried the damp and the storm around with him like some guilty memory or the promise of more bad weather.

There were other dangers on the Voyage apart from that of being turned into lunch. Take our species, for instance. Once we'd boarded and were tucked away, we felt pretty smug. This was, you understand, long before the days of the fine syringe filled with a solution of carbolic acid in alcohol, before creosote and metallic naphthenates and pentachlorphenol and benzene and para-dichlor-benzene and ortho-di-chloro-benzene. We happily did not run into the family Cleridae or the mite Pediculoides or parasitic wasps of the family Braconidae. But even so we had an enemy, and a patient one: time. What if time exacted from us our inevitable changes?

It came as a serious warning the day we realized that time and nature were happening to our cousin *xestobium rufo-villosum*. That set off quite a panic. It was late in the Voyage, during calmer times, when we were just sitting out the days and waiting for God's pleasure. In the middle of the night, with the Ark becalmed and silence everywhere – a silence so rare and thick that all the beasts stopped to listen, thereby deepening it still further – we heard to our astonishment the ticking of *xestobium rufo-villosum*. Four or five sharp clicks, then a pause, then a distant reply. We the humble, the discreet, the disregarded yet sensible *anobium domesticum* could not believe our ears. That egg becomes larva, larva chrysalis, and chrysalis imago is the inflexible law of our world: pupation brings with it no rebuke. But that our cousins, transformed into adulthood, should choose this moment, this moment of all, to advertise their amatory intentions, was almost beyond belief. Here we were, perilously at sea, final extinction a daily possibility, and all *xestobium rufo-villosum* could think about was sex. It must have been a neurotic response to fear of extinction or something. But even so . . .

One of Noah's sons came to check up on the noise as our stupid cousins, hopelessly in thrall to erotic publicity, struck their jaws against the wall of their burrows. Fortunately, the offspring of 'the Admiral' had only a crude understanding of the animal kingdom with which they had been entrusted, and he took the patterned clicks to be a creaking of the ship's timbers. Soon the wind rose again and *xestobium rufo-villosum* could make its trysts in safety. But the affair left the rest of us much more cautious. *Anobium domesticum*, by seven votes to none, resolved not to pupate until after Disembarkation.

It has to be said that Noah, rain or shine, wasn't much of a sailor. He was picked for his piety rather than his navigational skills. He wasn't any good in a storm, and he wasn't much better when the seas were calm. How would I be any judge? Again, I am reporting what the birds said – the birds that can stay in the air for weeks at a time, the birds that can find their way from one end of the planet to the other by navigational systems as elaborate as any invented by your species. And the *birds* said Noah didn't know what he was doing – he was all bluster and prayer. It wasn't difficult, what he had to do, was it? During the tempest he had to survive by running from the fiercest part of the storm; and during calm weather he had to ensure we didn't drift so far from our original map-reference that we came to rest in some uninhabitable Sahara. The best that can be said for Noah is that he survived the storm (though he hardly needed to worry about reefs and coastlines, which made things easier), and that when the waters finally subsided we didn't find ourselves by mistake in the middle of some great ocean. If we'd done that, there's no knowing how long we'd have been at sea.

Of course, the birds offered to put their expertise at Noah's disposal; but he was too proud. He gave them a few simple reconnaissance tasks – looking out for whirlpools and tornadoes – while disdaining their proper skills. He also sent a number of species to their deaths by asking them to go aloft in terrible weather when they weren't properly equipped to do so. When Noah despatched the warbling goose into a Force Nine gale (the bird did, it's true, have an irritating cry, especially if you were trying to sleep), the stormy petrel actually volunteered to take its place. But the offer was spurned – and that was the end of the warbling goose.

All right, all right, Noah had his virtues. He was a survivor – and not just in terms of the Voyage. He also cracked the secret of long life, which has subsequently been lost to your species. But he was not a nice man. Did you know about the time he had the ass keel-hauled? Is that in your archives? It was in Year Two, when the rules had been just a little relaxed, and selected travellers were allowed to mingle. Well, Noah caught the ass trying to climb up the mare. He really hit the roof, ranted away about no good coming of such a union – which rather confirmed our theory about his horror of cross-breeding – and said he would make an example of the beast. So they tied his hooves together, slung him over the side, dragged him underneath the hull and up the other side in a stampeding sea. Most of us put it down to sexual jealousy, simple as that. What was amazing, though, was how the ass took it. They know all about endurance, those guys. When they pulled him over the rail, he was in a terrible state. His poor old ears looked like fronds of slimy seaweed and his tail like a yard of sodden rope, and a few of the other beasts who by this time weren't too crazy about Noah gathered round him, and the goat I think it was butted him gently in the side to see if he was still alive, and the ass opened one eye, rolled it around the circle of concerned muzzles, and said, 'Now I know what it's like to be a seal.' Not bad in the circumstances? But I have to tell you, that was nearly one more species you lost.

I suppose it wasn't altogether Noah's fault. I mean, that God of his was a really oppressive role-model. Noah couldn't do anything without first wondering what *He* would think. Now that's no way to go on. Always looking over your shoulder for approval – it's not adult, is it? And Noah didn't have the excuse of being a young man, either. He was six hundred-odd, by the way your species reckons these things. Six hundred years should have produced some flexibility of mind, some ability to see both sides of the question. Not a bit of it. Take the construction of the Ark. What does he do? He builds it in gopher-wood. *Gopher*-wood? Even Shem objected, but no, that was what he wanted and that was what he had to have. The fact that not much gopher-wood grew nearby was brushed aside. No doubt he was merely following instructions from his role-model; but even so. Anyone who knows anything about wood – and *I* speak with some authority in the matter – could have told him that a couple of dozen other tree-types would have done as well, if not better; and what's more, the idea of building all parts of a boat from a single wood is ridiculous. You should choose your material according to the purpose for which it is intended; everyone knows that. Still, this was old Noah for you – no flexibility of mind at all. Only saw one side of the question. Gopher-wood bathroom fittings – have you ever heard of anything more ridiculous?

He got it, as I say, from his role-model. What would God think? That was the question always on his lips. There was something a bit sinister about Noah's devotion to God; creepy, if you know what I mean. Still, he certainly knew which side his bread was buttered; and I suppose being selected like that as the favoured survivor, knowing that your dynasty is going to be the only one on earth – it must turn your head, mustn't it? As for his sons – Ham, Shem, and the one beginning with J – it certainly didn't do much good for their egos. Swanking about on deck like the Royal Family.

You see, there's one thing I want to make quite clear. This Ark business. You're probably still thinking that Noah, for all his faults, was basically some kind of early conservationist, that he collected the animals together because he didn't want them to die out, that he couldn't endure not seeing a giraffe ever again, that he was doing it for *us*. This wasn't the case at all. He got us together because his role-model told him to, but also out of self-interest, even cynicism. *He wanted to have something to eat after the Flood had subsided.* Five and a half years under water and most of the kitchen gardens were washed away, I can tell you; only rice prospered. And so most of us knew that in Noah's eyes we were just future dinners on two, four or however many legs. If not now, then later; if not us, then our offspring. That's not a nice feeling, as you can imagine. An atmosphere of paranoia and terror held sway on that Ark of Noah's. Which of us would he come for next? Fail to charm Ham's wife today and you might be a fricassee by tomorrow night. That sort of uncertainty can provoke the oddest behaviour. I remember when a couple of lemmings were caught making for the side of the ship – they said they wanted to end it once and for all, they couldn't bear the suspense. But Shem caught them just in time and locked them up in a packing-case. Every so often, when he was feeling bored, he would slide open the top of their box and wave a big knife around inside. It was his idea of a joke. But if it didn't traumatize the entire species I'd be very surprised.

And of course once the Voyage was over, God made Noah's

dining rights official. The pay-off for all that obedience was the permission to eat whichever of us Noah chose for the rest of his life. It was all part of some pact or covenant botched together between the pair of them. A pretty hollow contract, if you ask me. After all, having eliminated everyone else from the earth, God had to make do with the one family of worshippers he'd got left, didn't he? Couldn't very well say, No you aren't up to scratch either. Noah probably realized he had God over a barrel (what an admission of failure to pull the Flood and then be obliged to ditch your First Family), and we reckoned he'd have eaten us anyway, treaty or no treaty. This so-called covenant had absolutely nothing in it for us – except our death-warrant. Oh yes, we were thrown one tiny sop – Noah and his crowd weren't permitted to eat any females that were in calf. A loophole which led to some frenzied activity around the beached Ark, and also to some strange psychological side-effects. Have you ever thought about the origins of the hysterical pregnancy?

Which reminds me of that business with Ham's wife. It was all rumour, they said, and you can see how such rumours might have started. Ham's wife was not the most popular person in the Ark; and the loss of the hospital ship, as I've said, was widely attributed to her. She was still very attractive – only about a hundred and fifty at the time of the Deluge – but she was also wilful and short-tempered. She certainly dominated poor Ham. Now the facts are as follows. Ham and his wife had two children – two male children, that is, which was the way they counted – called Cush and Mizraim. They had a third son, Phut, who was born on the Ark, and a fourth, Canaan, who arrived after the Landing. Noah and his wife had dark hair and brown eyes; so did Ham and his wife; so, for that matter, did Shem and Varadi and the one beginning with J. And all the children of Shem and Varadi and the one whose name began with J had dark hair and brown eyes. And so did Cush, and Mizraim, and Canaan. But Phut, the one born on the Ark, had red hair. Red hair and green eyes. Those are the facts.

At this point we leave the harbour of facts for the high seas of rumour (that's how Noah used to talk, by the way). I was not myself on Ham's ark, so I am merely reporting, in a dispassionate way, the news the birds brought. There were two main stories, and I leave you to choose between them. You remember the case of the craftsman who chipped out a priest's hole for himself on the stores ship? Well, it was said – though not officially confirmed – that when they searched the quarters of Ham's wife they discovered a compartment nobody had realized was there. It certainly wasn't marked on the plans. Ham's wife denied all knowledge of it, yet it seems one of her yakskin undervests was found hanging on a peg there, and a jealous examination of the floor revealed several red hairs caught between the planking.

The second story – which again I pass on without comment – touches on more delicate matters, but since it directly concerns a significant percentage of your species I am constrained to go on. There was on board Ham's ark a pair of simians of the most extraordinary beauty and sleekness. They were, by all accounts, highly intelligent, perfectly groomed, and had mobile faces which you could swear were about to utter speech. They also had flowing red fur and green eyes. No, such a species no longer exists: it did not survive the Voyage, and the circumstances surrounding its death on board have never been fully cleared up. Something to do with a falling spar ... But what a coincidence, we always thought, for a falling spar to kill both members of a particularly nimble species at one and the same time.

The public explanation was quite different, of course. There were no secret compartments. There was no miscegenation. The spar which killed the simians was enormous, and also carried away a purple muskrat, two pygmy ostriches and a pair of flat-tailed aardvarks. The strange colouring of Phut was a sign from God – though what it denoted lay beyond human decipherability at the time. Later its significance became clear: it was a sign that the Voyage had passed its half-way mark. Therefore Phut was a blessed child, and no subject for alarm and punishment. Noah himself announced as much. God had come to him in a dream and told him to stay his hand against the infant, and Noah, being a righteous man as he pointed out, did so.

I don't need to tell you that the animals were pretty divided about what to believe. The mammals, for instance, refused to countenance the idea that the male of the red-haired, green-eyed simians could have been carnally familiar with Ham's wife. To be sure, we never know what is in the secret heart of even our closest friends, but the mammals were prepared to swear on their mammalhood that it would never have happened. They knew the male simian too well, they said, and could vouch for his high standards of personal cleanliness. He was even, they hinted, a bit of a snob. And supposing – just supposing – he had wanted a bit of rough trade, there were far more alluring specimens on offer than Ham's wife. Why not one of those cute little yellow-tailed monkeys who were anybody's for a pawful of mashed nutmeg?

That is nearly the end of my revelations. They are intended – you must understand me – in a spirit of friendship. If you think I am being contentious, it is probably because your species – I hope you don't mind my saying this – is so hopelessly dogmatic. You believe what you want to believe, and you go on believing it. But then, of course, you all have Noah's genes. No doubt this also accounts for the fact that you are often strangely incurious. You never ask, for instance, this question about your early history: what happened to the raven?

When the Ark landed on the mountaintop (it was more complicated than that, of course, but we'll let details pass), Noah sent out a raven and a dove to see if the waters had retreated from the face of the earth. Now, in the version that has come down to you, the raven has a very small part; it merely flutters hither and thither, to little avail, you are led to conclude. The dove's three journeys, on the other hand, are made a matter of heroism. We weep when she finds no rest for the sole of her foot; we rejoice when she returns to the Ark with an olive leaf. You have elevated this bird, I understand, into something of symbolic value. So let me just point this out: the raven always maintained that *he* found the olive tree; that *he* brought a leaf from it back to the Ark; but that Noah decided it was 'more appropriate' to say that the dove had discovered it. Personally, I always believed the raven, who apart from anything else was much stronger in the air than the dove; and it would have been

just like Noah (modelling himself on that God of his again) to
stir up a dispute among the animals. Noah had it put about that
the raven, instead of returning as soon as possible with evidence
of dry land, had been malingering, and had been spotted (by
whose eye? not even the upwardly mobile dove would have
demeaned herself with such a slander) gourmandizing on
carrion. The raven, I need hardly add, felt hurt and betrayed
at this instant rewriting of history, and it is said – by those with
a better ear than mine – that you can hear the sad croak of
dissatisfaction in his voice to this day. The dove, by contrast,
began sounding unbearably smug from the moment we dis-
embarked. She could already envisage herself on postage stamps
and letterheads.

Before the ramps were lowered, 'the Admiral' addressed the
beasts on his Ark, and his words were relayed to those of us on
other ships. He thanked us for our cooperation, he apologized
for the occasional sparseness of rations, and he promised that
since we had all kept our side of the bargain, he was going
to get the best *quid pro quo* out of God in the forthcoming
negotiations. Some of us laughed a little doubtingly at that: we
remembered the keel-hauling of the ass, the loss of the hospital
ship, the exterminatory policy with cross-breeds, the death of
the unicorn ... It was evident to us that if Noah was coming on
all Mister Nice Guy, it was because he sensed what any clear-
thinking animal would do the moment it placed its foot on dry
land: make for the forests and the hills. He was obviously trying
to soft-soap us into staying close to New Noah's Palace, whose
construction he chose to announce at the same time. Amenities
here would include free water for the animals and extra feed
during harsh winters. He was obviously scared that the meat
diet he'd got used to on the Ark would be taken away from him
as fast as its two, four or however many legs could carry it, and
that the Noah family would be back on berries and nuts once
again. Amazingly, some of the beasts thought Noah's offer a
fair one: after all, they argued, he can't eat all of us, he'll
probably just cull the old and the sick. So some of them – not
the cleverest ones, it has to be said – stayed around waiting for
the Palace to be built and the water to flow like wine. The pigs,

the cattle, the sheep, some of the stupider goats, the chickens ... We warned them, or at least we tried. We used to mutter derisively, 'Braised or boiled?' but to no avail. As I say, they weren't very bright, and were probably scared of going back into the wild; they'd grown dependent on their gaol, and their gaoler. What happened over the next few generations was quite predictable: they became shadows of their former selves. The pigs and sheep you see walking around today are zombies compared to their effervescent ancestors on the Ark. They've had the stuffing knocked out of them. And some of them, like the turkey, have to endure the further indignity of having the stuffing put back into them – before they are braised or boiled.

And of course, what did Noah actually deliver in his famous Disembarkation Treaty with God? What did he get in return for the sacrifices and loyalty of his tribe (let alone the more considerable sacrifices of the animal kingdom)? God said – and this is Noah putting the best possible interpretation on the matter – that He promised not to send another Flood, and that as a sign of His intention He was creating for us the rainbow. The rainbow! Ha! It's a very pretty thing, to be sure, and the first one he produced for us, an iridescent semi-circle with a paler sibling beside it, the pair of them glittering in an indigo sky, certainly made a lot of us look up from our grazing. You could see the idea behind it: as the rain gave reluctant way to the sun, this flamboyant symbol would remind us each time that the rain wasn't going to carry on and turn into a Flood. But even so. It wasn't much of a deal. And was it legally enforceable? Try getting a rainbow to stand up in court.

The cannier animals saw Noah's offer of half-board for what it was; they took to the hills and the woods, relying on their own skills for water and winter feed. The reindeer, we couldn't help noticing, were among the first to take off, speeding away from 'the Admiral' and all his future descendants, bearing with them their mysterious forebodings. You are right, by the way, to see the animals that fled – ungrateful traitors, according to Noah – as the nobler species. Can a pig be noble? A sheep? A chicken? If only you had seen the unicorn ... That was another contentious aspect of Noah's post-Disembarkation address to those still loitering at the edge of his stockade. He said that God, by giving us the rainbow, was in effect promising to keep the world's supply of miracles topped up. A clear reference, if ever I heard one, to the scores of original miracles which in the course of the Voyage had been slung over the side of Noah's ships or had disappeared into the guts of his family. The rainbow in place of the unicorn? Why didn't God just restore the unicorn? We animals would have been happier with that, instead of a big hint in the sky about God's magnanimity every time it stopped raining.

Getting off the Ark, I think I told you, wasn't much easier than getting on. There had, alas, been a certain amount of ratting by some of the chosen species, so there was no question of Noah simply flinging down the ramps and crying 'Happy land'. Every animal had to put up with a strict body-search before being released; some were even doused in tubs of water which smelt of tar. Several female beasts complained of having to undergo internal examination by Shem. Quite a few stowaways were discovered: some of the more conspicuous beetles, a few rats who had unwisely gorged themselves during the Voyage and got too fat, even a snake or two. We got off – I don't suppose it need be a secret any longer – in the hollow tip of a ram's horn. It was a big, surly, subversive animal, whose friendship we had deliberately cultivated for the last three years at sea. It had no respect for Noah, and was only too happy to help outsmart him after the Landing.

When the seven of us climbed out of that ram's horn, we were euphoric. We had survived. We had stowed away, survived and escaped – all without entering into any fishy covenants with either God or Noah. We had done it by ourselves. We felt ennobled as a species. That might strike you as comic, but we did: we felt ennobled. That Voyage taught us a lot of things, you see, and the main thing was this: that man is a very unevolved species compared to the animals. We don't deny, of course, your cleverness, your considerable potential. But you are, as yet, at an early stage of your development. We, for instance, are always ourselves: that is what it means to be evolved. We are what we are, and we know what that is. You don't expect a cat suddenly to start barking, do you, or a pig to start lowing? But this is what, in a manner of speaking, those of us who made the Voyage on the Ark learned to expect from your species. One moment you bark, one moment you mew; one moment you wish to be wild, one moment you wish to be tame. You knew where you were with Noah only in this one respect: that you never knew where you were with him.

You aren't too good with the truth, either, your species. You keep forgetting things, or you pretend to. The loss of Varadi and his ark – does anyone speak of that? I can see there might be a positive side to this wilful averting of the eye: ignoring the bad things makes it easier for you to carry on. But ignoring the bad things makes you end up believing that bad things never happen. You are always surprised by them. It surprises you that guns kill, that money corrupts, that snow falls in winter. Such naïvety can be charming; alas, it can also be perilous.

For instance, you won't even admit the true nature of Noah, your first father – the pious patriarch, the committed conservationist. I gather that one of your early Hebrew legends asserts that Noah discovered the principle of intoxication by watching a goat get drunk on fermented grapes. What a brazen attempt to shift responsibility on to the animals; and all, sadly, part of a pattern. The Fall was the serpent's fault, the honest raven was a slacker and a glutton, the goat turned Noah into an alkie. Listen: you can take it from me that Noah didn't need any cloven-footed knowledge to help crack the secret of the vine.

Blame someone else, that's always your first instinct. And if you can't blame someone else, then start claiming the problem isn't a problem anyway. Rewrite the rules, shift the goalposts. Some of those scholars who devote their lives to your sacred texts have even tried to prove that the Noah of the Ark wasn't the same man as the Noah arraigned for drunkenness and indecent exposure. How could a drunkard possibly be chosen by God? Ah, well, he wasn't, you see. Not *that* Noah. Simple case of mistaken identity. Problem disappears.

How could a drunkard possibly be chosen by God? I've told you – because all the other candidates were a damn sight worse.

Noah was the pick of a very bad bunch. As for his drinking: to tell you the truth, it was the Voyage that tipped him over the edge. Old Noah had always enjoyed a few horns of fermented liquor in the days before Embarkation: who didn't? But it was the Voyage that turned him into a soak. He just couldn't handle the responsibility. He made some bad navigational decisions, he lost four of his eight ships and about a third of the species entrusted to him – he'd have been court-martialled if there'd been anyone around to sit on the bench. And for all his bluster, he felt guilty about losing half the Ark. Guilt, immaturity, the constant struggle to hold down a job beyond your capabilities – it makes a powerful combination, one which would have had the same ruinous effect on most members of your species. You could even argue, I suppose, that God drove Noah to drink. Perhaps this is why your scholars are so jumpy, so keen to separate the first Noah from the second: the consequences are awkward. But the story of the 'second' Noah – the drunkenness, the indecency, the capricious punishment of a dutiful son – well, it didn't come as a surprise to those of us who knew the 'first' Noah on the Ark. A depressing yet predictable case of alcoholic degeneration, I'm afraid.

As I was saying, we were euphoric when we got off the Ark. Apart from anything else, we'd eaten enough gopher-wood to last a lifetime. That's another reason for wishing Noah had been less bigoted in his design of the fleet: it would have given some of us a change of diet. Hardly a consideration for Noah, of course, because we weren't meant to be there. And with the hindsight of a few millennia, this exclusion seems even harsher than it did at the time. There were seven of us stowaways, but had we been admitted as a seaworthy species only two boarding-passes would have been issued; and we would have accepted that decision. Now, it's true Noah couldn't have predicted how long his Voyage was going to last, but considering how little we seven ate in five and a half years, it surely would have been worth the risk letting just a pair of us on board. And after all, it's not our fault for being woodworm.

Jeanette Winterson

Psalms

If you've ever tried to get a job as a tea-taster you will know as intimately as I do the nature of the preliminary questionnaire. It has all the usual things: height, weight, sex, hobbies new and old, curious personal defects, debilitating operations, over-long periods spent in the wrong countries. Fluency, currency, contacts, school tie. Fill them in, don't blob the ink and, if in doubt, be imaginative.

Then, on the last page, before you sign your name in a hand that is firm enough to show spirit, but not enough to show waywardness, there is a large empty space and a brief but meaningful demand.

You are to write about the experience you consider to have been the most significant in the formation of your character. (You may interpret 'character' as 'philosophy' if such is your inclination.) This is very shocking, because what we really want to talk about is that time we saw our older sister compromised behind the tool shed, or the time we very deliberately spat in the communion wine.

When I was small, I had a tortoise called Psalms. It was bought for me and named for me by my mother in an effort to remind me continually to praise the Lord. My mother had a horror of graven images, including crucifixes, but she felt there could be no harm in a tortoise. It moved slowly, so I could fully contemplate the wonders of creation in a way that would have been impossible with a ferret. It wasn't cuddly, so that I wouldn't be distracted as I might with a dog, and it had very little visible personality, so there was no possibility of us forming an intimate relationship as I might with a parrot. All in all, it seemed to her to be a satisfactory pet. I had been agitating for

a pet for some time. In my head I had a white rabbit called Ezra
that bit people who ignored me. Ezra's pelt was white as the
soul in heaven but his heart was black . . .

My mother drew me a picture of a tortoise so that I would
not be too disappointed or too ecstatic. She hated emotion.
I hoped that they came in different colours, which was not
unreasonable since most animals do, and, when they were all
clearly brown, I felt cheated.

'You can paint their shells,' comforted the man in the shop.
'Some people paint scenes on them. One chap I know has 26
and if you line 'em end to end in the right order you get the
Flying Scotsman pulling into Edinburgh station.'

I asked my mother if I could have another twelve so that I
could do a tableau of the last supper, but she said it was too
expensive and might be a sin against the Holy Ghost.

'Why?' I demanded as the man left us arguing in front of the
gerbils. 'God made the Holy Ghost, and he made the tortoises,
they must know about each other.'

'I don't want the Lord and his disciples running round the
garden on the backs of your tortoises. It's not respectful.'

'Yes, but when sinners come into the garden they'll be taken
aback. They'll think it's the Lord sending them a vision.' (I
imagined the heathen being confronted by more and more tortoises; they weren't to know I had thirteen, they'd think it was
a special God-sent tortoise that could multiply itself.)

'No,' said my mother firmly. 'It's Graven Images, that's what.
If the Lord wanted to appear on the backs of tortoises he'd have
done it already.'

'Well can I just have two more then? I could do The Three
Musketeers.'

'Heathen child,' my mother slapped me round the ears. 'This
pet is to help you think about our Saviour. How can you do that
if you've got The Three Musketeers staring up at you?'

The man looked sympathetic, but he didn't want to get involved
so we packed up the one tortoise in a box with holes and went
to catch the bus home. I was excited. Adam had named the
animals, now I could name mine. 'How about The Man in the

Iron Mask?' I suggested to my mother, who was sitting in front of me reading her *Band of Hope Review*. She turned round sharply and gave a little screech.

'I've cricked my neck, what did you say?'

I said it again. 'We could call it Mim for short, but it looks like it's a prisoner, doesn't it?'

'You are not calling that animal The Man in the Iron Mask, or anything for short, you can call it Psalms.'

'Why don't I call it Ebenezer?' (I was thinking that would match Ezra.)

'We're calling it Psalms because I want you to praise the Lord.'

'I can praise the Lord if it's called Ebenezer.'

'But you won't, will you. You'll say you forgot. What about the time I bought you that 3-D postcard of the garden of Gethsemane? You said that would help you think about the Lord and I caught you singing "On Ilkley Moor Baht'at".'

'Alright then,' I sulked. 'We'll call it Psalms.'

So we did, and Psalms lived very quietly in a hutch at the bottom of the garden and every day I went and sat next to him and read him one of his namesakes out of the Bible. He was an attentive pet, never tried to run away or dig anything up, my mother spoke of his steadfastness with tears in her eyes. She felt convinced that Psalms was having a good effect on me. She enjoyed seeing us together. I never told her about Ezra the demon bunny, about his ears that filtered the sun on a warm day through a lattice of blood vessels reminiscent of orchids. Ezra the avenger didn't like Psalms and sometimes stole his lettuce.

When my mother decided it was time for us to go on holiday to Llandudno she was determined to take Psalms with us.

'I don't want you being distracted by Pleasure,' she explained. 'Not now that you're doing so well.'

I was doing well; I knew huge chunks of the Bible by heart and won all the competitions in Sunday School. Most importantly, for an evangelical, I was singing more, which you do, inevitably, when you're learning Psalms. On the train my mother supplied me with pen and paper and told me to make as many separate words as I could out of Jerusalem. My father was dispatched for coffee and she read out loud interesting snippets from her new paperback, *Portents of the Second Coming*.

I wasn't listening; practice enabled me to pour out the variations on Jerusalem without even thinking. Words slot into each other easily enough once sense ceases to be primary. Words become patterns and shapes. Tennyson, drunk on filthy sherry one evening, said he knew the value of every word in the language, except possibly 'scissors'. By value he meant resonance and fluidity, not sense. So while my mother warned me of the forthcoming apocalypse I stared out of the window and imagined that I was old enough to buy my own Rail Rover ticket and go off round the world with only a knapsack and a penknife and a white rabbit. A white rabbit? I jumped a little at this intrusion into my daydream. Ezra's pink eyes were gleaming down at me from the frayed luggage rack. Ezra wasn't invited on this trip, I had been determined to control him and make him stay behind. In the box next to me I felt Psalms fidgeting. My mother was oblivious.

'Just think,' she said enthusiastically. 'When the Lord comes back the lion will lie down with the lamb.'

But will the rabbit come to terms with the tortoise?

Like Psalms, I was feeling nervous, as one would when one's fantasy life gets out of control. Ezra's eyes bored into my soul and my own black heart. I felt transparent, the way I do now when I meet a radical feminist who can always tell that I shave my armpits and have a penchant for silk stockings.

'I'm trying to be good,' I hissed. 'Go away.'

'Yes,' continued my mother, all unknowing. 'We'll live naturally when the Lord comes back, there'll be no chemicals or aerosol deodorants. No fornicating or electric guitars.' She looked up sharply at my father. 'Did you put saccharine in this coffee? You know I can't drink it without.' My father smiled sheepishly and tried to placate her with a packet of Bourbons, which was a mistake because she hated anything that sounded foreign. I remembered how it had been when my auntie had come back from Italy and insisted on having us round for pasta. My mother was suspicious and kept turning it over with her fork and saying how much she liked hot pot and carrots. She didn't mind natives so much or people who lived in the jungle and other hot places because she felt they couldn't help it. Europe, though, was close enough to Britain to behave properly and, in not behaving properly, was clearly perverse and due to be rolled up when the Lord came back. (In the Eternal City there will be no pasta.)

I tried to distract myself from her gathering storm by concentrating on the notices in our carriage. I took in the exhortation to leave the train clean and tidy and felt suitably awed by the dire warnings against frivolously pulling the communication cord. Ezra began to chew it. Tired and emotional, though fondly imagining we shared a common ground other than the one we were standing on, we reached our boarding house at nightfall and spent the holiday in various ways. One morning my mother suggested we take Psalms with us to the beach.

'He'll enjoy a change of air.'

I hadn't seen Ezra for a couple of days otherwise I might have been more alive to the possibilities of catastrophe. We set off, found a patch that wasn't too windy, said a prayer and my father fell asleep. Psalms seemed comforted by the sand beneath his feet and very slowly dug a very small hole.

'Why don't you take him to that rock in the breakers?' My mother pointed. 'He won't have seen the sea before.' I nodded, and picked him up pretending I was Long John Silver making off with booty. As we sat on the rock sunning ourselves a group of boys came splashing through the waves, one of them holding a bow and arrow. Before my eyes he strung the bow and fired at Psalms. It was a direct hit in the centre of the shell. This was of no matter in itself because the arrow was rubber-tipped and made no impression on the shell. It did make an impression on Psalms, though, who became hysterical and standing on his back legs toppled into the sea. I lunged down to pick him out but I couldn't distinguish between tortoise and rocks. If only my mother had let me make him into one of The Three Musketeers I could have saved him from a watery grave. He was lost. Dead. Drowned. I thought of Shelley.

'Psalms has been killed,' I told my mother flatly.

We spent all afternoon with a shrimping net trying to find his corpse, but we couldn't and at six o'clock my mother said she had to have some fish and chips. It was a gloomy funeral supper and all I could see was Ezra the demon bunny hopping up and down on the prom. If it had not been for my father's devotion and perseverance in whistling tunes from the war in a loud and lively manner we might never have recovered our spirits. As it was, my mother suddenly joined in with the words, patted me on the head and said it must have been the Lord's will. Psalms's time was up, which was surely a sign that I should move on to another book of the Bible.

'We could go straight on to Proverbs,' she said. 'What kind of pet would be proverbial?'

'What about a snake?'

'No,' she refused, shaking her head. 'Snakes are wily, not wise.'

'What about an owl?'

'I don't want an owl in my room. Owls are very demanding and besides when your Uncle Bert parachuted into the canal by mistake, it was an owl I saw just before I got the telegram.'

Death by water seemed to be a feature of our family, so why not have something that was perpetually drowned? 'Let's get some fish, they're proverbial, and they'll be quiet like Psalms was, and they'll remind us of the Flood and our own mortality.' My mother was very taken with this, especially since she had just eaten a fine piece of cod. She liked it when she could experience the Bible in different ways.

As for me, I was confronted with my own black heart. You can bury what you like but, if it's still alive when you bury it, don't look for a quiet life. Is this what the tea board wants to know about? Is it hoping to read of tortoises called Psalms?

I don't believe it. They must have an identikit picture of what constitutes a suitable forming experience, like playing quarterback in the school team and beating Wales, or saving a rare colony of worker bees from extinction.

My mother bought some brown ink in Llandudno and sketched Psalms on a few square inches of stiff card. She caught

his expression very well, though I still feel the burden of being
the only person who has ever seen what emotion a tortoise can
express when about to drown. Such things are sobering and
stretch down the years. I could have saved him, but I felt he
limited my life. Sometimes I take out the sketch and stare at his
mournful face. He was always mournful, though I think that
was a characteristic of the breed because I have never met a
jubilant tortoise. On the other hand, perhaps I never made him
happy. Perhaps we were at emotional odds like Scarlett O'Hara
and Rhett Butler. Perhaps a briny end was better than a gradual
neglect. I ponder these things in my heart. My mother, always
philosophical in her own way, enjoyed a steady stream of biblical
pets: the Proverbial fish, Ecclesiast the hen who never laid an
egg where we could find it, Solomon the Scotch terrier and,
finally, Isaiah and Jeremiah, a pair of goats who lived to a great
age and died peacefully in their pen.

'You can always depend on the prophets,' declared my mother
whenever anyone marvelled at the longevity of her goats. The
world was a looking glass for the Lord – she saw him in everything. Though I do warn her, from time to time, never to judge
a bunny by its pelt ...

Biographical Notes

KINGSLEY AMIS (b. 1922) Born in London. Poet and novelist. Came to prominence in 1954 with his first (and most famous) novel *Lucky Jim*, which embodies a post-war spirit of principled philistinism and wry comedy. His *Collected Stories* was published in 1980.

BERYL BAINBRIDGE (b. 1934) Born in Liverpool. Her first novel *Harriet Said* was completed in 1958 but not published until 1972, by which time its two successors were already in print. She is, to date, the author of eleven novels and a volume of stories, all of which are praised for a quirky realism and the blackest humour.

JULIAN BARNES (b. 1946) Born in Leicester. First novel *Metroland* published in 1981; best known for *Flaubert's Parrot* (1984), which gained its author considerable international acclaim. 'The Stowaway' is one of the interlocking stories that make up *A History of the World in 10½ Chapters*.

H. E. BATES (1905–74) Novelist and short-story writer, best known for his books about the Larkin family, of which *The Darling Buds of May* is typical. His style, at its best, is lively and diverting.

SAMUEL BECKETT (1906–89) Irish novelist and playwright, and exponent of a kind of nihilism. Started as a disciple of James Joyce but soon branched out into a manner of his own. Lived in France for most of his life; his famous *Waiting for Godot*, like much of his work, was originally written in French. His collection of stories, *More Pricks than Kicks*, was published in 1934.

MAX BEERBOHM (1872–1956) Born in London. Essayist, parodist, caricaturist and aesthete. His only novel, *Zuleika Dobson* (1911), is an extravaganza, and it was followed a year later by the literary parodies that make up *A Christmas Garland*. Famous for his whimsicality and aplomb.

ELIZABETH BOWEN (1899–1973) Born in Dublin. Anglo-Irish novelist and short-story writer. Author of many complex and stylish works, with a considerable talent for social comedy. Her best-known collection of stories is *The Demon Lover* (1945), which explores to the full the atmosphere of wartime Britain.

RICHMAL CROMPTON (1890–1969) Born in Lancashire, one-time classics mistress and creator of the unruly eleven-year-old William Brown (*Just William* of 1922 was followed by another thirty-eight titles). The William stories were originally written for adults, but quickly became a staple of English childhood reading lasting until the late 1950s, when their popularity began to wane (and the quality of the stories dropped off). William, as a character, is firmly within the tradition of English humour, midway between Dennis the Menace and Basil Seal.

E. M. DELAFIELD (1890–1943) Pseudonym of Edmée Elizabeth Monica de la Pasture. First novel *Zella Sees Herself* published in 1917; achieved fame with her 'Provincial Lady' diaries, which were issued in instalments in *Time & Tide* from 1929 on, before being published in book form. A social commentator with the lightest possible touch, and an expert in self-mockery.

KATHLEEN FITZPATRICK Author of one collection of related stories, *The Weans at Rowallan*, published in 1905 and later reissued as *They Lived in Co. Down*. Later editions have introductions by Walter de la Mare and C. Day Lewis.

MICHAEL FOLEY (b. 1947) Northern Irish poet, short-story writer and critic, and author of one novel, *The Passion of Jamsie Coyle* (1977).

MICHAEL FRAYN (b. 1933) Novelist, playwright and *Manchester Guardian* and *Observer* columnist in the 1960s. Creator of many comic characters such as Horace and Doris Morris the suburban couple, and the three boring brothers Howard, John and Ralph.

STELLA GIBBONS (1902–89) Author of a single 'classic modern satire', *Cold Comfort Farm* (1932), and many subsequent novels which failed to match the comic inspiration of the first. Celebrated as the creator of the Howling Starkadders. Aunt Ada Doom, Flora Poste and all. The title story from the collection *Christmas at Cold Comfort Farm* likewise displays a zest which is absent from the rest of the book.

ROBERT GRAVES (1895–1985) Poet, novelist and man of letters. Born in London, lived in Majorca for the greater part of his life. His *Goodbye to All That* (1929) is a classic account of the changes effected by the First World War; *The White Goddess* explores the world of mythology and poetic lore. Also the author of some entertaining stories.

HENRY GREEN (1905–73) Born in Gloucestershire. Masterly and idiosyncratic novelist who deals in a deadpan way with the oddities of everyday life; in *Party Going* (1939), for example, we keep coming back to an old lady washing a dead pigeon in a public lavatory. Green's peculiar resonance and unique angle on things place him among the most striking authors of the mid-century.

GRAHAM GREENE (b. 1904) Distinguished novelist and short-story writer, born in Berkhamsted, Hertfordshire. Famous for his evocation of seedy locales, his posing of moral dilemmas, sheer narrative power and off-key Catholicism. His *Collected Stories* was published in 1986.

JAMES KELMAN (b. 1946) Born in Glasgow, and has been praised for the quality of 'grim Glaswegian humour' that pervades his writing. His subjects are unemployment, the DHSS, drunkenness and disaffection. His collection of stories, *Greyhound for Breakfast*, came out in 1987.

BENEDICT KIELY (b. 1919) Born in Co. Tyrone, Northern Ireland. Novelist, short-story writer, journalist, broadcaster and university lecturer now living in Dublin. An especially colourful and exuberant author. *A Letter to Peachtree and Other Stories* was published in 1987.

RUDYARD KIPLING (1865–1936) Born in India. Journalist, poet, short-story writer and man of letters, whose first collection, *Plain Tales From the Hills*, was published in 1888. Seen as an apologist of the British Empire, Kipling fell out of favour in the more liberal climate prevailing between the wars; but, for all that, his best work remains exceptionally lively and vivid.

GEORGE MACDONALD FRASER (b. 1925) Born in Scotland. Served in the British Army between 1943 and 1947; then worked as a journalist in England, Scotland and Canada. His first novel, *Flashman*, was published in 1969.

AMANDA MCKITTRICK ROS (1860–1939) Born Co. Down, Northern Ireland. Achieved fame as 'the world's worst novelist' after the publication of *Irene Iddesleigh* in 1897. Much given to alliteration and malapropism. Became a cult figure during the early part of the century, with admirers including Aldous Huxley and Sir Desmond McCarthy. An 'Amanda Ros' club was set up in London.

JULIAN MACLAREN ROSS (1913–64) Author of a good many stories affording enticing glimpses into army life and the slightly seedy London of the early post-war years. Closely associated with the Soho–Fitzrovia set-up. Worked as an army clerk, and later became a script-writer in films. Published a volume of autobiography, *The Weeping and the Laughter*, in 1953. Best known for his *Memoirs of the Forties*, which was unfinished at the time of his death.

KATHERINE MANSFIELD (1888–1923) Born Wellington, New Zealand. First collection of stories, *In a German Pension*, published in 1911, by which time she was living in London and associated with A. R. Orage's magazine *New Age*. Died in France at the age of thirty-four, having written eighty-eight stories (some uncompleted).

W. SOMERSET MAUGHAM (1874–1965) Novelist, short-story writer, dramatist and critic. Began with *Liza of Lambeth* (1897). His *Complete Short Stories* was published in 1951. Acclaimed for the forcefulness and realism of his writing.

JOHN MORROW (b. 1930) Born in Belfast, left school at fourteen and became a shipyard worker, later moving on to insurance and the Arts Council. A racy and distinctive comic writer. *Northern Myths and Other Stories* was published in 1979.

V. S. NAIPAUL (b. 1932) Born in Trinidad; came to England in 1950, and has been a writer of short stories, novelist and essayist since 1954. Very highly acclaimed for his mastery of all the nuances of social behaviour and his psychological insight.

FLANN O'BRIEN (1911–66) One of the pseudonyms of Brian O'Nolan, who was also famous as a newspaper columnist under the name of Myles na gCopaleen, and an unerring satirist and wit. Born in Strabane, Co. Tyrone, but spent most of his life in Dublin. His first and most famous novel, *At Swim-Two-Birds*, was published in 1939.

FRANK O'CONNOR (1903–66) Born in Cork, and long regarded as one of the great exponents of the short story; adroitness and ease of manner make him especially enjoyable. Among the earliest writers to cast a cold eye on Irish pieties. Also a notable critic and translator of poems from the Irish.

SAKI (1870–1916) Pseudonym of Hector Hugh Munro. Born in Burma, and (like Kipling) educated in England. Political commentator and foreign correspondent, before publishing his first collection of stories (*Reginald*) in 1904. Very highly regarded for his singular inventiveness and edgy approach to comic writing. Killed on the Western Front in November 1916.

WILLIAM SANSOM (1912–76) Novelist and short-story writer who contributed to many periodicals including *Horizon*, *New Writing* and the *Cornhill*. Served as a fireman during the Blitz on London, and his first collection of stories – *Fireman Flower* – came out in 1944. A writer of flair and originality.

MURIEL SPARK (b. 1918) Born in Edinburgh. Came to prominence in post-war London, first winning an *Observer* short-story competition (1951), and going on to write a highly accomplished first novel, *The Comforters* (1957). One of the most outstanding stylists in English fiction, and a writer of great depth and ingenuity.

J. I. M. STEWART (b. 1906) Novelist, short-story writer, retired Oxford don and – under the name of Michael Innes – distinguished contributor to the detective genre. Highly regarded for his versatility and wit. *Our England is a Garden and Other Stories* was published in 1979.

DYLAN THOMAS (1914–53) Born in Swansea. Poet, prose writer, dramatist and script writer. Famous for the richness (some would say over-richness) and evocativeness of his poetry, but also a short-story writer of verve and charm. His *Portrait of the Artist as a Young Dog* came out in 1940. Died while on a poetry-reading tour of the USA.

GWYN THOMAS (1913–81) Born in the Rhondda, in south Wales. Novelist, short-story writer, dramatist, broadcaster and humorist, he helped to point up the strengths of the regional element in English fiction during the 1940s and 1950s. His autobiography, *A Few Selected Exits*, was published in 1968.

SYLVIA TOWNSEND WARNER (1893–1978) Born in Harrow, daughter of a schoolmaster. Author of poems, essays, a biography, seven idiosyncratic novels and eight volumes of short stories, all showing her singular imaginative power and narrative gifts.

Biographical Notes

WILLIAM TREVOR (b. 1928) Born in Co. Cork. Novelist, short-story writer and TV and radio dramatist. One of the most subtle, ironic and highly regarded of contemporary authors. *The Day We Got Drunk on Cake and Other Stories* was published in 1967.

EVELYN WAUGH (1903–66) Celebrated novelist and satirist who extended the range of English comic writing with such works as *Scoop*, *Put Out More Flags* and *The Ordeal of Gilbert Pinfold*. 'Basil Seal Rides Again' is the last and funniest of his stories.

FAY WELDON (b. 1933) Born in New Zealand. Novelist, short-story writer, stage and screen writer. Her custom is to subject the lot of women to sardonic and audacious scrutiny. The didactic element in her writing is tempered by wit and whimsy. *Polaris and Other Stories* was published in 1985.

ANGUS WILSON (b. 1913) Highly acclaimed novelist and short-story writer. From *The Wrong Set and Other Stories* (1949) on, has shown himself to be adept in the field of social comedy.

JEANETTE WINTERSON (b. 1959) Born in Lancashire. Her diverting first novel, *Oranges are Not the Only Fruit*, won a Whitbread award in 1985, taking a wry and disabused attitude to her evangelical up-bringing. It was followed by *The Passion* (1987) and *Sexing the Cherry* (1989).

P. G. WODEHOUSE (1881–1973) Probably the most famous English comic writer of the century, and a superb entertainer, with his stories of aristocratic pig-enthusiasts, inane young blades and the imperturbable Jeeves. Began as a school-story writer, but soon moved on to the world of clubs and country houses, on which he imposed the fullest frivolity and sparkle.

Acknowledgements

Thanks are due to the copyright holders of the following stories for permission to reprint them in this volume:

KINGSLEY AMIS: to Jonathan Clowes Ltd, London, on behalf of Kingsley Amis, and Random Century Group for 'Moral Fibre' from *Collected Short Stories* (Hutchinson, 1980; first published in *Esquire*, 1958), © 1958 Kingsley Amis

BERYL BAINBRIDGE: to Gerald Duckworth & Co. for 'People for Lunch' from *Mum and Mrs Armitage* (Duckworth, 1985)

JULIAN BARNES: to the author, Jonathan Cape Ltd, Alfred A. Knopf, Inc. and Random House Canada for 'The Stowaway' from *A History of the World in $10\frac{1}{2}$ Chapters* (Jonathan Cape, 1989), copyright © Julian Barnes, 1989

H. E. BATES: to Laurence Pollinger Ltd and Graywolf Press for 'Silas the Good' from *My Uncle Silas* (Cape, 1939)

SAMUEL BECKETT: to John Calder (Publishers) Ltd and Grove Press for 'Fingal' from *More Pricks than Kicks* (Chatto & Windus, 1934)

MAX BEERBOHM: to Mrs Reichmann for 'A Mote in the Middle Distance' from *A Christmas Garland* (Heinemann, 1912)

ELIZABETH BOWEN: to the Estate of Elizabeth Bowen, and Alfred A. Knopf, Inc. for 'The Cheery Soul' from *The Demon Lover and Other Stories* (Cape, 1945), and the *Collected Stories of Elizabeth Bowen*, copyright © Curtis Brown Ltd, literary executors to the estate of Elizabeth Bowen, 1981

IAIN CRICHTON-SMITH: to the author for 'Mr Heine' from *Murdo & Other Stories* (Gollancz, 1981)

RICHMAL CROMPTON: to Macmillan Publishers Ltd for 'William and the Young Man' from *William's Crowded Hours* (Newnes, 1931)

Acknowledgements

E. M. DELAFIELD: to Peters Fraser & Dunlop Group Ltd for 'The Provincial Lady in Wartime' from *Time & Tide*

MICHAEL FOLEY: to the author for 'Dympna'

GEORGE MACDONALD FRASER: to Collins Publishers Ltd and John Farquharson Ltd for 'Monsoon Selection Board' from *The General Danced at Dawn* (Barrie & Jenkins, 1970)

MICHAEL FRAYN: to Elaine Greene Ltd for 'Through the Wilderness' from *On the Outskirts* (Collins, 1964), copyright © Michael Frayn, 1964

STELLA GIBBONS: to Curtis Brown, London for 'Christmas at Cold Comfort Farm' from *Christmas at Cold Comfort Farm & Other Stories* (Longman, 1940), copyright by Stella Gibbons 1940

ROBERT GRAVES: to A. P. Watt Ltd for 'Period Piece' from *Collected Short Stories* (Casell, 1965)

HENRY GREEN: to the Estate of Henry Green, and Chatto & Windus/ The Hogarth Press for 'The Lull' from *Pleasures of New Writing* (1952), edited by John Lehmann

GRAHAM GREENE: to Laurence Pollinger Ltd and International Creative Management for 'A Shocking Accident' from *Collected Stories* (Bodley Head, 1967)

JAMES KELMAN: to Heinemann/Secker & Warburg Ltd for 'Renee' from *Greyhound for Breakfast* (Secker & Warburg, 1987)

BENEDICT KIELY: to A. P. Watt Ltd, Random House, Inc. and David R. Godine, Publisher, for 'Eton Crop' from *A Letter to Peachtree & Other Stories* (Gollancz, 1987), copyright © 1987, 1988 by Benedict Kiely

RUDYARD KIPLING: to Doubleday & Co. for 'The Last Term' from *Stalky & Co*

JULIAN MACLAREN-ROSS: to Alan Ross for 'Funny Things Happen' from *Better Than a Kick in the Pants* (Lawson & Dunn, 1945)

KATHERINE MANSFIELD: to Alfred A. Knopf, Inc. for 'Germans at Meat' from *The Short Stories of Katherine Mansfield,* copyright by Alfred A. Knopf 1926 and renewed 1954 by John Middleton Murry

W. SOMERSET MAUGHAM: to Heinemann/Secker & Warburg Ltd and A. P. Watt Ltd on behalf of the Royal Literary Fund for 'The Facts of Life' from *The Complete Stories of Somerset Maugham* (Heinemann, 1951)

JOHN MORROW: to The Blackstaff Press for 'Walk Tall, If You Dare' from *Northern Myths* (Blackstaff, 1979)

V. S. NAIPAUL: to Aitken & Stone Ltd for 'The Night Watchman's Occurrence Book' from *A Flag on the Island*

FLANN O'BRIEN: to the Estate of Flann O'Brien for 'The Martyr's Crown' from *Envoy* (February, 1950)

FRANK O'CONNOR: to Joan Daves Literary Agency and Alfred A. Knopf, Inc. for 'The Drunkard' from *Collected Stories* (Knopf, 1981; first published in the *New Yorker*, 3 July 1948), © 1951 by Frank O'Connor

AMANDA MCKITTRICK ROS: to the Estate of Amanda McKittrick Ros for Chapters 10 and 11 from *Helen Huddleston*, edited by Jack London (Chatto & Windus/The Hogarth Press, 1969)

WILLIAM SANSOM: to Elaine Greene Ltd for 'Time Gents, Please' from *Lord Love Us*, copyright by William Sansom 1954

MURIEL SPARK: to David Higham Associates Ltd for 'The First Year of My Life' from *The Stories of Muriel Spark* (Bodley Head)

J. I. M. STEWART: to A. P. Watt Ltd for 'Teddy Lester's Schooldays' from *Our England is a Garden* (Gollancz, 1979)

DYLAN THOMAS: to David Higham Associates Ltd and New Directions Publishing Corporation for 'Where Tawe Flows' from *Portrait of the Artist as a Young Dog* (Dent, 1940)

GWYN THOMAS: to Felix de Wolfe for 'An Ample Wish' from *The Lust Lobby* (Hutchinson, 1971)

SYLVIA TOWNSEND WARNER: to the Executors of the Sylvia Townsend Warner Estate for 'A Pair of Duelling Pistols' from *One Thing Leading to Another* (Chatto & Windus/The Hogarth Press, 1984)

WILLIAM TREVOR: to Peters Fraser & Dunlop Group Ltd for 'Raymond Bamber and Mrs Fitch' from *The Day We Got Drunk on Cake* (Bodley Head, 1967)

EVELYN WAUGH: to Peters Fraser & Dunlop Group Ltd for 'Basil Seal Rides Again' from *Work Suspended and Other Stories* (Chapman & Hall, 1967)

FAY WELDON: to Anthony Sheil Associates Ltd and Hodder & Stoughton Publishers for 'Horrors of the Road' from *Polaris and Other Stories* (Hodder & Stoughton, 1985)

Acknowledgements

ANGUS WILSON: to Heinemann/Secker & Warburg Ltd and William Morrow & Co., Inc. for 'Crazy Crowd' from *The Wrong Set*

JEANETTE WINTERSON: to Peters Fraser & Dunlop Group Ltd for 'Psalms' from *Close Company*, edited by Christine Park and Caroline Heaton (Virago, 1987; originally published in the *New Statesman*, 1985)

P. G. WODEHOUSE: to A. P. Watt Ltd on behalf of the Trustees of the Wodehouse Trust No. 3 and Random Century Group for 'Goodbye to All Cats' from *Young Men in Spats*

Every effort has been made to obtain licences from copyright holders. The publishers would be interested to hear from any copyright holders not fully acknowledged.

FOR THE BEST IN PAPERBACKS, LOOK FOR THE

In every corner of the world, on every subject under the sun, Penguin represents quality and variety – the very best in publishing today.

For complete information about books available from Penguin – including Puffins, Penguin Classics and Arkana – and how to order them, write to us at the appropriate address below. Please note that for copyright reasons the selection of books varies from country to country.

In the United Kingdom: Please write to *Dept E.P., Penguin Books Ltd, Harmondsworth, Middlesex, UB7 0DA.*

If you have any difficulty in obtaining a title, please send your order with the correct money, plus ten per cent for postage and packaging, to *PO Box No 11, West Drayton, Middlesex*

In the United States: Please write to *Dept BA, Penguin, 299 Murray Hill Parkway, East Rutherford, New Jersey 07073*

In Canada: Please write to *Penguin Books Canada Ltd, 2801 John Street, Markham, Ontario L3R 1B4*

In Australia: Please write to the *Marketing Department, Penguin Books Australia Ltd, P.O. Box 257, Ringwood, Victoria 3134*

In New Zealand: Please write to the *Marketing Department, Penguin Books (NZ) Ltd, Private Bag, Takapuna, Auckland 9*

In India: Please write to *Penguin Overseas Ltd, 706 Eros Apartments, 56 Nehru Place, New Delhi, 110019*

In the Netherlands: Please write to *Penguin Books Netherlands B.V., Postbus 195, NL–1380AD Weesp*

In West Germany: Please write to *Penguin Books Ltd, Friedrichstrasse 10–12, D–6000 Frankfurt/Main 1*

In Spain: Please write to *Alhambra Longman S.A., Fernandez de la Hoz 9, E–28010 Madrid*

In Italy: Please write to *Penguin Italia s.r.l., Via Como 4, I-20096 Pioltello (Milano)*

In France: Please write to *Penguin Books Ltd, 39 Rue de Montmorency, F-75003 Paris*

In Japan: Please write to *Longman Penguin Japan Co Ltd, Yamaguchi Building, 2–12–9 Kanda Jimbocho, Chiyoda-Ku, Tokyo 101*

FOR THE BEST IN PAPERBACKS, LOOK FOR THE

PENGUIN OMNIBUSES

The Penguin Book of Ghost Stories

An anthology to set the spine tingling, including stories by Zola, Kleist, Sir Walter Scott, M. R. James and A. S. Byatt.

The Penguin Complete Sherlock Holmes   Sir Arthur Conan Doyle

With the fifty-six classic short stories and the plays *A Study in Scarlet*, *The Sign of Four*, *The Hound of the Baskervilles* and *The Valley of Fear*, this volume is a must for any fan of Baker Street's most famous resident.

Graham Greene: Collected Short Stories

The thirty-seven stories in this immensely entertaining volume reveal Graham Greene in a range of moods: sometimes cynical, flippant and witty, sometimes searching and philosophical. Each one confirms V. S. Pritchett's statement that 'there is no better story-teller in England today'.

The Collected Novels of Franz Kafka

'Kafka is important to us because his predicament is the predicament of modern man' – W. H. Auden. This volume contains the three novels – *The Trial*, *The Castle* and *America* – of this century's most enigmatic and influential writer.

The Claudine Novels   Colette

Claudine at School, *Claudine in Paris*, *Claudine Married*, *Claudine and Annie*: seldom have the experiences of a young girl growing to maturity been evoked with such lyricism and candour as in these four novels. In the hands of Colette, Claudine herself emerges as a true original: first and most beguiling of the twentieth century's emancipated women.

FOR THE BEST IN PAPERBACKS, LOOK FOR THE 🐧

PENGUIN HUMOUR

The Unabashed Alex   Charles Peattie and Russell Taylor

Alex is the *Independent*'s daily strip-cartoon. With its characters drawn
from every tax bracket – bullish Alex, bearish Clive, decidedly boorish
Vince and their yuppie molls – and its lowdown on the downside of today's
wealth generation, it chronicles the City's most exciting era ever.

Un Four-Pack de Franglais   Miles Kington

Les quatre hilarious volumes de Franglais dans one mind-boggling livre!
Avec cet omnibus vous pouvez relax avec le knowledge que vous won't be
stuck for quelque chose à dire anywhere in the Franglais-speaking monde,
et cope avec any situation, n'importe quoi, either side de la Manche, or
even in it.

Milligan's War   Spike Milligan

The best bits of the greatest war memoirs in the English language in one
volume, featuring Harry Secombe, crabs, the dreaded Cold Collation and
Spike's underwear collection as just a few of the secret weapons that won
the war. 'Desperately funny' – *Sunday Times*

Imitations of Immortality   E. O. Parrott

A dazzling and witty selection of imitative verse and prose as immortal as
the writers and the works they seek to parody. 'Immensely funny' – *The
Times Educational Supplement*. 'The richest literary plum-pie ever con-
fected ... One will return to it again and again' – Arthur Marshall

How to be a Brit   George Mikes

This George Mikes omnibus contains *How to be an Alien*, *How to be
Inimitable* and *How to be Decadent*, three volumes of invaluable research
for those not lucky enough to have been born British and who would like
to make up for this deficiency. Even the born-and-bred Brit can learn a
thing or two from the insights George Mikes offers here.